**Karen Miller** was born in Vancouver, Canada, and came to Australia with her family when she was two. Apart from a three-year stint in the UK after graduating from university with a BA in Communications, she's lived in and around Sydney ever since. She started writing stories while still in primary school, where she fell in love with speculative fiction after reading *The Lion, The Witch and the Wardrobe*. Over the years she's held down a wide variety of jobs, including: customer service with DHL London, stud groom in Buckingham, England, PR officer for Ku-ring-gai Council, lecturer at Mount Druitt TAFE, publishing production assistant with McGraw Hill Australia and owner/manager of her own spec fi/mystery bookshop, Phantasia, at Penrith. She's written, directed and acted in local theatre, had a play professionally produced in New Zealand and contributed various articles as a freelance journalist to equestrian and media magazines. *The Innocent Mage* (Book One) has gathered many fans for 'Kingmaker, Kingbreaker', Karen's first fantasy series – she fervently hopes it won't be the last.

For more information about Karen Miller visit www.karenmiller.net

To find out more about Karen Miller and other Orbit authors register for the free monthly newsletter at www.orbitbooks.net

BY KAREN MILLER

*Kingmaker, Kingbreaker*
The Innocent Mage
The Awakened Mage

KAREN MILLER

# THE AWAKENED MAGE

KINGMAKER KINGBREAKER
BOOK TWO

www.orbitbooks.net

ORBIT

First published in Australia in 2006 by Voyager
HarperCollins*Publishers* Pty Limited
First published in Great Britain in 2007 by Orbit
Reprinted 2007



*All characters and events in this publication, other than those clearly in the public domain, are fictitious and any resemblance to real persons, living or dead, is purely coincidental.*



A CIP catalogue record for this book
is available from the British Library.

ISBN 978-1-84149-605-4

Papers used by Orbit are natural, recyclable products made from wood grown in sustainable forests and certified in accordance with the rules of the Forest Stewardship Council.

Typeset in Sabon by Palimpsest Book Production Limited,
Grangemouth, Stirlingshire

Printed and bound in Great Britain by Mackays of Chatham plc
Paper supplied by Hellefoss AS, Norway

Orbit
An imprint of
Little, Brown Book Group
100 Victoria Embankment
London EC4Y 0DY

An Hachette Livre UK Company

www.orbitbooks.net

*For Mary,*
*who always liked Gar best*

## ACKNOWLEDGEMENTS

First, last, and all the stops in between – my incomparable editor, Stephanie Smith.

Julia Stiles, copy editor extraordinaire.

The entire HarperCollins Voyager team, most especially Robyn Fritchley and Samantha Rich.

Fiona McLennan for friendship, feedback and excellent website advice.

The Orbit team and David Wyatt for the cover.

Elaine and Peter, again, for more beta reading above and beyond the call of baby Kate.

The Purple Zone crew, whose enthusiasm for Book One made me smile and smile and smile.

All the folk who gambled on me with their dollars, then made a point of letting me know they didn't consider the money wasted. Thank you.

And last, but never least, the wonderful booksellers who convinced them to take that gamble. Thank *you*.

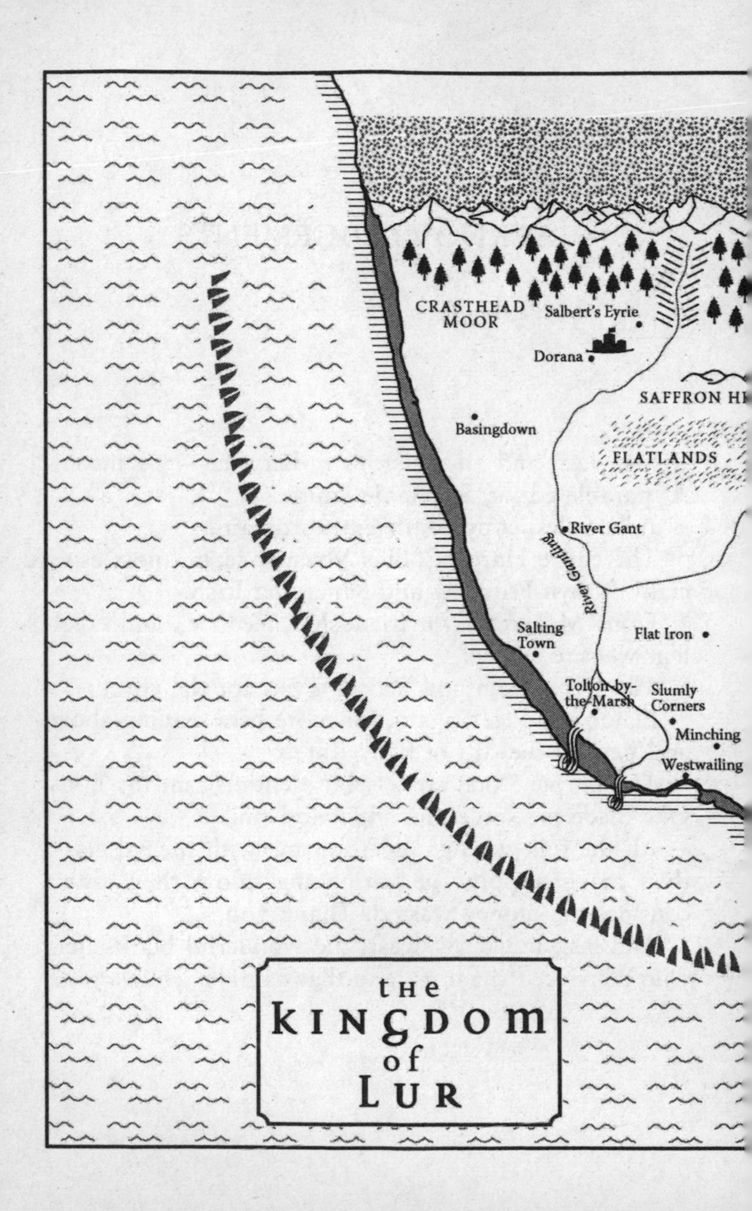
CRASTHEAD MOOR
Salbert's Eyrie
Dorana
SAFFRON
Basingdown
FLATLANDS
River Gant
River Gantling
Salting Town
Flat Iron
Tolton-by-the-Marsh
Slumly Corners
Minching
Westwailing
THE KINGDOM of LUR

BEYOND THE WALL
BARL'S WALL
BARL'S MOUNTAINS
THE BLACK WOODS
Sapslo
Jerring
Colford
THE DINGLES
Struan Caves
Dinfingle
Schoomer
Rillingcoombe
Bibford
Restharven
Dolphin Head
Chevrock
DRAGON TEETH REEF

# PART ONE

# CHAPTER ONE

With one callused hand shading his eyes, Asher stood on the Tower's sandstone steps and watched the touring carriage with its royal cargo and Master Magician Durm bowl down the driveway, sweep around the bend in the road and disappear from sight. Then he heaved a rib-creaking sigh, turned on his heel and marched back inside. Darran and Willer weren't about, so he left a note saying where Gar had gone and continued on his way.

The trouble with princes he decided, as he thudded up the spiral staircase, was they could go gallivanting off on picnics in the countryside whenever the fancy struck and nobody could stop them. They could say, 'Oh look, the sun is shining, the birds are singing, who cares about responsibilities today? I think I'll go romp amongst the bluebells for an hour or three, tra la tra la.'

And the trouble with working for princes, he added to himself as he pushed his study door open and stared in heart-sinking dismay at the piles of letters, memorandums and schedules that hadn't magically disappeared from his desk while he was gone, damn it, was that you never got to share in that kind of careless luxury. Some poor fool had to care about those merrily abandoned responsibilities, and just now that poor fool went by the name of Asher.

With a gusty sigh he kicked the door shut, slid reluctantly into his chair and got back to work.

Acridly drowning in Meister Glospottle's pestilent piss problems, he didn't notice time passing as the day's light drained slowly from the sky. He didn't even realise he was no longer alone in his office until a hand pressed his shoulder and a voice said, 'Asher? Are you dreamstruck? What's her name?'

Startled, he dropped his pen and spun about in the chair. 'Matt! Y'daft blot! You tryin' to give me a heart spasm?'

'No, I'm trying to get your attention,' said Matt. He was half grinning, half concerned. 'I knocked and knocked till I bruised my knuckles and then I called your name. Twice. What's so important it's turned you deaf?'

'Urine,' he said sourly. 'You got any?'

Matt blinked. 'Well, no. Not on me. Not as such.'

'Then you're no bloody use. You might as well push off.'

The thing he liked best about Matt was the stable meister's reassuring aura of unflappability. A man could be as persnickety as he liked and all Matt would ever do was smile. The way he was smiling now. 'And if I ask why you're in such desperate need of urine, will I be sorry?'

Suddenly aware of stiff muscles and a looming headache, Asher shoved his chair back and stomped around his office. Ha! His cage. 'Prob'ly. I know I bloody am. Urine's for gettin' rid of into the nearest chamber pot, not for hoardin' like a miser with gold.'

Matt was looking bemused. 'Since when did you have the urge to hoard urine?'

'Since never! It's bloody Indigo Glospottle's got the urge, not me.'

'I know I'll regret asking this, but how in Barl's name could any man have a shortage of urine?'

'By bein' too clever for his own damned good, that's how!' He propped himself on the windowsill, scowling. 'Indigo Glospottle fancies himself something of an *artiste*, y'see. Good ole-fashioned cloth dyein' like his da did, and his da's da afore him, that ain't good enough for Meister Indigo Glospottle. No. Meister Indigo Glospottle's got to go and think up *new* ways of dyein' cloth and wool and suchlike, ain't he?'

'Well,' said Matt, being fair, 'you can't blame the man for trying to improve his business.'

'Yes, I can!' he retorted. 'When him improvin' his business turns into me losin' precious sleep over another man's urine, you'd better bloody believe I can!' Viciously mimicking, he screwed up his face into Indigo Glospottle's permanently piss-strangled expression and fluted his voice in imitation. '"Oh, Meister Asher! The blues are so blue and the reds are so red! My customers can't get enough of them! But it's all in the piddle, you see!" Can you believe it? Bloody man can't even bring himself to say piss! He's got to say *piddle*. Like that'll mean it don't stink as much. "I need more *piddle*, Meister Asher! You must find me more *piddle*!" Because the thing is, y'see, these precious new ways of his use up twice as much piss as the old ways, don't they? And since he's put all the other guild members' noses out of joint with his fancy secret dyein' recipe, they've pulled strings to make sure he can't get all the urine he needs. Now he reckons the only way he's goin' to meet demand is by going door to door with a bucket in one hand and a bottle in the other sayin', "Excuse me, sir and madam, would you care to make a donation?" And for some strange reason, he ain't too keen on that idea!'

Matt gave a whoop of laughter and collapsed against the nearest bit of empty wall. 'Asher!'

Despite his irritation, Asher felt his own lips twitch. 'Aye, well, I s'pose I'd be laughin' too if the fool hadn't gone and made *his* problem *my* problem. But he has, so I ain't much in the mood for feelin' amused just now.'

Matt sobered. 'I'm sorry. It all sounds very vexing.'

'It's worse than that,' he said, shuddering. 'If I can't get Glospottle and the guild to reach terms, the whole mess'll end up in Justice Hall. Gar'll skin me alive if that happens. He's got hisself so caught up in his magic the last thing he wants is trouble at Justice Hall. Last thing *I* want is trouble at Justice Hall, 'cause the way he's been lately he'll bloody tell me to take care of it. *Me*! Sittin' in that gold chair in front of all those folk, passing judgement like I know what I'm on about! I never signed up for Justice Hall. That's Gar's job. And the sooner he remembers that, and forgets all this magic codswallop, the happier I'll be.'

The smile faded from Matt's face. 'What if he can't forget – or doesn't want to? He's the king's firstborn son and he's found his magic, Asher. Everything's different now. You know that.'

Asher scowled. Aye, he knew it. But that didn't mean he had to like it. Or think about it overmuch, either. Damn it, he wasn't even supposed to be here! He was supposed to be down south on the coast arguing with Da over the best fishing boat to buy and plotting how to outsell his sinkin' brothers three to one. Dorana was meant to be a fast-fading memory by now.

But that dream was dead and so was Da, both smashed to pieces in a storm of ill luck. And he was stuck here, in the City. In the Tower. In his unwanted life as Asher the bloody Acting Olken Administrator. Stuck with Indigo bloody Glospottle and his stinking bloody piss problems.

He met Matt's concerned gaze with a truculent defiance. 'Different for him, but not for me. He pays me, Matt. He don't own me.'

'No. But in truth, Asher, the way things stand for you now – where else could you go?'

Matt's tentative question stabbed like a knife. 'Anywhere I bloody like! My brothers don't own me any more than Gar does! I'm back here for now, not for good. Zeth or no Zeth, I were born a fisherman and I'll die one like my da did afore me.'

'I hope you do, Asher,' Matt said softly. 'There are worse ways to die, I think.' Then he shook himself free of melancholy. 'Now. Speaking of His Highness, do you know where he is? We've a meeting planned but I can't find him.'

'Did you look in his office? His library?'

Matt huffed, exasperated. 'I looked everywhere.'

'Ask Darran. When it comes to Gar the ole fart's got eyes in the back of his head.'

'Darran's out. But Willer's here, the pompous little weasel, and he hasn't seen His Highness either. He said something about a picnic?'

Asher shifted on the windowsill and looked outside. Late afternoon sunshine gilded the trees' autumn-bronzed leaves and glinted off the stables' rooftops. 'That was hours ago. They can't still be at the Eyrie. They didn't have that much food with 'em, and it only takes five minutes to admire the view. After that it's just sittin' around makin' small talk and pretendin' Fane don't hate Gar's guts, ain't it? Prob'ly they went straight back to the palace and he's locked hisself up in the magic room with Durm and forgotten all about you.'

'No, I'm afraid he hasn't.'

Darran. Pale and self-contained, he stood in the open doorway. Nothing untoward showed in his face, but Asher felt a needle of fright prick him between the ribs. He exchanged glances with Matt, and slid off the windowsill. 'What?' he said roughly. 'What're you witterin' on about now?'

'I am not wittering,' Darran replied. 'I've just come back from business at the palace. The royal family and the Master Magician are not there. Their carriage has yet to return.'

Again, Asher glanced out of the window into the rapidly cooling afternoon. 'Are you sure?'

Darran's lips thinned. 'Perfectly.'

Another needle prick, sharper this time. 'So what're you sayin'? You sayin' they got lost between here and Salbert's Eyrie?'

Darran's hands were behind his black velvet back. Something in the set of his shoulders suggested they were clutched tightly together. 'I am saying nothing. I am asking if you can think of a reason why the carriage's return might have been so severely delayed. His Majesty was expected for a public park committee meeting an hour ago. There was some . . . surprise . . . at his absence.'

Asher bit off a curse. 'Don't tell me you ran around bleatin' about the carriage bein' delayed! You know what those ole biddies are like, Darran, they'll—'

'Of course I didn't. I'm old but not yet addled,' said Darran. 'I informed the committee that His Majesty had been detained with Prince Gar and the Master Magician in matters of a magical nature. They happily accepted the explanation, the meeting continued without further disruption and I returned here immediately.'

Grudgingly, Asher gave a nod of approval. 'Good.'

'And now I'll ask you again,' said Darran, unimpressed by the approval. 'Can you think of any reason why the carriage hasn't yet returned?'

The needle was stabbing quick and hard now, in time with his pounding heart. 'Could be a wheel came off, held 'em up.'

Darran snorted. 'Any one of them could fix that in a matter of moments with a spell.'

'He's right,' said Matt.

'Lame horse, then. A stone in the shoe, or a twisted fetlock.'

Matt shook his head. 'His Highness would've ridden the other one back here to get a replacement.'

'You're being ridiculous, Asher,' said Darran. 'Clutching at exceedingly flimsy straws. So I shall say aloud what we all know we're thinking. There's been an accident.'

'Accident my arse!' he snapped. 'You're guessin', and guessin' wrong, I'll bet you anything you like. What kind of an accident could they have trotting to Salbert's Eyrie and back, eh? We're talking about all the most powerful magicians in the kingdom sittin' side by side in the same bloody carriage! There ain't an accident in the world that could touch 'em!'

'Very well,' said Darran. 'The only other explanation, then, is . . . not an accident.'

It took Asher a moment to realise what he meant. '*What*? Don't be daft! As if anybody would – as if there were even a reason – y'silly ole fool! Flappin' your lips like laundry on a line! They're late, is all. Got 'emselves sidetracked! Decided to go sightseeing further on from the Eyrie and got all carried away! You'll see! Gar'll be bouncing up the staircase any minute now! You'll see!'

There was a moment of held breaths, as all three of them waited for the sound of eager, tapping boot heels and a charming royal apology.

Silence.

'Look, Asher,' said Matt, smiling uneasily, 'you're most likely right. But to put Darran's mind at rest, why don't you and I ride out to the Eyrie? Chances are we'll meet them on their way back and they'll have a good old laugh at us for worrying.'

'An excellent suggestion,' said Darran. 'I was about to make it myself. Go now. And if – when – you do encounter them, one of you ride back here immediately so I may send messages to the palace in case tactless tongues are still wagging.'

Scowling, Asher nodded. He didn't know which was worse: Darran being right or the needle of fright now lodged so hard and deep in his flesh he could barely breathe.

'Well?' demanded Darran. He sounded almost shrill. 'Why are you both still standing there like tree stumps? *Go*!'

Twenty minutes later they were cantering in circumspect silence along the road that led to Salbert's Eyrie. The day's slow dying cast long shadows before them.

'There's the sign for the Eyrie,' shouted Matt, jerking his chin as they pounded by. 'It's getting late, Asher. We should've met them by now. This is the only road in or out and the gates at the turn-off were still closed. Surely the king would've left them open if they'd gone on some where else from here?'

'Maybe,' Asher shouted back. His cold hands tightened on the reins. 'Maybe not. Who can tell with royalty? At least there's no sign of an accident.'

'So far,' said Matt.

They urged their horses onwards with ungentle heels, hearts hammering in time with the dull hollow drumming of hooves. Swept round a gradual, left-handed bend into a stretch of road dotted either side with trees.

Matt pointed. 'Barl save me! Is that—'

'Aye!' said Asher, and swallowed sudden nausea.

Gar. Lying half in the road, half on its grassy border. Unconscious . . . or dead.

As one he and Matt hauled against their horses' mouths and came to a squealing, grunting, head-tossing halt. Asher threw himself from his saddle and stumbled to Gar's side, as Matt grabbed Cygnet's reins to stop the horse from bolting.

'Well?'

Blood and dirt and the green smears of crushed grass marked Gar's skin, his clothes. Shirt and breeches were torn. The flesh beneath them was torn.

'He's alive,' Asher said shakily, fingers pressed to the leaping pulse beneath Gar's jaw. Then he ran unsteady hands over the prince's inert body. 'Out cold, though. Could be his collarbone's busted. And there's cuts and bruises aplenty, too.' His fingers explored Gar's skull. 'Got some bumps on his noggin, but I don't think his skull's cracked.'

'Flesh and bone heal,' said Matt, and dragged a shirt sleeve across his wet face. 'Praise Barl he's not dead.'

'Aye,' said Asher, and took a moment, just a moment, to breathe. When he could, he looked up. Struggled for lightness. 'Bloody Darran. He'll be bleating "I told you so" for a month of Barl's Days now.'

Matt didn't laugh. Didn't even smile. 'If the prince is here,' he said grimly, his horseman's hands white-knuckled, 'then where are the others?'

Their eyes met, dreading answers.

'Reckon we'd best find out,' said Asher. He shrugged off his jacket, folded it and settled Gar's head gently back to the cushioned ground. Tried to arrange his left arm more comfortably, mindful of the hurt shoulder. 'He'll be right, by and by. Let's go.'

Remounting, he jogged knee to knee with Matt round the next sweeping bend. Battled fear and a mounting sense of dread. Cygnet pinned his ears back, sensing trouble.

They found Durm next, sprawled in the middle of the road. As unconscious as Gar, but in an even bloodier and broken condition.

'Busted his arm, and his leg,' said Asher, feeling ill as he ran his hands over Durm's limbs. The Master Magician's body was like a wet sack filled with smashed crockery. 'Damn. Make that both legs. There be bits of bone stickin' out everywhere. And his head's laid open like a boiled egg for breakfast. It's a miracle he ain't leaked out all his blood like a bucket with a hole in it.'

Matt swallowed. 'But he's alive?'

'For now,' Asher said, and got wearily to his feet. Looked further down the road for the first time – and felt the world tilt around him.

'What?' said Matt, startled.

'The Eyrie,' he whispered, pointing, and had to steady himself against Cygnet's solid shoulder.

Not even approaching dusk could hide it. The splintered gap in the timber fence at the edge of the Eyrie

– wide enough for a carriage to gallop straight through.

Matt shook his head. 'Barl save us. They can't have.'

Asher didn't want to believe it either. Sick fear made him more brutal than Matt deserved. 'Then where's the carriage? The horses? The family?'

'No. No, they *can't* have,' Matt insisted. He sounded years younger, and close to tears.

'I reckon they did,' Asher replied, numb, and dropped his reins. Obedient, resigned, Cygnet lowered his head and tugged at the grass verge, bit jangling. Asher broke into a ragged run towards the edge of the lookout.

'Don't,' said Matt. 'We're losing the light, you fool, it's too dangerous!'

The voice of reason had no place here. He heard Matt curse, and slide off his own horse. Shout after him. 'Asher, for the love of Barl, stay back! If they are down there, we can't help them. If they went over the Eyrie they're dead for sure! *Asher*! Are you listening?'

Heedless, he flung himself to the ground and peered over the drop. 'I can see somethin'. Maybe a wheel. It's hard to say. At any rate there's a kind of ledge, stickin' out.' He wriggled backwards and sat up. Stared at Matt. Now standing behind him. 'I don't reckon they went all the way to the bottom. I'm goin' down there.'

Appalled, Matt grabbed his shoulders, tried to drag him to his feet. 'You *can't*!'

He wrenched himself free and stood. 'Get back to the Tower, Matt. Tell Darran. Get help. We need pothers, wagons, ropes. Light.'

Matt stared. 'I'm not leaving you alone here to do Barl knows what kind of craziness!'

Damn it, what was wrong with the man? Couldn't he *see*? 'You got to, Matt,' he insisted. 'Like you say, we're losing the light. If they are down there and they ain't all dead, we can't wait till mornin' to find out. They'd never last the night.'

'You can't think anyone could *survive* this?'

'There's only one way to find out. Now what say you stop wastin' time, eh? Might be they are all dead down there, but we got livin' folk hurt up here, and I don't know how long that maggoty ole Durm's goin' to keep breathing without a good pother to help him. I'll be fine, Matt. Just *go*.'

Matt's expression was anguished. 'Asher, no . . . you can't risk yourself. You mustn't. I'll do it.'

'You can't. You're near on a foot taller than me and two stone heavier, at least. I don't know how safe the ground is on the side of that mountain, but a lighter man's got to have a better chance.' Matt just stared at him, begging to be hit. 'Look, you stupid bastard, every minute we stand here arguin' is a minute wasted. Just get on your bloody horse, would you, and ride!'

Matt shook his head. 'Asher—'

Out of time and patience, he leapt forward and shoved Matt in the chest, hard. 'You need me to make it an order? Fine! It's an order! *Go*!'

Matt was beaten, and he knew it. 'All right,' he said, despairing. 'But be careful. I've got Dathne to answer to, remember, and she'll skin me alive if anything happens to you.'

'And *I'll* skin you alive if you don't get out of here,' he retorted. 'Tie Cygnet to a tree so he don't follow you. I ain't keen on walkin' back to the Tower.'

'Promise me I won't regret this,' said Matt, backing away. His scowl would've turned fresh milk.

'See you soon.'

Matt stopped. 'Asher—'

'Sink me, do I have to throw you on the damned horse mys—'

'No, wait!' Matt said, holding up his hands. '*Wait.* What about Matcher?'

He lowered his fists. 'What about 'im?'

'He's got a family, they'll worry, start a fuss—'

Damn. Matt was right. 'Stall 'em. Send a lad with a message to say he's got hisself delayed at the palace. That should hold his wife till we can—'

'You mean *lie* to her? Asher, I can't!'

Barl bloody save him from decent men. 'You have to. We got to keep this as secret as we can for as long as we can, Matt. *Think*. If we don't keep her fooled for the next little while—'

'All right,' said Matt. 'I'll take care of it. I'll lie.' His face twisted, as though he tasted something bitter. Almost to himself he added, 'I'm getting good at it.'

There wasn't time to puzzle out what he meant. 'Hurry, Matt. Please.'

He watched his friend run back to the horses, anchor Cygnet to a sturdy sapling then vault into his own saddle. The urgent hoof beats, retreating, echoed round the valley. Then, under a dusking sky lavished lavender and crimson and gold, Asher eased himself over the edge of Salbert's Eyrie.

It was a sinkin' long way down to the hidden valley floor.

*Don't look, then, you pukin' fool. Take it one step at a time. You can do that, can't you? One bloody step at a time.*

The rock-strewn ground at first sloped gradually, deceptively. Beneath his boot heels gravel and loose earth, so that he slipped and slid and skidded, stripping skin from his hands as he grappled stunted bushes and sharp-sided boulders to slow his descent. His eyes stung with sweat and his mouth clogged dry with fear. The air was tangy and fresh, no crowded City smells tainting, flavouring. It struck chill through his thin silk shirt, goosebumping his sweat-sticky flesh.

Further down into the valley he went, and then further still. Every dislodged rock and pebble rang sound and echo from the vast space below and around him. Startled birds took to the air, harshly protesting, or scolded him invisibly from the Eyrie's dense encroaching foliage.

He reached a small cliff, a sheer-faced drop of some five feet that looked to give way first to a sharply sloped terrace and from there to a natural platform jutting out over the depths of the valley. Most of the platform itself was obscured by shadow and rocky outcrops, but he was sure now he could see the edge of a wheel, tip-tilted into the air.

If the carriage had landed anywhere other than the hidden valley floor, it would be there. Beyond the edge of the platform was nothing but empty space and the shrieking of eagles.

Five feet. He'd jumped off walls as high without thinking twice. Jumped laughing. Now, belly-down and crawling, he eased himself feet first and backwards over the edge, tapping his toes for cracks in the cliff face, burying his ragged, bloody fingernails in the loose shale as he scrabbled for purchase.

If he fell . . . if he fell . . .

Safely down, he had to stop, still holding onto the cliff edge, sucking air, near paralysed with fright. That sharp little needle had returned and was jabbing, jabbing. His ribs hurt, and his lungs and his head. All the cuts and scratches on his fingers, his palms, his cheek and his knee burned, bleeding.

Time passed.

Eventually recovered, the needle withdrawn and his various pains subsided, he let go of the cliff. Turned inch by tiny inch to press his shoulderblades against the rock and look where next to tread . . . and felt his heart Crack wide with grief.

So. His eyes had not misled him.

It was indeed a wheel, and more than a wheel. It was two wheels, and most of an ornate, painted carriage. It was a brown horse, and sundered harness, and a man, and a woman, and a girl.

He closed his eyes, choking. Saw a broken mast and another broken man.

'Da,' he whispered. 'Oh, Da . . .'

Ice cold to the marrow, shaking, he continued his descent.

There was blood everywhere, much of it spilled from the shattered horse. Splashed across the rocks, pooled in the hollows, congealing beneath the stunted, scrubby bushes that clung to life on this last ledge before the dreadful drop to the valley floor, it soaked the air in a scarlet pungency.

Staring over the platform's edge Asher saw treetops like a carpet and the white specks of birds, wheeling. There was no sign of the second carriage horse or Coachman Matcher. A fine fellow, he was. Had been. Married with two children, son and daughter. Peytr was allergic to horses and Lillie had the finest pair of hands on the reins the City had ever seen.

Or so said Matcher, her doting father.

Despairing, he turned away from the pitiless chasm yawning at his feet and faced instead the death he could see. Smell. Touch.

Borne was pinned beneath the splintered remnants of the carriage. His long lean body had been crushed to a thinness, and one side of his face was caved in. He looked as though he wore a bright red wig. Dana lay some three feet to his left, impaled through chest and abdomen by branches smashed into javelins. The impact had twisted her so that she lay half on her side, with her fine-boned face turned away. It meant he couldn't see her eyes. He was glad.

And Fane . . . beautiful, brilliant, impossible Fane had been flung almost to the very edge of the narrow rock shelf; one slender white hand, unmarked, dangled out into space, the diamonds on her fingers catching fire in the sun's sinking light. Her cheek rested on that outstretched arm, she might have been sleeping, only sleeping, anyone finding her so might think her whole and unharmed . . . if they did not see the jellied crimson pool beneath her slender torso, or the eerie translucence of her lovely unpowdered face. Her eyes were half open, wholly unseeing; the lashes, darkened by some magic known only to women, thick and long and bewitchingly alluring, as she had been alluring, lay a tracery of shadow upon her delicate skin.

There was a fly, crawling between her softly parted lips.

For the longest time he just stood there, waiting. *In a moment, one of 'em will move. In a moment, one of 'em will breathe. Or blink. In a moment, I'll wake up and all this will be nowt but a damned stupid ale-born dream.*

*In a moment.*

He came to understand, at last, that there were no more moments. That not one of them would move, or breathe, or blink again. That he was already awake, and this was not a dream.

Memories came then, glowing like embers at the heart of a dying fire. '*Welcome, Asher. My son speaks so highly of you I just know we'll be the greatest of friends.*' Dana, Queen of Lur. Accepting his untutored bow and clumsy greeting as though he'd gifted her with perfumed roses and a diamond beyond price or purchase. Her unconstrained laughter, her listening silences. The way her eyes smiled in even the gravest of moments, a smile that said *I know you. I trust you. Trust me.*

Borne, his sallow cheeks silvered with tears. '*What does my kingdom hold that I can give you? He is my precious son and you saved him. For his mother. For me. For us all. You've lost your father, I'm told. I grieve with you. Shall I stand in his stead, Asher? Offer you a father's words of wisdom if ever you need to hear them spoken? May I do that? Let me.*'

And Fane, who smiled only if she thought it might do some damage. Who never knew herself well enough to know that beneath malice lay desire. Who was beautiful in every single way, save the one that mattered most.

Dead, dead and dead.

Bludgeoned to tearless silence, he stayed with them until to stay longer would be foolish. Stayed until the cold and dark from the valley floor crept up and over the lip of the ledge and sank icy teeth into his flesh. Until he remembered the last living member of this family, who had yet to be told he was the last.

Remembering that, he left them, reluctantly, and slowly climbed back up the side of the mountain.

# CHAPTER TWO

There were hands to help him over the broken railings at the top of Salbert's Eyrie.

'Easy does it,' said Pellen Orrick, holding his elbow with firm fingers. 'Catch your breath a moment. Are you all right?'

Bent over and heaving air into his lungs, aware of stinging scrapes and strained muscles, Asher nodded. 'Aye. Where's Matt?'

'Minding his own business back at the Tower.' Orrick frowned, and released his grasp. 'You know, Asher, some folk might say you were mad to climb down the side of the Eyrie. I might even be one of them. Was it worth the risk?'

Breathing easier, he slowly straightened. Some Doranen or other had conjured glimfire; a floating flotilla of magical lights turned the new night into a pale imitation of day. He looked into the Guard captain's shadowed, hatchet face and nodded again. 'Aye.'

Orrick's expression tightened. Then the tension left him and he sagged, just a little, and only for a heartbeat. 'You found them.'

There was nobody else within earshot. Orrick had set a line of guards to keep everyone away from the Eyrie's treacherous edge and further calamity. Beyond them, by the side of the road, clustered a group of agitated Doranen. Staring, Asher recognised Conroyd Jarralt and Barlsman Holze; Lords Daltrie, Hafar, Sorvold and Boqur: Jarralt's General Council cronies. No sign of Gar or Master Magician Durm, though. Doubtless they'd been rushed back to the palace and the eager bone-bothering of Pother Nix.

Further along the road stood two wagons, a fancy Doranen carriage and one of Orrick's men guarding coils of rope. With a pang of relief he saw Cygnet, still safely tied. An uneasy silence muffled the scene, broken only by the stamp of a hoof and snatches of sharp speech from the gathered Doranen lords.

'Asher?' said Orrick.

'Aye,' he said. 'I found 'em. The family, any road. Coachman Matcher's lying at the bottom of the valley, I reckon, along with one of his precious horses.'

'And you're certain they're dead?'

He laughed. Was he certain? *Red blood and white bone and black flies, crawling* . . . 'You want to go see for yourself?'

With a deep sigh, Orrick shook his head. 'Can their bodies be retrieved?'

He shrugged. 'Maybe. Reckon it'll take a hefty dose of magic and some luck, though.'

'Their position is precarious?'

'They're on a bit of a ledge stickin' out over the valley. You tell me if that be precarious or not.' Swept by a sudden, obliterating tide of exhaustion, Asher felt all the blood drain from his face and staggered where he stood. 'Damn,' he muttered.

'Easy now,' said Pellen Orrick, once more taking his arm. 'You've had a nasty shock.'

The captain's kindness was almost his undoing. Grief and rage and a hot swelling helplessness blurred his sight. He could feel his heart's brutal beating, solid blows against his ribs like the tolling of a funeral drum. The cold night air seared his struggling lungs and his teeth began to chatter like bones in a breeze. He felt wetness on his cheeks and looked up. Was it raining?

No. The starry sky was clear of cloud. And anyway, how could it be raining? Lur's WeatherWorker was dead. Furious, he blinked back the burning tears. *Tears*? Fool. Tears were for folks with time on their hands . . .

A shout went up from the cluster of Doranen dignitaries. Lord Hafar had spotted him. Pointing, he tugged at Conroyd Jarralt's brocade sleeve. Jarralt turned, frowning, mouth open to snap or snarl. Then he saw too. His chin came up, his shoulders braced and his teeth clicked closed. Vibrating with angry self-importance he broke away from the group . . . and so revealed its centre.

Revealed Gar.

Awoken to a fragile consciousness, the prince – no. Not any longer. Not after today. The *king* was sitting on a cushioned stool at the side of the road, draped in a blanket with a hasty bandage wound tight about his head. His left arm had been bound hard against his battered body to safeguard the broken collarbone. In his right hand he held a mug of something steaming, and stared into its depths as though it contained all the secrets of the world.

Conroyd Jarralt took another step forward, his jewelled fingers fisted at his sides. 'Asher!'

The sound of his name rang like a chapel bell calling for silence. The lords' muttering voices faltered. Stumbled.

Stilled, as step by step Asher shrank the distance between himself and his friend. His king.

Gar looked up. One pale eyebrow lifted, seeing him. And he realised there was no need for anything so crude as words. The truth was in his tears, still drying amidst the dirt, and the telltale pallor of his cheeks, nipped as cold as frostbite.

He reached the tangled knot of Doranen lords. Reached Gar, who looked into his rigid face with an air of calm enquiry. A polite patience. An absence of anything more powerful than a mild curiosity. He stopped and dropped to his knees. There was pain as his bones met the unyielding road. It scarcely registered. Hands by his side, shoulders defeated, filthy with dirt and sweat and little smears of other people's blood, he bowed his head.

'Your Majesty.'

From the watching lords, gasps. A cry, quickly stifled. A sob, smothered.

Somebody snickered.

Asher snapped up his head, disbelieving.

Gar was laughing. His face was mirthless, and his eyes, but still he laughed. The blanket around his shoulders shivered free. The scarce-touched contents of the mug slopped over its sides to splash dark stains on his ruined breeches. His nose began to run, and then his eyes, tears and mucus reflecting glimfire, glittering like liquid diamonds. And still he laughed.

Jarralt turned on him. 'Stop it!' he hissed. 'You disgrace yourself, sir, and shame our people! Stop it at once, do you hear?'

He might as well have saved his breath. Ignoring him, Gar continued to laugh, not stopping until Barlsman Holze came close to touch his unhurt shoulder with gentle fingertips.

'My boy,' he whispered. 'My dear, dear boy. Hush, now. Hush.'

Like an Olken toy running down its clockwork, the giggles bumped erratically into silence. Asher dragged a kerchief from his pocket and held it out. For some time the former prince just sat there, staring at the square of blue cotton. Then he took it and wiped his face. Handed back the soiled kerchief and said, 'I want to see them.'

The lords broke into a babble of protest.

'Don't be ridiculous,' snapped Conroyd Jarralt. 'It's out of the question.'

'Conroyd's right,' added Holze, and tried to lay a calming hand on Gar's arm. Gar shook him free, heedless of the pain, and stood. His expression was ominous. 'Truly, the idea is most unwise!' Holze persisted. 'Dear boy, think of the danger. You heard what Pother Nix's assistant said! You need warmth. Rest. More rigorous physicking. We must get you indoors, immediately. Come now. Listen to your elders, Your Hi – Your Ma – Gar. Be wisely guided, and leave this unfortunate place.'

The other lords echoed the demand. Asher, aware of Pellen Orrick now standing close behind, grunted to his feet and exchanged uneasy glances with him as the lords closed ranks about Gar and raised their voices in ever more vehement argument.

Gar let the storm of words rage unchecked. Seemed almost not to hear his clamouring subjects. His frowning gaze was focused somewhere distant, pinned to something only he could see. Then, at last, he stirred. Lifted his hand.

'Enough.'

Ignoring him, the lords continued their clamour.

'*Enough*, I said!' The lords fell back, shocked. Stared

at the glimfire flaring from Gar's fingertips as his newly focused gaze swept all their dumbfounded faces. 'Is this how you speak to your king?'

Conroyd Jarralt stepped forward. 'You presume a title not yet conferred, Your *Highness*.' He turned to Asher. 'You.'

This was no time for lord-baiting. Asher bowed. 'Sir.'

'Borne's death is not in doubt?'

He shuddered. 'No. King, queen and princess. They're all dead down there.'

Grief rippled through the Doranen. Jarralt, the only one unmoved, stared at him with eyes like frozen silver. Then he glared at Gar. 'Even so. Until both councils have met and the proper ceremonies been observed, you are yet a prince, sir. Not king.'

Gar clenched his fingers and the glimfire died. 'You challenge my claim?'

'I challenge your presumption. Scant hours have passed since your father's death. Before the succession is settled there are questions to be asked, and answered, in the matter of His Majesty's destruction.'

'What questions?'

Jarralt waved an impatient hand. 'This is neither the time nor the—'

'I disagree,' said Gar. 'It is the only place, and if you don't ask here and now I swear you never will.'

Holze insinuated himself between them. 'Gar, Conroyd, please. This is unseemly, the bodies cannot yet be cold. Desist, I implore you, in Barl's—'

'No,' said Gar. 'I would hear Lord Jarralt's question.'

Jarralt's lips thinned in an angry smile. 'Very well. Since you insist. How is it that you survived the accident barely touched when the rest of your family is so dreadfully perished?'

Gar's answering smile was winter cold. 'You forget Durm.'

'Our esteemed Master Magician is unlikely to live through the night. Come the dawn, I warrant, there will be only you.'

'You accuse me of *murder*, Lord Jarralt? Of killing my father, my mother, my sister—'

'Your unloved sister,' said Jarralt. 'Who scant days ago tried to kill you.' He nodded at the edge of bandage peeping beyond Gar's shirt cuff. 'I believe the wound is yet unhealed.'

'So, Conroyd. You are a man who listens to servants' gossip,' said Gar. 'How . . . disappointing.'

Jarralt's face darkened. 'It pleases you to insult me. Very well. But how long will your arrogance last once I have undertaken enquiries as to precisely how this accident unfolded? When I—'

'As to that, my lord,' said Pellen Orrick, 'any investigation into these, deaths falls to me. As Captain of the City it is my right, and my responsibility.'

'Indeed?' said Jarralt, skewering Orrick with contempt. 'And why should I trust your impartiality? Or your competence?'

'Because the late king trusted them, sir,' Orrick said quietly.

'And if you discover foul play, Captain?' said Holze. 'What then?'

Orrick's hatchet face sharpened. 'Then I will pursue the murderer to the ends of the kingdom. He or she will find no escape and receive no mercy . . . regardless of rank, social status or privilege.'

Gar nodded. 'Satisfied, Conroyd? Good. Now if you'll move aside, I intend to visit a while with my family!'

Alarmed and helpless, Asher watched Gar take two staggering steps towards the edge of the Eyrie. Unbidden, Lords Daltrie and Sorvold reached for his arms in an effort to restrain him.

It was a mistake.

'*Let be*!' Gar shouted. A golden light shimmered into life around him. The lords unwisely touching him cried out and snatched their hands away.

Conroyd Jarralt's hand went to the sheathed knife on his hip. 'You see?' he demanded. 'He uses magic as a weapon! Prince Gar is unfit for any kind of authority! He knows nothing about being a true Doranen! He is a precocious, undisciplined child who cannot be trusted with the power so newly come upon him!'

'You're the one who can't be trusted!' Gar spat. 'All your life you've coveted my father's throne and now he's dead you think to take it! Well, think again, Conroyd. There was more kingship in my father's little finger than you possess in all your body. I'll see this kingdom a smoking ruin before ever I see you on its throne!'

Jarralt raised a shaking fist. 'Just like your father, you overstep all bounds. Magic or no magic, you're not fit to rule! You're nothing but the unnatural offspring of a selfish and short-sighted fool!'

Gar's golden aura deepened. Flared crimson, like a fire fed fresh fuel. Jarralt was forced half a pace backwards. 'Stand in Justice Hall and say that, Conroyd,' Gar whispered. 'I dare you. Stand in Justice Hall and see what the people reply.'

Conroyd Jarralt sneered. '*The people*. That undisciplined rabble of Olken? That's who you'd call for your support? You wretched boy, if they are all you can rely upon then—'

Dismayed, Asher jumped as Pellen Orrick leaned close and whispered urgently, 'Do something, Asher, quick, before the fools go too far.'

'*Me*?' He stared. 'Why *me*?'

'Because you're the only one here the prince'll listen to.'

Gar was shaking, his face screwed up against every kind of pain. 'Is this disaster your doing, Conroyd? Is your appetite for power so ravenous you'd *kill* to feed it? My father, my mother—'

'*Kill your mother*?' Heedless of Gar's crimson mantle of power, of his torn flesh and broken bone, Jarralt grabbed him by the shirt front and dragged him to his toe-tips. 'You pathetic little worm, I *loved* your mother!' he cried. 'I love her still! If she'd married me she'd be alive this minute! If she'd married me I'd have given her a *real* prince! A son she could be *proud* of!'

'My lords!' shouted Asher, and threw himself at Jarralt. Snatched at the incensed man's hands and dragged them free of Gar's shirt, then shoved Gar in the chest, heedless of the danger, sending him staggering back two paces. 'For *shame*, sirs, both of you! The royal family dead and you brawling like drunken sots in an alehouse!'

Jarralt turned on him, snarling. 'Lay hands on me again and I'll see you strung from a gibbet before sunrise!'

Holze chimed in, parchment-grey with distress. 'No, Conroyd, no, the boy's right. You must control yourselves – this dreadful business – set an example—' The elderly cleric's eyes were full of tears. Behind him the other Doranen lords dithered, paralysed by protocol and surprise. 'His Highness is overwrought, he spoke out of grief and shock, you can't think he'd believe that you

– that *anyone* – would deliberately harm our king and his family! And you, Conroyd, you spoke unthinking too. This terrible tragedy – we are all of us in dreadful disarray. Your Highness—'

The crimson glow around Gar was fading fast. His face had emptied too, of fury, of passion, leaving only pain. He looked confused. Bewildered. 'My lords – I don't – I feel—' An enormous shudder racked him head to foot, and he blanched dead white. 'Barl help me,' he murmured as his eyes rolled back in his head.

Asher leapt and caught him before he thudded to the road. 'Gar!'

The prince was a sprawling dead weight, he had to let him go, let him sag to the ground despite his wounds and broken bone.

'His Highness shouldn't be here,' Asher said to Holze as the cleric knelt and took Gar's unharmed wrist to chafe. 'He needs to go home.'

'He needs a good physicking first,' said Holze, and looked about him. 'Conroyd . . .?'

Without a word, Jarralt came forward. Dropped to one knee, slipped his arms beneath Gar and stood easily, the prince cradled against his chest.

'Into the carriage with him, Conroyd,' said Holze, regaining his feet with Asher's help. 'He must be seen by Nix as soon as possible. The rest of us will have to make do in one of the wagons. I'm sure the experience won't kill us.' Realising what he'd said, he flinched.

'You ain't goin' back with him?' said Asher, surprised.

Holze shook his head. 'No, no. There are things to do here first. A shrine. A prayer candle. I brought all the necessaries with me.'

Asher nodded. 'Reckon Gar'll appreciate that. And the king.'

'Yes, well . . .' For a moment, fresh grief threatened. Then Holze mastered himself and flapped a hand at Jarralt. 'Don't just stand there, Conroyd! Go!'

Trailing after them, Asher waited until Gar was stowed safe and silent in the lushly upholstered vehicle with Conroyd Jarralt by his side. 'Take His Highness to the palace infirmary, my lord,' he said as the carriage door was pulled shut between them. 'I reckon Nix must be waiting for him on pins and needles.'

Jarralt's handsome face was all sharp lines and smooth planes. Cold. Remote. Like the Flatlands in the depths of winter. 'Yes. I expect he is.'

'My lord . . .' Asher hesitated, then plunged on. 'I can't believe this weren't a terrible accident, but if Captain Orrick finds otherwise . . . you have to know. Gar ain't the one responsible.'

For a little while Jarralt sat in continued silence. Then he turned his head, just enough, and met Asher's gaze directly. 'Nor am I.'

Asher nodded. Lied. 'I believe you. Sir.'

Jarralt's look was icy enough to freeze a man solid where he stood. 'And what makes you think I give one good damn about what you do or don't believe?' His hand slapped the carriage door's painted panel. 'Coachman! To the Tower!'

Pellen Orrick patted Asher's shoulder as he joined him in the middle of the road. Together they watched the glimlit carriage disappear around the first bend. 'Well done, Asher,' he said. 'A nasty moment neatly turned. If ever you get tired of life in the prince's employ I'm sure I could find a place for you in the Guard.'

'I got to go,' said Asher. His head was aching so badly he thought it might explode. 'There's folks back at the Tower wondering what's amiss, and prob'ly ready to raise the roof by now. What are you goin' to do about the bodies?'

'Tonight?' Orrick shrugged. 'Nothing. Even with magic and glimfire it's too dangerous to retrieve them in the dark. I'll leave the lads here to keep watch and return with help at first light.'

Cautiously, Asher nodded. 'Just one problem with that. You're forgettin' Matcher. We got his wife and family sittin' at home as we speak, expectin' him to walk through the door any minute. And then there's the lads at the palace stables. They'll miss the horses.'

'Damn,' said Pellen Orrick. 'Yes. All right. Leave it to me. I'll send senior officers. Make sure the news doesn't spread.'

'Fine,' he said, relieved. 'So I'll be off, then. See you tomorrow some time.'

Orrick nodded. 'Yes. You will.'

Asher trudged away. Cygnet was anxiously pleased to see him, all snorts and whickers and impatient stamping. Holze conjured a small ball of travelling glimfire to light his way home and blessed him with unsteady hands.

'You served Barl well tonight, young man,' the cleric said as Asher hauled himself into the saddle. 'I shall remember you in my prayers.'

Looking down at him, Asher nodded. 'Reckon we're all goin' to need prayin' for by the time this mess is sorted.'

'Indeed,' Holze said soberly. 'Indeed.' And stood back as Asher clapped his heels to Cygnet's sides and bounded away.

It wasn't till he was long past Jarralt's sedately travelling carriage and almost back at the Tower that Asher realised he'd spent the last little while giving orders to some of the most powerful Doranen in the kingdom . . . and the Doranen had obeyed him.

Arrived at last in the Tower stable yard, after handing Cygnet over to Boonie for a rubdown and his mash, he found Matt tending a colt that had kicked its way out of a transport cart and was pincushioned with splinters for its trouble. A look and a headshake were all he needed to give the bad news. Matt's face lost some colour, and his hands shook a little as he eased another spike of wood from the injured colt's neck.

'Barl bless them,' he said, dropping the splinter into the basin at his feet. 'We'll talk later?'

'Aye,' said Asher, turning away. 'Later.'

It was a short walk from the stables to the Tower. Hollow, dreading the confrontations to come, he dragged his feet through the pathway's raked gravel and thought it might be nice to drop down dead of a seizure just about now. So he wouldn't have to open the Tower's front door. Wouldn't have to go inside. Wouldn't have to see the faces of the people he knew were waiting there, for him, for news. Waiting to be told not to worry, it were all a false alarm.

Waiting in vain.

The Tower's front doors stood slightly ajar. He took a deep breath. Wrapped his fingers around each brass handle. Pushed hard and stepped inside.

'I sent everyone home,' said Darran, rising from his chair at the foot of the staircase. 'It seemed pointless to keep them loitering about here for hours on end.'

'Pointless,' Asher said slowly, shoving the doors shut behind him. 'Aye.'

Fingers laced precisely across his concave middle, Darran took three steps forward then stopped. 'Well?'

Anyone who didn't know him would think he was in complete control of his emotions. 'Is he dead?'

Adrift in the middle of the empty foyer, Asher blinked. 'No.' All of a sudden he was feeling very tired. He needed a chair. Hadn't there been more chairs in here this morning? 'Just banged up a bit. Jarralt's takin' him to see Pother Nix now.'

'*Lord* Jarralt,' said Darran automatically. 'Asher?'

He dragged his sagging eyelids open. 'What?'

'Is anybody dead?'

He turned away. The maggoty ole fool was goin' to go *spare* when he heard.

'*Asher.*'

Turning back, he shoved his hands into his pockets. Forced himself to look into Darran's haggard face. 'Not Durm. Durm's alive. Or he was when I saw him last.' He shrugged. 'Just.'

'I don't care about Durm,' said Darran.

'You should. 'Cause if he don't pull through and speak up for Gar's magic I reckon we're all in a mess of trouble.'

Darran hardly seemed to hear him. 'Who else? You said not Durm. Very well. Who else lives . . . aside from him and Gar?'

It was the first time he'd ever heard the ole scarecrow refer to Gar as anything other than 'the prince' or 'His Highness'. It frightened him. 'Nobody,' he said, brutal. 'All right? His whole family's dead. Oh, and Matcher too. And the horses. Better not forget the poor bloody horses, eh? All of 'em dead. Lyin' in bits and pieces on the side of Salbert's Eyrie. Now, were there anythin' else you wanted to know?'

A thin, disbelieving moan escaped Darran's alarmingly blue lips. His fingers unlaced. Clutched at his chest. He began to sag at the knees.

Asher leapt at him. 'Don't you dare! You fart, you bugger, you silly cross-eyed crow! Don't you bloody *dare*!'

Grunting with the effort he lowered Darran to the tiled foyer floor and wrenched open the sober black coat and the weskit beneath. Scrabbled at the old man's plain cravat, loosening its knot, then tugged open the pristine white shirt. The old fool's chest heaved for air, thin as a toast-rack covered with a tea towel. There were tears in his eyes, welling and welling like a magic fountain. He needed a pillow or something to rest on. Asher looked around, grabbed a cushion from the solitary foyer chair and rescued Darran's head from the floor.

Then, helpless, he chewed at his lip. Now what? He weren't a pother, he had no idea what to do next. Dimwitted ole fart, sending away all the staff, even the messenger boys. He grabbed Darran's right arm, shoved back the coat and shirt sleeves and chafed the blueveined wrist, thin and pale and knobbly.

'Come on, now,' he said desperately. 'There's been enough death around here for one day, you ole crow. Gar won't thank you for peggin' out on him. He's to be king now, he'll need you for that. If you ain't here to keep him organised they might ask Willer, and that little sea slug couldn't organise a piss-up in a brewery!'

Darran tried to frown. His lips worked soundlessly for a moment, then he whispered, 'Willer – my assistant – you show respect—'

'That's more like it,' he said, grinning with relief. 'Just you lie there and breathe, Meister Scarecrow. In and out, in and out, and don't you dare think of stoppin'.'

Darran's eyes fluttered closed, but his chest continued to rise and fall. Asher released the old man's wrist and sat back on his heels. He could feel sweat trickling down his spine and gluing his hair to his scalp. He needed a bath. And food. His empty belly growled at the thought. But bloody Darran had sent the cook away. He'd have to risk her wrath and raid the kitchen for whatever was lying about. And he would, too . . . just as soon as he could be sure Darran wasn't going to cause him even more trouble than usual by dying.

Then he looked up, because the Tower doors were swinging open. It was Gar. On his own two feet and walking. A step behind him, Conroyd Jarralt. They saw Darran and halted.

'Barl save me,' said Gar. Looking and sounding like a man who'd lost his last hope of happiness. 'Is he—'

'No,' he said, scrambling off the floor. 'What are you doin' here, you're s'posed to be on your way to see Nix!'

'I came to tell Darran what happened.'

He spared Jarralt an accusing glance, then said, 'Aye, well, I already told him. Can you get him to Nix? Now?'

Not looking at Jarralt, Gar nodded. 'My lord?'

In searing silence Jarralt helped Asher get the groggy old man out to the waiting carriage. Gar followed behind, somehow managing to keep his own self upright.

'You need me?' said Asher, once Darran was settled against the plush velvet cushions and Gar had climbed in beside him.

'Yes,' said Gar.

'Ride with the coachman,' said Jarralt curtly, and climbed into the carriage.

Biting his tongue, Asher obeyed.

The Royal Infirmary was located in a wing off the palace's main building, with its own driveway and entrance and courtyard for privacy and peace. Willing hands assisted Darran inside. Offered to help Gar and were coldly rebuffed. No longer required, Jarralt departed with little more than a correct bow. Gar nodded austere thanks, Asher heaved a sigh of relief and the infirmary assistants barely noticed.

A carry-chair was produced for the ailing old man to rest in and a couple of servants summoned to do the carrying. A spare pother, hastily produced, took one look at Darran and Gar, tut-tutted, and trotted them off to the person who knew best how to handle difficult patients.

Asher, hovering close by Gar in case of another collapse, prayed hard under his breath for strength. The smells in this place were making his head swim. If he didn't get out of here sooner rather than later the infirmary's manky bone-botherers were going to have one more patient on their hands.

After a short trip along narrow, quiet corridors they found Nix standing in some kind of three-sided reception area, complete with desk and chairs and several potted plants. There was a closed door in each wall, each painted a different colour: blue, green and deep crimson. The Royal Pother stood before the crimson door, washing his bloodied hands in a basin held by one assistant, while dictating notes to another.

'—twice hourly, with a goodly compound of urval, goatsfoot and stranglepus rubbed well into the unstitched wounds,' Nix recited, his eyes half-closed in thought. Reaching for the towel draped over the basin-holder's forearm, he pursed his lips. 'For the stitched wounds, dust every four hours with powdered grassle. In an hour we'll—' Suddenly aware of a wider audience, he stopped drying his hands and refocused his attention. Saw Darran slumped in the carry-chair, tossed aside the towel and went to him.

'Well?' said Gar.

Nix looked up from his gentle examination. 'He'll do.'

'And Durm?'

Nix turned to the basin-holder. 'Wulf, fetch Pother Tobin.' To the chair-carriers he said, 'Take His Highness's secretary into the green chamber.'

'Tobin?' said Gar, watching Darran's departure. 'No. I want you to—'

'Tobin will see your Darran right, never fear,' said Nix. 'He's had a heart spasm but he's in no immediate danger.'

'Very well,' said Gar after a moment. 'Then take me to Durm.'

Nix shook his head. 'Not yet.'

Beneath the churning pain in Gar's eyes, a flare of heat. 'It wasn't a request, Nix.'

'Not yet,' said Nix stubbornly. 'He needs quiet, not company. Think of him, sir, not yourself.'

Asher risked a touch to Gar's rigid, uninjured arm. 'Durm's in good hands. Get yourself seen to. You're set to fall arse over eyeballs any moment.'

Gar's glance was like a whiplash. 'Did I ask you?'

'No,' said Asher, holding his ground. 'Don't mean I'm wrong, though.'

Nix held out his hand. 'Come, Your Highness.' His voice was gentle now. Coaxing. 'Let me heal you. And then I'll take you to Durm.'

Swaying on his feet, Gar capitulated. Allowed himself to be led away like a docile child.

Uninvited, Asher followed.

# CHAPTER THREE

Nix led the way to his book-lined, herb-infested office. The chamber's air was thick with hints of potions past, reluctantly swallowed. Cheerful flames leapt in a small fireplace; the room was stiflingly warm.

'Right then,' he said, planting himself between desk and scarred workbench. 'Now that we're beyond sight and sound of nuisance, let's see the truth of the matter, shall we, Your Highness? Time to strip, please, down to your skin.'

Too battered and weary for further protest, Gar let Nix and Asher between them ease him out of his hasty bandages and ruined, bloodstained clothes. With memories of his own past hurts resurfacing, Asher was as gentle as he could be, wincing as the full extent of Gar's injuries were revealed. Breathing unevenly, Gar cradled his left arm with his right hand and waited for the ordeal to end.

'Hmmph,' said the pother, inspecting the prince like a man at a horse auction. A frown pinched his bushy grey and yellow eyebrows together as his blunt fingers skimmed the surface of Gar's insulted body, marking each cut, each scrape, each ripening bruise. Air hissed between Gar's clenched teeth as Nix's fingers lightly traced the irregular line of the broken collarbone.

He felt Gar's skull, took his pulse, listened to his heartbeat and breathing, checked the coating on his tongue and the clarity of his eyes. 'Any idea how long you were stunned out of your senses?'

'No,' said Gar. 'I remember – I think I remember – flying through the air. Hitting the ground. I know I woke twice. Tried to get up, go for help . . . I couldn't even stand.'

'It were mid-morning when you left,' said Asher. 'And dusk when me and Matt found you.'

'Hmmph,' said Nix. 'A goodly brain rattling, then. You'll need a day or three in bed, to guard against conniptions.'

'Bed?' Gar pulled a face. 'I think not.'

'Did you know I've an excellent cure for an argumentative patient, sir?' Nix asked, eyes narrowed. 'It involves needle, thread and meals sucked through a straw.'

'Spare me your dubious wit!' retorted Gar. 'Your king is dead and his heir with him! It falls to me now to continue his legacy. Do you tell me I can do so from my *bed*?'

Suddenly pale, and with tears in his eyes, Nix jabbed Gar's chest with a pointed finger. 'I tell you, sir, that as Royal Pother I am charged with the gravest responsibility: the care of this kingdom's physical wellbeing in the body of its WeatherWorker. With Borne's death, may Barl keep him, that body is now yours. From this day forth you belong to Lur, first and foremost. And in the pursuit of my sacred duty as your pother I will allow you no secrets, grant you no privacies, spare you no shame and brook no argument. If I say you must rest you *will* rest. For upon your health depends the welfare of Barl's Wall and the kingdom it protects. The lives of every last man, woman and child. Because of this your health is *my* kingdom and in this room *I* am king. Do you understand?'

As Gar stared at Nix in silent shock, Asher sighed. 'He's right. And no, you didn't ask me.'

'I didn't have to,' said Gar. His voice was a strangled whisper. 'Of course he's right.'

Gentle again, Nix lightly touched Gar's shoulder. 'Sit, sir, while I collect what's needful.'

There was a chair close by. Asher helped Gar into it, then stood back. More than anything he wanted to drape himself over the desk or lean against a handy stretch of wall, but protocol dictated otherwise. And Nix would probably throw something at him for making a mess.

The pother went to his office door, pulled it three inches wide and barked through the opening: 'Kerril! Fetch me a quarter-cup of janjavet with two drops of dursle root essence added after pouring. Also a measure of bee-blossom. Quickly!'

While he waited for his subordinate to bring him the requested potions, Nix rummaged in a cupboard and withdrew four cork-sealed pots, a bluestone mortar and pestle and a small clear vial of something green and viscous. After depositing them on the crowded bench he rolled up his dangling sleeves and got to work. The smell as he pounded each ingredient in the pestle was vile.

Gar stirred and looked up, his expression apprehensive. 'You expect me to swallow that?'

A tap on the door indicated Kerril's return. 'No,' replied Nix as he pushed the door shut and handed Gar one of the cups Kerril had given him. 'This.'

Gar sniffed the liquid suspiciously. 'What is it?'

'Something to dull the pain while I fix that broken collarbone,' said Nix, standing over him. 'Bone-knitting's not the gentlest of healing magic.'

The pother's expression was sympathetic but unyielding. Gar spared him a single burning look then shuddered and tossed the potion down his throat.

'Barl's mercy!' he gasped, and started gagging. 'Are you trying to poison me?'

'I'd advise you not to vomit, sir,' said Nix, returning to his mortar and pestle. He added the bee-blossom and resumed pounding. 'You'll only have to drink another lot and I'm told it tastes even worse the second time. Now just sit quietly while it takes effect and I finish this ointment.'

Still gagging, Gar dropped the cup and hunched over, fisted fingers pressed to his mouth. A few moments later, Nix was ready.

Eyes closed, words whispering under his breath, the pother laid his hands on Gar's broken collarbone. At his touch a spark of light ignited. Became a flame. His fingers began to dance up and down the bone's irregular length, drumming lightly, and the flame danced with them.

Asher had never seen a Doranen bone-knitting before, although he had friends who'd required it after a squall off Tattler's Ear Cove rattled them like thrown knuckle-bones from bow to stern in their fishing smack. 'Hurt like blazes,' Beb and Joffet had told him with identical grimacing shudders.

Clearly, Gar would agree. Even with the pain-dulling potion his face was salty white and shiny with sweat, and his breathing came hard and harsh. Small grunts escaped him, and his right hand spasmed on the arm of the chair.

'Nearly done,' Nix murmured. The flame beneath his fingers was a furnace now; Asher imagined he could feel the heat of it in his own flesh, and winced. 'Take a nice deep breath,' said Nix. 'And hold – hold – hold—'

With a final burst of light and a sharp command the broken bone beneath the pother's hands snapped back into place. Gar shouted, and would have flung himself out of the chair if Nix hadn't restrained him. Flinching in sympathy Asher watched the healer cradle Gar hard against the magic's tormenting aftermath, patting his back and clucking like an old hen.

'There now, there now, that's the worst over, I swear it.'

Slowly, Gar recovered. Straightened, and pushed Nix away. 'I'm fine, stop fussing,' he muttered.

Nix returned to his bench and retrieved the mortar of stinking ointment. 'Stand up for me, Your Highness. We'll just test that arm first, then take care of your bumps and scrapes.'

His breathing still a little unsteady, Gar stood. Lifted his left arm above his head, waved it in circles, clenched his hand to a fist and pulled his elbow tight to his side.

'Excellent,' said Nix. 'Another day and you'll never know it was damaged. Now for the rest of you.'

In swift silence he daubed his pungent green concoction onto Gar's hurts. Seconds after touching the damaged flesh it melted out of sight. The dried blood faded, and with it the ointment's eye-watering smell. A thin protective film now coated each wound.

'There,' said Nix at last. 'Better?'

Gar touched cautious fingertips to his cut forehead. Pressed them against his torn hip, thigh, ribs. 'Better.' He let his hand rest on Nix's arm for a moment. 'My thanks.'

Nix nodded. 'You'll take the ointment with you. Apply it morning and night for three days. You'll be healed by then.'

'Yes,' said Gar. 'I'll do that. But as for staying in bed, Nix . . .'

The pother heaved a disgruntled sigh. 'I know. I know. The burden of kingship cannot be laid down.' He turned to Asher. 'I charge you to keep a close eye on him. Send for me at the slightest suspicion of weakness, or collapse.'

Asher nodded. 'I will.'

'And now,' said Gar, 'I will see Durm.'

Asher looked at him sidelong. 'Dressed like that?'

Gar's reply was to close his eyes, frame four silent words with still-colourless lips, and with the fingers of his left hand trace in the chamber's warm air a complicated sigil. Two heartbeats later he was holding shirt, trews and a weskit in his arms.

The effort dropped him back to the chair.

'You didn't let me finish,' said Nix, reproving. 'No magic for a week.'

Stippled with sweat, Gar shook his head. 'I must. The WeatherWorking—'

'Will wait. Schedules can be adjusted. Performing magic in your condition could cripple you.'

*Cripple*. It was a word laden with bitter memory.

'Fine,' Gar said curtly. Shakily he stood again and, with slow deliberation, began to dress.

Nix busied himself emptying the rest of the mortar's ointment into a small jar. 'And you, Asher,' he said. 'There's blood on your hands.'

Asher looked. True, there was. Not all of it his, though. Most of it not his. But how could he say that, in Gar's hearing? He shrugged. 'Scraped knuckles. I'm fine.'

'Show me.'

He shoved his hands under Nix's nose. The pother ran his experienced gaze over the cuts, dabbed them with ointment, then stoppered the jar with a cork and held it out. 'There's enough here for you, too. Both of you use it, or I'll know the reason why.'

Asher looked up from his tingling hands. 'Yes, sir.'

Behind them Gar fastened the last button on his weskit. 'Durm,' he said. His face and voice brooked no opposition. 'Now.'

Pother Tobin was waiting for them in the reception area. When she saw Gar, she bowed.

'Your secretary is resting comfortably, Your Highness. He's been given a good strong dose of heartsease and should be well enough for visitors come the morning.'

Gar nodded. 'My thanks.' As the pother bowed again, retreating, he turned to Nix. 'Where is Durm?'

Nix nodded at the reception area's crimson door. 'In there. But before you see him, I must caution you. His injuries are grave, his appearance . . . unsettling. I have done all I can for him. What happens now is up to his constitution, and Barl's mercy.'

Gar didn't reply immediately. His gaze wandered round the hushed reception area for long moments, touching on the bright-painted doors, the windowless walls, the potted plants. His expression was distant. Unmoved. 'Will he live?'

Nix pursed his lips. 'I'm a healer, sir. Not a soothsayer.'

There was a pother in Durm's room, seated in a chair beside the patient's bed. She stood as they entered the windowless chamber. Glimfire sconces threw small shadows onto the cream-coloured walls and a fire kept any chill at bay. At a signal from Nix she left them, closing the crimson door behind her.

Supported by mysterious pother magic, Durm floated some eight inches above a high, wide platform fitted on all four sides with wooden railings. To Asher it seemed there wasn't a single square inch of the man's naked skin that wasn't stitched or stained or stretched with splints. Indeed, the massive head wound was embroidered so thickly his hairless scalp looked infested with caterpillars. His eyes, once as cold and piercing as spears of ice, were now invisible, consumed by the bloated purple flesh of his face.

Gar checked when he saw him, one hand coming up in a fierce denial. 'Barl have mercy,' he whispered, a small wounded sound in the silence. 'If I didn't know it was him . . .' He managed a step closer. 'Why haven't you knitted his bones, Nix? You can't leave him broken like this!'

'Bone-knitting would most likely kill him,' said Nix. 'We'll get to that, in time.' *If he lives*. The words hung unspoken between them.

'His stupor . . .'

'A result of the head injury. It is . . . severe.'

'Will he wake?'

'Perhaps.'

'With his wits?'

Nix shrugged. 'Unknown.'

'How long? Before he wakes? Before you do know.'

Nix frowned, but answered. 'Days, certainly. Most likely weeks.'

Reluctantly, Gar dragged his gaze away from the monstrosity hovering over the bed. 'But not months. It can't be months, Nix. The WeatherWorking. My succession. This kingdom needs him! *I* need him!'

'I know that,' said Nix. 'And if he can be healed, sir, I will heal him and return him to you.'

'*If?*'

Nix sighed, and clasped his hands behind his back. The unspoken words would have to be spoken. 'You must forgive my plain speaking, Your Highness, but I see no point in prevarication. To be blunt, I hold little hope.'

Gar's face was chilled and chalk-white. Staring wide-eyed at Durm he said, 'But little is not the same as none.'

'No,' Nix replied after a cautious pause. 'No, it's not.'

Asher watched as Gar moved to Durm's bedside like a man entranced. When the prince spoke, his voice was the merest thread.

'I loved him once, and then I hated him. Now I don't know what I feel . . .' He fell silent, struggling for words. 'Except fear. I've known him all my life. He is as much my family as my father, my mother, my sister. If he dies . . . I am truly alone.'

He sounded bereft. Knifed to the soul.

Nix stepped forward and rested his hand on Gar's shoulder. 'No, sir,' he said, his voice rough with tears. 'Not alone. Never alone while there is breath in my body.'

Asher cleared his throat. Banished tears of his own. *Da. Da.* 'Nor mine,' he added. 'Gar . . . let's go. There ain't nothing you can do for Durm . . . and you need sleep.'

Gar's stricken gaze continued to feast on the unconscious Master Magician. 'No. No, I can't leave him.'

Nix's fingers tightened. 'You can't stay,' he said gently. 'Indeed, your presence might well hinder, not help. I will send for you the moment there is any change.'

For a moment Asher thought Gar would fight them.

Then the prince – the king – sighed deeply. Touched two fingertips to his lips and pressed them lightly to Durm's cheek.

'Come back to me, Durm,' he whispered. 'I can't go on without you.' Then he let Nix shepherd him to the chamber's crimson door.

Asher followed them out, and didn't look back.

*Trapped in his prison of spoiled and spoiling flesh, Morg screams and screams. Wherever he is, he is not alone. There are voices somewhere close, nearby, but they click-clack on the edge of hearing and he cannot reach them or understand what they say. Struggling like a spider tangled in its own web he battles to make sense of this new reality.*

*Durm's body is broken and bleeding. Only his own indomitable will keeps the fat fool's flesh alive, his spirit from oblivion. The sluggish blood is soaked in drugs, enveloping and deadening and holding him fast, but still he is assaulted by pain. It is centuries since last he felt such a sensation. It is insulting.*

*His predicament is insulting.*

*He is Morg, far beyond the pettiness of physicality in all its incarnations, yet he is caught. Against every expectation, and in the face of all his power, he is bound to this lump of sundered meat. Shackled to its fate. Slave to its destiny. If Durm dies, he dies.*

*The shock is enough to threaten his reason.*

*How can this be? he wails. I am Morg! I am invincible!*

*Death, his bitter and once-beaten enemy, is laughing at him. Waiting in the shadows and laughing. It rubs its greedy hands with glee as it waits for the fat fool's body to die. For the spell to fail, and so release Morg's spirit to destruction.*

*No, cries Morg. You have not won. I will not die. I am Morg and my name means Victory! You cannot defeat me. You will never defeat me. There is a way. There has to be a way. Am I not immortal? Immortal beings cannot die! I cannot die!*

*Yes, you can, says Death. In this place and time, you can.*

*Morg knows Death speaks the truth, and despairs. For the first time in centuries, he is desperate. Faced with circumstances he did not create and cannot control. For the first time in centuries, he feels fear. The damage done to this borrowed body is dire. Even with his vast powers it still might plunge into Death's greedy abyss, taking him with it.*

*And if not – if he does manage to keep the fat fool alive – what if Durm is permanently crippled? His faculties deranged? If the pothers cannot mend this broken frame it will be no use at all. What then? Will he be forced to endure eternity inside Durm's ruined body?*

*Morg howls at the thought, twisting and turning and beating the bars of his cage. Durm's sickly flesh rebels at his fury. The failing heart fails further, and the labouring lungs deflate. Panicked, Morg abandons profitless emotion and focuses his will. Beat, heart! Breathe, lungs!*

*Resentfully, dying Durm obeys him.*

*Morg reflects. He is in this place for one reason only: to tear down Barl's Wall in all its golden glory and grind her treacherous heart's descendants into the dirt so he might claim the last square inches of the world for his own. To do that, he needs a host. And if Durm can no longer serve that purpose, he must find another host who can.*

*Another host . . .*

*He has no idea if such a transfer is even possible.*

*I will make it possible, vows Morg. I am limitless, and I will finish what I started. After that, fat Durm can die, and welcome. Along with all his friends.*

*Time marches, and with it the events he has set in motion. Soon the black toad magic planted within the cripple's mind will warp, and shrivel, and die. He must be there to see it. He must be alive to savour the moment, nectar on the tongue, and birth the bloody days that will usher in the end of the world as these poor fools have known it.*

*I am Morg, he sighs. Immortal and invincible. I feel no pain. I feel no fear. Reaching out his mind, he wraps the fraying thread of Durm's life around his fisted intellect and bends his will towards eternity.*

*Live, Durm, he croons into the echoing spaces around him. Live, fat fool. For I am Morg, and I'm not done with you yet.*

Matt sighed, then stretched his back. It had taken far longer than he'd thought, but at last the injured colt was plucked free of splinters, sticky with ointments and drowsing in the deep straw of its stable. Finally done with physicking he smoothed his hand down an unspoiled length of dappled grey neck, then leaned against the nearest wall. He was alone now, and waiting, all the lads dismissed for the night. It was just him and his horses, the way he liked it best. The colt flicked its ears at him and he stroked it again, seeking comfort in the warmth of living flesh beneath his hand.

Pushed far away where he couldn't feel it, pain lurked like a wolf in the woods. All the royal family save Gar was dead, and tomorrow the City would wake to a world unimagined. What this meant for him and Dathne, for Veira and the rest of the Circle, for Gar, for Asher, he had no idea. He was too tired now to think of it. Too tired, and too afraid. The shadows in his life had crept much closer, were touching him now with chilly darkness and surprise. He'd been looking for them, and still they'd caught him unawares.

Silence settled inside the stable and out. Matt closed his eyes and let himself settle with it. Let himself breathe, just breathe, and sought out the subtle shift and sway of the energies swirling invisible through the night air. Unfurled his gift and asked it to taste the flux and flow of magics in the world.

Something was different. Something was . . . missing.

Frowning, he tried to pin down the sensation. What was its cause? Not death, though the death of King Borne was momentous. Powerful Doranen had died before now and he'd not detected any great change in the world. The silence their passing created was soon smothered by the voices left behind.

No. This had something to do with the other change he'd felt. The one that had stood the hair on the back of his neck in a kind of creeping horror the first time he'd noticed it. The one he couldn't begin to explain, to Dathne or himself. A single discordant note in the choir of Lur's magic, thin and sharp and sour. Poison, to a man with his knack of feeling the world.

That note had fallen silent. After weeks of hearing its soft, malevolent voice he'd almost grown accustomed; its sudden absence now sounded louder than a shout.

But *why*? Why had it disappeared, as abruptly as first it arrived? Entirely disconcerted, he stretched his senses to their limits in an effort to find the answer.

An edgily amused voice said, 'You look like a man sniffing milk to see if it's gone off.'

Matt sighed and opened his eyes. 'Dathne.'

Small and straight in the stable doorway, her head and shoulders covered in a green wool shawl, she raised her eyebrows. 'Your call through the crystal sounded shrill. What's happened?'

The colt stirred, disquieted by their voices. Matt soothed it with a touch and a murmured reassurance then eased his way out of the stable. The lamplit yard was hushed, just the normal sounds of horses in their beds and owls in the surrounding trees, hooting. His lads were upstairs in their dormitory, sleeping or playing cards. It was safe to talk.

Even so, he kept his voice down. 'Borne's dead. The queen, too. And Fane. Durm as good as, and might not last the night.'

Shocked silence. In her face a wealth of surprise, which meant she hadn't dreamed this. Strangely, he was comforted. If she'd known and kept it from him . . .

'Jervale defend us,' she said at last, her voice a fervent whisper. '*How*?'

'An accident.'

'And what of Gar?'

'He's injured too. But in no danger.'

She seemed unable to grasp the enormity of it. He was having some trouble there himself. She said, still stunned, 'They're dead? You're certain?'

He shrugged. 'Asher is. He saw them for himself and told me.'

'*Asher* saw . . . ?' Her thin face blanched. 'He was there? Involved? Is he injured? Is he—'

He put a hand on her shoulder to calm her. 'He's fine.'

She shook her head. Tugged her shawl tight. 'Tell me everything.'

When he was finished she stepped closer, her face flushed with angry colour, and shoved him hard in the chest. 'You *fool*! What were you thinking, letting him do anything so rash, so dangerous? Climbing into Salbert's Eyrie? That's madness! What if he'd fallen? What if he was lying there dead like the rest of them? What then?'

He caught her hands as she lifted them to shove him a second time. 'I tried to stop him. But he was determined and I had no good reason to keep on arguing. Not one I could share. You bade me hold my tongue, remember?'

She pulled free. 'So it's my fault? Why didn't you go climbing down there yourself?'

'I offered to but he wouldn't listen. Dathne, why are we fighting? He isn't dead.'

'No, but he could be! You had no right to risk him!'

'And you haven't risked him?' he retorted. 'By not telling him what he should know of himself? And that business with the fireworks and Ballodair the day we first met, you don't think *that* was risking him?'

'That was different and you know it. I had to put him in the prince's way, I had to get him into the Usurper's House!'

'And I had to let him see if any of the royal family were left alive,' he said. 'Or risk stirring his suspicions. Asher was beside himself, Dath. Ready to go right through me. What would you have done if you'd been there instead of me?'

Furious, resenting his logic, she glared up into his impatient face. Then, without warning, her hot gaze shifted. Focused somewhere behind him. Melted into relief and sorrow and something else. Something he didn't want or dare to think about.

He turned, knowing already who it was he'd see. Asher. Trailing into the yard like a man at the end of a week's marching over unforgiving ground.

He heard her gasp. Stepped aside and watched her go to him. Stand before him, thin and worn with worry. 'Matt's told me,' she said. 'Are you all right?'

The question seemed to surprise Asher, as though the last thing he expected was concern for himself. He shrugged. 'Aye.'

'And the prince?'

'He'll live. I've put him to bed up in the Tower.'

'Praise Barl.' She looked at her feet, and then into his face. 'And it's true? They're really dead?'

'Aye,' he said again. 'They're really dead.'

As though speaking the words out loud were some kind of catalyst, his stolid composure fractured. His face crumpled, lost years, became the face of a boy in unbearable pain. Matt felt his own face twist in sympathy.

Dathne held out her arms and welcomed Asher to her breast. He went to her gladly, fiercely, holding her like a man in fear of falling. Her holding of him was no less desperate.

The sight of their embrace sank Matt's untouched heart, and roused a host of fears. Dathne's face was hidden from him, and he was glad, because he could see Asher's . . . and it told him everything he needed to know. More than ever he'd wanted.

'Jervale have mercy,' he said aloud . . . but softly, so they wouldn't hear him. 'Please. And then tell me what to do now.'

# CHAPTER FOUR

Asher woke the following morning fully clothed and sprawled face down across his bed. For long moments he just lay there, groping for his bearings. His head felt heavy, wooden, and his mouth tasted like barnacle scrapings. His hair was tacky with dried sweat, making his scalp itch. There was dirt under his chipped fingernails. Dirt on his shirt sleeves too, along with dried blood. His back ached, and his shoulders, and his hands were scabbed with cuts. What the—

And then a wave of memory crashed over him, tumultuous with fragmented images. *Borne. Dana. Fane. The dead brown carriage horse. Gar's face. Dathne . . .*

He groaned, rolling over to stare at his pale blue bedchamber ceiling. Groaned again as muttering pains roused to a roar. Everything hurt. The room tip-tilted about him and he clutched at his blankets, waiting for it to steady right side up so he could think more clearly.

After the stables, and Dathne – *the way she'd held him, soothed him, the warmth of her hand against his cheek and the tickling rush of her breath across his skin* – he'd staggered back to the Tower. Gar had demanded to be left alone, insisting he was all right, but he'd wanted to make sure. Nobody could lose their entire family in one blow and still be all right, not even a man as habitually cool and self-contained as the Prince of Lur.

But Gar had locked his suite's main doors and wouldn't answer no matter how hard the bell rope was pulled or how loudly the carved wood was banged upon. Truth be told, he'd not been sorry. He'd had his fill of grief for one night.

So he'd gone all the way downstairs and underground to the deserted Tower kitchen and filled his empty belly with this and that from the cook's precious pantry. Then he'd staggered up to his room, intending to sit a while and try to think this calamity through. Unravel all its implications and decide what it might mean, to himself and the kingdom.

Instead, he must have fallen asleep.

No reason to feel guilty, he told himself sternly. The dead were dead. The living still had to sleep, didn't they? Aye, and eat and work and fight and love . . .

Love.

*Dathne.*

Pushing the thought of her aside, because he didn't begin to know what last night might mean and lacked the energy right now to untangle the puzzle, he sat up. Swung his still-booted feet to the floor, twitched open the bedside window's curtain and looked outside.

It was late. Maybe half-nine. From this high up he could just make out the tail end of the morning's second exercise string: six immaculate horses heading out from the stables towards Spindly Copse. Looked like Willem bringing up the rear; the boy always liked to ride Sunburst, and he'd know the chestnut colt's broad backside anywhere.

In his imagination he heard the stable lads' laughter and scoffing catcalls as they rode out to the Copse, and was greenly envious. Lucky bastards. What he wouldn't give to be one of them again, far from the glare of public service and the intimacy of lives shattered by disaster.

A battering of fists against his apartment's outer doors startled him. Then came a voice, raised in impatient demand: 'Asher! Asher, get out here at once!'

Willer. *Bastard.*

For one single, luxurious moment he contemplated deafness, or insensibility, or even self-inflicted death. Any or all were better than dealing with Willer at half-nine in the morning on a growlingly empty stomach after a day and a night like the ones he'd just lived through.

But no. Somebody had to take charge of the Tower till Darran was released from Nix's clutches, and if he didn't do it Willer would. Which meant that by eleven o'clock he'd have *everybody* running around killing themselves.

Scowling ferociously he flung wide his apartment doors. 'Keep the noise down, you bloody great fool! You want to wake the prince?'

Blinding in purple satin, Willer stared at him, took one horrified breath and immediately fished for his kerchief. 'Barl preserve me!' he said through pale mauve silk. 'You *stink*! And you're filthy! What is going on? And where is Darran? He sent all the staff home yesterday over my strenuous objections and now he's nowhere to be found and the maids are milling about like hens!'

'Darran's been taken poorly. He—'

'Poorly?' Willer dropped the silk kerchief and lunged. 'What do you mean? What have you done to him? I swear, Asher, I *swear*, if you've harmed so much as a hair on Darran's head I'll—'

With some difficulty Asher fended him off. 'I ain't done nowt to the ole crow! Now shut your trap so's I can tell you what's what, or I'll push you head first down my water closet!'

Willer hurriedly stepped back. 'Lay a finger on me and I'll have you arrested.'

'You could try,' he said with an evil, relishing grin. 'Now listen. Seein' Darran's in his sickbed you'll need to stand in for him today, Barl save us all.'

'Of course I shall stand in for him!' Willer snapped. 'Who else could be entrusted with such an important task? Certainly not you.'

He throttled the impulse to kick the little pissant where, on reflection, it wouldn't do much damage. 'Look, you, stop flappin' your bloody lips and *listen*. There's an important announcement to be made on another matter. Get the staff together in the foyer while I—'

'Announcement? About what? Asher, I *demand* you tell me—'

'*Listen*, I said! Or are you deaf as well as a dimwit? Get the staff together, grounds folk and stable as well as Tower, while I see how the prince wants to proceed. All right? Understand? Or do I have to draw you little pictures?'

'And who are you to give such orders?'

'I'm the man who's goin' to punch you in the nose if you don't do as you're told!'

The sea slug's eyes narrowed in fury. 'You have no authority over me.'

'Want to bet? If you don't about-face right now and get the staff assembled, I'll see you dismissed and chucked out of here on your pimpled fat arse. And don't think for a moment Gar won't back me up, 'cause we both know he will.'

'You arrogant, insupportable *bastard*. One day,' said Willer, wheezing with rage, 'there will be a reckoning for you! One day I shall strip you naked before the world and you'll be seen for the rotten, pernicious, power-hungry—'

Closing the door in Willer's face made him feel a lot better. A hot bath and some food for his empty belly would've made him feel better still but there wasn't time for that. So he washed quickly out of his privy basin, haphazardly scraped the bristles off his face with a razor one stropping short of sharp, brushed the worst of the sweat and dirt from his hair, hauled on clean clothing and went upstairs to rouse Gar.

This time when he knocked on the royal suite's front doors they swung open on soundless hinges. There was nobody on the other side.

'Smartarse,' he muttered, and entered. Crossed the empty sun-striped foyer and took the stairs up to Gar's bedchamber. With a brief knuckle-rap on the closed door he opened it, and was confronted with darkness.

'Gar? You in here?'

All the bedroom's curtains were drawn: only the merest silver of sunshine slid between them to leaven the gloom. Asher banged and bruised and cursed his way to the nearest window and pulled back the brocade hangings.

'If I'd wanted light,' said Gar, 'I would've made some.'

He was slumped in an overstuffed armchair, still dressed in the clothes he'd pulled on last night in Durm's office. His pale hollow cheeks were stubbled with gold; grief was smeared into dark shadows beneath his half-closed eyes. The sumptuous bed was unslept in.

Asher crossed his arms and bumped his backside onto

the windowsill. 'When Nix said rest, I think he meant in a bed.'

'And if I'd wanted company,' Gar added, eyebrows lowering, 'I would've sent for someone.'

He shrugged. 'Darran says a good servant anticipates his employer's wishes.'

Gar let his bruised, unbandaged head fall against the padded chair back. 'I'm sure he does. But since when do you give a fat rat's fart what Darran has to say?'

'I don't. How are you feelin'? Collarbone all right?'

Gar lifted his left arm. Waved it overhead, and let it drop back to his lap. 'Fine.'

'Your bumps and bruises?'

'Also fine. Nix is an excellent physician.'

'Good.'

An awkward silence fell. Asher took refuge in it, frowning at the carpet. Gar looked bad. Brittle, as though one word too many, one breath too deep, would shatter him.

But he couldn't say nothing.

He looked up. Felt his eyes burn, his throat tighten. With eyes wide open saw again the blood. The bodies. He took a deep breath and let it out, shakily. 'Gar. About yesterday. Your family. I—'

'*Don't*,' said Gar, one hand swiftly raised. 'I can't afford your sympathy, Asher. Not now. Not yet.'

He blinked. 'Oh.'

'If you want to help . . . then help me stay strong.'

'I can do that.'

A little of the bleakness eased from Gar's face. 'Thank you.' He pushed to his feet. 'Now I must make myself presentable. The staff—'

'I got 'em waiting downstairs. Will you make the announcement, or d'you want me to—'

'I'll do it. Tell them I'll be with them shortly, would you?' He pulled off his weskit and tossed it over the back of the armchair. 'Give me ten minutes.'

Nodding, Asher slid off the windowsill. Started for the chamber door, hesitated, and turned back. 'Gar . . .'

Impatient, Gar glanced at him. 'What?'

Still hesitant, he took another step closer. Brittle or not, grieving or not, there were things Gar needed to hear. Things that couldn't wait. 'Nix may be a good pother, but he ain't got the power to make a man live if his body's hurt past healing. Or mend a mind that's broken. I know this is hard, but—'

Gar paused in the middle of undoing his buttons, his eyes abruptly cold. 'No.'

'You don't know what I'm goin' to say yet!'

'I know exactly what you're going to say,' Gar replied, and returned to his unbuttoning. 'The answer is no. I have a Master Magician.'

'Gar . . .' He closed the gap between them a little more. 'I know Durm's your family now, but you can't let that make your choices for you.'

Gar stripped off his shirt and threw it at the chair. Despite Nix's stinking green ointment, his torso looked like a mad painter's palette. 'I'm not.'

'You are! You got to look at this the way the people will,' he insisted. 'All your life they've known you as Gar the Magickless. Gar the Cripple. And it never mattered because there was your da, and your sister, two of the best magicians this kingdom's ever seen. The smallest spratling in Restharven knew the kingdom was safe, because of them.'

'The kingdom is still safe!' retorted Gar, stung. 'I am Gar the Magickless no longer!'

'I know, but it's only been weeks! *Weeks*, Gar, after

all those years. Folks have barely got used to the idea that you're a magician, and now you want 'em to see you as king? As *WeatherWorker*? You may be as powerful as Fane ever was, but you're not trained. Not the way you should be. You said it yourself, Durm still had so much to teach you!'

'And he shall teach me,' said Gar, eyes bright with temper. 'As soon as he recovers.'

'You don't know he will!'

'And you don't know he won't!' snapped Gar. 'Unless we are now to number physicking amongst your many talents!'

Asher shoved his hands in his pockets, sorry he'd ever opened his mouth. But he had, and it was too late now to take back what he'd said. 'I ain't the one holdin' out little hope, Gar. That's Nix. His words, not mine. You can't pretend otherwise just because—'

'I'm not pretending anything!' said Gar, and turned his back. 'And neither am I continuing this conversation. The subject is closed.'

Asher reached out, grabbed Gar by the arm and spun him around. 'No, it ain't. Like it or not, you have to face facts. You need a Master Magician. You can't leap into WeatherWorking on your own, without some other trained magician to guide you. It's too difficult. Too dangerous! You can't—'

Gar raised a warning finger. 'Say "can't" to me one more time and I promise you'll be sorry!'

'Sorrier than if you charge pig-headed into WeatherWorking and bring the Wall crashing down around our ears?' he said, ignoring the raised finger, and the dangerous light in Gar's eyes, and everything save the need to make the fool see sense. 'I don't think so.'

'I have no intention of destroying Barl's Wall!'

retorted Gar. 'Or of appointing Conroyd Jarralt my Master Magician!'

'You have to! Who else is there powerful enough to manage the job? You have to appoint him Master Magician, even if it's only for a while! Until Durm gets better, since you're so sure he won't die or wake up an addled wreck. 'Cause if you don't, if you try WeatherWorking alone, without help, and somethin' goes wrong, that more'n likely means you'll be dead and Jarralt'll be king and then what'll the rest of us do?'

'Are you deaf?' cried Gar. 'I will not do it! I have a Master Magician!'

'No, Gar! What you've got is a lump of bloody meat held together with catgut and pothering and prayers and you can't—'

'*Enough*!' Gar shouted, livid with pain. His arm came up, fingers fisted – and the room was filled with furious power.

Asher felt the magic hit him. Felt it lift him and toss him like a bundle of kindling on fire from the inside out. He flew backwards. Hit the bed. Bounced off it again, slammed into the wall, then slid into a crumpled heap on the carpet. Every sleeping bruise woke and started screaming. Deafened, he lay there feeling warm blood trickle from his nose, his mouth. Smelling scorched air. Beneath the pain there was fear.

Bleached white and still as stone, Gar stared back at him. Watched as he groped his way to his feet and half sat, half collapsed onto the bed. Watched as he touched the blood on his face and considered his crimsoned fingertips.

'Asher,' he said at last. 'I—'

Asher lifted a hand and Gar fell silent. Turned on his heel and disappeared into his privy closet. There came the sound of water running into a basin. The opening and closing of a cupboard. Then he came out again carrying the basin and a soft white cloth. Closed the immeasurable distance between them and waited.

Silently Asher took basin and cloth and cleaned his face of blood. The sharp pounding pain subsided, but the fear remained. Translated slowly into anger. Still unspeaking, he handed back the basin and stained white cloth, stood and pushed past Gar to stand once more at the window. His bones ached. Looking outside he saw a horse and rider draw to a halt in the Tower's front courtyard. Saw a liveried servant – Daniyal – appear and take the animal's reins.

He knew that horse. Knew its rider, too.

'Pellen Orrick's here,' he said, not turning around.

'Asher . . .'

'I'll go down and see what he wants while you finish tidying yourself ready to speak to the staff. After that you'd best get over to the infirmary. See how Durm's doin' this morning. And Darran. The ole man'll howl like a girl if you don't make a fuss over 'im, take him some flowers and a box of sweetmeats.'

'*Asher* . . .'

Still he refused to turn round. Couldn't trust what his face might show. 'Reckon that'll be the first and last time you ever raise a hand to me, Gar. Reckon you do it again, with magic or without, and that'll be the end of that.'

Subdued, his voice small in the large round room, Gar said, 'Yes. Asher, I'm sorry. Forgive me.'

Now he risked revealing his face. Looked at Gar for long moments and saw that the prince's contrition was genuine. He nodded. 'You're grievin'.'

'That's no excuse.'

He didn't want to talk about it. Wanted to forget it had happened, forget that this Gar, magician Gar, wasn't the man he'd made friends with in Dorana's market square a lifetime ago. That this man was about to become a king, and contained in his fingertips the power to kill. 'Anythin' you need me to say to Orrick?'

Gar shook his head. In his eyes understanding and a reluctant acceptance. 'No. Not that I can think of.'

'Fine,' he said, and headed for the chamber door.

'Asher!'

He slowed. Stopped. Waited.

'I'll think on what you said. About Durm. And Conroyd Jarralt.'

'Good.'

'And I truly am sorry. It will never happen again, I swear.'

He nodded, and kept on walking.

Pellen Orrick was waiting halfway down the Tower's front steps. Immaculate and self-contained as ever, the Guard captain looked at him closely and said, 'Are you all right?'

'Aye,' said Asher, meeting his sharp gaze full-square. 'Why wouldn't I be?'

'No reason,' said Orrick after a brief hesitation. 'Beyond the obvious, that is.' Beneath the spit and polish he looked weary. Sick at heart. 'We got the family up safe and sound, just after dawn. Barlsman Holze took them to the palace directly. The infirmary.'

With an effort, Asher blotted out memory. *Red blood and white bone and black flies, crawling*. 'No sign of Matcher, I s'pose?'

'I'm sorry.'

He'd known before asking. Had to ask anyway. 'So, what now?'

Orrick shrugged. 'Now we wait for the results of the physical examination. Holze, my men and I combed the accident site before retrieving the bodies, looking for any sign of tampering. Anything that could suggest that someone somehow sent the carriage over the Eyrie on purpose, with or without magic. We found nothing.'

'That's good. Ain't it?'

Another shrug. 'That depends. People like explanations for things, Asher. That's their nature.'

'I s'pose. Nix is lookin' at the bodies now, you say?'

'Nix and Holze.'

'And they really can tell if there's been magic used?'

'Holze says so,' said Orrick. He was silent a moment, inspecting the nearby treetops. Looking for crimes? Probably. The law was Pellen Orrick's bread and butter and blankets. 'He kept vigil all night. He's a good man. A holy man. If we can't trust his findings, and Nix's, we're all in trouble.'

'D'you reckon they will find anythin'?'

'No,' said Orrick, grimacing. 'Borne was a great king. Revered by everyone. The queen was loved. Princess Fane respected, and accepted by all as the WeatherWorker in Waiting. There's not a soul in Lur who'd want them dead.'

Asher looked at him sidelong. 'Gar might.'

'*What*?'

'Don't tell me you ain't considered the idea, Captain. Gar's got his magic now. Might be he decided he'd make a better WeatherWorker than his sister and didn't want all the folderol and kerfuffle of a schism over the matter.'

Pellen Orrick fell back a pace and stared at him, his expression a mixture of disbelief and horror. 'Asher, are you serious? Do you truly want me to consider His Highness responsible for this tragedy? Is it what *you* believe? Don't forget, it's only by Barl's grace that he and the Master Magician survived!'

'Could be it was planned that way.'

Orrick seized his arm. 'Asher, I charge you straight: if you have any proof or knowledge that this was no accident, you cannot stay silent. *Was* it deliberate murder? Tell me!'

Pulling free, he said, 'I ain't got the first idea, Captain. I don't reckon so. But even if it was, there's no way Gar were involved.'

'*Not* involved?' Orrick glared. 'Then why in Barl's blessed name would you—'

'Because I can think of at least one man who'll say it's possible!' he said. 'Maybe even likely. Can't you?'

Some of the angry colour faded from Orrick's face. His eyes narrowed and he folded his arms across his chest. 'Lord Jarralt.'

'Exactly. And you need to be ready for him, Captain. He'll stir up trouble if he can. Claim the kingdom needs a seasoned magician as Weather Worker. And without Durm to stand behind Gar as the heir, things could get real nasty real fast.'

'What do you mean, without Durm? I'd not heard the Master Magician was dead.'

'He ain't. Not yet, any road. But between you and me and the anchor, it ain't lookin' good. And Durm dead'd suit Conroyd bloody Jarralt right down to the ground. So I'm just sayin', Captain. Keep your eye on him. Don't let him bully you into makin' a findin' that suits him more than you or the kingdom.'

Now the faintest of smiles was curving Orrick's thin lips. 'For a fisherman, Asher, you display a remarkable grasp of politics.'

'Aye, well, I'm a fast learner,' he said, scowling.

'Speaking of His Highness,' said Orrick after an appreciative pause, 'how is he this morning?'

He shrugged. 'Fine.' Orrick's eyebrows lifted. With an effort, silently cursing the Guard captain's instincts, he smoothed his tone. 'Grievin', of course. Looks a bit the worse for wear, which is only to be expected. But he's fine.'

'I'm glad to hear it,' said Pellen Orrick. 'Because the kingdom needs stability, Asher. There's nothing a man in my line of work likes less than a lack of stability. It tends to make people . . . frisky.'

From inside the Tower came a loud lamentation, voices male and female raised in disbelieving shock and pain. Daniyal, still holding Orrick's horse at a discreet distance, looked around, alarmed.

Asher winced, then sighed. 'He's told 'em. Now we're in for it.'

Orrick clasped his shoulder briefly. 'I must get to the palace. With luck Holze and Nix will know by now if there was magical foul play. Will you tell His Highness the bo – his family is safely retrieved?'

Asher nodded. 'Aye.'

'He'll want to see them, of course. Tell him that provided Holze and Nix have finished their examinations, I have no objection.' Orrick frowned. 'I hope Nix thinks to . . . put them to rights. His Highness shouldn't have to see them . . . like that.'

'No,' he said after a moment. 'He shouldn't.'

'Good morning then,' said Orrick. He collected his horse, mounted neatly, economically, and trotted away.

Daniyal came slowly up the Tower steps, looking to Asher for instructions.

'Go inside,' Asher told him. 'The prince has news for you.'

Daniyal ran. Asher stayed on the Tower steps, letting the sunshine soak into his bones. Willing it to melt the shards of ice still chilling him to the marrow. Familiar footsteps sounded behind him and he turned.

'So. That's done,' Gar said grimly. Dressed head to toe in unrelieved black, his hair had been confined in a tight plait. Black ribbon was threaded through the braiding. 'What did Orrick want?'

Asher told him. Gar took the news in silence.

'You goin' along to the palace now?' said Asher.

'Once I've eaten. You'll join me?'

'S'pose,' he said, shrugging.

Gar's icy expression fractured, revealed a churning of emotion. 'I've said I'm sorry. I've sworn it won't happen again. What else do you want from me?'

What he wanted, Gar couldn't give him. Nobody could. The dead were dead and couldn't be brought back to life, nor an unfamiliar world made trustworthy once more. Gar was staring at him. Angry. Fearful. Uncertain. He shook his head. Smiled, just a little. 'Griddle cakes, berry syrup and hot buttered toast.'

Gar's face flooded with relief. 'I think I can manage that. Come on. We'll eat in the solar, quickly, and then go to the palace. There's a lot to be done today.'

Aye, there was. And none of it pleasant. In silence, he followed Gar back into the Tower, where the house-maids were weeping and even Willer's tongue was stilled.

One of Nix's myriad assistants came forward to greet Gar and Asher as they entered the Royal Infirmary's reception room. She bowed low then clasped her hands behind her back. The green badges on her collar, denoting her status as a fifth-year apprentice, winked in the bright glimlight.

'Your Highness.' Her voice was calm, her face smooth, polite, but there was a horrified sympathy deep in her eyes. 'I'll tell Pother Nix you're here.'

She withdrew, and some moments later Nix joined them. He looked exhausted; Asher realised that the sagging, wrinkled blue robe he wore this morning was the same one he'd worn last night.

'Your Highness,' said the pother, and offered a perfunctory bow. 'How are you this morning?'

'Well enough,' said Gar. 'How is Durm?'

'Still with us, sir. His will is extraordinary. I think any other man would have succumbed to his injuries by now.'

Some of the tension eased from Gar's face. 'Not if he had you as his pother. May I see him?'

'Perhaps later. To be truthful, there was some agitation during the night. We've got him quiet again, well dosed with calming herbs. I wouldn't like to see our good work fly out the window quite so soon.'

'Agitation? Do you mean—'

'I'm sorry, Your Highness,' Nix said, and pressed a hand to Gar's arm. 'No sign of awareness, as such. Just an excitation of the nerves. It's to be expected, with this kind of injury.'

'I see,' said Gar, and cleared his throat. 'Well, you know best, Nix. And you have my complete confidence.'

'Thank you, sir. I'll do my utmost to ensure it's not misplaced.'

Gar nodded, and banished the last betraying emotion. 'So. If I can't see my Master Magician, can I at least pay a visit to my secretary?'

'Certainly you may,' said Nix, and smiled his relief. 'Indeed, you'll make the old gentleman's morning.'

'He is well?'

'Well enough to leave us soon, I believe. If you'd care to follow me?'

As Nix moved towards a nearby corridor, Asher touched Gar's elbow. 'I don't need to see Darran too, do I? Like as not one look at my face'll drive the ole crow straight into a relapse and Nix'll have my guts for garters. Why don't I just go and—'

'No,' said Gar. 'I've got something important to say to both of you, and I want you in the same room when I say it. Don't worry. I'll protect you from Nix. Now come along. We don't want to keep the good pother waiting.'

Swallowing a groan, Asher fell into step.

Darran had been removed to a small private chamber a short walk from the reception area. Propped up in bed and looking ridiculous in a pale pink nightgown, when he saw the prince the faint colour in his cheeks faded altogether.

'Oh, sir! Sir!' he cried, struggling to throw back his blankets.

As Nix withdrew, closing the chamber door behind him, Asher propped himself against the wall and Gar moved to the bedside. 'Lie still, old friend. Nix tells me you're doing well and might even escape confinement later today – provided you do nothing foolish.'

'I fancy I've been foolish enough already,' murmured Darran, sinking back against his pillows. One thin veined hand stole out, fingers brushing against Gar's black silk sleeve. His expression was beseeching. 'Oh, sir. Dear sir. Tell me it isn't true. Tell me your ruffian friend there has played a cruel trick on me. It would be like him, after all. Tell me anything . . . except that they're dead.'

Gar shook his head. 'I wish I could. I'm sorry.'

Darran burst into gulping, gasping tears. Gar sank to the edge of the bed beside him and opened his arms. Clutching, coughing, Darran continued to weep, his face buried against Gar's shoulder.

'I'm sorry – I'm so sorry—'

Gar patted his back, stroked his hair. 'I know, Darran. I know.'

Skewered with pity, Asher looked away. He had no time for scarecrow Darran but even so . . . the ole fool's grief was genuine. Was a knife, opening half-healed wounds. *Red blood and white bone and black flies, crawling . . . a friend, addled and drooling . . . a tired old man broken by a mast, alone and abandoned and calling his name . . .*

Imagination lashed him like a whip. Smarting, he shoved his hands deep into his pockets and set his jaw. He wasn't going to cry, he wasn't, he wasn't. Tears were nothing but a waste of good saltwater.

At last the old man stopped his ragged weeping. Stared into Gar's tearless face and whispered, 'Oh, sir. Sir. What are we going to do?'

'What we must, Darran. Go on without them.'

'Without them?' Darran echoed. Fresh tears spilled. 'Dear sir . . . I'm afraid I don't know how.'

Gar reached into his tunic, withdrew a black handkerchief and held it out. Speechless, Darran blotted his sallow cheeks dry and let the damp crumpled silk fall to his lap.

'In truth, Darran, neither do I,' Gar said. 'But there must be a way. And if there isn't, we'll have to make one. The kingdom needs me, and I need you. More than I ever have before. Can I count on you?'

'Sir!' said Darran. 'As if you need to ask!'

Gar smiled and patted his hand. 'I don't want to take

you for granted. Darran, I have a huge favour to beg of you. One that will tax your loyalty and endurance to their very limits, I fear. But I wouldn't ask such a sacrifice of you if I didn't think it was important. Will you hear me out? Please?'

The old man flushed faintly pink, like a maiden at her first Festival dance. 'Well, of course, sir. You must know there's nothing I won't do for you.'

Asher rolled his eyes. Silly ole fool . . .

'Thank you, Darran,' said Gar. His pale face was settling into new and unaccustomed lines. He looked years older now, and grim. 'Asher?'

Suspicious, he took a reluctant step towards the bed. 'Aye?'

'I know there's scant love lost between you two,' Gar began carefully. 'That you take great delight in puncturing each other's consequence, as often and as publicly as possible. There is fault and provocation on both sides, though I think you'd rather die before admitting it. But I also know you both love me, and I hope you know that love is returned, as for a crusty old uncle, say, and an irascible brother.'

Asher raised an eyebrow. 'We s'posed to guess which one of us is which?'

'Hold your tongue, you impertinent guttersnipe!' snapped Darran. 'His Highness is speaking!'

'*Please*!' said Gar, glaring.

Instantly contrite, Darran lowered his head. 'Your Highness.'

'Sorry,' Asher muttered.

Darran snorted. '*That* was convincing.'

'Barl save me!' cried Gar. Overhead, the air beneath the chamber ceiling thickened. Darkened. A flickering tongue of lightning licked the underbelly of the looming cloud and the chamber's glimfire lamps sparked and sputtered. 'Must I find bandages to stuff in your chattering mouths? *Listen* to me! This kingdom faces its gravest crisis since Trevoyle's Schism. *I* face the darkest, most demanding days of my life, and I'd rather not face them alone.'

'You are not alone, sir,' said Darran, offended. 'You have me, for as long as there's breath in my body.'

'I know, but it's not enough!' Gar slid off the bed and began to pace the small chamber. 'Don't you understand? I need *both* of you! I've always lived a public life, but this will be different. As Weather Worker I will be scrutinised as never before. I may be my father's legitimate heir but my journey has been, to say the least, unorthodox. With every eye upon me I can't afford the slightest stumble. For if I fall, not one Doranen hand will reach out to help me to my feet. Instead they'll clutch the sleeve of Conroyd Jarralt, the only other magician we have who's capable of wielding Weather Magic. It is the last thing my father would've wanted. I *can't* let Conroyd win! If he wins—'

'Er . . . Gar?' said Asher.

Gar turned. 'What?'

He considered the cloud-obscured ceiling. 'Are you s'posed to do that?'

*'What?'*

'That,' he said, and pointed.

Gar stopped. Looked. 'Oh.' He frowned. 'Probably not.' He snapped his fingers and the incipient thunderstorm vanished. 'Asher—'

Damn, damn, damn. This was going to give him ulcers, he just *knew* it. 'I get it,' he sighed. 'You need a united household. Me and Darran singin' the same song.'

Gar's expression softened. 'Precisely. I don't ask you

to love each other – I'm not that much of a fool – but I do ask you to support each other, at least in public. Because in supporting each other, you support me. And Barl knows, in the weeks and months ahead I shall need all the support I can get!'

Asher heaved another sigh. 'No need to fret yourself. Reckon I can stomach playin' nice with Darran here, at least till all this upset's settled down. Provided we ain't talkin' years.'

'Not exactly a ringing endorsement, but I'll take what I can get,' Gar murmured, faintly smiling. He turned his head. 'Darran?'

Darran had the look of man who had bitten into an apple and found half a worm. 'Your Highness?'

Returning to the bed, Gar rested a hand on the old man's blanketed knee. 'Please. I know he's a ruffian and a reprobate and a thorn in your side . . . but he's not all bad. Would I have him for a friend if he was?'

Darran's thin fingers hovered for a moment, then curled around Gar's hand. 'Of course not, sir. Never fear. I will do precisely what you ask, no matter how difficult—' He flicked a dark look sideways. '—or painful – the task proves to be.'

Leaning down, Gar pressed his lips to Darran's forehead. 'Thank you.'

'I want to return to work,' said Darran. 'Will you tell Nix to release me?'

'No,' said Gar. 'You'll stay in that bed until you're quite recovered.'

Defeated, Darran slumped against the pillows. 'Then can you at least do something about his dreadful medicine?'

Gar nearly laughed. 'No, Darran, I'm sorry to say I can't. I can call lightning from a clear sky, snow from a sunbeam and rain from a red dawn, but I am powerless in the face of those bloody awful potions.'

Darran heaved a lugubrious sigh. 'That's most unfortunate, sir.'

'It is, isn't it?' said Gar, smiling, and touched his fingers to the old man's cheek.

Nix was waiting for them in the reception area. 'Your Highness.'

The warmth and brief amusement had disappeared from Gar's face. 'I understand my family was brought here for examination by you and Barlsman Holze.'

'Yes, Your Highness.'

'Your examination is complete?'

'Yes, sir.'

'I wish to see them.'

'Certainly, Your Highness. Allow me to—'

'No need,' said Gar. 'I know the way.'

Asher swallowed a groan and started after him. As Nix fell into step beside him he glanced sidelong at the pother and muttered, 'You sure? They weren't exactly portrait material last time I saw 'em.'

Nix's face spasmed in an uneasy mix of anger and understanding. 'To the best of my ability, that has been rectified. What do you take me for?'

Asher grimaced. 'A good pother,' he admitted, and let Nix hurry him along in Gar's impatient wake with an imperious wave of his hand.

# CHAPTER FIVE

The palace's dead room was located underground, two floors below the infirmary wing. The chill was pronounced, the silence complete. Two City guards stood sentinel by the double-doored entrance. They stepped aside as Gar approached and bowed as he and Nix swept past unseeing. Asher, who shared a weekly pint at the Goose with both of them, acknowledged each with a nod and followed Gar into the dead room's antechamber, where he drifted into a cold white corner and held his tongue.

Holze was lighting the Barlscandle in the chapel nook cut into one stark white wall. Dressed in his most dignified crimson, cream and golden robes, he looked wan of face and grossly old, almost transparent with grief and weariness. As though his cape of office was too heavy to bear. He turned at their entrance. 'Your Highness!' With an effortful puff he blew out the taper, discarded it on the floor and approached Gar with outstretched arms. 'My dear, dear boy. How are you this sad morning?'

Gar suffered Holze's embrace of peace without protest, but stepped back once the elderly cleric released him. 'Well enough, sir. Yourself?'

Tears welled in Holze's red-rimmed eyes. 'Indeed, my heart is heavy.'

'What did your examination of my family's bodies reveal?'

Holze exchanged a discomfited glance with Nix. 'Ah . . . yes. The examination. Pother Nix . . . ?'

Nix cleared his throat. 'Captain Orrick has charged us to keep our findings secret until his final report is complete.'

Gar nodded. 'Asher. Send to Captain Orrick and command him to make his report to the existing Privy Council two hours hence. I'll want you there too. Dress appropriately.'

'Me?' he said, startled.

Gar ignored him. 'Nix,' he continued, 'as far as the conduct and findings of the examination are concerned, Holze will speak for you both. Your duty lies at Durm's bedside. Return to him now, and do not leave him again unless it's to tell me he's awake and ready to fulfil his role as my Master Magician.'

Struck dumb, Nix gaped. 'Your Highness,' he said at last, faintly.

'I would have privacy now,' said Gar, raking his cold gaze over all their faces. 'Leave.'

There was only one other door in the dead room's antechamber. Gar opened it, entered the chamber beyond and thudded the door shut behind him.

In the silence that followed, Pother Nix blew out his cheeks and said, '*Well*! Of all the high and mighty—'

'Poor boy,' said Holze, shaking his head. 'He's clearly undone with grief. Careful handling, that's the key. Barl knows he's a fine young man but he does have a temper, though he's seldom shown it. I wonder how best we can convince him to . . .'

As one, they exchanged glances then turned and stared at Asher.

He folded his arms across his chest and stared back, unimpressed. 'Don't you go lookin' at me,' he advised them sourly. 'I ain't got a death wish. You're his spiritual advisor, Barlsman Holze, and you're his official physicker, Pother Nix. Those are sacred callings, ain't they. Me? I just work here. Now I suggest you do like the good prince said, eh? Unless you're looking for new positions and a change of scenery.'

And with that sage advice he left them to their business, so he might attend to his.

Privy Council? *Privy Council*? Ha! *Now* what was Gar up to?

The dead room was cold. Well, it had to be, didn't it? Dead flesh rotted. Even when magically preserved, in the end it still rotted. Best not to give nature a head start, then. Best to beat back the ravages of decay for as long as possible, with whatever weapons came to hand.

Cold was the first.

Shivering, Gar stood with his shoulderblades pressed to the chamber's heavy door and kept his eyes closed. One glimpse of those three shrouded figures had been enough. They were here in the dead room, laid out on plain wooden tables. What else did he need to know? To see?

*Their unsmiling faces. Their unmoving lips. Their still, unbreathing bodies.*

If he didn't, would he ever believe this nightmare was real? Or would he spend the rest of his life waking each and every morning to think, no, no, it's all right! It was just a dream!

The idea was unbearable. He had to look. No matter how dreadful, how haunting, how unspeakable the images might be, he had to look his fill until truth overcame hope. Until he could begin to accept the inescapably altered landscape of his life.

Slowly, he opened his eyes. The first thing he truly saw was colour. Vases of sweet pink pamarandums stood in niches cut into the white-washed walls. Their scent danced in the air. Tickled his nose. Cloyed in his mouth.

He was going to be sick.

Somehow he swallowed the flooding bile, just as last night he'd swallowed Nix's gross potion. Ah, the things one did when one was a king.

Was nearly a king.

'I know you never believed me, Fane,' he said to the smallest of the shrouded shapes before him, 'but I really don't want to be WeatherWorker. I wish there'd been time to convince you I was telling the truth. Do you believe it now, wherever you are?'

Silence.

He stepped away from the door. Folded his arms across his black silk chest and tucked his fingers into his armpits. Taking another step, then another, he found himself standing not quite an arm's length away from his family, lying so still beneath their kindly covering sheets. As part of his ritual offices Holze had laid a twisted strand of Barlsflowers on each breast. That each small bouquet sat undisturbed and unmoving hammered home, like a nail through his heart, the fact that they were dead.

'I don't know what to say to you, Father. Mama. Little sister. You died and I didn't. What can I say, faced with a truth so ugly? "Sorry"? It hardly seems adequate.'

There was something . . . wrong . . . with the shape

of his father's hidden body. From the shoulder region down it looked strangely flat.

Imagination stirred. Recoiled. He wasn't going to think about that.

'Durm survived too,' he said. 'Nix says his hopes are slim, but I don't think he'll die. I'd have to appoint Conroyd his successor if he died and Durm won't want to give him the satisfaction. I know I bloody don't.'

He held his breath, then, waiting to hear his mother's loving, scolding voice. '*Don't swear, darling. It isn't nice.*' The silence persisted. He stared at her shrouded silhouette, willing her to speak. A lock of her hair had escaped the confining sheet. It shimmered in the dead room's glimlight, just as once, only yesterday, so long ago, it had shimmered in the sunshine as she laughed. He longed to touch it. To wind that gentle curl about his fingers and tug, teasing, as once he'd tugged and teased as a boy.

He couldn't. What if that glorious golden hair felt dead, as she was dead? What if it came away in his hand like straw severed from the living earth? It would be a desecration . . .

His lungs were clamouring. He let out his pent-up breath in a sobbing rush and sucked in cold pamarandum-tainted air. The scarlet spots dancing before his eyes dimmed, and his frantic heart eased.

He knew then he couldn't look at them unshrouded. Couldn't bear to poison living memory with dead flesh. All he could do was accept their passing. Be true to their hopes and dreams for him, for the kingdom they had loved their whole lives, and pledge his own life to its ceaseless service.

'Pellen Orrick is investigating, but I think this was just a terrible accident,' he told them. 'Barl would never let it be otherwise. For six and a half centuries she's watched over us. Protected us. There's no reason she'd abandon us now. This was an accident.'

Faintly, through the room's solid door, he heard voices. The heavy tread of booted feet. The City Guard, changing over. Four souls among the thousands now resting in the palm of his hand. But was his palm big enough to hold them all safely? Heart pounding anew, he examined that palm. Every line of it. Every crease. And thought . . . *perhaps not.*

The palm became a fist, shaking. In his blood the power burned, yearned, yammered for freedom.

It was big enough. It had to be.

'And it *was* an accident,' he said. 'Wasn't it?'

The shrouded figures before him didn't answer.

He sighed. Relaxed his fist and tucked his cold fingers away again. The hunger in his blood receded and, with its siren song silenced, he was able to think more clearly.

He wasn't crying.

This was his family, laid out like butcher's kill for housewifely perusal. Why was he so calm? So detached? Surely that couldn't be right. Shock didn't last this long, did it? Here he was, face to face with his family's broken bodies, decaying even as he stood there watching. Shouldn't he be feeling *something*? Something other than physical, fleshly cold?

And oh, dear Barl preserve him, he was cold. Cold to the fingertips, cold to the marrow. Cold to the centre of his heart.

Is that what had happened to his tears? Were they frozen? Unable to flow? He'd wept, surely, the last time he'd thought his father dead. He was certain he remembered weeping then. In that barn. Buried in straw.

Yes, yes, he'd wept then. Quietly, so Asher wouldn't hear him.

So shouldn't he be howling now, like a dog? With his father and mother and sister smashed to pieces on a mountain, scraped piecemeal off the rocks, brought here to this cold white room of death, shouldn't he be *howling*?

'I'm sorry,' he whispered to his rotting flesh and blood. 'I don't know what's wrong with me.'

In less than two hours' time he would face Conroyd Jarralt in the Privy Council. Lay the matter of these deaths to rest so that his family might rest too. In peace. Forever. In less than two hours' time he would be named the next king of Lur.

So soon. So dreadfully soon. Fear, soft and secret, fluttered in the pit of his belly.

'Can I do this, Father? Am I even a shadow of the man you were? If not, the fault is mine. All that's good and true in kingship I learned by watching you. I'll do my best not to betray that legacy. I promise.'

But what if it was a promise he couldn't keep? What if his best efforts proved inadequate to the task? What then? In his imagination he heard Fane's laughter, scornful and scouring.

*'Then, brother dear, our parents and I won't be alone for long.'*

Shuddering, he dropped to his knees. Grasped the end of his father's wooden table with desperate fingers.

'No,' he whispered. 'You're wrong, Fane. You were always wrong. I will not fail. As Barl is my witness . . . *I will not fail.*'

In the sun-shafted Privy Council chamber, Conroyd Jarralt looked at Pellen Orrick with guarded dislike and an imperfectly disguised disappointment. 'An accident? You're certain?' His tone implied that only an idiot could believe such a thing.

Asher let his gaze march along the council chamber's velvet-burdened curtain rails. Poor bloody Orrick. His back was so stiff and straight you could snap a tree trunk across his spine with a single blow, and his face was blank, battened down like Restharven Harbour in a storm. Seemed like the captain enjoyed Privy Council meetings just as much as he did.

'As sure as I can be, my lord. Certainly I've found no evidence or proof of deliberate malice,' Orrick replied.

Asher looked at him then, marvelling how he could stay so calm in the face of Jarralt's hostility. Just a little something in the eyes, mayhap. Some flash or flicker of distaste.

Jarralt sneered. Of them all he seemed to be the only one who'd enjoyed a tranquil night's sleep. Still handsome, still arrogant, wrung by neither grief nor despair, even his clothing was ostentatiously bright: forest green instead of black. There was lace at his throat and a diamond winking like a strumpet in one ear. 'How hard have you looked? It's not quite a day since it happened. I find it difficult to believe you could have reached your conclusion of "accident" so swiftly.'

'My lord, I have exhausted all avenues of enquiry,' Orrick replied evenly. 'There are, after all, only two possible explanations for what happened. Either it was an accident or a murderous attack. Quite apart from the fact that nobody in his or her right mind would attempt to slaughter our entire royal family, the Eyrie was closed to the public yesterday. There is only one road in or out and two of my guards were posted at the turn-off to warn away the general citizenry. Nobody approached them.'

Holze said, 'Why didn't they raise the alarm when the family failed to return in good time?'

'Because Her Majesty dismissed them, sir,' replied Orrick.

'The criminal, or criminals, might already have been hiding at the Eyrie, or somewhere close by,' said Jarralt.

Asher cleared his throat. 'I don't reckon so, my lord. The picnic was decided on the spur of the moment. Nobody knew ahead of time.'

Jarralt burned him with a look. 'So you say.'

'And I,' said Gar. 'If that is of any interest to you, Conroyd.'

'Everything about this business interests me,' said Jarralt. Then added, after a pause just long enough to be insulting, 'Your Highness.'

Pellen Orrick cleared his throat. 'Furthermore, both Barlsman Holze and Royal Pother Nix assure me that no trace of arcane interference can be found in or on the bodies.'

'That's exactly so,' said Holze. 'Nix and I examined them most rigorously. No taint of magic was present.'

Jarralt scowled. 'I wish to examine them myself. As a Privy Councillor, I have the right.'

A frozen pause. Asher didn't dare look at Orrick, or Gar. Then Holze rested admonishing fingertips on his colleague's indecently decorative sleeve. 'It may well be your right, Conroyd, but I doubt it would be wise. Or well received.'

Face darkened with blood, Jarralt snatched his sleeve free. 'Is that an accusation?'

Holze sighed. 'No, old friend. It's a warning.'

'Of what? For what?' demanded Jarralt. 'Am I a Privy

Councillor or not? Do I have the right to satisfy my concerns or don't I? The king is *dead*, Holze!'

The cleric flushed. 'I know that, Conroyd. I held his poor broken body in my own two hands! Kissed his cold brow with my own lips! I know that he is dead!'

'Then you of all people should want this matter investigated thoroughly!'

'I'm sure it has been,' Holze said wearily.

'But I—'

'*Think*, Conroyd! There are only two people in all the kingdom who can be considered worthy of the WeatherWorker's crown. You and Prince Gar. Surely you see it's impossible for you to involve yourself in any investigations. Instead you must trust that I, Pother Nix, and our good Captain Orrick here, have ascertained the truth of the matter. Without any fear or favour.'

Asher glanced sideways at Orrick. The man's hatchet face was sharper than ever as he watched the confrontation with eyes that drank in every gesture, every hesitation, and gave away not a single thought of his own. Crafty bugger.

Jarralt's teeth were clenched, muscle leaping along the line of his sculptured jaw. 'Holze—'

'Conroyd, *please*!' said Holze, so moved that he thumped a fist to the tabletop before him. 'Do you think I'd not be thorough? I assure you, I was. While at the Eyrie I examined the remains of the carriage horse *and* what was left of the carriage. I also did a casting of the area around the lookout. Now while I'm the first to admit I'm no Durm, still I fancy my skills are sufficient for these tasks. Not to mention the fact I am Barl's devoted servant, dedicated to truth and justice. I would solemnly swear on my chapel's altar in front of all the kingdom, neither the horse nor the carriage nor any of the royal family were tampered with, and I support wholeheartedly Captain Orrick's findings. This dreadful event was caused by a caprice of fate, and not by any malignant human agency. Barl, in her infinite, unknowable wisdom, has called Their Majesties and Her Royal Highness home. It is not for us to question why.'

Jarralt's lips twisted. 'I'm sorry, Holze, but I find that hard to believe.'

'Nevertheless,' said Gar, stirring in his dead father's seat, 'you will believe it. Unless you wish to accuse Barlsman Holze, Pother Nix and Captain Orrick of corruption and conspiracy? Perhaps even murder? If so, I hope you have the proof. Barl's Laws are pointed in the matter of baseless allegations, sir. Some might even say unforgiving. As you well know.'

'What I know,' said Conroyd Jarralt, 'is that this matter is far too serious for sweeping under the nearest convenient carpet with a havey-cavey enquiry and a mouthful of religious platitudes.'

'Meaning, my lord?' asked Orrick, scrupulously polite.

Jarralt spared him a scant look. 'Meaning the account of yesterday's . . . accident . . . is incomplete.'

Gar regarded him through narrowed eyes. 'Conroyd, how many more times must I tell you? You asked me last night if I remembered what happened and I said no. You've asked me here, twice, and still the answer is no. Can you honestly believe a third asking will magically elicit a different answer? Perhaps Durm will be able to satisfy your curiosity when he—'

'When?' scoffed Jarralt. 'Don't delude yourself. The man is—'

'Alive,' said Gar softly. Dangerously.

Jarralt smiled, an unpleasant baring of teeth. 'But for how long?'

'Nix tells me there's hope.'

'Nix is a fool who tells you what you want to hear,' said Jarralt.

Asher stirred. 'That ain't true. He's a good man with the kingdom's best interests at heart. If he says there's hope for Durm, you can believe it, my lord. And even if there ain't, it's the prince's decision who gets made Master Magician next. Nobody else's.'

The council chamber fell utterly silent. Jarralt turned his head, eyes glittering with rage. 'You dare? You *dare* to speak to me like that?'

Before Asher could answer, Gar said, 'He speaks as my friend . . . and a member of this Privy Council.'

'*What*?'

Horrified, Asher looked at Gar. 'Wait a minute. Sir. I never—'

'I need you,' Gar said, his eyes not leaving Jarralt's furious face. 'As I need you, Conroyd. And Durm.'

With an effort everyone could see, Jarralt thrust aside the issue of an Olken on the Privy Council. 'I've seen Durm,' he spat. 'It's a miracle his brains weren't spilled on the road as well as half his blood. Even if he lives, you can't think he'll be of any use? That he can continue as the kingdom's Master Magician? If he lives he'll be nothing but a witless fool and you know it.'

Still reeling, Asher caught his breath. Felt his heart constrict and heard a distant echo of tipsy laughter. *Jed.* Pellen Orrick looked at him, one eyebrow raised in query; he shook his head. Forced himself to breathe again, quietly, and made his fingers unclench in his lap. Orrick looked away.

Gar said, 'I said I need you, my lord. I didn't say in what capacity. I have no intention of appointing a new Master Magician today.'

'I wasn't aware we'd decided you had that authority,' retorted Jarralt. 'Orrick has yet to satisfy me that we are indeed dealing with an accident.'

Gar shoved back his chair, stood and began to pace the chamber. 'Barl give me strength, Conroyd! Do you truly believe I murdered my family? If so, say it. Here and now, with these good men as witnesses. And then perhaps you can explain how I managed to do so while nearly getting killed myself!'

'Even the best of plans can go awry. Or . . . perhaps it's that you had an accomplice!'

'An *accomplice*? What madness are you pursuing now, my lord? Who in this kingdom would—'

'Who do you think?' cried Conroyd Jarralt, and flung out an accusing arm. '*Him*, of course! Your upstart Olken!'

Asher leapt out his chair so fast he nearly fell over. '*Me*? Are you raving? Me, kill the king? The queen? Princess Fane? Not to mention poor bloody Matcher and his horses, who never hurt a soul in their lives! You got no call to go accusin' me, nor no proof of anythin' neither! The only things I ever killed in all my days were fish and fleas! You take that back, Jarralt! You take that back right now!'

Jarralt slid from his chair like a well-oiled eel. Swallowed the distance between them in three swift strides and backed Asher into the nearest wall. One elegant manicured hand, its fingers laden with rings, flattened itself to his chest. '*Lord* Jarralt, you vermin-ridden interloper,' he corrected, his voice a virulent whisper. 'You misbegotten whelp. You stinking piece of Olken offal. You're behind all this, aren't you? How did you do it, hmmm? Who did you suborn with promises and lies to perpetrate this foul deed? The palace staff?

A greedy minor Doranen lordling? Or was it the prince himself you bewitched into this murder? And what, in the name of all that's good and holy, did you hope to achieve by doing it? And did you really think I'd not *discover* you?'

Speechless, gaping, Asher stared into Jarralt's eyes, into bottomless blue wells of such obliterating hatred he thought he felt his heart stop beating. 'You are mad, Jarralt. You're stark bloody raving.'

'That'll do, my lord,' said Pellen Orrick. His hand came down on Jarralt's shoulder and his fingers tightened in a warning, and a threat. 'Let's all draw breath and talk like the calm custodians of the kingdom we are. Or should be.'

With a wordless snarl Jarralt stepped sideways, breaking the captain's grip.

Asher looked at Orrick. 'I never hurt 'em,' he said. 'My life on it.'

'I know,' said Orrick. 'I have a dozen witnesses to place you at the Tower when the carriage went over the Eyrie.'

'Witnesses?' He didn't know whether to be relieved or outraged. 'You mean you *checked* on me?'

Orrick sighed. 'Of course. I checked on you all. Even Barlsman Holze, may Barl excuse me.' One by one he looked at them, his expression exasperated and uncompromising. 'Gentlemen, I am Captain of this City. It is my sworn and sacred duty to uphold Barl's Laws and bring miscreants to justice. If I thought a man had done this thing I wouldn't rest until I had him in my hands. Not if he were the lordliest lord in all the kingdom. Not if he were a king himself.' His hard gaze rested on Gar. 'Nor even a king's son.'

Gar nodded. 'As well you should not. This kingdom

expects no less of you, and the men who serve under your command. Orrick, you've said you think these deaths came about by misadventure, not murder. Upon peril to your very soul, I'll ask you for the last time: do you still stand by that conclusion?'

Orrick squared his shoulders and clasped his hands behind his back. 'Your Highness, I do.'

'Very well,' said Gar. 'You have the gratitude of this Privy Council for your swift and thorough examination of these events. Be advised, however, that should any new facts come to light and cause you to rethink your conclusion, we expect to hear of them immediately.'

Orrick nodded. 'You will, sir.'

Gar turned to Jarralt, a series of thoughts shifting behind his cold green eyes. When at last he spoke his tone was mild, polite, but with an undercurrent of ice. 'My lord, it's no secret we've had our differences. But I believe that honest dissent is no bad thing. If our decisions cannot withstand scrutiny then we don't deserve the authority to make them. I have accepted Captain Orrick's finding in this matter. The tragic deaths of my father, my mother and my sister – this realm's king, queen and WeatherWorker in Waiting – did not come about by any human agency. If ever I did impugn your honour in relation to this, I say now I was in error. And I offer you my hand in token of a new beginning between us.'

To accept the prince's apology Jarralt had to step closer. Yield his position. Asher held his breath. If the bastard didn't do it, if he persisted in his mad claims of conspiracy and murder, the kingdom'd go up in flames, near enough . . .

'A new beginning,' said Conroyd Jarralt, as though the words were broken glass in his mouth. He stepped forward and grasped Gar's forearm.

His fingers tight on Jarralt's sleeve, Gar smiled. 'So you accept Captain Orrick's conclusion? Neither I, nor my assistant Asher, nor any man, woman or child associated with or known to me or him, did plan or execute the murder of my family, or the attempted murder of Master Magician Durm.'

Jarralt's answering smile was complicated. 'I accept Orrick has no evidence or proof of it. I accept he made a genuine attempt to uncover the truth of the matter. I accept . . . the role of honest dissenter.'

Gar stared at him. 'And do you also accept I am my father's true and lawful heir to the throne of Lur? To the title of WeatherWorker? Speaking bluntly, sir: do you, Lord Conroyd Jarralt, in this place and at this time, before these witnesses, accept that I am, by Barl's great mercy, your king?'

# CHAPTER SIX

Jarralt's head went back, as though bracing for a blow. Asher stared, holding his breath. If Jarralt chose to fight . . .

But he didn't. Instead he offered Gar a curt nod. 'Yes. In this place and at this time, I accept you as king. Your Majesty.'

The challenging light in Gar's eyes faded. Releasing his grip on Jarralt's arm he let his lips soften into a reserved smile. 'Excellent. It seems we understand one another at last, sir.'

Asher nearly swallowed his tongue. Was Gar suntouched? Did he think one brief arm clasp and a grudging admission meant the end of Jarralt's opposition? Of his enmity, and his likely crusade for the crown? Did *any* of them here think that?

Bloody Holze clearly did . . . or wanted to. He was beaming like a maiden aunty at the birth of a new nephew. Orrick? Well, who could tell? Orrick's inscrutable face revealed nothing except, perhaps, a smidgin of grave approval. For himself, he'd as soon believe he could vault straight over the Wall. And as for Gar—

Gar was still smiling. Self-contained and seemingly satisfied. No warmth in his eyes, though. He wasn't fooled, not he, after a lifetime with these people. For there was no warmth in Jarralt's eyes either, if ever there had been or could be. This was just a breathing space in the battle. A momentary pause in hostilities. Because Conroyd Jarralt would no sooner give up his dreams of a crown than – than – the late and unlamented Princess Fane would've kissed a commoner in the street, and Gar knew it.

'And now we have that settled,' he said, 'we must turn to other pressing matters. Gentlemen, let us resume our seats.'

Asher waited for Gar to sit, then Jarralt, before sliding back into his own chair. Was it a trick of the light or did Captain Orrick spare him the merest hint of an approving nod as he, too, sat down again? Uncertain, he folded his hands primly on the table before him. Lowered his eyelids to half-mast and let his gaze discreetly rest on Gar's face as he tried to work out what was coming next.

Gar sat in silence, collecting his thoughts. He looked remade. Gone was the magickless prince, fallible and vulnerable and endearingly human. In the space of a few scant hours tragedy had remoulded Gar into a portrait of untouchable, unreachable monarchy, as distant and unknowable as any daubed onto canvas in the last six hundred years. Asher thought it was like looking at a stranger, and felt a chill shiver through him.

'Obviously, the first order of business is to inform the kingdom of yesterday's tragic events,' Gar said. 'I will need you all to assist in this difficult task.'

Jarralt was asked to inform members of the General Council. Barlsman Holze would see that the kingdom's

Barlsmen and women were told and encouraged to offer all words of comfort to their grieving chapel districts. Asher was appointed the task of telling the palace staff and helping to coordinate the dozens of couriers and heralds required to spread the news throughout the City and the rest of the kingdom. Pellen Orrick was commanded to assist Asher in that detail, and also see to it that strict law and order was maintained in Dorana once the sad news broke.

'What about Matcher's widow?' said Asher. 'She's been sittin' at home under guard since last night.'

For a moment Gar looked nonplussed, as though he'd never heard of the royal coachman. Then: 'Yes. Of course. Dismiss the guards and present yourself to the lady, Asher. Extend to her my deepest sympathies for her bereavement. Assure her she need have no fears of hardship; there will be a generous pension. And thank her for her discretion in this delicate matter.'

Asher swallowed a groan. More grief, more tears . . . 'Aye, sir.'

With Durm indisposed, Gar continued, Barlsman Holze would announce his ascension to WeatherWorker that afternoon on the steps of Justice Hall, once the Barl's Chapel bells had tolled for the late royal family. 'While there is no question of my fitness or right to assume the throne,' he said, not looking at Jarralt, 'the last WeatherWorker to die without first publicly declaring an heir was Queen Drea. That was more than two centuries ago. Therefore, above all, we must forestall any misgivings amongst the population: they should know their lives will continue in safety and prosperity, no matter whose head supports the crown.'

'An excellent idea,' Holze approved. 'And what of your coronation?'

Gar frowned at his laced fingers. 'Tradition dictates a WeatherWorker be crowned in the presence of his or her Master Magician.'

'Then it would appear,' said Conroyd Jarralt, smoothly, 'we have a problem. Your Majesty.'

'Not yet we don't, Conroyd.'

'But as you rightly point out, you cannot be crowned WeatherWorker without—'

'Yes, I can,' said Gar, glaring. 'It's tradition, not law.'

'That's true,' conceded Jarralt. 'At least as far as the coronation is concerned. However, it is stated in law that a WeatherWorker cannot rule without the guidance of a Master Magician. And while Durm draws breath today, each moment might be his last. Admit that much, at least. Your Majesty.'

'I'd be a fool not to consider the possibility,' said Gar, his voice thin with leashed temper. 'But that's all it is: a possibility. For the good of the kingdom I shall be crowned WeatherWorker at midnight on Barl's Day after next, whether Durm is revived or not. Two weeks after that I shall reconsider his position.'

Hungry as a hunting cat, Jarralt leaned forward. 'Against all urgings and advice, Durm has neither named nor trained his successor. The choice will be yours.'

'He felt that to prematurely appoint his own heir would be to invite . . . unrest,' said Gar coldly. 'There is historical precedent for his concern. My father was satisfied with the decision, therefore—'

'Your father did not foresee the current crisis. If he had, then we wouldn't—'

'Conroyd!' said Holze, shocked. 'Please!'

Gar raised a quelling hand. 'It's true our lives would be simpler had Durm made his choice before now. He didn't. And as he still breathes I have no intention of replacing him or usurping his right to name his successor. At least not until I must. His life rests in Barl's hands now, gentlemen. I suggest we wait and see what she intends to do with it before we visit this matter again.'

Holze cleared his throat, breaking the charged silence. 'There is one other thing we should touch upon, if only briefly.'

'The funerals,' said Gar. 'Yes. My family shall lie a month in state, Holze, in the palace's Grand Reception Hall, so that all in the kingdom who wish to do so might pay their final respects. After that time they shall be interred privately in our house vault. Asher—'

He sat up. 'Sir?'

'I'm charging you, Darran and Captain Orrick with the responsibility of arranging the public viewings.'

'Sir,' he said, and swallowed a sigh. He didn't mind the prospect of working closely with Orrick. But with *Darran*? 'What about the actual interment? You want me to—'

Gar shook his head. 'I'll worry about that. Holze, you and I will meet to discuss the matter.'

'Certainly, sir,' said Holze. 'At your convenience, naturally. And your removal to the palace? When can we expect that?'

'The business of good government does not require my nightgown to be hung in a palace wardrobe,' said Gar. 'When I am more accustomed to my new estate I shall revisit the matter of leaving the Tower. Not before.'

Holze, no fool, could recognise a door when it was slammed shut in his face. He nodded. 'Certainly, Your Majesty.'

'And the Wall, Majesty?' asked Jarralt. 'The weather, and its Working?'

'Aren't matters you need be concerned with, my lord,' replied Gar. 'Thanks to Durm's prudence and foresight I have the necessary skills at hand.'

'But lacking a Master Magician, sir, and yourself . . . unpractised, in the art of WeatherWorking, surely—'

'I am my father's son, Conroyd,' said Gar. 'I need no more qualification than that.' He stood. 'Gentlemen, you have your assigned duties. Apply yourselves to their commission without further delay.'

Scrambling to his feet with the rest of them, Asher watched Gar leave the Privy Council chamber like a slender, haughty cat. Watched Conroyd Jarralt frown, wait a moment, then leave and turn out of the doorway to walk in the opposite direction. Watched Holze sigh, and smooth his unadorned braid with unhappy fingers, and follow Jarralt.

'So,' said Pellen Orrick once they were alone. 'Meister Privy Councillor now, eh?'

He swallowed bile. 'It weren't my bloody idea!'

'I know,' said Orrick. 'I saw your face when he said it.'

Resisting the urge to spit sour saliva on the chamber floor, he said, 'About yesterday. Your findings. Was it really an accident?'

'Why?' said Orrick. 'Do you doubt my competence now, along with our good Lord Jarralt?'

He scowled. 'Course not. Just . . . it seems wrong, somehow, all those powerful magicians brought low by an *accident*.'

'I see,' said Orrick, amused. 'Feeling a touch mortal, are you?' He shrugged. 'Doranen die, Asher, just like we do. Their magic can't protect them from everything. I've known Doranen who choked on a fishbone. Broke their necks falling down a flight of stairs. Drowned in their bathtub. Death has no rhyme or reason. It comes for us all, making up its own mind as to when and how.'

Still scowling, Asher scuffed at the chamber floor with his boot heel. 'I know, but—'

'But you want it to make sense.' Orrick laughed. 'I was right last night. You do have a guardsman's mind.' Sobering, he stared out of a chamber window. 'If you're asking whether I think these deaths out of the ordinary, then yes, I do. But beyond that? I have neither reason nor proof to question Pother Nix and Barlsman Holze's findings. Nor your innocence, or His Majesty's, or even that of Lord Conroyd Jarralt, though as a man I find him . . . distasteful.'

Surprised, Asher stared at Orrick. 'That ain't very discreet of you, Captain.'

Orrick stared back. 'Why? Are you a tattle-tongue?'

He just snorted and shook his head. 'Gar – His Majesty, I mean, he seems—'

'He's a king without warning, Asher. A young man whose whole family has just died in violent, sudden circumstances. He wears his royalty like a suit of armour, to keep emotion at bay.' Orrick smiled then, mockery and sympathy combined. 'Are you feeling slighted?'

'No,' he said, affronted. 'Reckon I'm feelin' . . .' *Sorry. Scared. Uncertain. Overwhelmed.* 'Hungry.'

'Then eat.'

'Ha. Who's got time, Captain?'

'Call me Pellen. Since it seems we're to be working hand in glove, for a while at least. And speaking of which—'

'Aye?' he said.

'I'd like to sit down with you, once I've prepared my men for what's coming,' said Orrick. 'Look at calling an urgent meeting of all the guilds' representatives.

When this sad news breaks, the streets will be awash in tears, I think.'

Asher nodded. 'And the guilds are in a better position than we are to keep their members under control. That's good thinking, Cap— Pellen.'

'When you've a moment to scratch yourself send a runner down to the guardhouse,' said Orrick. 'I'll come up as soon after as I can.'

'Provided you ain't had to lock me up for throttlin' that ole biddy Darran. 'Cause I'm tellin' you, Pellen, it ain't beyond the bounds of possibility.'

'Well, don't hold back on my account,' said Orrick, straight-faced. 'We could meet in your cell, then, which would save me a trip to the Tower.'

It took him a moment to realise the joke. Who'd have thought it? Hatchet-faced Orrick with a sense of humour.

'Ha!' he said, warmed, and headed for the door. 'Very funny.'

Pellen Orrick fell into step beside him. Smiled, swiftly and with a dry amusement. 'I thought so.'

Undisturbed by customers, Dathne was tidying shelves when she heard the first faint, wailing cries from the street outside her bookshop. Turning, she looked through the display window to see her alarmed neighbours spilling out of their premises like ants from a stick-stirred nest, pushing and shoving in a cluster round Mistress Tuttle from the bakery five doors along. Mistress Tuttle was flapping her hands in a frenzy as she spoke, her oven-flushed cheeks streaked with tears.

Dathne felt her breath catch as relief warred with sorrow. So. The news was out then. Which meant she could put down one burdensome secret, at least, and worry instead about what next Prophecy would send to try her. Not more death, she fervently hoped. Three lives – well, four if you counted poor Matcher – and five if you included Asher's father – had already been sacrificed for the sake of an uncertain future. To ensure that whatever must come to pass would come to pass, so Asher might be reborn as the Innocent Mage.

*Why, Veira?* she'd asked the old woman the previous night, after telling her of the royal family's fate. *Why would Prophecy need to kill so many?*

Veira's reply through the Circle Stone had been typical. *We don't know it is Prophecy's doing, child. But if it is then you should know there is a reason. Even if we can't see it for shadows.*

As the uproar in the street outside intensified, Dathne starting shoving a new shelf of books into line. Reason or not, it seemed to her that Prophecy was being needlessly harsh. Surely events might have been managed without bloodshed, and suffering, and the look on Asher's face as he fell into her outstretched arms.

Snared in memory she felt again the weight of him against her, his bone-deep trembling beneath her spreading hands. Heard for the thousandth relived time the way he exhaled her name like a prayer and drank her face down with his eyes. Fresh longing rose sharp within her like sap in the trees after winter . . .

*No.* He was the Mage and she was the Heir. It was true they walked the same path at the same time, but they must journey alone, their hands never touching, their hearts unentwined. What she felt was sentiment, pure and simple, and Prophecy had no time or use for sentiment. *She* had no time or use for it. Sentiment would kill a lot more people than Prophecy ever could.

But oh . . . how hard it was to deny him. Hard, and

day by day getting harder, for now she knew him. *Really* knew him, not simply as the living embodiment of Prophecy but as a man.

She knew he liked malt ale better than hop. Roast chicken, not sauced duck. Liked to sing, but out of mercy refrained in public. His favourite colours were green and blue. He thought play-acting in the theatre was a ragtaggin' bloody great waste of time but would stand in front of a puppet show for an hour and never notice the time fly past. He was impatient of pretension, self-opinion and the puff-and-ruffle of guild meisters and their lackeys, yet gave his time, favours and sometimes money freely to those guild members he found in need. Complained bitterly if asked to read any kind of history book, but snuck peeks at the brightly illustrated fairy tales left lying about the shop for children to discover.

He was rude and crude and caustic and compassionate. Loyal, implacable, honest and fair. His skin against hers was a benediction, his voice at her doorstep a song.

'*Damn* you, Asher! Why couldn't you have been hateful? Or – or married, or ugly, or old? Why couldn't you have been anyone but yourself?'

'Who are you talking to, dearie?'

Startled, Dathne turned. Pushed her hands into her skirt's capacious pockets and blanked her face. 'Meister Beemfield! I'm sorry, I didn't realise I had a customer. Can I help you?'

Meister Beemfield's hat was askew on his head and there were tears in his faded blue eyes. 'Oh, dearie,' he quavered, lost, bewildered. 'Have you heard? It's the king, lass. And the queen too, and that pretty daughter of theirs. Dead, dead, all dead. The heralds are crying it throughout the City!'

'No!' she gasped, suitably shocked, and tried to squeeze out a surprised tear or two. Failing, she groped for her handkerchief and hid her face. 'How awful!'

Meister Beemfield was shaking his head. 'You'd best shut up your shop for the day, dearie. There'll be nobody buying books this afternoon. The heralds say there's to be an announcement at five o'clock on the steps of Justice Hall. If you like I'll escort you there now. The streets are fair thronged and there's no saying what could happen when folks are ramshackled with dismay.'

He was the one who wanted to go, she realised. Wanted, and was perhaps afraid, feeling frail and overwhelmed by tragedy. Certainly he wasn't wrong about the streets. One glance through the window showed her a solid mass of townsfolk streaming along in the direction of the City's central square. One misstep, one stumble, and the old man might well be thoughtlessly trampled. For herself she could easily miss the gathering. Whatever the announcement she'd learn of it soon enough. But it meant so much to Meister Beemfield, and he was an excellent customer . . .

And there was a good chance Asher would be there.

'That's a very kind offer, sir,' she said. 'Let me get my shawl.'

Lady Marnagh had been weeping. Her pale grey eyes were bloodshot and puffy and her lower lip persisted in trembling. Every so often, when she thought Asher wasn't looking, a finger crept up to capture an errant tear. He would've offered her a kerchief but still felt in awe of her. Besides, she probably had her own. Probably, she was trying to be discreet.

They stood with the rest of Justice Hall's staff inside the building, as Barlsman Holze graced the steps beyond the open double doors and prayed before the gathered multitude in the square. The mood in the hall was sombre, the silence almost complete. A muffled sob here, a shuddering sigh there: they were the only sounds aside from Holze's measured, stately voice. Magic carried his words through the air and into the hearing of the City's inhabitants, who'd crushed themselves into the square so tightly Asher doubted you'd fit even a feather in there with them. More folk crowded at the windows of the various buildings lining the square. He thought they might even have tried crowding into the guardhouse, if Captain Orr – Pellen – had let them.

Staring at all those listening people he found himself counting heads. So many yellow, so many black. From up high like this he could see they formed a pattern. A lot of the yellow heads were gathered right up the front, around the base of Justice Hall's wide marble steps. Others were thick around the edges of the square, so it looked like a pie: golden pastry edges with a thick blackberry filling.

It occurred to him he'd be hard-pressed to put a name to most of the Doranen faces out there. The only Doranen he could claim to know, even slightly, were Barlsman Holze and Conroyd Jarralt. Lady Marnagh. And a few of the Doranen on the General Council. Jarralt's cronies. And only then because he couldn't avoid them. Beyond that, Doranen society was a mystery to him. Like oil and water his folk and Gar's sloshed around inside Dorana's walls, touching frequently but never quite mixing. Even as Assistant Olken Administrator he'd never had to deal with the City's Doranen. On the rare occasions over the past year or so when a Doranen was involved in Olken business, Gar had taken care of it. And when one of them invited Gar to dinner they never saw fit to include an Olken fisherman at the table. Even one who'd learned the hard way which fork to use when.

With an unpleasant shock he wondered if *Gar* could put a name to all their faces. The only times the prince mixed with his own folk was when duty or royal protocol meant he couldn't escape the encounter, or when Darran's protests and pleadings wore him down and he grudgingly accepted one of those invitations to dinner or the races or some other kind of exclusive Doranen entertainment.

Now though, thanks to disaster, that was about to change. Magickless Prince Gar could avoid his peers, but WeatherWorker King Gar was suddenly one of them. About to go sailing into strange and unfamiliar waters. And, like a rowboat tethered to a smack, Asher of Restharven was about to go sailing into them with him.

Asher bit his lip in dismay. How would the Doranen react to the notion of their almost invisible prince upon the throne of Lur? To a once-crippled outcast, more at home with the Olken than his own people, suddenly become the beating heart of all their lives? And how would they react when they realised he expected to marry one of their daughters so he might breed himself an heir?

Before the accident Gar had felt nervous at the thought of unveiling himself to them as a prince reborn. So how would it be now? He was an untried, untested magician, famous for all the wrong reasons, and now he was the king. The WeatherWorker. All that stood between Lur and the unknown dangers beyond the Wall. And not one of his own people knew if he was up to the job. To be honest, even Gar didn't know. And if he stumbled, even once, even slightly, Conroyd Jarralt and his cronies would be on him like cats on a mouse.

Asher felt his heart sink like an anchor. *Barl bloody save me! I ain't a bloody guard dog!*

Holze had finally finished entreating Barl's mercy and protection. Now he waited as the echoes from the crowd's final response died away. Feeling Lady Marnagh's disapproving gaze, Asher wrenched his attention back to the moment at hand and managed to mutter something appropriate at the tail end of the Hall's employees' heartfelt murmuring. Then he took a small step forward, the better to see the crowd and waited, hardly breathing.

'Now, good people of Dorana City, it falls upon me to answer the greatest question of all,' said Holze. He wore his finest vestments; the lowering sun struck multicoloured fire from threads of gold and silver, from rubies and emeralds and deep purple amethysts. There were so many fresh blossoms tied into his braid he could've opened a flower shop. 'Tradition dictates it is the Master Magician who names our next WeatherWorker. But our dearly beloved Durm still recovers from his injuries, so it falls upon me to stand in his place. Barl, in her infinite and mysterious wisdom, has decreed we must live our lives henceforth without the loving guidance of King Borne or the expectation of his glorious daughter Fane's reign thereafter. But in her magnificent adoration of us, her children, Barl has yet kept the promise made to our forebears and ensured our continued peace, prosperity and safety. Therefore in her great name I give you His Majesty King Gar, WeatherWorker of Lur!'

As a swell of sound surged from the crowd, Asher heard shocked gasps behind him. He turned and there was Gar himself, walking through the gap between the gathered Justice Hall staff. Still dressed in unrelieved black, his bruised head bare of circlet or crown, his face was pale and set in grim lines. As though completely alone he passed between his staring subjects, straight by Asher, out through the open doorway and onto the steps of Justice Hall.

When the crowd saw him the noise threatened to shatter the sky. Shrieks. Shouts. Great cries of welcome, and of woe. Somewhere in the gathered press of flesh a man's voice screamed, 'King Gar! King Gar! Barl bless our King Gar!'

Another voice echoed him. Then another. And another. Then two voices in unison. Three. Ten. Thirty. Fifty. Louder and stronger, man, woman and child, the chant leaping from throat to throat like flames in a wheatfield.

*'King Gar! King Gar! Barl bless our King Gar!'*

There were Doranen voices raised out there, along with Olken. They were raised in here, too, Asher saw. Not as loudly as the folk outside, but with the same amount of passion. In the faces of the gathered staff he saw love, relief and a transcendent joy. Lur had a new WeatherWorker. They could go to bed tonight feeling safe, protected, knowing the world could continue unchanged, and for that they gave thanks. Which was all well and good and a nice way to finish the day, but how long would joy and gratitude last if Gar wasn't ready?

Holze had dropped to his knees, head bowed to his chest in homage to the new king. Gar left him there for three heartbeats, then bent and drew the elderly cleric to his feet. Embraced him. The crowd's chanting doubled in fervour and volume. Asher could feel his bones vibrating. The noise was so loud he thought it might bring the roof of Justice Hall down on all their heads and tumble the City's buildings into rubble and dust.

On the steps outside, Gar released his hold on Barlsman Holze and turned to face the crowd. His hands lifted high overhead and a stream of golden light burst forth from his outstretched fingertips. Up and up and up into the air it poured, and suddenly the world smelled of freesias and jasmine and all sweet things. The crowd fell raggedly silent, watching, as the raw magic coalesced over their heads, becoming a thick golden cloud.

Gar clenched his fingers into fists. The golden cloud shivered. Shuddered. Collapsed into thousands and thousands of flower petals that rained onto all the upturned faces of his people. As the crowd gasped in wonder, Asher swallowed his own surprise. It was hard to get used to Gar doing magic. It was like watching a crippled bird spread its wings and fly effortlessly, casually, the way it should've flown from birth.

'Citizens of Dorana!' Gar cried. 'Yesterday there walked among you a man known in this kingdom as His Royal Highness Prince Gar of Lur. Yesterday that man died, along with all his family, and today is reborn as your king. Your servant. Barl's instrument in the world, whose only ambition is to maintain and nurture the strength of her Wall. Whose only reason for living is to keep you as you are: loved and safe and obedient to her will. Yesterday I was a prince with one father, one mother, one sister. Today I am a king with more fathers and mothers and sisters than I can count. Yes, and brothers too, aunts and uncles and cousins and children. For the people of Lur are my family now. And I will love my family unto death, and defend them from any who would wish them harm. In Barl's name I swear it, and may magic desert me if my heart and oath are not true!'

A breathless hush. A quivering silence. Then:

'*King Gar! King Gar! King Gar!*'

Asher felt the small tight knot in his gut unravel just a little. Gar had sounded calm. Confident. At peace with himself and the burden Barl had placed, for no good reason, on his unready shoulders.

He'd sounded like his dead father. Like a king.

As Asher watched, weak-kneed with relief, Gar started down the steps of Justice Hall. Holze reached out a hand to him, saying something in an alarmed undertone; the words were lost in the crowd's cries of adoration and acclaim. Gar ignored him. Asher pushed forward to the doorway, incredulous. Was Gar mad? He couldn't just saunter into that mob on his own! Not that he was in danger, not from any deliberate unlawful act. But all those people! The unbridled emotion! They'd want to touch him, talk to him, he'd be overwhelmed. Horrified, Asher stared at Holze and Holze stared back, his hands spread in helpless disbelief.

'Do something,' he hissed. 'Start up another prayer or a hymn, quick! We can't let him—'

But it was too late. Gar had reached the bottom of the marble steps. Was stepping into the crowd. The Doranen before him fell back, pushing against the people behind them. A hesitant middle-aged Doranen man in blue brocade spoke to him. There were flower petals caught in his unbound yellow hair. Gar replied, then nodded and rested a hand on his shoulder. The man stared at Gar, speechless, then burst into sobs. Gar embraced him. Held him close for a heartbeat, then let go.

The simple gesture broke the stunned silence and the crowd's uncertain stillness. Suddenly Gar was surrounded by eager, reaching hands, Doranen and Olken both, seeking to touch their miracle king. To comfort and be comforted in this time of pain and loss and new beginnings. His aura glowing like a candle,

Gar moved through the press of bodies in the square, embracing and being embraced, and his people made way for his progress. Welcomed him into their arms and their hearts and laid the ghosts of his family to rest.

Asher watched in silence for a time, then turned again to Holze. 'Well. Seems he knows what he's doin' after all.'

There were tears on Holze's seamed cheeks. 'He is indeed his father's son,' he whispered, hungry eyes following Gar's slow progress through the square. 'For the first time since I saw that terrible gap in the Eyrie's fence, I am not afraid.'

Asher bit his lip. 'Don't s'pose you know where Lord Jarralt is, do you? Thought he'd be here for this.'

'I have known Conroyd Jarralt all his life, Asher,' Holze said softly. 'He is many things, not all of them comfortable, but a heretic and a traitor he is not. Conroyd loves this kingdom. He would never do anything to harm it. If you believe nothing else, believe that.'

There was no point arguing. Asher nodded. 'Aye, sir.'

'I'll return to Barl's Chapel now, and pray for their late Majesties and Her Highness. If His Majesty should need me for any reason, send a runner.'

'Aye, sir,' said Asher again, and stood aside to let Holze pass. Before following him back into the hall, he cast a last look over the crowd and his king. Likely Gar would be out there for hours yet, the way every last Olken and Doranen was trying to lay a hand on him. Which meant it looked like another late night for one Meister Asher, formerly of Restharven.

Hooray.

A cleared throat behind him distracted his frowning attention. He turned.

'Is the staff dismissed then, Asher?' asked Lady Marnagh. 'May I send them home?'

She'd never deferred to him like that before, not in all the time he'd known her. Yet he wasn't the one who'd changed. Was this what he could expect from everybody now? Some of Gar's kingly lustre rubbed off on him? He nodded. 'Might as well, m'lady. Ain't no work to be done, and they'll be wanting their families, most like.'

'What about you?'

He shrugged. 'Reckon I'll be stayin' on for a bit, till that crowd out there's seen its fill and gone home. Might be something the king wants doing.'

'Yes, of course.' She hesitated, and fresh tears brimmed in her eyes. 'Will you tell His High— His Majesty how sorry I am? How sorry we all are.'

'Aye.'

She brushed her fingertips across his sleeve. 'Thank you. Good evening to you, Asher.'

'And you, Lady Marnagh.'

He watched as she gathered her staff together and herded them towards the rear doors. Outside, voices in the crowd swelled and crested like the restless, roaring ocean. Abruptly reminded, suddenly homesick, he turned on his heel and followed the tail end of Marnagh's staff out of the Hall.

# CHAPTER SEVEN

In the Hall stables where Cygnet had been left to browse on hay, Asher found Ballodair dozing in the box beside Cygnet, and a single stablehand polishing brass.

'You can go, Vonnie,' he said. 'Since there ain't no other horses to mind. I'll wait here till His Majesty returns and see the horses come to no harm.'

Shy Vonnie nodded his thanks, lit the stable-yard lanterns against the creeping dusk and scarpered. Asher found an empty water bucket, upturned it and sat with his back braced against the wall between the two occupied stables. Passingly curious, Cygnet whuffled in his hair. Asher patted his nose. With no apples forthcoming the horse lost interest and withdrew to doze in the deep straw. Asher stretched out his legs, folded his hands in his lap and followed suit.

He woke some time later when somebody kicked him in the ankle. 'Ow!' he said, and opened his eyes. It was dark and he was cold. 'Where's Gar?'

'He's still out there,' said Dathne. She was buttoned into a black woollen jacket and carried a cloth-covered basket in one gloved hand. 'Hungry? I brought dinner.'

He creaked to his feet. 'What time is it?'

'Nearly half-seven.' She put down the basket and uncovered it. The air filled with the scent of hot cornbread; he sniffed appreciatively, suddenly ravenous.

As Dathne busied herself with the basket's contents she added, 'The square's still straggled with people. They won't go home till they've touched their new king, and he won't send them away, even though he must be exhausted by now. People are singing his praises up street and down. If they were afraid before, or uncertain, they aren't any more.'

He held out his hand and took the napkin-wrapped food she was offering. 'How'd you know I was here?'

Her smile was brief and affectionate. 'Where else would you be but nearby, waiting for him?'

He shrugged, his mouth too full for speaking. The cornbread was soaked in butter; he nearly moaned aloud at the taste. She smiled again, enjoying his enjoyment, and took a dainty bite of fried chicken wing. He had melted butter running down his chin and inside his sleeve. He didn't care. She'd thought of him and brought him dinner.

She said, 'Tell me, if you can: how is Master Magician Durm? Really?'

'Not dead,' he replied, reaching for a plump seasoned drumstick. 'Were you out in the square then? When Holze announced Gar king and he gave his pretty speech?'

'It was a pretty speech. It made a lot of people cry.'

He sucked butter and chicken fat from his fingers, watching her face. 'You?'

'Would you like more?' she asked, and bent to the basket. 'There's plenty.'

He held out his napkin and she filled it again. Bloody

woman. If she had cried, she'd never tell him. Did that mean she'd never be his, if she couldn't even share that much of herself? He thought it might. Despair chilled him. He could feel his dreams and desires for her, for them, fading like mist in the morning. Once, just once, he wished he could know her true heart.

'What?' she said, staring.

He shook his head. 'Nowt. This is good,' he answered, and filled his mouth with more hot sweet cornbread before he said something else. Something he could never take back and would go to his long-distant grave regretting.

'Everything's going to change now,' she said, bending again to fuss with the basket. 'Have you thought about that?'

Every bloody moment, waking and sleeping, since the horror of Salbert's Eyrie. 'A bit.'

'He'll have no time for Olken administrating now. The WeatherWorking will swallow him alive, just like it swallows all of them.' She straightened. 'I imagine he'll ask you to take over for him for good. Olken Administrator Asher. Asher of Dorana, instead of Restharven.'

The words were a harpoon between his ribs. 'You sound like bloody Matt,' he said, more roughly than he intended, or wanted. 'So I'll tell you what I told him. Dorana's my home for now, not forever.'

'Fine. But while it is "for now", what are you going to do?' she demanded. 'If the king asks you to serve him as his Olken Administrator, what will you say?'

He dropped his chewed chicken bone and the butter-stained napkin into the basket. 'What d'you reckon? I'll say what I always say when he asks me to do things,' he muttered. 'I'll say yes.'

She reached out and touched his hand. Smiling now, temper forgotten. A shock blazed through him, lightning in a hot sky. 'Don't be so gloomy. There are worse ways to pass the time.'

'No, there ain't,' he said, fighting the urge to take the fingers that had touched him and hold them captive till the end of time. 'Cause it means I got to work hand in hand with that bloody ole Darran like he and I never wanted to kill each other every day from the first day we met. And since we did – we do—'

She laughed. 'Oh dear. Sounds to me like you need an assistant. Somebody to save you from him . . . or him from you.'

'Of course I need a bloody assistant!' he said, glowering. Reaching again to the basket he helped himself to more hot cornbread, lukewarm now, and chewed savagely. 'I've needed one ever since Gar got his magic and I been left to pick up the pieces of everything else.'

'Will I do?'

It took a lot of red-faced coughing and a few well-placed blows on his back to dislodge the cornbread that had gone down the wrong way. Eyes streaming, chest heaving, he stared at her. '*You* be my – ha! That's very funny, Dath!'

Her smile was unsettling: cool and contained and faintly challenging. 'It's not a joke.'

He looked more closely and realised, no, it wasn't. 'What about your bookshop?'

She shrugged. 'What about it? I can hire someone to sell books for me. I've been selling them myself for a long time now, Asher. Perhaps I'd like to do something different.'

He wiped his hands up and down the front of his breeches, heedless of grease stains. If she'd sprouted hooves and a tail he doubted he'd feel more surprised. Dathne as the Assistant Olken Administrator. *His* Assistant Olken Administrator. It was crazy. She'd want to run back to her books inside of a week. All that petti-fogging detail and dealing with the guilds. She'd lose her temper and bite them on the nose at the first sign of contrariness . . .

'I handle people as much as I handle books, Asher,' she said, reading him. Drat her. 'You're not the only one who has to deal with the guilds, you know. And flibbertigibbet shillyshalliers who couldn't make up their minds if their lives depended on it. Plus I'm an excellent record keeper, and well known in the City. Not to be immodest, but I'm well liked too. I could be very useful to you, in all sorts of ways.'

She meant it. She really was offering herself as his assistant. 'It ain't great pay,' he warned her. 'It's long hours and lots of argy-bargy and aggravation and no matter how hard you try you almost never please everybody. And nobody thinks you got a life of your own, they think you're there to listen to all their problems any hour of the night or day and then fix 'em with a snap of your fingers. And when you can't, or won't, they pout and whinge and threaten to lay a complaint.'

She grinned. 'Don't you think I know all that? After a year of listening to you moaning into your ale down at the Goose, Asher, don't you think I know exactly what this job entails?'

'And you still want to do it?' When she nodded, he threw up his hands. 'See? You are mad.'

'If you don't want me, you can say so. But don't think I'm not serious.'

'What does Matt say?'

'What's Matt got to do with it?'

He grimaced. 'Seems to me you talk to him about practically everything. Seems to me every time I turn around there's you and him nose to ear in a corner somewhere, whispering. Thought you'd've asked his opinion on this afore scarin' the life out of me with it.'

'This has nothing to do with Matt,' she snapped. 'It's about you and me, and whether or not you want me as your assistant administrator. So. Do you?'

Did he want her? Barl save him, he wanted her so much he sometimes feared his bones would melt. The thought of working with her . . . of having her with him every day . . . hearing her voice, smelling her hair, watching her glide through a room, dividing the air like a beautiful knife. It meant he'd have all the time in the world, then, to learn that secret heart of hers. To coax it out of her close keeping and hold it in his careful hands.

'What?' she said as he cloaked intemperate desire in a fresh fit of coughing. 'What's wrong, are you all right?'

'I'm fine,' he said, and banged his chest. Grinned. *Every day . . . every day . . .* 'Indigestion. Must be somethin' I ate.'

That made her laugh, and smack the side of his head. 'Ungrateful lump! That's the last time I—' And then she stopped, the smile vanishing. Sober, serious, she dropped to the ground in a deep curtsey. 'Your Majesty.'

He spun about. Gar. Looking exhausted and exultant and subtly not himself. 'Sir,' he said, and bowed.

'You waited,' said Gar.

'Course I bloody waited. You all right?'

Gar's eyebrows lifted. 'Shouldn't I be?'

Dathne took a hesitant step forward. 'Sir, if I may –

if it's not presumptuous – I'm sorry. Your family was deeply loved, and will be sorely missed. I know you'll make a fine king, I don't mean – it's just – oh dear—'

It was the first time Asher had ever seen her tongue-tied. Disconcerted, he watched as Gar stepped close, kissed her gently on the cheek and said, 'I know. Thank you, Dathne. Now you should go home. It's late, and I have more work for Asher.'

She curtseyed again, then snatched up her basket. 'Yes, sir. Thank you, sir. Asher, we'll speak again soon?'

'Aye,' he said. 'Soon.'

In silence they watched her hurry away. With his head still turned, Gar said, 'Do you know the worst thing about all this?'

He folded his arms across his chest. 'No.'

'Everyone is so sorry. In such pain. For me, for themselves. I tell you, I've been wept on so much tonight my tunic is soaked right through. They tell me how their hearts are broken, they tell me how wonderful my family was, they think they're giving me comfort but what they really want is for me to comfort them.' Gar laughed softly. Ballodair stuck his head over the stable door and whickered. Crossing to him, Gar smoothed a tangle from his forelock and gently tugged one curving ear. 'So I do. I hold them in my arms, even though I know Darran for one would faint at the thought, and I let them weep against my chest and tell me how hurt they are that my family is dead. And then I give them the kiss of peace and promise that no harm will come to them or their children now that I am king. And they smile at me, because that's really what they came to hear, and they go back to their living family and someone else steps forward to take their place.'

'The *Doranen* do that?' he said, staring.

Gar's sideways smile was derisive. 'What do you think?'

After an uncomfortable pause, he cleared his throat. 'You know I'm sorry, right?'

Gar nodded. 'Of course.'

Another pause. He inspected his shirt cuffs, wondering what Gar was waiting for. 'That were quite the show you gave them out there tonight.'

Gar shrugged. 'I had to do something. They had to see I'm a cripple no longer. But sparkly lights and flower petals won't hold them forever, Asher, Olken or Doranen. They believe in me now because they're shocked and grieving and, as you say, I put on a convincing show. Unfortunately their belief won't last long. Not without something more . . . tangible . . . to back it up.'

He pulled a face. Gar was right, drat it. 'Ain't much you can do about that.'

'On the contrary,' said Gar. 'I can call rain. And not just here in Dorana, but all over the kingdom.'

He choked. 'All over the *kingdom*? Are you mad? You ain't never even called rain in a teacup!'

'Not in a teacup, no. In a test globe. The principle is the same, it's just a question of degree.'

'Of degree? Have you lost your wits? Not even your da made it rain over an entire kingdom! You'll kill yourself! Why not wait a day or so? See if Durm comes round. If he does, you can ask him what—'

Gar's look was dagger sharp. 'I can't afford to wait that long. I can't afford to wait at all. If I don't do something definitive the people will cease to believe in me and Lur will crumble into chaos and despair. Conroyd Jarralt will make his move and I'll lose the crown my father spent his life serving. I'm calling rain, Asher. Tonight. And I want you with me when I do.'

*'Me?'*

'Who else?'

He stepped back a pace, aghast. 'Anybody but me!'

'You'll be quite safe, I promise.'

'You don't know that! You ain't never done this before!'

'True,' Gar conceded after a lengthy silence. 'But for all things there must be a first time. For me, for WeatherWorking, tonight is that time. Asher, I can do this alone. I just don't want to.'

And what about *me*? he wanted to shout. What about what *I* want? He half turned away, hands clasped to the top of his head. As usual, what he wanted was about to go overboard with the fish guts. He turned back. 'All right. Just this once. But you better not think I'll be makin' a habit of it, 'cause—'

'Good,' said Gar. 'Now let's hurry. I want the sky full of rain within the hour.'

In silence they rode back to the palace, but instead of continuing to the Tower they branched off towards a wooded expanse in the old palace grounds, where gardeners and lawn keepers no longer toiled and nature ran riot. Washed with pale travelling glimlight, the horses picked their cautious way along a narrow path that led directly into the heart of the tangled trees and undergrowth.

'Here,' Gar said at last, and drew rein. 'It's best if we go on foot the rest of the way. The path is narrow and the trees grow quite thickly. Besides, horses are sometimes – disturbed – by the Weather Chamber.'

'Oh, aye?' said Asher, sliding to the ground. 'And what about fishermen?'

Gar flung his leg over the pommel and jumped. 'I wouldn't know.'

'Well, I bloody would,' he said, and tied Cygnet's reins to the nearest sturdy tree branch. 'Fishermen are even more disturbed than horses. And don't dismount like that, it's dangerous. You could break your bloody neck.'

Gar sighed. 'I've been dismounting like that for years, Asher. Does my neck look broken to you?'

'No, but there's a first time for everything,' he retorted. 'Or so I been told.'

Gar tugged on Ballodair's knotted reins and gave the horse a brisk pat. 'Come on. The night's not getting any younger.'

Side by side they hurried along the narrow grassy path. The thin air had sharp nipping teeth, but Asher didn't feel them. Noticing his shivers, Gar had conjured a coat for him right out of his wardrobe in the Tower and handed it over with such a look of self-satisfaction he'd had to grin, even though circumstances dictated that amusement was in pretty poor taste.

Of course, so was arguing with the recently bereaved in pretty poor taste, but some things couldn't be helped.

'I still ain't convinced this is a good idea.'

'Of course it is. You said it yourself just this morning. I shouldn't attempt WeatherWorking alone.'

'But what if something goes wrong?'

'You'll fetch help, of course.'

'Help. Right,' he said slowly. 'Only, I reckon there might be a problem with that.'

Gar looked mystified. 'A problem?'

'Aye! 'Cause after they've helped you, it's *me* they'll be helpin', right into the nearest empty cell down at the guardhouse.' Still Gar looked mystified. Asher could've hit him. 'It's forbidden for Olken to meddle in magic, or had you forgotten that? I mean, has the name Timon Spake completely slipped your mind? 'Cause I'll tell you right now it surely ain't slipped mine!'

Gar stopped. 'I forget *nothing* about that day. And it offends me that you'd think I would.'

'Well, I'm offended by the idea of gettin' my head chopped off!' he retorted, wheeling round to face his idiot king.

'Barl save me!' Gar snapped. 'Nobody is going to chop your head off! And you won't be meddling in magic, you'll be protecting me while I perform my sacred duty as Lur's WeatherWorker. You fool, you're more likely to be awarded a medal!'

'Tell that to Conroyd Jarralt!'

With an impatient hiss Gar grabbed Asher's arm with one hand and with the other pointed upwards. 'Look at the gift Barl gave us. Go on. *Look* at it.'

Heaving a sigh, scowling, Asher tilted his head back and looked up at the Wall. At the great and glowing wash of gold soaring into the star-studded sky beyond the treetops. Remote. Mysterious. Magnificent.

'All right,' he said sourly, and tugged his arm free. 'I'm lookin'. So what? It's the Wall, Gar. Same as it's always been.'

'Yes. The same, for more than six hundred years. And you've grown completely used to it, haven't you? Hardly give it a thought from one week to another. And do you know why? Because you've never had a reason to doubt it would be there when you looked for it, any more than you doubt there'll be air to breathe when you open your eyes after a good night's sleep.'

'Gar—'

'What does the Wall mean to you, Asher? What do you see when you look at it?'

'I don't know,' he said, baffled. 'Safety. Prosperity.' He shrugged. 'Magic.'

Gar stared up at the golden mountains. 'I see the altar upon which my father sacrificed his life. Upon which all of Lur's WeatherWorkers have sacrificed themselves, generation upon generation, all the way back to Blessed Barl herself, whose life was given in the making of it. I see a sword, which starting tonight will cut me and bleed me one day at a time, until I have no blood left to shed. I see my life, and my death, and the pain-soaked days in between, offered as payment for the taking of a land that wasn't ours, and the visitation of a danger that should have passed your people by and didn't. Because of mine.' His gaze slid sideways then, before returning to the Wall. 'That's what I see, Asher.'

Asher frowned. Again, abruptly. Gar was a stranger. An unfamiliar spirit housed in prosaically familiar flesh. He shoved his chilly hands into his coat pockets. 'D'you really reckon you can make it rain all over the kingdom?'

With an effort, Gar tore his gaze away from that glowing wash of gold. 'I reckon that if I don't try, we'll never know.' He started walking again and Asher fell into step beside him.

Half a mile later the path ended, spilling like a riverlet into a small clearing . . . at the centre of which stood the kingdom's Weather Chamber. Seeing it, Asher felt his feet stumble and his heart thud hard.

According to history, Barl herself had built it from her own design and spent her last living days there as she invented and perfected the Weather Magic and the Wall that would keep Lur safe from predation until the end of time. Made of the same stone as Gar's Tower, it was crowned with a domed glass roof and an uninterrupted view of the sky. There was no other palace building within sight or earshot. Light from the Wall seemed nearer here, brighter and more dense, as though the Chamber had some power to call it close. It splashed over the ancient bluestone blocks, roaring them to midnight life.

He looked around. 'There ain't any guards.'

Gar shook his head. 'There's no need. The Chamber's steeped in magic. My father used to say it feels . . . alive. Somehow it knows when it's not alone. If any visitor comes here with ill will the door won't open and no magic known to us can make it otherwise.'

He stepped into the clearing. Asher took a deep, shuddering breath and followed.

The chamber's door was plain, unvarnished wood. No handle, no knocker, no keyhole or lock. Gar frowned, dredging memory.

'I was just a child the last – the only – time I came here,' he murmured. 'Durm had intended to bring me back soon, to expand my education . . .' His lips tightened and he wiped his palms down the front of his black tunic. 'Another plan smashed to pieces, along with everything else.' Throwing his head back he slapped his hands to the timber and pushed.

The door remained shut.

'It's just stuck,' said Asher, breaking the white-hot silence. 'Damp's got it or somethin'.'

'What damp?' said Gar through clenched teeth. 'I haven't made it rain yet.'

He pushed again, harder. Again the door resisted him, creaking a little. Releasing a sobbing breath, Gar stepped back. Stared at the door, perplexed and angry and a little afraid. 'Give way, damn you! I am the king and I *will* be admitted!' He struck the timber a blow with his fist. '*Admit me*!' And then he stepped close once more.

Rested his forehead against the door and stroked his fingers down the weathered grain like a coaxing lover. 'Please,' he whispered. 'Please . . . let me in . . .'

Discomforted, Asher laughed. 'It's a door, Gar. Wood. It ain't really alive. And even if it is, I don't see any ears stickin' out anywhere, do you? No way it can bloody hear you. I'm tellin' you, it's the damp.' To prove his point, he shoved against the closed door himself.

It opened.

'Bloody thing,' he said, scowling. 'Playin' hard to get, that's all. If it is alive, I bet it's female.'

Gar tugged at the hem of his tunic. 'No. It was some lingering damp, as you say.'

Asher looked up. 'How many stairs to the top, do you reckon?'

'One hundred and thirty.'

'Oh, my achin' legs.'

Gar sent the travelling glimfire ahead of them into the chamber's entryway, and in muscle-burning silence they climbed to the solitary glass-domed chamber at the top of the tower. Gar opened its door unhindered, nodded Asher through and followed him inside. The bobbing glimfire cast their shadows on the floor in long thin lines. With a wave of his arm Gar swung the door closed again, then ignited fresh glimfire in the sconces attached to the curving walls. Shadows vanished and the chamber was revealed.

The room was clean and cold, smelling faintly, lingeringly, of rain. The parquetry floor gleamed a dark red-brown, hundreds of timber strips laid end to end and side by side in a subtle, intricate pattern. Perhaps some fifty couples dancing would fit beneath the domed glass ceiling . . . that was if the centre of the floor had been empty.

It wasn't. Directly beneath the domed ceiling sat something that to Asher's fascinated gaze looked like an overgrown child's toy.

'The Weather Map,' said Gar, his expression avid. Hungry. Tinged with awe, and fear. 'Barl's incredible power laid bare. It's a magical representation of the kingdom, down to the last hamlet and village.'

Cautiously approaching, Asher saw he was right. There were Barl's Mountains, with the Black Woods clustered at their feet. There was Dorana with its high, encircling wall, and the River Gant spreading silver fingers. The Saffron Hills. The Flatlands. All the places he and Gar had visited or passed through on their trip to Westwailing, as well as the kingdom's other towns, villages, farms and hamlets, its orchards, vineyards and fields of wheat and barley, recreated in perfect miniature. He leaned closer and felt his stomach clench. There, exquisite and touchable and utterly out of reach, was his beloved Restharven.

Without looking up, not wanting to tear his eyes away from even this small taste of home, he said, 'How does it work?'

'To be honest, I'm not exactly sure,' Gar admitted.

Now he did look up. 'You ain't *sure*?'

'Not about the how, no,' said Gar. He sounded defensive. Looked annoyed. 'Durm and I didn't get this far.'

Too bad. 'But you're sure it works.'

Gar walked around the edges of his inherited kingdom, his gaze greedy. 'Oh yes. It changes, even as the kingdom changes. Newly cultivated fields spring up, fallow fields fall into slumber. Land is sold, boundaries change, and you'll know it just by looking here. Whatever happens in the land is reflected in this map.' Annoyance forgotten, his fingers skimmed the air above the toy towns, the wheatfields, the open meadows and the wooded glens. 'Isn't it magnificent?' he whispered.

There was something so naked in his face Asher felt embarrassed. Love . . . longing . . . avarice . . . desire . . . or some strange alchemical blending of all those difficult emotions. It was too intimate a moment for observance.

He looked up. Whether it was his imagination or some trick of the crystal-clear glass arching overhead he didn't know, but the stars looked close enough to touch. The Wall too. Silver and gold, crushing him with beauty. He had to look down again, it was too much to bear. Gar still circled his little kingdom like a cat contemplating a bowl of cream, lost in a private reverie with his soul stripped bare, so he found something else to look at.

The Chamber's curving walls had long ago been soothed smooth and white with plaster, and fitted from floor to waist-height with sturdy cherrywood bookshelves and a single, double-doored cupboard. The shelves were burdened with leather-bound books, some thick, some slender, some ancient, some nearly new. The space between the ceiling and the first crammed shelf was covered like a child's scrapbook with calendars, charts, diagrams, hand-scrawled notes on yellowing scraps of parchment, sketches, jottings . . .

Skimming their circular surface, he saw they were all in some way connected with the weather. Rainfall patterns, wind patterns, seasonal guides, planting guides, snowfall indicators. Notes concerning what crops were harvested when, and where, and how, and what each farmer needed to get the job done in a timely fashion. How much rain was needed to lush the grass in the horse-breeding Dingles district. How much snow the icegrape growers felt was just enough to nurture their precious vines. How deep down the River Gant should freeze for the very best of winter skating, and what was the best temperature for its careful melting come the spring. Not a single facet of Olken or Doranen life was missing. Everything thought of, everything cared for.

When he'd come full circle, he looked at Gar. Shook his head. 'I had no idea . . .'

'Why should you?' said Gar. He'd stopped prowling round the map and was watching him instead. His face was comfortable again, all private feeling decently tucked away. 'WeatherWorking isn't an Olken concern. It's not even a Doranen concern. Only the WeatherWorker is required to shoulder this burden. To know its weight and import in the world. The balance is too delicate, the scope for disaster too great, for it to be otherwise.' He smiled. 'A boat is less likely to capsize with only one hand on the tiller.'

'It's too much,' said Asher. 'Too much for one man. Or woman.' He waved his hand at the crowded wall. 'You thought Fane could do this? Little Fane? She never would've been strong enough. I could've near snapped her in half with my bare hands!'

Gar's pale face stilled, so it looked like a mask of marble. Asher, realising what he'd just said, cursed under his breath. 'Gar – I didn't mean – look—'

'It's all right. In the end she did break easily, didn't she? But that was just flesh and bone. What we have here is a matter of power. And Barl knows, Fane had more of that than most.'

'More than you?'

Gar shrugged. 'It's moot. The only question that counts now is do I have enough?'

'And do you?'

'That's what we're here to find out, isn't it?'

Again Asher looked at the Chamber's wall with its burden of knowledge, of history. Of expectations. 'You got any idea what all this means?'

'Some,' Gar admitted. 'But I'm not so worried about that. See those books in the bookshelves? They're the diaries of every WeatherWorker who ever lived, all the way back to Barl herself. Contained in those pages is everything I need to know about the weather, and the Wall, and how they work to keep each other strong. All I need to do is read them and remember. And we both know I'm very good with books.'

Asher looked away. Books, aye. Gar had never had trouble with books. But this? This was different. This was all their futures, their health and their happiness and the ordered life of Lur . . . and it rested in the hands of a man not so far past his majority and only recently come into his magical birthright. A man alone, bereft of an older, experienced voice to guide him when he doubted, to support him when he stumbled.

To save him if he failed.

Suddenly he was feeling sick again. 'Maybe Jarralt's right. Durm should be here. What help will I be if something goes—'

Gar's face tightened with impatience. 'How often must I say it? Nothing will go wrong! This is my *destiny*, Asher. How can I be doomed to disaster when Barl herself has placed me on her throne?'

'I don't know,' he said unhappily. 'But there's more than one fisherman who's set out to sea under clear skies and never come home again. Sometimes storms break without warning, Gar.'

'Westwailing was an accident,' Gar said curtly. 'The unfortunate result of illness. I am meant to be here. Nothing will go wrong.'

Asher shoved his hands in his coat pockets. 'Why couldn't you stop the horses?'

'*What*?'

'There were five magicians in that *carriage*, Gar. You tryin' to tell me one of you couldn't have used magic to stop the horses from gallopin' over the edge of Salbert's Eyrie?'

Gar stared at him. 'The art – if you can call it that – of magically influencing another living thing is long lost to us. Barl forbade it, and with good reason. Can you imagine what might happen if one magician could crawl inside another's mind and work his will unhampered?'

Asher turned away. He could imagine it, aye, and bloody well wished he couldn't.

Gar's voice pursued him. 'What are you really trying to say? I thought the accident was behind us. I thought we had moved on from uncertainty and suspicion. Was I mistaken? Do you still have doubts? Do you doubt *me*?'

# CHAPTER EIGHT

'*No*!' said Asher, turning back. 'But it's all happenin' so fast! This time last night we're standing at the edge of Salbert's Eyrie. I've just crawled up from seein' your poor dead family, and you're there tellin' the world it was Conroyd Jarralt who killed 'em. A day later it's all decided what happened were an accident, you're proclaimed king and here we are in the most secret, sacred place in the kingdom ready for you to make it rain and me to save you if it all goes arse over eyeballs! I'm dizzy, Gar! I just want to *stop*, just for a minute, so's I can get my bearings! Sink me, I'm a *fisherman*! I never came to Dorana for *this*!'

Gar's face was riven with stresses he'd never asked for. Never deserved. 'And I never expected to be king. Barl have mercy! Don't you think I'd sacrifice every last drop of magic in me if it would turn back time and save them? Do you think I *wanted* this?'

'Of course I bloody don't! Nobody in his right mind would want this.'

'But I have it,' Gar said grimly. 'Want it or not, it's mine.'

'But not mine!' he said, and thumped his chest. 'I'm

Olken, your magic's got nowt to do with me. And if this does go arse over eyeballs I don't want to be the one left behind to explain what you're doing lyin' stone dead on the floor!'

A ringing silence. Then Gar flicked a finger and the chamber door swung open. 'Of course. I should've realised. I'm sorry.'

Expecting argument, or rebuke, Asher blinked. 'Gar—'

'No. It's all right. Only fools never feel fear.' A bleak smile. 'I'm so afraid right now I could vomit. But that's not your concern. You're right. This Weather Chamber is no place for an Olken.'

Torn between relief and guilt he shoved his hands back into his pockets. 'See, Gar, you got to be careful now. Jarralt could use me bein' here as a way to undermine you.'

With a flash of unfamiliar arrogance, Gar lifted his chin. 'He could try.'

'That's the point. He would. He will.'

'No. The point is that I've been selfish. In the time since we first met, I've come to think of you as the brother I never had. I suppose I hoped – thought – you felt the same way.'

Gar his *brother*? Asher stared. He had enough damned brothers to last him a lifetime. Did he really want another one? One with blond hair, a crown and enough trouble trailing in his wake to start a dozen fistfights down at the Goose?

The answer came slowly, but with certainty. Yes. He did. Because, despite all the aggravation and the irritation, the heart-stopping catastrophes and the niggling spats, in a little over a year Gar had given him more, trusted him more, leaned on him more, laughed with him more and cared about him more than his flesh-and-blood brothers had in a lifetime.

The realisation must have shown in his face because Gar smiled. 'I'm glad. Now go.'

'Go?' he echoed. 'But—'

'Brothers don't burden each other unfairly,' Gar said. His expression was contrite. Earnest. 'Get some rest, you look exhausted. But before you retire send a message to Conroyd Jarralt asking him to join me. I'll wait till he arrives.'

Asher cleared his throat. Good. This was good. He didn't belong here, in the fiery heart of Doranen magic. No Olken did. 'You're sure?'

Gar nodded. 'Yes. It has to be Conroyd.'

He took a hesitant step backwards. Battled his better judgement, lost, and said, 'If you really want me to stay, I'll—'

'What I want isn't important. Go, Asher. I'll see you in the morning.'

Guts churning, he turned and walked towards the open door. He was relieved, he was affronted, he was thrilled, he was furious. *Bastard*. Why couldn't Gar have argued? Why did he have to be so – so – understanding? So *reasonable*. Did Gar think he *couldn't* do it? That he wasn't strong enough to take whatever WeatherWorking could dish out, even as a bystander? Somewhere deep inside did Gar think the Olken were *weak*?

That *he* was weak?

He reached the door, fingers touching the unpainted timber. He stopped.

*Was* he weak?

'*Damn* it!' he shouted, and slammed the chamber door closed in his own face. Whirled around to glare at watchful, waiting Gar. 'You always know what to say, don't you! Always know which strings to pull so's you can get your own way! I should've known – I've watched you do it day in day out as the bloody Olken Administrator! Mind you, can't say I ever expected to find you administratin' *me*!'

Gar flushed. Folded his arms across his chest. 'Well? Did it work?'

'Of course it worked, you devious bastard! I'm on this side of the bloody door, ain't I?'

The first true, unfettered smile since the accident lit Gar's face. 'Don't expect me to apologise.'

He snorted. 'Don't worry. I'm dumb, but I ain't that dumb.'

'I know I'm asking a lot,' Gar said, the bright smile fading. 'It seems I'm always asking a lot from you. But don't expect me to apologise for that either. You're a man with many gifts, Asher. Gifts best used for the good of this kingdom, and if you think I'll stop using them just because the idea makes you uncomfortable, or me, then you really should walk away now.'

'No. I already got one friend harmed for life 'cause I walked away.' *Jed.* Asher folded his arms against the bruising memory and thudded his shoulderblades to the door. 'I'm stayin'.'

Gar nodded. 'Good.' He returned to the map of Lur, his expression now revealing uncertainty. Caution. A wary hope. 'It's like a dance,' he whispered. 'One with a set pattern that hasn't changed in over six centuries, that's been passed from WeatherWorker to WeatherWorker since the Weather Magics were born. All I have to do is find the right place to join in . . .' He frowned. 'The transfer of incantations from the Orb was . . . difficult. Painful. Durm said it was to be expected, but . . .'

'You think it didn't work?'

'No, no, it worked,' said Gar. 'The Weather Magics are in me. If I close my eyes I can see their shapes. Taste the words. The sigils tingle my fingertips, eager for release.'

Asher shrugged. 'Then let's not keep 'em waiting.'

'No. Let's not.' Stepping slowly, walking widdershins around the map, Gar raised his right hand and traced a figure in the air. Its shape glowed, burned bright as fire, then faded. At the same time he pronounced a single word: '*Luknek*.' Another shape, with the left hand this time. Another word: '*Tolnek*.' Bright fire burned, and faded. Right hand. Word. Left hand. Word. Right hand. Word. Left hand. Word. Out of nowhere a wind, rising. It centred around Gar, stirred his clothing as he walked and spoke and drew burning patterns in the air.

Still leaning against the closed door, Asher felt his skin prickle and saw a faint blue shimmer dance along his forearms, then disappear.

The power was building.

As he watched, caught between fear and fascination, small clouds thickened over the map's model Dorana City. Touched by a shadow he glanced up and saw clouds through the glass-domed ceiling, spinning into life out of the clear night sky.

Buffeted more strongly now, Gar continued to circle the map, sweating as he traced more sigils in the air and uttered the words of power, faster and faster. The wind increased in strength, began to howl like a live thing trapped and tortured. Three more turns around the table and he could walk no further: the wind was too strong. The power too great. So he stood, braced against its might and fury, arms raised, fingers battling to make the signs that would call the rain. His eyes were screwed tight closed and his mouth was open in a silent gasping, as though he were being torn apart.

The writhing clouds above the map billowed outwards to cover the entire recreation of Lur. Tiny forks of lightning flickered in their depths, to be echoed a heartbeat later in the clouds above Chamber and City. Thunder rumbled, inside and out.

Blue light like little fingers of flame danced the length of Gar's body. Unravelled his disciplined hair and whipped it round his face as though the long blond strands were alive and in torment.

At its raging peak the power ignited into a wild blue firestorm, roaring and crackling and feeding on itself, with Gar at its greedy heart. Blood burst from his eyes, from his nose, his ears, his mouth, and his whole body flailed and shook. He opened his mouth and screamed like a man on fire. Horrified, Asher started forward then stopped, indecision a knife at his throat.

'Gar!' he shouted. 'Gar, are you all right? Is this normal or not? What should I do? For Barl's sake, tell me what to do!'

But Gar was far beyond hearing. In the nightmare leaping of blue flame and golden glimlight his blood-slicked face looked inhuman. Unreachable. Unknown.

Then, as had happened at the height of the storm in Westwailing, an enormous explosion of sound rent the air. Asher cried out and clapped his hands to his ears. Gar echoed him, screaming as though he'd been pierced by a sword . . .

. . . and overhead the blotting clouds wept their summoned rain like a benediction over Dorana City and all the lands of Lur.

Conroyd Jarralt was entertaining friends to dinner. Only the heads of the best houses, naturally. Those closest in status to his own. The Doranen might be illustrious by nature, but still, some families were more illustrious than others. Sorvold. Boqur. Daltrie. Hafat. Direct descendants of the great exiles from Old Dorana, those wise magicians who'd seen the way the wind was blowing and fled before Morgan's madness destroyed them as it destroyed hundreds of other, less perspicacious magicians. They were names to be proud of. Histories that would embarrass no one, most particularly their host. And they were all senior members of the kingdom's General Council too, with their busy fingers pressed against any number of pulses.

A man could be a friend and useful at the same time. In fact, it was better if he was.

Of course, Council service or not, none of those names was as illustrious as his own. Conroyd Jarralt of House Jarralt, founded by Lindin Jarralt, one of the finest magicians the Doranen race had ever produced. Only the royal house could boast a better pedigree, more exceptional magicians, and even that was subject to debate. After all, would House Jarralt have bred up a cripple as heir to the throne?

No. It most certainly would not.

Were it not for the treachery and mischance his family had suffered during the turbulence of Trevoyle's Schism, it would be WeatherWorkers born of House Jarralt, not Torvig, who ruled the Kingdom of Lur. Dusty memory had power still to boil his blood; the degree of kinship between his ancestor and the madman Morgan had been slight. Hardly worth mentioning. Good for the merest footnote in the annals of history, if that. More importantly, there had never been so much as a breath of an allegiance between the insane sorcerer and his twice-removed cousin Lindin. As Barl was his witness, Lindin had been one of the first to voice concern over Morgan's experiments! Could Borne Torvig have claimed the same of his own ancestor? No, he could not.

But that, seemingly, counted for nothing. Morg's shade haunted them all. Tainted him still in some eyes, though no one would dare say so to his face.

Only now, with the near extinction of House Torvig, did blighted House Jarralt have a chance to assume its rightful place in Doranen history. Why, if Gar had been killed along with his family, or if the miracle flowering of his magical birthright had never happened, it would be Conroyd Jarralt who stood today as king.

But Gar wasn't dead, and his late-born powers appeared formidable. Which meant that yet again House Jarralt was to be denied its proper place in the world.

Fate could be monstrously unfair.

Not for the first time, Jarralt regretted his lack of a daughter. He could have married a daughter to the fate-favoured scion of House Torvig and died less unhappily, knowing his blood flowed through the veins of Gar's child, the kingdom's next WeatherWorker. But no. Even that small consolation was denied him. Two children he'd been granted, like most citizens of Lur. Even if dispensation could be arranged for the birth of a third child it was far too late now and just as likely his dull and dutiful wife would waste the effort on another son.

Still. Where the prospect of rightful glory was concerned, not *all* hope was lost. Fat Durm's hold on life was yet precarious, or so discreet enquiries informed him. With the Master Magician's successor carelessly unnamed, Gar would be forced to make the appointment himself. And it was clear that in all the kingdom there was no one better bred, better qualified or more deserving of the honour than Lord Conroyd Jarralt.

'My dear,' a voice beside him murmured. 'The wine.'

Jarralt blinked and watched his surroundings swim back into focus. His dining room, lavishly appointed. His wife, lavishly jewelled. His friends, waiting patiently for his next unimpeachable pronouncement. 'Wine?'

The immaculate Olken servant standing at his elbow bowed and held out a bottle for his inspection. 'As requested, my lord. Vontifair Icewine, vintage 564. Chilled for precisely forty minutes.'

Nole Daltrie wagged a finger. '564? Cuttin' it a bit fine there aren't you, Con? Icewine don't hold its bite for more than eighty years. Any longer than that and you might as well pour us a glass of piss and vinegar.'

*Con.* Jarralt hid his irritation behind a bland smile. 'Don't worry, Nole. The eightieth anniversary of this vintage's bottling isn't until tomorrow.'

Daltrie hooted and slapped the table. 'Vintage icewine and vintage Conroyd! What an evening!'

Jarralt nodded at the servant, who broke the bottle's de-warded seal and splashed a mouthful into the next course's wineglass. The icewine's thin, snow-laden tang sliced through the dining room's lingering redolence of honey-baked lamb, muscatel venison and spiced pork; Jarralt's guests sighed and licked their lips. He rested the rim of the glass against his teeth, subduing greed, and permitted a trickle of clear blue indulgence into his mouth.

It cleansed his jaded palate like magic.

'Perfect,' he said, lowering the glass, and nodded again at the servant. The other glasses were scrupulously burdened with three inches of icewine, not a hair's-breadth more; the disappointment-laced avarice in his guests' eyes almost made him laugh out loud. Waiting, he travelled his gaze around all their guzzling faces. When the servant had withdrawn and they were again alone, he remarked, 'So. A new day dawns for our beloved kingdom.'

As though invisible cords had been cut his fellow diners let out silent sighs of relief and relaxed in their chairs. Morel, Sorvold's robustly handsome wife, fluttered her jewel-crusted fingers. 'I must say, Conroyd dear, it's all terribly disconcerting. I mean, the boy's a *child*. In magic, at least, if not in fact, and even there he's still young. What kind of a king will he make? Does anybody know? Does anybody know *him*? I certainly don't!'

Iyasha Hafar was nodding her vigorous agreement; her diamond pendant earrings prismed the chandelier's glimlight and scattered rainbows across the tablecloth. 'Exactly! Why, he's practically a stranger! I think he's only ever attended one of my garden parties and I'm sure even then it was under sufferance! I'd swear you could count on the fingers of one hand the number of invitations he's accepted in the last year.'

'Doranen invitations,' her husband added dryly. 'As far as I can make out, he's always available for carousing with the Olken.'

Tobe Boqur replaced his emptied wineglass on the table and belched. 'Don't be too hard on him, Gord. For a start it's been his job to mix with Olken society, and for another—'

'For another,' said Madri Boqur, smiling at her husband as she finished his sentence for him in her irritating little-girl whisper, 'I don't imagine he ever felt comfortable around his own kind. Not while he was—' She blushed. 'You know.'

'I think the word you're avoiding is "crippled",' Jarralt replied. 'No, no, my friends, please don't look like that. I assure you, he applied the term to himself often enough. Borne's son is nothing if not a realist.'

'You'd know, serving with him on the Privy Council,' said Payne Sorvold. 'What else is he, do you think?'

'Our king,' said Lynthia Daltrie. Her sharply jutting chin looked more stubborn than ever. Nole had long since lost the battle to control her; such a pity. 'As ordained by Barl and therefore above reproach. I have to say I liked his speech in the square today. It showed heart. Courage. I think his father would've been proud.'

A reflective silence fell. Jarralt waited for his wife to break it: Barl save him, she was a woman who couldn't abide a room without words in it.

'All I know,' Ethienne said peevishly, 'is that it will feel most peculiar, addressing that unfortunate young man as "Your Majesty". He's younger than both of my boys!'

'I suppose he's got what it takes to *be* king,' Madri said uncertainly. 'I mean to say . . . Barl wouldn't allow an incompetent to inherit the throne. Would she?'

Almost as one their gazes flicked to the glass balcony doors through which gleamed the Wall's distant golden haze. Jarralt hid a smile at the sight of their apprehensive expressions. Even tediously devout Lynthia had her doubts. As well she should have. Lur was in greater danger now than ever before, even during the schism. How lucky for his friends and their children that Conroyd Jarralt was at hand. Watching their silent dismay, the way they tried not to look at each other or reveal unflattering fear, he again wanted to laugh out loud.

Ah, dear. They were good enough people, these friends of his, but as transparent as his dining-room windows. Lacking any kind of real ambition or inner fire. They represented the best that Doranen society had to offer, yet not a one of them was strong enough to wield real power. To balance the kingdom in the vital role of Master Magician, or wear the crown of the WeatherWorker.

Only he was. And praise Barl for that. For if Gar's power should prove insufficient . . . if the strain of WeatherWorking killed him sooner rather than later, as had happened more than once in the past . . . if he should fail to produce an heir or sired one as crippled as he himself had used to be . . .

Well.

Thunder boomed over their heads, rattling the windowpanes and the emptied wineglasses on the table. Jarralt's secret smile died. 'What was that?' he demanded, pushing to his feet.

Ethienne pointed at the sky beyond the doors. 'Look! Clouds!'

'And lightning!' added Tobe Boqur. The words had hardly left his mouth when the room strobed a second time as, outside, spears of blue-white fire streaked earthwards from the rapidly thickening atmosphere. Even as they watched, the Wall's golden glow dimmed, dimmed, and disappeared.

Gord Hafar stood and crossed to the doors. Flung them open and thrust his hand outside. He looked back over his shoulder. 'It's going to rain,' he announced. 'The air's alive with it. You never told us Gar had been given the Weather Magics, Conroyd.' Gord sounded accusing. In his eyes, a shadow of hurt surprise.

Fool. Just because he shared his icewine did Gord think he'd share his secrets, too? 'You didn't need to know,' he replied brusquely. 'Before the accident there was still a question mark over the succession. There was no way of telling who would prove to be the stronger WeatherWorker, Fane or Gar, without testing them first.'

Payne Sorvold cleared his throat, his expression

disapproving. 'You took a risk, Conroyd. The law is clear on the matter. Only two people might possess Weather Magic at the same time: the WeatherWorker and the WeatherWorker in Waiting. Such action was a recipe for another schism. As Privy Councillor you should have stopped it.'

Jarralt spared the man an impatient glance, inwardly seething. Who was Payne Sorvold to task *him*? 'Exceptional circumstances require the taking of risks and the bending of law. As Privy Councillor it's my duty to recognise that. Besides, the danger of schism was Borne's doing, not mine. If he hadn't bullied his way into a dispensation for a second child we never would've faced a divided succession in the first place. If you're going to criticise anyone, Payne, why not start with the General Council for weakly acquiescing to—'

'The General Council,' Nole said loudly, his flabby cheeks reddening, 'weakly acquiesced to nothing! We did what had to be done for the good of the kingdom. We acted according to law *and* with Barl's blessing!'

'And why we're arguing about it now, nearly twenty years later, I cannot begin to understand!' added Lynthia. 'The point is moot!'

'As is the question of Gar receiving the Weather Magic,' said Jarralt. His gaze remained fixed upon the curdling sky. 'With the death of his sister he is once more an only child. The line of succession is clear, and the law stands.'

'On a sprained ankle, if you ask me,' muttered Nole.

'Nobody did, dear,' said Lynthia, and patted his arm. 'Never mind. As Con says, what's done is done. All that really matters is we have a WeatherWorker and the kingdom is safe.'

As if to punctuate her words a thunderclap like the

end of the world boomed over their heads. The women shrieked. The men shouted. Jarralt laughed. Beyond the open glass doors the murky cloud-covered sky gushed rain like a woman whose waters have broken.

King Gar, WeatherWorker of Lur, was born.

Jarralt eased away from his dining table. Crossed to the doors leading out to the uncovered balcony. Stepped over the threshold and into the rain.

'What are you doing, Conroyd?' Ethienne demanded breathlessly. 'You can't stand out there, you'll be soaked! All your clothes will be ruined! Come back inside. Conroyd? Conroyd, are you listening? *Conroyd*!'

He ignored her. Ignored the surprised protests of his dinner guests. Walked to the very edge of the balcony, six tall storeys above the ground, braced his widespread hands on the balustrade and looked out across the City. Looked further, beyond the City's encircling wall to the invisible horizon. The view was exactly the same: rain, rain, rain. The weeping clouds went on forever.

His new silk brocade tunic was sodden, a dragging weight against his shoulders. Rivulets of water ran down his arms, his chest, his legs, and pooled in his brand-new shoes. Yes, Ethienne, all ruined.

He tipped back his head and felt more water from his soaking hair run down the back of his neck. Eyes open, mouth open, he lifted his face to the pouring rain. Drowned himself, blinded himself, in the miracle of Gar's calling.

Every droplet was a needlepoint of acid etching him with bitterness and despair, in his flesh, his bones, his bowels. In his heart, and the secret places of his soul.

*Borne ... you bastard. You bastard. You've beaten me again.*

* * *

Released at last from the Weather Magic's merciless grasp, Gar swayed drunkenly, bloodily, then collapsed unstrung to the floor beside the map of Lur where the little clouds dropped tiny vanishing raindrops from the mountains to the sea. Groaning, retching, shaking, he began to laugh.

Asher dropped to his knees beside him. 'It ain't funny!' he shouted, fright shattering his voice. 'You maniac! You great ravin' *lunatic*! What are you laughin' for? It ain't bloody funny!'

Flopping like a landed fish, Gar stared up at him through a mask of blood. 'It worked!' he gasped, spitting scarlet bubbles. 'Did you see? It *worked*! I made it rain! *Everywhere*! Fane never managed that!'

'Aye, aye,' Asher muttered, scrabbling in his pockets for a handkerchief. 'You made it rain and you made a mess and you took ten years off my life, you daft bastard. Hold still!'

'You know . . . that hurt,' Gar wheezed as Asher mopped the worst of the gore from his face. 'A lot. But it was incredible! The *power*. I never knew – I never *dreamed* – oh, Asher! Aren't you sorry you'll never know what it's like? That you'll never command a power like it? Aren't you . . . I don't know . . . jealous? You can tell me. I won't mind. I'll understand.'

Asher stared down at him. At his shivering, shuddering, pain-racked body. 'Oh aye. I be so jealous I could spit.'

Gar grinned redly and stared up at the glass-domed ceiling, enchanted. 'Look,' he whispered. '*Look* what I did.'

'Aye,' he said as the rain fell from the quietly clouded sky. The sound of it striking the transparent ceiling woke gentle echoes in the chamber below. 'Look what you did, Now shut your trap while I find somethin' to clean you up proper. 'Cause if you go back to the Tower lookin' like this and Darran sees you, sure as sharks the ole crow'll find some way to make this all *my* fault.' And then, relenting, added roughly, 'Your da'd be proud right now, I reckon. And your ma too.'

Fresh tears gathered in Gar's bloody eyes. 'I hope so,' he whispered, triumph extinguished, lurking grief ascendant once more. 'Oh, I hope so.'

Asher cursed. *Fool. Damned fool. Just when you got him smilin' again . . .*

'Come on,' he said. Slipping an arm beneath Gar's shoulders, he levered the exhausted king upright. 'Scoot yourself backwards and lean against the wall till you're feelin' better.' Looking around the chamber, he scowled. 'Why ain't there any chairs in here?'

'I don't need a chair,' said Gar, sliding by inches across the parquetry floor. He reached the wall, slumped against it and groaned. 'I'm fine.'

Asher stood. 'You don't look fine. You look like shit.'

Eyes half closed, Gar raised a finger. 'Now, now. Remember to whom you speak.'

'Excuse me,' he said. 'You look like royal shit.'

Gar's lips twitched. 'That's better.'

'Does it still hurt?'

'Oh, Asher . . .' Gar blinked his eyes open again. 'You have no idea.'

But he did. Some idea anyway. He'd heard Gar's screams, after all. Watched helpless as his friend writhed inside the power. Convulsed. Wept blood even as he laughed.

'Well . . .' Uncertain, he folded his arms. 'For how long? For always? I mean, is this your life now? Nowt but blood and pain?'

With an effort, Gar pulled his knees up to his chest and wrapped his arms around them. 'Yes.'

'But . . . you can't do this every day,' he said, appalled. 'You can't bleed and hurt like this every day. How will you stand it?'

Gar shrugged. 'The same way my father did, and my grandfather, and my great-grandmother, back and back and back till the dawn of our days here.'

'But you *can't*!'

'I must. What's the alternative? Shirk my duty and hand the crown to Conroyd Jarralt?' Gar pulled a face. 'I don't think so. Besides, it's not every day. Well. Not always. As I recall, my father sometimes had two days respite at a time, between Callings. Three even, in winter.' He smiled, remembering. 'Winter is good.'

'Gar, nowt happens in winter. What about spring?'

The remembering smile faded then and Gar frowned at his knees. 'Oh, spring. Yes. Spring is . . . not so good.'

'You fool, spring'll *kill* you if this is just a taste of what's to come!'

Gar shook his head. 'No, it won't. You're forgetting this wasn't a normal Working. Tonight I made it rain from one end of the kingdom to the other, and that's not the way it's usually done. Not even in the spring. You're worrying over nothing. I'm fine, or I will be soon enough.' He stretched a hand out in front of him and flexed his fingers with only a small grimace. 'See? The pain's easing already.'

Asher snorted. 'Even if you poked my eyes out I could tell you were lyin'. Gar—'

The outstretched fingers became a fist. '*Don't.*' Then Gar's icy gaze melted and the fist became a hand, became vulnerable fingers, trembling. 'I am who I am, Asher. I was born for one reason and one reason alone. You can't change that.'

Asher kicked one boot-heel against the floor, scuffing the polished parquetry. 'All right,' he muttered grudgingly. 'If you say so. You're the king.'

'Yes,' said Gar. 'I am.' In his voice, echoes of pain and a tired, replete satisfaction. 'And now the king says, time to go home.'

'Not till I clean up the rest of that blood. You look like a slaughterhouse apprentice.' His gaze fell on the Chamber's single cupboard. On impulse he crossed to it, opened the doors and inside found a pile of soft rags, a bowl and a stoppered vial. Looking back at Gar he said, 'Seems like your da kept himself prepared.'

'Or Durm,' agreed Gar. 'Bring them here.'

'There ain't any water.'

Gar smiled. 'Give me the bowl. I'll take care of the water.'

He handed it over, then sank cross-legged to the floor and watched as Gar closed his eyes, spread his hand above the empty vessel and whispered something under his breath. A blue spark ignited in the space between clay and flesh. Gar grunted, his face contracting against new pain. The blue spark briefly danced then died . . . and the bowl began to fill with water from the bottom up, as though an invisible spigot had been opened.

Asher laughed. 'How'd you do that?'

Gar gave him back the bowl. 'Do you really want to know?'

Abruptly, he remembered who he was, and where he was, and what the penalties were for asking those kinds of questions. 'No.'

'It's all right,' said Gar. 'I'll answer. If you want the

truth, it'll be a relief to talk about it. With Durm . . . unwell, there's nobody else to listen.'

Asher dipped his fingers in the water. It was warm. Wetting one of the soft cloths, wringing it out, he said, 'Holze'd listen.'

Gar shook his head. 'I can't talk to Holze. Not about this. Not about any kind of magic. I can't talk to any of them.'

He held out the cloth. 'I s'pose not.'

'Holze may be a cleric, but he's also on the Privy Council and friends with Jarralt,' said Gar, his voice muffled as he cleaned his face. 'With all the prominent Doranen. If there was even the smallest suggestion I was unsure about the WeatherWorking, about *anything* . . .'

He sighed. 'I know. Goodbye King Gar, hello King Conroyd.' With a grunt, he unstoppered the vial from the cupboard. A pungent, eye-stinging stink wafted into the chamber. He spat out the cork, choking.

'I'm not drinking that,' said Gar.

Cautiously, Asher sniffed. 'One of Nix's little concoctions. It pongs a bit like the one he gave me after gettin' back from Westwailin'. Your da must've kept it here, for afterwards.' He held out the vial. 'You might as well. I mean, you're so weak right now I could just pinch your nose shut and tip it down your throat, but that'd be a mite undignified, I reckon. You know. Seein' as how you're king and all.'

Glaring balefully, Gar held out his hand. 'I don't know when, and I don't know how, but I swear I'll get you for this.'

Asher grinned. ''Course you will. Just one swallow, mind. We got no idea how strong that muck is.'

Gar swallowed. Gagged. Thrust the vial blindly in Asher's direction and scrubbed at his mouth with the bloodstained rag. 'And after I've got you,' he panted, spitting and hawking, 'I'll bloody well get Nix too!'

Asher restoppered the vial then inspected his friend. Whatever was in the pother's vile sludge it was doing the trick. A little colour was returning to Gar's complexion and his hands were steadier. 'Better?' he asked.

Gar grimaced. 'Yes.'

Into the fallen silence, as the magic rain clouds thinned into memory over the map of Lur, he said, 'So. Seems you are a WeatherWorker, just like your da.'

The faintest of smiles ghosted over Gar's face. 'Yes. And you know what that means.'

Asher let his head drop. Here it came. 'I got a sneakin' bloody suspicion.'

'There's no one else I'd trust to be Olken Administrator,' said Gar. 'And no one else I need more on my Privy Council. But I promise you this, Asher. When Durm is well again and I am settled into my rule, when I am married and the succession is assured, if you want to go back to your precious ocean I'll make no attempt to stop you. And when you do leave, it will be as a fabulously wealthy man.'

Asher turned his head to stare at tiny Restharven, where tiny boats made of magic danced in the tiny harbour. With money and power and King Gar's blessing his brothers would never stand in his way again. He'd return home inviolate, able to dictate his own destiny without interference.

And Dathne had offered to be his assistant . . .

He grinned. 'Ah, sink it. Restharven ain't goin' anywhere.'

'Does that mean you accept?'

'Aye,' he said. 'I accept.'

# CHAPTER NINE

From her privileged position as a member of the elite royal staff, Dathne sat on her cushioned seat in Justice Hall and watched Barlsman Holze crown Gar as Lur's new king.

A temporary dais had been erected at the front of the Hall, where usually the Law Giver sat and pronounced sentence. Draped in gold velvet, it shimmered richly in the glimlight called for the occasion.

Hands meekly clasped before him, Gar knelt on a crimson cushion at Holze's feet as the Barlsman prayed over his bowed head. In contrast to the cleric's jewel-crusted green and gold and crimson brocade robes, his gold-laden cap and the various holy rings clasping his fingers, Lur's almost-crowned king was dressed starkly in white. He looked like a sapling willow stripped bare of bark. Young. Vulnerable. Unready for the burden fate had thrust upon him.

Beside her, dressed in the finest silks and brocades she'd ever seen him wear, Asher watched the ceremony in anxious silence. Fretting, she suspected, on things going wrong at the very last moment. Worrying that all his hair-tearing work with Darran would somehow come to naught. She let her fingers drift to his arm and lightly squeezed. Smiled when he glanced at her. He smiled back, but without enthusiasm.

Holze spread his arms wide and tipped back his head. 'O Blessed Barl, look down upon this man, your child in magic, and hear now his solemn oath, sworn in this place before you and all his people. Anoint him with your beneficence, pour your strength into his heart and guide him to truth and wisdom all the days of his life.'

Gar looked up then. Folded his hands across his heart. 'Blessed Barl, from whom all life flows, I solemnly swear to serve you and the kingdom you gave us, Doranen and Olken alike, unto my last living breath. I will keep your children in peace and prosperity, Working the Weather, keeping your great Wall strong and upholding your laws without exception until my last drop of blood is shed. May magic desert me if I am untrue.'

Holze nodded at a waiting acolyte. The robed assistant stepped forward, bearing the WeatherWorker's crown. Handed it to him. Dathne held her breath as the intricately wrought silver and copper and gold was lowered onto Gar's bowed, waiting head.

Booming from the square outside, the City's great Barl's Clock tolled the stroke of midnight. Signalling the end of night . . . the start of day.

It was all very *symbolic*.

A great sigh went up from the gathered witnesses: City guild meisters and mistresses, Captain Orrick, the General Council's Doranen lords and ladies, mayors and mayoresses from the kingdom's larger towns, select royal staff. Dathne saw in their faces the raw relief bubbling like stew in a lidded pot. *Praise Barl, praise Barl, now life can get back to normal* . . .

She felt profoundly sorry.

Barlsman Holze began reciting the traditional WeatherWorker's Blessing above the head of still-kneeling Gar. Glancing sideways, she saw Darran wipe away a surreptitious tear, dear old fusspot that he was. A stickler for protocol, inevitably irritated by someone like Asher, but a good man.

Not like Willer.

Further along the pew in which they sat, Willer hunched in his finery like a dyspeptic peacock. Still sulking, the repellent little tick. Everything Asher had ever said about the slug was true. That he could actually think he'd be named Olken Administrator, or even the assistant! Was he mad as well as horrible? And the way he'd acted ever since the announcement of her appointment. Snide. Sneering. Uncooperative. He'd better get over his snit soon or Asher would dismiss him no matter how many more excuses Darran found for him.

Sick of the sight of him, she let her gaze wander elsewhere. Darran wasn't the only one moved to tears: royal staff who'd known their new king as a babe in his cradle, as a toddler tumbling about the corridors of the palace and getting into mischief like any normal small child; guild officials who'd come to know him so closely this past year, and maybe mourned his loss to magic; noble Doranen, perhaps regretting that late-blossoming power and the madcap dreams it killed . . . or dreaming instead of a nubile daughter's chances of being crowned queen. They all had tears on their cheeks.

So many faces. So many hidden thoughts. So many lives that would wildly unravel once Prophecy was fulfilled.

Her grim musings were interrupted as Holze reached down and drew Gar to his feet. Turned the new king to face his silent subjects. Raised his arms and cried:

'Behold a miracle! Behold our virtuous king, by Barl's great grace, Gar the First, WeatherWorker of Lur!'

Now the assembled witnesses were getting to their feet, cheering. Well. Mostly cheering. Dathne scrambled to copy them.

Beside her, clapping along with everybody else, Asher leaned close.

'Barl bloody save me,' he said as, moved almost to tears, King Gar stood before them and accepted the rapturous acclaim. '*Now* life's goin' to get interesting!'

The unkempt, ill-favoured denizens of the Green Goose were in diabolical form, rollicking and carousing and tipping their mugs of beer over their shrieking neighbours' heads then laughing as though they'd just done something terribly clever and hysterically funny.

*Funny*? Willer sank further into his obscure corner seat, hugged his fourth tankard of ale closer to his chest and sneered. It wasn't in the least bit funny. It was puerile. Juvenile. No, no, that was far too old for this unruly mob. It was infantile. Yes. Infantile and . . . and . . . mortifying. These rowdy sots were royal servants. His colleagues, loosely speaking. *Very* loosely. Supposedly they were the cream of Lur's Olken population. Yet here they were carrying on like ignorant farmhands at a barn dance, getting drunk and singing bawdy songs out of tune and generally making fools of themselves.

Morg smite them all, was this any way to celebrate the crowning of a king?

And what was there to celebrate anyway? The day Gar's family had carelessly fallen off the side of a mountain more than just a carriage had been wrecked. More than people had died. He hadn't realised it at the time, but he knew it now. His future had been wrecked too. His dreams had died, as bloodily as any king.

Quivering with overwhelming indignation, Willer swallowed another mouthful of his admittedly excellent ale.

He couldn't understand it. How could Barl have *done* this to him?

Another inebriated toast to the new king rattled the inn's smoke-soaked rafters. He winced. What in Barl's name had brought him into this den of iniquity? He didn't belong in here, he belonged in the Golden Cockerel where the only interruption one ever experienced was the gentle throat-clearing of the waiter, asking if sir required more wine. There was violin music in the Cockerel. There was an exquisite silk-swathed soprano in the Cockerel. There was cut glass and polished silverware and fine dining in the Cockerel. What had he been *thinking*, coming here?

A sly little voice inside his head answered, *You were thinking that in here you'd be safe. In here, you wouldn't have to laugh, and smile, and wear a brave face. In here, you could be invisible.*

Which wasn't the case at the Cockerel. He was well known there. Lauded and fawned on and minced after, importuned and flattered and visible. Anonymity there was impossible. Worse, waiting for him in the refined atmosphere of the Cockerel were his genteel royal colleagues, the other secretaries and assistant secretaries and undersecretaries and junior royal apothecaries who also frequented Dorana's most fashionable establishment.

The ones who even now were saying:

*'Poor Willer. Passed over twice. First in favour of the fisherman and then for that odd woman – you know the one, all skin and bone, hangs on the stableman's sleeve, the bookseller. Yes, her. Without even his own precious superior to argue his case.'*

*'No! You mean to say Darran supports the appointments? Gracious! Ah well. They do say every man finds his level, and it seems poor Willer has found his. But who'd have thought it would be so low?'*

Moaning, he took another deep swallow of ale.

Of course it was foolish to feel hurt by Gar's decision. He should have expected the slight; *everyone* knew that where Asher was concerned, the pri— the king had all the perspicacity of a newborn babe.

What he *hadn't* bargained for was Darran's betrayal. After three years of faithful service, of uncomplaining drudge-work and utterly reliable discretion, of forgone private pleasures and curtailed private plans, to be publicly humiliated like that. To be ranked as just another dispensable pen-pusher. To see Darran standing shoulder to shoulder with that unspeakable Asher, their mutual implacable foe, and hear him praise the lout without stint or sarcasm. '*Our good friend Asher, who'll serve His Majesty and the kingdom superbly as Olken Administrator.*'

Trembling with rewoken outrage, Willer tried to drown tormenting memory with more ale but instead spilled the tankard's remaining mouthfuls down his shirt front.

'Damn!'

He tried in vain to catch the eye of one of the Goose's three slatternly barmaids, but the useless wenches were too busy inviting Matt's stable lads to ogle their dubious charms. Defeated, he slumped further in his seat and brooded into the emptied depths of his ale pot.

Somebody squeezed into the corner booth with him. Without asking. The cheek! 'Kindly find another place to sit,' he said haughtily, not looking up. 'I do not care for—'

A full tankard of ale thudded onto the benchtop

before him. Now he did look up, into a face unknown to him. Long, thin, middle-aged. Olken. Unpleasant. The face smiled. 'Evening to you, Meister Driskle.'

He frowned at the impertinent oaf. 'Do I know you, sir?'

'No,' said the man. His clothing was covered by a long grey cloak, and in one hand he held a matching tankard of ale. 'But I know you.'

'Many people know me. I am a well-known man.'

'You are,' agreed the stranger. 'And an honour it is to be sitting here with you.' He nodded at the tankard he'd placed on the bench. 'Will you share a toast with me, Meister Driskle? To our new king, may Barl bless his days among us!'

Well. One could hardly refuse to toast the king . . .

'And to the memory of his family, Barl give them rest!'

Or his late parents and sister . . .

'And to the swift recovery of our revered Master Magician!'

Not even Durm, though life was surely more peaceful without him.

Feeling a trifle bleary, Willer squinted at his new friend. 'Who *are* you?'

The man smiled. 'The servant of someone who'd like a word or three, Meister Driskle. If you've the time just now.'

He sniffed. 'If this is some clumsy attempt to weasel a favour from a man with royal influence, then—'

'Oh no, Meister Driskle,' the man in grey said. His eyes were amused.

'Then what does this "someone" want? Does he have a name? I'll not set one foot outside this wretched tavern if you won't tell me who—'

The man smiled. Lifted a finger and pulled down the

edge of his cloak to reveal his collar. It was embroidered with a black and silver falcon: the emblem of House Jarralt.

Willer thumped backwards in his seat. 'What is going *on* here?'

The man smiled more widely still and winked. His finger crooked, beckoning. Dumbfounded and mizzled with ale, Willer struggled from behind the bench and followed House Jarralt's grey-cloaked servant out of the rackety inn and into the street, where a dark, discreet carriage drawn by four dark, discreet horses stood by the kerb. The servant opened the carriage door, and Willer peered inside the curtained, glimlit interior.

There was only one occupant.

'Lord Jarralt!' he gasped. Snatching off his hat, he hastily offered an awkward, unbalanced bow. 'How may I be of service, sir?'

Lord Jarralt was dressed in sober greys and blacks. He waved one ringless hand, indicating he desired his visitor to join him. Awed, Willer clambered up the carriage steps and bumped himself onto the empty black velvet seat opposite the Privy Councillor. His heart pounded painfully beneath its muffling layers of flesh.

'You may leave us, Frawley,' the lord said to his grey-cloaked servant.

Willer flinched as Frawley clicked the carriage door shut. There came the crack of a whip, the slip-sliding clatter of shod hooves on wet cobbles, and the carriage moved off. To where or in what direction it was impossible to tell.

'My lord,' he said, breathless, 'I don't understand. Is something the matter? The king, is he—'

Jarralt lowered his upraised, silencing finger. 'For the moment our beloved king is unharmed. Willer. And may

I say how well it becomes you, that your first thought was for him and his safety. I am . . . impressed.'

Willer nearly swallowed his tongue. He didn't know which was more exciting: that Lord Conroyd Jarralt knew his name, that he was sitting in the grand man's carriage or that he'd just been paid an extravagant compliment by one of the most powerful and prestigious Doranen in the kingdom.

He cleared his throat. 'Thank you, my lord. How may I serve you? Your man was most circumspect . . .'

'I am pleased to hear it,' said Lord Jarralt. 'Our business is of a private nature. I wouldn't like to think of it as . . . food for public consumption.'

Was that a warning? Yes. Yes, of course it was. 'Oh, sir, you may rely on my complete discretion! I know the value of silence, I assure you. Why, in my capacity as private secretary to His Majesty, I—'

'Silence,' said Lord Jarralt. 'Yes. Silence is often useful and so frequently underrated. It can even be a weapon, if wielded wisely. Do you follow me, Willer?'

He snapped shut his teeth and nodded eagerly.

Lord Jarralt smiled. 'Excellent.'

Questions crowded Willer's mouth like pebbles. Why am I here? Where are we going? What is it you want of me? Why are we meeting in secret? He was choking on curiosity, could barely breathe. His hands clutched the brim of his hat so tightly he thought his knuckles would crack.

Lord Jarralt said, 'You don't like Asher, do you.'

It wasn't a question. Still unspeaking, he shook his head.

'You're not alone. Tell me . . . were you asked to describe him, what would you say?'

What would he say? What *wouldn't* he say? Feeling

oppressed by all the savage words clamouring to be set free, he tittered. 'I'd say he's – he's a bilious headache, my lord.'

That made Lord Jarralt laugh out loud. 'A bilious headache! Yes. How true. But he is more than that. He is a noxious weed grown rampant and unchecked in our garden, this precious Kingdom of Lur. I'm told he's been appointed Olken Administrator. A tragedy, to be sure.'

Willer swallowed. 'Yes, my lord.'

'To be truthful,' Lord Jarralt mused, fingers tapping idly on one knee, 'I thought it might be you, but . . . alas. Doubtless Asher is to blame. He's poisoned the king against you.'

A pang of hope seized Willer's heart. He leaned forward, his crushed hat falling heedless to the carriage floor. 'Oh, my lord,' he breathed. 'I'm so afraid. His Majesty is so good, so kind, so trusting. I fear he has nurtured a viper in his bosom unawares. While Darran thought as I do I had some hope of Asher's villainy finally coming to light, but now *Darran* has fallen under his spell too. I don't like to seem immodest but I think I am the only one who can see—'

'Modesty is best reserved for those who have much to be modest about,' said Lord Jarralt. 'For men like us, Willer, men of accomplishment and vision, it is a pointless conceit. You have no need to fear. You are not the only one who sees Asher for what he truly is.'

Willer released a silent sigh of ecstasy and sat back in his seat. The cold void within him was gone now, filled to overflowing with a bubbling warmth. *Men like us*. 'My lord, I am relieved beyond words to hear you say so. But what can we do? We are two lone voices, crying in the wilderness.'

'I know,' said Lord Jarralt, and smiled so sadly Willer

thought his heart might break. 'It is a lonely road we walk, Willer. I take it you love our new king?'

Willer gasped. 'Of *course*!'

Lord Jarralt twitched aside the curtain from the carriage window and for a long moment stared through it into the night-dark landscape beyond. Where they were now, Willer had no idea. The horses' hooves no longer pounded cobblestones, he could tell that much. It meant they must have travelled beyond the City. Did it matter? Not at all. This incredible conversation had already taken him further than he'd ever gone in all his life.

'Gar is of an age to be my own son, you know,' said Lord Jarralt, sounding almost wistful. 'It's how I've always thought of him. And like any father, I worry. Imagine a host of dangers that might at any moment befall him.' His gaze flickered. A warning, or an invitation?

Willer took a deep breath to calm his booming heart. 'You think the king is in *danger*, my lord?'

Jarralt let the curtain fall again. 'What do you think?'

Willer stared. 'I – I don't know.'

'I think you do. You said it yourself. A viper in the bosom.'

'Yes . . . I did . . .' He frowned. 'But Asher saved his life in Westwailing.'

Lord Jarralt smiled. 'Or so we're told.'

'I suppose,' Willer said slowly, 'the story could be untrue. We only have Asher's word, after all. The king's recollection can't be relied upon, he was drowning at the time. And the truth is a mirror, isn't it? What you see in it depends very much on who's looking, does it not?'

Lord Jarralt sighed. 'I am a plain man, Willer. Plots and puzzlings and devious designs are foreign to my nature. Therefore allow me to speak plainly, in the hope that you will speak plainly in your turn.'

'I will, sir.'

'Speaking plainly, then, I am afraid Asher wields an undue influence over the king. I am afraid His Majesty has been duped. Deceived into believing the lout is harmless. On the contrary, he is baleful. He holds the Doranen, Barl's own people, in contempt. And now that his power is unparalleled in the kingdom I am afraid he will use it to manipulate our gentle, trusting new king for his own ends.'

'What ends, my lord?' he said, trembling.

Lord Jarralt shrugged. 'What is the ambition of every noxious weed?'

The question seemed to suck all the air out of the carriage's interior, so that Willer struggled to keep his lungs inflated. He felt hot and cold, terrified and vindicated, brave and confronted, all at the same time. 'To take over the garden,' he whispered.

'Exactly.'

'But, my lord . . .' He was anguished. 'We have no proof.'

'What is proof, my friend, but a coat of paint required by fools who cannot see that a house unvarnished is still a house?'

'I know . . . I know . . . but His Majesty will never believe us without it.'

'That's true,' Lord Jarralt admitted. 'So we must find it. Or, should I say, you must find it.'

He sat back. 'Me, my lord? How? I have no magic, no authority. I'm a mere Olken, a cog in the royal wheel, I—'

Lord Jarralt smiled. 'Willer, Willer . . . don't sell yourself so short. You are far more than that. You are brave.

Wise. Dedicated. Most importantly, you are *there*. Within the royal household. In the right place at the right time to do what must be done. To discover the proof that will rescue our dear king from this monstrous Olken. I know it will be difficult, torture even, but you must slay your pride. Swallow your repugnance for Asher, mask your legitimate loathing of him, and stay as close as you can so his actions might be observed. Can you do this, my friend? Tell me you can. Tell me I am not mistaken in your nobility, your dedication to doing what is right no matter the personal cost.'

He could scarcely breathe. 'You are not, sir, I swear you are not!'

'You will report every discovery, every suspicion, to me and me alone,' Lord Jarralt cautioned. 'No one else can know what we are about. In time, Asher's true nature will be revealed, of this I have no doubt. But for now he has the king – indeed the kingdom – hoodwinked.'

'Hoodwinked and bamboozled,' Willer agreed. 'To my daily pain.'

'But not forever,' said Lord Jarralt. 'One day, Barl grant it be soon, Asher will stumble and you will be there to witness it. You, Willer, will save our king and kingdom from disaster and so earn the love of all men unto the end of time. But only if you say yes. If you don't, we shall see calamity unknown since the days of Morg and you will be known throughout eternity as the man who helped to kill a kingdom. As Blessed Barl is my witness, I know this to be true. So now we come to it, Willer. Now we reach the point of no return. Will you serve our beloved Lur, my friend? Will you join me in this holy quest to slay the monster Asher?'

'Yes, my lord,' said Willer, still breathless with emotion. 'Oh, *yes*. I will!'

# PART TWO

# CHAPTER TEN

*Drifting on a drug-soaked sea, Morg cradles Durm's fragile life tenderly, like a mother her babe in arms, and sings to it a song of survival. The fat fool's flesh is reluctant to heal. With every laboured breath Durm fights him, willing himself to die. Morg sweats and strives to deny him the victory.*

*Pother Nix is his unwitting ally, as determined as Morg to see this ruined carcass claw its way back from the brink. The tiny part of Morg not consumed by the battle is amused; would Nix fight so hard if he knew who it was he struggled to save?*

*Little King Gar is also an ally. Every day he comes to sit with Durm. Pours love and hope and healing into Durm's slumbering ears and prays out loud for a miracle.*

*Morg prays with him, and hopes dead Barl is listening.*

*Durm is listening. Durm weeps, even as he hardens his weakened heart against the king's entreaties and continues to strive for death.*

*Nix says to his king, Do not give up, sir. For where there is life is also hope.*

*Morg devoutly hopes that he is right. Marshals his strength, and continues his war.*

With a shuddering sigh Gar released Durm's flaccid hand. Sorrow and despair were weights on his chest, pressing his lungs flat and crushing his heart. 'Sometimes I think coming here is a waste of my time, Nix.'

The pother pressed his shoulder briefly. 'Not at all, Your Majesty. I believe our good Durm draws strength from your loving presence.'

'But he's struggling. Isn't he?' he said, frowning at the Master Magician's waxy, fallen face. 'Why? Why must he fight so hard? I thought you said his injuries were healing.'

Nix fussed at a vase of mixed lilies and sweetums on the windowsill. 'They are. Slowly.'

The man's evasiveness was a naked flame to dry grass. Anger ignited, consuming royal restraint. '*Too* slowly!'

'Everything that can be done is being done, sir. He is dosed on the hour with the freshest, most potent herbs from the infirmary garden and hothouse. All of my magical skill is dedicated to his recovery.'

'Then why is he not *healed*? Why does he lie here day after day in this stuporous daze, never once speaking to me or even opening his eyes!'

Nix spread his hands wide. 'If I could answer that, sir, I'd be the greatest pother in history. But he *is* making progress. It just takes time.'

Gar pushed out of his chair and began to pace Durm's small and airy chamber. 'I'm being pressured, Nix. My Privy Council would have me decide Durm's fate sooner rather than later. He was my father's dearest friend. Is a Master Magician beyond compare. I need him. Already

I've stalled my advisors twice. I can't procrastinate forever. My kingdom requires a Master Magician in more than name. When will I have one?'

Nix crossed his arms and tucked his hands into his sleeves. His expression was disappointed and reproving. 'Your Majesty, you know better than to ask me that.'

Stung, Gar folded his fingers into fists and stared through the room's small window. In the gardens outside men and boys toiled amongst the flowerbeds, laughing in the early morning sun. How he envied them their untroubled lives. If he couldn't at least point to a tangible, touchable improvement in Durm's condition by the end of the week he'd have no choice but to abandon all hope of keeping Conroyd out of the Weather Chamber.

Even worse, it would be the right thing to do.

'I'm sorry, Nix,' he sighed. 'I don't mean to slight you. I know you can't make that kind of pronouncement, or give me promises Durm's body might not be able to keep.'

The pother's severe expression eased. 'If I might presume on a lifetime's acquaintance, sir?'

'Presume away.'

'Don't let yourself be bullied by men who have a vested interest in Durm's slow recovery. Or by those whose honest concern is the kingdom's welfare, but who have yet to fully accept your new status. *You are the king*. Sanctified by Barl, blessed with the Weather Magic. Don't forget that . . . or let those who are sworn to serve *you* forget it either.'

Surprised into silence, Gar stared at Nix. Then, as the pother's words sank slowly home some of the crushing weight eased and he could breathe more comfortably. 'No,' he said at last. 'I won't.'

'You should get some rest,' Nix said abruptly. 'I spent more years than you've been alive watching what WeatherWorking did to your father. It's a cruel business. Be miserly with your energy, sir, or you'll not live to see your own child follow in your footsteps.'

Gar closed his teeth on a stinging rebuke. The man was obeying the impulse of his own sacred duty . . . and he was right, damn him. WeatherWorking was proving to be everything his mother had complained of, and more. Despite the pother's revolting restorative his head ached all the time and his bones felt strangely friable. Likely at any moment to crumble into dust. If not rigorously disciplined, his thoughts floated like thistledown on an errant breeze, impossible to catch. And he trembled inside, as though a thin cold wind blew ceaselessly beneath the surface of his skin.

'It's only been three weeks,' he said. 'In time I'll adjust, as my father adjusted before me, and his before him. Barl would not have given me the crown without also imparting the strength to wear it.'

Expression circumspect, Nix nodded. 'Indeed.'

Gar let his gaze drift to Durm's still body. Rested it there, aching. 'I must return to work. If he should in the smallest way stir . . .'

'Of course,' said Nix, and opened the chamber door for him. 'At once.'

As he made his way through the palace to Durm's desolately empty apartments, he thought: *Let him stir soon, Barl. I'm running out of time.*

It felt strange, almost . . . indecent . . . to be sitting in Durm's hushed, private study, holding one of his jealously hoarded magic texts. This room so belonged to the Master Magician he felt like a trespasser. He could almost hear Durm's deep and disapproving voice demanding to know what he thought he was doing . . .

The book he balanced so carefully in his lap contained the spells he needed to shape the marble effigies destined to grace his family's coffins. There were Doranen in the City who could do it, of course. Who performed the magic for any citizen with the money and a need for such reminders. Where the royal family was concerned, though, tradition dictated the task be reserved for the Master Magician.

With Durm insensate, he'd do it himself. A last, loving service for those he had capriciously survived.

He let the book fall open and searched through its age-mottled pages until he found the incantation. Read the words, felt the sigils unfold, and marvelled anew at the difference within him.

Years ago he'd studied nursery spells, struggling to make them come alive in his mind. Had failed, because without magic he'd been as successful as a deaf child trying to hear music by reading a score. Now incantations sounded in his head like a choir and the magic in his blood danced to hear them.

Banishing exhaustion, lost to the slow march of daylight past the curtained window, he sank himself beneath the surface of wonder and let the magic sing.

According to the notices outside the palace hall where the royal family lay in state, public viewing stopped at six o'clock. Asher stood in the shadow of a deep-set doorway and listened to the plaintive protests of stragglers as Royce and Jolin, the guards on duty, kindly but firmly chivvied them out. It was nearly half-past the hour. After a day locked up in consultations he was tired. Hungry. Worn to frazzlement with other people's problems and dreading the night's WeatherWorking to come. He could think of at least three other places he'd rather be.

And yet, here he was.

Tear-stained and still complaining the stragglers wandered past him, unseeing. He waited till they'd left the palace completely, then stepped out of concealment.

'Leave that,' he said to Royce and Jolin as they started to close the hall's double doors. 'Go home. I'll stand watch till the next shift arrives.'

Surprised, they stared at him. 'You sure?' said Royce.

He made himself grin. 'When did you know me not sure, eh? Go on. Scarper. Or I'll report you to Orrick for insubordination.'

Jolin grinned back. 'No need. We're away. Why not join us down the Goose later for a pint or three? Or are you too grand now, Meister Olken Administrator?'

'Not too grand. Just too busy. Have one for me.'

Laughing, they agreed to suffer on his behalf and departed. He watched them for a moment, envious, then entered the huge hall where Gar's family lay in all their silent splendour.

The room was gently glimlit, casting shadows, softening death. Three velvet-draped biers stood end to end in the centre of the room: Borne, Dana, Fane. Crimson ropes formed a cordon around them, protecting them from extravagant grief. Their faces were uncovered, serene; their bodies buried in a riot of hothouse blooms whose scent tinted the air with summer.

He shivered, suddenly cold. Closed the distance between himself and Borne and made himself look into that blank, uninhabited face. The king's hair was gold again. Washed clean with soap, or magic. Flooded with relief, he realised some part of him had expected blood. Stupid.

He took a deep breath. Released it slowly through

gritted teeth. 'Well, Your Majesty, here's a thing. You dead. Durm still makin' up his poxy mind. Gar figurin' out your fancy Weather Magic as he goes along. And me . . . me seein' and doin' things no Olken's got business stickin' his oar into. It's all a bloody mess, ain't it?'

The hall's ceiling was so high his voice echoed. His throat felt sore, his chest tight. A tic in the muscle beside his eye twitched wildly.

'So. Dead or not, sir, you got to do something. He's my friend but he's your son and I'm tellin' you straight, I don't know how to help him. I can't tell if he's doin' your magic right or not. I mean, it rains. It snows. Freezes where it's s'posed to. I think. At least nobody's complainin'. But it's *killin'* him. He says it's s'posed to hurt, it's the price he has to pay, but *this* much? I can't believe that. It's like he's burnin' alive. Bein' cut with a thousand knives. He bleeds and bleeds. At this rate I don't reckon he'll last *one* year, let alone a lifetime. And I ain't any use to him, all I can do is watch. You asked me to take care of him, and I'm tryin', but . . . you need to tell me *how*!'

No reply. He shifted slightly. Looked instead at Dana and Fane. Beautiful once more, all cruel deformities hidden beneath sweet petals of pink and blue and yellow and mauve. Burnished with glimlight, preserved with powerful magic, their pale skin glowed, lifelike.

Revolted, despairing, he flung himself away.

Silhouetted in the doorway Dathne said, 'I thought you weren't going to come here.'

His heart was pounding. 'Changed my mind.'

She came forward, slowly. The day's hard work showed clearly in her tired eyes. She looked pale. 'Why?'

*Because Gar's killin' himself with magic and I don't know how to stop it.* But he couldn't tell her that, so he chose a different truth. 'Thought if I saw 'em like this, all clean and covered in flowers . . .'

'You'd be able to stop seeing them all broken and bloody?'

He nodded. Who'd've thought he'd start bad dreams at his age? 'Somethin' like that.'

'And is it working?'

Without warning her face blurred and he was looking at her through a prism of tears. 'No.'

'Oh, *Asher* . . .'

He wrapped his arms so tight about her he thought he heard her ribs creak, but she made no complaint. Didn't pull away. Just threaded her long thin fingers through his hair and murmured nonsense words of comfort against his skin. Pain was a rising tide he was too weary to hold back.

'I miss my da,' he whispered into her hair. 'I never got to say goodbye. My damn brothers – they wouldn't even tell me where he's buried . . .'

Her warm hands framed his face. 'They're bastards. *Bastards*. Don't think of them.'

'I don't. I didn't. Not until now.'

'Let it go, Asher. Your father was mortal. He was always going to die.'

Her sudden brutality shocked him. Prising her hands free he nodded at Gar's perished family. 'Like them?'

'Yes! Like them. We're none of us immortal, Asher. Death lies at the end of every journey. What matters is how we travel the road.' Then her fierce eyes softened, and her fingers touched his cheek. 'This isn't just about your father, is it? Something else is troubling you. Can't you tell me what it is? We're friends. I can help.'

He closed his eyes. If only he could tell her. Share the burden. The weight of it was crushing him. The fear that something terrible was happening to Gar and he was powerless to prevent it. 'It's . . . complicated, Dath.' Reluctantly, he stepped away from her. His skin where her fingers had rested was warm; the rest of his body felt like ice. 'Maybe one day.'

'You look exhausted.'

'I am.'

'Then stop tormenting yourself in here. Go home to bed. You've another full day of appointments tomorrow, you'll need your wits about you.'

He shuddered. 'Don't remind me. I got a last-ditch meeting with Glospottle and the Dyers' Guild. If I can't make 'em see sense it's all goin' arse over eyeballs into Justice Hall.'

A glimmer of amusement amid the concern. 'Do you need me?'

If he told her how much, he'd frighten her away. 'I'll be fine. You got enough on your plate as it is.'

'I can reschedule my meetings, I can—'

He pressed a finger to her lips. 'No. The Bakers' Guild can't wait, or the Vintners', or Lord Daltrie's taxation committee. You want to help me? Keep the whole bloody pack of 'em far, far away and I'll love you forever.'

*Love*. The unguarded word fell between them like a rock. Silently he cursed himself and took his finger from her lips. She turned away. Fumbled at her tunic.

'I'll do my best.'

'Dathne—'

'I should go,' she said, glancing at the open doorway. 'I'm meeting Matt in the Goose. Did you want to—'

His turn to look away. 'Can't. Somewhere to be.'

Her relief was imperfectly disguised. 'Another time then.'

'Aye,' he said, heart heavy. 'Another time.'

She was smiling, but her eyes were troubled. 'If we don't cross paths tomorrow between meetings, good luck with Meister Glospottle.'

'Thanks. I'll need it.'

She left him then, and he watched her go with his fists clenched hard at his sides. Fool. *Fool.* Of all the stupid things to say . . .

*Please, Barl. Please. Don't let me have chased her away.*

Not long after Dathne's abrupt departure, Colly and Brin arrived for their turn at guard duty. He left them to it and made his brooding circuitous way on foot to the Weather Chamber. Entered, and waited upstairs for Gar to arrive. Stood helplessly by, again, as Lur's king screamed and bled and fed the land its rain and magic.

Sickened, shaking, he held the dose of restorative to Gar's blue and bloodstained lips, coaxing it into his mouth. 'Send for Jarralt, Gar! Make him Master Magician before this kills you and he takes it all.'

Feebly, Gar pushed the cup away and slid sideways down the wall until he was prone on the parquetry floor. His shirt was soaked through with the sweat of his efforts. Convulsive shudders racked him from head to toe. He looked like a man in the last stages of some desperate illness.

'No.'

He threw the cup across the room. '*Damn* you! What am I s'posed to *do*?'

Gar closed his sunken eyes. 'Nothing. I am my father's son. This cannot kill me.'

'Well, it's bloody near killin' me!'

The faintest of smiles touched Gar's face. 'Poor Asher. I'm sorry.'

Abruptly ashamed, he dropped to the floor. 'No.

No. Don't mind me. I'm scared for you, is all.'

Grimacing, Gar forced himself to sit up. Leaning against the wall, chest heaving, he gave Asher's shoulder a clumsy pat. 'Don't be.'

*Don't be*? What kind of sinkin' stupid thing was that to say? Fear transmuted to fury. '*Gar—*'

'You should go,' Gar said. 'We don't want—' He broke off, coughing harshly, a terrible tearing rasp of sound suggesting lung-rot. 'Go,' he whispered. 'I'll be fine. I just need to rest a while.'

'No, Gar, you—'

'Shall I make it a royal command? *Go*!'

He stood. 'You're mad, y'know that? Stark staring crazy.'

Gar just shook his head. 'I'll see you tomorrow.'

The long walk back to the Tower was chilly, and haunted with ugly images. What to do? Perhaps a confidential hint dropped in Pother Nix's ear . . .

Willer, a satchel hugged under one arm, was leaving the Tower just as he arrived. 'Asher!' The sea slug's face contorted into a peculiar expression of nervous ingratiation. 'Fancy meeting you this late. Don't tell me you've not stopped working yet?'

Mindless chatter with Willer was the last thing he needed. 'No.'

Willer stepped a little sideways, blocking him. 'Me, either. Darran needs these papers delivered to the palace as a matter of urgency. You know, I thought we worked hard when Gar was just a prince, but—'

Asher raised an eyebrow. 'Gar?'

'I mean His Majesty,' said Willer hastily. 'Sorry. No discourtesy intended.'

*Sorry*? What the – 'Willer, was there somethin' you wanted?'

The pissant's fat pink cheeks flushed. 'No. Well, yes. Nothing imp – that's to say – look. Asher. I've been thinking. I know we've never quite seen eye to eye.' An embarrassed titter. 'As much my fault as yours, I expect. I'd like to start over. Show you I'm not such a bad fellow after all. In fact, I'll show willing, shall I? Darran's got me working from sun-up to sundown and beyond, but I'd be happy to place myself at your disposal. Work alongside you, as another assistant. Who knows? We might even turn out to be friends!'

Barl save him. His night was going from bad to worse. 'Friends? You and me?'

'Yes. After all, lots of people get off on the wrong foot to start with and then realise they were wrong about each other. Why not us?'

Why *not*? He didn't know whether to laugh or vomit. 'Willer—'

'Oh, please, Asher. At least think about it. Consider the idea of us making a fresh start.'

'Sure. I'll consider it.' *Once I'm dead and buried . . .*

Willer beamed. 'Oh, that's wonderful. Thank you. I promise you won't regret it.'

He was regretting it already. 'Fine. Grand. Goodnight, Willer.'

He left the little slug babbling his gratitude on the Tower's front steps and took himself up to bed. Sent down for a supper of soup and hot bread then sat stubbornly in his cosy parlour, fighting sleep, until he heard Gar's ragged footsteps on the staircase beyond.

Only then did he crawl into bed himself.

Gar woke late the next morning, grudgingly. The merest sliver of light between his drawn bedchamber curtains was like a scythe slicing through his head. His chest hurt and his screwed-tight eyes. His skin. His bones. His whole body overflowed with a grinding, remorseless pain.

Which was nothing compared with the exquisite torment of last night's WeatherWorking.

*Asher's right, damn him. This really does have to stop . . .*

Tentatively, he uncurled his clenching of limbs beneath the blankets and eased his eyelids open. The room tilted. Spun like a top. His empty belly heaved, spasming. Good thing he'd forgone dinner or he'd be thrashing in its stinking remains right now . . .

With infinite reluctance, the violent nausea passed. Drenched in sweat he lay in his tangle of bedclothes and stared at the light-dappled ceiling until he could no longer ignore his nagging bladder.

His face in the privy closet mirror was horror enough to give little children nightmares.

Haphazard bathing and an unsteady shave lifted his spirits, marginally. More than anything he wanted to crawl back into bed and blot out the world for a day . . . a week . . . forever . . . but he had a sacred duty to perform.

No matter how ill and old he was feeling.

Breakfast was out of the question, so he dressed and went downstairs. Bad luck crossed his path with Darran's in the Tower's empty foyer. His secretary looked up from perusing some newly delivered message and didn't quite stifle his shocked gasp.

'I know,' he said, forestalling a spate of consternation. 'Death warmed over and so on and so forth. Consider it said and the conversation closed. Where's Asher?'

Darran cleared his throat. 'In meetings all day, sir. Did you wish me to—'

'No. No. Doubtless I'll catch up with him in due course.'

'And you, sir? Where will you be, if you're needed?'

'The family crypt. I'm going to create their effigies today, Darran. Immortalise them in marble. Assuming of course that the templates have been delivered?'

A reflection of his own pain shimmered in Darran's eyes. 'Yesterday, sir. While you were otherwise engaged. I did leave a note for you on your library desk, did you not—'

'I haven't set foot in there for weeks.' After all this time he'd hoped to have made a start on the precious few books saved from Barl's lost collection, but events had galloped past him.

'Never mind, sir,' said Darran gently. 'Your books and scrolls aren't going anywhere. When you're ready, they'll be waiting for you.'

He was so tired an old man's kindness could touch him to tears. He patted Darran's arm in passing and left him to his duties.

House Torvig's crypt had been built in the grounds of the palace just after Trevoyle's Schism. Its architect was his first royal ancestor, King Cleamon, who'd won the right by Duel Arcana for himself and all his descendants to call themselves WeatherWorker, live in the palace and inter their dead in an opulent marble sepulchre crowned with the newly redesigned house emblem: a thunderbolt crossed with an unsheathed sword.

The chamber he'd chosen for his family's final resting place was small. It seemed . . . fitting. They'd been close in life, after all. Why not rub shoulders in death, too? He bumped around it now like a fly in a honey pot, heedless of bruising his hip on the corner of one open, waiting coffin. Trying not to look at the three templates the undertakers had left here, propped on wooden sawhorses, ready for magical moulding. One male figure, suitably kinglike. One female, dressed like a queen. And of course the lovely young girl's body, representing Fane. He shuddered. These marble approximations were even more unsettling than his family's actual bodies.

Abruptly tired, he dropped onto the bench seat cut into the chamber's far wall and hid his face in his hands.

He was afraid.

The task awaiting him, a magical creation of their living faces in lifeless stone, was the last thing he'd ever do for them. Years from now, when he too was dead and sleeping beside them in this small cold place, strangers yet unborn would look upon what he wrought here today and believe that what they saw was true.

He lifted his head to stare at the effigy that would become his sister. Its marble face was a blank white expanse, a clean slate, a held breath. The features he gave it here and now would *be* Fane, forever; he could give her a hook nose, bulbous lips, beady eyes or a lumpen, misshapen brow. He could pouch her cheeks like a greedy squirrel's. Reduce her chin to a querulous afterthought. He could make her as ugly on the outside as she'd been on the inside and nobody could stop him. She certainly couldn't. She was dead.

Vivid as a crack of lightning he saw her: silver-gilt hair gleaming in the sunshine, limpid blue eyes sparkling with mischief, or maybe malice; the sound of her laughter rang in his head more clearly than any silver bell.

He stood. Moved to the lump of carved rock that must become his sister and, ignoring all pain and illness and bone-deep fatigue, summoned the transformation spell.

Untamed, untrammelled, the words surged through his mind like a storm tide, burst from his mouth like snow melt released, sweeping aside all fear. Power cascaded from the secret place inside, raged through his bloodstream, poured out of his fingertips and into the chilly waiting marble. Stone turned to cream beneath his hands, softened and slipped and slithered as memory and magic transformed rock into remembrance.

When at last it was done and Fane lay sleeping before him, beautiful and whole, he pressed his cold flesh lips to her warm stone forehead. Let his cheek rest against hers, and whispered into her immaculate ear.

'I could have made you ugly and I didn't. Remember that, little sister. Remember I still love you, and this as well: you haven't won. The magic remains mine. I did not seek this power and yet it came to me. I did not yearn to be WeatherWorker, but that is who I am. All of it Barl's doing, not mine. I'm sorry you're dead but I won't betray our father by rejecting her gifts just because you couldn't bring yourself to share.'

The pain behind his eyes was fierce now. Unforgiving. Feasting on the flickers of remaining magic in his blood. He ignored it. Glory was in him, and triumph, and a burning determination to see this sacred duty done.

His mother's face came less glibly, exhaustion threatening her defeat. Grimly he beat back the scarlet tide even as he felt his face distort in a rictus of torment. When at last she lay before him, eyelashes curling, lips curved in a secret smile, he pillowed his aching head upon her breast and let his trembling fingers caress her hard white hair. In the crypt's swaddling silence he thought he heard her singing, an old sweet lullaby of love and loss. He could have stayed there forever, except his task was not complete.

Stern and joyful, gentle and bold, his father waited.

This time the magic came forth snarling, like a cur dog dragged from the gutter. No riotous gushing but a mean trickle, dregs dripped from a guzzled keg. Panting, sweating, that thin keen wind beneath his skin howling now like one of Asher's sea storms, he wrestled his reluctant power, screamed at it, cozened and commanded and demanded its obedience. The marble beneath his frenzied fingers seethed and surged, and in his mind's eye the memory of his father's face refused to stand still. Slipping and sliding and shifting its focus, it wouldn't let him see, wouldn't let him remember, wouldn't let him offer this last loving gesture in honour of the man he'd adored.

'I will do this! I *will*!' he shouted. '*Electha toh ranu*! *Ranu*! *Ranu*!'

The ancient words of compulsion shuddered the crypt's glimlit air. He felt the magic sear his veins like acid, excoriating his flesh. Something deep inside him twisted, tore, ripped his thoughts asunder with monstrous claws. In their place an endless emptiness, unfurling like a fledgling seed.

A profound silence. Then a fist of darkness crashed upon him and the world ended.

# CHAPTER ELEVEN

Halfway up the stairs to her apartment after double-checking Poppy's bookwork for the day, Dathne heard the banging on the back door and groaned.

'Go away!'

The banging continued. Cursing, she started down the stairs again.

'I'm coming, I'm *coming*!' she protested, and flung open the door. '*What*?'

Asher, resplendent in green velvet and dull gold brocade. She felt her heart constrict as betraying colour flooded her cheeks.

'Oh. It's you.'

He carried a sealed wine jug. Holding it up, tightly smiling, he said, 'Care to help me drown my sorrows?'

For a moment she didn't follow. Then, remembering his last meeting of the day, his meaning dawned. 'Oh no.'

'Oh yes,' he replied. 'Glospottle refused to see sense, and so did his poxy guild. So it's arse over eyeballs and tits over toenails all the way to Justice Hall.'

It wasn't funny, it truly wasn't, but she had to press her lips hard together for a moment. 'I'm so sorry.'

He shoved the wine jug at her. 'Not as sorry as me. Just don't laugh.'

'I wouldn't dream of it.' She took the jug then looked past his shoulder into the small yard behind her shop. 'Where's Cygnet?'

'Snug in his bed. I walked. Needed the exercise, and the time to think.'

'I'm not surprised.'

'So you goin' to ask me in then, or just take my wine and shut the door in my face?'

Again, she felt her cheeks heat. Stepping back, she said, 'Sorry. Of course. Come in. Have you eaten?'

'Not lately,' he said, crossing her threshold. 'Is that an invitation to dinner?'

'Yes,' she said after a moment. 'I suppose it is.'

Three steps inside her tiny living room he stopped and stared around him, unabashedly curious. He'd never been inside her home before. Keeping him at a friendly arm's length had always been her best defence.

It didn't seem to be working any more.

The tiny dining table was set for one, so after putting the wine jug in her equally tiny kitchen she fetched cutlery for him and a napkin.

He sniffed appreciatively. 'Somethin' smells good.'

'Rabbit stew,' she said, trying not to notice how easily he fitted into her home. 'Not as fancy as the meals you're used to these days, but—'

'It's perfect,' he said. 'Want me to pour some of that wine?'

She wished he wouldn't smile like that: warmly, intimately . . . lovingly. 'Why not? You've got those sorrows to drown, after all. Glasses are in the cupboard beside the sink.'

He went rummaging. 'I'd rather drown Indigo bloody Glospottle.'

How many times could she straighten a knife and fork before she looked ridiculous? 'In a big smelly vat of his own urine.'

That made him laugh, but the sound trailed off into a groan. He reappeared in the doorway, holding two glasses of palest green icewine. 'Don't bloody tempt me.' He shook his head. 'Barl save me, Dath. I'm goin' to *Justice Hall.*'

She took the glass he offered her. 'And not in chains, which is the biggest surprise of all.'

That made him laugh too. It felt good to know she had the power to amuse him. *Careful, careful*, her inner self warned. But she didn't want to be careful. The icewine was superb, tart and full of fruit. She took a second swallow then put the glass on the dining table. 'Have a seat. I'll dish up.'

It felt odd, sitting opposite him at the table she usually shared with no one. Circumspectly, from beneath her lowered lashes, she watched him eat. Even that had changed about him. So much polish he'd acquired. He wore his expensive clothing now as though it was just another part of him, like his hair. Once, she vividly remembered, he'd walked around inside velvet and brocade as though at any moment he expected them to bite him. He'd never seemed to her precisely young, just rough . . . but not any more. Grave responsibilities had aged him. Seasoned him, like green timber long soaked in sunshine and rainstorms. She didn't know whether to be pleased, or to feel sorry for the fisherman stranded so long on dry land.

Upon closer examination, sorrow won. The Glospottle crisis had intensified the strain she'd sensed in him yesterday evening, not replaced it. Whatever had bothered him then continued to bother him now. He was being gnawed by a secret; the pain of it was in his eyes, his voice, his stubbled face.

She dabbed her lips with her napkin. 'And how is our new king? He's not been seen in public since his coronation. You must know people are starting to wonder.'

Asher tipped the last of his wine into his mouth. 'He's fine.'

'Are you sure?'

He shrugged, an irritated twitch like a horse dislodging flies. 'You think I'm lying?'

'I think you're withholding the truth, which is lying's kissing cousin.'

'*Damn* it, Dathne!' Shoving his chair back, he let his knife and fork clatter to the plate and went to her curtained window. Twitched the faded coverings open and stared into the street. 'I told you last night, it's complicated. Stop bein' such a . . . a . . . slumskumbledy wench!'

'I do know what that means,' she said primly. 'Matt told me.'

'Matt wants to keep his tongue between his teeth.'

Appetite stifled, she folded and refolded her napkin. 'I'm only trying to help you.'

'You can't.'

'How do you know if you won't let me try?'

'Don't you understand? I'm tryin' to *protect* you!'

Damn him and his quaint notions of decency. She had to *know* . . . 'I never asked for your protection.'

'You would if—' He turned back to the window, hiding again. 'This ain't a game, Dathne. We're talkin' laws and consequences and things best left alone. I'm grateful for your friendship. I enjoyed your rabbit stew. I can't repay that by puttin' you in danger.'

He sounded so torn. So tempted to confide and make her part of his secret. Here then was the moment. If she could break him now, he'd truly be hers. She slid out of her chair, joined him at the window and let her palms rest flat against his back. He flinched, tension thrumming through him. The flesh beneath her hands was as hard as marble.

'It's my choice, Asher,' she whispered. 'My decision. If you can risk this danger, whatever it is, then so can I. Let me help you. *Please*. No one should be this alone.'

He sighed, a deep and shuddering breath. Broke away and went back into the kitchen. When he came out again he was drinking from the jug of icewine.

'Don't know if I can do this sober,' he said, almost apologetic, and held out the jug to her. 'Don't know if you can either.'

She set the jug aside. '*Tell me*.'

Eyes stricken, expression agonised, he dithered like a horse on the edge of a ditch too wide to safely jump. 'Dathne . . .'

She smiled, as invitingly as she knew how. 'It's all right. I'm not afraid.'

He leapt. 'I been goin' with Gar to the Weather-Working.'

'Oh,' she said, after the silence between them had stretched beyond bearing. Clasped her hands behind her back so they wouldn't start beating him about his stupid wooden head. 'And whose bright idea was that?'

'His – at first.'

'But then you adopted it as your own?' Try as she might, she couldn't keep the acid sarcasm from her voice.

'Someone's got to be there,' he said, stung. 'You got no idea what it's like! The bloody magic *guts* him, Dath. He bleeds like a butchered hog, he ain't able to walk for an hour after. Sometimes longer. He can't face that alone.'

She wanted to shake him till his teeth fell out. Centuries of waiting dribbled down to these last weeks and days and he was risking everything the Circle lived for, *everything*. 'And you can't face it with him! It's death to dabble in their—'

'I ain't dabblin'!'

'But you're *there*, Asher!' she cried. 'Witness to their most secret, sacred magic! To everyone else it'll mean the same thing. If this comes out—'

'How can it come out? I ain't tellin', Gar ain't tellin'. Are you about to—'

'No, of *course* not!' Hammered with fear, she wrapped her fingers round the end of her plait and tugged until her scalp screamed for mercy. She hadn't seen this coming. Why had she not seen this coming? All of Prophecy's plans at risk because of his friendship with Gar! 'Asher—'

He flung himself away from the window and began a ragged pacing. 'You reckon I *want* to be there, holding the bowl as Gar vomits his guts out night after night? You reckon I enjoy washing all the blood off him, and me? That I like having to sneak about the Tower prayin' like a Barlsman that bloody Willer don't stumble across me comin' when I'm s'posed to be goin', or goin' when I should already be gone?'

'But it's not fair, what the king's asking. How he's putting you at risk. I don't believe there's not a single Doranen he can't call upon to aid him until Durm either recovers or is replaced.'

He stopped then, and dropped into her shabby armchair like a deer struck with an arrow. With his elbows braced on his knees he let his head fall heavily into his hands. 'Who? Not Nix. That sends the kind of message Jarralt's just itchin' to read. Not Holze. He'd see it as his moral duty to say somethin' *for the good of the kingdom*. There's nobody, Dath. Nobody he can trust to see him like that, except me.'

He sounded so defeated. She sat on the arm of his chair, fighting the urge to thread her fingers through his hair. He wore it longer now than once he had. 'I'm sorry I shouted,' she said softly. 'I'm glad you told me.'

'It's the only way I can help him, Dath,' he said, and slumped sideways a little to lean against her. 'I don't know what else to do. All he ever talks about is avoiding another schism. How that'd be a betrayal of his da. He's convinced that if Conroyd Jarralt ever learns how hard it is for him to control the Weather Magic, the bastard'll challenge him as unfit. And he would too. Jarralt couldn't care less about a schism if it means stickin' the crown on his own head after.'

'But if Gar truly isn't strong enough—'

He jerked away. 'We don't know that! Look what's happened to him in the last two months! First he gets his magic, then he's nearly killed gettin' thrown from a runaway carriage. And losin' his family on top of it – there ain't been a WeatherWorker in history who's come to the throne like that. It's a bloody miracle he can do it at all.'

He slumped again, anger spent. Unbidden, her hand drifted to rest on the nape of his neck; he made a pleased little sound deep in his throat and closed his eyes. She let her hand stay where it was, thinking hard.

Another schism. That would surely usher in the Final Days foretold by Prophecy. Indeed, for a time the Circle in Trevoyle's time had thought *they* were the ones to face the fire. The idea made sense. Fitted all too neatly with her visions of death and destruction. A battle between mages for the crown, for the control of Barl's Wall, would swiftly see the magical balances of the kingdom upset. And Asher would be in the middle of it, standing at Gar's right hand as he fought to keep control, to stay king. Yes. It all made horrible sense.

What she couldn't see was how Asher was supposed to stop it from happening. Not with Olken magic, which was a soft and subtle thing, cajoling and persuasive. Not when he hadn't even discovered its existence within himself yet.

The not knowing was killing her. *What about a hint, Jervale*, she silently pleaded. *Just a little hint* . . .

No reply, and none truly expected. She'd have to learn the truth of things another way. Since Gar seemed at the heart of the mystery, and Asher was close to Gar, then she'd have to get closer to Asher. In the name of duty. In the service of Prophecy.

*Yes, yes*, she answered the critical voice within. *And because I want to.*

Beside her, Asher stirred. 'I should go,' he muttered.

'Why? Is there a WeatherWorking tonight?'

'No. But he was all set to create his family's effigies today. He'll take it hard. I should—'

'Leave him be,' she advised. 'Let him grieve without an audience.'

He pressed his fingers to his eyes. 'Aye . . . maybe . . . but you don't want me clutterin' up your livin' room. I'll—'

She drifted her hand from his nape to his shoulder, almost caressing. 'Did I say that?'

Dark colour flushed his weathered skin, and in his face she saw the deepening, the maturing, of all the feelings she'd seen there that night outside the Goose when he'd asked her to leave Dorana with him and go gallivanting off to Restharven. Uncertainly he said, 'I thought—'

'You need to ease your mind, Asher. Like it or not you aren't a fisherman any more. You're a man of power and responsibility. A solver of problems, even unlikely ones drowning in piss. Gar's not the only one who needs a friend to look out for him. Stay. Rest. Forget about Gar's problems, and Justice Hall, and all the other worries weighing you down. Stay. Your company's no hardship to me.'

She watched hope flare in his eyes. Felt guilt, and a wicked flaring of her own, and smothered them both. Some of the strain eased from his face. He smiled and her heart turned over. 'All right,' he said. 'I'll stay. But only for an hour.'

In the end he stayed two hours, and took his leave in a far better mood than when he'd arrived. He hadn't chased her away. If anything she seemed closer to him now than she'd ever been before. As though something inside her had surrendered to the feelings she fought so hard to deny.

He didn't know why, and he didn't much care.

*She's mine, she's mine, and soon I'll hear her say it.*

He jogged back to the Tower, invigorated. Made it all the way up to his suite, had his fingers on the door handle, damn it, when a peremptory voice called out: 'Asher! A moment if you please!'

Swallowing a groan, he turned. Darran stood on the landing below him, a frown pulling his face into tight lines of concern.

'Darran, it's late,' he said, looking down through the staircase railings. 'Whatever it is, can't it wait till morning? I'm fair bloody knackered. What are you still doin' here anyways? Nix'll have your guts for garters if you keel over again after all his pills and potions. He'll say you're makin' him look bad.'

'I'm not interested in Pother Nix's reputation,' replied Darran. 'And if it's all the same to you I'd rather not stand here bellowing like a fishmonger in the markets. Kindly come down to my office where we can converse like civilised men.' Forestalling argument, he disappeared.

Swallowing another groan, Asher trudged downstairs. Just to prove a point he didn't actually enter Darran's office but leaned against the doorjamb instead. 'You must be feelin' poorly, callin' me civilised.'

Darran looked up from behind his desk. 'I was being polite.'

'No need to bother on my account.'

'Clearly not,' said Darran snippily. 'Now do stop being obstreperous, at least for five minutes. Or is that too much to ask?'

Despite his crushing weariness, Asher grinned. 'Prob'ly.' Then, to avoid a tongue-lashing, he did as he was asked. Kicked the door shut behind him and dropped into the nearest chair. 'Well?'

Darran steepled his fingers against his chin. 'I'm worried about His Majesty.'

He could've screamed. 'Gar's fine.'

'He is *not* fine,' said Darran. 'He needs a Master Magician.'

'He's got one.'

'The one he's got is broken. He needs a new one.'

'He doesn't want a new one!'

'This isn't about what he wants, Asher! It's about what's best for him!'

Asher got up and started pacing, his heels thumping the carpet as though he were killing cockroaches. All the lovely lingering glow of pleasure from Dathne's company was vanished. Now he felt prickled and badgered and shoved in a corner, hot and bothered and bullied.

'In case you hadn't noticed, Darran, I ain't a Doranen. I can't snap my magic fingers and make everything all right.'

'Perhaps not, but you can talk to him. Use your dubious influence. Make him see he must—'

'Don't you think I've *tried*?'

'Then try harder!'

'How? What d'you want me to do, Darran? Lock him in a room alone with Willer till he begs for mercy and promises anything to be let out again?'

Darran slapped his desk. 'If that's what it takes, yes! Asher, are you blind? Have you seen how dreadful he's looking?'

'Of course I bloody have.'

'Then *do* something. Don't you understand? You're the only person he'll listen to! In short, I fear you are his only hope!'

'I don't want to be his only bloody hope!'

'And that makes two of us!' Darran shouted back, surging to his feet. 'But what we want is irrelevant! All that matters is our king!'

Asher threw up his hands. 'All right! All right! I'll do it! Anything to shut you up! Barl's mercy, you bang away like a bloody woodpecker, don't you?'

Darran's lips curved in a mocking smile. Slowly, he sat again. 'Given you possess all the sensitivity of a tree stump, I thought it the wisest tactic.'

'Oh, ha ha,' he muttered, and threw himself back in the chair. A fresh headache was building behind his eyes, thunderous as a storm.

Now Darran's smile was mordantly amused. 'I hear you're to preside in judgement at Justice Hall. Extraordinary. I must say Barl has a strange sense of humour.'

'You're tellin' me.'

'Such an undertaking will involve a great deal of preparation. You'll require assistance.'

'I got assistance.'

Darran pulled a disapproving face. 'As a legal expert I'm sure Mistress Dathne makes a very fine bookseller.'

He felt his face heat. 'I never said it was Dathne.'

'You didn't have to. And while I'm sure she performs her duties as Assistant Olken Administrator quite adequately, clearly this is a very different situation. Therefore, in the interests of not disgracing His Majesty, *I* shall coach you in the duties and protocols expected of you in the matter of Glospottle and the Dyers' Guild. No, no,' he added, lifting a hand. 'There's no need to thank me.'

'Trust me,' Asher said grimly. 'I weren't about to.'

'Have you set a date for the hearing?'

'Not yet.'

'Best to make it sooner rather than later. This ridiculous Glospottle business has dragged on for far too long,' said Darran with a severe sniff. 'We can begin work tomorrow morning. After you've spoken with the king. Yes?'

He glared. Darran smiled. Still glaring, he stumped

out of the ole crow's office and slammed the door as hard as he could behind him.

The loud bang of timber against timber didn't relieve his feelings, or help his headache, in the slightest.

He tried to speak to Gar first thing the next morning. But Gar wasn't in his apartment suite, or the solar, or anywhere in the Tower. Mildly disconcerted, he wandered out to the stables, where he found Ballodair eating breakfast. Which meant the king wasn't out for an early ride. So where was he?

'What's amiss?' said Matt, behind him.

He rearranged his expression and turned. 'Nowt. Just stretching my legs.'

Matt was grinning. Pulling on his gloves, ready for riding. 'I hear your little meeting with Glospottle and the Dyers' Guild nearly came to blows. Make sure you save me a seat in Justice Hall, eh? I wouldn't want to miss the sight of you in your crimson robes.'

'Sink me bloody sideways! Who told you?'

'It was the talk of the Goose last night. If you weren't famous before, my friend, you will be after! An Olken sitting in judgement at Justice Hall? You're a man of hidden talents, Asher.'

'I'm a man of many headaches, is what I am. I'll see you later, Matt. I got some business to attend to.'

As he left the stable yard, frowning, a nasty thought occurred. Yesterday Gar had gone to his family's crypt to create the effigies. But that wouldn't have taken all day and night. Not unless—

—unless something had gone horribly wrong.

Brisk walking turned into a fast jog, then an all-out run as he headed for House Torvig's private burial vault. He was panting, streaming sweat, by the time he reached it. Glimfire still burned in the passageways; not a good sign. He took four wrong turns before finally stumbling into the small glimlit room Gar had selected to house the coffins.

He found his king sprawled face down on the flagstoned floor.

'Gar!'

There was a pulse, praise Barl, and slow, measured breathing. Gar's skin was dry, cold, his eyes gently closed. Even as Asher poked and prodded and shouted his name he stirred. Coughed. Woke and stared around him, confused.

'Asher?'

'Barl bloody save me,' Asher muttered, and helped him to sit up. 'Are you all right? What happened? Don't tell me you decided to *sleep* in here! 'Cause that's takin' reverence for the dead just a—'

'No, no,' said Gar, and pressed a hand to his head. 'I was moulding the effigies and – I can't remember – there was pain, and a bright light, and—' His expression changed, confusion to caution to sudden fear. 'Help me stand.'

With a grunt Asher hauled him to his feet. Gar swayed for a moment, finding his balance, then looked at the three coffins. Sucked in a great gasp of air and blanched fish-belly white.

'Barl bloody save me,' Asher said again, and this time it was a prayer. Serene, peaceful, exquisite: the faces of the queen and her daughter slept side by side, a song and its echo. But Borne's face was a monstrosity.

On the left side it was perfect. An immaculate representation of the man. The right side, though, was twisted. Melted. The stone eye in its socket had boiled and burst, dribbling marble tears down the sunken cheek. It was as though the effigy were made of wax, not stone, and some mad magician had breathed on it with fire.

'What happened? What went wrong?'

'I don't know,' Gar whispered. 'It's all a jumble. Barl have mercy, Asher. His *face*!'

Asher stepped between Gar and the dead king's coffin. 'Don't look at it. Just listen. This happened 'cause you're coming apart at the seams, Gar. Nix's bloody potion ain't fixing you, it's just been keepin' you glued together. Except now even that ain't working. And folk are startin' to notice.'

'What folk? What are you talking about?'

'Darran's been on at me. He can see how poorly you're looking, and so can everyone else.'

Gar frowned. 'Don't. Not in here.'

'Where then? Gar, it's time you came to your senses. Durm's no closer to gettin' out of bed today than he was three weeks ago and a blind man can see you need a Master Magician *now*.'

'Must I make it a royal command? I said I won't discuss it!'

'You have to.' Heart thudding, Asher shoved his fists in his pockets. 'You're so bloody worried about betraying Durm. What about him?' He stepped aside, revealing Borne's disfigured face. 'If you work yourself unconscious or worse, into a fit that *kills* you this time, you'll be givin' this kingdom giftwrapped to Conroyd Jarralt. And if that ain't a betrayal of your da I don't know what is!'

For a moment he thought Gar was going to hit him. Then fury faded, and Gar turned away. 'I know.'

'You need help. With the WeatherWorking, your magic. You need someone who understands what it means to be Doranen. I can hold your coat for you while you make it rain, and mop you up with cloths and water afterwards, but I can't tell you how to control your power.'

'I know that too,' said Gar, and turned round again. He looked shattered. 'I know I've been postponing the inevitable. And I know it has to stop.' He looked again at his father's ruined effigy and flinched. 'This is a sign from Barl, I think. A warning.'

'Then take the hint.'

Gar nodded. 'I will. Tomorrow. Today I must rest. There's WeatherWorking tonight and I need to regain my strength. If what happened here should happen while I'm in the midst of a Working . . .' He shuddered.

'Fine,' said Asher, and started backing towards the chamber door. 'Tomorrow. And don't think I won't hold you to it. That bloody Darran'll never let me hear the end of it otherwise.'

Pale again, and sombre, Gar followed. As he passed his father's coffin he paused, bent low and pressed his lips to the cold, marred stone of his brow. 'I'm sorry, Father. I'll return soon and make this right. I promise.'

'Course you will,' said Asher, waiting in the doorway. 'It only happened 'cause you're tired.'

'Yes,' said Gar, still staring at his father's face. 'I expect so.'

Something in the way he said it prickled Asher's skin. He took a step back into the chamber. 'Gar?'

'I'm fine. It's just—'

'Gar, don't. Magic ain't like the spotty blisters. You don't catch it then get over it. Even I know that much. If you start thinkin' like that—'

'Like what?'

'Like maybe . . . maybe . . .' He couldn't say it. If the words remained unspoken . . .

Gar's lips twisted. 'Like maybe my magic is failing?'

*Damn.* 'No! That's daft. How can magic fail? It's magic. I mean, you're the historian, Gar. Has there ever been a case of a Doranen's magic failing? Running out? Drying up?'

Slowly, Gar shook his head. 'No. But then there's never been a case of it manifesting at such a late age either.'

'So now you're not just studyin' history, you're makin' it,' he said, itching to shake sense into him. Shake out fear, and doubt. 'You're *tired*, Gar. That's all. For the love of Barl, don't you start lookin' for things to fret on! We got problems enough as it is.'

Gar sighed. 'You're right. I'm sorry.'

'Aye, well, don't be sorry. Just be walkin', eh? Some people have got work to do.'

That made Gar laugh. 'You are so rude.'

He grinned, flooded with relief. 'I ain't rude. I'm just me.'

'Yes, you are,' said Gar. 'And praise Barl for it.'

# CHAPTER TWELVE

After seeing Gar safe and sound to his apartments, and narrowly avoiding both Darran and Willer, Asher lost himself in yet another day crammed top to bottom and side to side with meetings. Decisions. Authority. Things he was getting used to, but slowly. He saw Dathne only in passing. She smiled at him, her eyes warm, and his spirits lifted. Telling her his secret was dangerous but he couldn't be sorry. Nothing would make him regret feeling closer to her.

The day ended, at last. He ate his dinner down at the Goose, suffering with as much goodwill as he could muster the whooping and hollering and ribtickling about his upcoming appearance in Justice Hall. Matt's lads promised to fill his boots with manure for good luck. Behind all the joshing and jibing, though, was genuine admiration. A kind of rough-spun awe. He was one of them, one of their own, and yet he was different. Not better. Just . . . special.

The idea made him laugh. *Tell that to my brothers.*

With several hours to go before he was due to meet Gar for WeatherWorking he distracted himself playing darts with Matt and a few of Pellen's lads. Hoped Dathne might stop by for a pint, but she didn't show. Just before closing he paid out the money he'd lost in wagers, said his goodnights and made his circumspect way to the Weather Chamber.

Gar arrived some ten minutes after he did, brisk and rested and uninviting of personal enquiries. 'Any crises occur today I should know about?' he asked, conjuring pale gold glimfire.

'None I couldn't handle.'

'Darran told me about Glospottle,' Gar said with a sly smile. 'Don't worry. I'll see you through Justice Hall.'

Asher nodded. 'Appreciate it. What's on the menu tonight then?'

'Rain on the Flatlands. Snow in the Dingles. And the River Tey is overdue for freezing.'

So. A long hard night then. Wonderful. Swallowing a sigh, Asher settled himself in the armchair conjured for his comfort and waited for the show to begin.

Braced for the coming onslaught, Gar raised his left hand. Closed his eyes, murmured a brief prayer and traced the first sigil on the waiting air. The magic ignited, feebly. Asher frowned.

'Gar . . . that were the wrong sigil.'

Gar's look would have burned stone. 'It was not.'

'You just drew the third sigil for the right hand. Not the first for the left.'

'I did *not*.'

He sighed. 'I've watched you call rain enough times now that could I teach the incantation in a classroom. That were the wrong sigil. And you didn't walk widdershins.'

'Asher!'

He sat back. 'Fine. You're the king.'

Walking this time, Gar started again. Waved his hand

through the incorrect sigil, dispelling its energy, and this time drew the proper one. '*Tolnek*.'

He winced. *Luknek*, Gar was supposed to say *luknek* first. 'Gar . . .'

'*Be silent*!'

Asher bit his tongue.

Breathing heavily, Gar raised his right hand and drew the fifth sigil, not the second. Instead of burning brightly it hung wraithlike for mere seconds, then faded. On a stifled curse he tried again, and this time managed the correct sign.

Increasingly uneasy, Asher watched Gar stumble through the rainmaking incantation. This was *wrong*. By now the power should be rising, but the atmosphere in the chamber was unstirred. Instead of painting the sigils smoothly on the canvas of waiting air, Gar's fingers clawed the shapes without grace or commitment. All his precision was gone, and with it his accuracy. His confidence. This Working was a mishmash of meaningless gestures, a litany of misremembered words. A travesty.

At last he could bear it no longer. He got to his feet and moved to intercept Gar's disjointed procession. Held out his hands and said, rough with compassion, 'Stop. Gar, just stop.'

'No,' Gar said, and shoved him aside.

Stepping in front of him a second time he said, 'You ain't rested enough. Leave it. The rain can wait.'

'It can't wait. Without the Weather Magic the Wall will fall.'

'In one night?'

Gar dragged a shaking hand down his face. 'You'll have to help me.'

'*What?*'

'The words are in here!' said Gar, rapping his

forehead with his fingers. 'And the sigils. But I can't quite see them . . . grasp them . . .'

'Me, help?' He tried to swallow, but his mouth was too dry. 'With magic? Are you mad?'

Impatient, Gar looked at him. 'You said it yourself: you know the incantations back to front and inside out. Guide me through them. Say the words and draw the sigils so I can copy them.'

'You are mad,' he whispered.

'Weren't you *listening*?' Gar's eyes were feverish. 'I can't remember the incantation's proper sequence! If you don't help me then it won't rain tonight and that will be all the provocation Conroyd needs to challenge my fitness as WeatherWorker.'

'And if I do, and he finds out, that's *my* head usin' a wooden block for a pillow!'

'How would he find out?'

Asher opened his mouth. Closed it. Glared.

'I'm not asking you to break Barl's First Law,' Gar said with quiet intensity. 'I'm asking you to help your king.'

Shit. *Shit*. He could just see the look on Dathne's face if he told her about *this*. 'I don't know.'

*'Please.'*

Stomach churning, he took refuge in movement. Stamped back and forth across the chamber, anger fuelled by resentment. He could feel Gar's eyes on him. His tension and barely controlled fear. Echoing in memory, a promise to an unwell man. *I'll look after him*. He stopped.

'All right. I'll do it, on one condition.'

Gar couldn't hide his wild relief. 'Name it.'

'First thing in the morning you go see Nix and tell him you're sickenin' for something. You drink whatever disgusting muck he puts in your hand. And then you pay a visit to Conroyd Jarralt and congratulate him on his promotion.'

A long silence. A reluctant nod. 'Very well,' said Gar.

He looked as though his heart was breaking. Asher didn't care. 'Then let's get this over with. Before I come to my bloody senses.'

'How do you want to do this?' said Gar, frowning. 'Long-winded explanations won't work.'

He shrugged. 'You ever play a mirror game?'

'When I was three!'

'You got a better idea? 'Cause I'm all ears!'

They stood face to face beside the Weather Map, arms outstretched and fingertips touching. Torn between fear and feeling stupid, Asher closed his eyes. 'You ready?'

'Yes. When the power ignites, be sure to get out of the way.'

He snorted. 'Like I need tellin'.'

Stepping slowly sideways they began the Weather-Working dance. Not exactly meaning to, with his inner eye Asher saw the Flatlands in full sunshine. The rolling hills and the nodding grasses, burdened with tiny birds. Tasted the clean tang of open air and heard the curlews crying. Closing his eyes he commanded from memory the exact sequence of signs that would summon the rain. Then, hesitantly, he raised his left hand. Gar's hand lifted with it. Together, they drew a picture in the air. His voice whispered, '*Luknek*.' Gar echoed him. Walk, walk, walk. Raise the right hand. Draw the second sigil. '*Tolnek*.' Another echo. Walk, walk, walk. Raise the left hand. Draw the third sigil. It was getting easier somehow. '*Luknek*.' Again, the echo. Asher frowned. Was it his imagination or did his fingers just tingle? No. It was nothing. The blood not getting to his fingertips properly, that was all. '*Tolnek*.'

Gar cleared his throat. 'Asher . . .' His voice sounded strange.

'Shut up, I'm trying to concentrate,' he growled. What was the next sigil? Oh. Aye. Confident, now, he drew it. '*Luknek*.'

A rising breeze trailed hot fingers across his face and his silk shirt whispered. Deep in his blood, a seething sizzle. '*Asher*!' Gar said urgently. '*Look*!'

Sweating, he halted and unclenched his eyelids. Gar was untouched, but blue fire was dancing over *his* hands and up his arms. Even as he watched, Gar let his fingertips drift away. Let his arms fall by his sides. Stepped back.

But the blue fire kept on dancing.

'Sink me bloody sideways!' he choked out, and stumbled away from the map until he hit the wall, hard. It was the only thing that stopped him from falling.

Silence. The thickened air above the map slowly uncurdled. Asher stared at it.

'What was that?'

'Start the incantation again,' said Gar, his voice thin and strained. 'By yourself this time.'

'No bloody way!'

'Please.'

'*No*! No more please, no more help! I'm gettin' out of here!'

He headed for the door, but Gar got there first. 'Asher. Start the incantation again.'

He was so afraid he thought he might suffocate. 'Get away from the door, Gar. Or so help me I'll knock you on your arse and step over you on my way out.'

'Asher . . . I think there's magic in your blood.'

'No, there ain't!'

Gar pointed at the map. 'Then how do you explain what just happened?'

'I don't! And neither do you! It didn't happen. I ain't never been here. I'm goin' home to bed and I ain't never comin' back!'

He shoved Gar aside and wrenched wide the chamber door. Gar's cold, unfriendly voice said, 'Leave and I'll have you arrested.'

He stopped. Couldn't turn round. 'You're *threatenin'* me?'

'I'm asking you to stay. I'm telling you we have to learn the truth. Here. Now. Don't you understand? If you have power, *everything* changes!'

He felt dizzy. 'I don't want it to!'

'Our personal private desires don't count. Asher, on the night of Timon Spake's death—'

He turned. 'I don't want to remember that!'

There was no colour in Gar's face now. No emotion either. He looked as human as one of those marble effigies in his family crypt. 'On that night,' he said, relentless, 'I called Barl's First Law stupid and senseless because Olken couldn't do magic. But it seems you can. And that explains everything. Why Barl made that law, why your people must die if you break it. Because there's only room for one race of magicians in this kingdom. Mine.'

'That's fine with me.'

'But not with me! Don't you understand?' said Gar, entreating. 'We stole more from you than land! We stole your magic! For six hundred years your people have been living a lie! One that my people forced upon you somehow.'

'And do we look like we're sufferin' because of it?' Asher demanded. 'No. Gar, it don't matter. Who cares what happened six hundred years ago?'

'*I* care! And so should you!'

'Well, I don't. I ain't you, a romantic in love with the past. I'm a practical man livin' in the here and now. Let this go, Gar. Pretend it were a dream. If you don't it'll only end badly for both of us.'

'I can't,' Gar whispered. 'Please. Try the spell again. Perhaps I'm wrong and you don't have magic. Perhaps it was just an odd kind of Transference, because our fingers were touching.'

He nodded. 'Fine. That's what it was. Problem solved. Good—'

Gar put his arm across the open doorway. 'But if I'm right . . . Asher, you say you can forget this but we both know that's a lie.'

*Damn* him. Damn *everything*. Why had he come to this wretched bloody City? Why hadn't he just left well enough alone, stayed in Restharven and worked something out with his brothers? Or he could've upped stakes and shifted to Rillingcoombe. Bibford. Tattler's Ear. What had possessed him to abandon his safe life on the coast for *this*?

He had *magic* inside him? How could that be?

It had to be a mistake.

*Damn* it. Gar was right about one thing, the bastard. Until he knew for sure, he'd never get a good night's sleep again.

Cursing, terrified, he returned to the Weather Map.

This time he kept his eyes open. Felt an odd kind of tugging sensation, drawing his mind and imagination to the map's recreated Flatlands. He watched his shaking fingers draw the sigils as a voice he scarcely recognised as his own recited the rain-calling incantation. Watched the sigils burst into fiery life. Saw blues flame dance up and down his arms. Felt magic's wind rise, gently at first, then stronger and stronger till it buffeted him like storm breath racing inland over the open sea. His blood bubbled with an unfamiliar power that remembered the ocean. He couldn't have stopped even if he'd wanted to.

Barl save him, he didn't want to. How was this *possible*?

The air above the map begin to thicken. Darken. The unwanted power he'd raised gave tongue in rumbling thunder and tearing cracks of lightning. He was hot and cold all at once. Shaking and utterly still. His body tingled, like the kissing of a hundred pretty girls. His hair spat sparks, and his fingers, and all the world shimmered bright and blue.

Then the rain burst forth . . . and the world washed blue to red in a heartbeat as his blood exploded through the confines of his flesh, poured burning from his eyes, his nose, his mouth. And everywhere he turned there was pain.

He fell, screaming. Consciousness receded on a scarlet tide. When it flowed back again he was propped against the chamber wall. His face was tacky with blood and Gar was pressing a cold cup to his lips.

'Drink. It will help.'

Dazed, confused, he swallowed. Gagged. Then opened his eyes as Nix's foul concoction burned through the fog in his aching head. 'Tell me I'm dreamin',' he whispered. 'Tell me I didn't just do that.'

Gar put down the cup. 'I wish I could.'

Humiliatingly, he wanted to whimper. 'Sink me, that hurt.'

'I know.'

Yes, he knew, but so what? It was *supposed* to hurt him, he was Doranen. The WeatherWorker. *I'm a bloody Olken, I'm s'posed to get hurt stubbin' my toe, not workin' magic!*

'Gar, this ain't right. It can't have happened. We *have* to be dreamin'!'

Gar shook his head. 'Sorry. It was no dream.' He grimaced. 'A nightmare, perhaps . . .'

'But . . .' He struggled to sit up. 'Barl bloody save me. What do I do now?'

'Now?' Gar straightened out of his crouch and looked down at him, all emotion buried. 'Now you drop snow on the Dingles and freeze the River Tey.'

The words stole his breath like a gut punch. 'I can't.'

'You must.'

'I *can't*, I—'

'If you don't there'll be questions. I can't afford questions, Asher. Not until I've had time to think.'

He never knew fear could make a body physically sick. Sweet-sour saliva flooded his mouth, and his belly churned. Now Gar looked almost . . . angry. 'This ain't my fault. I never asked for this.'

'I never said you did. Just . . . finish what you started, Asher.'

'And then it's finished?'

Gar nodded. 'Yes. Then it's finished.'

His body still thrumming with pain, he clambered to his feet and did as he was told. He called the snow, and he froze the river, and when it was done he was a twitching, blood-spittled heap of unstrung bones on the floor.

He felt Gar's hand press his shoulder. 'I'm sorry. I'm sorry. Thank you.'

He couldn't have opened his eyes if his life had depended on it. But even with them shut he could feel the warm golden wash of Barl's Wall through the chamber's glass ceiling. The touch of it made him want to vomit.

'Go away.'

Gar went. Alone at last, he surrendered to tears.

'Barl bloody save me . . . who am I? *What* am I? And why did this happen to me?'

'Damn!' Pother Nix cursed explosively. 'And he was doing so well!'

Beside him, young Kerril gasped as a writhing Durm banged a violent fist to his forehead. The blow reopened an almost-healed wound. Blood spattered his hand, his face, the sheets.

'Now, now, Durm, that's enough,' Nix grunted, pressing his palms to the Master Magician's heaving shoulders. 'Tincture of ebonard, Kerril, quickly, before he breaks his bones a second time!'

She obeyed, fumbling a little in her haste. At the door to Durm's chamber crowded the other pothers on duty, the ones who'd come screaming for help when the Master Magician's convulsions first started.

The ebonard fumes from the cloth Kerril pressed to Durm's nose and mouth were taking effect. His thrashing slowed, became more feeble. His eyelids flickered. A crescent of white showed, rolling.

'Good girl,' said Nix. 'Now a lozenge of ebonard and tantivy. You can administer it. Use a spatula or you'll lose your fingers.'

She was an excellent student. Deftly she slid the wooden stick between Durm's teeth and tucked the dark green drug under his tongue to dissolve. As they waited for the soporific to calm him completely, Nix looked again to the gaggle of pothers in the doorway.

'Well? Your duty's done here. Be about your business.'

They retreated in silence, but their exchanged glances said it all. Even staunch Kerril looked doubtful.

'Go,' he told her. 'I'll sit with him till I'm satisfied he'll stay sleeping.'

She nodded and withdrew and he sat there with his fingertips pressed to Durm's erratic pulse, his mouth bitter with the taste of impending failure. He couldn't maintain the charade any longer; this fit had stripped him of all final, fading hope.

Durm was dying. It was merely a matter of time now, before the Master Magician's weakening will succumbed.

'I'm sorry,' he sighed, and patted Durm's slack wrist. 'I tried. Please believe me, I tried.'

*So close, so close to breaking free, Morg feels the drug seep into his prison of blood and bone and cries aloud his fury and despair. Barl's Weather Magic burns him like a brand. It means the cripple still has his unnatural magic . . . but how can that be? Gar's artificial powers should have failed him by now! They were explicitly designed to fail!*

*Thrust into the shadows, Durm the dunghill rooster crows his temporary triumph. Morg snarls at him, revealing all his terrible teeth, and Durm wisely shuts his beak and cowers.*

*Satisfied, Morg bends his mind and will towards victory. He must escape this fleshy cage. He must discover why the cripple's magic still holds sway. He must bring his exile to an end.*

*Let me out! Let me out! Let me out!*

Matt felt the change roar through the world like fire. The ferocity of it sat him bolt upright in his bed, shattering sleep, scattering dreams. Heart pounding, he lit his bedside candle and stared around his tiny bedroom.

Everything looked exactly the same.

There was sweat on his face, stinging his eyes, trickling through his stubble. Dragging up the sheet he blotted himself dry and waited for his thundering pulse to ease.

Was it Asher? Had something happened to him? He couldn't tell. Sight wasn't his gift, and for the first time in his life he regretted its lack.

As always when he was troubled he sought solace in his horses. Safety lamps burned throughout the night beside each stable, casting shadows. Overhead, the cold stars shone like chips of living ice and the Wall glowed gold as steadily as ever. He trod across the yard softly, slippers whispering, mindful of every step. His lads were good lads, well trained; they'd wake at the first sign of upset or the sound of unexpected feet crunching gravel.

Poor neglected Ballodair roused from dozing and chumbled sleepily over his stable door, curved ears flicking. Patting him, petting him, Matt promised to make sure the king rode him more often or else let him go away for a time to the countryside, where a horse could be a horse and kick up his heels at will.

Wheeling like rooks disturbed, thoughts and questions crowded his aching head. Something momentous had just occurred. The balance of Lur's magic was changed, upset, disordered. Turned arse over eyeballs, as Asher would say.

He frowned, letting Ballodair's tidy forelock thread through and through his busy, distracted fingers.

Was it Asher behind this change? And if so, did that mean they'd truly reached the end of waiting? In the last year there'd been so much tension. Anticipation. He felt as though he'd been holding his breath forever beneath a lowering sky, watching lightning flicker, listening to the thunder roll, expecting it to rain now . . . now . . . now . . .

Was *this* now? Had the first hard raindrops finally fallen? Had the Innocent Mage lost his innocence at last?

'Matt!' a soft, breathless voice called from the shadows. '*Matt*! Did you feel it?'

Dathne, as though summoned by his questioning thoughts.

He hurried to her, mindful of how clearly voices carried on the cool night air. 'What are you doing here?' he whispered, hustling her out of the stable yard proper and into the gardens beyond. 'Are you mad?'

She was panting, as though she'd run all the way from her apartment to his stables. Even in the palest of moonlight he could see her wildly shining eyes. 'Did you feel it?' she said again, her fingernails digging into his arm. 'Like an explosion of fireworks! A hundred times stronger than when I felt him first arrive! Do you know what this means? Asher's power has woken!'

So. The Final Days were upon them at last. 'Then it's time to tell him the truth.'

She shook her head. 'No.'

'*No*?' He took hold of her. In his grasp her shoulders felt so breakable. '*Think*, Dathne! We might not be the only ones who felt him wake. If the Doranen learn of him they'll kill him within the hour and tell everyone he died in his sleep. Then they'll turn on the rest of us. We *have* to tell him! Tonight. He must've felt it too, he must realise something's changed in him. We have to explain before he does something stupid out of fear or ignorance. What if he reveals himself before we're ready?'

Frowning, she held up a silencing hand. Matt felt his heart thud: he knew that look. She was searching within, listening for that small voice that only she could hear. That spoke to Jervale's Heir and no-one else. These were the times she became a stranger. Her hair was unruly, loosened for bed. It billowed round her sharp face in a soft cloud. Made her look younger than her years . . . and she was hardly old to begin with.

'No. We have time yet,' she said at last, stirring.

He wanted to shake her till her teeth fell out. 'Please, Dathne, *please*. For once in your life be guided. He's the *Innocent Mage*. This kingdom's only hope. We can't risk him, we can't leave him ignorant any—'

'I'm Jervale's Heir!' she hissed at him, like a cat. 'I can do whatever I see fit!' She pointed to the Wall, their silent golden witness. 'Does the damn thing look unsteady to you? Trembling on the brink of destruction? No. Which means Prophecy is incomplete. I still have time.'

'To do *what*?'

She looked away. 'To convince Asher he can trust me with all his innermost secrets. With *this*.'

He decided to take a risk then. 'You know he's still in love with you.'

She wasn't a stupid woman. She heard the silent criticism. The implied accusation. Her jaw tightened and she folded her arms across her narrow chest. 'Of course. Why else do you think he'll tell me what I need to know?'

A hundred words, a thousand protests, clamoured for release. He beat them back. Took another risk and let his hand return gently to her shoulder. 'Be careful, Dathne. You think you're oh-so-clever – and in some ways you are – but he's not the only one in love.'

He'd shocked her. Her mouth opened. Closed. Opened. Her sharp eyes dulled with surprise and all the passionate colour fled from her face. 'My feelings are none of your business, Matt. I'm Jervale's Heir. I know what I'm doing. And anyway, I don't have any feelings.'

Defeated, as always, he shoved his hands in his pockets. 'If you say so.'

'I say so. And this too: don't question my judgement again.'

'All right. If that's what you want.'

Her eyes were cold. 'Yes. It's what I want.'

He thought she knew herself well enough to understand it was a lie. And that she knew him well enough, too, to realise he had no intention of holding his tongue if he thought he had to speak. This was a matter of saving face, of soothing hurt. She thought she'd kept her love hidden and was angry to discover she was wrong.

'Fine. I'll go back to bed then,' he said. 'If that's all right with you.'

'More than all right,' she snapped. 'If anything else happens, I'll let you know. Probably.'

'Aye, Dathne,' he said, walking away. 'You do that.'

The memory of her pale, furious face chased him into sleep. Worry and dread made sure it wasn't peaceful.

Gar walked back to the Tower in the dark, without benefit of glimfire. He was too afraid of what might happen should he attempt its conjuration. His chest felt tight, hooped with iron bands. His palms were sweaty, his eyes hot and dry.

*Asher made it rain. Asher made it snow. Asher froze a river.*

*And I couldn't.*

Some sound caught in his throat then. A sob, or another expression of distress. Breathing was suddenly painful, as though the air had turned to knives.

He'd fallen into the habit of visiting his unburied family of a night-time, once the public were safely elsewhere. He couldn't face them tonight. Not after such a catastrophic failure. Fane would jeer at him and call him names and his father . . . his father . . .

He stared at Barl's magnanimous Wall, serenely shining in the distance. Emblem of his sacred oath. Victim of his inadequacy.

'Sweet lady, Blessed Barl,' he whispered, dropping to his knees beneath the indifferent sky. 'Tell me how I've failed you. Show me how to make amends. From earliest boyhood my only desire has been to serve you. Why did you gift me with magic if not to make me your voice in Lur? Why did you take back the gift? Is my service now distasteful? Did I falter, or did you?'

Holze would say the question flirted with blasphemy, and perhaps it did. Too bad. He still wanted – *needed* – an answer.

None came.

A different question then. 'Where does Asher's magic come from? You? Or was it always in him? Is it in all his people? If so, what does it mean? And what should I do about it? If Conroyd Jarralt ever finds out Asher is a dead man and perhaps all his people with him. Is that what you want? The Olken dead? *Asher* dead?'

Still no answer. A sudden wave of fear and fury drove him to his feet. 'Well, I won't have it! I won't let you kill him!' he shouted to Barl's last lingering presence, her Wall, implacable and uncaring. 'I defy your First Law, madam! I defy *you*! No matter how I came to it, I am Lur's king and I shall do what I must to protect it from harm. To protect the Olken from harm. From you, if I have to. Do you hear me, Barl? I would even protect them from *you*!'

He returned to the Tower. Stripped and fell into bed to dream wildly of flood and fire and women weeping. Exhausted, he woke hours later to daylight and a dreadful understanding that needed nothing so crude as manifested proof.

Once more, he was empty. His magic was gone.

# CHAPTER THIRTEEN

Willer had already been hard at work for nearly three hours when his prey finally deigned to come into the office. Ever since his . . . arrangement . . . with Lord Jarralt, that was how he'd thought of Asher. And of himself as the wily hunter, poised to bring him down.

But as prey, damn him, Asher was proving elusive.

Hidden in the false bottom of the right-hand drawer in his desk were his notebooks, filled cover to cover with the lout's transgressions. He remembered them all. He'd practically crippled himself these last few weeks, painstakingly listing each and every crime. Just as soon as he could he was going to pass them along to Lord Jarralt. Lord Jarralt would find them fascinating reading, he was sure. They'd go a long way to seeing that Asher got his deserved comeuppance, he was certain.

Almost certain.

Because while they were damning, they weren't precisely . . . treason.

What he *really* needed was to catch Asher in the middle of committing an act so heinous, so treacherous, so clearly illegal, that not even his nauseating friendship with the king could save him. It was the only way to save His Majesty.

Tragically, though, catching the bastard red-handed was proving harder than he'd anticipated. Asher was slippery, and disinclined to let anyone close. He doubted now if his offer of assistance would get him where he needed to be. Perhaps he'd have better luck working on the stupid bookseller; a woman that plain and unapproachable would surely be grateful for the attentions of a well-set-up and influential young man.

He did know one thing for certain. If he didn't soon come up with some kind of evidence to seal Asher's fate, Lord Jarralt would turn elsewhere for aid. Someone else would be the key to Asher's destruction. Someone else would get the glory.

He thought he'd rather die.

Some twenty minutes later Asher finally made an appearance in the office, looking ill and strained and altogether drained of his irritating arrogance and energy. He moved as though his head might topple from his shoulders at any moment. As though every muscle pained him, separately and in chorus. Willer felt his pulse quicken. The bastard had been drinking. To excess, to look as poorly as this. And now here he was, determined to make vitally important decisions that would affect hundreds of lives.

Splendid.

'Gracious me,' he said, unctuously concerned. 'Are you quite well, Asher? You look positively *green*.'

Asher barely glanced at him. Eased himself by inches into the nearest chair and scowled. 'When's Darran meetin' with the market committee again?'

'Tomorrow.'

Asher grunted. 'Make sure I get a copy of last month's figures by end of day then.'

Willer swallowed a scream. 'Certainly.'

'Have you seen Dathne?'

'I believe she had a meeting with the Midwives' Guild this morning. I'm so sorry, I thought you knew.'

Asher's expression was filthy. 'Midwives' Guild. Aye. That's right. Course I knew.'

*Liar*. Willer knocked a pen to the floor and dived beneath his desk to retrieve it. When he could trust his face again he sat up. 'Is there anything else I can help you with? Preparations for the upcoming hearing in Justice Hall, perhaps?'

'No.'

Watching the bastard screw his thumb tips into his eye sockets, watching him wince, Willer felt his fingers tighten to crushing point around the pen. Rude, ignorant, arrogant . . .

Hurrying footsteps sounded on the staircase outside. Then a junior messenger, pink-cheeked and breathless, appeared in the open doorway and bowed. 'Meister Asher, sir, His Majesty's compliments and you're to join him in the stable yard. Dressed for riding, he said.'

'Riding?' said Asher ungraciously, lowering his hands. 'Now?'

The messenger darted a glance at Willer. 'Yes, sir.'

Asher cursed under his breath. 'Go back and tell him I can't, Toby. Tell him—' Another curse. 'Damn it. Tell him I'll be there directly.'

'Sir!' squeaked the shocked messenger boy, and fled.

With an effort, Willer schooled his face to solicitude. 'I'll tell Mistress Dathne you've been called away, sir, shall I? When she returns? And Darran? They'll need to rearrange your appointments.'

'Rearrange 'em?' snarled Asher, hoisting himself to his feet. 'For all I care they can—' He stopped himself, just. Favoured Willer with a look of intense dislike, and headed for the door. 'Aye. Do that.'

Willer waited for the sound of his feet on the staircase to fade into silence, then indulged in a gust of silent, excited laughter. Refusing a royal summons. Was there no end to Asher's arrogance? How perfect for his purpose. And before a witness, too! Messenger boys' tongues waggled faster than their knobbly little knees did when they ran. This story would be all over Tower and palace by sundown.

Lord Jarralt was going to be *thrilled* . . .

Swearing viciously, Asher yanked off his fine indoor clothes and pulled on his riding leathers, boots and a second-best shirt. Meet Gar in the stable yard! As if he had time for riding! As if he felt well enough, with every inch of his body still screaming bloody murder after – after—

He could scarcely bring himself to think it. When he'd woken a scant hour before sunrise, cold and stiff on the Weather Chamber floor, his face crackling with dried blood and his fine shirt ruined, he'd snivelled like a spratling, a girl, so monstrous was his fear and confusion and dread.

And now Gar wanted to talk about it.

Well, he didn't. What was there to talk about? Nobody could ever know what had happened last night. They must never speak of it, not even when they were alone. That's what he'd tell Gar while they were out riding through the poxy countryside.

And that would be the end of it.

The horses were saddled and waiting in the stable

yard. Matt was holding them, chatting with Gar. Seeing Asher, his eyebrows flew up and his lips pursed in a soundless whistle. 'I've seen healthier-looking drowned cats. What's amiss?'

Smoothly, Gar answered for him. 'Asher is proving himself my most hardworking and loyal subject.' Beneath the surface pleasantry, Asher saw he was brittle as sugar-glass.

'That's our Asher,' Matt agreed, handing over Ballodair's reins. 'Dedicated to a fault. Now you have a good ride, Your Majesty, and mind yourself, because he's feeling a bit fresh this morning.'

Proving the point, Ballodair humped and cow-kicked when Gar swung himself into the saddle, then bounded stiff-legged across the stable yard. As Gar fought to control him, gasping, Matt turned to Asher.

'You do look bloody awful,' he said, grabbing hold of the offside stirrup leather to keep the saddle steady.

Asher pulled himself aboard his patient Cygnet and nodded his thanks as Matt slid his boot home in the stirrup iron. 'Too many meetin's, not enough fresh air.'

'Ready?' Gar called out, Ballodair momentarily subdued.

Matt stepped back, frowning. 'Come see me when you've done riding. We'll talk.'

'Ain't got time for talkin' these days, less it be with poxy guild meisters and the like,' Asher replied, giving Cygnet a nudge with his heels. Then he dredged up a smile, because Matt was looking right down in the mouth. 'But thanks.'

And he followed Gar out of the yard.

They cantered side by side for miles along the barren Black Wood Road, not speaking, until they reached the turning for Crasthead Moor. Gar kicked Ballodair onto it, urging the stallion to go faster, faster. Standing in his stirrups, Cygnet's long silver mane flogging his face, Asher pounded in their wake. Under clean blue skies, with cold air whipping their cheeks to colour, they rode into the heart of desolation. When at last the rock-strewn moor spread bleakly in every direction, Gar lifted his hands and eased Ballodair back to a canter, then a trot, then a walk and finally a steaming halt. Panting, sweating, Asher gentled Cygnet to a standstill opposite, keeping his distance.

A wary silence filled the space between them. When it became unbearable, Gar spoke.

'We can't pretend it didn't happen.'

Asher blinked away wind-whipped tears. 'I can.'

'No,' said Gar, his expression as cold and remote as the moor. 'You can't. You see, we have a problem.'

'You reckon?' he said, and laughed. A pluming of breath echoed his derision.

Gar's gloved fingers tightened on his reins. 'If you laugh again I'll pull you from your horse and beat your head to a bloody pulp with a rock.'

He looked Gar up and down. 'You could try.'

With a cry of frustration Gar wheeled Ballodair in a churning of mud and small stones. The horse snorted, resenting the rough treatment. 'Asher. Don't. It doesn't help us.'

He settled his gaze on the distant horizon. 'True. There's only one thing can help us. Me leavin'.'

Ballodair pawed at the wet ground, grunting his impatience. Gar jerked the reins hard. 'You can't.'

'I can,' he said, fear stirring. 'I will. I—'

'Asher, I've lost my magic.'

Somewhere in the distance, a faintly crying curlew.

Beneath him, Cygnet snorted and swished his tail. He cleared his throat. 'I don't know what that means.'

Gar's eyes were terrible. 'Yes you do. We both do. Gar the Magickless has returned.'

'That ain't possible.' A dreadful premonition was beating black wings about his head. He tried to fight it off with words. 'You're just exhausted. Imagining things.'

'*Imagining* things?' Gar shouted. 'How dare you say so? How *dare* you after all I've lived through? Do you think I could forget what twenty-four years of barrenness felt like after a mere few *weeks* of magic? I am *empty*, Asher. Devoid of all power, and even its memory. Whereas you – *you*—'

Asher flinched as Gar's furious glare burned him. Jerking up his hands, closing his calves against Cygnet's sides, he backed the horse two paces. 'Don't say it.'

Gar was implacable. 'I must. And you must hear it.'

'*No*. I can't – you can't ask me – expect me—'

'But I can, Asher. I do. I may not in conscience be king any longer, but I'm still my father's son. Custodian of his legacy. The last living link to House Torvig, caretakers of this kingdom for nearly four centuries. I have a duty and I will fulfil it. Regardless of the cost, or consequences.'

'To you?' Asher laughed, unamused. 'There ain't no cost or consequences to you! Cost and consequences are for ordinary folk like me and Timon Spake!'

Gar just looked at him. 'Last night, Asher, you made it rain. So don't you sit there and prate to me of ordinary folk. You are anything but *ordinary*.'

'I am if I say I am!' At the tone of his voice Cygnet tossed his head, ears pinned. 'You think I *want* this? Magic? Ha! If there was a way to get rid of it right here and now I would!'

'Really?' said Gar, taunting. 'Are you sure? Don't tell me you didn't feel magic's glory last night, as well as its agony. I saw your face, Asher. I know *exactly* what you felt.'

Shocked speechless, shaking with outrage, he could only stare. The thin wind blew chill and bitter in his face, biting all the way to bone. Cygnet jittered, haunches swinging left and right, ready to bolt. 'That ain't my fault. I never asked for it.'

Gar's lip curled. 'Maybe not. But you've got it.'

'And you're so jealous you could spit, ain't you? Well, damn you, Gar,' he said at last, and wheeled Cygnet away.

Gar spurred Ballodair forward, blocking his escape. 'I'm sorry,' he said harshly. His face was filled with a monstrous pain. 'You must understand. I thought I was my father's son in more than name, but I'm not. Oh Asher, don't you *see*? You *have* to help me. If it's discovered I've lost my magic, there'll be chaos!'

'And if it's discovered I found it, there'll be chaos anyway! Not to mention an execution!'

Gar shook his head. 'That won't happen.'

'Why?' he sneered. 'Because you'll protect me?'

'Yes.'

'Ha! Like you protected Timon Spake?' It was a low blow, but he didn't care. As Gar recoiled, silenced, he jerked Cygnet back a pace. 'Don't ask me to use Weather Magic again, Gar. I can't do it. I *can't*.'

Recovered, Gar ignored him. 'Barl's Wall cannot survive without it. And if the Wall falls this kingdom and all the innocent people in it will be destroyed. Is that what you want?'

'I ain't the only one who can do it! There's Conroyd Jarralt, for a start. And he's Doranen. He's *supposed* to!'

Gar's face twisted. 'Oh yes. King Conroyd: a thought

to ice the blood. But there are others, too, with sleeping dreams of majesty. If my failure is made public wild ambition will rule the day and we'll be wading hip-deep in blood before the week is out. Trust me, Asher. I'm an able historian and I know what the promise of power can do.'

Asher's fists were clenched so hard on the reins that his gloved fingers were going numb. 'So . . . don't tell me. Let me guess. You want to go on wearin' the crown while I take care of the WeatherWorkin'? Is that the plan?'

Gar looked him full in the face. 'I'm desperate.'

'Well, *I* ain't! And I ain't scraddled in the head neither! You'd never keep this secret, Gar! Sooner or later folks'll notice you ain't doin' magic in public any more. There'll be talk. Questions. Polite at first, but in the end they'll be demands. The truth'll come out, and when it does I won't be the only Olken in strife! You can't ask me to put all my people at risk. You can't!'

Silence. Gar stared again at the bleak and dreary moor. Asher, slowly freezing to his marrow, tucked his fingers into his armpits and waited. A sparrowhawk soared overhead, wings outstretched. Spying something amongst the grassy tussocks below, it abruptly halted, feathered wingtips snatching at the clear bright air. A plummeting dive, a shriek of triumph and it wheeled away again, death dangling from its talons.

'You're right,' said Gar at last, rousing from reverie. 'We can't keep it secret forever. But we can keep it secret for a month.'

'And what good'll *that* do?'

'Asher, your people weren't safe during Trevoyle's Schism. Hundreds died. And if the kingdom schisms again, hundreds more will join them. Maybe thousands, this time. You can stop that. In a month I should be able to read every medical and magical text we have, to see if there's a cure for what afflicts me. There might even be something in Barl's lost library. I never got the chance to look through it completely.'

'So you're saying there's a cure now?'

Gar shrugged. 'There might be.'

'And if there ain't?'

Another shrug. 'If by the end of a month I've failed to find a remedy, or if Durm is still unconscious – or dead – and can be no help at all, I'll go to Conroyd and Holze. Tell them my magic has failed. Name Conroyd king and Holze the new Master Magician. Conroyd will receive the Weather Magic, undertake his first WeatherWorking and then be publicly presented as king. No uncertainty. No schism. No death.'

A month. Rain and snow and blood. *Magic*. 'Don't wait,' he said, his belly churning. 'Do it now.'

Gar shook his head. 'Not while there's even the slimmest hope I might still keep this kingdom from Conroyd.'

'Then choose someone else!'

'There is no one else.'

'Barl bloody *save* me!' he cried, and spun Cygnet about so he wouldn't have to look at Gar's quiet despair a moment longer. 'I wanted to be a fisherman, Gar. I wanted nowt but a boat and the ocean and an open sunlit sky—'

'And I wanted magic,' said Gar. 'Not every man gets what he wants, Asher. Most men just get what they're given.'

Asher stared over the moor, unwilling to trust his voice. Afraid that a single word might shatter him entirely.

Gar said distantly, 'I was going to be married. I was going to be a father. It's funny, isn't it, how you can tell yourself you don't want something so often you actually begin to believe it.'

Crasthead Moor blurred. Anguished, he blinked it clear again. Found his voice. 'How can you ask me to do this?'

'How can I not?' said Gar.

It was a demand. A plea. A millstone round his neck.

He slipped his feet free of the stirrups and slid from the saddle. Dropped his reins and walked away, head down, boots squelching in the wet.

He'd always lived a dangerous life. A man went out at dawn, there was no saying he'd come back at sunset. Fishing was an unchancy way to spend your days. He'd grown up with that. Accepted that. He understood fishing.

But this? How could he understand this?

*I got magic in my blood.*

Where had it come from? How did it get there?

*How do I get rid of it?*

One sip of Weather Magic had been enough. No man should have that much power, not for any reason. Not even to do good. His bones still ached with the memory of it. With the glory, and the pain.

Behind him, the sound of boots thudding to the muddy ground. The slap and squelch of Gar approaching. A familiar, frustrating presence at his back.

He didn't turn around. 'What if I ain't the only one, Gar? What if there's other Olken like me?'

'Then I pray they stay safely hidden.'

'I'm *scared*!' he said, and felt his gloved hands become fists.

'So am I.'

Asher turned, then. Took a deep, hurting breath and let it out. Gar didn't look scared. His face was a mask, all feelings smothered.

'If this goes wrong—'

Gar shook his head. 'It won't.'

'It *might*! And if it does—'

The mask slipped. 'Then they'll have to kill me too,' Gar said. His voice was low and shaking. 'They'll have to kill me first. I swear it, Asher. On the bodies of my father and my mother and my poor misguided sister. They will have to kill me first.'

Stirring words, honestly meant. He wanted to believe them. Gar believed them. But was that enough? If the unthinkable happened and this mad scheme was discovered, would the oath of a magickless king be enough to save him?

When he'd asked Gar's dead father how best he could help, this wasn't what he'd had in mind . . .

Gar said quietly, 'Please, Asher. Do this. I think our kingdom is doomed if you don't.'

For one long moment he forgot how to breathe. A terrible interior pressure swelled and swelled, dancing black spots before his eyes and threatening to crush his lungs. The desolate moor smeared red and orange and gold. He flung away from his tormentor, his friend, his king. Bent double, closed resentful fingers around a wet grey rock and hurled it into the melting distance. Hurled another, and another, and another, his bones vibrating with an incoherent rage. When he could stand it no longer he opened his mouth and screamed, bellowed, vented all his fear and fury into the wide, uncaring sky. And then stood there, his head bowed to his chest. Emptied and resigned.

Gar's gentle hand came to rest on his shoulder. 'Thank you, Asher. I promise you won't regret it.'

The return ride from the moor to the Tower stables was completed in silence. Back in the stable yard, Gar threw

Ballodair's reins to young Boonie and walked away. Asher watched him go, not the least sorry they were to be separated for a while.

He needed time to think.

Jim'l offered to take care of Cygnet, but Asher refused. Good honest labour, that's what he was after. Distraction, and sweat born of muscles, not magic. He returned Cygnet to his stable, untacked him, then collected a spare grooming box and busied himself with the soothing task of making the silver stallion beautiful.

Solitude didn't last long.

'Have a good ride then?' Matt asked, leaning over the stable's closed half-door.

He glanced up from untangling Cygnet's tail hair by hair. 'Aye.'

'You should go out more often. Cygnet needs the exercise, and you need the fresh air.'

'Aye, but when? Ain't enough hours in the day as it is.'

'Early,' suggested Matt. 'Before breakfast. It'll give you an appetite.'

'Give me a heart spasm more like,' he said, briefly grinning.

Matt frowned. 'That's not funny. Asher, what's wrong?'

He freed the last tangle in Cygnet's tail and reached for a dandy brush. 'Nowt.'

'Why don't I believe you?'

Damn. Too sharp by half, was Matt. He made himself look up. 'Nowt you can help with.'

'It's a big job you've taken on, this Olken administrating,' Matt said after a moment. 'Before, you could hide in the prince's shadow. Now he's king and you're in full sunlight. If you're not careful you could get burned.'

An observation too close for comfort. He swapped the dandy brush for a soft-bristled body brush and started scrubbing at the dried mud on Cygnet's flanks. The horse swished its immaculate tail, and he thumped its rump in warning. 'I'll be fine.'

'I'm sure you will,' said Matt, looking unhappy. 'Just mind your step, will you? Don't do anything stupid.'

What, like make it rain? To hide the thought he swapped sides from Cygnet's left flank to his right. 'Fuss, fuss, fuss. Ain't you got work to do?'

Matt slapped the stable door. 'Yes. I just wanted to tell you the horses to pull the royal hearse arrive sometime today.'

'His Majesty'll want to inspect 'em. Let me know when they get here.'

'Of course,' said Matt.

Alone again, Asher indulged himself in another half-hour of horse-primping then surrendered to the promptings of duty and returned to the Tower. Where Darran was waiting, armed with a four-foot-high stack of legal books and an evil smile.

In his weaker, less honourable moments, Asher found himself wishing that Darran had . . . all right, maybe not *died*, but remained ill enough after his collapse for Nix to have made him retire. To the country. At the other end of the kingdom. And forbidden him long carriage rides.

'You got to be bloody joking,' he said, stopping in his office's open doorway. 'And that's *my* desk you're sittin' at, in case you hadn't noticed.'

Darran unfolded himself from the chair. 'I've taken the liberty of conferring with Lady Marnagh. Given the vexatious nature of the dispute between Indigo Glospottle and his guild brethren, and despite the fact you're a jurisprudential ignoramus, we thought it wise to gazette the hearing for early next week. That's after the funeral, and should give me enough time to prepare you adequately.' He sniffed. 'Now kindly take a seat. We have a great deal of work to get through before—'

Asher slouched into his office. 'Not we. Me. I can read, Darran, and I don't need you turnin' the pages for me. If I run into trouble I'll ask Gar.'

Darran's eyebrows lifted. 'You can't possibly bother His Majesty at a time like this! *I* will—'

'Mind your own business,' he said, and tugged Darran out from behind the desk. 'He's burying his family this Barl's Day, Darran. Don't you reckon he might welcome somethin' else to think on?'

An expression of grudging acknowledgement crossed Darran's face as he pulled his arm free. 'Perhaps.'

'Glad you agree. Now if there ain't anythin' else—'

'There is. Apparently there are several matters pending at Justice Hall that require the attentions of a Master Magician. Lady Marnagh feels the issue is becoming . . . urgent. If you could mention as much to the king?'

Coward. 'Aye,' he said, and sat down. 'I'll mention it. Now close the door on your way out.'

Alone at last, he eyed the pile of legal books with weary distaste. After the madness of Crasthead Moor he couldn't be less interested in Glospottle's pissy piss problems.

*Barl save me. What have I done?*

The office door opened, admitting Dathne. 'I've finally settled that business with the Midwives,' she said, hanging her cloak and satchel on the corner coat rack. 'I doubt we'll have any more trouble now.'

He couldn't remember what the problem was but smiled anyway. 'Fine.'

'Oh – and His Majesty asked me to give you this.'

He leaned across his desk and took the note she held out to him. Cracked the crimson wax seal and read it.

*See me. The crypt. Two hours after sunset.*

Barl save him, what now? What else could there be for him to sacrifice on the altar of Gar's desperate dedication to Lur?

Dathne was watching him closely. 'Trouble?'

'No,' he lied, sliding the note into his pocket.

She dropped into the chair opposite his desk and nodded at the pile of books Darran had left behind. 'A little light reading?'

'More like a recipe for headaches,' he said, and let himself look at her, just look at her. Since joining the Tower staff she'd unwillingly exchanged her comfortable bookseller cottons and linens for the stiffer formality of silk and brocade. The expensive fabrics suited her. Brought out the sheen in her thick black hair and softened her lean angularity. Damn, she was so beautiful . . .

Even when she was frowning. 'You've got a headache now, haven't you?'

He rubbed his throbbing temple. 'Does it show?'

'Only to me.' Returning to her satchel, she rummaged for a moment and withdrew a small stoppered pot.

'No potions!' he protested. 'You're as bad as bloody Nix. Just you keep away from me with that muck.'

Affectionately scornful, she moved to stand behind him. 'Gossoon. It's a salve, not a potion. Now be quiet.'

The smell from the pot as she unstoppered it was almost pleasant, hinting at mint leaves and honey and other things, unknown but soothing to the senses. Her ointment-smeared touch on his skin was a benediction, a tingling taste of what could be. Should be.

Would be, if fate just once was kind.

Kneading, stroking, her strong and supple fingers smoothed his temples, his neck, slipped inside his shirt collar to flirt with his shoulders. 'You're so tense,' she murmured. 'No wonder you've got pains . . .'

He sighed and let his head fall back to rest against her blue brocade chest, soft and welcoming: a pillow long desired. Her fingers roamed freely, wandered upwards to dally through his hair.

'You'll make me smelly,' he complained, drowsy and only a little serious. 'Like that pissant Willer.'

A soft chuckle. Slender fingers waking fire. 'Barl forbid. Now—'

A sharp rat-tat of knuckles on the office door. 'Asher!' said Matt, barging in. 'Those horses are – oh.' Foolishly he stood in the middle of the office, staring, and foolishly Asher stared back. Behind him he could feel Dathne stiffen.

'Asher's busy, Matt,' she said, all amusement fled from her voice. 'Go away.'

'Busy,' said Matt, still staring. 'Yes. I can see that.'

Asher sat forward, a tide of heat washing through him. 'I had a headache. Dathne was helping.'

The strangest look passed over Matt's abruptly pale face. 'Yes, well, she's a very helpful woman.'

'Matt!' said Dathne sharply. 'Don't you—'

Asher raised one finger and she fell silent. A miracle, of sorts. He stood. Stared Matt full in the face. 'That'll do. Horses in good fettle?'

Matt nodded. 'They are.'

'Good. The king'll come see 'em directly. Anything else?'

'No.'

'Fine. Then you can go.'

Another nod. 'Very good. Sir.'

Dathne broke the awkward silence Matt left in his wake. 'I should go. More meetings. You know how it is. I'll leave the ointment here, shall I? You can rub it in yourself if the pain returns.'

*No*, he wanted to cry. Stay. Tell me what you meant by this, tell me I ain't dreamin', tell me if you felt what I felt when you touched me.

'All right,' he said. 'You have any trouble, you let me know. I got to make a start on these bloody legal books.'

Her smile was fleeting, and impish. 'Good luck. If I finish my meetings in time I'll help you with them, shall I?'

He shrugged. 'If you like.'

'No promises, mind,' she warned.

*No Promises.*

For some reason, the comment made him shiver.

# CHAPTER FOURTEEN

The day dragged on, and at long last died in a fiery sunset. Dathne didn't come back. He wasn't hungry but he ate dinner anyway. Cluny would read him a lecture if he didn't, then for good measure badger the cook into serving him a dessert of offended complaints and insulted imprecations. He didn't have the stomach or the energy to hear them. His headache had returned with a vengeance.

*See me.*

Hiding in his private sitting room, he stared through the uncurtained window and watched the world outside dwindle into dusk, into darkness. Even the glow of Barl's Wall seemed faded. Tarnished. Or was that just fear, pulling a deadening veil across his eyes?

*See me.*

When it was time he fetched a coat from his wardrobe, shrugged it on and let himself out of his apartments. The Tower was hushed. The faintest murmuring of voices drifted downwards from the staircase over his head: Cluny and her hardworking housemaid friends tending the stairwell candles. A door banged. Someone laughed. Someone else shouted two floors down, sounding disgruntled. He thought it was Willer. With a sigh, needing support, he took hold of the handrail and began his reluctant descent. Slipped unseen from the Tower and made his way to the palace grounds.

Gar was outside the crypt, holding a candle-lantern and looking annoyed. 'At last. Two hours, I said. Have you forgotten how to count?'

'I ain't that late.'

'Late enough. Come on.'

He pushed open the crypt door and went inside. Asher stared after him, apprehension like a sea swell rising to swamp all other, harsher emotions. Then he followed.

In the royal family's chamber three more candle-lanterns had been lit and placed around the small, chilly room. Flickering shadows danced up the white walls and over the flagstone floor. Balanced on Borne's incomplete effigy was a creamy-white globe.

'What's that thing?'

Gar glanced at it. 'The Weather Orb. Come in, would you?'

Fascinated, repelled, Asher took half a step closer. 'There're colours in there . . .'

'That's the Weather Magic,' said Gar, withdrawing a battered, ancient-looking book from a satchel on the floor.

Asher nodded at it. 'And what's that?'

'A collection of spells and incantations specific to the role of Master Magician. I took it and the Orb from Durm's study this afternoon. The rest of his books and papers are being boxed up and delivered to the Tower tonight. One month isn't long, Asher. I don't intend to waste a minute of it.'

He felt his guts cramp. 'So you pinched Durm's stuff. What's that got to do with me?'

'Everything,' said Gar, impatient. 'If you're going to

preserve Barl's Wall you have to take on her Weather Magics. Or try to, anyway. I've no idea if the Transference will work with you saying it instead of a Master Magician. I've no idea if it'll work on you at all, given you're Olken. Still, we don't have a choice. The attempt must be made. And in secret . . . hence us meeting here.'

Mouth dry, heart racing, he stared at the Orb. 'And if this Transference don't work? What happens to me?'

Gar shrugged. 'I don't know that either. But these magics come from Barl herself. I can't believe she'd let them hurt someone. Kill them.'

Beneath the fear, a spark of anger. 'She's six centuries dead, Gar, and you never knew her. You got no idea what she would or wouldn't let happen.'

Gar frowned at the floor, then looked up. 'Are you having second thoughts?'

'Wouldn't you?'

'Probably.'

He tried to smile. 'What about third?'

'Asher—'

'Ah, sink it!' he said, and scrubbed a hand across his face. 'Let's just get it over with, eh?'

Gar nodded. 'Agreed.'

They sat facing each other on the flagstones. Gar held the Weather Orb and balanced the open spell book in his lap. 'It's only fair to warn you . . . this might hurt.'

He rolled his eyes. 'Now he tells me.'

'Since you can't read Ancient Doranen I'll recite the spell and you can repeat it after me. If what happened in the Weather Chamber holds true, that should trigger the Transference.'

'And if it don't?'

A wintry amusement touched Gar's face. 'Then it's hail King Conroyd.'

Asher glared at the pretty pearl-white Weather Orb. 'Hurt how much, exactly?'

'I survived,' said Gar, and gave him the Orb.

It felt peculiarly heavy. Almost alive. Or aware. The colours swirling beneath its skin made his senses swim. Without conscious thought his fingers formed a cradle.

'That's right,' said Gar. 'Hold it just like that. No tighter, no looser. Close your eyes. Breathe. Good. Now . . . are you ready?'

Asher felt the crypt's cold air catch in his throat. Ready? No, he wasn't bloody ready. How could anybody be ready for something like this? He grunted.

'All right,' said Gar, softly. There was a rustling of pages, a slithering of leather, as he picked up Durm's book. 'Repeat after me: *Ha'rak dolanie maketh* . . .'

Heart booming, head spinning, Asher licked his dry lips and repeated the tongue-twisting words. '*Ha'rak dolanie maketh* . . .'

As he whispered the last syllable the Orb trembled in his grasp. He felt warmth. A humming energy. He opened his eyes, stared down at the maelstrom of gold and green and purple and crimson magics he held between his hands . . . and fell headlong into it. From some impossible distance he heard Gar's voice and he echoed it, repeating the words he had no hope of understanding.

Deep within, some secret place he never knew existed seemed to . . . open. Unfold, the way a rose unfolds its petals at the first kind kiss of the sun. The Orb was glowing so brightly he shouldn't have been able to look at it, but he could. He could see right into the heart of it, and it felt like staring into the heart of magic itself. Images poured into the newly opened space within him, and with them came words . . . knowledge . . .

Power.

He could feel his chest heaving, his breath rasping. The Orb's heat and light burst free of their shell, rushed through his skin like hot sweet wine through cheesecloth and now he was the Orb, glowing with magic, his bones were burning with it and the world had turned crimson and gold.

There was no pain.

Gar was still speaking; standing on the rim of this brand-new world he could hear his friend's voice, drifting towards him from a vast distance. He let the words float into his ambit. Breathed them in and breathed them out again as though they were incense, or the smoke from one of Dathne's scented candles. The power pouring into him swelled like a wave racing in from the ocean, deep and strong and impossible to control. He felt like a child again. Remembered the time Da tossed him over the side of their fishing boat and into the water, so he'd learn how to swim.

*'Don't fight her, boy! You'll never win! Let go, just let go! She'll hold you like a woman if you let her! Let go . . .'*

He let go now, as he had then. Let the wave of power take him, lift him, drag him deep under and throw him up high. He heard himself cry out, a sound of wonder and despair. A fountain of words welled into his mouth and he shouted them for all the world to hear. A final surge of magic speared him like a javelin of fire. For one brief, exulting moment he knew himself invincible . . .

. . . and then the fire faded. The power snuffed out like a pinched candle. He was a man again, not magic made flesh, and the Orb in his trembling hands was nothing more than a bauble.

He could have wept.

When at last he stirred, Gar was staring at him as

though they'd never met. 'There was no pain for you . . . was there?'

He shook his head. Slowly, awareness returned. That was a lantern. He sat on the floor. Above him lay the quiet stone faces of dead people. He felt light enough to fly. Weighed down with impossible knowledge.

'Do you know that at the end you were saying the last words of the Transference spell with me, not after me?'

Carefully, he returned the Orb to Gar. 'If you say so. I can't remember . . . it's a blur.'

Gar stood. His face was cold, all emotion smothered like a river under ice. 'There's one more thing we have to do.'

He slumped against the nearest coffin, groaning. 'What? Gar, I don't want to do anythin' else. Not tonight. I'm knackered. All my insides are turned upside down and my head's near to burstin' open there's so much stuff been crammed in it.'

Gar's answer was to look in his satchel and remove a small pottery bowl filled with damp soil. 'There's a seed in here,' he said, holding it out. 'Make it sprout.'

'Make it sprout?' Asher stared. 'Why?'

'As a test. We need to be sure the Transference worked.'

'I ain't a bloody gardener! I don't know how to—'

'Yes, you do!' said Gar. Leaned down, grabbed him by one arm and hauled him to his feet. 'It's *in* you now, as it once was in me.'

'Ow! Leave off!' he protested as Gar tapped him ungently on the side of the head to make his point.

'Just think of the seed, Asher. Imagine it bursting into life. Magic will do the rest.'

Scowling, he snatched the dirt-filled bowl and glared into it. His mind was blank. *Think of the seed.* He held his breath, screwed up his face and imagined green and growing things. Words floated to the surface of his mind and flirted there like sea foam on the ocean.

*Talineth vo sussura. Sussura. Sussura.*

He parted his lips and let them escape.

Melting heat. A javelin of fire. A flaring of crimson and gold. The bowl vibrated. Even as he gasped in pain, felt something warm and wet trickle from his nostrils and over his lips, the moist dirt shivered. Shimmered. Erupted like a waterspout. Something slender and green unfolded from the dark earth, leapt to life in a riot of yellow and blue. He cried out. His fingers lost their tenuous hold of the bowl, let it slip and fall. It shattered on the crypt's stone floor, spilling dirt, spitting shards of clay.

The flower he'd given birth to kept growing. Breathless and disbelieving he watched as its stem broadened, budded, as the buds opened, as the blue and yellow petals uncurled and doused the air with perfume, as its tangle of roots tangled further. At long last it stopped growing and instead lay like a miracle at his feet.

'Barl save me,' breathed Gar. 'Germinate the seed, I said, not turn the crypt into a greenhouse.' He shook his head in wonder, and envy. 'Who are you, Asher? *What* are you?'

Asher stared at the flower, feeling such a brangle of things – fear, elation, horror, joy – that for a moment he forgot how to speak. 'You're the history student,' he said when his tongue at last obeyed him. 'You tell me.'

Gar's face tightened. 'I wish I could.'

He busied himself collecting the Orb and the book and stowing them safely back in the satchel. Turned then to picking up the shards of broken pottery and putting them in there too. His movements were savagely self-controlled.

Asher bent to help him. Gar struck his hand away. 'I'm not helpless.'

He stepped back. 'I never said you were.'

'But you thought it!'

'I never did. Gar—'

'Helpless! Useless! Defective!' On the last word Gar's voice cracked, his face twisted and he turned away.

Knotted with unwanted sympathy, all Asher could do was wait. Gone was the proud and powerful king who'd walked amongst his people in the market square, comforting and being comforted, wearing his magical birthright like a mantle of crimson and gold. In that man's place this born-again cripple, brought low by grief and fate and a bewildered anger that his life could take such an unkind turn. That against every belief and expectation an Olken could possess the magic he'd longed for so passionately all his life. That had manifested without warning then deserted him without rhyme or reason, leaving him emptied, hollowed, not even a shadow of his other, grander self.

At long last Gar regained his self-control. 'I'm sorry.'

Asher patted Gar's shoulder, feeling awkward. 'Don't be.'

'It's late. We should go. But first . . .' Painfully, Gar looked at his father's mutilated marble face. 'The effigy. If I gave you the incantation would you . . . I don't want anyone to see . . . it's dangerous. For both of us. And disrespectful to him.'

Asher sighed. He didn't want to. The less magic he used, the happier he'd be. But—

He let Gar give him the words he needed and remoulded Borne's disfigured features as though they were made of butter, not marble. Then he banished the spilled dirt and the riotous plant he'd created into the woods that ringed the crypt.

'Thank you,' said Gar. Subdued. Withdrawn. 'I'm grateful.'

'Prove it,' he said. 'Find me a way out of this.'

Gar nodded. Touched his fingertips to his father's perfect effigy. 'I'll try.'

Deaf to all of Darran's entreaties, Gar had decided upon a private interment for his family. Six sober City guards removed the bodies from the palace's east wing, watched by Conroyd Jarralt, members of the General Council, Pellen Orrick and a host of palace and Tower staff who'd gathered in silent respect on the lawn bordering the gravel driveway.

Asher, standing with Dathne and Darran and Willer, chewed on his lip and bullied his face into some semblance of stern discipline. Bloody funerals. He hated them. He and Dathne had attended Coachman Matcher's four days after the accident as official representatives of the king, and what a weeping and a wailing that had been. The dreams he'd had that night. His mother's funeral. His father's death and the funeral he'd been denied. Poor addled Jed, as good as dead.

Now this.

Holze walked behind the sad procession of coffins, weighted down with his most ornate robes of office, offering his prayers for the dead royals in a clear, carrying voice. Beside him walked Gar, silent, swathed head to toe in deepest black. For the first time since his ascension to the throne his clothes were embroidered with the sword-and-thunderbolt symbol of House Torvig. On his collar points, his shirt cuffs and over his heart. Another battle with Darran, that had been, one Gar had wisely lost. The reigning monarch always wore his or her house insignia. *Always*.

Even if it did make him feel like a fraud.

As the lowering sun threw shadows across the surrounding gardens, Pellen's boys slid the three coffins neatly into the back of the glossy black hearse, closed its rear doors, then fell into place well behind Gar and Holze. Matt picked up the black horses' reins and his whip and soberly moved away from the palace, down the tree-lined drive that would lead them, eventually, to the crypt. Equally sober, Gar, Holze and the guards followed in its wake. Holze was still praying.

As soon as they were gone from sight, sobs broke out amongst the crowd. Asher glanced around, saw weeping Olken, weeping Doranen. Not Jarralt, of course. Even if he was genuinely grieved he'd never lower himself to show it in public. But the Doranen members of the General Council, they seemed not to have such scruples. They grieved without reservation, as did the Olken guild leaders. There were even tears on Pellen's cheeks. Of course the royal staff were awash with misery. Beside him, Willer had surrendered to soggy hiccups and Darran was practically howling into his handkerchief.

Dathne, her eyes bright, touched his sleeve. 'They're sheep in search of a shepherd, Asher. You should say something.'

He didn't want to. Hated drawing attention to himself, especially with Conroyd Jarralt watching, but she was right. And Darran was in no fit state, blubbing like a baby.

'My lords and ladies, good guild meisters and mistresses, gentlefolk all,' he called, raising a hand to attract their attention. 'This sad day sees the end of an era in our kingdom. As His Majesty goes to bid his private farewells, let us remove to the palace's Hall of Meetings to partake of refreshments and shared memories in honour of King Borne, Queen Dana and the Princess Fane.'

A moment of surprised silence, of exchanged looks and lifted eyebrows. Then those nearest the palace began to drift towards it. Darran, damply composed now, plucked at his elbow. 'That was well said, Asher. Very well said indeed.'

'You sound surprised.'

Darran's chin lifted. 'I am. Now—'

'Asher,' said Conroyd Jarralt, suddenly at his elbow and icily civil. 'A word.'

He bowed. 'Of course, my lord.'

'In private.'

'Certainly.' He turned to Dathne. 'I'll see you inside.'

She withdrew, taking Darran and Willer with her and sparing him a swift, sympathetic smile over her shoulder. He didn't dare acknowledge it. Instead he surrendered to Jarralt's frigid scrutiny.

Contemptuous of social niceties, Jarralt said, 'When does the king intend to appoint his new Master Magician?'

'My lord, he has one already.'

Jarralt's colour heightened. 'Durm is nothing but a breathing carcass.' His voice was pitched low, for intimacy. 'And Gar's sentimental attachment to him places all of us in danger. You have his ear, fisherman. Bend it. Advise our king that further delay in the matter of Durm's replacement will lead to questions I'm sure he'd prefer weren't asked.'

Asher clasped his hands behind his back, so Jarralt wouldn't see fists. 'Is that a threat?'

'A warning,' said Jarralt, and smiled. 'I will not see

this kingdom imperilled by a boy whose judgement has already proven . . . questionable. He gave an undertaking before witnesses that this matter would be resolved.'

'And it will be, my lord. In his time. Not yours.'

The smile widened. 'Indeed. But time is not infinite. Time . . . runs out. Listen carefully, Meister Administrator. That sound you hear is the swift approach of a last chance.'

Bastard. *Bastard*. Asher manufactured a smile of his own. 'Really? Seems more to me like the sound of a man puttin' a noose round his own neck.'

Jarralt laughed. 'Were I you, Asher, I'd not be so swift to speak of nooses and necks. You have my warning. Do with it what you will . . . and be prepared to reap the consequences.'

Fighting nausea, he watched Jarralt saunter across the manicured lawn and into the palace.

It was some time before he could bring himself to follow.

Flickered by candlelight, Gar listened to Holze's footsteps retreating. To the crypt's inner door banging closed. To the faint echoes of the heavy brass-bound outer door booming shut. He crossed the small, crowded chamber and pushed its heavy oak door until it thudded home against the jamb. Then he turned and slumped against it.

'So. Here we are then. Alone at last.'

Someone giggled. After a startled moment he realised it was him. He slapped a hand across his mouth to stifle the shocking sound.

The cold stone coffins, full-bellied now with bodies, graced with those beautiful marble effigies, sat silent before him.

'I won't stay long,' he said after a little while. 'I know

you want to sleep. It's just . . . there's something I'd like to ask you. Just a little matter I'd like to see cleared up. Now that you're safely here, in your new home, and we're sure not to be overheard. You don't mind, do you? No, I didn't think you would.'

With an effort he pushed himself away from the door. The chamber shimmered softly in the candlelight. No glimfire now, not unless he asked Asher to conjure it for him. He felt his guts twist. *Like a child, running to its nurse for sweetmeats. Please, Asher, may I have some glimfire? Please, Asher, can you make it rain?*

Fane's stony sweet face mocked him . . . and all his rage broke free.

'I don't understand it!' he shouted at them. 'Did you *know* this could happen? Asher made it rain, he made it snow, he fixed your face, Father! And you'd have me repay him with *death*?'

Unmoved, unmoving, his father's face slept in the gently flickering light.

'I helped you murder Timon Spake! I forced Asher to watch! *Why*? To make sure we maintain our stranglehold on power in this land? To keep the Olken ignorant of their magic? To continue this shameful legacy of lies and deception? We didn't *save* Lur, we *stole* it. Conquered it. Somehow managed to bury the truth of the Olken's own magical birthright. Robbed them of their heritage and history. Do you know what that makes me? The inheritor of a criminal crown, no better than the monster Morg!'

No one answered him.

'And now we are punished. *I* am punished. What do I do next? How do I proceed? My magic is extinguished. Vanished as though it had never existed. Durm remains unconscious, teetering still on the brink of death, and

Conroyd . . .' He took a deep, shuddering breath. 'Conroyd is circling and he won't wait forever. All that stands between your kingdom and disaster, Father, is an uneducated Olken fisherman! How did this happen? Why did it happen? Tell me, please, *what does it mean*?'

His anguish echoed in the small stone chamber, bounced from wall to floor to ceiling in concentric circles of grief.

Flinging himself to the floor beside his mother's coffin, he seized her cold stone shoulders in his hands and willed her spirit to hear him.

'Mama . . . Mama . . . I grew to manhood watching you treat everyone you met with grace and courtesy, no matter who they were or how they lived. Baker, butcher, nobleman or nurse, Doranen or Olken, they were all the same to you. Everything I know of living Barl's legacy, of honouring her teachings and upholding her laws, I learned from you! And now I've learned it was likely all a lie. So what do I do now, Mama? Guide me, I beg you! I swore an oath to protect this kingdom and its sacred laws with my life! If I hold true to that oath I have to kill Asher. And in killing him I'll kill our kingdom with him. So no matter what I do, I'm forsworn! Is that what you want for me?'

Releasing his mother, he turned again to Borne. 'You were never ambitious for ambition's sake. If you'd wanted this kingdom's future placed in Conroyd's hands, if you'd trusted he'd do right by *all* the people, not just our own, you *never* would've bullied the Councils into giving you Fane. You'd have named him heir, to us if not to the population. But you didn't. I know you don't want me to abdicate. I know you don't want Conroyd as king.' He stared into his father's marble features, searching for answers. For hope. 'I suppose I could be wrong. It could be that Asher is the only Olken who can do magic. And if that's so, isn't it some kind of miracle? That he's with me now, in my darkest hour? Doesn't it mean he was born special for a reason? Don't I have to keep him secret, and safe, even if it means breaking Barl's Law myself?'

He glanced over at Fane. 'I know what you'd do, sister dear,' he said, derisive. 'You'd say the risk was too great. You'd round up every last Olken and put them in prison. Or send them to the axe, just in case he's not the only one. You'd say it was what Barl wanted but I won't believe that. How can he be Barl's enemy, our enemy, and also be the key to the kingdom's survival?'

Fane stayed silent. She always did, when the questions proved not to her liking. Exhausted, he let his body slump against her coffin. His head was aching badly. 'And if Durm does wake, what then? Where will his loyalty lie? With Barl? The kingdom? With the memory of a dead king he loved like a brother . . . or with the crippled failure his friend left behind as heir?'

He pressed his hands to his face. 'I'm so tired, Father,' he whispered. 'I'm confused. Afraid. I've no one to talk to. Asher's the only man I can trust now and he's more frightened than me. Barl save me, I wish you were here. I wish I knew what you wanted me to do . . . what *you* would do . . .'

His father didn't answer, which might have meant any number of things.

At length, chilled and hungry and empty of answers, he returned to the Tower where, mercifully, people left him alone. After a half-hearted meal he crawled into bed, fell asleep . . . and dreamed of Fane, laughing. Of a scarlet sky bleeding red rain. Of the Wall's demise.

Try as he might, he couldn't wake.

# CHAPTER FIFTEEN

Pother Nix sat in an easy chair, rereading his notes on the applied uses of lorrel seeds. A peculiar piece of flora, lorrel, good for gangrene and bloody flux. Found only along Lur's savage east coast, where it clung precariously to life along the barren cliff tops; just one of many unique Olken plants. Without magic, their healers relied on natural remedies and for that he was profoundly grateful. Like it or not, and most Doranen abhorred it, magic could only do so much. Olken herb lore had saved many a Doranen life, and praise Barl for it.

In the bed beside him, wasted and wan, Durm shifted, sighing. Nix glanced up, anxious, but it was dreaming only. No new fit or seizure. He released a grateful breath.

Praise Barl for herb lore indeed. He thought it was the only thing keeping Durm alive, for his healing magics had long since reached their limits. Durm stirred and sighed again, bald head rolling on the pillow. Nix reached out an absentminded hand, intending to check his patient's pulse—

Durm's fingers curled around his own.

'Barl save me!' cried Nix, and leapt to his feet. Durm's

eyes were open. Unfocused, but open. 'Kerril! Kerril, to me!'

The chamber door flew open and Kerril practically fell into the room. 'Sir? Are you—'

'He's awake! Barl be blessed, he's awake! Fetch me a wet cloth, quickly!'

As Kerril fled, Nix sought the pulse point in Durm's throat. It thrummed beneath his fingertips, fast but strong.

'Mmneeugh,' said Durm, struggling to speak. 'Hwheee . . .'

'Hush, hush,' he soothed. 'You're safe, man. Lie still.'

Despite their best endeavours, Durm's lips were dry and chapped with flaking skin. When Kerril returned, followed by the inevitable gaggle of colleagues, Nix took the cloth she handed him and pressed its wetness to the Master Magician's mouth.

At its touch Durm's gaze sharpened. Breathing harshly, he tried to sit up. Nix restrained him. 'No! Durm, no! You must stay still!'

Durm frowned, tugging his scars into tangled new shapes, and his lips framed soundless words. He stared around the healing chamber, searching for something, or someone. 'Borne,' he gasped, his voice harsh, guttural. 'Borne!' Tears leaked from his bloodshot eyes.

'Somebody fetch the king,' said Nix.

As Kerril bolted, scattering pothers like so many skittle-pins, Durm spoke again. 'Nix? Nix, help me!'

'I'm trying,' Nix told him, and felt tears of joy, of shock, pricking his own eyes. 'But you must lie *still*.'

Durm shuddered, a mighty convulsion that lifted his shoulders from the mattress. His eyes opened wide, and his mouth, and the most extraordinary expression of triumph and ecstasy and virulent relief washed over his face. '*Awake*!' he roared. 'At last, at last, *awake*!'

'Yes, awake, but poorly yet!' said Nix. 'You must—'

'Let me up,' Durm demanded, and struggled to throw aside his blankets. 'I have wasted too much time here, I have spent more of myself than I can spare, healing this rotten carcass. Let me *up*, I say! Or be blighted where you—'

Heedless of newly knitted flesh and bone, Nix threw himself across Durm's chest. 'Fetch me ebonard! *Now*!'

As someone scuttled to do his bidding, he spread his right hand flat and pressed it against Durm's thundering heart. '*Quantiasat*! *Boladuset*!' It was a calming invocation, useful when a patient was conscious but agitated. '*Boladuset*, Durm, Barl curse you with hives! Be *still*!'

The invocation caught, and Durm flopped back against his pillows. Somebody thrust a vial of ebonard into Nix's hand; he tossed the contents into Durm's gaping mouth and slammed closed his jaw for good measure.

Durm swallowed. Gagged. Snorted. His staring eyes rolled, fogged, and a foolish smile melted over his face. Nix sagged, then turned to scowl at his goggling underlings.

'Be off with you! His Majesty will arrive soon.'

But it wasn't the king who answered his summons.

'What's amiss?' demanded Asher, striding into the sick man's chamber as though he owned it. Nix, staring, remembered the rough-spun young Olken he'd once treated for a split eyebrow and thought he'd not have achieved a more perfect transformation with magic.

He stood. 'I requested His Majesty's presence.'

'His Majesty ain't available. Why do you need him?'

In the bed between them, momentarily forgotten, Durm shifted and sighed and said, 'Borne . . .'

'He's *awake*?' said Asher, incredulous.

Nix smiled. 'Awake, and seemingly with all his faculties.'

Still staring at the recovered Master Magician, Asher said, 'I'll fetch the king,' and left as abruptly as he'd arrived. Nearly half an hour later he returned, this time accompanied by His Majesty.

Gar looked worn to the nub and ripe for dropping. Not surprising, perhaps, since he'd interred his family only yesterday. Still . . .

Nix bowed. 'Your Majesty.'

Gar barely acknowledged him. Pushed straight past and dropped into the chair beside Durm's bed. Snatched up Durm's fleshless hand and pressed it to his lips.

'Durm. Durm, I'm here.' When Durm didn't respond, Gar looked up, displeasure unhidden. 'What is this? You said he was *awake*!'

Nix exchanged a glance with Asher and cleared his throat. 'He became agitated, sir. I was forced to gentle him with ebonard. He'll stir again presently, I'm sure.'

Unmollified, Gar turned back to Durm. 'You had no business drugging him, Nix. You *know* I need him alert and—'

In the bed, Durm sighed. Stirred. Dragged his eyelids open. 'What . . . what . . .'

Breathing hard, Gar leaned close. 'Praise Barl. Durm, can you hear me? Do you know me?'

Durm smiled into Gar's anxious, waiting face. 'Of course,' he said. His voice was soft and slurring. 'You're crippled Gar, Borne's runting regrettable offspring.'

Nix stepped forward. 'Ebonard is a powerful soporific, sir, and oft tickles the tongue to unfortunate utterances. It would be unwise to—'

Gar's face was bleached of blood. 'You think I'd hold a sick man's words against him?'

Another exchange of glances with Asher. This time the king's friend frowned and shook his head. Nix abandoned remonstrance. 'Of course not, Your Majesty.'

Durm stirred again, querulous now. 'Borne? Where is Borne?'

Subdued, Gar leaned close. 'He can't be here at the moment. But he sends you his love.'

Durm smiled. 'Borne. My friend. Give my love to him. Tell him I shall see him soon.' He sighed and slid again into sleep.

Gar released Durm's hand, stood and moved to the window. 'He has no memory of the accident?'

'It's too soon to say for certain,' replied Nix. 'But given his injuries . . . likely not. Once he's strong enough I'll—'

'No. I will tell him.'

'As Your Majesty desires.'

'How soon before he can return to his duties?'

Nix hesitated. Everything about this grieving young man urged caution. 'Sir . . . it's a miracle Durm lives at all. Perhaps it's not wise for us to look too far into the future.'

Gar glanced over his shoulder, a cold look. 'You know I need him, Nix.'

Caution was all very well, but he'd not be bullied into harming a patient. Not even by a king. 'I know that whatever your needs may be, Your Majesty, Durm's will always come first.'

'The king knows that,' said Asher. His tone was conversational, his eyes sharp. 'Just do your best, eh, to bring Durm about as fast as possible. That's all we're askin'.'

*We*. Nix felt the faintest stirring of unease. 'Your Majesty?'

Gar turned. 'That's right. Of course you must protect his health. Protect, but not coddle. I'm asking for him as much as myself, Nix. Durm is not an idle man. He'll heal faster knowing there's work to be done. Knowing he's needed.'

It was a fair observation. Still, Nix felt unsettled. Some new stress was carved into Gar's face. Something apart from WeatherWorking. 'To be sure. And how does Your Majesty? You seem to me a trifle . . . peaked.'

'I'm fine.'

To satisfy himself, Nix reached for Gar's wrist and laid a palm to his forehead. The king suffered his swift, impersonal touches with a thinly veiled impatience. When he was done, and grudgingly satisfied, Nix retreated. 'You should rest more. I warned you, these first weeks of WeatherWorking will break you if you let them.'

'I'm fine, I told you,' Gar snapped. 'Save your energies for Durm.'

He risked a smile. 'I have enough energy for both of you, sir.'

Gar stepped forward, furious. 'You think this *amusing*?'

'Majesty, no. I—'

'*Heal him*, Nix! Or I'll not be answerable for the consequences!'

Shaken, Nix watched him leave. Frowned, affronted, as Asher, on the king's heels, gave him a look of filthy disgust.

In his bed Durm slept on, smiling like a babe.

Conroyd Jarralt was in his bath when the message arrived. *Durm has woken and is in his right mind.* So great were his rage and disappointment that the cooling water began to bubble with heat and he had to leap out naked before he scalded himself.

'Tell Frawley to wait in the library,' he told the flustered maidservant. 'I'll see him directly.'

'Sir!' she gasped, and fled.

He wrapped himself in a rich brocade robe, dried and ordered his hair with an impatient finger-snap, then descended the stairs to meet with his henchman.

'My lord,' said Frawley, bowing low. Wrapped in his customary grey cloak, hat pulled low to his forehead, he looked, as ever, usefully nondescript.

'Our fat friend sent you a note, I take it?'

Frawley shook his head. 'No, sir. He tracked me down to the Whistling Pig and accosted me in the privy.'

'Were you observed?'

Frawley looked hurt. 'My lord.'

He couldn't care less about Frawley's feelings. 'Is that all he said?'

'Yes, my lord.'

Jarralt sat at his desk and drummed his fingers. 'Willer is laggardly in his task.'

'I did mention you were eagerly awaiting good news, my lord,' said Frawley. Uneasy now, he pulled off his hat and let his fingers nibble at the brim. 'I made a point of telling him.'

'I think it's time he was reminded of his mission's urgency,' said Jarralt. 'Where is he now?'

'His lodgings, most like, sir, this time of night.'

'Find him. Escort him to the west gate of the City Barlsgarden. I will meet you there.'

'My lord,' said Frawley, and took his leave.

Ethienne was amusing herself at her spinet in the music room. 'I'm going for a walk,' Jarralt told her.

'A walk?' she said, astonished. Mercifully she stopped playing and stared at him as though he'd sprouted wings. 'At this hour? But you've just had your bath.'

'Please don't distress yourself in staying up till I return. I feel a trifle restless this evening. I might well walk for some time.'

She stretched out a hand to him. 'Oh, Conroyd. Are you still so very sad?'

'We live in sad times, my dear.' For many reasons, and one more just added to the list.

'But you got over loving Dana years ago,' she said, pouting just a little. 'And you never had a fondness for Borne. Not as a man, I mean. As our king, of course, you revered him, as did we all.'

She'd have to know, sooner or later. 'Durm has woken. I just received word.'

And now his second-best wife understood. 'Oh, *Conroyd*!'

'Yes,' he said softly, and indulged in the thinnest of smiles.

Ethienne rallied. 'We cannot despair,' she announced, rising from her music stool. 'Awake is one thing. Unimpaired and able to function as the Master Magician is quite another. My dear, do not abandon hope. You will be Master Magician one day, I know it.'

She had no idea of his true ambition, of course. He would never dream of confiding in a woman like her. She was challenged enough to keep her mouth shut on his supposed desire to take Durm's inferior place at Gar's side.

He shrugged. 'Whatever happens, it will be according to Barl's will.'

Flushing, she fingered the holy medal on its chain around her neck. 'Of course.'

'Pray continue with your music-making, my dear,' he added, nodding at the spinet. 'And I shall see you in the morning at breakfast.'

He escaped her enthusiastic butchery of a popular dance tune and exchanged brocade robe and slippers for sober-hued tunic, trousers and boots. Muffled in a black cloak, with a low-brimmed hat to encourage concealing shadows, he left his townhouse and made his brisk way out of the exclusive Old Dorana residential district and towards the City Barlsgarden.

The night was clear, with no rain set to fall. According to the current Weather Schedule – Borne's last – there'd be no rain in the City for another five days. The temperature was due to start dropping, though. Gar would need to take care of that soon, or the River Gant wouldn't freeze over and there'd be no skating parties. He'd not stay popular long if that annual delight was unforthcoming.

The idea made him smile.

Amusement faded swiftly, however. His window of opportunity was fast sliding shut. Ethienne's optimism was little short of wishful thinking. If Durm had survived this far it would be just his luck for the man to make a full recovery. And if that happened any hope of discrediting Gar would disappear. Durm would safeguard his dead friend's son to the death. Even to the extent of protecting that miserable Asher.

No. If he was going to strike . . . seize the throne . . . seize his destiny, it would have to be soon.

He passed a pair of patrolling City Guards. They stared hard, recognised him, and nodded their heads politely as they continued on their way. He ignored them.

The Barlsgarden wasn't far on horseback or by

carriage; on foot, it took him over half an hour and he was sweating by the time he reached the west gate. So much for his bath. The flower-infested patch of ground lay in the City's somnolent religious district. No shops or taverns or restaurants here, just the sprawl of Barl's Chapel seminary, hospice and modest accommodation for clergy too old or infirm to continue their religious duties abroad in the kingdom. It was the perfect place for a meeting best kept private. No foot traffic, no inconvenient horses or carriages carrying people who had no need to know his business. All the little novices and Barlspeakers would be safely tucked into their beds or on their bony knees by now, praying. He was safe.

The Barlsgarden had a high wrought-iron fence all round it, punctuated with four gates, but to the best of his knowledge they were never shut. He slipped into the grounds through the west gate and waited.

'My lord! My lord?'

Frawley. Panting at his heels pudgy Willer, streaming sweat and stinking of garlic. The reek of it warred with the Barlsgarden's sweet winter jasmine, and won. Jarralt resisted the urge to press a kerchief to his nose and mouth, and stepped into the faint pool of light cast from a distant glimlamp.

'Lower your voice, Frawley,' he ordered. 'Sound carries. You extracted Meister Driskle without comment?'

'Sorry, sir. Yes, sir. Nobody saw me take him.'

Willer, his expression a distasteful conglomeration of anxiety and eagerness to please, bowed untidily. He was still struggling for air. 'My . . . lord! How can I serve you? Frawley says he passed . . . along my message. I'm afraid I don't know any more than that, concerning . . . the Master Magician's condition.'

Jarralt looked down his nose at him; it was a useful technique for intimidation. 'Yes. It is your lack of knowledge that brings us here.'

The fat little Olken paled. 'My lord?'

'When we first met, Willer, you gave the impression of a man urgently desirous of saving our precious kingdom from calamity,' he said, letting his displeasure show. 'Yet all I have received from you so far are vague hints, unsubstantiated suspicions and a list of transgressions that, while they may perfectly illuminate Asher's unsatisfactory character, hardly advance our cause of proving he's a danger to the crown. Can it be I was mistaken in you, sir?'

'My *lord*!' the little man squealed. 'I'm doing my best, I swear it! But it's not easy. Asher's so damned secretive!'

Jarralt allowed his expression to ice over. 'So. When you assured me you were perfectly placed to uncover Asher's misdeeds, you were in fact . . .' He stretched the pause to screaming point. 'Exaggerating?'

'No, no! And I wasn't lying either! I *am* perfectly placed, my lord! My life on it!' the Olken protested in a gasp. 'It just might take a little longer than I – than *we* – thought. But I'll do it. I swear I'll do it!'

'Neither my time nor my patience, Willer, are infinite.'

Cringing like a whipped cur, the Olken dared to touch a fingertip to Jarralt's sleeve. 'My lord, I'm sure I could learn more if only I could get access to Asher's private papers. To his office and all his desk drawers.'

'You suspect Asher of hiding incriminating evidence in his office?'

For a moment the fat man struggled with his reply. Then he shrugged unhappily. 'My lord, I can't in honesty say so for certain. But if he keeps it anywhere, I'm sure it's there. Or in his private apartments. If only I could get inside when he wasn't around, I know I could find the evidence we require. But he keeps all his doors locked and I don't have keys. Darran does but he won't let me—'

The flowerbeds were lined with small round river pebbles, black and white in turn. Jarralt stooped and selected one of each colour. Enclosing the black one in his right fist, he whispered an incantation against his folded fingers and waited for the humming buzz against his flesh that would signal the spell's success. A flash of heat, a sizzling thrill, and it was done.

'This will unlock any door or drawer,' he said, holding the pebble out to his pawn. 'Use it wisely. I will know where it has been.'

With eyes like a greedy child's the Olken took the pebble and slipped it into a weskit pocket. 'My lord.'

Next he enchanted the white pebble and held it out. 'This one will give you an hour's feeble glimlight. Enough to see by, but not be seen. Rap it once against a hard surface to activate the spell, once again to turn it off. When you have found what it is we require throw both pebbles into the nearest well and send to Frawley immediately, no matter the hour. Is that understood?'

The white pebble disappeared into another pocket. 'My lord, I will not betray your trust,' fat Willer promised. 'We will apprehend this miscreant, you have my solemn word. The kingdom will be saved.'

Clearly, he was expecting some kind of response. A compliment, possibly, or a heartfelt declaration of faith and gratitude. Jarralt looked at Frawley. 'Escort him back to his lodgings by a different route. Avoid the guards and any other late-night pedestrians.'

Frawley bowed. 'My lord.' Taking the repellent man's black woollen sleeve, he hustled him away.

Jarralt watched them go, waiting till they'd rounded a corner out of sight, then pulled his own cloak a little closer and struck out for home. Smiling, he allowed a little of Ethienne's optimism to warm him.

Soon. Soon now, despite Durm's tiresome attachment to life, he would have Borne's wretched son and the inconvenient Olken at his mercy. A brief unpleasantness, a minor upheaval. A short period of public mourning, and then a new day would dawn.

*Bow down, you people of Lur. Make way. Pay homage. Here is your new liege, King Conroyd the First.*

Dathne propped her elbows on her dinner table and frowned. 'I thought you liked my cooking,' she said. She sounded puzzled. Maybe even a little hurt.

Seated opposite her, Asher looked at the muddle of carrot, spinach and spicy mince on his plate and pulled a face. 'Sorry. Guess I ain't got much of an appetite.'

She reached for the bread, tore off a fresh hunk and mopped up her leftover gravy. 'What's wrong?'

He loved to watch her eat. Such swift, precise movements. All her formidable personality focused on taste and texture. 'There's a WeatherWorking set for tonight.'

Displeased, she wiped her fingers on her napkin. 'If it disturbs you so much, don't go.'

'Dath . . .' He sighed. 'Don't.'

'I won't pretend to like it just because you want me to,' she said tartly.

'You'd rather I lied?'

'I'd rather you stayed here!'

'Aye, well, so would I, but we both know I can't.'

She pushed away from the table and began clearing the plates. 'Won't.'

Damn. He'd come here for respite, not reproaches. He stood. 'I can't do this, Dathne. Not tonight.'

She beat him to the door. Pressed her back to it and held her palms out. 'Wait. Wait.' Her hands came to rest on his chest. 'I'm sorry. Don't go. Not until you have to. I didn't mean to nag. It's just – I worry about you.'

His heart beneath her hands beat hard and fast. 'I know. But with any luck I'll not be involved much longer. Now Durm's turned the corner—'

'Is it certain? Nix thinks he'll make a full recovery?'

'He's . . . hopeful.'

He watched the doubt shift behind her eyes. Saw her take a breath, ready with more pesky questions he couldn't answer without telling more lies. He stopped her mouth in the only way he could think of: with his own.

Shocked, she tightened her fingers on him, clutching at his shirt. He heard her muffled protest. Felt her stiffen and begin to pull away. Giddy, he put his arms around her, crushing her close. She tasted of wine and spices and surprise. Just as he thought he'd misread her entirely, ruined everything, she surrendered. Became pliant in his arms. Kissed him back, with passion.

When at last they parted she stared at him, panting. He managed to smile. 'Not goin' to hit me, are you?'

Her soft lips curved in a smile. 'I should.'

'For takin' liberties? Aye. Prob'ly. Specially since I ain't sorry.' He felt his own smile fade then. 'Are you?'

She answered him with a kiss that stole his breath as completely as he'd stolen hers. Then she released him, and reached up to frame his face with her hands. Her eyes were fierce. 'I understand why you do it, Asher. Gar's your friend and you love him. But don't let love blind you to danger. Or lull you into false security. He may be your friend but he's the king first and he'll not forget that. Don't you forget it either.'

Her words cut too close for comfort. To hide his face from her he pulled her to him in another embrace. Sighed as her arms slid around his neck and her fingers ran through his hair. 'It's all right, Dath,' he whispered. 'I know what I'm doing.' And hoped she'd believe him. Wished he could believe himself. For the briefest, maddest moment he wanted to reveal his impossible secret.

She pulled away, half smiling, half frowning. 'What? What is it?'

No. It was impossible. To tell her would be monstrous. Selfish. Unkind, and dangerous. How could he love her and risk her life? He shook his head. 'Nothing. I should go. Rest up a bit, before the Working.'

'Rest here.'

'Dath, if I stayed I doubt either of us'd get much rest.'

She punched him. 'Speak for yourself! I know what's right and what isn't.'

He rubbed his smarting chest; she had a hard fist when she felt like it. 'No. I meant that sooner or later you'd start on at me again about Gar and then we'd be branglin' and I don't want to spoil things.' He traced the sharp clean line of her cheek with his finger. 'Spoil this.'

Capturing her hand in his, she touched her lips to his knuckles. 'You won't.'

'I know I won't, 'cause I'm leavin',' he said. 'I wanted to see Matt any road. Clear the air after the other day. We been avoidin' each other.'

'Don't worry about Matt,' she said, pulling a face. 'He'll get over it.'

'Aye, but I won't. I'm a sensitive flower, me,' he said, and laughed when she punched him again. 'Ow. See?'

She pulled free of him and opened the door. 'Fine. Off you go then, Meister Flower. I'll see you in the morning.'

'What, you ain't goin' to walk me out?'

'I would if you deserved it.'

He kissed her again for that, swiftly, and let the expression of shy pleasure on her face warm him all the way home. Where, since he'd been telling the truth about Matt, he went straight to the stable yard.

Matt was still at work, mending a broken bridle in his office. The pot-bellied stove in the corner belched heat and bubbled a kettle on its lid. Asher kicked the office door closed and went to the cupboard. Fished out a mug and the tea jar and set about brewing himself a cup. Matt threaded his needle with a fresh length of waxed thread, mute as a swan.

He sighed. Added a dollop of honey to his tea and said, stirring, 'You told me you weren't in love with her.'

'I'm not,' Matt answered, after a moment.

'Then why does it matter if I am?'

'Did I say it matters?'

Exasperated, he threw down his spoon. 'You didn't have to! It was written all over your face. So d'you want to tell me what's goin' on?'

Still Matt stared at his stitching. 'Nothing's going on.'

'Is that so?' Carefully, he put down his mug. 'Then why won't you look at me, Matt? What are you scared I'll see in your eyes when you say "I don't love her"?'

Matt did look at him then. Stabbed his needle into the ball of waxed harness thread and stood. 'Nothing. It's none of my nevermind, Asher, you've made that clear. Now why don't you go about your business and leave me to—'

A crashing from the stable yard spun him about, last words forgotten. As one they leapt for the office door. Matt reached it first, wrenched it open. All the horses were jostling now, roused to whickers and kicking by the panicked banging and thrashing in their midst.

Matt swore. 'That bloody animal, it's been nothing but trouble – grab the long line, Asher. I'll need your help.'

The grey colt that had hurt itself on the way to Dorana was cast in its stable. As the startled lads rushed downstairs into the yard, hauling on boots and jackets as they came, Matt caught the rope Asher threw him and led the way to its box.

'Stand back, boys,' he ordered the lads. 'We don't want to panic him further.'

Asher looked over the stable door. The colt had rolled up against the wall. Legs half folded between belly and timber, it was trapped and half mad with terror. He could see blood already. Horses had killed themselves like this; they didn't have much time.

Without speaking, not needing to, he and Matt entered the stable. The colt began to thrash again. He went to its head, held its cheek to the straw with one hand and pressed its neck flat with his knee. Restrained, the colt grunted and groaned but couldn't move. Swiftly Matt looped one end of the rope around the colt's front legs, the other around its hind. With the knots secure, he looked across and nodded.

'On three. One – two – *three*!'

He pulled, and Asher guided the colt's head and neck, rolling it over and away from the wall. As soon as it was clear Asher pinned the colt down again and Matt untied the rope. Young Jim'l, always fast on the uptake, slid the bolt on the stable door and held it open just wide enough. Then they threw themselves out of the stable as the sweaty colt lurched to its feet, then bucked and reared and stamped its rage.

Safe in the yard, blotting sweat, Matt said, 'Thanks. Damn bloody thing.'

Asher grinned. 'Me or the horse?'

Matt's answering grin was . . . complicated. 'What do you think?'

They had an audience of goggling stable lads; it was no place for a private, painful conversation. 'I think I need to get goin'. We'll talk later, eh?'

Coiling up the rope, again Matt wouldn't look at him. 'If you insist.'

Baffled, hurt, he shoved his hands in his pockets. 'You sayin' there's nowt to talk about?'

Then Matt did look up. His face was weary. Sad. 'I'm saying I doubt it'll make much difference.'

Stung, Asher turned on his heel and started walking. Said over his shoulder, 'Aye . . . well . . . don't do me any favours, Matt.'

Despite his anger, he hoped Matt might come after him. Call after him, at least. Make *some* kind of effort.

Nothing.

So – sink it. If Matt wanted to play the sore loser, let him. He had other friends, and other things to worry about.

Like WeatherWorking.

# CHAPTER SIXTEEN

Two hours later, as the burning magic faded, Asher let his legs fold beneath him and thudded to the Weather Chamber floor. Through barely open eyes he watched gentle rain tumble onto the fallow apple orchards of the Home Districts, and snow feather itself over the icewine region of Fairvale.

'Here,' said Gar, and held out a cup of Nix's disgusting potion. Hand shaking, Asher took it and drank the vile sludge of herbs and vinegars concocted to keep body and soul together. His belly heaved, protesting, but he managed to keep it down.

Gar reached for him with a damp cloth. 'Now your face—'

'I can do it,' he mumbled. 'Don't need a bloody nurse-maid.'

He could feel Gar's worried gaze on him as he dabbed at his blood-sticky skin. 'You shouldn't try to do so much at once,' Gar said. 'Olken aren't meant to endure this kind of power.'

He dropped the stained cloth and dragged himself to his feet. He couldn't stand unaided, though; the Weather Magic still ate him like acid. He shuffled sideways and leaned against the chamber's circular wall, his head viciously pounding. 'I got no choice. Can't afford to spend all night on it. I still got work to do, back at the Tower.'

'Can't it wait?'

'No.'

Gar busied himself shoving cloth, basin and potion back in the cupboard. Slammed its doors. 'I know this is hard,' he said, his voice low. 'But what would you have me do? I'm reading Durm's books. I'm searching for a cure.'

He pulled a face. 'Read faster.'

'I can't! The books are *old*, Asher, recorded in ancient dialects, obscure codes! If I translate them incorrectly, if I let haste overcome scholarship, I'll make a mistake, one that will kill you or me or everyone in Lur! Is that what you want?'

'I want this to be *over*!' he retorted, goaded to desperation. 'I want my life back the way it was before!'

Gar turned on him. 'Before what? Before when? There is no "before", Asher! There's only now, from this minute to the next, holding on tight and hoping the sky doesn't fall on our heads.'

Asher stifled a groan. His bones were chalk, ready to snap at the smallest exertion. He'd left exhaustion behind days ago. 'When we said a month, I thought: that ain't such a long time. I can do that. But now I ain't so sure. Right now an hour feels like forever.'

'I know. I'm sorry,' said Gar. He was stricken with guilt. 'Look. I'm supposed to draft a new Weather Schedule soon. There might be some arrangements I can change. Stretch things out a bit, give you more time between Workings.'

'You'll have a queue of farmers and suchlike bangin' on the door with complaints.'

Gar frowned. 'The WeatherWorker's word is law. If I can adjust the rain and snowfall frequencies without adversely affecting the crops . . .'

'Try,' he said. 'Please?' It shamed him, begging; but the magic was breaking him. He could feel the fissures spreading.

The gentle shush and splash of snow and rain on the relief map was easing. With a sharp, deep breath he pushed himself away from the wall. Made himself stand up straight.

'I'll do, now. You should get on back. I'll wait a bit, then follow.'

Gar shook his head. 'You're in no fit state to walk alone. And we shouldn't risk you falling asleep in here. We'll go back together. It's late enough now that no one should notice.'

It wasn't a good idea, but he didn't have the strength to argue. 'Fine,' he said. 'You're the king.' And even let Gar help him down the stairs, one arm strong and steady about his shoulders.

They returned to the Tower in silence. Gar went on up to his apartments and Asher, reluctant, headed for his office. The worst of the pain and nausea had passed, he was mostly tired now, and light-headed. An hour longer, he'd work, and that should keep nagging Darran satisfied.

Light spilled from beneath his closed office door. He opened it, and there was Dathne. 'What are you doin' here?'

'You and that damned WeatherWorking. I couldn't sleep,' she said, apologetic and truculent at once. 'And there was work to do. I didn't think you'd mind.'

He came inside and closed the door. Shrugged out of his jacket and hung it on the coat rack. 'No. I don't mind.'

'Good,' she said, and smiled. Then relief faded as she looked more closely at him. 'Asher – there's blood on your weskit.'

He looked down. Damn. So there was. 'It's nowt.'

'Nowt?' She came round from behind her desk. 'Since when is blood nowt?'

Barl save him, he was too tired for this . . . 'Dath, don't fuss. I got a bit too near to Gar when he was WeatherWorking, is all; I told you, it's a bloody business.'

'*His* bloody business. So how is it *you're* the one looking half dead?'

'I'm *fine*,' he insisted.

She stepped back. 'No. You're not. There's something you aren't telling me.'

The hurt in her eyes was like a knife wound. 'Don't do this, Dath,' he whispered. 'Please. Can't you understand? I've made promises.'

She was silent for a moment. Staring. Thinking. Then she moved close to him again and touched her fingertips to his weskit, where blood had turned cream to crimson like magic. 'You should go to bed. You really do look dreadful.'

He felt dreadful, all his sleeping pains rewoken. 'Can't. Glospottle's hearing is the day after tomorrow and I ain't nowhere near ready. I still got a pile of books to read through and make notes on.'

'Then I'll stay and help,' she said, smiling. 'Two heads are better than one.'

A tempting offer, but it was late and his defences were weakened. If she asked him again to confide in her, he might not have the strength to resist. Especially since he was feeling so desperately alone. 'Dath—'

She rested her palm above his heart. 'Let me stay. Please?'

He shouldn't . . . he shouldn't . . . 'All right,' he said. 'But only for a while.'

At her suggestion they took the books he needed up to his apartment library, which had sofas on which they could comfortably recline. She took one half of the pile, he took the other, and they settled down to reading.

Time passed. Soon he forgot about 'just an hour' and 'only for a while'. It didn't matter that he was weary or that his eyes felt gritty. Scented pine burned cheerfully in the fireplace and it was so cosy, so domestic, to be sharing silence with her in his private apartment, working.

Curled up on the other crimson leather sofa Dathne sighed, used a finger to mark her place in the book she was studying and scratched some more notes on the already crowded piece of paper beside her. Her expression was one of grave concentration. The very tip of her tongue poked out from the corner of her mouth as she wrote, and there was an ink smudge on the end of her nose. He felt his heart turn over.

She looked up, sensing his regard. 'What?'

He couldn't say it. Said instead, 'I been thinking. Don't reckon I can do this.'

'What? Preside over the hearing?' She returned to her notes. 'Of course you can.'

'No, I can't. It's *Justice Hall*, Dathne! Legal folderol and footlin' about! I don't understand that claptrap!'

She grinned. 'Which is why we're sitting here in the small hours of the night studying when all sensible people are in their beds. Have you finished *Tevit's Principles of Jurisprudence* yet?'

Tevit's tedious bloody Principles of Juris-bloody-prudence lay open and abandoned on his chest. The first three paragraphs on page one had given him a thumping headache and it had gone downhill from there.

'No.'

*'Asher . . .'*

He pushed the book to the carpeted floor, where it landed with a satisfying thud. 'Can't I just throw Glospottle and the rest of the Dyers' Guild into prison instead?'

Another grin. 'I'm sure Pellen Orrick would love that.'

'I know I bloody would,' he said, glowering. A yawn overtook him; when it was done twisting his face inside out he let his head thud onto the sofa's padded arm roll and closed his eyes. Exhaustion was like a blanket of warm snow, weighing him down. 'I just reckon the world's gone mad if a no-account uneducated fisherman from Restharven can sit on that throne in Justice Hall and tell folk he hardly knows what they can and can't do with their own urine.'

'You don't give yourself enough credit,' said Dathne, her voice coming closer. 'Next to our king you're the most important man in Lur.' She was bending over him. He could feel her soft breath fanning his face. 'I thought you'd realised that by now.'

'What I realise, Dathne, is that I—'

Her warm, soft lips suffocated the rest of his sentence. Shocked silent, he lay there drowning in exquisite sensation. After an age she released him, and he breathed again. He opened his eyes.

'Now who's takin' liberties?'

'Me,' she whispered and kissed him again, smelling of passion and perfume. Tasting of the honey-mints she liked to nibble when she thought no one was looking. He lifted his hands to the nape of her neck and unpinned her thick black hair. It fell about his face in lavender-scented disarray. Her fingers were framing his face, holding him, caressing him. Shivering his skin and setting it on fire. Even through a barricade of brocade and silk he could feel her breasts against his chest. All the blood left his head in a dizzying rush, making a beeline south.

'Asher? What is it? You're not enjoying this?' she murmured against his mouth.

'Yes! Yes!' he whispered frantically.

Her fingers tightened. 'Then kiss me back, damn you!'

He was her obedient slave. His arms crept around her back, encircling the fragile ribcage, home to her thundering heart. At last they broke apart, sobbing for breath. Her stunned eyes were enormous, her lips wet and swollen. He pressed his fingertips against them and shuddered as she touched him with her tongue.

'Don't,' he groaned, and captured her hand in his. 'If you do that again I might—'

'What?' she whispered, and trailed her other fingers across his bare chest. Bare? When had his shirt come unbuttoned?

'You know what! Dathne, we can't *do* this!'

'But I want to do this,' she said, and kissed him yet again.

Head swimming, senses blazing, he let himself respond. Let the whirlwind take him, blind him to sense and reason. Her skin was silk and cream beneath his questing fingers. She moaned his name, trembling at his touch. He felt like a king.

They slid from couch to carpet and she fell beneath him, crying aloud as he kissed her breasts, a small shocked sound of pleasure.

He stopped, panting. 'We can't. We mustn't. We're not married, Dathne.'

Her scented skin was damp, her hair the wildest tangle. She smiled. 'Then marry me.'

Disbelieving, he stared into her passion-blurred face. '*What*?'

'There must be a Barlsman awake somewhere in this City.' She smoothed his cheek with her fingertips. 'Let's go find him.'

She was serious. Closing his fingers around her wrist he tugged her free. 'You said you didn't love me.'

She wouldn't look at him. 'I lied.'

'Why?'

'I was afraid.'

'Of what?'

She sat up. Buttoned her blouse, her fingers unsteady. 'Nothing. Everything. It doesn't matter now.'

'It matters to me.'

She touched her lips to his, lightly. 'It shouldn't. What's important is that I've come to my senses.'

'Why now?'

'I realised I could lose you.'

'*Lose* me?'

Her gaze flickered sideways. 'Don't tell me you've not noticed all the fond Olken mamas as you ride through the City. They point you out to their unmarried daughters and tell them to smile as you pass by. You could start a florist's shop ten times over with the roses that get thrown at you on public occasions. There must be a hundred girlish hearts breaking in Dorana, all for love of you.'

He didn't know whether to kiss her or shake her silly. 'Dathne, since when have I noticed fond mamas or their husband-hunting daughters? For one thing it ain't been nowt but work, work, work ever since I got to this bloody place, and for another . . .'

'Yes?' Her voice wasn't quite steady. 'For another?'

'Yours is the only girlish heart I'm interested in.'

Tears spilled down her cheeks. This time their kiss was delicate, dulcet. When it ended he folded his fingers around hers.

'But it don't mean I can marry you. At least not yet.'

Her eyes widened in pained surprise. 'Why not?'

She was a fiercely bright woman. Married to him, living with him, she'd discover the truth. If things went wrong and he couldn't protect her . . . 'The kingdom's only just out of mourning, Dath. And Gar—'

'Must marry soon himself,' she said. 'Haven't you heard Darran on the subject?' She pulled a face. 'Why should the king care if we stand before a Barlsman and exchange our vows? Or is he so churlish he'd begrudge you a marriage born of love instead of duty?'

Right now, with his own hopes for love and family cruelly blighted. Gar might well begrudge any kind of marriage. And even if he didn't, it would be equally cruel to flaunt happiness under his nose.

Something else he couldn't tell her. 'Dathne . . . it ain't as simple as that.'

'It could be,' she said, and withdrew her fingers from his. 'Perhaps you don't love me after all.'

He answered her calumny with a kiss that stole all the air from their lungs and left them gasping. 'Believe me now?'

With her head on his chest and one hand crept inside his shirt to lie against his ribs she said, 'Yes. But you'll put duty first.'

Ever since they'd met she'd been his sympathetic sounding board, his sage advisor, his blunt and brutal mirror. It cut him to the quick, repaying her honesty with half-truths and lies. 'I'm sorry,' he whispered.

She smiled painfully. 'Don't be.' Bending low, she kissed the ropy scar along his forearm. 'I know a little about duty myself.'

He didn't deserve her. Couldn't believe he'd won her. What a courtship he'd endured . . .

She kissed him again. Soaring, he lost himself in sensation. Kissing was so much better than thinking. Or worrying. Or trying to come to grips with *Tevit's Principles of Jurisprudence*. Who'd have thought a floor could feel so comfortable? Or a spare and angular body so soft? Kissing Dathne was a homecoming.

Breathing hard, they sat on the floor in tangled silence. Then Dathne stirred. Her fingernails traced circles on his chest, raising goosebumps. 'Do you know how we Olken married before the Doranen came?'

He rested his cheek on the top of her head. 'No.'

'We stood together, witness for each other. We declared our desire to be handfast and faithful. And we were married.'

'Just like that?'

She nodded. 'Yes, my love. Just like that.'

*My love*. Dizzy, he tilted her head back with a finger beneath her chin and gazed into her heavy-lidded eyes. 'That were a long time ago, Dath. There were reasons things changed.'

She pouted. 'I know, I know. Marriages need to be recorded, babies can't be born willy-nilly. We must never outgrow the land we have here. But I'm not saying we won't ever stand before a Barlsman, Asher. When you think our public happiness won't hurt the king we can have our marriage entered in the registry. But why should we deny ourselves our private joy till then? If we were any other people, living anywhere else in Lur, we could marry in a heartbeat. I'm sorry for the king's sorrow, truly, but why must we suffer because of it?'

Her words struck a deep chord. Unbidden, buried resentment stirred. Why indeed? He was already sacrificing so much for Gar. Risking so much. He deserved something in return, didn't he? Some small spark of happiness. He and Dathne couldn't live together of course. Not at first. Maybe not for months. Might only have a handful of stolen moments, like this one. But the moments would be theirs. Joy would be theirs. And in her arms he could mercifully, hopefully, forget his other, unjoyful secrets.

Harsh practicality doused his daydream. 'But what about babies? You know there can't be any babies, Dath, not until—'

'Hush,' she said, and pressed a finger to his lips. 'Babies are women's business. Leave that to me. We'll have no babies till the time is right.'

Relieved, he gathered her close. 'Even married, you know there'll be things I can't tell you. Private business 'tween Gar and me that can't go further. It don't mean I ain't mad in love with you. I am. Reckon I always have been. But—'

She kissed him. 'I know. I understand.'

'And we'd have to be bloody careful. There'll be folks around all the time. Noticin' types like Darran and pissant Willer. They can't suspect a thing. Can you live a secret life like that?'

Tears welled in her eyes. 'I think so.'

He frowned, then. 'And you can't tell Matt either.'

'Don't worry,' she said. 'Matt's the last person I'd want to tell.'

Jealousy stabbed. 'So he *is* in love with you.'

'No. *No*. But he'd . . . disapprove. We'd argue. And

this is my choice, not his.' She kissed him, hard. 'Matt is a friend, Asher. You're the only man who's ever moved me.'

The simple declaration stunned him. 'You really want to do this?'

Her answer was to break away from him. Bemused, he watched her lock the library door, pad to the fireplace and heave fresh logs into the dying flames, then retrieve a pale gold silk-weave scarf from the depths of her satchel.

'Hold out your hand,' she said, so he did. She sank to the carpet before him and matched his move, palm kissing palm, and laced her fingers with his. Then, frowning lightly, she bound their flesh together with the scarf. He said nothing, feeling giddy, feeling dreamlike.

They were getting married.

The ritual binding complete, she sat on her heels and considered him. The heat of her hand was like magic in his blood. 'I am Dathne Jodhay, a maid of good conscience and unsullied name. I take this man, Asher, to be my husband and swear to him my love and loyalty until I die.' She smiled then. 'Your turn.'

'I am Asher of Restharven,' he replied. In his own ears his voice sounded . . . breathless. 'I'm a man of good conscience and unsullied name, except if you ask Darran or Willer or Conroyd Jarralt and why would you? Dathne Jodhay is my woman, my wife, and if anybody looks so much as sideways at her I'll knock their bloody block off.'

Dathne was shaking with silent laughter. 'Oh, Asher, you're such a romantic!'

'Sink romance,' he growled, and pulled her to him hard enough to make her gasp. 'Are we married?'

'Oh yes,' she said, and toppled him to the floor. 'We're married.'

And then there was no more talking, as clothes peeled from flesh like shedding skin. Laughing, groaning their mutual needs, hands roamed, tongues touched, fingertips coaxed forth bonfires of delight.

Suddenly disconcerted, lost in a wilderness of pleasure, Asher fumbled to a halt. Lifting his lips from her breast, he gazed into her chaotic eyes. 'Uh, Dath. You know I ain't never . . .'

More laughter. Wicked hands, holding. 'It's all right,' she promised him, trembling. 'Neither have I. But I reckon we'll work something out.'

The minute he laid eyes on them, Matt knew. Stepping back into the shadows between the stallion stables and the feed room, watching them creep into the stable yard like conspirators, he felt his heart turn over.

*Dathne, Dathne, what have you done?*

It was early yet, not quite a half-hour past dawn, and the lads were only just rousing from their beds. Smeary with sleep, he'd abandoned his own blankets nearly two hours ago to check on the grey colt, and stayed up to finish mending that broken bridle. To worry about Asher and the rift sprung up between them that he didn't know how to close. Now his stomach was growling for breakfast and there was a pain behind his eyes and all he wanted was hot tea and sizzling bacon and a moment just to sit, and rest, and not think about anything.

What he *didn't* want was another argument with Dathne. But now, having seen her, seen Asher, how could he stay silent? Pretend he'd not seen anything? She'd lost her mind. The strain of being Jervale's Heir must've upset her judgement, tipped her right over the edge of reason. And while he owed loyalty to her, and paid the debt gladly, there was an even greater claim on his conscience. He had a duty to the Circle. To Prophecy.

And somebody had to save her, even if it was from herself.

They weren't holding hands, not exactly. But their fingertips were touching as they tiptoed to the tack room and she was looking into his face with her unlocked heart in her eyes. He was grinning, happier than the City had ever seen him.

She waited as he slipped into the tack room and emerged a moment later with Cygnet's saddle, saddle-cloth and bridle. The horse had recognised his step and was hanging over its stable door, ears pricked, nostrils fluttering a welcome. He saddled up and she draped herself over the door, watching. Giggling softly. *Dathne*? It was hard to believe. When he was done, she swung open the door for him and stood aside as he led Cygnet into the yard.

'Ride carefully now,' she admonished him, her voice hushed. 'The kingdom needs its Olken Administrator in one piece.' Her hand was on his arm. There was something terrifyingly possessive about the simple gesture. She smiled, her expression wicked and suggestive and heartbreakingly intimate. 'And so do I.'

His hand slid round her waist, down to her hips, down even lower, and he pulled her to him with a grunt of satisfaction.

'Stop fratchin' at me,' he said. 'Cygnet and me've been out early every morning this week and ain't come to harm. It's the only time I get to m'self these days, and I ain't about to give it up.' He nipped at the soft skin between her jaw and throat. 'Not even for you.'

Their kiss was molten, passion unleashed. Matt

watched it, despairing. There wasn't enough common sense in all the kingdom to douse this. When they parted Dathne stepped back, unsteady on her feet, and Asher was flushed.

'Now get away from me, woman,' he said, throwing the reins over Cygnet's head, 'afore I go off like a rocket. I'll see you back at the Tower sharp at nine.'

'Yes,' she said. 'There's the rest of Tevit to get through today.'

'Sink Tevit and his bloody *Principles of Jurisprudence*,' said Asher, grinning. He swung himself into Cygnet's saddle and sat there, staring down at her. 'I love you.'

'And I you,' she replied. 'Now go if you're going. Matt and the lads will be downstairs any minute.'

She watched him ride out of the yard, then turned to leave through the main entrance's archway. Her face was shuttered again, closed down and self-contained. Matt took a deep breath and stepped out of the shadows.

'Dathne.'

Startled into silence she stared at him. Then: 'Matt. You're about early. And stealthy, too. You should mind where you creep, my friend. You might give some poor soul a seizure.'

Closing on her, he took her upper arm in his callused fingers. 'Are you mad, Dathne? Have you abandoned all sense? You're *futtering* with him?'

She jerked her arm from his grasp, glaring. 'I'm married with him. It's not futtering when you're married, Matt.'

'You're *married* . . .' Speech failed him. Aghast he looked at her, this sudden stranger, and struggled to find the words. '*Dathne*—'

The door leading up to the staff dormitory flew open

and the chattering stable lads tumbled into the yard. 'Not out here,' she said grimly, and stalked to the office. He followed her inside and closed the door behind them.

'You're married with him,' he said, despair reducing his voice to a whisper. 'Does Veira know?'

'Not yet.'

'*Why*, Dathne?' he asked her. 'Why did you do it?'

'Because I had to. Because I need him bound to me, body and soul. He's holding something back, Matt. Something important. I must know what it is.'

He collapsed into the office's dilapidated armchair and rubbed his hands across his face. 'You *are* mad. You told Asher you loved him, Dathne. I heard you.'

Her cheeks tinted pink. 'That conversation was private.'

'Dathne! Love won't save you when he finds out you've used him!' Outrage and dismay churning through him, he pushed to his feet and began pacing the small office. Outside in the yard the horses were neighing and banging their stable doors, demanding breakfast. The lads laughed and joked, gravel crunching beneath their boots and buckets rattling as they crisscrossed from feed room to stables and back again. 'When did you marry?'

She was watching him closely, chin up, arms folded across her chest. 'Last night.'

'Who witnessed? Holze?'

There was a moment's hesitation before she answered. 'Nobody.'

'*Nobody*?' he said, incredulous. 'You mean you just exchanged vows with each other? No Barlsman? Whose crazy idea was that?'

The heat in her cheeks deepened. 'Mine.'

He wanted to scream. Stamp. Throw mugs at the wall and watch them shatter. 'Of course it was. Dathne, you're a fool! If there wasn't a Barlsman then you *aren't* married and it *is* futtering and if anybody finds out—'

'They'll only find out if you tell them!' she retorted. 'Save your breath, Matt. It's done and you can't undo it. And I was right. Whatever he's hiding, he almost told me last night.'

'Before or after you futtered him?' he said bitterly.

She slapped him, hard enough to burst stars before his eyes. 'Don't you dare.'

His face throbbed, but he ignored the pain. 'You say I'm your compass, but what good's a compass if you don't follow its directions? Ever since he came here I've said he should be told.'

'And he will be!'

'But only when it's too late! After this, after what you've done, when he finds out the truth he'll spit on you and walk away!'

'No, he won't.'

'Yes, he *will*. He'll walk away and Prophecy will fail and our lives will've been for *nothing*!'

There was fear in her face now, crowding out her defiant anger. 'You're wrong. He understands duty, Matt. And sacrifice. He wouldn't be the Innocent Mage if he didn't!'

'He may be the Innocent Mage, Dathne, but he's also a man! He's a man before he's anything else, and if you think a man can so easily forgive this kind of betrayal then it wouldn't matter if you'd futtered a *hundred* Ashers, you'd still be an ignorant girl!'

He was ready for her this time and caught her wrist before her hand reached his face.

'Let go of me,' she said, her voice a deadly whisper.

'Dathne—'

'*No*!' Her eyes were glittering. 'It's over, Matt. You're no use to me any more. I'm telling Veira you've stepped aside. Can I trust you'll hold your tongue? Say yes. You must know by now there's nothing I won't do in the service of Prophecy.'

'No,' he whispered back. 'Nothing. Not even strumpeting yourself.'

The office door swung open and in walked Asher, talking all the while. 'You in here, Matt? There's half a tree come down on the fence round Crooked Paddock and all the three year olds are out. Thought I'd best ride back and warn you, seein'—' He stopped, all friendliness freezing. 'What's goin' on? Dathne?'

Before she could answer, Matt turned on him. 'And *you*! Are you as mad as she is? You're the Olken Administrator! Don't you know what scandal there'll be if you're found to be futtering out of wedlock with your assistant? Not even the king will save you then!'

Incredulous, Asher stared at Dathne. 'You *told* him?'

'He saw us.'

'No, he didn't,' said Asher, and slammed the office door. 'He didn't see nowt. He don't know nowt. And if he values his bones unbroken he'll let go of you right now.'

Matt released Dathne's wrist and stared at the livid white marks his fingers left on her flesh. 'Tell him you made a mistake, Dathne. Please. Tell him everything.'

'What everything?' said Asher. His expression was ugly. 'What's he on about, Dath?'

She stepped forward, barring Asher's progress. 'Nothing. It's nothing. It doesn't matter. We were just talking.'

He didn't believe her. Gently he pushed her aside and came closer. Matt made himself meet his friend's unforgiving eyes. 'I asked you once if you had feelings for Dathne,' said Asher. 'You said no. Seems to me you lied, Matt.'

He turned to her. 'For Barl's sake, Dathne—'

'I'm sorry, Matt,' she said, and threaded her arm through Asher's. Her eyes were pitiless. 'I wish I could care the way you want me to, but it's Asher I love. Not you.'

*'Dathne!'*

'Look, Matt,' said Asher, voice and face thawing slightly, 'I'll make this easy on you. You're dismissed.'

He stared, stupid as a scarecrow. 'I'm what?'

'Dismissed,' said Asher. 'Let go. Relieved of your duties. I'm reassigning you to His Majesty's stud farm down the Dingles. I'll get Ganfel from over the palace stables to step in for now. He's a good man with horses, he'll see the place don't fall apart till I can decide who'll take over here.'

He shook his head. 'You can't—'

'I can,' said Asher. 'I have. It's done.'

Still, he couldn't believe it. 'But . . . but . . .'

'*It's done.*'

There was no fellowship in Asher's face now. No amusement or warm understanding. Matt wasn't sure he knew this man at all. 'I thought we were friends.'

Asher smiled. Stepped closer and lowered his voice. 'We are. Which is why you're walkin' out of here on your own two legs.' The smile vanished. 'You put your hand on her in anger, Matt. Ain't another man in all this kingdom who'd do that and walk away.' He stepped back again. 'Now, why don't you go see to them pesky sightseein' three year olds, eh? After that you can report to Darran. He'll help you with the particulars of gettin' resettled down to the farm.'

Matt turned again to Dathne. 'You're just going to stand there and let him—'

'I'm sorry, Matthias,' she said. She never called him Matthias. 'I do believe it's best this way.'

Her denial of him hurt worse than Asher's anger. Almost, he opened his mouth and blurted out the truth and Jervale's Heir be damned. But he couldn't do it. He'd sworn a sacred oath to obey her . . . and he'd keep it, no matter what that cost.

'What if I fight you?' he said to Asher in a strangled whisper. 'I could fight you.'

Asher shrugged. 'You'd lose. I never came to this dratted City lookin' for power, Matt, but it seems I ended up with it anyways. Ordinarily I ain't one for throwin' my weight around but for this I'll make an exception. Dath's right, even if you don't see it now. And you'll do fine down in the Dingles. Maybe you'll not be as high up the ladder there as you are here, but you're young yet. You'll manage.'

*You're young yet*, from a man six years his junior. Feeling like he'd been turned to solid wood, he nodded again. 'Yes, sir.' He allowed himself a pinch of sarcasm. 'Thank you, sir.'

Asher's eyes narrowed. 'Off you go then.'

Without looking back, without saying another word, he went.

# CHAPTER SEVENTEEN

Darran and Willer were already at work in their office when Asher returned to thc Tower, his hopes of a morning ride dashed to pieces. Cluny and her house-maid friends bustled about the foyer, putting fresh flowers in the vases, straightening the paintings on the walls. They dimpled and curtseyed as he strode in. It wasn't their fault he was in a killing mood, so he smiled and nodded and pretended not to notice the wary surprise in their eyes.

'Asher!' Darran called as he pounded up the stairs on his way to change clothes. 'A moment, please!'

'I'm busy,' he called back without stopping. 'I'll be down directly.'

A scuttling of footsteps behind him. A plump hand, plucking at his sleeve. 'Darran says it's urgent,' Willer gasped. 'It's about the weather.'

He pulled his arm free. 'What about it?'

There was definitely something . . . furtive . . . about Willer these days. He smiled too much, and in the wrong way. His familiar belligerence was drowned in sugar syrup and yet somewhere beneath the sticky sweetness a sharpened knife blade glinted, waiting. These days

Willer put his teeth on edge in a whole new and unpleasant way.

'Please come,' the sea slug said, his eyes wide and earnest. 'Darran needs you.'

And thanks to yet another promise to Gar, what Darran wanted Darran got, all in the name of nauseating bloody unity. Swallowing a string of curses, Asher followed Willer back down the stairs and into the secretary's office.

'What?'

Darran looked up from his desk. The sun had barely started its long slow crawl up the sky and there he was, crisp and shaven and immaculate in black, distressingly healthy, surrounded by ink pots and parchments and piles of important papers.

'As a matter of urgency I require the new Weather Schedule,' he said. No 'good morning', or 'sorry to interrupt you,' or any such common-and-garden pleasantries. Bloody ole crow. 'And a firm idea of how often His Majesty intends to prepare one. The palace informs me the late king drafted the weather patterns some six weeks in advance. Does His Majesty intend to maintain the same routine? Or does he anticipate an alteration? If so, I must know. I'm getting messages from all over the kingdom wondering when the next schedule will appear. People are agitating, Asher. I would much prefer they didn't.'

'Ask Gar. It's weather business, that is,' said Asher. 'Ain't none of my nevermind.'

'I'm making it your nevermind,' said Darran, and not without a gleam of malicious pleasure either, the miserable geezer.

'Sink me bloody sideways,' he muttered. His head was aching already and dawn was only five minutes ago. 'All right. When I get a minute I'll—'

'Now,' said Darran. 'If you please.'

Clearly, there was no escape. And anyways the ole crow was right, drat him: the last thing Gar needed was widespread agitation over a delayed Weather Schedule. That'd suit Conroyd bloody Jarralt right down to the ground, that would.

Willer was goggling at him, fat lips pursed in a smile. He scowled. 'What are you bloody lookin' at, eh?'

Willer's smile widened. 'Why, nothing at all, Asher. I promise.'

'Well, go look at it someplace else. You're makin' me seasick!' And on that mildly satisfying note he headed for the door . . . only to turn back halfway, remembering. 'Matt's transferrin' down to the Dingles stud farm, Darran. Draft me a letter of recommendation to sign, would you? Lots of compliments. And send a runner to the Treasury so's he can take his money with him, and one to the palace for Ganfel to take over just now.'

Darran exchanged a surprised look with Willer. 'Matt is leaving? Why?'

'Personal reasons. Nobody's business but his own. I'll tell the king. No need for you to bother him about it. He don't need to be fratched with anythin' else just now. Right? That means you too, Willer. Not a bloody word.'

Frowning, Darran said, 'Willer knows the meaning of discretion as well as I do, Asher. Matt's departure shall not be mentioned outside this room.' He sighed. 'But I think it a great pity. His Majesty's very fond of him.'

Asher felt a stab of pain. *And so was I fond of him, before he laid hands on Dathne* . . . Then he shrugged, and continued to the door. 'Folk move on, Darran. You can't hold onto 'em.'

He overtook Cluny on the last flight of stairs up to Gar's suite. She was carrying the king's breakfast tray, and dimpled when she saw him.

'Morning, Asher.'

The wafting aromas of bacon, fried potato, scrambled eggs and hot bread teased his empty stomach and doused his mouth with saliva. 'Morning. Want me to take that up for you?'

'Oh, would you?' said Cluny, pink-cheeked and grateful. 'Only we've a maid with the collywobbles and there's ever so much to do.' She thrust the covered breakfast tray into his hands, dimpled again, enchantingly, and flew back down the stairs. Despite all his aggravations, he smiled after her. He liked Cluny. A lot. If it hadn't been for Dathne . . .

His blood stirred, thinking of her. *We're married . . . we're married!* Thinking of all they'd done the night before and soon would do again, he hoped. With that warm pleasure to sustain him, crowding out all dark thoughts of Matt, he headed on up the stairs.

Gar was in his library, barricaded behind towers of books. Asher kicked the door shut behind him and wandered over to stand in front of the desk.

'Breakfast.'

Gar grunted and kept on working. Asher sat down, tray in his lap, uncovered a plate and filched a crispy slice of bacon. Kicking his boot heels onto a handy table he sat back with a sigh, crunching. Then noticed what was different about Gar's crowded, chaotic library.

There was a new painting on the far wall.

Well. Not new new. But new to the Tower. Sucking bacon grease from his fingers he studied the enormous portrait. The royal family stood beside a spreading djelba in full bloom; the velvet pink petals looked real enough to touch. Behind them the pristine white walls of the palace, jewelled windows glinting in the sunshine. And behind the palace Barl's Wall, soaring triumphantly into the cloudless sky. It was a masterful painting, commissioned from one of the kingdom's finest Doranen artists. Lord Someone-or-other. Short, skinny, busy fingers, temper like a sex-starved tomcat. *Bracan.*

He'd caught his subjects seemingly between breaths. Borne was smiling, Dana seemed ready to laugh. Fane looked so beautiful it broke a man's heart. Remembering them, he felt his throat close hard and tight. Painted Gar stood beside his sister, one hand resting on her shoulder. Posed by Bracan, doubtless. You'd never catch them touching on purpose, unless it was to slap or stab. Gar was smiling too, but his eyes were sad. As though he knew something the others didn't. As though he could see the future, and was sorry.

'We were a handsome family, weren't we?' said Gar.

Asher nodded, melancholy settling like a mist. 'Aye.'

Gar turned away from the painting. 'I miss them so much,' he said, his voice low. Unsteady. 'Even Fane.'

'I know.'

'I just received word from Nix,' Gar said, and flicked a discarded note with one fingertip. 'Durm is awake again and much improved. He's asking to see me.'

Damn. Unsettled, Asher drank some of Gar's teshoe juice. 'You goin'?'

'Of course.'

'When?'

'Soon.'

He chewed his lip. 'Durm know about your family yet?'

'No.' Gar examined an ink stain on his finger. 'When I tell him, and he learns I'm now the king, he'll ask about my magic. The WeatherWorking. And if he senses something's wrong – if my lies don't fool him – well. It doesn't bear thinking about.' Then he frowned. 'Is that my breakfast you're eating?'

'Aye.' He held out the tray. 'You want it?'

'Not anymore.' Elbows resting on the desk, Gar considered him. 'You all right? You had me worried last night.'

He helped himself to a slice of toast. Bit. Chewed. Swallowed. 'I'm fine.'

'Really? You look . . . angry. Are you having second thoughts? I wouldn't blame you if you were. Last night's Working was hard.'

Asher scowled at the breakfast tray. He had bigger problems than the WeatherWorking just now. If he told Gar about Matt, things would get very messy very fast. Doubtless Gar would order his stable meister's reinstatement, and Matt needed putting in his place. Deserved some punishment for so distressing Dathne. A month or two in the Dingles would serve him right. He could come back after that. After he'd had time to cool his heels and accept the fact that Dathne would never be his.

None of which he could tell Gar. Far better to let Matt slip away quietly and then tell Gar after the event. He shook his head. 'Darran's been jawin' at me, is all. Wants the new Weather Schedule. Today.'

'I don't have time today.'

'Then make time,' he said, scowling. 'You said you'd fix things so the WeatherWorkin'd go a bit easier on me. Here's your chance.'

Gar waved a hand at the books on his desk. Waved again at the books piled on the carpet beside his chair. 'I know what I said. But Asher, I can do the Weather Schedule or I can keep on ploughing through Durm's library in search of the solution to our problems. I can't do both, and you're the one complaining I'm not reading fast enough.'

With a rattle of plates and cutlery Asher dumped the breakfast tray on the floor. 'Gar—'

'I'm serious!' said Gar. 'With Durm awake again we could have less time than we planned. If his recovery proceeds swiftly – if he's able to return to his own apartments before our month is up—'

All the books would have to go back. And Durm, learning of their removal, might suspect something was wrong. Questions could be asked – secrets revealed—

Abruptly his pilfered breakfast curdled in his belly and hot fear rose in his throat. 'Then we'll be in the shit, won't we?'

Gar sat back, regarding him steadily with narrowed eyes. 'You *are* having second thoughts.'

'One of us has to!' Restless in his chair, he stared through the nearest window. 'With your da gone Durm's the strongest magician in the kingdom now, ain't he?'

'Yes.'

'Pity you can't declare him king.'

Gar shook his head. 'It's against the law. No one can be WeatherWorker and Master Magician both.'

'Then give him the crown and find another Master Magician.'

'It would have to be Jarralt,' Gar pointed out. 'Which doesn't help us much. Anyway, Conroyd would never accept the lesser prize. Not in favour of Durm. And Durm's not married, he's childless and has no prospect of an heir. It's grounds for a challenge, Conroyd knows it, and we're back to schism again.'

Damn. It seemed every way they turned there was Conroyd bloody Jarralt standing in the way. He scowled at his boots, thinking. 'Look,' he said at last, 'I know you don't want to hear this, Gar, but I don't reckon you got much choice. With Durm awake it's too dangerous for us to keep on the way we've been. Go to him today. Tell him what's happened, that your magic's failed.'

'I can't tell him about you!'

'Of course you bloody can't!' he said, alarmed. 'You'll have to lie, won't you? Say your magic failed last night. And if he can't fix you and Jarralt has to be named king, at least he'll be there as Master Magician to keep him in line.'

'Only if he makes a full recovery,' said Gar. 'And if Conroyd is content for him to stay Master Magician.'

'That ain't his decision, is it?'

'Technically, no,' said Gar, pulling a face. 'But in truth I'd not put it past Conroyd to push Durm from power. He knows too well Durm's opinion of him. And that Durm's loyalty will always be first and foremost to House Torvig.'

'Durm knows that, though. He won't let Jarralt shuffle him off without a fight. And Jarralt won't raise a public ruckus over it – he'd lose support in a heartbeat.'

Gar's expression was mulish. 'I don't care. This is all speculation, Asher. So long as Durm doesn't know what's happened I still have a chance to find a cure on my own and remain king. The second we make my infirmity known, it's over. Now you promised me a month. Do you keep that promise, or walk away from it?'

*Bastard.* He'd never gone back on a promise in his life, and Gar knew it. 'All right,' he said, not caring how surly he sounded. 'But here's fair warning. One month and not a day or even an hour longer. That's our agreement and that's what I'll hold you to. Even if you drop to your knees and beg.'

'I won't,' said Gar, unsmiling. 'I have my honour, as you have yours. My word is my word and won't be broken. Do you doubt it?'

'No. Just want my position understood, is all.'

Gar nodded. 'It's understood. Now leave me so I can get back to these wretched books. If you want to be useful, go see Durm in my stead. Give him my regards. Find out from Nix how his recovery proceeds.'

Asher stood. Drifted towards the door, eager to be gone. 'And if Durm asks when he'll see you?'

'Soon,' said Gar. Picking up his pen, he returned his attention to his parchments. 'Tell him he'll see me soon. And, Asher?'

Hand on the door latch, he turned. 'Aye?'

'Tell Nix to break the news about my family.'

'Right,' he said, after a moment. And closed the door gently behind him.

Morg glared at the gormless young pother attempting to foist upon him yet another dose of herbal muck. 'Unless you desire ears like a rabbit I suggest you go away!'

The nitwit blanched. 'I'm sorry, sir, it's Pother Nix's orders.'

'Then fetch me Pother Nix so I might rescind his ridiculous orders!'

'Sir,' the nitwit said faintly, and scuttled away.

Groaning, Morg lay back upon his raft of pillows. Damn this broken body. With Durm at last defeated, safely silenced and caged once more, he'd thought his mastery complete.

But no. Chained to the vagaries of a corporeal existence, he found himself still weak. Still hostage. Twice this morning he'd tried to rise and twice Durm's mangled remains had defeated him. The situation was intolerable. There had to be another way . . .

The chamber door opened, admitting Nix. He looked displeased. 'Durm, I must insist you don't frighten my staff. They are merely acting upon my instructions. Do you wish to make a full recovery or don't you?'

Morg bared his teeth. He had no time for a full recovery. This body was old and weakened, first with excess, now with injury. And he had lingered in this place for far too long.

In the doorway behind the pother, unnoticed, lurked crippled Gar's pet Olken. He pointed. 'What is he doing here?'

Nix turned. Saw the upstart and raged. 'I told you to wait outside, Asher! The Master Magician is not ready for vis—'

'Sorry, but I got orders from the king,' the upstart said stubbornly. 'A message.'

Because Durm was not supposed to know of Borne's death, Morg struggled against his pillows and let his voice tremble. 'From Borne? I don't understand. Why does he not deliver his message in person?'

As Nix glared, murderous, the Olken stepped forward. 'It's all right, Nix. Gar said to tell him.'

Morg let his voice grow faint. 'Tell me? Tell me what?'

Rage relinquished, the pother sighed and folded his hands. 'I'm sorry, Durm. We kept the news from you for fear it would be too much to bear. Borne is dead. The queen, too, and Princess Fane.'

'Dead?' Morg whispered, and let Durm's grief well into his eyes. Dribble down his cheeks. 'No . . . no . . . may Barl have mercy . . .'

'Gar is our king now,' Nix murmured. 'The Wall stands strong in his stewardship.'

Yes, but *why*? Morg raged behind his mask of tears. *How*, when his magic should have died long since? 'Poor boy. To be orphaned and crowned in such swift, unkind succession,' he said brokenly. 'I must see him. I beg you, Nix, send for him at once. I will not rest until I can—'

'I'm sorry, sir,' said the upstart Olken. 'I'm here to give you His Majesty's regards and say he will come, soon.'

'But not now?' Morg dashed Durm's tears from his cheeks and let himself sag, frail and pathetic, against his pillows. 'Why not now? Is something wrong? Is the WeatherWorking too hard for him? Does his magic not hold?'

The Olken stiffened. Watching closely, Morg saw something flicker in his eyes. And knew that whatever words next fell from his lips would be a lie.

'Why would you wonder that, sir? His Majesty's magic holds strong and true. He's his father's son, right enough. He'll tell you so himself just as soon as he can.'

Nix said sharply, 'And if that is your message delivered, Asher, you may leave. The Master Magician has enough to contend with for now.'

Gar's pet bowed. 'Sir.' Bowed again to Durm. 'Sir. You got any message for the king? Reckon he'd be heartened by a word or two. No disrespect intended, but he's been frettin' for you somethin' fierce.'

Morg squeezed out another tear. 'The dear, dear boy. Tell him this, Asher. I love him, and grieve with him, and promise him this: that together we shall see our kingdom reach its glorious destiny, ordained on the day Barl came over the mountains.'

The Olken exchanged a baffled glance with Nix and bowed again. 'Aye, sir. I'll tell him.'

He departed. Nix too, after more fussing. Ablaze with triumph, Morg allowed himself a raucous, silent crowing.

The cripple was failing. The time at last had come.

All he needed now was a way out of Durm's used-up, useless body . . . and the victory would be his.

Conroyd Jarralt walked downstairs to the musical strains of Ethienne berating a servant. 'I particularly asked for *yellow* roses, you useless girl! Are you colour-blind? Or just stupid, like the rest of your Olken friends?'

The servant was on the brink of tears; brimming eyes, flushed cheeks and a trembling lower lip. Ignoring her, he slid an arm around his ranting wife's shoulders and smoothly swept her with him along the hallway to the foyer and front door. 'That's enough, Ethienne. They're flowers, not a matter of life and death.'

She pouted. 'But, Conroyd—'

He tightened his encircling arm, squeezing her to silence. 'Like little starlings in their nest, my dear, Olken servants twitter. And with the Olken lout so close to the throne and wielding influence I would prefer he received no fourth-hand reports claiming I permit the mistreatment of his people under my roof. Understood?'

She wriggled and he let her go. Watched as she smoothed her hair with immaculately manicured fingers. Jewelled rings flashed in the afternoon sunshine filtering through their townhouse's tall windows. Her ageing, perfectly made-up face was sulky. 'Yes, Conroyd.'

He kissed her scented cheek. Softened his manner, because Ethienne always responded most readily to coaxing. 'I have business with Holze. Shall I bring you home some yellow roses?'

She reached up and flattened the folds of his silk

cravat. Echoes of the flirting girl he'd married. 'Very well. And don't be late! The Daltries and the Sorvolds are guesting here this evening, remember?'

He did. And with luck he'd have news for them that would add extra spice to the meal. 'Of course, my dear,' he said, and kissed her cheek again. 'Till this evening.'

He closed the front door on her simpering laughter and ensconced himself in his bright blue carriage, the one with his house emblem blazoned proudly on both doors. The horses drawing it were blood bays, caparisoned with equal pride.

This was not a day for stealth. At least, not overtly.

Dorana's mood was elevated, he noted, as the carriage rumbled briskly from his townhouse to the centre of the City. The gloom of the past weeks was gone, doubtless washed away by Gar's proficient WeatherWorking. The Doranen and Olken faces he passed were smiling, carefree. Relieved. Death's shadow had blotted out the sun, but only for a moment.

He let the carriage curtain fall back to cover the window and rested his head on the cushions behind him. Despite Durm's inconvenient recovery and Willer's failure to uncover malfeasance beneath Gar's roof, still he refused to abandon hope. There was one last weapon in his battle for power that he'd yet to lay his hands upon . . .

He found Holze in the cleric's Barl's Chapel study. It was a small room, unadorned save for the ubiquitous portrait of Barl hanging above a perpetual candle. Warm light flickered across the saviour's grave young face, her golden hair, the long plait that trailed over her left shoulder. The chamber's atmosphere bordered on the unpleasantly chill.

Holze was reading a religious text and making notes.

'Conroyd!' he said, looking up from behind his plain desk as an acolyte ushered his visitor into the room. 'Gracious. Am I expecting you? I don't recall—'

'Efrim,' said Jarralt, deliberately genial. 'No. I came in the hope you'd be free and able to spare me some of your valuable time.' He threw a pointed glance at the acolyte. 'On matters of state.'

'Of course, of course.' Holze closed his religious text, disposed of his pen and dismissed the acolyte with a smile and a nod. 'Have a seat.'

For reasons best kept to himself Holze didn't believe in comfortable chairs. Jarralt arranged himself in the uncompromising wooden stool-and-back arrangement beside the cleric's desk and folded tranquil hands in his lap.

'I realise any reservations I express regarding our kingdom's current circumstances will be seen by some as nothing more than the mouthings of an ambitious, embittered man. But I hope you'll see them for what they truly are: an honest concern for Lur's future.'

Advancing age had failed to dull Holze's wits. His eyes were sharp and his expression astute as he said, 'You're here about Durm. And the king.'

Jarralt nodded. 'Yes. And while you and I haven't always agreed, still I think you know me as a man who loves this kingdom, Efrim, and wants only what is in its best interests.'

'Yes, Conroyd. I do.'

'Please believe me, what I have to say gives me no pleasure. But to stay silent would be a betrayal of everything I hold dear.' He kissed his holyring. 'Of Blessed Barl herself.'

Holze sighed. 'Go on.'

'I am trying to remember that His Majesty is young

and recently bereaved,' Jarralt said, frowning. 'And that Durm has devoted his whole life to Lur's prosperity. But I am deeply worried and have no one else to whom I can, in confidence, turn to for advice.'

'Unburden yourself, Conroyd,' Holze said gently. 'Share your misgivings with me and together we'll find a way to ease your troubled mind.'

Jarralt resisted the urge to resettle himself on the uncomfortable chair, and instead schooled his expression to one of sober, sombre confession. 'Borne was a great king. We weren't close, for obvious reasons, but I would never deny his power as a WeatherWorker. Question his domestic decisions, yes. And the way he used his influence, his charisma, to further his dynastic ambitions. That in particular I deplored. But it was done, and ratified, and even I could see that Fane was something out of the ordinary.'

'Gar is hardly mundane either,' Holze pointed out.

'But for all the wrong reasons, Efrim. He was a cripple for most of his life. Magical as a rock. And then, without warning, his power burst upon him and nobody questioned it. Nobody thought it was odd. They were too busy celebrating the miracle.' Hearing his own bitterness, he took a moment to moderate his tone. 'And now with Borne dead, Fane dead, he's our WeatherWorker. Charged with the most sacred magic in the kingdom. And nobody thinks to ask if he's suitable. Or stable. Nobody has thought to wonder if that capricious magic might leave him as suddenly as it arrived.'

Holze's fingers stroked the rat-tail Barlbraid on his shoulder. 'Durm said his legitimacy as a magician is beyond reproach.'

It was no good. He could tolerate the chair no longer. Pushing to his feet, he paced the small, cool chamber.

'Durm was the closest thing Borne had to a brother. Borne loved him uncritically and trusted him without question – feelings that were returned tenfold. I doubt there is nothing Durm wouldn't do if it meant protecting his dead friend's dynastic claim to the throne.'

'That . . . is a serious accusation, Conroyd,' said Holze. He looked and sounded troubled.

'Don't mistake me, Efrim!' he said, raising one hand. 'Durm would never break the law or act against the interests of the kingdom. Not consciously, at least. But I have come to wonder whether his judgement is to be trusted where Borne's son is concerned. And now . . . with these terrible injuries . . . the ravages of grief . . . can we be certain there's been no permanent damage? Is it safe, or wise, to trust him without question?'

Holze nodded slowly. 'I confess, Conroyd . . . these are matters I have myself been pondering.'

Jarralt smothered unseemly elation. 'And there is yet another matter. More disturbing even than Durm's precarious position. Asher.'

Holze let his gaze settle on Barl's portrait. 'You've never much cared for him. Or his people.'

'Perhaps not, but that doesn't mean my concerns aren't legitimate. This Olken has the ear of our king, and the power to persuade him towards actions that might not be in our best interests. He's been made a Privy Councillor! Are you at ease with this? For I'm not!'

'No,' said Holze eventually. Unhappily. 'I, too, find Gar's deepening reliance on Asher . . . disturbing. Barl gave the Olken into our keeping. They are a simple people, ill-equipped to deal with matters of magic or high government.'

Tasting victory, he crossed to Holze's side and dropped to one imploring knee. 'Then, Efrim, we can stay silent no longer. You are Lur's most senior cleric. Both of us serve as Privy Councillors. Gar's fitness as ruler is demonstrably questionable. For the good of the kingdom we *must* act. We owe Borne's memory nothing less.'

Holze's elderly face crumpled. 'Conroyd, Conroyd, I fear you're talking about a second schism.'

'*No*!' he said, and rested an urgent hand on Holze's reluctant arm. 'I'm talking about saving our people from a compromised king and his questionable Master Magician before it's too late and our moral cowardice destroys us all.'

Holze turned his face away, distress in every frail line of his body. 'How do you suggest we proceed?'

'Then you're with me? When I take this matter to the General Council, you'll add your voice to mine?'

'Don't you mean, will I champion you as Lur's next king?' Holze said bitterly, his face still averted.

'Only if that is Barl's will. Perhaps you should ask her, Efrim.'

Holze sighed. 'I already have. Change is coming, whether we welcome it or not.'

Heart singing, face grave, he again kissed his holyring. 'Then may Barl's will be done. And thank you for your support.'

'I don't see I have a choice Conroyd,' Holze whispered. 'Even though I fear we'll break two hearts with this.'

He stood. 'Better two hearts than a whole kingdom, Efrim. Remember that when your conscience pricks you.' He adjusted his coat and cravat. 'I'll go now to the infirmary. Speak with Durm and assess his condition. After that we'll talk further. Agreed?'

Reluctantly, Holze nodded. 'Agreed.'

* * *

Morg floated beneath the surface of awareness like a fly drowning in honey. Damned Nix and his damned potions, thrusting him yet again into helpless impotence. Rage was somewhere. Desperation too. And Durm. Gibbering witlessly now, the force of his personality diminished to a thinness, a shadow, a mere suggestion of his former self. How he longed to let the fat fool die . . . but the risk was too great. Body and soul were still tied, and if the connection were broken there was some small chance the carcass would vomit its unwelcome lodger into the ether, and death.

It wasn't a chance he was prepared to take.

He heard – felt – the door to his chamber, his prison, open. Footsteps. Voices. The door closed again. He tried to open Durm's eyes, struggled to impose his weakened will on the drugged flesh that enveloped him tighter than a virgin's body. The drugged flesh defeated him, again.

'There, my lord. You see?' The pother. Sounding irate. Affronted. 'As I told you, the Master Magician is still sleeping. He cannot speak with you!' A wicked man, Nix, overflowing with pestilent herb lore. Interfering, meddlesome. There'd come a day soon when Pother Nix would choke himself to a bloody froth on a *banquet* of herbs . . .

'My apologies, Nix, if I appeared to question your competence, or honesty.' And that was Conroyd Jarralt. Blood called to the memory of blood. Echoes of ancestry. Hope, stirring. The blossoming of a germinated idea . . .

'If it is so important that you confer with him, my lord, perhaps when he wakes I can ask him if—'

'Good pother,' said little lord Jarralt. 'May I speak my mind to you? Trusting of course in your absolute discretion?'

'You may, my lord.'

'Your word as a pother on it?'

'Certainly!'

A sighing silence. Then: 'It's no secret, Nix, to those of us whose business it is to know such things that Durm's injuries were savage.'

'They were.'

'So savage his survival is a miracle?'

'Yes.'

'So savage that to think he might regain his former strength and power undiminished is . . . regrettably . . . little more than a daydream?'

A long hesitation. 'My lord . . .'

'Say no more,' said Jarralt, all sweet sympathy. 'Your face answers all.'

'Lord Jarralt—'

'It is a delicate matter. I understand.' Such kindness in that warm molasses voice. 'And painful. You answer to a king who perhaps has . . . lost perspective.'

Struggling to surface, Morg thrashed feebly against the weight of Nix's damnable drugs. There was ambition here, he could smell it like a demon scenting birth-blood. Ambition and a ruthless will to win at all costs. *Splendid.* This Jarralt was strong . . . and now more than ever he required strength. Had been kept prisoner by weakness for long enough.

Jarralt was the answer to a prayer.

The pother cleared his poxy throat. 'My lord, you know I am constrained—'

'Of course,' soothed his ambitious descendant. 'I understand you perfectly. Be not alarmed, Nix. We are cut from the same cloth, you and I. Men of honour sworn to serve this kingdom above all else, even the bonds of personal attachment. Durm is my friend. We've served together on the Privy Council for many years and his fall from greatness breaks my heart. Yet despite that, I'll do what's necessary to safeguard Lur from harm. As will you, I'm sure. Now I wonder if I might have a little time alone with my friend? Affairs of state have kept me from his side and I would lend him whatever strength he can use.'

'Certainly, my lord,' said the mewling pother. 'But I warn you, he's heavily sedated. If he should wake be good enough to send for me at once.'

Morg heard the chamber door open. Close. Heard footsteps come closer to the bed. Heard Conroyd Jarralt laugh softly. Seductively. A man on the brink of conquest.

'Well, Durm. Now it is just we two alone,' he whispered. 'And I shall tell you how the story ends . . .'

# CHAPTER EIGHTEEN

It wasn't the voice of a friend. It echoed with avarice, with deep dislike and ambition long denied.

Suddenly Morg realised he was in danger.

He thought his mind would twist apart then, so frantically did he try to break the stuporous bonds holding him prisoner. With outraged astonishment he recognised the acid emotion: fear.

*Fear*?

When was the last time he'd felt such a thing? Had he ever felt it? He couldn't remember. No, no. It wasn't possible. Morg – the supreme power of the world – *afraid*?

Never.

Or . . . never before now. But now he was helpless, trapped, at the mercy of this man who stank of a desire for death. Durm's death. *His* death, for so long as he remained in Durm's body. He'd thought to house himself in Jarralt next. In a day or two, once Durm was finally free of drugs and he could act unhindered.

But here was the vessel now, fattened with plottings of its own and suddenly there was no *time* . . .

There came the sound of timber scraping tile as a chair was pulled closer to the bed. A sighing creak of springs, a swish of silk against silk. Cool fingers touching fevered flesh.

'I never liked you, Durm,' said Jarralt. The molasses was melting, revealing the naked blade within. 'And you never liked me. Yet we continued to play our silly game of pretend, didn't we, in order to keep Borne happy. To keep the people happy and ensure unadulterated peace. You always thought I loved myself more than this kingdom, but you were wrong. If that had been true I would have challenged Borne's right to rule long ago.'

With a greater force of will than he'd ever before exerted, Morg calmed his raging spirit. Experienced another unfamiliar emotion: shame, that he could so completely forget himself, if only for a moment. It was a contaminant, this flesh. It polluted the purity of the unfettered mind, shackled it to urges and impulses and infirmity.

He couldn't wait to leave it behind.

Jarralt was softly laughing. 'Notice I'm referring to you in the past tense, old man. Broken man. Defeated man. Your tenure as Master Magician is over. Soon I will take your place, but not for long. Before the year is out I'll have the means to bring down brave House Torvig, brick by rotten brick. Then Conroyd will be king. As I should've been king twenty-five years ago. What do you think of *that*, Durm?'

In the depths of his cage, Durm was also struggling. Morg felt some fleeting sympathy. Focusing his will, drawing his weakened powers close about him like a cloak, he saw himself as a lance of fire poised to pierce the veil of Nix's cloying, thwarting drugs. The flame consumed itself, consumed the remaining strength he'd not used up in his fight to live despite Durm's mangled body.

'Were I so inclined I could smother you here and now,' crooned Jarralt. 'Shall I do it? Do I dare? The way your body's ruined it might even be a mercy. You were never one for weakness. You'd have smothered Gar if you could. Would Borne have loved you, I wonder, had he known? Had he seen in the depths of your eyes what I saw the day his son's crippledom was made public?'

Morg felt his spirit shudder. Heard Durm's sickbed creak as Jarralt leaned upon it. A warm, sweet breath fanned Durm's flaccid face. Soft, strong hands clasped close the hollowed cheeks. As he struggled to escape Durm's useless body he heard a gloating whisper.

'There's a shadow falling over you, Durm. Do you feel it? It's the shadow of House Jarralt, plunging you deep into an endless dark . . .'

The hands resting against Durm's face tightened. Thumbs hot as coals pressed hard against his eyeballs, burning through tissue-paper lids. Morg felt his spirit spasm, felt a great leap of power to power, like to like, a song of lust and greed and unslaked thirsts. From far away he heard Durm's dreadful wail of anguish.

'Look at me, you drug-soaked carcass!' hissed Jarralt. 'Look at me and see how I have won!'

Blinding brightness, as Jarralt's thumbs forced open Durm's pain-sunken eyes. Morg gloried in it, revelled in it, felt the final surging flare of his strength and will break through the barrier between himself and the wider world. The clammy bonds of failing flesh snapped at last and he was free of Durm's broken body, free of that terrible prison, free to pour himself into a new host, a perfect host, a vital, vigorous, voracious host.

Jarralt opened his mouth to scream – and Morg poured into him. Flowed through arteries and veins, soaked skin and sinew, suffused Jarralt's muscle and bone and brain until no single cell remained that was not himself. Left Durm behind and dying, his tongue tied tight against utterances of *Morg*.

Pulling away from abandoned Durm like a man who has unwittingly handled offal, Morg strutted the confines of the infirmary chamber and revelled in the glory of his new host: a man in his prime, fit and lithe and fabulously handsome. At last, flesh worthy of his spirit! Captive deep inside himself Jarralt shrieked and scrabbled and clawed.

In the bed, propped up by pillows, Durm breathed slowly, heavily, dragging air into his lungs with reluctance.

Morg smiled. 'Fat fool. A pity you'll not be here to see my final triumph.' The sound of his words wrapped in Jarralt's exquisite voice was a shock. He'd grown used to Durm's unromantic gravelling. Reaching, he touched a slender finger to the ruined man's flabby, sallow cheek. Prepared to extinguish his sputtering life.

The chamber door swung open and Nix cleared his throat. 'My lord, forgive me, but Durm is in need of further physicking. You may return tomorrow, if that's your desire.'

Morg straightened. 'I would like that, Nix. Affairs of state permitting.'

'Of course, sir,' said the pother. 'I hope you derived some comfort from your visit, my lord?'

He gave Durm's pillows a hearty pat, as though he were concerned with the care and comfort of the patient, and swung about to smile at the pother.

'Comfort? Dear Pother Nix,' he said, in that magical, musical voice, 'you have no idea.'

* * *

Feeling perverse, not even waiting for his palace replacement Ganfel to arrive, Matt packed up his small hoard of belongings, cleared out of his stable yard accommodation while the lads were busy elsewhere, and took a room at Verry's Hostelry. He needed time alone to absorb what had happened that morning and decide how best to go on from here.

Asher had dismissed him. And Dathne had stood by, letting it happen. Hadn't lifted so much as a *finger* to save him . . .

The pain of that calamitous confrontation was savage. Jervale save him, could he have handled matters any worse? He was a *fool*. He should've waited. Should've tackled Dathne somewhere, *anywhere* else. Should've given himself time to calm down. Think things through. *'She's a racehorse, not a brood mare.'* That's what he'd told Asher. And then, forgetting all his own sage advice, like the clumsiest clot-head apprentice stable lad he'd tried to ride roughshod over her. Knowing full well she was mad in love with Asher. Seeing with his own two eyes that she was newly risen from a night in his arms, all aglow with passion and in no mood for sober chiding.

*And you wonder why sometimes she doubts your wisdom?*

Well, the milk was all spilled now and the jug smashed to pieces for good measure. She'd made her decision quite clear.

*'Go away, Matt. You're not wanted any more.'*

Well, he might not be wanted but he'd damn well be needed. Forget Asher's high-handed decree. He couldn't bury himself down in the Dingles, it was too distant. Trouble was, he couldn't stay here in Dorana either. He needed somewhere else, somewhere safe, where he could watch over Dathne and her Innocent Mage without fear of discovery.

Feeling like a traitor he rummaged through his hastily packed belongings and unearthed the chip of crystal he'd never before had to use. Never imagined he'd need to use. That he'd never told Dathne he possessed.

Veira answered almost immediately. Her surprise was shot through with sudden alarm. *Matthias? Is that you?*

'Yes, Veira. It's me.' And was surprised himself to feel the pricking of unexpected tears.

She sensed them, and her manner gentled. *What's happened, child?*

Quickly, stumbling a little with nerves and emotion, he told her.

*I should have suspected it*, Veira replied slowly. *I knew she loved him and of late she's been . . . evasive. Wound tight as tight, with Prophecy's slow progress. Can you not speak with her? Find your way back to understanding?*

'No. She's got the bit between her teeth, Veira. The only voice she hears right now is Asher's. If I stay, if I try and force a reconciliation, I fear I'll just drive her further away. And she needs me still, I know it.'

*As do I, child, and all our precious Circle. So you must come to me and together we'll wait for Prophecy's wheel to turn again. Don't despair, Matt. Jervale will not abandon us now.*

Relief was so great it was almost like pain. He wasn't alone. He had somewhere to go. A job still to do. 'All right, Veira,' he said. 'I'll make arrangements and leave at first light.'

*On a cherry blossom day in the Royal Gardens, Gar chases his giggling sister between and around the cultivated pansy beds, the rows of quiet peters, brilliantly blue, the sapling trunks of youthful flowering pim-pim trees. He chases, but not too closely. Her baby legs are chubby, her unshod baby feet stomp the grass with delight, but unsurely. In the radiant sunshine her hair is a crown of gold thistledown, suggesting another crown yet to come.*

*'Can't catch me, Gar! Can't catch me!'*

*He's not even trying, but she doesn't know that. He pretends to be winded and pants at her, 'You're too fast for me, Fane!'*

*Somewhere close by, just out of sight, their parents are watching. He knows they worry about him. Worry he might not love his little sister for having in abundance the magic he was born without. They needn't, but he can't tell them that. They think he doesn't know why shadows lurk behind their smiles.*

*They're his parents, Lur's king and queen, but still, they are mistaken. He knows.*

*Up ahead, his sister stumbles. Her baby legs buckle and she tumbles headlong to the ground. Grass stains smear her pretty pink frock, her petal-soft skin. There is a moment of shocked silence and then she begins to cry.*

*He swoops. Gathers her up in his big strong nine-year-old arms. Cuddles her to his green and bronze weskit, brand new, a present from Mama. For why? Just because.*

*Because he is different . . . less . . . and not supposed to know it, or feel less loved.*

*Fane sobs against his chest in rage as much as fright. Her rosebud hands make small knobby fists and she beats them against the air. She's a feisty one, his little sister. She'll have the world her way or not at all. Two years of age just gone, she is, and everyone who knows her knows that.*

*'It's all right, Faney, please don't cry,' he begs her, rocking and jigging to lull her to laughter. 'I'm here. I've got you. You don't have to cry.'*

*She hiccups. Swallows furious grief. Tips back her small head, looks into his face and smiles . . . and smiles . . . and smiles . . .*

'Fane,' said Gar, and opened his eyes. His face was wet with tears.

Behind his bedchamber's heavy velvet curtains, a glow of mid-morning sun. A new day, beset with old problems.

Durm again was deeply stuporous.

Telling him yesterday evening, Nix had been nearly incoherent with despair and disbelief. He couldn't understand it. The Master Magician had been fine all morning. Had accepted, grudgingly, the need for more rest in the afternoon. Had swallowed his medicine and gone straight to sleep. Not even Lord Jarralt's brief visit had disturbed him. Everything about him appeared as it should . . . And yet he would not wake.

Most like would never wake now. It was time to accept the unacceptable: Lur's Master Magician would not recover.

Nix blamed himself, of course, but it wasn't anyone's fault. People died, whether you wanted them to or not.

Swaddled in a cocoon of blankets, Gar brooded at the pale green ceiling. If he could swallow that bitter pill he could swallow another one, too. Had to swallow it, because that's what kings did. They faced unpalatable truths.

His charade as WeatherWorker was over.

With Durm mere days – maybe hours – away from dying, he had nowhere left to turn. Conroyd would now demand he be made Master Magician and with no reasonable way of denying the appointment the truth of his magical blighting would come out. There was no way he could hide it any longer.

He'd gambled, and he'd lost.

Duty demanded he go to Conroyd this very morning, admit his magic had deserted him, and offer the man his crown. His kingdom. To do otherwise would not only be a betrayal of his sacred oath, it would put Asher in danger of discovery.

And that was out of the question.

Making Conroyd king. The merest thought of it was enough to close his throat, stifle his lungs, make him sweat and sweat. Everything within him resisted, strenuously, the idea of making Conroyd king.

Groaning, he rolled out of bed. Relieved himself – it reminded him of Indigo Glospottle, and coaxed a fleeting smile – scraped overnight stubble from his chin and cheeks, fumbled his hair into a rough-and-ready plait then found clothes to cover his nakedness. His belly rumbled but the thought of food made him nauseous. He sat in an armchair and returned to his brooding.

What would his father do, faced with this dilemma?

The answer came swiftly. *Fight.*

Borne would fight this, as he'd fought when his son's lack of magic could no longer stay a secret. The law was clear on the question of royal children. *One* heir to the throne. But Borne had known then what his son knew now: that to meekly submit to the law meant the ascension of House Jarralt and the fall of his own. Meant surrendering the care of the kingdom and its peoples to a man half convinced that Olken weren't people at all. Just slightly intelligent cattle. They weren't. And to treat them so would lead to civil war.

So Borne sidestepped the law. Fought with his councils, both Privy and General, until they saw things his way and gave him an heir, not an error.

Yes. Faced once more with the prospect of Conroyd as king, Borne would do anything, everything, to thwart the lord's burning ambition. But what? *What*? What could Borne's son do that might deny Conroyd the crown?

Shining in the darkness, a glimmering, ghostly idea.

Perhaps . . . risk a schism?

Chewing on a thumbnail Gar let his thoughts race along unfamiliar paths. He'd always assumed that, as the acknowledged, superior magician, Conroyd must be named king. And that to widen the field of candidates for the crown would be to invite disaster. His father had believed so. And he trusted his father's instincts implicitly. Accepted his conclusions without question.

But Conroyd had two sons. Give him the crown and he would have to choose his heir. Elevate one . . . disappoint the other. Be it now or later, schism was again the likely outcome.

Could there be another choice for WeatherWorker? Someone other than Conroyd? Was there in his kingdom a Doranen of another house fit to wear the crown? A magician of sufficient power to wield and control the tormenting Weather Magic? Who might . . . just might . . . share Borne's affection and respect for the Olken and so preserve amity between the races?

He had no idea. Only Durm would know. As Master Magician he knew intimately the strengths and weaknesses both magical and personal of every Doranen living in Lur. It was from them he would appoint his own successor. It was his duty to know.

A pity he'd not also thought it his duty to record his

conclusions for posterity in writing, so someone else might read them and use the information to avert disaster.

If he could find someone other than Conroyd . . . assure himself beyond all doubt that he or she was fit to rule . . . he could sidestep Conroyd altogether. Crown this unknown Doranen in private and present Privy Councillor Lord Jarralt with a king or queen he couldn't replace.

'I think I have it, Father,' he said to his empty bedroom. 'A solution that answers all dilemmas . . . and shows, perhaps, that I'm still your son.'

It meant he'd have to see his Master Magician today. Bully Nix into rousing the dying man long enough to get some idea of where to find this Doranen paragon, this uncrowned monarch of Lur. Because one thing at least was certain. The longer he delayed taking action, the more likely it was that Durm would die unconsulted.

And that would be . . . unfortunate.

Fired with a desperate enthusiasm, but still mindful of what else was happening today, Gar went downstairs to find his Olken Administrator.

Asher was in his apartments, vomiting.

'I don't know why you're letting yourself become so overwrought,' Gar told him, watching as he blotted his pale sweaty face with a towel. 'You've been in Justice Hall a score of times. And it's not as if Glospottle's case is a matter of life and death. It's *piss*, for Barl's sake. The dispute never should've gone this far in the first place!'

Asher straightened, glaring. 'You sayin' this is *my* fault?'

Gar raised a placating hand. 'No. You handled the matter as well as anyone could have. Glospottle's a stubborn fool and the guild is just plain greedy. This was always going to end up in Justice Hall.'

Pausing in the middle of changing shirts from green silk to blue, Asher snorted. 'Wish you'd said so sooner. I'd've chucked it all in and gone back to Restharven.'

'Why do you think I didn't?'

That earned him a sharp look. 'What's amiss now?'

He didn't want to say too much in case his idea came to nothing. 'I've had a thought. About how to extricate ourselves from the mess we're in without risking discovery.'

'Aye? And?'

'I'll tell you later . . . if it works out. If it doesn't, I don't want to look foolish.'

Asher's lips twitched. 'Bit late for that, I reckon.'

In all his life, nobody ever spoke to him like Asher. Like he was just another man. An equal. A worthy target for easy teasing. It made all the darkness . . . bearable.

He cleared his throat. 'I received a note from Conroyd last night. Requesting an urgent meeting with himself and Holze in their capacity as Privy Councillors.'

Asher finished pulling on boots buffed to an eye-searing shine. 'Privy Council meeting? I weren't invited.'

Gar smiled wryly. 'I noticed. Which is why I'm yet to respond. I don't know for certain what they're after but I think I can guess. I'm going to ignore them for as long as I can.'

'Ignore them forever!' said Asher, indignant. 'Who's the bloody king around here, eh?'

'Yes . . . well . . . that's the thorny question, isn't it?' Gar allowed himself a brief and bitter smile, then changed the subject. 'I'm sorry I can't be with you at the hearing today. I'm sorry I wasn't more use in helping you prepare.'

'Don't fratch it,' said Asher, shrugging into an opulent gold and peacock weskit. 'You had more important things to think on, and I had help enough. Besides, Dathne weren't about to let me set foot in Justice Hall without I was stuffed full to indigestion with folderol and jurisprudery.'

He saw the way Asher's eyes warmed at the mention of her name, and took refuge in a little gentle teasing of his own. 'When are you going to do something about that woman? Declare your intentions? Sweep her off her feet? It's clear to anyone with half an eye you're as mad as maggots about her.'

Asher flushed. 'Don't know what you're talkin' about,' he muttered, and dragged his best dark blue velvet coat off its hanger. 'I got to get goin'. Bloody Darran's insistin' I ride in a coach all the way to Justice Hall. Silly ole crow.'

'That was my idea,' Gar confessed, and laughed out loud at the look on Asher's face. For a moment, just a moment, the ache in his chest eased a little. 'It's an historic day, Asher. An Olken, Law Giver in Justice Hall. I wish we could celebrate it the way you deserve.'

'Ha!' said Asher, rolling his eyes. 'I'm bloody glad we can't. There's been enough botheration already.'

Gar shook his head. Struggled for words that wouldn't sound maudlin but reflected how he felt. 'I owe you so much. I doubt there's another man living who'd have done what you've done. Risked what you've risked just because I asked it. I want you to know it's appreciated. And one day – I don't know when or how – I'll back up my words with deeds.'

He held out his hand. Asher stared at it, his expression a muddle of exasperated pleasure. Such a rough-mannered man, his fisherman friend. Brusque and bullish, impatient of so much, and so many. But with a heart as strong and as grand as his beloved ocean, and possessed of a courage as unbreakable as Barl's blessed Wall itself.

'Get away with you,' said Asher and, to Gar's surprise brushed his hand aside to clasp him in a brief and rib-bending embrace. 'Stop wastin' my time, eh? You want history to show I was late to my first big performance at Justice bloody Hall?'

Gar stepped back. 'Of course not. Go. Good luck. You can give me a blow-by-blow account over a cold ale before dinner.'

Heading for the door, Asher grinned over his shoulder. 'Provided you're payin'.'

'Just do me a favour. Make sure the blows aren't literal?' he added. 'And Asher?'

Asher whirled. '*What?*'

'There's a Working tonight. Remember?'

All the warm amusement fled Asher's face. Stilled, chilled, he nodded. 'You think I could forget?'

And then he was gone.

Abruptly sobered, harshly reminded of everything he most wanted to wipe clean from recollection, Gar returned to his apartments to prepare for his meeting with Durm.

Asher looked so resplendent in his Justice Hall finery it was all Dathne could do to stop herself from throwing her arms around him in front of all the Tower staff, shouting for everyone to hear: 'He's mine, he's mine, all mine!'

Instead she allowed herself to meet his questing eyes with a single, burning look, and laughed to see it kindle fire in his face.

'Let me see now, let me see,' fussed Darran, bustling to meet him at the bottom of the Tower's spiral staircase. 'Olken Administrator or not, Law Giver or not, I won't let you set one foot outside if you're a disgrace to His Majesty.'

To Dathne's surprise Asher bore the old man's wittering with unpolished good grace. Let him tweak at his weskit, smooth down his sleeves, repin the diamond at the centre of one expensive lapel. With half a smile and exaggerated patience he looked down his nose at Darran and asked him, drawling, 'Well?'

Darran sniffed. Stepped back, thin hands folded across his black silk middle. 'You're as gaudy as a popinjay, but I suppose you'll do.'

The maids, the messengers and the extra clerks Darran had requested from the palace broke into enthusiastic applause. Willer just smiled a strange, frozen little smile and fluttered his fingers, which could have meant anything. Miserable little sea slug. For herself, Dathne clapped until her palms were stinging.

'All right, all right,' said Asher. 'Ain't you lot got work to do?' Pretending to be cross with them, but inwardly tickled pink. If he was hurt by the conspicuous absence of the stable lads he didn't show it. They weren't speaking to him, on account of Matt.

Briefly, sharply, she felt a pang of guilt. If only she hadn't lost her temper. If only Matt hadn't lost his. If Asher had stayed out on his ride, instead of returning unexpectedly and catching them in conflict.

She hadn't told Veira yet. Couldn't bring herself to expose her lack of judgement.

*I am the Heir. I should've known better.*

But it was done now, and too late for undoing. Matt hadn't left for the Dingles yet, she knew that much. His letters of recommendation were still with Darran, uncollected. She'd give it another day and then go see him. Mend their broken fences. Convince him to stay longer while she eased Asher back to the idea of him being here. He couldn't really believe Matt was in love with her. The idea was ridiculous. He'd see that himself, once cooled completely of temper. He had to.

And Prophecy would continue unhindered, taking its own sweet time as usual.

As the staff departed, chattering, Darran said, 'The coach is waiting out front for you. Willer and I will see you in the Hall.'

Asher stared. 'I don't need you there.'

'Nevertheless.' Darran smiled. 'We are attending.'

'Fine,' said Asher. 'But don't think I'll sit still for a review after.' He looked at Dathne then and held out his hand. 'Coming?'

She wasn't expecting that. 'Me?'

'To go over the last-minute details.' His voice and face were proper and polite, but his eyes promised wickedness. Her blood became honey, warm and voluptuous.

Ignoring Willer's jealous glower and Darran's avuncular simper, she pretended to boredom. Waved away Asher's outstretched hand. 'Very well. If you insist.' And marched off without him towards the foyer doors.

He followed, laughing.

As the carriage rolled down the driveway, Asher drew the curtains tight closed and stole her breath in a kiss. She let him thieve from her again, just once, then pulled away and wrenched the curtains open. The carriage had just turned out of the main palace gates and was heading down the long slow street to the City centre.

'Oy!' he protested.

'There'll be time for dalliance later,' she said severely. 'For now, you look outside this carriage then tell me the curtains should stay shut!'

'Sink me bloody sideways,' said Asher, awestruck, and stared at the passing pavements. 'What d'they think they're *doin'*?'

It seemed there wasn't an Olken man, woman or child in the City not crammed on the pavements to see him go by. They were shouting. Waving. All the young girls brandished flowers. Reaching across him she slid down the window and the crowd's excitement poured into the carriage like a waterfall.

*'Asher! Asher! Asher!'*

'Don't just sit there,' she scolded, laughing. 'Wave to them. They're your people, they're proud of you. For the first time since the coming of the Doranen we have one of our own at the pinnacle of power.'

'Did I say I wanted to be a bloody pinnacle?' said Asher, scowling. 'Barl bloody save me!'

She watched him put his face to the window. Heard the roaring crowd roar louder, seeing him. Knew that this was right, felt it in her bones as she'd not felt anything so strongly since that morning – a lifetime ago now – when she'd woken to know that at last he was within her reach. The ties of blood and magic making her Jervale's Heir rejoiced.

The Olken in the streets scant feet from their carriage, the Olken shouting and laughing and calling his name, they adored Asher for being their Olken Administrator. How much more would they adore him when he was revealed as their Innocent Mage?

Suddenly she no longer cared that she couldn't see how that would happen. No longer cared that dreams and visions had fallen into slumber. Her desperate need to know had died. It was enough that she was here, beside him, in a royal carriage headed for Justice Hall where he would sit in the seat of the Law Giver and solemnly uphold the law. Enough to know that she had done her part in guiding him to this place, at this time, when the world trembled on the brink of change.

Enough that he was her husband and she his wife.

If Matt had been here he'd be moping. Frowning. Worrying that Prophecy had more to say than just there was an Innocent Mage. He'd be reminding her of danger, too. That Asher was born to face a fearsome darkness. That Prophecy was vague on what, or who, or how, and could be she should think on that.

She was tired of thinking on that. She'd thought on that for years of her life and what had it got her? Sleepless nights and a belly full of dread. A small and shabby apartment above a shop full of books and no one in the bed beside her.

Asher was here. Prophecy's child. Soon enough he'd confide the last of his secrets to her, because he loved her. Trusted her. It was meant. Prophecy unfolded and they would do its bidding.

Asher took her hand, shaking her free of reverie. 'Pellen told me there'd be a ruckus but I didn't believe him. Now I owe him a beer, the bastard.' He laughed. 'There's even Doranen out there! Come to see *me*! What would my da say, eh, if he could see this?'

Daringly, she raised his fingers to her lips. 'He'd say he was proud,' she whispered. 'As I am proud.'

The carriage trundled onwards.

# CHAPTER NINETEEN

'I'm so sorry, Your Majesty,' said Pother Nix unhappily. 'I've seen this happen before, and there is no explanation for it that I or any pother can give. When a man is this grievously injured, logic oft disappears. For reasons known only to itself Durm's body has given up the fight to live.'

Sitting close beside the bed, Gar chafed Durm's cold lax fingers; it was like rubbing a bundle of sticks. 'And you're quite sure there's nothing more you can do to save him?'

'Sir, as I told you last night, I have fed him every herb under the sun, in more combinations than I thought were possible,' said Nix. 'And exhausted my supply of healing spells and incantations. Alas, for all his formidable skills, Master Magician Durm's injuries have proven greater than his ability to survive them.'

Gar rested his gaze on Durm's sunken, retreating face. On the graceless folds of emptied skin draped across jutting cheekbones, the thinned and shrunken lips, the pouched, sagging jowls. He'd never been a handsome man, Durm, but there'd been power in his face. A blunt brutality of character. Now there was merely absence.

A fast-fading reminder of the man who once had lived there.

'How long does he have, can you say?'

Nix spread his hands. 'No, sir. He's in Barl's keeping.'

'Is he like to wake again, before the end?'

'Perhaps. I cannot say for certain, Your Majesty.'

Gar chewed at his lip. Now matters could become a trifle . . . difficult. 'Nix, I must speak plainly. I'm sore in need of Durm's counsel before he dies. There's the question of who he wished to succeed him, and other matters I'm not at liberty to discuss. Is there a way of . . . encouraging his waking? Some stimulating herb or incantation you can apply, that will rouse him enough to speak?'

Nix's indrawn breath was loud in the hushed chamber. 'Your Majesty! Such interference would violate every—'

'Nix.' The pother flinched. Gar released Durm's quiet hand and stood. 'I have all solemn respect for your calling, you know that. But I am king of a curious country. One whose balance may be disturbed more easily than any man can know. If these past weeks have taught me anything of kingship it's that there's no sacrifice too great it can't be made. No principle too inviolate it can't be slain in the service of the greater good. I have learned that there's theory and then there's practice, and a king who can't place pragmatism above all the other virtues is a king unworthy of his crown. *I need to speak with Durm*. Can you make that happen?'

The room was cool, but a bead of sweat trickled down Nix's cheek. In his face, a terrible struggle. 'Your Majesty – I can try. If you can swear to me on the most holy thing you know there is truly no other way.'

'Then on the stilled hearts of my family, I swear it.'

Nix slumped and a deeply sorrowing sigh escaped him. 'There is an herbal paste which should achieve your desired outcome. It will take me a moment to prepare.'

'Go, then,' Gar said, and sat again. 'Durm and I will be waiting.'

Nix departed, the chamber door closing softly behind him. Gar recaptured Durm's fingers with his own and squeezed. 'I know you approve,' he said, trying to smile. 'All my life you've despaired of my softness. My easily bruised emotions. You should be proud now, old friend. Old enemy. For what could be more ruthless than taking a dying man by the heels and dragging him backwards from the brink?'

Only the fractional rise and fall of Durm's chest betrayed his fragile hold on life. Not by so much as a flicker of his eyelid did he show that he could hear or feel a presence by his side. Gar let go of the dying man's hand and pressed hard fingertips to his eyes. His head was aching. It always ached, these days. His head . . . his heart . . .

Behind him the chamber door opened again. Closed. Nix padded to the bedside, a small mortar in one hand. A stinging smell, sharp like the depths of winter and acrid as smoke, burned the air.

'I dare not use too much of this,' Nix cautioned as he scooped a little of the stimulant onto the tip of a tiny wooden spatula and smeared it into the portal of Durm's left nostril. 'I wish I dared not use it at all.' He flicked a glance over his shoulder; in it Gar saw concern. Anger. The bitterness of necessity.

'You use it at my bidding,' he said, gently. 'There is no blame attached to you, Nix.'

'If I were a knife in your fist, perhaps,' retorted Nix. Now he was smearing more of the blue paste against the mucous membranes of Durm's lips and gums. 'But I'm flesh, not steel, and I have a mind of my own and a conscience I must answer to.' He hesitated. 'Don't burden it with more than is necessary, Your Majesty.'

Gar let his gaze ice over. 'Rest assured, Royal Pother, that whatever your burdens they are minuscule compared to mine.'

Rebuked, Nix dropped his gaze to the floor for a moment, then looked up again. 'If the stimulant works at all, and I don't guarantee it will, you'll see a change in the next few minutes. If he does rouse then for pity's sake ask your questions quickly, don't press him further than he seems able to go and spare him as soon as you can.'

'I will,' he said. 'Now go. Bolt the door behind you, and seal the chamber against sound,' Seeing the surprise in Nix's eyes he added, 'It's a question of solemn secrecy and the need to husband my powers for the WeatherWorking. I would not spend them except in that service.'

Nix bowed. 'Your Majesty.' With a lingering, potherly look at Durm, he withdrew.

It felt as though centuries passed before Durm showed any response to Nix's stinking concoction. His shallow breathing deepened. His fingers twitched. His head shifted on the pillow. Heart pounding, Gar leaned forward.

'Durm,' he whispered. 'Durm, can you hear me?'

The faintest of moans, little more than a sigh. A gathering frown in the scarred face. A spindle of spittle, oozing from the corner of his lips. Beneath the translucent eyelids, a turgid roll of eye.

'Durm,' he whispered again, more insistently. 'Please?'

Now the moaning sigh became a groan, and Durm's chest rose and fell more vigorously. In his formless face surfaced some echo of the personality housed within his failing body. A grunt. A snuffling snort. Blue mucus oozed and bubbled from his nostril and over his parting lips.

'*Durm*!'

Durm's eyelids lifted, barely. His slitted gaze dragged through the air as though burdened by invisible anchors. '*Gar . . .*'

He pulled the armchair closer. Leaned further in till his lips were almost touching Durm's ear. On the tip of his tongue was the question he'd come here to ask.

Instead he asked something else, because not to ask it was impossible. He'd never have another chance. When Durm died his last hope of recovery, of keeping his kingdom, would die along with him.

'My magic's failed, Durm. Is there a cure? An answer in your library, or Barl's? Do you know a way to save me?'

In a gravelled whisper Durm said, 'No.'

The word was like a sword thrust in his side. His breath hitched. His eyes burned. 'Are you certain?'

'No cure.'

'Then who can I crown instead of Conroyd? I need a different heir!'

Durm coughed again, his face gathering tight in a monstrous frown. His bed began to tremble gently, echoing the larger tremors now racking his reunited limbs. He opened his mouth and screamed.

'No!' cried Gar, and leapt up to press Durm's shoulders to the mattress. 'Not yet! Hold on, Durm! I need you!'

Another gargling scream.

He captured Durm's thrashing head between his hands and forced the maddened eyes to meet his own, even as the wasted, frantic body of his father's best friend struggled and writhed.

'Help me, Durm! *Help me*!'

'The diary!' Durm shouted, bucking and twisting beneath his blankets. 'Barl's diary! Your only hope!'

Heart pounding, he leaned closer still, willing the dying man to hear him. 'Barl left a *diary*? When? Where? Do you have it? *Durm*!'

A terrible convulsion shook the Master Magician. Blue froth bubbled between his lips and his eyes rolled back in his head. Panting, Gar pulled juddering Durm into a desperate embrace.

'Did you tell my father about it? Did you give it to him?'

A terrible sound, then. Durm was laughing. Wasting the last of his life. 'He doesn't know . . . I hid it . . .'

'Oh, Durm . . . *Durm*!' Dying or not, Gar could have strangled him. 'Where is it now? Where will I find it? Why is it our only hope? Hope for what? For me? Can it give me back my magic?'

Tickling his skin, a fading breath. In his ear, a failing whisper. 'Conroyd . . . beware Conroyd . . .'

The convulsions ceased. He lowered Durm gently to the mattress, the pillows, and looked into the waxen face. 'I know,' he said sadly. 'I do. Durm . . . where is the diary?'

Hollowed, emptied, Durm parted blue-stained lips. 'Borne . . . forgive me. I couldn't stop him . . .'

He cupped his hand to Durm's fleshless face. 'You're forgiven. Durm, where have you hidden the diary?'

But it was useless, and he knew it. He wept, despairing, even as Durm's chest rattled with air like a child's toy. The light behind the half-lidded eyes dwindled. Tears brimmed. Even as he watched, the final dregs of colour drained from Durm's cheeks, leaving them like living parchment, and his eyelids closed completely. Whatever strength Nix's stimulant paste had lent him it was failing fast.

'Never mind, Durm,' he said softly. 'It's all right. Go in peace, and Barl's great grace attend you.'

Some dark shadow flitted over Durm's waxy face. 'Barl,' he murmured. 'The bitch, the slut, the treacherous whore.' His eyelids fluttered. Lifted. Revealed confused and clouding eyes. The rattle was in his throat now; an ominous portent. 'Gar . . .'

A butterfly's shout would sound louder.

'Hush,' he whispered. 'I'm here. I'm with you.'

The vivid personality behind Durm's eyes was utterly defeated. '*Forgive me* . . .'

He kissed Durm's cold and clammy forehead. 'For everything.'

Another inwards breath, rattling. A long pause. A bubbling exhalation.

Then nothing.

Gar called Nix into the room. 'He's gone. Do what is needful, but make no public mention of his passing. Bind your staff to strictest secrecy on pain of dire retribution. I will announce this disaster in my own good time.'

Nix bowed, his expression frozen. 'Yes, Your Majesty. If I may ask – did you get what you needed, before . . . ?'

'No,' he said, after a moment. 'No, I did not.'

Outside the palace, the day continued cool and bright, just as Asher had ordered. Scarlet warblers whistled in the trees. Squirrels scampered. The Wall soared clean and bright and golden into the cloudless sky.

Carefully, so carefully, he made his way back to the Tower. Asher needed that new Weather Schedule. He could do that at least. And when it was done, he would look for Barl's diary . . . for all the good it could do them.

Lady Marnagh pounced on Asher the moment he walked through the rear doors of Justice Hall. With his ears still ringing from the shouting, the shrieking, the screaming of his name – *Asher! Asher! Asher!* – and his lips tingling from Dathne's last swift kiss, he dived into the Hall's shadowed silence like a parched man finding water.

Marnagh escorted him up to the private screened Law Giver's gallery. Robed him in the Law Giver's crimson robe. Settled the Law Giver's crown firmly on his head. He closed his eyes, not wanting to see the thunderbolt. Still resistant to all it implied.

Then she guided him onto the magical platform that would deliver him to the madness waiting below. The minute his shiny black boots became visible the restless ocean of sound filling the Hall crashed into waves of fresh and unstinting acclaim. Shouts, applause, cries of 'Praise Barl' and 'Bless our Administrator' dinned his ears as the platform drifted downwards.

He opened his eyes and, for a heartbeat, let his mouth hang open. The hall was *packed*. Mostly with Olken, but there were some Doranen mixed in there as well. Conroyd bloody Jarralt, hoping he'd make some terrible mistake most like. Olken members of the General Council. Conroyd Jarralt's cronies, Daltrie, Sorvold, Hafar and Boqur, the ones who'd been with him that night at Salbert's Eyrie. Even Holze was there. The cleric saw him staring and smiled, his eyes watchful, his expression ambiguous.

Dathne had squashed herself into a front pew between Darran and Willer. She waved at him, just a little.

He fought the temptation to wave back.

There was Indigo bloody Glospottle, trouble's architect, tall thin streak of piss that he was. His face was the colour of piss, too, as though finally, *finally*, he realised what he'd got them all into. On the other side of the aisle from him the Dyers' guild meister, red-faced and bloated with consequence, not looking at all happy about being here.

That'd teach him to be greedy.

Amongst the clamouring Olken faces were dozens more he recognised. Cluny, and the rest of the house staff from the Tower. Some of the palace staff he was coming to know. Pellen Orrick, grinning like a loon, the bastard, and waggling his eyebrows like this was *funny*. Lads from the guardhouse, off-duty and mashed in shoulder to shoulder to watch their old drinking mate make a ninny of himself. Guild meisters and mistresses, some of whom he'd offended and others just mildly irritated. Many, though, who thought of him as friend. Aleman Derrig and his daughters. Folks he knew to smile at in the street, that he'd never met but who knew him because he was the Olken Administrator, and important.

No Matt, of course. He was sorry for that. Sorry for losing his temper, too. But he'd put it right soon enough. Go all the way down to the Dingles if he had to and set the matter straight. Long silences could easily get filled with calamity . . . and one Jed in a lifetime was enough.

The platform came to a stop, bumping him free of memory. The tumult of welcome intensified, vibrating his bones. He almost turned tail and ran. But then he saw Lady Marnagh at her Recording Table, glaring daggers at him from behind a polite mask. Reading his mind. He took a deep and gulping breath then stepped onto the Law Giver's dais. Sat in the Law Giver's chair and struck the golden bell three times.

He might as well have pissed into the wind.

So he stood, raising his arms for silence. His Olken audience only shouted louder. He waved his arms, burningly aware of Conroyd Jarralt, of Barlsman Holze, the Doranen General Councillors. Of what this looked like to them and how easily they might take it out on Gar. On him. On the Olken in general.

He looked at the nearest City guard, pulling a mad face. Stifling a grin, Jolin rapped his pike-butt on the tiled floor in warning. The other guards joined in.

His Olken admirers, drat 'em, ignored the summons to silence.

On a deep breath, his heart pounding, he jumped onto the Law Giver's red velvet seat. 'Sink me bloody sideways!' he bellowed. The hall's magicked acoustics amplified the shout, delivering it sharply to every attendant ear. 'Would you bloody well *pipe down*?'

Laughter. A few shocked gasps. A tail-ending of 'Praise Barls' and 'Hail Ashers'. Then a ragged hush descended. He leapt lightly off the chair.

'Right,' he said, tugging at his weskit through his crimson velvet robe. 'So now *that's* sorted, let's get down to business.'

Indigo Glospottle spoke first. Although most of the City by now must have known the bones of his complaint, given how his tongue wagged at every opportunity, even so the Olken in the audience hung on his every word as though they sat in the theatre, not Justice Hall, and this was a grand fine entertainment laid on for their amusement.

Asher supposed, swallowing a grin, that in many ways it was. The crimson velvet chair was comfortable. He sat back, chin sunk in one hand, and tried to look as though Glospottle's groanings were exciting news to him.

Eventually, after much huffing and puffing and hand-waving, Glospottle's tale of hard-done-by and persecution dribbled to an end. Which meant that Guild Meister Roddle rose ponderously to his feet and argued in the opposite.

Ten minutes later, Asher had had enough of the over-dressed dyer's droning. He raised a warning hand. 'Wait a minute. Just . . . wait. Seems to me this is all startin' to turn a bit hedgehog.'

Roddle blinked. '*Hedgehog*?'

'Uncomfortably prickly,' he explained, as yet another titter of amusement rippled round the crowded hall. He ignored it. 'Now, Meister Roddle—'

'*Guild* Meister Roddle.'

'For now,' he said, and bared his teeth. 'Provided you don't fall into the habit of interruptin' me. Now I just spent the last two days reading your guild's rules and statutes and chartered articles and what-not and I don't recall seein' mentioned anywhere as to how new techniques belong to the guild and not the man or woman who invented 'em.'

Roddle cleared his throat. 'The tradition is long-standing, sir,' he said stiffly. 'The actual amendment to ratified guild charters is more recent.'

Asher narrowed his eyes. 'How recent?'

Roddle's face flushed a dark purplish red. 'This morning.'

The spectators muttered loudly as Indigo Glospottle leapt to his feet. 'That's *outrageous*!'

'Shut up, Indigo!' said Asher. 'You've had your say.' Indigo subsided, spluttering. 'This morning, eh?' he continued. 'That smacks to me of cheating, Roddle. Did you see the whacking big sword on the outside of the building as you came in? You recall Barl's opinion on little things like cheating?'

'We are not *cheating*!' the guild meister protested. 'Indigo Glospottle is a *thief*, sir, he steals from his guild brethren, he—'

'And you can shut up too,' he said, and waved his hand in dismissal. 'Reckon I've heard all I need to. It's my turn to flap lips now.' From the corner of his eye he caught the look on Lady Marnagh's face as she dutifully supervised the magical recording of the proceedings. He suspected she wasn't sure whether to hit him or hug him.

'Sir,' said Roddle faintly, and resumed his seat. The spectators held their breaths and sat forward, waiting.

Asher slid out of his chair, stepped off the dais and began pacing back and forth the full width of the hall. Against every and all expectation he was enjoying himself.

'Our kingdom's a place of rules and regulations. We've got ourselves so used to 'em I reckon we've near forgot how many there are. Rules for marriage and for bearing children. Rules for schooling and religion. Where we work, how we work, what we work towards. What jobs the Olkens do, what jobs the Doranen do. Who uses magic and who doesn't.' His voice dried up momentarily and he had to wet his lips before he could continue. He hadn't meant to say that last bit. 'Any road. Lots of rules. And then we got the guilds. The guilds are important. They enforce a lot of our rules. Help keep this kingdom runnin' sweet and smooth just as much as any WeatherWorker ever did. Without the guilds binding us all together, could be we'd find ourselves in a right mucky mess.'

A murmur from the audience. Exchanged glances between Jarralt and his cronies. Holze, nodding in slow agreement. Pellen Orrick, his eyebrows lifted, watching everything and everyone with his melted-ice eyes.

'And for a long, long time now,' Asher continued, still pacing, 'nowt much has changed around here. The way we brew beer. The way we milk cows. The way we grow cotton and card wool. Harvest grapes. Raise horses. I reckon turn the clock back a hundred years, two hundred, and no one'd notice the difference.' He stopped pacing then, right in front of a transfixed Indigo Glospottle, and shook his head. 'But then along comes a man with an idea. An idea for bluer blues and redder reds, and the next thing you know the apple cart's turned arse over eyeballs and there's pippins all over the street. And here's me, s'posed to be pickin' 'em up without a one bein' bruised.' Lifting his gaze, he swept it over the packed Hall. 'Sorry, folks. That ain't about to happen. Nobody upsets an apple cart without there bein' a few apples spoiled.'

'All right then!' a voice shouted from the midst of the throng. 'So what're you goin' to do about it?'

He grinned. 'Well now, I'm glad you asked me that question, Willim Bantry, and that'll be three trins in the Barlsbox if you please, for speakin' out of turn.'

A gust of laughter. Asher's grin widened.

'So. Guild Meister Roddle wants the secret to Indigo Glospottle's superior piss handed out willy-nilly to every guild member, even though they did nowt to deserve the money they'll make off it. And Indigo Glospottle wants to keep his secret piss a secret and get rich off it all on his lonesome. And if they won't let him do that, he wants to leave the Guild.' He sighed and shook his head. 'Well, I can't be having that. The guilds keep us strong. I ain't about to weaken 'em, Indigo, by lettin' you run about on your own undermining the Dyers' Guild's authority.'

Glospottle pouted.

'*But*,' he added, with a burning look at Roddle, 'I ain't about to sit back twiddlin' my thumbs as *you* get rich off another man's invention. So here's my ruling. Indigo gives the Guild his secret piss recipe, and for every bolt of fabric sold that was made with that same recipe the guild gives Indigo a tithe. Five trins sounds about right to me.'

As Indigo Glospottle broke into excited laughter Guild Meister Roddle rose shouting to his feet. 'I object, sir! I *object*!'

'You don't get to object, you whingeing bloody ninny-hammer!' roared Asher, closing on him. 'If you'd stuck by the first agreement, that Indigo'd keep his secret to hisself and pay the Guild a tithe from every sale, we wouldn't be here now! But you didn't and we are and now I've made my ruling! So get out of my sight afore I knock you on your pimpled arse and make you drink a *pint* of Glospottle's secret bloody piss! *Hot*!'

The hearing concluded immediately thereafter, amidst much confusion, cheering and acclaim.

With her ribs still aching from laughter Dathne hovered at the rear of Justice Hall and waited for Asher to emerge. Half an hour after his riotous conclusion to the trial and still he'd not escaped. Guild Meister Roddle had come out, ashen-faced and spluttering, supported by a bevy of guild members, after signing the paperwork that entered the ruling into law. Indigo Glospottle had come out too and hugged her, weeping with relief. Pellen Orrick had come out briskly, raising his eyebrows at her in passing.

Pellen Orrick's risen eyebrows spoke untold volumes.

At long last Asher emerged, all alone. He saw her and smiled. 'Take me away from here, woman,' he said limply, and let her hustle him into the small, anonymous hired carriage she'd paid to wait round the side of Justice Hall. The official carriage she'd dismissed with a coin for the coachman and a conspiratorial smile.

'You fool,' she said, and kissed him. 'I'm afraid to imagine what you'll think of next.'

They went back to her apartment over the bookshop and watched the sun go down from the rooftop. When hunger stirred she fetched them roast chicken and baked potatoes and soaking sweet honey cakes from Meister Hay's cookery down the street, and they gorged themselves to hiccups.

Then she took him by the hand and led him to her bedroom.

'You know I can't stay,' he said. There was honey smeared in the corners of his mouth.

'Not the whole night,' she agreed, kissing him clean. 'But for a while.'

Falling breathless into each other's arms, onto her creaking old bed, they let pleasure have its way with them. Afterwards he slept, and she sat up in the bed and watched him, marvelling. Eventually she drifted into dozing sleep and woke only when something cold and feather-light kissed her on the cheek.

It was snowing.

Heart-stopped and speechless she stared at the whirling ice flakes as they fell from the lacy white cloud beneath her bedroom ceiling. In the bed beside her Asher muttered and moaned, his eyes closed tight. The merest thread of blood trickled meanly from beneath his lashes, like a tear.

She nearly suffocated, she held her breath so long.

It was over soon enough. The snowfall stopped, the lacy cloud dispersed. He began to stir. Alarmed, she slid under the blankets beside him and pretended she was sleeping. She felt him slip from the bed. Heard the swish of silk and leather over skin as he pulled on his clothes. Shivered as his warm lips touched her mouth.

And then he was gone.

Alone and still shivering she lay in her bed and rocked like a child, stunned beyond the release of weeping.

Of all the things she'd ever imagined, she'd never imagined *this*.

# CHAPTER TWENTY

Close to panic, Willer turned away from shuffling the papers and parchments on top of Asher's desk and began to rummage through its drawers instead. He *had* to find something incriminating tonight. This was the fifth time he'd crept into Asher's office, he couldn't fail again! Lord Jarralt was losing his patience, there'd been harsh words outside Justice Hall today after the Glospottle hearing and besides, the whole business was so *dangerous*.

Nothing in the first drawer. Or the second. What about the third . . .

Just as he reached for the last drawer he heard a pair of muffled voices. A key, scraping in the office door's lock. He swallowed a shriek. Snatched Lord Jarralt's lightstone from the desktop and smacked it against the timber until the tiny glow extinguished. Fumbling it into his pocket he made a dive for rat-faced Dathne's desk just as the office door swung open. Heart pounding, runnelled with sweat, he wrapped his arms about his head and waited for the axe to fall. A flare of conjured glimlight splashed shadows on the carpet and lit up two pairs of passing legs.

'—extraordinary discovery,' the king was saying, voice hushed. 'I can scarce believe Durm kept it secret. Who knows what might be in it? A cure, perhaps . . .'

Then keep on bloody lookin' for it if you reckon it's so important!' said Asher, stamping across the carpet to his desk. 'Or go back to readin' Durm's books. I told you, I don't need you there. I can manage for one night on my own.'

'No, you can't,' the king retorted. 'It's too dangerous.'

Shuffle, shuffle, as Asher searched through the papers scattered all over his desk. 'It ain't no more bloody dangerous now than it was the night before last. I survived then, I'll survive tonight. All I want from you is a way out of this! I want to come back from the Weather Chamber and hear you say: "That's it, Asher. That was the last time. No more WeatherWorking for you."'

In the silence that followed, Willer stuffed his coat sleeve in his mouth to stifle a horrified cry. *Asher* was *WeatherWorking*? How could that *be*?

The king said, very quietly, 'Don't you think I want that too?'

Asher's reply was swift and scathing. 'Well, wantin' ain't enough, Gar. We've gone a bloody long ways past wantin'. Durm can't help us now, he's dead. It's just you. One way or another you got to fix this, 'cause every day that goes by with you pretendin' to be king and me pissin' blood to make it rain and snow is one more day someone could find out the truth. How many bloody times do you need to hear it? I can't do this much longer!'

Willer was afraid they'd hear his heartbeat, pounding in his chest like a madman's hammer. Durm was dead? When? How? Don't say Asher had *killed* him!

'I promise,' the king said after a long and tension-filled pause. 'You won't have to. I know as well as you this has to stop.'

The sound of Asher's palm slapping timber was so loud, so unexpected, Willer almost hit his head on the underside of Dathne's desk. 'Are you sure you left the new Weather Schedule in here?'

'I put it on your desk myself,' said the king. 'Let me look.' More slithery sounds of paper and parchment shuffling. 'Here it is. You buried it under your notes for Glospottle's hearing.'

'No, I didn't! I ain't been – oh, never mind!' said Asher, and Willer let out a sigh of silent fright. 'Bloody Darran prob'ly snuck in here snoopin' while Dathne's back was turned. Now, you're sure you got this right? I ain't goin' to send snow where there should be rain, and ice where there ought to be snow?'

'It's right,' the king said. 'I may have lost my magic, but I can still read and count.'

For a moment Willer thought he might faint dead away. King Gar had *lost his magic*?

'Glad to hear it,' said Asher. 'Now you get back to your books and I'll take care of this.'

'All right then,' said the king, reluctant. 'But for Barl's sake, be careful. Don't overtax yourself. And make sure you drink Nix's potion after.'

'Nag, nag, nag,' said Asher nastily. Oh, he was *such* a nasty man . . .

There came the sound of parchment, rolling. Two pairs of booted feet, leaving. Willer held his breath until the door clicked closed behind them and Asher's key scraped again in the lock.

Alone again, and undiscovered, he stayed under Dathne's desk and shook so hard he thought his teeth would shatter like glass. Durm dead . . . the king unmagicked . . . and Asher of Restharven a criminal. The man who just that very morning had stood up in Justice Hall and dared, *dared*, to lecture on the welfare of the kingdom. The sanctity of Barl's great Laws.

He was *WeatherWorking*. Even more incredible, he was doing it with King Gar's knowledge! His blessing, even. How could that be? *Gar* wasn't evil. There was only one explanation: Asher must have bewitched him, somehow. Ensorcelled him into doing his wicked bidding. Perhaps even stolen his magic in the first place.

Monstrous. *Monstrous.*

And then horror slowly gave way to a dawning joy. How this had all happened was no longer important. It had happened, and that was more than enough.

*Praise Barl!* he wept in silent ecstasy. *Praise Barl and all her mighty works! My prayers at last are answered!*

Then, unexpected, within his transcendent triumph chimed a thin sharp note of fear.

When the kingdom learned all he knew – when Asher's perfidy and the king's blind foolish faith were revealed – there would be chaos. The uproar following Timon Spake would be nothing, *nothing*, to the crisis brewing now. It was inevitable: all Olken would in some way, large or small, pay for Asher's crime. Even though they were innocent. Even though this wasn't their fault.

Imagining it, he felt his courage falter. He held their lives in the palm of his hand. Would be, once he told Lord Jarralt of this discovery, the immediate cause of their unjust suffering. People would know it. And *blame* him. He swallowed more tears. Oh, how unfair. How *unfair*.

One more crime to lay at Asher's feet.

And yet, he had no choice. He had to speak. For the

good of the kingdom, he could not stay silent. Asher must not escape punishment. The king must be freed from his pernicious, evil influence, no matter the cost. No matter that poor Willer, Barl's blameless instrument, would yet carry some of the blame. History would redeem him. In time, he'd be seen as a hero. A champion for right, and justice.

*That's what I am, Barl. I'm your champion!*

When he judged enough time had passed, he unlocked the office door with Lord Jarralt's magical key, crept unseen from the Tower and made his way towards the Weather Chamber. He didn't want to report this momentous news to Lord Jarralt until he'd witnessed with his own eyes the filthy stinking depths of Asher's crime.

He got lost twice. Royal staff knew in theory where the Chamber was located but none had cause to visit it. Snow began to fall just after his second wrong turning. When at last he stumbled onto the right pathway, he was cold, wet and out of breath, his pantaloons were torn and his left hand was scraped to blood from when he'd tripped over a tree root and gone ungainly sprawling.

The Weather Chamber was awe-inspiring. Terrifying. It was a wonder Asher dared stain it with his shadow, let alone defile it with his presence. A strange glow flickered at its very top, flashes of blue and silver-white and scarlet.

Willer crept closer, jumping at every whisper in the grass, every creaking in the trees. The mournful hoot of a low-flying owl nearly made him piss his pants. Hot-faced, gasping, he fell against the Chamber's door. He almost couldn't hear over the pounding of blood in his head.

To his surprise it was unlocked. He felt his lip curl.

Sunk deep in arrogance, Asher thought himself inviolate. Undiscoverable. He couldn't wait for the look on the bastard's face when he realised how wrong he'd been.

He entered the Chamber. Not daring to use the lightstone he fumbled his way up the stairs in the dark, stubbing his toes and chewing his lip to stop himself from crying out at the pain. There were tight iron bands clamped about his chest. He was going to have a seizure, his legs were about to burst into flame.

Just as he thought he really would die the endless stairs came to an end and he was outside the Weather Chamber itself. The door was open the merest sliver. Through the hairline crack he could see a fierce bright light and hear strange and horrible sounds. Someone was screaming, a garbled gobbling of extreme distress, and buried within was a string of unintelligible words.

Willer felt the hair stand up on the back of his neck.

As he stood there, dithering, the screaming rose to a ragged crescendo and abruptly stopped, as though cut with a knife. A moment later came the thud of a body hitting the floor.

Trembling, hardly breathing, he pushed wide the door and looked his fill.

An austere room papered with complicated charts and diagrams. Shelves crammed with ancient books. In its middle a miraculous thing, a model of the kingdom, and above it tiny clouds twinkling snowflakes. Unmoving beside it, Asher. Smeared and dribbled with blood. Dead then? Please not. *Please* not, for he must live to face his crimes, to kneel at the feet of his vanquishing foe. To be stripped naked before all the City, the kingdom and seen for the monster he was, knowing full well who'd unmasked him.

He crept closer. Asher was breathing. Shallowly, groaningly, with lines of pain cut deep in his flesh. Blood caked his eyelashes, clogged his nostrils, glistened redly on his lips. He was deeply, gloriously insensible.

Stealthily, Willer withdrew. Used Lord Jarralt's charm to lock the door behind him and used it again on the door at the foot of the staircase.

And then he ran.

'Conroyd! Conroyd, wake up, dear, wake *up*!'

Morg opened his eyes. Who – ah yes. His gormless, wittering wife . . . at least for now. 'Ethienne?'

'Oh, Conroyd!' she said, querulous and pouting. 'There is a *dreadful* little Olken downstairs and he won't go away no matter *what* I say! He insists you must see him and he won't leave the premises till you do!'

Morg stretched, revelling in the oiled ease of his glorious new body. 'Did he give you his name?'

'Willim. Or Wolton. Or something beginning with "w",' said Ethienne, still pouting. 'Do make him go away, Conroyd, please? It's the middle of the night and he really is quite awful!'

Morg flung back the blankets. '*Willer*?'

'Yes, that's it. Willer. What in Barl's name have you to do with such a—'

He leapt out of bed, cursing. 'Be silent, you ridiculous old hag!' And ignored her gobbling shock as he flung on Jarralt's dressing-gown and hurried from the room.

Willer waited in the foyer, dishevelled and bloodied and muddied and gross. 'My lord!' he cried, and scuttled across the carpet to meet him at the foot of the stairs. 'Oh, my *lord*! The Master Magician is dead, and . . . and . . .'

Morg seized him by the shoulders and shook him. 'And what, man? Is it Asher? Tell me quickly, is it Asher?'

The fat little Olken's eyes were shining like stars. 'Oh, my lord, yes, it's Asher! At last, sir, at *last*! Lord Jarralt, *we have him*!'

# PART THREE

# CHAPTER TWENTY-ONE

Pellen Orrick sighed and took another thoughtful sip of tea. Beyond the window of his guardhouse office, silent snow continued to drift through the air and settle on the sill, the garden, the gateposts and the street. The glow of glimfire from the City streetlamps turned white to gold, a constant reminder of magic.

Deep silence surrounded him. The guardhouse cells downstairs were free of guests, for the moment, and the lads on night call were sleeping peacefully in their cots. Business as usual, now that the City had emptied of mourners and life was slowly falling into its new rhythms. Gar on the throne. Asher the Olken Administrator.

The thought of Asher tipped his mouth into a smile. Outrageous. The man was outrageous. Today's – no, yesterday's – performance in Justice Hall would be gossip fodder for weeks. Months. He'd thought Guild Meister Roddle would drop dead of a seizure on the spot. He'd nearly had a seizure himself from trying not to laugh out loud.

Reprobate Asher had climbed onto the Law Giver's *chair*. The chair that had cradled royal law-giving rumps for years. But then that was Asher all over, wasn't it?

Always climbing onto things. Yes, and over them too. Benches. Tables. Obstacles. Restrictions. Traditions. Shredding pomp and consequence with all the finesse of a cheese-grater.

A silent convulsion of laughter shook his bones. Indigo Glospottle's name would live on for generations now. Asher had seen to that. So much authority resting on those broad and brawny shoulders. If it had been anybody else standing on that Law Giver's chair he knew he'd not be laughing, but worried. Power like that could turn a man's head more easily than the lilting walk of a pretty girl passing by. But not Asher's. If ever he'd met a man entirely unimpressed with the trappings of power, it was Asher.

Sparks spat in the fireplace as a log broke apart, crumbling into coals and ash. The room was warmed with magic, of course, but he still kept a fire burning through winter. Most people did. Even the Doranen loved the sound and smell of fresh burning pitty-pine. The romance of leaping flames.

Orrick stifled a yawn. Middle of the night, he should be sleeping, but paperwork couldn't tell the time and he'd let it lapse of late. Extraordinary. He was a man of strict and proper procedure. He couldn't remember the last time he'd left this office without the daily report being finished and filed for future reference. And here he was with a full week's worth of reports undone. It wouldn't do.

Sound and movement in the street below his window caught his attention. The hollow clopping of hooves on cobbles. A carriage, drawing to a halt at the guardhouse gates. Two cloaked figures alighting.

Pellen Orrick put down his pen and went to investigate.

'Lord Jarralt!' he said, betrayed into showing surprise. He stood back from the guardhouse front door. 'Please, my lord. Enter.'

The king's Privy Councillor was attended by Willer Driskle, from the Tower. The palace. Wherever it was he worked these days. A blameless man, but not well liked. Unpopularity wasn't a crime, though, so the guard had no cause to know him. Orrick nodded politely and closed the door behind them.

'Your office,' said Lord Jarralt, stripping off his gloves. 'Now.'

Such a chilly man. Orrick bowed, taking no offence; it was pointless. 'My lord.' With a quelling look at young Piper, on overnight front desk duty and struggling not to gape, he led his visitors upstairs.

Jarralt refused the chair that was offered him. Willer almost accepted, caught the lord's cold eye and changed his mind. Orrick, not inclined to be intimidated in his own office, took his chair behind the desk and sat back, observing.

'Tell him,' said Jarralt, slapping his gloves across one palm as though his flesh offended him. 'All of it.'

'Yes, my lord,' Driskle said, and planted his fists on the desktop. There was something eager, *lascivious*, in the way his eyes were shining. Something predatory.

Disliking him, Orrick stared at the encroaching hands till the fat little man withdrew them and stood back. 'Tell me what?'

'Captain Orrick, you must arrest Asher of Restharven at once. He has broken Barl's First Law and attempted magic!'

He laughed. '*Asher* has? Are you *mad*?'

'*Tell him*,' said Lord Jarralt grindingly.

He listened in growing disbelief as Driskle spewed

forth a tale as horrifying as it was unlikely. 'I don't believe it,' he said at last, once the man was done with his litany of accusations.

'I do,' said Lord Jarralt.

Orrick shook his head. There was a hot buzzing in his ears and his eyes were fogged with shock. 'But Olken can't do magic.' He turned to Willer. 'You *saw* him call the snow?'

'I saw the snow falling and went into the Weather Chamber. He was alone. Unconscious on the floor and covered in blood. And I heard him and the king talking about WeatherWorking. I *told* you,' whined Driskle. 'Asher's a criminal and he has to die!'

Feeling sick, Orrick ignored that. 'How were you in a position to overhear anything of a private nature discussed between Asher and His Majesty?'

'That is not your concern,' said Lord Jarralt.

He stood. 'Forgive me, but it is. These are grave accusations. I won't proceed against Asher on nothing but the word of a man who, if I may be blunt, appears to have a personal stake in his downfall.'

'You will proceed, Captain,' snapped Jarralt, 'or find yourself relieved of duty. Master Magician Durm is dead, and you are questioning the orders of his successor.'

Jarralt's eyes were frightening. Pale, pale blue and colder than any winter ever called. Flickering in their depths, a scarlet thread. Or was that just his imagination? Orrick didn't know. It took every skerrick of strength in him not to cower beneath that burning stare.

'Dead, my lord? I had not heard so.'

'The news is not yet public. You will consider it privy, and not to be repeated.'

'Of course. My lord, His Majesty trusts Asher implicitly,' he said, still fighting, even though he knew he was lost. 'What Driskle suggests is madness. And as for this nonsense about magic, even if it were possible, which it isn't, to say that Asher would so imperil himself, this kingdom—'

Lord Jarralt smiled. 'You speak most eloquently in his defence, Captain. Should I be questioning *your* loyalty?'

He felt his face bleach white. 'I am as true a subject as ever lived.'

'Really? I always felt you accepted the explanation for the late king and his family's unfortunate deaths somewhat readily, Orrick,' said Jarralt. 'Perhaps that is a matter which in due course would pay further investigation.'

'My lord, I protest! I do my duty without fear or favour!'

Smile vanished, Jarralt's eyes were deadly. 'Indeed? Then rouse your men, Captain, and tell them nothing of magic. That information you may regard as secret, on pain of death. Am I understood?'

'Yes, my lord,' he said. His mouth was dry.

'You and your officers will accompany me to the Weather Chamber. Then we'll see how willing you are to yoke your future to Asher's short, bloody and painful one.'

He was Captain of the City Guard. He had no choice. He bowed. 'My lord,' he said, and went to wake his men.

Tossing restlessly on the hard floor of the Weather Chamber, shot through with sizzling sparks of pain, Asher dreamed.

*Sick and dying in her bed, Ma holds out her arms to him. Thin white arms, which once had been so plump and brown. 'Give me a hug now, Asher, and promise you'll be a big strong boy once I'm gone,' she says in her foam-thin voice, which only a month before had been as strong as the ocean itself. 'Your da's goin' to need his little man soon and I know you won't do nowt to fratch or disappoint him, will you? You'll never let him down.'*

*He cries, oh how he cries, as they lay her in the cold salty ground and sing the Farewell above her head.*

*Standing at the graveside in his best brown homespun shirt and trousers that Ma made, he can't believe the sun is shining and the sky is so blue, as blue as her favourite blouse that only last night Zeth cut up into pieces to grease the hinges on the fish trap in his boat. How can the sun be shining on such a terrible day?*

*As he weeps, dark clouds race in from all directions, tumbling and tearing and clogging the sky until all the light is gone, the bright yellow light, and it begins to rain.*

*'What be you doin', Asher?' his brothers angrily shout. 'You ain't s'posed to make it rain! We'll have to give you a damn good straightenin' if you think it be your business to make it rain, a no-good Olken fisherman like y'self!'*

*And Zeth undoes his copper-studded belt. Slides it free of his narrow waist and cracks it double against his leathery palm. In his eyes such a yearning for blood . . .*

*'Stay clear of me, Zeth!' he says, backing away. 'Da, don't let him! Don't let him, Da!'*

*But Da's not listening, Da's on the ground with a heavy great mast across him, split in two, and the rain's washing all the blood out of him, all Da's blood is running into the grass, onto the grave, soaking away to be with Ma.*

*The rain falls harder, bits of ice in it now, the clouds have turned as black as pitch and purple like bruises and there's thunder, thunder, boom boom boom . . .*

Asher woke, gasping, to the hollow echoing tread of feet on the stairs leading up to the Weather Chamber. Mazed with dreaming, with woken pains both old and new, he was only halfway to his feet when the door burst wide and Willer gabbled in, pointing. At his heels were Pellen Orrick and Conroyd Jarralt.

'See? See? I told you he was here! *Now* will you believe me?'

Pellen's face was bloodless, his eyes narrow with pain. A truncheon hung from his belt. 'Asher? What are you doing here? Don't tell me this repulsive little popinjay was *right*?'

A terrible wave of anger and despair crashed over him and he took a wild step forward, fists clenched. 'You fool, Willer! You farting bloody *fool*! You've gone and ruined *everything*!'

Willer was grinning like a numbskull, dancing on the balls of his ugly flat feet. 'Not ruined! *Saved*! I've saved the kingdom and soon everyone will know it!' he crowed. 'There are guards downstairs with chains and rope to bind you hand and foot. It's over, Asher! You're done with!'

Asher leapt on him. 'You sinkin' idiot!' he shouted, pummelling and kicking and clawing in fury. 'You slime-ridden, shit-eating, runting, putrid *sea slug*, you—'

Pellen stepped forward and clubbed him on the head. Still fragile and vulnerable from the Weather Magic, he was brought to his knees by the blow, retching.

'Don't believe him, Pellen,' he choked, red pain rolling through him. 'You *know* me. I ain't a criminal *or* a traitor!'

A face carved from ice would look warmer. 'How can I not believe, Asher? You're inside the Weather Chamber, where you ought not to be.'

He groaned. 'Send for the king. He'll explain everything, he'll—'

'What are you doing here?'

He was so afraid he wanted to vomit. 'I ain't sayin',' he whispered. 'I want to see Gar.'

Pellen's eyes were devoid of hope, or pity. 'Asher of Restharven, in the name of our king and by the authority granted me as Captain of this City, I arrest you for the capital crime of breaking Barl's First Law.'

'Well done, Captain,' said Conroyd Jarralt, and let one smoothly gloved hand fall on Pellen's shoulder. Beside him Willer still danced his little victory jig, shining like a greedy child on Grand Barl's Day morning. 'I can see I need doubt your loyalty no longer. Now call up your men and make sure this traitor's bound fast. There are many questions to be asked . . . and answered.'

They locked him in the same cage Timon Spake had occupied in the hours before his death. When one ignorant Asher of Restharven had blithely said, '*Chop off the bastard's head.*' He swallowed black laughter, and tears.

*I wanted nowt but a boat and the ocean and an open sunlit sky . . .*

Gar's answer, echoing, taunted him from a distance of days that felt like years now.

*'Not every man gets what he wants, Asher. Most men just get what they're given.'*

Again, the threat of morbid amusement.

*Fine. So can I give it back?*

Stifling a groan he tried to ignore his body's insistent pains. The guards had ripped off the gag and choking hempen noose they'd thought was needed to get him here from the Weather Chamber but had left his arms tied to breaking point behind his back. His elbows thrummed, his wrists stung, his swollen hands throbbed and his shoulder sockets burned. His mouth tasted like ashes and dried blood. His head ached, and his ear, where Pellen's truncheon had clubbed him.

He was desperate to sit but they'd taken away the bench and straw that Timon Spake had enjoyed, and the floor held no attraction; even through his booted feet he could feel the flagstones' chill.

Even more desperate was his need for a pot: his bladder was full to bursting. But even if they'd left him one he couldn't unbutton his trousers, so when he couldn't hold it any longer he just let go; the hot piss running down the inside of his right leg was the only warm thing in the place. That and the shame that burned him like coals.

Shame, but not fear. He refused to be afraid. Gar had promised he'd be protected, and Gar was the king.

Time passed. He wondered why his release was taking so long; surely they'd wake Gar for this, even if it was still dark outside. Was it still dark outside? He couldn't tell.

When the outer cell door finally opened it was to admit Conroyd Jarralt, with Pellen behind him. Asher straightened. 'Where's His Majesty?'

'Snoring sweetly in his bed, I presume,' said Jarralt.

'You ain't *told* him?' He turned to Pellen. 'You got to tell him, Pellen, you—'

'Captain Orrick.'

'What?'

Pellen's expression was rigid. 'You will address me as Captain Orrick.'

He took a moment to breathe slowly, carefully. To subdue fear. 'All right. Captain Orrick. I know how this looks but I swear if you rouse the king and ask him to come, he'll explain—'

'It's your explanation we're interested in,' said Orrick. 'Your presence in the Weather Chamber is a capital crime, punishable by death. Attempting to implicate His Majesty will not save you.'

'I got nothing to say! Not till you get Gar down here!'

With a gentle sigh, Jarralt stepped forward. 'You may leave us, Captain. I require private conversation with the prisoner.'

Orrick shook his head. 'No, my lord. He's in my charge and is my responsibility. Traitor or not he has certain rights. I must stand witness.'

Jarralt's face spasmed with rage. 'Need I *again* remind you, Captain, that I am—'

'With due respect, the Master Magician has no jurisdiction over criminal investigation,' said Orrick, unflinching. 'Only sentencing, once guilt is established.'

Asher stared. Master Magician? Since when? 'You're gettin' ahead of yourself, Jarralt. Durm ain't even cold yet, and Gar—'

'*Silence*,' hissed Jarralt. He glared at Orrick. 'Captain, I commend your diligence. But we deal with matters beyond mere law-breaking. This business strikes at the very heart of our kingdom and touches upon questions of magic, which are of no concern to you.'

Orrick hesitated. Asher, fear flaring, pressed his face to the prison's bars. 'Don't go, Pellen. Captain Orrick. Don't leave me alone with him. *Please*.'

'Fear not, Captain,' said Jarralt expansively. 'I have

no intention of cheating the axeman of his fee.'

'Very well, my lord,' said Orrick. 'But I shall hold you to your word.' The door closed behind him.

Jarralt smiled. The malice in him stepped Asher back three paces. 'I ain't sayin' nowt till Gar gets here.'

'Really?' Something deep in the Doranen lord's eyes flared scarlet. '*Pain*,' he whispered.

And pain cut through Asher like a scythe. Doubled him over and stole his breath. 'Barl rot your entrails, Jarralt,' he grunted, still bent in half. 'I ain't tellin' you *nowt*.'

'Wrong, filth,' said Jarralt. 'You'll tell me everything.'

And he did, in the end. Once he'd finished screaming. He couldn't stop himself. Jarralt's mind winnowed his like a grain thresher, reducing all thoughts of resistance to chaff.

Eventually, emptied of words, he fainted.

For the fifth time since his early arrival at the Tower that morning, Darran got up from his desk and poked his head through his open office doorway. Looked down. Strained his hearing for any sign of his tardy assistant. But no, *still* no Willer. Where could the wretched man be? They had *oceans* of work to swim through . . .

And then he heard the Tower's front doors open and Willer's imperious voice demanding, 'Berta! Is Darran arrived yet? We have urgent business!'

*We*?

As the maid replied he caught a glimpse of Willer, and the man he ushered up the staircase before him.

Lord Jarralt.

He returned to his desk. When Willer flounced into the room on Lord Jarralt's heels he was busily reading the day's schedule. He stood and bowed. 'My lord.'

Then he fixed his attention on his assistant. 'You are fearsome tardy this morning, sir. Might I ask where—'

'At the guardhouse,' said Willer. 'Engaged on matters of state.'

'At my behest,' added Lord Jarralt. 'I presume you have no objection?'

Matters of state? *Willer*? Darran bowed again. 'Of course not, my lord.' He cleared his throat. 'Did you require something of me, my—'

'Asher of Restharven is arrested,' said Lord Jarralt. Anyone would think the announcement was unexciting to him, provided they weren't looking at his eyes.

'Arrested?' Darran said faintly. 'On what charge?'

'No charge, but proven treason!' said Willer. 'His guilt is beyond all doubt! He—'

'Willer,' said Lord Jarralt mildly.

Willer's mouth sprang shut like a mousetrap.

'I must see the king,' Jarralt continued. 'Take me to him.'

Darran shifted uneasily. 'My lord, His Majesty called snow last night. The WeatherWorking taxes him, he often remains late abed the following—'

'Now,' said Lord Jarralt.

Clearly, argument was out of the question. 'My lord,' he said, then turned to eye Willer quellingly. 'I shan't be long. Kindly prepare for me the notes for today's session with—'

'No,' said Willer. He was grinning. 'I don't work for you any more. I've accepted Lord Jarralt's offer of a position on his staff.'

'You've done *what*?'

'You're a fool, Darran,' Willer said spitefully. 'Asher took you in along with everybody else. Even the king. But not me. *I* saw through him. I stayed loyal to Barl

– and Lord Jarralt knows it. You'll have to find yourself another errand boy.'

His hand itched to slap the insolent smile from Willer's face. 'I see,' he said thinly. 'Congratulations. Make sure you remove any personal items from your desk before you depart.'

Willer looked around the room, his gaze sticky with distaste. 'There's nothing I want from here.'

'Then repair to my townhouse,' said Lord Jarralt, 'and await my return.'

'My lord,' said Willer with an extravagant bow, and withdrew.

The pompous, ungrateful little – little *turd*. Darran watched him go with ill-concealed loathing, then stepped from behind his desk. 'My lord? If you would follow me?'

Heart pounding, head awhirl with shock and speculation and a burning desire to know what Asher had done, he led Lord Jarralt up the spiral staircase to the door of His Majesty's suite.

Gar was woken from slumber by a rough hand shaking him and a dazzling assault of sunlight.

'Stir yourself, boy,' said a curt, unwelcome voice. 'Your sins have found you out.'

He sat up, incredulous. '*Conroyd*? What is the meaning of this? How did you get *in* here?'

Outlined in sunlight Conroyd Jarralt stood beside the bed, his golden head a glowing nimbus. 'Your secretary admitted me.'

'Then he's dismissed. Darran, do you hear me? You're dismissed!' He screwed up his eyes and squinted round the room. 'Where are you, you damned interfering old woman?'

'Not here,' said Conroyd. 'What I have to say is for your ears alone.'

Sliding back under his blankets, he rested a forearm across his face. It felt as though he'd fallen asleep mere moments ago. Hours and hours spent searching through Durm's borrowed books, and not even a sign of Barl's diary.

'I'm not interested. Now get out.' When Conroyd made no move, he sat up and shouted. 'Are you deaf? Your king just gave you a command! *Get out!*'

Conroyd smiled. 'Your tame Olken is arrested and sitting in a cell, and you are called upon to clarify certain matters arising from his apprehension.'

He half climbed, half fell out of bed. Reached for his dressing-gown and covered his nakedness. '*Arrested*? On whose authority? Yours? How *dare* you? Free him! *Immediately*! And then take his place in the guardhouse!'

Conroyd considered him, unmoved. 'You don't ask why he's arrested. Can it be you already know?'

*Barl save them . . . Barl save them . . .* 'I don't care why! All that matters is you've laid hands on a fellow councillor without recourse to your king! You'd never have done this while my father was alive and you won't do it now that he's dead!'

'Asher has broken Barl's First Law,' said Conroyd. 'Where else should he be if not in prison?'

*Conroyd knew*. Stunned into silence, he felt his blood turn to ice. *Somehow, he knew*.

Conroyd sneered. 'You puling cripple. Did you truly think you could succeed? Against *me*? Did you actually believe you could deny me my destiny? My rightful possession of this land? You're just like your father, a weakling and a—'

'*Don't you speak of my father*!'

Conroyd ignored him. 'Criminal. Asher has confessed, boy. Magic has failed you and your complicity in his crimes is beyond doubt.'

'Do you *hear* yourself, Conroyd?' he said, his voice low and shaking. His empty stomach roiled and bile burned his throat, his mouth. *Asher was arrested.* '"Your rightful possession of this land"? You arrogant bastard. Father was right: given the chance you and your heirs would elevate the Doranen to godhood and reduce the Olken to slaves! Is it any wonder I'd do anything, risk anything, to keep House Jarralt away from the throne?'

'You pathetic earth-sodden worm!' Conroyd screamed in a whisper, backing him into the wall. 'Are you truly this blind, this *stupid*? You've given an Olken magic! Given a subhuman race of cattle *power*!'

'Let go of me, Conroyd,' Gar said as fingers twisted in the brocade of his dressing-gown. 'Let go and get out.'

'How did you do it? Who was it helped you?' Conroyd hissed. 'The filth didn't know. Was it one of my so-called *friends*? Is that how you did it? Did you promise Daltrie power, or Boqur? Sorvold? Hafar? Promise them riches in return for—'

'I promised nothing to no one!' he shouted, and wrenched himself free. 'And that was assault upon your king – so now *you're* the traitor.'

But Conroyd wasn't listening. Motionless, the hectic colour fading from his face, comprehension dawned behind his eyes. 'It was *in* him?' he said slowly. Almost disbelieving. 'The Olken has magic of his *own*?'

Heart thumping, Gar pushed past him. Stumbled against the corner of the bed and nearly fell. 'Go home, my lord. Consider it house arrest. I will—'

'Do nothing!' said Conroyd, and laughed. 'Little crippled king, do you not understand? It is *over*. Your secret is revealed, your failure discovered. Asher of Restharven is destined to die . . . and you are powerless to save him.'

*But I promised him . . . I promised* . . . Fighting nausea, he made himself look into Conroyd's hateful, hating face. 'Anything Asher did was because I asked it. Because he is my friend.'

Conroyd smiled. 'Then he is a fool. And his lack of discrimination will kill him.'

Gar wondered if this was how his father had felt when the carriage hurtled over the edge of Salbert's Eyrie. 'I'll make you a bargain, Conroyd.' His voice sounded thread-thin and distant. 'Release Asher and I'll give you the crown.'

Conroyd laughed. 'The crown is mine already, boy, and all the kingdom with it! Instead of bargaining you should get on your knees and *beg*!'

'For what? Asher's life?' he dropped to the carpet. 'Very well, then. I beg.' He winced as strong fingers, heavy with rings, imprisoned his face.

'Too late,' said Conroyd.

Something dreadful was burning in the man's eyes. Gar forced himself not to quail before it. Made himself meet that incendiary gaze. 'If you kill him, Conroyd, I'll shout from coast to coast that the Olken are as magic as we. I'll destroy the lie our people have lived here these past six hundred years. I'll tell the truth and let it cost me my life.'

Conroyd's cruel fingers tightened to gasping point. 'Breathe one word of Olken magic, cripple, just one, and I'll bring House Torvig down on your magickless head. By the time I'm done history will remember your father as an ignorant, impotent, cuckolded king. And your mother? Your mother will be known as the Strumpet Queen who sullied her marriage bed with some rutting Olken farmhand, your true father, and then foisted her blasphemous spawn upon an unsuspecting kingdom. Your house will be reviled, its crypt will be struck open and the corpses of your family cast into the wilderness. And your sister? I'll erase her from Doranen memory as though precious, precocious Fane never lived. When I am done with it all that will remain of House Torvig is the cuckold, the strumpet and the half-breed cripple. Is that the legacy you want to leave, boy? Shall that be the sum of your dynastic achievements?'

'You wouldn't,' he choked, fighting the urge to retch. 'You loved my mother!'

'*Loved* her?' echoed Conroyd. 'Your mother was a bitch, a slut, a treacherous whore!'

Guts heaving, Gar knocked the grasping fingers aside and stood. 'I promised Asher I'd protect him. To break that oath would be to destroy House Torvig myself. So do your worst, Conroyd. But be warned: my house stands stronger than you know . . . and you're not as loved as you think.'

Conroyd's face twisted. 'I could kill you, worm, before you had the chance to open your mouth.'

'You could, but you won't,' he retorted. 'Without me to endorse your succession there will be a schism, Conroyd, with no guarantee you'd emerge victorious or even alive at the end of it. Be sensible. Spare Asher and I'll abdicate in your favour and keep secret his use of magic. Kill him . . .'

A moment of blazing silence. 'Well, well, well,' said Conroyd softly. 'So the worm has a spine.'

'How often must I tell you? I am my father's son.'

Conroyd's eyebrows lifted. 'And as your father's son how will you react, I wonder, when I declare a purge upon the Olken?'

*'What?'*

Now Conroyd was smiling. 'Unless you abdicate *and* sign a proclamation publicly condemning Asher of Restharven to death as a criminal, a traitor and a breaker of Barl's Law, I promise he'll be but the first Olken to die. For the sake of the kingdom, and to uphold our sacred laws, I shall launch a purge the likes of which this land has never seen, and when I'm done if there are enough Olken left living to fill a single village then I'll say that I have *failed*!'

Bludgeoned to a disbelieving silence, Gar stared at Conroyd. 'You're mad,' he said at last. 'The General Council would never let you. *Holze* would never—'

'Stop deluding yourself!' Conroyd said brutally. 'Do you think there's a Doranen breathing who wants to see an Olken with magic? And if you think Holze would try to stop me, you've sadly mistaken the depth of his devotion to his precious Barl and her Laws!'

Abruptly, his legs would no longer bear his weight. Collapsing onto his bed Gar turned his head away so Conroyd wouldn't see his despair. His defeat.

'Is there no human feeling in you?' he whispered. 'Does a king's word mean nothing? Asher *trusted* me. Trusted my promise I'd keep him safe.'

'Then he is twice a fool. It was a bargain you had no business making. A promise you knew full well you could never keep, didn't you?'

No. *No*. At least . . . not a promise he thought he'd have to keep. Damn it, they'd been so *careful*.

'The choice is a simple one,' said Conroyd, relentless. 'Do as I say or drown in a flood of Olken blood.'

Gar made himself look at his tormentor. 'You'd truly do it, wouldn't you? You'd kill them all.'

'I have said so,' said Conroyd. 'Do you at last believe it?'

Yes. He believed it, and wondered, sickened, if his father had ever once suspected the truth of this man. The hatred and the violence that slept behind his eyes.

'And what of me?' he asked dully. 'What happens to me once I've signed my name to your filthy lies? A convenient accident?'

Conroyd shrugged. 'Not unless you lose your senses and try something . . . unwise. You'll remain here in the Tower. In seclusion. Withdrawn from public life, your health sadly ruined by the loss of your family and your magic. By the betrayal of one you so stupidly trusted.'

'The people—'

'Won't miss you for long. The Doranen barely noticed your existence before your mistaken elevation to king. And as for the Olken . . .' Another disdainful shrug. 'They were never people in the first place.'

Gar pressed a fist against his heart. There was a pain in him so dreadful, so deep, he thought he should die of it. He wished he could. Kill Asher . . . or kill a kingdom full of his innocent brethren. Whatever he decided, he'd be stained with blood forever.

*Oh, sweet Barl, forgive me . . .*

'Bring me your proclamation then,' he said, and could hardly recognise his own voice. 'I will sign it. And may Barl damn you, Conroyd, in this life and the next.'

# CHAPTER TWENTY-TWO

After a sleepless night, Dathne rose with the sun, washed and dressed and ate a half-hearted breakfast, then drifted downstairs to the bookshop. Dusting shelves was a mindless antidote to worry, and anyway it needed to be done. Young Poppy, hired to run the place day to day, was perfect with customers but seemed allergic to cleaning.

There was something soothing about books. Even the newest Gertsik romance calmed her riotous nerves. Made her smile. Safe amongst her silent shelves, pretending it was still her old life that she lived, she dabbed and drifted and tried not to remember the touch of snowflakes on her skin.

But memory would not be denied.

*Asher made it snow.*

Her hands shook, and she dropped her dusting cloth. She'd never dreamed his power would come like this. Weather Magic was Doranen magic. She'd never known of an Olken who could wield it.

'Fool,' she berated herself savagely, retrieving the duster. 'He's the Innocent Mage and born of Prophecy. What did you think he was? Just another Olken?

Oh, Asher, *Asher*. If only you'd *confided*!'

Failure burned her. She'd been so sure that if she seduced his body his mind would surely follow.

She wasn't used to being wrong.

'I'm Jervale's Heir,' she whispered to a shelf crammed full of histories. 'I'm in the business of being *right*.'

Clearly, the time had come to tell him. To spirit him somewhere to safety and show him to himself at last. Reveal to him his destiny and purpose. Veira would know best where he could be hidden, which meant she could no longer avoid talking to the old woman. And if that meant a scolding for her silence, so be it.

Decided at last, Dathne tossed aside the dusting cloth, turned for the door leading back to her apartment – and was startled by an urgent tapping on the bookshop window. It was young Finella, Mistress Tuttle's apprentice, on her way to work at the bakery. The girl's eyes were popping-wide in her pale face. She waved her hand, pointed round the corner, then disappeared from view.

Frowning, Dathne unlocked the shop's back door and slipped into the tiny courtyard behind. 'Yes, Finny?'

The girl was on the brink of tears. 'Oh, Mistress Dathne, I saw you in there as I was passing and I thought perhaps I should tell you but now I don't know, I don't want to get in trouble, but you work with him, you're friends with him, and you've always been so kind to me . . .'

*Asher*. Resisting the urge to shake the wretched child, Dathne forced a smile. 'It's all right, Finny. Take a deep breath and tell me what's amiss.'

'Oh, Mistress Dathne!' Finny whispered. 'Meister Asher's been arrested!'

'Arrested?' she said sharply. 'Nonsense. Where did you hear such a poppycock tale?'

Finella shrank back. 'From my brother Deek! He was

street-cleaning in the alleyway opposite the guardhouse and he saw them bring Asher in. All tied up he was, with a cloth over his face and a noose round his neck! But the cloth slipped and Deek saw him. It was awful, he said! Captain Orrick was there, and Lord Jarralt too.'

*Arrested* – and in such a skulduggery fashion. She could hardly think straight for the frantic pounding of her heart. 'And did they see Deek spying there?'

Finny coloured, indignant. 'He wasn't spying, he was doin' his job! But no, he says they never saw him 'cause he made sure to stay quiet as a mouse. Deek says a smart man who comes across that kind of business is deaf and dumb and blind!'

'And yet he told you?'

'I'm always the first one up, on account of starting so early in the bakery,' said Finny, shrugging. 'He said he had to tell someone, he was feeling all wobbly, and he knew I'd hold my tongue. And I will too! I'm only telling you 'cause I know you're Asher's friend!'

Trembling, Dathne hugged her. 'And I'm right grateful, Finny. Now off you go to Mistress Tuttle's before you get docked for lateness. And, Finny – not a word about this to *anyone*. Promise?'

Finny nodded vigorously. 'Oh yes, I promise. Mistress Dathne, is Asher going to be all right?'

She forced a smile. 'Of course he is. I'm sure it's all a terrible mistake.'

Reassured, Finny hurried away. Breathless with fear, Dathne contacted Veira.

*Arrested*? the old woman repeated. The link connecting them vibrated with her shock. *Do you know why?*

'No,' said Dathne. 'But, Veira . . . he has the Weather Magic. I fear he's been discovered.'

Veira swore.

'I'm sorry!' Dathne wailed. 'This is all my fault! I should've told him who he was weeks ago, I should've listened to Matt, I should *never* have—'

*We can lay blame later. Pack all that might betray you, child, and leave the City at once.*

'Leave?' she said. 'Veira, no! I have to save Asher, I have to—'

*You can't, child. Not on your own. And the City won't be safe for you now. Come to me and together we'll find a way.*

Smearing the tears on her cheeks with a shaking hand, Dathne nodded. 'All right. Where are you?'

The knowledge sped from Veira's mind to hers through the Circle Stone link. 'The Black Woods? You're not so far away then.'

*Far enough. Don't risk a horse, for fear of attention. Cloak yourself and slip out of the City sideways. Walk as fast as you can. The Black Woods Road is lightly travelled this time of year. If you do see someone, hide till they pass. I'll meet you on the way.*

She wasn't alone . . . the relief was overwhelming. And then she sat up sharply, remembering. 'Matt! Veira, I have to warn Matt.'

*Leave Matthias to me. Think only of yourself, child. If you stay there much longer the next knock on your door could be a guardsman with inconvenient questions.*

Numbly, she stared into the pulsing heart of the Circle Stone. 'Asher will think I've abandoned him,' she whispered. 'He'll think I never meant a word I said.'

*Maybe he will and maybe he won't*, said Veira. *That's not for you to say. Now hurry!*

Fat with satisfaction, Morg scattered salt on the wet ink of the proclamations that Gar would shortly sign then sat back in his chair. Beyond the closed door of Jarralt's private library he could hear voices as the lord's household bustled.

At last his plans were fruiting. And with inconvenient Asher soon to be dead, the cripple off the throne, and himself as king and free to tamper as he willed, Barl's cursed Wall would quickly be a memory.

Knowing how close he'd come to failure, fury stirred. First Durm's injuries, then the unexpected interference of that Olken filth. A tremor of hatred, of livid frustration, shook his fine-knit limbs. He was so *sick* of this place. Sick of this exile behind Barl's Wall. Of being cut off from his vast reservoir of power, trammelled and confined in these prisons of meat, vulnerable to mere *accident*. Forced to wait and plot and connive and scheme instead of reaching out his will and *taking* what he wanted the instant that he wanted it!

To be thwarted by an Olken? It was enough to make him vomit! He wanted to kill them all. Slaughter every last Olken and yes, the Doranen too. Rid this pretty kingdom of its cattle and renegades. Cleanse the land with blood and fire.

But no. As an infinite intellect trapped in finite flesh, he dared not risk it. Alarm and alert the kingdom's magicians and united they might defeat him. Caution was the key. The moment Barl's Wall was destroyed he could abandon this body and reunite with his larger, immortal self. But until then he had to be careful. Until then, Morg could still die.

A whisper from his deeply prisoned host. *Yes, yes, die!*

He smiled. Fool Conroyd, who'd fancied himself a mage to be reckoned with. Who only now began to understand the meaning of ambition. Of mastery. Of power.

The parchments dry now he rolled them, secured

them with a ribbon from the desk drawer and tucked them under his arm. Fat Willer was waiting patiently on a bench outside the library door.

'My lord!' he cried, lumbering to his feet. 'What now?'

A useful little toad, this. Disappointed poisonous men were always useful. 'Return to the Tower. Inform that black streak of misery Darran that I wish him to announce an emergency session of the General Council for two o'clock this afternoon.'

Willer bowed. 'Yes, my lord.'

Next Morg ordered Jarralt's carriage and directed it to the City Chapel, where he found wittering Holze in the midst of leading a morning service.

'Conroyd!' the Barl-sodden cleric exclaimed once the caterwauling was over and the congregation had emptied from its seats. 'You look quite perturbed! Is something the matter?'

Morg arranged Jarralt's austerely beautiful face into lines of tragedy and woe. 'Alas, dear Efrim, I'm afraid it is. Can we talk? Privately?'

'Of course! Come, we can speak in my office.'

Smiling quietly, Morg followed him out of the chapel. As they passed yet another portrait of his dearly beloved dead whore, he blew her a kiss.

When Asher roused from his stupor he found himself still on the floor of his cell in the guardhouse, unbound, and Pellen Orrick sitting in a chair outside it reading reports. The pain Jarralt had inflicted was gone but the memory of it dried his mouth and threatened to start him shaking all over again.

Unsteadily, he sat up. Leaned against the nearest bars. 'I want to see Gar,' he croaked. 'I got a right.'

Orrick looked at him. Nobody would ever describe

the captain as forthcoming, but they'd fallen into the habit of easy, joking conversation in the last long weeks. He'd been halfway to thinking the man might become a friend. Now, though, the warm flicker of appreciation in Orrick's pale eyes was extinguished and his face was set like stone.

'Don't speak to me of rights, Asher. Not after what you've done. And don't go trying to change your tune now, either. You *confessed*, to Lord Jarralt and then to me! You're condemned out of your own mouth!'

He'd confessed to Orrick? He didn't remember that. Pain had stolen his last hour or so. 'I only did what Gar asked me to do.'

Orrick grimaced. 'So you say.'

'I'm a liar now, am I?'

'Asher, I'm afraid to think what you are,' said Orrick and stood, turning away.

He wrapped his fingers round the cell bars and hauled himself to his feet. 'Jarralt ain't told you, has he?'

Reluctantly, Orrick turned back. 'Told me what?' he asked at last, grudging.

'Gar's lost his magic.'

Another silence, longer this time. Then Orrick shook his head. 'That's impossible.'

'No. It's true.'

'Then you stole it,' Orrick retorted, 'though Barl alone knows how.'

'*Stole* it? Do I look brainsick to you?'

'You look like a traitor.'

It was no good, he couldn't stand up any longer. Stifling a groan, he slid back to the floor. 'Well, I ain't.'

'You broke Barl's First Law!'

'And Jarralt broke the Second! He hurt me with magic, Pellen! Do you care about *that* law? Or doesn't hurting me count?'

For the first time a shimmer of uncertainty crossed Orrick's obdurate face. 'I have no bias in the law, Asher,' he said stiffly. 'I agree Lord Jarralt was . . . misguided. But he was also sore provoked!'

'And so was I bloody provoked!' he shouted. 'D'you think I did this *willingly?* Gar begged me, Orrick. You got any idea what that's like, being begged by a king? He was desperate to keep Lur out of Jarralt's hands and I was stupid enough to let him convince me. *Ask* him, Pellen. He'll tell you I ain't lyin', I *swear.*'

Orrick ran a hand over his face. Listening, but not convinced. 'You didn't steal His Majesty's magic?'

*'No.'*

'Then where did it come from?' Orrick whispered. He looked torn between fear and fury. 'Olken are taught from the cradle: we don't have magic. So where did yours come from if not the king?'

'I don't know and I don't care! All I know is Gar swore to protect me if the truth came out. Well, Pellen, it's out. And instead of actin' like the City's Captain and askin' the king yourself whether or not I'm tellin' the truth, you're runnin', about like Conroyd Jarralt's lapdog! Takin' his word unchallenged – a man who tortures with magic. A man who's coveted this kingdom's crown for the best part of his life. Who'd do just about anythin', I reckon, to snatch it off Gar's head and put it on his own.'

Orrick glared, seething. 'I am no man's lapdog!'

Muscles screaming, Asher forced himself onto his knees. Hanging onto the bars, harshly breathing, he looked Pellen Orrick full in the face. 'Prove it.'

Orrick stayed silent as a thousand thoughts rolled behind the glassy surface of his eyes. Slowly, the outright rejection in his face faded to wary suspicion. 'Why should I? You're the one in prison, not me.'

'Today,' Asher agreed, feeling ill. 'But if you let this injustice stand without raising a finger against it there won't be a single Olken safe in all of Lur. Don't you see, Pellen? If Jarralt dares hurt *me* with magic, who of us won't he touch?'

Still suspicious, Orrick tapped a knuckle to his lips. 'You must see, Asher. What you claim strains all bounds of credibility.'

It was a struggle, but he kept his voice steady. He was so close to begging . . . and he'd never begged for anything in his life. 'I can't help that. What I did was for Gar, and the Kingdom. I swear it. Pellen, you know me. You *know* me. I ain't a traitor.'

Like the first hint of sunlight on snow, Orrick's expression softened. 'Before today, I confess I'd have laughed to hear you called one.'

Asher swallowed. 'And nowt's changed. But without your help I'll never prove it.'

'Lord Jarralt has laid it strict upon me I'm to keep this coil a secret,' said Orrick, frowning. 'I'm not to step foot outside the guardhouse till he returns.'

He'd never known hope could hurt so much. 'Then send Gar a message. Private and sealed. If you ask him, he'll come. He'll fix this, I know it. He promised.'

Orrick turned away from the cell. With his hand on the outer door's latch he said, not looking back, 'I promise nothing.'

'But you'll try?'

The longest moment of silence he'd ever lived through. A fractional dip of Pellen Orrick's head. White knuckles on the door latch. 'Yes, Asher. I'll try.'

When Conroyd Jarralt returned to the Tower and was shown into Gar's library, he wasn't alone; Holze stood at his shoulder. One look at him and Gar knew Conroyd had told all. Eyes grim, mouth pressed thin and unforgiving, there was little of the kindly, welcoming cleric about the royal spiritual advisor now. Instead he looked like a man made of iron, against which all gentle things must shatter.

Pinned to his chair by Holze's hard, heavy gaze, Gar felt himself diminish. Weaken. Falter.

In the time between his rude awakening and this moment he'd managed to gather his scattered wits. Smother dismay and bolster courage. Let Conroyd bluster and bully as he liked, he was not king. His threats were the rantings of a man unhinged by thwarted ambition, nothing more. No Doranen of conscience would stand by and let him slaughter innocent Olken. No cleric who followed Barl's merciful teachings would countenance such uncivil discord. Holze would never side with Conroyd. Holze would understand that what his king had done was done for the good of all.

Or so he'd told himself as he bathed and dressed and recovered his balance. But now Holze was here before him, with all his thoughts clear in his face.

'Your Majesty,' he said. 'I scarcely know where to begin.'

Gar stood. There must yet be hope. 'Holze. Efrim. I thought you of all men would understand.'

'Understand what?' said the cleric, a whip-snap in his voice. 'That you placed personal ambition above a sacred oath? That you suborned blasphemy in the pursuit of worldly power? That you conspired to pervert the course of law and justice, of Barl's holy word, which you were sworn to uphold? No, sir. I do not understand. I will never understand. And I praise Barl your father did not live to see the day his son committed such sins against the kingdom in whose sweet service he spent his life.'

'How can the truth be blasphemous?' he demanded. 'Holze, don't you understand? We've been living a lie, all of us. The Olken are possessed of magic. Learning this, how can we in good conscience—'

'The question of Olken magic is irrelevant!' said Holze. 'The only arbiter of conscience is Blessed Barl and her Laws and they are crystal clear on the matter. Magic is reserved for the Doranen, custodians of Barl's kingdom. As king you but hold this land in trust. A trust you have grievously betrayed.'

Gar looked from Holze to Conroyd Jarralt. Until now, he'd never thought hate could be a thing you tasted, like wine gone sour in the jug. 'Congratulations, Conroyd. Somehow you've managed to convert a good man to your deceitful cause.'

Conroyd smiled. 'The only deceit was yours. Now hold your tongue. All we require from you is a signature on these proclamations. Your opinions have ceased to carry weight in this kingdom.'

'Whilst yours have assumed all the heaviness of a crown?'

'In due course.'

The bastard was unspeakably smug. Feeling sick, his ill-advised breakfast churning in his belly, Gar held out his hand to receive the first roll of parchment. Untied the ribbon encircling it. Read its contents.

He looked up. 'I can't sign this.'

Holze exchanged glances with Conroyd. 'Why not?'

'Because it's a lie!' he said, and tossed the parchment aside. 'Asher didn't steal my magic. There was no Olken conspiracy to dislodge me from the throne, or usurp Doranen authority in the kingdom. Asher did what he did because I asked him to and for no other reason! Isn't it enough that you want me to kill him? Must I kill his memory also, and all the good he did as well?'

'If you do not sign it, you leave open the possibility that some misguided Olken fool might question the validity of his condemnation,' said Conroyd. 'He is popular, this monster you created. To uncreate him you must paint him blacker than he's painted himself and so ensure he is remembered not with love but with loathing. His destruction must stand as a beacon till the end of time, a warning to any Olken who would dare disturb the quietude of this kingdom.'

As well talk to a wall as to Conroyd Jarralt. He looked to Holze. 'Can't you see this is wrong? How can you support it? Ask me to support it? I thought you loved me!'

'I loved a boy who loved his family,' said Holze, unmoved. 'I loved a man who loved this kingdom, who bore misfortune with fortitude and spent his life in service to others. I don't know the man I see before me today. And how can I love a man I do not know?'

Gar felt his legs give way, fold him once more into his chair. Suddenly it was hard to breathe. 'I can't do this.'

'You must,' said Holze. 'Asher is a canker, poised to kill a kingdom. He must be cut from its heart before his poison spreads. If you do not see it there is as little hope for you as there is for him.'

He'd never imagined soft-spoken Holze could sound so harsh. 'But he is innocent. Blameless.'

'Hardly innocent,' said Conroyd. 'By your own admission he broke the law!'

Again, he looked to Holze. 'Do you know what Conroyd threatened, to make me agree to this perfidy?

Did he tell you what he swore he'd do if I refused to conspire with him in Asher's murder?'

Holze was shaking his head. 'Lawful execution is no murder.'

'He said he'd despoil my family's legacy!'

'You've done that yourself.'

'He said he'd slaughter thousands of guiltless Olken!'

'If it's discovered there are other Olken – other traitors – with pretensions to a power denied them by Barl herself then certainly they will die,' Holze replied. 'But that is hardly slaughter.'

Conroyd smiled. 'Accept it, boy. Your reign is over. You threw power away when you yoked yourself to Asher of Restharven. Sign his warrant of execution and this, your intent to abdicate, then get down on your knees and praise Barl that for the sake of this kingdom's peace you're to be spared a more *rigorous* accounting of your actions.'

Gar stared at the second roll of parchment and for one last mad moment considered defying them. Considered spitting in Conroyd's handsome, hateful face and trusting himself and Asher to Barl's mercy. To the love of his kingdom's people, both Doranen and Olken. To their forgiveness of his frailty, his failure as a magician, his desperation as a king.

Somehow, Conroyd read his mind. 'They might – *might* – forgive you, boy. They will *never* forgive Asher. He is dead already. He was dead the moment you convinced him to defy Barl's First Law. And if you're honest, if you're even capable of honesty, you know I speak the truth.'

He felt a peculiar inner breaking then, as though his bones were made of glass and Conroyd's words were hammers, striking. He nodded. 'Yes. I know.'

There was pen and ink in the desk drawer. He fetched

them and signed the proclamations. Wrote carefully, with a steady hand, using all his names and titles. *Gar Antyn Bartolomew Dannison Torvig, Scion House Torvig, Defender House Torvig, WeatherWorker of Lur.*

Traitor . . . betrayer . . . and breaker of oaths.

'Don't forget your personal seal,' prompted Conroyd. 'The finishing touch, so to speak.'

A stick of sealing wax lay in another drawer. Conroyd melted it for him with a word, smiling just a little. He pressed his signet ring into each blood-red pool and completed his act of treachery. Watching, it was as though a stranger's hand did the deed.

Conroyd took the signed proclamations and rolled them swiftly. 'As for the rest . . .'

'Rest?' he said, dully. 'What rest?'

'My elevation to the throne. I've called an emergency General Council meeting at which you'll announce your abdication and withdrawal from public life. You'll declare me your lawful heir. Lur's new king and WeatherWorker. Then you'll return to this Tower and not set foot beyond its grounds until such time as I give you permission.'

This was a dream, it had to be. 'Today? You want me to abdicate today?'

Conroyd was pulling on gold-stitched gloves. 'Why postpone the inevitable? Without magic you cannot be king. And Lur needs its WeatherWorker. Barl only knows what damage was done by that creature you let meddle with the Wall.'

'Asher did no damage.'

Conroyd sneered. 'How would you know? You're a magickless cripple.'

He flinched. Felt corrosive self-hatred, like acid. His father would *never* so meekly submit . . . he *had* to keep fighting . . .

He made himself stand. 'For all you know there might be a cure for me, Conroyd. I demand consultation with Pother Nix. I demand—'

'Nothing,' said Conroyd. 'Not now, not ever. And besides, there is no cure. Now, as to the dispersal of your household.'

'Dispersal? What do you—'

Conroyd ignored him. 'In keeping with your newly reduced role in the kingdom, and to minimise your burden on the royal purse, the majority of your staff will be reassigned. Only Darran will remain to take care of your modest daily needs. I hope he can cook. And clean.'

'One man?' Gar said, incredulous. 'To care for all this Tower? Darran is elderly, and recently infirm! You can't expect him to—'

'But I can,' said Conroyd, smiling. 'I do. Perhaps you could in some small way shift for yourself? Barl knows you'll have the time.'

'Conroyd,' Holze murmured disapprovingly. Standing to one side. Doing nothing, *nothing*, to stop this.

Unheeding, Conroyd continued. 'Your stables of course will be emptied; horses and equipment sold off.'

Fresh pain stabbed. 'Sold? Ballodair? No! He was a gift from my father, you have no right to—'

'Your expenses must be defrayed somehow. And given you'll not be riding anywhere in the near future, what need have you of horses? The animal will be sold, along with all the rest.' Conroyd stepped closer, pale eyes glittering. 'You dare to complain? Don't. Mercy has its limits. You are free on sufferance, boy.'

'Free?' he said, and laughed. 'I'm your prisoner.'

Holze cleared his throat heavily. 'If this Tower has become your cell, then it's a cell of your own making.'

'And as cells go, it's not without comfort,' Conroyd added. 'I'm sure your unfortunate Olken would be pleased to change places.'

Gar felt his belly spasm. 'He's not to be touched, Conroyd. You've got your wish. He's in prison and condemned to die. That should be enough even for you.' When Conroyd stayed silent, he turned to Holze. 'Barlsman, I'm begging you. Restrain Lord Jarralt. If not for me, then for the love you bore my father.'

Holze's face twisted. 'Your purse is empty of that coin, sir.'

'Your purse is empty of all coin,' said Conroyd. 'Save the cuicks I let fall in your path. Remember that. Remember also the Olken stand hostage to your good behaviour and silent tongue. If word of Asher's exploits leaves this room, there will be consequences.'

'I see,' said Gar, when he could trust himself to speak. 'I disobey and someone else suffers?'

Conroyd's smile was pure poison. 'Exactly. Now, I suggest you spend the next while penning a short, crowd-pleasing speech for our esteemed General Council. As for the meeting, I'll return to collect you for it later this afternoon. Don't keep me waiting.'

With an effort, he bit back a response. Instead looked to Holze. 'About Durm—'

'I go now to the palace infirmary,' the Barlsman said. 'He shall be afforded all rites and respect. None of this mess is of his making.'

Was that true? He wished he knew. Wished, desperately, that he'd had more time to quiz the dying Master Magician. To learn more of Barl's diary and what use Durm had made of it, if any, and how it was their only hope. He had to find the thing. If there was an escape from this nightmare, perhaps he'd find it there . . .

'Thank you, Holze,' he said stiffly. 'For myself, and my father.' He looked again at Conroyd. 'You will need to choose his successor.'

Conroyd shrugged. 'Certainly. At some point.'

'No. Now. The law is quite clear, you must—'

'Law?' Conroyd laughed. 'You sit there and lecture me on *law*? Hold your tongue, brat. Remember your new position in the kingdom.'

He stood, feeling most peculiar. Disconnected and likely to float right out of his body. 'I shall. Are we done?'

'For now.'

'Then get out.'

Conroyd's golden eyebrows lifted. 'Get out, *Your Majesty*.'

He opened his mouth to say something catastrophic, but was stopped by Darran's flustered entrance. 'Forgive me, Your Majesty, but an urgent message has come from the City Guardhouse. It's from Captain Orrick. The runner is awaiting your reply.'

Conroyd held out his hand. 'Give it here.'

Darran hesitated. 'My lord, it is addressed to the king.'

'*Give it here.*'

Gar nodded as, uncertain and unhappy, Darran glanced at him. The message was handed over. Conroyd broke the seal, read the note. Refolded it and slipped it into his pocket. 'Tell the runner to inform Captain Orrick I shall arrive at the guardhouse in due course.'

Darran took a step towards him. 'Sir . . . ?'

Gar stared at the floor. 'Do as Lord Jarralt says, Darran.'

'Yes, sir,' said Darran, and withdrew.

What did it say?' he asked.

Conroyd shook his head. 'Nothing that concerns you any longer.'

Jarralt and Holze departed, taking the signed proclamations with them. Aimless, emptied of thought and feeling, Gar wandered around the room like a boat set adrift on a lowering tide. Darran returned and hovered in the open doorway.

'Your Majesty . . .'

'Leave me be.'

Darran took a step forward. 'Sir, Lord Jarralt is issuing orders. He says—'

'I know what he says,' he whispered, and ran gentle fingers along a shelf-line of books. 'Lord Jarralt is a voluble man.'

Darran's lined face was a picture of confusion and dismay. 'Sir . . . he says you're no longer the king.'

'He's right. I've had a busy morning, Darran, though you might not think so to look at me.'

'Your Majesty . . .'

*'Don't call me that!'*

A shocked silence. Darran crept a little closer. 'Sir?'

'Do you know what I've done since opening my eyes?'

It was Darran's turn to whisper. 'No, sir.'

'Then I'll tell you. I've eaten breakfast, renounced the throne and murdered my friend. And look, it's not even midday! Quick, Darran, find me a baby and I'll strangle it before lunch!'

'Sir!'

It came as a shock to realise he was crying. Hot tears, falling from cold eyes. Springing from a cold and killing heart.

'Just get out, would you?' he shouted. 'Get out of here, old man, old fool! Get out and leave me alone!'

Darran fled.

* * *

It felt like years had passed, but finally Orrick returned. When the cell's outer door opened again Asher grunted to his feet and stepped to his cage's locked door.

'Pellen!' he said eagerly, craning to see past the captain's shoulder. 'Did you fetch him? Is he coming? Is it all sorted out? What's that scroll you got there? Is it my pardon?'

Pellen gave him a look so cold, so hard, it was like being struck in the face with a bar of iron.

'Be silent.'

He felt his heart jolt. 'Pellen? What is it, what's—' And then he stopped, because entering the outer cell was Conroyd Jarralt. He carried a slender poker, tapping it against one boot as he walked. At his heels Willer, bloated and shining with triumph. And behind him came two guards, manacles dangling from their fists. Ox Bunder and Treev Lallard, casual darts and drinking mates down at the Goose.

He felt the blood drain from his face, leaving him dizzy and sick, and stepped unsteadily backwards. 'Pellen? What's goin' on?'

Ignoring him, Orrick looked at Jarralt. Jarralt nodded. Orrick unrolled the scroll and began to read.

*'Insofar as he has been apprehended in the midst of a blasphemous and criminal act, with witness unimpeachable, and insofar as this act is named the breaking of Barl's First Law: I, King Gar the First, WeatherWorker of Lur, hereby condemn Asher of Restharven to lawful death.'*

Numbly disbelieving, he let the words wash over him like so much salty water. '*. . . suspicion of baleful influence upon his king . . . instigation of Olken conspiracy to usurp the throne . . . Furthermore, let it be known that said criminal Asher of Restharven has acted in a fashion* *suggestive of further miscreancy . . . authorised to question by whatever means necessary . . .*'

Orrick stopped reading. Confused, Asher stared. 'No. That ain't right. Gar wouldn't – that ain't right! It's a forgery! Jarralt—'

Orrick stepped forward and flattened the parchment against the cell bars. '*It is no forgery.*' His voice was harsh with rage and pain. 'Or don't you recognise the signature? The seal?'

They were Gar's.

'So what?' Asher said, starting to shake. 'That don't prove nowt. Gar wouldn't abandon me like this, make up that pack of lies about conspiracies and usurping. This is Jarralt's bloody bastardry! Gar would *never*—'

'That's *enough*, Asher!' Orrick shouted, snatching back the proclamation. 'His Majesty has renounced you. It's over.'

Conroyd Jarralt cleared his throat. 'Well . . . not quite, Captain. Before death comes discomfort. Unless of course Asher would like to reveal here and now the names of those who helped him?'

'Nobody helped me,' he said. 'There was nowt to help with! There ain't no conspiracy!'

'The king says there is,' said Conroyd Jarralt. 'And that's good enough for me. Guards?'

The cell door was unlocked. Bunder and Lallard entered. Shackled him with the manacles, fixed the chains to the sides of the cell and stretched him out like a scarecrow in a field.

'Excellent,' said Jarralt. 'Now leave us.'

'What about a trial?' demanded Asher as the outer door banged shut. Already his shoulders were burning. He saw Willer step closer to the cage, eyes alight with eagerness. 'Don't I get a trial? Timon Spake got a trial!'

'You're not Timon Spake,' said Jarralt. 'The king himself has corroborated your confession and condemned you out of hand.'

'He wouldn't! He *promised.*'

Jarralt ignored him. Instead turned to Orrick. 'Captain, it's likely this traitor's co-conspirators will be found amongst his intimate acquaintances. Seek them out and arrest them quietly before they have a chance to flee justice.'

*Dathne.* Asher choked back a cry of protest. *No.* Oh, to be able to warn her. There'd be a way with magic, if only he knew what it was.

Bloody magic. It had to be good for more than causing trouble.

Orrick was nodding. 'Yes, my lord.'

'Willer?'

'My lord?'

'Assist Captain Orrick. You'll know best who to look for and where they can be found.'

Willer's disappointment was almost comical. 'My lord? I wanted to stay, to assist you in—'

'*Willer.*'

Cringing, the slug retreated. 'Yes, my lord. Of course, my lord.'

'And Willer? Captain? One last thing.' With the snap of his fingers and a softly spoken word, Jarralt froze Orrick and the slug where they stood. 'Attend. Asher was apprehended attempting magic, not performing it. There is no power in him. This is what you know and will remember.'

'That's a lie,' said Asher. The blankness in Pellen Orrick's face made him feel sick. It was as though the man's soul had been wiped away. Willer's too . . . if the little turd possessed one. 'I can do magic. I'd bloody kill you with it if I could!'

The look in Jarralt's eyes was frightening. 'You couldn't. But in the short time remaining to you, dare hint to anyone that you could try and I'll kill them. Their families, too. Is that clear?'

Nauseous, believing him absolutely, Asher nodded. 'Aye.'

'Good.' With another snap of his fingers, Jarralt released his frozen victims. 'Carry out your orders then. And see to it I am not disturbed hereafter, Captain.'

Orrick bowed. Seemingly he'd taken no harm from whatever Jarralt had done. 'My lord.' Without a backward glance he left the cell, a subdued Willer at his heels.

Asher watched Jarralt pass his hand before the outer cell door. Saw the air shiver blackly. Felt a brief pressure against his chest. Jarralt turned. Smiled. Approached.

'Alone at last.'

Asher felt his lungs hitch. 'Gar never signed that proclamation.'

Lounging in the open cell door, Jarralt raised his eyebrows. 'Of course he did.'

'No. You faked it. You—'

'*Asher*.' Jarralt's smile twisted into something more complicated. 'He signed it.'

Asher believed him. For a moment he couldn't breathe at all. Rage . . . grief . . . terror . . . his heart was barely beating.

'You know I did this on my own,' he protested. 'You know there ain't a conspiracy. You were inside my head. You know *everything*.'

Jarralt raised the poker and eyed its slender strength. 'True.'

'Then why—'

'Because I want to. Because your simple axe death will not satisfy. You interfered, little Olken, and I brook no interference. So I'm going to punish you . . . the good, old-fashioned way.'

There was sweat rolling down his back. His face. Asher blinked the stinging saltwater from his eyes. There was something . . . different about Conroyd Jarralt. He'd always been a smug bastard. Impatient. Contemptuous. Superior. Utterly unlikeable. But now he was something else. Something more. It rolled off him in thick stinking waves. Blood-curdling, stomach-churning . . .

*Evil.*

'Gar was right about you,' he whispered. 'Borne, too. You're bad. Rotten bad, all the way through. You can't hide it any more. And when your Doranen friends see the truth of you, they'll not let you keep your stolen crown. This kingdom'll tear apart, Jarralt. It'll die, and you'll have killed it. Is that what you want?'

'Yes. Now save your breath,' Jarralt advised him kindly. 'You'll need it for screaming. And when you're done with screaming – after I've reduced your throat to a raw and bloody wasteland – Orrick and his men will take you to the centre of the City Square, where you'll be chained in a cage for all the world to see and spit upon. And at midnight on Barl's Day next, a suitably dramatic moment you'll agree, before as large a crowd as can be contrived, your head will be hacked from your shoulders, your body will be fed to the swine, the swine shall be butchered and fed to the dogs, and the dogs will be shot dead with arrows.'

Languid and unexcited, Jarralt strolled into the cell. Spoke a single, knife-edged word. The poker's brass tip caught fire. In his pale ice eyes pleasure flickered, and something else. Something dark and dangerous and soaked in blood. He smiled. Touched.

Asher's world disappeared in a scarlet sheet of flame.

# CHAPTER TWENTY-THREE

With a small self-satisfied sigh Darran covered His Ma— His Highness's lunch tray with a damask napkin. The prince's silence since Lord Jarralt's abrupt departure and his own unkind ejection from the library had been absolute and ominous. Luncheon gave him the excuse he needed to make sure everything was all right.

Well. As all right as it could be, given recent appalling developments.

With a last look about the kitchen he picked up the tray and headed for the door. It was perhaps a good thing Mistress Hemshaw had been dismissed; if she could see the place now, after his distracted efforts at cooking, she'd have gone into strong hysterics.

He was tempted to go into strong hysterics himself.

How empty the Tower felt with all its people forcibly removed. Aching with sorrow and regrets he climbed stair by silent stair up to Gar's suite of apartments. Passing by Asher's floor, he shuddered. Closed his mind to a calamity of images and kept on climbing.

The prince was still in his library, sitting in the armchair he'd shifted to face the uncurtained window.

'I've brought you some luncheon, sir,' Darran said, standing just inside the doorway.

'I'm not hungry.'

'Hungry or not, you should eat,' he replied, forcing his voice to a cheerful chiding. Hesitantly, he entered the room. 'If you fall ill it'll be Pother Nix's potions you'll be swallowing, and while my cooking isn't perfect I can promise you it does taste better than that.'

'Leave it on the desk then,' said Gar. His voice sounded dull. Lacklustre. His left hand was just visible, dangling over the arm of the chair. It looked dead.

Darran frowned, and shook his head even though the prince couldn't see him. 'Now, sir, you don't want it to get cold.'

'I said *leave it on the desk*!' Gar shouted, and flung himself out of the chair. A sapphire-studded dagger dangled from the fingers of his right hand and his eyes were frightening.

Darran stepped back, his grip on the lunch tray tight enough to hurt. 'Sir, the weapon isn't necessary. I assure you the chicken is quite deceased. I roasted it myself.'

With a roar of rage Gar threw the dagger across the room. It struck the doorjamb and stuck there, quivering. 'I care naught for your chicken, old man! Take it away! And if you can't do as I tell you, don't come here again!'

He would *not* look at the dagger. Instead he put down the tray on the nearest flat surface and approached his prince. 'Enough, sir,' he said, hands raised palm out like a man reasoning with madness. 'You're going to hurt yourself.'

Gar laughed. 'Hurt myself? You old fool, I never hurt myself! Only other people! My parents – my sister –

Durm – yes, he's dead now too.' He groaned, and dropped slowly to the floor. 'Asher . . .'

Darran knelt beside him, deaf to complaining muscles and creaking bones. 'You're talking nonsense. You didn't cause the accident that killed your family and our poor Master Magician, Barl rest him.'

'How can I be certain?' demanded Gar. 'I don't remember what happened! It might have been me, Darran. It might have been my damned capricious magic. No physical agency for the accident was ever discovered, was it? And clearly my power was never right. It was flawed, as I am flawed. If I wasn't I'd still possess it. I'd still be the WeatherWorker and Asher would . . . Barl's *tits*, Darran. I swore I'd protect him, I swore he'd be safe, and instead I signed his death warrant. I betrayed the only friend I've ever known, a man who saved my life, who tried to save my kingdom when I couldn't. I am *pathetic. Disgusting*. I wonder how you can bear to be in the same room with me.'

Distressed by his distress and closing his ears to the blasphemy, he seized Gar's hand and held on tight. 'Don't say such things, sir!'

'Why not? They're true. So what if Conroyd threatened me? I should've found a way to defeat him. To save Asher!'

He stared. Gar's hand felt so cold. *He* felt so cold. 'Lord Jarralt threatened you? How? Why?'

Gar pulled his hand free and let himself sag against the armchair. 'It doesn't matter. What matters is I've given our kingdom to that man. Handed it over without a fight. My father would be so disappointed . . .'

'No, sir! *No*,' he said fiercely. 'That's not true. Your father loved you and was proud of you every day of his life. He's proud now, I'm certain of it, as I am proud.

And nor is it true that Asher is your only friend. *I* am your friend, sir, and will remain so till the day I die.'

Gar looked at him. Tried to smile, and miserably failed. 'Then in the name of all that's merciful, Darran,' he whispered, '*leave me alone.*'

He sighed. Clambered to his feet, frowning. 'If I do, sir, will you promise me first that you'll eat?'

'I could,' said Gar. 'But my promises are a figment, Darran. Don't you know that yet? I shed promises the way a dog sheds fleas.'

'And *that's* not true either!'

Now Gar stood, only to slump on the arm of his chair. As though standing were a task beyond his strength. 'Isn't it? Ask Asher.'

He sniffed. 'I don't consort with criminals.'

'He's not a criminal. He's a sacrifice.'

'But he's arrested! Why would he be arrested if he's not a—'

'Darran . . .' Gar hesitated. Examined the carpet. 'If I tell you what's happened, why I'm deposed and the Tower emptied, Asher condemned—'

'Oh, I wish you would, sir! I can't make head or tail of anything!'

Now the prince looked up. His face was solemn, his gaze intent. 'You can never repeat it. Lives will depend on your silence. Not just yours and mine, but those of every Olken in the kingdom. Do you understand?'

Darran straightened. Let a little of his affronted pride show. 'I have spent the best part of my life in royal service, sir. I think I know the meaning of discretion.'

Faint colour washed into Gar's pale cheeks. 'Of course you do. Forgive me.'

'Certainly. Now please, sir. *Tell* me.'

By the time the prince finished Darran knew the world

he'd lived in was gone forever, or perhaps had never existed. He groped his way to the library's other chair and sat down.

'Barl have mercy,' he whispered. 'This is all my fault.'

The prince stared. 'Your fault?'

Hot with shame, he couldn't look at Gar. Stared instead at his manicured fingernails and longed hopelessly to be anywhere else in Lur, confessing anything but this. 'You see . . . I always encouraged Willer in his antipathy towards Asher. Allowed him to know the depths of my own disliking. For a whole year, longer, we carped and criticised and complained of his existence to each other. And then, after you asked Asher and me to work together for the good of the kingdom, I failed to take Willer into my confidence or explain my change in attitude. Instead I reproved him for bad behaviour. When you became king I think Willer was expecting some kind of promotion. But it didn't come – and then I was so busy – oh, sir. Willer never would've turned to Lord Jarralt, never would've spied for him, if I'd handled the matter with greater tact!'

After a long silence Gar sighed. 'You don't know that. I don't know that. And it hardly matters now. If it's any consolation, Darran, I don't blame you. I think Willer and Asher would've been enemies regardless. They're cut from different cloths.'

Subdued, Darran folded his hands in his lap. 'You're very generous, sir.' He cleared his throat. 'Is there nothing you can do for Asher?'

'No,' Gar said tiredly. 'I wish there was. I'd die in his place if Jarralt would let me. But the kingdom comes first, and your people must be protected. If Willer hadn't been set to spy on him – if our mad plan hadn't been discovered – we might have weathered this storm. Found a way to calmer waters, or a cure for my affliction. But it's too late now. I can't save Asher. I can't even save myself.'

Darran shook his head. 'It's beyond all comprehension sir. That an Olken could *do* such things . . .'

'I know,' said Gar. 'And now you must forget what I've told you. I should've held my tongue. Not burdened you with the truth. It's just—' His voice cracked. 'I don't want him to die without another person knowing the good he tried to do. Knowing that no matter what is said of him once he's gone, he was *never* a traitor.'

Darran moistened dry lips. 'Yes, sir. I understand. It's been a shock, I won't deny that . . . but I'm glad you confided in me.'

'Are you?' The prince shook his head. 'Let's hope that doesn't change.'

'It won't,' he promised. 'Sir . . . this is all indeed a tragedy, but nothing can be gained or changed by you making yourself ill. Please. Won't you eat?'

Gar sighed. 'I'll try. But I make no guarantees, Darran. I've a speech to write and the thought of it makes me retch. Leave me be, and I'll do my best with your damned chicken.'

'Yes, sir,' he said, his heart all in pieces, and left the prince alone.

The palace's Great Assembly Hall was humming with a score of different conversations as Morg made his eloquent entrance, cripple in tow, a few minutes before two o'clock. Once passed through the hall's open double doors he paused, considering the scene before them. Filling the left-hand pews were Doranen lords and ladies of varying talents and influence, who fondly imagined that a seat on the General Council equated with having some sort of power. He smothered a smile; ignorance could be such a comfort. Clustered together, as usual, in the pew closest to the speaker's chair were Nole Daltrie, Gord Hafar and Tobe Boqur: Jarralt's deluded friends. How disappointed they'd be to learn they weren't the kingdom's next Privy Council.

Gord saw him and raised a discreet hand in acknowledgement. Noticing, Nole and Tobe followed suit. He nodded back, briefly smiling.

The hall's right-hand pews were the province of the Olken guild meisters and mistresses. According to Jarralt's plundered memories they were normally a noisy crowd, but this afternoon they sat in silence or conversed in low, uneasy voices. Their cattle faces were tight with worry, their eyes shadowed, darting uneasy looks across the hall at their Doranen betters. They were magickless, but not quite stupid. Word of loutish Asher's arrest had clearly spread. Dealing a cruel blow to their pretensions and raising a host of fears.

They were right to be afraid.

Directly opposite the hall's entrance was the speaker's chair and behind that the specially reserved seats for the king and his Privy Council, placed on a raised dais. How bare it looked now, with only one other chair occupied. No Borne. No Durm. Only Holze, who'd arrived earlier and sat now in silence, his bare head bowed in prayer or sleep.

Such a reduction of power. A thinning of the ranks. But they'd get no fatter. King Morg would have no Privy Council, no chorus of fools. His rule would be absolute. No dissenting opinions, no bleating naysayers. Now . . . and once the Wall was fallen. One king. One voice. It was the only sure way to rule. Six hundred years of absolute mastery had shown him that.

Jarralt's other dear friend, Payne Sorvold, the current Council Speaker, caught their arrival and met them halfway across the hall's central floor space. 'Your Majesty. Conroyd. Welcome.'

The cripple nodded. 'Lord Sorvold.'

'Forgive me, sir, but we had not expected you. It was Lord Jarralt here who requested this extraordinary—'

'I know. I desire a brief word with the Council,' said the cripple. 'Before you attend to . . . other business.'

'Certainly, Your Majesty. Conroyd, if I might ask for an inkling of the matter you wished to raise, then—'

'Once His Majesty has had his say,' Morg explained, gently smiling, 'I think you'll find the other business self-explanatory.'

Sorvold's pale green eyes narrowed and his thin lips pursed. 'Indeed? All respect, but as Speaker I—'

'Should practise silence,' he said.

Flushed, taken aback, Sorvold turned to the cripple. 'Your Majesty, if I might have a brief word in private?'

'You may not,' said Morg before the cripple could answer. 'Call the Council to attention, Payne. We are all busy men.'

As Sorvold withdrew, offended, the cripple said, 'I'll thank you not to speak for me just yet. I'm still king here, Conroyd.'

He smiled. 'So jealous of your dwindling moments, little runtling?'

Leaving the cripple to make his way to the speaker's dais, Morg joined Holze. The Barlsman stirred at his arrival and sat up. His face was wan. Worn. Doubtless he'd come here direct from overseeing the disposition of dead Durm's body. There was grief in his eyes and in the way his hands clasped each other tightly in his lap. Such a wasteful emotion.

'Conroyd.'

'Efrim.'

Just below them, Sorvold picked up his little hammer and tapped it on the Assembly Bell. All around the hall surreptitious conversations ceased. Those standing assumed their seats. The air of restrained dread, of watchful curiosity, intensified.

With silence achieved, Sorvold sounded the Assembly Bell a further three times. Nodded to the young woman acting as secretary, so she might trigger the recording spell for the meeting's minutes, then cleared his throat.

'With the authority vested in me as Speaker of the Assembly I declare this meeting open. May Barl's mercy attend us, her wisdom guide us, her strength sustain us. All silence, please, as His Majesty now addresses this august body.'

'Thank you, Lord Sorvold,' said the cripple. His face too was wan, thoroughly bleached by the black tunic he continued to wear in honour of those dead fools, his family, and the thankfully abandoned Durm. 'My good councillors, I appear before you today with a heavy heart, bearing news I know you will not welcome, as I do not welcome it. But I trust in your restraint and acceptance of Barl's will . . . no matter how hard acceptance may be.'

Well, he certainly had their attention. Long denied a good piece of theatre, Morg sat back and prepared to enjoy himself.

'Firstly,' continued the cripple, his hands resting before him on the speaker's lectern, 'it is my sad duty to inform you that Master Magician Durm has passed from life and into Barl's mercy. I ask now for a minute's silence in honour of his greatness and a life spent in service of our kingdom.'

The minute passed, tedious slow.

'Thank you,' said the cripple. 'Of his life and dedication, more shall be said in due course. Secondly, I must now tell you that due to irreparable health concerns I forthwith abdicate our kingdom's throne and withdraw from public life indefinitely. Be it known I have chosen my lawful heir and successor, Lur's new king and WeatherWorker, and name him Lord Conroyd Jarralt.'

Sensation. Cries. Lamentations. Shock, and a rising furore of voices both Doranen and Olken crying, 'No! No! We do not accept this! You are our king!'

The cripple let them continue unchecked for a short time, then nodded at Sorvold, who again hammered his little bell. Gradually the uproar subsided.

'Good people,' said the cripple, hands raised in supplication. 'I can no longer serve you as your king. The magic that so lately flowered in my breast has withered and died. In memory of the love you bore my late and so lamented father – that you bear me, in his memory – I beg you to accept this decision without remonstrance and instead devote your loyalty to King Conroyd the First. And if anyone here should think to dally with notions of challenging his accession, be warned. It is my right and duty to name an heir and I have done so. A second schism hurts all and helps none. If you truly love me, be satisfied with my decision . . . and Barl's mercy on us all.'

More buzzing. Tears, and consternation.

'Lastly,' the former king said, raising his voice above the din, 'I would touch upon the matter of my Olken Administrator.'

And silence fell like the blade of an axe.

'As many of you doubtless know, Asher is arrested

for crimes against Barl and this kingdom and soon will pay the price in full. I think I need not say how grieved I am. What I will say is this: that no matter how heinous they might be, the actions of one Olken must *never* be counted the actions of all. To do so would be a gross injustice and a violation of Barl's intentions in this land. Guard against revenge and retribution, my lords, my ladies and dear gentlefolk. Guard against it at the peril of your souls. I know King Conroyd will.'

A ripple of whispers through the watching Olken. There were tears in the cripple's eyes now, leaking onto his cheeks. His hands were unsteady on the speaker's lectern.

'I hope you know how I have loved you,' he added, his voice breaking. 'Please believe that my actions today spring from that true devotion. Better that. I should die than any harm come to you and yours through me. Barl bless you all and guide King Conroyd to wisdom and mercy.'

One of the Olken leapt to his feet. 'Barl's blessing on you, sir! Barl's blessing on Prince Gar!'

The cry was taken up at once, shouted by Olken and Doranen alike. Morg watched, amused, as all the councillors leapt to their expensively shod feet and roared their acclaim as Gar made his way towards the hall's exit. Beside him, Holze said grudgingly, 'Well. He managed that quite acceptably.'

He patted the cleric's arm. 'Dear Efrim. Do you think so?' And left the fool staring as he descended to the floor of the hall, meeting the cripple by the large double doors. 'Thin ice, runtling,' he murmured. 'Very thin ice.'

'I'm glad you recognise your danger, Conroyd,' said the cripple. 'Are you a historian, sir? If not, I suggest you pick up a book. The past is peopled with unwise individuals who forgot that brute force leads to nothing but defeat. The name "Morg" springs to mind.'

Startled, he stared more closely at the runt. 'And what do you know of Morg, cripple?'

Gar shrugged. 'Only what any half-intelligent person knows. That he was a small man who tried to make himself larger with violence . . . and failed. I hope you learn from his example, for your sake.'

He laughed. Laughed until tears pricked his borrowed eyes, then patted Gar sharply on the cheek. 'The carriage is waiting. Return to your Tower, boy. When I want you again, be sure I'll send a lackey. And mind you remember the terms of your freedom, for I will not hesitate to change them. Defy me and I'll place guards at all your doors and grievously punish those who seek to aid you.'

For long moments the cripple stared at him. Then he turned his back and left. Morg watched him for a moment, still vastly amused, then forgot him. Basked instead in the music of obedience and acclaim soaring upwards to the hall's distant rafters.

'Hail our King Conroyd! Hail our King Conroyd! Barl bless our King Conroyd, WeatherWorker of Lur!'

Their desperate pleasure at his ascension floated him all the way to the dais the cripple had just vacated for the last time. Listening to their eager cries he felt a shrivelling contempt. They were all cattle, these peasants and their overlords. There wasn't a man among them worthy of anything but slaughter.

Standing before them, hands folded on the lectern, he let his gaze roam their animal faces as they continued to shout and stamp. Cattle? No. Even cattle had a semblance of purpose. The Olken and Doranen of this pallid kingdom were sheep. Willing to follow anyone who could promise them peace and an endless procession of magical days. It made him ill to see it. That a race as majestic and proud as the Doranen should come to *this*? This bleating, following, milling flock.

Whatever strength Barl's escapees had possessed it was bled to nothing here in their descendants. Their descendants were paper Doranen . . . destined all to burn.

He unfolded his hands and held them up in modest appeal. 'Good people, good people, I beg you: enough!'

Ragged silence fell. Those fools who'd leapt to their feet resumed their seats. Like penned sheep who heard the rattle of the gate unlocking, they stared and waited, hoping for food.

'My dear councillors,' he said, infusing his voice with sorrow. 'These are dark days indeed. Our beloved kingdom has come to a pretty pass. Brought to the brink of destruction by the actions of one misguided man. I know—' He raised one hand in warning. 'You loved your former king. Love him still as a prince and the sad representative of a fallen house. I commend your love, my subjects. I do. Your willingness to overlook his profound errors of judgement tells me all I need to know of your hearts. Good hearts. Stout hearts. But not, perhaps, as wise as Barl might wish them to be.'

A muttering now, and a flurry of exchanged glances. He waited a moment then rode roughshod over their objections.

'Blind devotion is a dangerous thing,' he told them. 'It was blind devotion that handed power to the traitor, Asher, furnishing him with the means to dabble in forbidden magic.' Another pause, as a gasp rippled its way through the flock. 'Only Barl knows the true intent of his black, unloving heart. Only Barl knows what damage he has wrought in the paradise she died to create.'

Nole Daltrie, always reliable, stood and cried out: 'What are you saying, Conr— Your Majesty? Do you think the kingdom's in danger?'

'The kingdom was in danger from the day Gar elevated that stinking fisherman to heights he didn't deserve,' he replied. Conroyd's belief that, fervently and passionately felt. Shared. 'Now I fear we face more than mere danger. I fear we face catastrophe.'

Not muttering now but cries of consternation. Daltrie exchanged horrified looks with the rest of Conroyd's councillor friends. 'Do you say the Wall itself is in jeopardy?'

The thought was so appalling it froze their voices in their throats. Stricken, Daltrie sank back slowly to his seat.

Morg nodded. 'Hard as I find it to say so, Lord Daltrie, yes. I fear it might well be.'

'*No*!' they shouted, thawed by terror. '*Save us*!' they begged him with tears in their eyes.

Holze stood, uninvited, and raised his voice above the lamentations. 'Councillors, control yourselves! In Blessed Barl's name, I command you, have faith!' As the noise subsided, he continued. 'Barl will not let her Wall be defeated. Has she not delivered us from Asher's evil and given us into the care of King Conroyd, in whom her power resides? Have faith, I tell you. And be guided by His Majesty.'

Ah, Efrim. Barl-sodden, but useful. Morg nodded to the cleric then turned back to the assembled councillors. 'I am your king,' he said quietly as Holze sat down. 'Of course I will save you. But I fear it won't be easy, Thanks to Asher's meddling, the balance of magical power in the kingdom is gravely disturbed. How badly the Wall is affected I don't yet know . . .

but we must face the bitter truth. It is affected.'

The Olken councillors were moaning. Covering their faces with trembling hands and rocking on their haunches. Every Doranen eye was upon them, and the looks were far from friendly.

'In his lust for a power that was never meant for him, Asher has endangered the life of every soul in this kingdom,' said Morg. Letting his words bite now, like the tip of a lash. 'And every Olken who encouraged him to think he was more than an Olken bears a share of his guilt. Fear not – I will not punish the undeserving. But I tell you here and now, guild meisters and mistresses of Lur: look hard at your people. Examine their behaviours. For henceforth I hold you accountable, and will see you answer for their sins.'

Not a sound from the Olken. And if any one of them had harboured some lingering affection for Asher, the looks on their faces told him it was stone dead now. He hid a smile.

Holze said, 'And what of the Wall, Your Majesty? What of the WeatherWorking?'

'History shows us we have a period of grace,' he replied. 'Some short time to live without WeatherWorking before we are undone. Therefore I shall withdraw from the public eye, that I might take into myself the Weather Magics and study how best to apply them. To undo the damage Asher has wreaked and avert a dire disaster.'

Now it was Payne Sorvold who spoke. 'You'll require a Master Magician . . . Your Majesty.'

He nodded. 'I shall appoint Durm's successor once this crisis is past, Lord Sorvold. For now all I need to help me restore our beloved kingdom is contained in his books and journals. Have no fear, sir. I shall prevail.'

Sorvold nodded. 'Yes, Your Majesty. And what of Your Majesty's Privy Council?'

He felt his expression harden. 'It too must wait until the crisis is past.' He unpinned his gaze from Sorvold's frowning face and swept it around the hall. 'Good people, do you not yet understand? By the merest whisper have we escaped a disaster of Asher's making. Life as once we knew it has changed. Perhaps forever. Listen, now, as I explain more fully what I mean . . .'

Carted back to the Tower like so much lumber, Gar stifled a groan when he saw Darran waiting for him on his palatial prison's front steps. Even dredged up a smile as the old man bowed and insisted on opening the carriage door for him. The gesture came hard, though. Any brief satisfaction he'd felt in defying Conroyd before the General Council, of warning him to leave the Olken alone, had faded. All he felt now was ill, and tired, and desperately sad.

'Well, old friend, it's done,' he said, as Conroyd's carriage rattled away. 'I am again Prince Gar the Magickless.'

There were tears in Darran's eyes. 'Yes, sir.'

He willed his own eyes to stay dry. Forced his voice to remain steady and strong. 'It's for the best. What can any of this be but Barl's will, after all? My magic is gone, and that's hardly Conroyd's fault. In truth, none of this is his fault. I may hate him, but I can't blame him. At least not for being the best remaining magician in the kingdom.'

'No, sir.'

'I'm going to the stables now. To say goodbye to the horses before—'

Darran touched his sleeve. 'I'm so sorry, sir. They're

already gone. Men from the Livestock Guild. I couldn't stop them, they had written orders from Lord Ja – from the king. It was all I could do to hide the little donkey. If we keep it in a pasture down the back no one will know we have it. I just thought . . . well . . . it may come in useful. As a lawn mower, if nothing else.'

Poor Darran. He looked so stricken, so brimful of guilt. 'It's all right,' Gar said gently. 'Of course you couldn't stop them.' *Ballodair. Oh, Ballodair*. 'Well, if there's no point visiting the stables I'll go for a walk instead. Don't fret if I'm gone for some time, Darran. I have a lot to think about.'

'Yes, sir,' said Darran. And, as Gar turned away, said, 'Sir?'

Gar looked back. 'Yes?'

'Be careful. Don't . . . walk too far. Don't give that man an excuse to take anything else.'

He smiled. 'What is there left for him to take, Darran?'

Darran stepped closer, his face screwed up with pain and trepidation. 'Your life.'

'My *life*?' He laughed. 'Ah yes. My life. Do you know something, Darran? I'm beginning to think he can have it, and welcome.'

'*Sir*!'

Relenting, he patted the old man's shoulder. 'It's all right,' he said, and started to back away. 'I was joking.'

Darran shook a finger at him, just as he used to when he worked at the palace and was scolding a younger, happier Gar. 'Really? Well, as jokes go it wasn't the least bit funny!'

Turning his back on Darran's disapproval he walked away and kept on walking, until his family's crypt appeared among the trees. Quite possibly he was breaking Conroyd's rules by coming this far but he didn't care. If Conroyd thought to keep him from his family he was very much mistaken.

As ever, the crypt was cool. Dark. Fumbling for lantern and matches, skinning his knuckles, he tried to forget that once light had been his for the asking.

The amplified candlelight cast attenuated shadows up the walls and across the faces of his family. He kissed his father, and his mother. Tickled his sister's feet. Arranged himself uncomfortably on the floor.

'I'm sorry,' he said into the silence. 'I'd have come sooner but . . . a lot has happened since you left.'

His mother whispered: *That's all right, dear. You're a busy man.*

'Not as busy as you might think,' he replied. 'Father, I have a confession. I've lost the two best things you ever gave me: your crown and your horse. It seems you raised a careless son.'

A father's disappointment. *Very. Can't you get them back again?*

*Of course he can't. He's useless.* A sister's angry scorn.

'I'm sorry,' he repeated. 'I did the best I could. Unfortunately my best proved inadequate to the task.'

Silence. Were they really speaking, or was his mind at last unhinged? And if it was . . . did it even matter?

*Typical*, he heard Fane sneer. *Whinge, moan, sigh. It's a wonder you didn't die years ago, drowned in a butt of self-pity. Don't just sit there, idiot. Do something.*

Even imagined, the sharp words stung. He grabbed hold of his sister's stone foot and hauled himself upright. 'Do *what*?' he demanded of her. 'I am powerless. Exiled in my own City. Discarded, irrelevant and alone. What would *you* do, if you were me?'

The answer came not in words but as a spearing shaft of memory. Of intent, abandoned.

Barl's diary. If Durm was right, their only hope. How or why, he had no idea. But he trusted Durm. He had to. He had nowhere else to turn.

Damn it, how could he have *forgotten*? He had to find that diary. Had to go back to the Tower, now, and search Durm's books again before Conroyd discovered their removal and took them away. No matter he'd searched the collection twice, without luck. The diary *had* to be there. Cunningly hidden, as was Durm's devious habit.

*Please, Barl, let me find it.* Show me a way out of this disaster.

He dropped a grateful kiss on his sister's cold stone cheek and ran all the way back to the Tower.

# CHAPTER TWENTY-FOUR

Blistered and weary, the knapsack on her back as heavy as an anvil, Dathne trudged along the empty road that led to the Black Woods. To Veira and her village, beating at their timber heart. There was dust on her face, turned streakily to mud by infrequent, unhelpful tears. She was chilled, she was hungry, she was eaten with despair. The sun had set two hours earlier, and weak moonlight was her only guide. She'd tripped and stumbled a dozen times, lost her footing completely and crashed to the roadway once. Her scraped knees and elbows stung viciously; her tired mind was one vast and aching bruise.

*Asher. Asher. Asher.*

She hardly recognised herself, so diminished felt her spirit. Misery was a crushing weight, compressing her bones to chalk. She never knew she could feel so small.

*Asher.*

That catastrophe seemed worse even than the now unstoppable onslaught of the Final Days. Asher was flesh and blood to her, he was laughter and whispers and callused fingers, touching. Pleasure like magic coursing through her veins. The Final Days were unimaginable. For all her frightened dreaming, she couldn't seem to make them real. But Asher was real. Asher was arrested. And unless some miracle intervened, Asher was dead . . . along with any hope for the kingdom's future.

The thought knifed pain through her whole body, so swift and severe she couldn't walk. Gasping, hurting, she braced her hands upon her thighs and waited for the torment to ease. A kind of wild rushing wind stormed through her mind, blotting out thought, obliterating memory.

She welcomed it.

Gradually the pain eased and reason returned. She straightened, inch by hesitant inch. The night stretched for miles around her, inhabited by stars, and trees, and small rustling creatures.

Then, carrying keenly on the thin cold air, new sounds. Horseshoes ringing hollow on hard-packed clay, slowing from a brisk jog to a cautious walk. A wooden creak of turning wheels. Approaching round the bend ahead, a looming shape framed in dancing torchlight.

Heart pounding, she waited for the cart to reach her. Watched as the shaggy brown pony pulling it slowed, slowed then stopped in a puffing cloud of breath. She looked up into the hooded, mysterious face of the person holding the pony's reins.

Gnarled hands pushed the hood back onto rounded, slumping shoulders. 'Dathne.'

She nodded. Tried to smile. 'Veira.'

'Well, child,' the old woman said, and sniffed. 'If you were a few years younger and my joints a little less creaky I'd fling your skirts up over your head and put you over my knees for this.'

Dathne stared at her, speechless.

In the torchlight Veira's face leapt and flickered with shadows. 'But you're a young woman, and I'm an old one, and I don't suppose a paddling would make either of us feel any better. So don't just stand there gawking. Come up here beside me and let's get you home to bed.'

They travelled in awkward silence for nearly three hours, along the narrow road that drew them deep into the Black Woods like a crooked, beckoning finger. At first the trees grew thinly, with spindly trunks and lacy foliage, but the further the pony ambled them into the gloom-ridden forest the more robust and vigorous the djelbas, honey-pines and weeping noras became. The air grew close and still as more and more of the star-strewn sky disappeared from view. Even though she was miles closer now to Barl's Wall and the mountains that anchored it, its golden glow was reduced to a smeary shadow. Anyone living within this sea of trees could easily forget the Wall existed.

She wished she could.

Her nose was tickled by the scent of rich rotting mulch. She caught the sound of trickling water somewhere to the left. Keeping herself distracted she let her gaze roam the encroaching forest as it rolled along beside her. Caught sight of a glowing orange fungus on a fallen tree trunk – newt-eye, good for enhancing concentration – and wished she could ask Veira to stop the cart. Newt-eye was hard to come by in the countryside round the City.

The City. Her home for six long years, but now a place of danger she could never visit again. At least not until . . . and always assuming there was anything left to visit afterwards. Was her absence noticed yet? Had anyone raised the alarm? Were they hunting for her even now? Well, let them hunt. Let them turn the City upside down. They'd find no clue to help them. No guiding trail of breadcrumbs. She'd escaped. She was safe.

She'd abandoned Asher behind her.

The passing forest blurred and she rubbed a hand across her face. If Veira saw it she didn't say so. All her attention was on the pony and the winding road ahead. Dathne pulled her coat more tightly round her ribs, wondering what would happen to her bookshop, that convenient mask she'd come to love, despite herself. And all her things, in her tiny rooms above it. Obeying Veira's command she'd brought with her only the items that might raise suspicion. Her Circle Stone. Her orris root, the tanal leaf, other herbs and simples not generally found in an Olken pantry. A few clothes, too, for necessity. A dragonfly in amber, gifted to her from Asher the first Grand Barl's Day after his arrival in Dorana.

She felt her heart hitch, and fisted her fingers in her lap. She *would not* think of Asher.

Beside her, Veira cleared her throat. 'Nother half-hour and we'll be there, near enough,' she said.

Dathne nodded. 'Good.'

It was strange to hear the old woman's voice out loud, a sweet and solid sound, after so long with nothing but Circle Stone communication, mind to mind. Even seeing her was a shock. In the link she'd seemed younger. Smoother. Less . . . wrinkled.

Aware of the scrutiny, Veira chuckled breathily and glanced at her sidelong. 'Told you I weren't no oil painting, child.'

She felt her cheeks heat. 'I'm sorry, I didn't mean to be rude, I—' Her fingernails were close to drawing blood, so tightly were they clenched against her palms. 'I'm sorry.' And not just for staring. She was sorry for everything.

'I know,' said Veira, and patted her on one blanketed knee.

She blinked her vision clear. 'You warned Matt all right? He's safe?'

'As safe as any of us,' said Veira.

'I handled that badly,' she whispered, pinning her fists between her knees. *The look on his face, as she sided with Asher* . . . 'I handled it all badly. I've no business being part of the Circle. Prophecy is falling to pieces and it's all my fault!'

In the flickering torchlight Veira's expression was a mystery. 'You don't know that, child. Best not to run ahead of ourselves. This business ain't done with till the Wall's fallen down, and last time I looked it was still standing.'

Then we're not lost? The kingdom can still be saved? Asher won't—' She couldn't finish the sentence out loud. Didn't even dare complete the thought.

'I hope not,' Veira said at last. 'We'll do our best to save him. Though I fear it will come at a terrible cost.'

'You have a plan?'

Another long silence.

'I have an inkling of a possibility,' said Veira without looking at her. 'I'll not be speaking of it yet. I've others to consult, and hard thinking to do first.'

And that sounded less than encouraging. Sounded frightening. Dangerous. Likely to fail. In Veira's comfortable voice, there tolled a premonition of sorrow.

She'd had enough sorrow for one day. 'I can't imagine living in a forest,' she said, staring at the branch-latticed sky.

Veira smiled, revealing crooked teeth. 'I can't imagine living anywhere else. Not any more.'

'Do you like it?'

'Well enough. A forest's cool. Quiet. And there's always fresh rabbit when the fancy takes me.'

'Yes, but what do you *do*? How do you live?' In all the time she and Veira had known each other, she'd never once asked. Once, it hadn't seemed important.

'I'm a truffle hunter,' said Veira. 'Means nobody asks me why I live so far out from the village. Why I spend so much time alone with my pigs.' A breathy chuckle. 'Mind you, the pigs is more for company. I got easier ways of finding truffles than parading about the forest with a pig on a leash. Good listeners, pigs. Better than most people I know.'

'And the other villagers? What do they do? Why would they choose to live in such isolation?'

Veira shrugged, and rattled the reins to keep the pony up to its bridle. 'It's only isolated from the Doranen. The village is a happy, close-knit place. Lively. And there's a mort of things to do in the Black Woods, child. Berrying. Mushrooming. Trapping. Herbals and dye-plants. Sweetsap. Woodcarving. Clockmaking. Bees – some of this kingdom's finest honey comes from our bees, you know. Oh yes. The Black Woods are full of bounty for those who aren't afraid of the dark.'

'Oh,' she said, feeling ignorant. Feeling helpless. She should have brought some books to sell . . . 'Well. I had no idea.'

'No reason you should do, child,' said Veira comfortably.

'Is the village large?'

'Large enough. A hundred and fourteen families, last count.' Veira pointed ahead of them, to the right. 'Over thataways, it is.'

'And how will you account for me? I've always been

told villagers are a curious lot. They'll want to know who I am, where I'm from . . .'

'No, they won't,' said Veira. 'I've done a tidy job of keeping myself a loner. Folks know me, but only as deep as I want 'em to, and only when I go to them. I discouraged visitors years ago.' Clicking her tongue, she once more rattled the plump pony's reins. 'Get on with you, Bessie. You ought to be smellin' home by now.'

Not long after that they turned left onto a rutted grass-grown roadway. Followed it in silence, and at last reached Veira's thatched stone cottage all alone in the wooded vastness of the forest. Warm light glowed through a curtained front window. The night air smelled of jasmine and moonroses, the flowers' perfume mingling with the spicy sweet scent of honey-pine smoke drifting out of the cottage's chimney.

Veira eased the cart to a halt by the open front gate. 'Bessie's bedroom's round the back. Get yourself inside, child, while I see the poor beast settled. Stir up the hob and put on the kettle like a good girl. I'm parched for some hot sweet tea.'

Oh yes, yes, tea. Clasping blanket and knapsack Dathne clambered out of the wagon and made her unsteady way up the garden path. She felt stupid with tiredness. More than anything she wanted quiet, and somewhere to rest her aching head. Just as she reached the front door, it opened.

*Matt*. Tall. Frowning. Swallowing all the space in the small doorway. Here? In Veira's cottage? She felt the knapsack slip from her fingers. Heard a tinkling crunch as something broke inside it. Or did the sound come from inside her? She couldn't tell. Couldn't speak. Could only stare, and stare, and stare . . .

'Hello, Dathne,' said Matt, unsmiling. 'Welcome to the Black Woods.'

When Asher groped his way back to reluctant consciousness he found himself in a different cage. This one was outside. On a cart in the middle of the City Square – just as Jarralt had promised. The straw beneath his huddled body was fouled and stinking. There were heavy iron manacles on his wrists and his ankles, connected by a short, heavy chain. The manacles' inner surfaces were rough and rusty. Chafing. The pain was small compared to the enormous hurting in the rest of his abused body. Jarralt had been thorough. And enthusiastic. *Bastard.* Who knew he'd wanted that damned King's Cup so bad, eh?

*Pity I didn't just let the mongrel have it. Might've saved me a lot of grief.*

It was dark. Late. Hovering glimfire splashed shadows and soft light. Standing at attention a few feet from the nearest corner of his cage, a poker-backed City Guard. If he'd wanted to he could've called the man's name out loud.

He didn't want to. Also as promised, his throat was raw and swollen. Only one thing kept him from surrendering to despair: they hadn't found Dathne. Orrick had returned to report his failure, refusing to look at Jarralt's bleeding, moaning victim hanging in his chains.

So. No Dathne, and no Matt either. It seemed that sulking out of sight somewhere after their quarrel had saved him.

Thwarted of more victims, Jarralt had been furious. Had returned to his vengeance with greater vigour. Asher shuddered, remembering. He would've died happily then, knowing she was safe – that they both were safe

– but Jarralt knew to perfection how to hurt, and hurt, yet keep him on the wrong side of death's door.

He blinked, shivering, trying to clear his pain-blurred vision. Unfolded his arms and legs, needing to ease his cramped muscles. His putrid straw bed rustled, pressing against his filthy shirt and trousers, his burned and bloodied flesh. From somewhere quite close, a shout.

'He's awake! The blasphemous bastard's awake!'

He lifted his head. Four guards, not one. Four men who once had been his friends, matched to each corner of his cage. He strained to see past their blue and crimson uniforms. Slowly, achingly, the world swam into sharper focus. What he saw stopped his heart, or so it felt. Beyond the cage, beyond the guards, beyond the wavering circle of glimlight, a sullen shifting mass of silent faces.

The Olken of Dorana City had come to feast their eyes on the traitor.

Wincing, breathing harshly through pinched nostrils and gritted teeth, he made himself sit up, even though it hurt so much he thought he might vomit again. There were faces out there that he knew. Guild meisters he'd counselled. Guild members he'd helped. Turning his head, looking over his shoulder, he saw more friends. People he'd drunk ale with down at the Goose. People who'd laughed to see him. Thrown roses without thorns. Flirted. Flattered. Boasted that he knew them and smiled at his approach. Screamed his name as he'd travelled the road to Justice Hall. Who'd witnessed him sitting in judgement in that grand place and applauded as though he was their hero.

Nobody was applauding now. Now he wasn't anybody's hero.

'Filthy blasphemer!' somebody called from the crowd.

'Liar!'

'Traitor!'

Somebody threw something. An egg. It burst against the bars of the cage to drip stinking, rotten and slimy to the floor. The stench mixed with the reek of excrement and vomit, clogging his blood-caked nostrils, churning his stomach with acid and bile.

'I ain't!' he croaked, and felt the split skin of his face crack and ooze. 'I ain't no more a traitor than you!'

As those in the crowd close enough to hear him burst into jeering laughter, the nearest guard turned and thrust his pikestaff into the cage in a single, economical jab. It caught him in the mouth, crushing his lip against his teeth, tearing his flesh even wider.

'One more word,' the guard said, 'and I'll cut out your tongue. Got it?' It was Dever. They played leapjacks together down at the Goose on the nights they found themselves there at the same time. Used to play. Dever wasn't grinning now, wasn't reaching out to slap him on the back, buy him a pint, bend his ear about the latest lady love.

Now he looked cold enough to kill.

Another egg came sailing out of the crowd. This one found its target. Hit him on the side of the head. The smell was gut-wrenching. Somebody else threw fresh cow shit. Lukewarm but still stinking, it burned his face where Jarralt had laid him open, searching for satisfaction.

The guards made no attempt to stop the rain of abuse. Only when something landed too close to them did they raise their pikestaffs and shout. There was no escape. All he could do was survive it, just as he'd survived Jarralt. In the end he curled up on his side and tried to ignore the shouts, the insults, the eggs, and everything else they threw at him. The pain. Concentrated instead on the one thing that would sustain him for as long as this ordeal endured. Hate. On the one name that fed his slow-burning fury.

*Gar.*

When he woke a second time it was again to glimlit darkness and the rise and fall of unfriendly voices, sibilant as the ocean, to the smoky scents of roasting meats as food merchants catered to the avid crowds of Olken still gathering to gloat and deride. So large had their numbers swelled that a barrier had been erected around the cart and cage, keeping the insomniac onlookers at bay; standing beyond it, pikestaffs at the ready, a different set of guards.

What was wrong with the bastards, eh? Didn't they have homes to go to? Children to care for? Did they have nothing better to do than stand around here feeding their faces on sheep fat and bile?

Well, no. Clearly not.

Groaning, swearing as all his hurts growled, biting, and colder than ever he could remember, he managed to force himself upright. 'Barl's ti—' he began to curse under his breath, then stopped. Stared. Closed his fingers into fists.

Willer stood outside the cage, smiling in at him. In his pudgy hands a hot beef sandwich, dripping bloody juices down the front of his apple-green jacket. He didn't seem to notice. His bloated face was shiny with grease, with triumph, and his eyes gleamed in the lambent glimfire.

'I told you I'd make you pay,' he said conversationally, around a mouthful of sloppily chewed bread and meat. 'Didn't I?' The gloating smile widened, like a toad's. 'This should teach you to disbelieve me.'

'Go away,' he said, even though he knew he was wasting his breath.

Willer shivered with pleasure. 'The executioner was in the guardhouse all afternoon, sharpening his axe. I went to watch. Zzzt, zzzt, zzzt. You'll never guess: the townsfolk are placing bets on how many strokes it'll take to do the job. They hate you, Asher. Thanks to you, Olken life is about to change for the harder. I'm hoping it'll take three strokes to kill you. Four, even. I'm hoping it hurts. A lot. You deserve to suffer. You deserve everything that's happening to you.'

'You're a fool, Willer,' he said tiredly. 'Such a damned bloody fool. You got no idea what you've done.'

'I know exactly what I've done,' said Willer, eyes bright with malice. 'I've helped bring a blasphemous traitor to justice.' Dripping beef forgotten, he stepped even closer to the cage. 'The guards say they heard you screaming. How I wish I'd been there to see it.' His voice was laden with longing. 'All those times you disrespected me. Abused me. Humiliated me. Insulted me with your very presence. Did you think I would forget? Did you think I would *forgive*? They say you shat yourself like a baby, that you—'

'Willer,' said Darran, stepping out of the shadows. 'That's enough. He knows you've won. Go home.'

Startled, Willer spun about. 'Darran! What are you doing here. You're supposed to be nursemaiding pathetic magickless Gar!'

Darran came closer. Smoothed out a wrinkle in the pissant's beef-stained coat. 'When I think I once felt affection for you, I could vomit,' he said, his voice low, shaking. 'Go home. Before I forget myself and make a scene.'

Uncertain, truculent, Willer knocked the age-spotted

hand aside. 'Why are you protecting him, Darran? You hate him as much as I do! You wanted him brought down as much as I did, don't try to deny it! "Give him enough rope and he'll hang himself", that's what you said. And then you preferred him over me, *me*, who served you like a son for years! *Why*?'

Darran shook his head slowly, like a teacher despairing of a backward student. 'Because Gar asked me to. Because, like you, I swore to serve him with faith and loyalty. Because *unlike* you I kept my word.'

Willer's jaw dropped. 'Asher's a traitor. A blasphemer! He broke Barl's First Law!'

'Yes, he did,' agreed Darran, nodding. 'And for that he'll die. But even so, he's a better man than you'll ever be.'

'Succouring a traitor is treachery in itself!' hissed Willer. 'I could have you arrested for that. I *will* have you arrested! I'm not your dogsbody any more. Now I'm a man of influence and I won't be trifled with!' He turned away, searching for the nearest guard, and his wet pink mouth opened wide, to shout.

Darran's fingers closed about his arm. 'I wouldn't, Willer, if I were you.' His voice was soft. More dangerous than Asher, watching and for the moment disregarded, could ever have imagined. 'For a man who prides himself on his memory you seem to have forgotten a thing or two. Even with all that's happened I'm not without influence myself. Remember Bolliton? I do. I also have proof. The right words in the right ear and—'

'*What*?' Sea slug Willer pulled free and backed away, his greasy face puce with fury, and fear. His elbow bumped the bars of the cage. 'How *dare* you threaten me? I'll tell the king what you've said, I'll see you thrown in prison for it, I'll—'

The fat fool had forgotten where he was. Despite his chains Asher touched his fingers to the back of the pissant's collar. Seized it and twisted savagely, cutting off Willer's air with a gurgle.

'You'll do nowt or I'll kill you here and now,' he whispered into Willer's ear. 'Think I can't? Think I won't? What can they do if I wring your neck? Chop my head off twice?'

With a strangled shriek Willer wrenched himself free. The nearest guard, finally noticing the prisoner had visitors, turned. Scowling, his pikestaff at the ready, he approached. Then, seeing who they were, hesitated. 'Meister Darran. Meister Driskle.'

The ole crow bowed. 'Good evening, Jesip.'

'Meister Darran, you shouldn't be here,' Jesip said unhappily. 'You neither, Meister Driskle. We got strict orders to—'

'Relax, guardsman,' said Darran with his oiliest smile. His hand fell on Willer's shoulder, fingers tightening. The sea slug closed his mouth, his expression pinched with pain. 'I've orders of my own.' Darran lowered his voice to a conspiratorial whisper. 'Confidential. A matter of state. You understand?'

Asher held his breath. Jesip was new. Young. Easily awed. And Darran had a reputation.

'Two minutes, Meister Darran,' said Jesip. 'Orders or no, I can't give you more than that.'

'Thank you,' said Darran. 'I'll make sure your co-operation is noted in the right circles.'

Jesip flushed. 'Just doing my job, sir.' He looked at Willer. 'And Meister Driskle?'

'Is with me,' Darran said smoothly. His grasping fingers tightened further. Willer squeaked. 'But he's not feeling well. A morsel of food gone down the wrong way.' He spared the slug a reproving look. 'One should never eat and speak at the same time, dear boy. There might be an unfortunate incident.'

As Willer gasped like a landed fish, Jesip nodded, one finger raised in warning. 'So it's two minutes, then. And only because you work for the palace.'

'Exactly,' said Darran.

'And once you're done, best mind you take care on your way home,' Jesip added. 'The mood's a mite unchancy round here just now.'

Darran nodded, smiling. 'Excellent advice. Thank you.'

As Jesip withdrew, Darran released his fearsome grip on Willer's shoulder. 'Run away now, Willer, and forget you saw me . . . or I swear there'll be a reckoning you'll not forget.'

Tripping over his own feet, cursing, Willer fled. Asher looked at Darran. 'Bolliton?'

Darran sighed. 'Alas, an unsavoury business. I reimbursed the prince's coffers from my own pocket. Kept various receipts . . . hidden. Allowed Willer less leeway afterwards. It seemed the prudent thing to do. In hindsight, however . . .'

'Prudent would've been dismissing the little turd,' Asher muttered. 'Might've saved a lot of heartache.' Without warning a fresh wave of pain assailed him. He slid down the cage bars again, into the filthy straw.

Darran didn't reply. Instead just stood there, silent, his eyes unreadable, his expression composed, as his measuring gaze took in the brutal evidence of Jarralt's displeasure. The dried manure and egg and other detritus, gifts from a grateful, adoring public. Asher looked away, not wanting to see his condition written plain in the old man's face.

'What are you doin' here, Darran? You come to gloat?'

The secretary shifted his gaze and stared at the crowd. 'Look at them all. By now I doubt there's a cradle-bound babe anywhere in this City who doesn't know you're arrested, and why. Within days they'll have heard it even down on the coast.'

Asher closed his eyes. 'That'll put a smile on my bloody brothers' faces.' Thinking of the coast, of the people there, he bit his lip. Made himself look at the ole crow. This was going to hurt worse than Jarralt's poker . . . 'Darran. I need a favour.'

Darran drew back. 'A *favour*?'

'It ain't for myself,' he added quickly. 'Not exactly. I got a friend. Jed. We grew up together in Restharven. He's hurt, on account of doing something I asked, and won't ever get better. Since we got back from Westwailing I been sendin' him money. Makin' sure he was looked after. When this is over . . . when I'm—' He took a deep, painful breath. Let it out. '—dead, can you make sure what's left of my savings finds him?

Darran's expression was a mingling of surprise and sorrow. 'Asher, all your money's been confiscated. Your possessions too. You don't have a cuick or a shirt to your name.'

He should have expected it. *Jed*. He swallowed anger. Thought of something else and sat up sharply, no matter the pain. His heavy chains rattled. 'Cygnet? What about Cygnet?'

'I'm sorry,' said Darran after a long pause. 'The stables are disbanded. Someone said – I truly am sorry, but Conroyd Jarralt has your horse now.'

It was a sharper agony than anything done to flesh and bone. He pressed his bloodstained hands to his face and felt salt sting the open wounds there. Felt his hard-pressed willpower break at last. His precious Cygnet, prey to that man's hands and heels, to cruel bits and crueller spurs.

Darran stepped closer. 'You should know, Asher, I've been told everything.' His voice was thinned to a whisper. 'Is it true? That you can – you know?'

Wrenching his thoughts away from Cygnet, poor Cygnet, he lowered his hands. 'What does it matter?'

'*Asher*! Is it *true*?'

He let his head rest against the cage. There was no point denying it now. 'Aye. But I wouldn't go repeatin' it if I were you. Jarralt'll kill you.'

Darran seemed torn between horror and fascination. 'Then if you do have . . . *power* . . . can't you free yourself?'

He'd asked himself the same question. He supposed it was possible. In theory. He could call down a freezing on the City, say, that'd turn all its citizens into ice statues. Leave him free to break out of this cage and run. But long before they'd frozen the guards would have clubbed him unconscious. Or dead. And anyway, there was nowhere to run to.

'No. I can't.'

Darran stepped closer still, so his face was near to touching the cage. 'I know why you did it.'

He let his eyes close. '"Why" don't matter. Not any more.'

'You did it because you love him.'

That made him laugh. He dragged his eyelids open. '*Now* you believe it?' He breathed hard, trying to dull the stabbing pain. 'Gar was more a brother to me than Zeth or Wishus or Bede or *any* of 'em. A hundred times I could've walked away. Should've. Wanted to. But I didn't. And I broke Barl's Law 'cause he asked me to. 'Cause he promised to protect me and I believed him. I thought his word meant something.' His hands fisted. 'Better watch yourself, ole maggoty man. Better take a good long look at what's happened here and ask yourself twice what you're doin', staying with him. 'Cause this is where loyalty leads you.'

Darran wrapped his fingers around the bars. 'Asher, listen.'

Beyond the cage Jesip and the other guards had drifted into a huddle round an open brazier to drink some ale and gobble meat pies. One of them stirred up the coals with a poker; the brazier's mouth glowed with a steady, scarlet heat. Searing memory stirred and he felt his muscles contract, his bowels loosen.

'Asher?'

Shame turned to anger. 'Go away, Darran. Ain't nowt you can do here and I'm sick of your manky ole face.'

Darran let go of the bars. 'Not before you've heard what I came to say.'

'I ain't interested.'

'This wasn't Gar's fault.'

He choked. 'Not his *fault*? Of course it's his fault! He said he'd protect me and look where I am!'

'If you'd let me explain, then—'

'Explain?' he said, incredulous. 'Explain *what*?' He wanted to howl, to scream, to tighten his fingers round Darran's scrawny throat and throttle him into silence. 'That it turns out Gar's gutless? I know that already!'

'Please, Asher, you must see his position!'

'I do see it! He's alive and I soon won't be. He's in his Tower and I'm in this cage. I saved his *life*, Darran! He's only breathin' today 'cause of me!'

'I know that,' said Darran, desperately whispering. '*He* knows that.'

'Then he has to stop this! He *owes* me, ole man!'

'Oh, Asher,' said Darran, his voice breaking. 'Don't you think he'd save you if he could? He *can't*. His hands are tied, he—'

'Tied?' he said savagely, and raised his manacled wrists. 'Well, mine are bloody *chained*!'

Darran stepped back, his face grey and drawn. 'He knows that too. And he's sorry, Asher. You've no idea how sorry he is. But there's nothing he can do. There were threats made. Dreadful threats. Against him . . . against the Olken people. He had to sign that proclamation.'

'He's the *king*, Darran! He can bloody *unsign* it!'

There were tears in Darran's eyes. *Tears*. 'Not any more. Haven't they told you? This afternoon he renounced his crown in favour of Conroyd Jarralt. Our new king has confined him to the Tower and stripped him of authority. For all the good he can do you now – for all the good he can do himself – Gar might as well be in that cage with you.'

Hope's last embers died. Despairing, Asher flung himself at the iron bars separating him from Darran and pressed his face against them.

'I wish he was! You tell him that, you stinkin' ole maggot! Tell him *he's* the traitor and it's *his* head they ought to cut off with their sharp and shiny axe! But since it'll be mine, tell him I hope he dies a long, slow death years and years from now, and that every minute of every day of every one of them years is *agony* and that every time he closes his eyes he sees my face! The face of the friend he *murdered*!' Exhausted, shuddering, he felt himself start sliding down the bars. 'Go on, you bastard! *Tell* him!'

Jesip must have heard him then, because he left his fellow guards, marched back to the cage and poked his pikestaff between the bars. Asher barely felt its sharp tip puncture his skin.

'Watch your mouth, traitor!' Jesip growled, then turned to Darran. 'I'm sorry, sir, but you've had more than two minutes and—'

'It's all right,' said Darran. 'I'm leaving now.'

'Right then,' said Jesip. He sounded relieved. 'Goodnight to you, sir.'

'Goodnight, Jesip,' replied Darran, turning. 'And . . . goodbye, Asher.'

He summoned a skerrick of saliva and spat. 'Piss on you, Darran. And piss on that treacherous shit in the Tower.'

Jesip hit him. Hit him again, and again, until all he could do was lie face down on the floor of the cage, breathing in the stench of shit and egg and vomit, grunting with each blow. Moments later the other guards joined in. The sounds of their dedicated fury mingled with the shouts and applause of the crowd.

Not soon enough, the world went away.

# CHAPTER TWENTY-FIVE

Morg stood before Conroyd's dressing-room mirror and admired the way his blue brocade dressing-gown brought out his eyes. Behind him, Conroyd's wife continued to wail.

'But you *can't* send me away!' Ethienne protested, perilously close to stamping her foot. 'I'm the *queen* now, Conroyd! I belong in the *palace*!'

He sighed and smoothed his unbound blond hair. She belonged in a coffin buried six feet deep. 'My dear, I know. And when the time is right the palace is where you'll be. Where we both will be, with the House Jarralt falcon flying proudly above it. But until that time I want you out of Dorana, safe on our country estate with our sons to look after you.'

'How am I unsafe here? You're the king!'

'I know,' he said, turning. Smiling. 'But until the traitor Asher is dead, the City will be filled with Olken from every corner of the kingdom, come to see him die and all doubtless unhappy with the curfew and other restrictions I've had to lay on them in the wake of his wickedness.'

She pouted. 'Who cares if they're unhappy? It's their

duty to obey you without question and if they don't they should be arrested!'

'And they will be, my dear. But you've told me yourself how this business has upset the staff, and it will only get worse before it gets better. There'll be no such upheaval on the estate. Besides,' he patted her cheek, 'I must concentrate on my new, important duties, and you know what a distraction you are.'

That had her simpering, the silly cow. 'Oh, Conroyd, dearest—'

'So, my pet, you'll go? To please me?'

'And what of my pleasure?' she retorted, folding her arms. 'I only like the country in the summer and anyway, I want to see that dreadful Asher die.'

Out of patience, he snapped his fingers before her petulant face. '*Obedience.*' All the lively argument drained away, leaving her pale and docile and, above all, silent.

What a shame he couldn't so ensorcel every other Doranen in the kingdom. It would make things so much easier. Unfortunately, that was impossible. He'd have to find another way. It was vital he get rid of as many Doranen from the City as he could; the fewer magicians he had around him the better, for even the most rudimentary practitioners would begin to notice the Wall's decline.

Provided, of course, he could achieve its demise. Unsustained by WeatherWorking it would fall, eventually, but that would take too long. And too many questions would be asked in the meantime.

The Doranen, sheep or not, would notice his lack of WeatherWorking. Holze would certainly begin to agitate. Demand proof of his proficiency and the appointment of dead Durm's replacement. And, if unsatisfied would doubtless rally the kingdom's magicians against him.

There was only one solution. He *had* to find a way to thwart Barl's will. To absorb her wretched Weather Magic into himself and unravel her Wall from within.

For if he didn't . . .

First things first, however. He turned again to Conroyd's wife. 'You are leaving for the country, Ethienne. Willingly and with enthusiasm, eager to begin preparations for the creation of a new Doranen court.' A happy thought occurred, and he laughed out loud. 'What's more, as soon as you arrive at the estate you'll invite as many of the City's Doranen as can be accommodated to join you there, that they might assist you in those preparations. Make it a royal decree. You'll enjoy that, and they won't dare refuse.'

Ethienne nodded, witless and smiling. 'Of course, Conroyd. Whatever you say, my dear.'

Not all the Doranen would go, of course. The damned councillors would stay, some of them, royal decree or not. Conroyd's friends, for certain. But many would obey the summons, greedy for the chance to make themselves indispensable to the new regime.

And that would give him the time and space he needed to devise a way around Barl's safeguards against him. To kill her Wall and her kingdom, once and for all.

Veira's kitchen was small and cosy. The walls were painted a buttery yellow. The drawn curtains were blue. The cupboards, the dresser, the table and chairs, all were crafted from mellow brown timber and carved with acorns and wheat sheaves and lambs. Dried herbs in bunches dangled invitingly overhead, scenting the air. Seated at the table, Dathne breathed in the muddled aromas of sage, of dilly-tip, rosemary, thyme and pods of tottle seeds, feeling oddly comforted. The stove in the corner wafted heat from its wood-filled pot belly. Standing before it, as though he'd grown up here, as though he belonged, Matt tipped fresh tea leaves into an old brown pot then filled it from a kettle boiling on the stove top. His back was to her, and he wouldn't turn around.

'I don't understand it,' she said, slumping partly against the wall, partly over the tiny table. The cushion on the chair was a blessing after the hard bench seat of Veira's wagon. 'Why didn't you tell me you were coming here?'

Matt said nothing. Veira, setting out plates, glanced at him. The look was as good as a poke with an elbow. He shrugged. Said, over his shoulder, 'We weren't on speaking terms, remember?'

She frowned, not liking the reminder. 'But how did you know where Viera lived? Even *I* didn't know where she lived! Not until she told me!'

'And I told him too,' said Veira. She'd shed her hooded cloak since coming inside; plump and comfortable, she was layered in a patchwork of blue cotton and black felt and bright scarlet sheep's-wool; her long grey hair was coiled round and round the back of her head like an elderly sleeping snake. Slivers of silver-bound jet dangled from her soft earlobes and her fingers were burdened with rings. Her eyes, dark brown and lively, were narrowed now in sharp consideration. 'Did you think you were the only one with a Circle Stone, child?'

Shocked, Dathne sat up. 'Well, of course not . . . but I didn't think—' She stared accusingly at Matt's stubborn back. 'You were *spying* on me?'

'Feh!' said Veira, disparaging. '*Spying*. Twice, I've spoken to Matthias since you and he fell in together. I called him, to make sure I could, and after that stayed silent, hearing not a whisper until he reached out and told me he needed to hide.'

She let her gaze rest broodingly between Matt's shoulderblades. Wanted him to feel its weight. 'And was that all you told her?'

He refused to turn. Pretended he had to guard the waiting mugs in case they sprouted wings and flew away. 'I told her everything. I had to. You wouldn't.'

She wanted to leap from her seat and beat her fists against him. 'You had no right! I'm the Heir, not you. It was for me to tell, in my own time and in my own way! You've resented my feelings for Asher ever since you learned of them. Maybe he was right. Maybe you *are* jealous! You—'

He did turn then, his face white with temper and tiredness. 'Jealous? Don't flatter yourself! Believe me, Asher's welcome to you, high-handed, self-opinionated slumskumbledy woman that you are! So convinced that you're invincible, just 'cause you're the Heir! Well, you're *not* invincible. You didn't see this coming. You didn't see he had their magic in him, and maybe none of ours. And you wouldn't listen when I said, over and over, he needed to be told. If we'd told him, he wouldn't be in this mess!'

For a moment she could hardly breathe. Matt *never* spoke to her like this. *Nobody* spoke to her like this. 'You don't know that!' she spat back at him. 'You don't know anything! Telling him might've made things worse!'

'How could they be *worse*?' he shouted. 'Asher's going to *die*!'

'Now that's enough,' said Veira, and slapped her palm down sharp on the table. 'Both of you. I'm too old for all this brangling and besides, it won't change what's happened. There's been mistakes on both sides that can't be unmade now.' Her kindly face was tight with disapproval. 'Dathne, you've no business flying at Matthias. Yes, he told me all your muddle-headed doings, and then spent twice as long again making excuses for you. He's been a good and loyal friend, my girl. Better than you've deserved.'

Hot with shame and angry embarrassment, Dathne stared at the knobbly pine-board floor. Couldn't bring herself to look at Matt. 'I'm sorry,' she muttered. Her voice sounded very small in the cottage's kitchen. Small, and unremarkable. Not the voice of an all-seeing prophet at all. She lifted her gaze. 'I'm just tired, and worried. I'm glad Matt came to you, Veira. He'd have been in danger, else.'

Veira sniffed. 'Oh, he's still in danger, child. We're all of us in danger.' She looked again to Matt. 'That tea ready yet, my boy?'

'Nearly,' he said, and pulled out a chair at the table for her. 'Sit. I'll do the rest. Biscuits as well?'

Veira settled herself in the seat with a sigh. 'Of course biscuits. Tea ain't tea without biscuits.'

Briefly grinning, he opened a nearby cupboard and pulled down a large corked clay jar glazed red and blue. Took a crock of honey from another, teaspoons from a drawer and a pitcher of milk from a cool-box set under the sink, and placed them on the table.

Dathne stared. 'Well! You've made yourself at home!'

Frowning again, he turned away to gently swill the tea inside its pot. 'I had to, didn't I? Seeing I was kicked out of my own.'

She flushed. 'Matt—'

Veira rapped her knuckles on the tabletop. 'No more, I said! Rivers don't flow backwards.'

Reproved, Dathne closed her lips tight and looked at Matt instead as he busied himself with pouring the brewed tea. Despite everything it was good to see him, large and practical in Veira's little kitchen. He'd lost his scent of horses. Smelled now of honey-pine and beeswax. His face was thinner, though, carved with lines she'd never seen before. And there was a sadness in him that was also new. Her doing. She felt her throat constrict, and turned to Veira.

'So . . . you know everything?'

Veira's eyebrows lifted. 'Everything Matthias knew, yes. Which I'll warrant's not the same as everything there is to know. I've no doubt there're things you kept from him as well as me.'

There was a look in Veira's eyes that made her squirm. 'Nothing important, I promise. Veira . . . what I did. It wasn't for me.' Handing out the tea-filled mugs, Matt made a small, disbelieving sound. Her cheeks burned. 'All right. Not wholly for me. I hoped that if Asher and I were . . . close . . . intimate . . . he'd believe he could finally trust me. Confide his secrets. Then I'd know how best to proceed. Prophecy's proven unreliable, Veira. Unclear, and even ambiguous. And it's never been constant. I couldn't see where it was leading us.'

'So you told yourself it led to that young man's mattress,' retorted Veira. 'Which is where you've always wanted to travel.'

'*Veira*!'

'She's right, Dath, and you know it,' Matt said sharply. 'We'll not solve a thing if we can't face the truth unflinching.'

She didn't want to think about that. 'You don't seem very surprised, Veira. That I – that we – Asher and me, that we—'

Shrugging, Veira peered into her steaming mug. Splashed in some milk and a dollop of honey. 'It's true I ain't the Heir no more than Matthias, but I've still got a good pair of eyes in my head and a knack or three of my own,' she said, stirring. 'I could tell which way the wind was blowing.'

'Then why didn't you stop me, if Matt's right and it was such a terrible thing to do?'

'Did I say he was right?' said Veira, and exchanged glances with him as he passed her a plate piled high with almond biscuits. 'Did I say it was terrible? I don't recall saying that. We still don't know where this will end.'

'We've got a pretty good idea,' Matt said, glowering, and leaned against the kitchen bench.

Instead of answering, Veira dipped a biscuit in her milky tea and ate it with lip-smacking relish. 'Drink up, child,' she said mildly. 'And then you'll do some scrying and we'll see what we can see.'

Dathne felt herself shrink with fear. She had no desire for tea. 'Scrying? For Asher? Veira, I can't. Not tonight. I'm so tired. Maybe tomorrow—'

'Yes, tonight,' the old woman said, eyebrows pulled low. 'Before sunrise. I've tried but I can't seem to find him. Matthias says you never fail, no matter what the distance.'

She glared at helpful Matt. He shrugged, his eyes cool and contained as he took a sip from his own mug. There was an empty chair beside her; he could've sat down if he'd wanted . . .

Pain, quick and sharp. Such a gulf between them, greater than ever before. Could they cross it? Rebuild their bridges? Or was their friendship dead and buried, as Asher might soon be dead and buried?

Of course she wanted to see where Asher was. How he was. She was desperate to know . . .

She was terrified of what she'd find out.

'You must, child,' said Veira, relentless. 'Knowledge is power.'

'All right,' she said grudgingly, making no effort to be pleasant. 'If you insist.'

They finished their tea and their biscuits and Veira brought out her scrying basin. Prepared the water, the tanal leaf, vervle, cloysies' tears and moon-rot. When everything was ready Dathne looked at her and at Matt and said, still tetchy, 'I'll make no promises in this. He might well be beyond me.'

'All I ask is that you try, child,' said Veira. 'That's all I'll ever ask.'

So she tried. A part of her so fearful, a part of her with hope. Deep in the tanal leaf's languorous grasp, she seasoned the scrying water and opened her heart. Sent forth her questing mind.

*Asher. Asher. Asher.*

Moments later she found him. Huddled. Hurting. Caged like an animal and abused by the very people he was born to save. Weeping, she told Veira and Matt what she saw in the basin and heard them gasp in turn. 'We must help him,' she whispered as the tears coursed down her face. 'We must save him. Can we save him? Is there time?'

'That's a question I can't answer,' said Veira as she put her arms round Dathne's shoulders. 'Not yet. But I promise you this much, child. We'll try.'

*'We must save him. Can we save him? Is there time?'*

Tossed and turned by Dathne's desperate questions, Veira rose before dawn and tiptoed into her little kitchen to make a cup of tea. How odd, to be creeping thief-like about the cottage she'd lived in solitary for twenty-seven years. But she knew already that Matthias was a light sleeper; years of living with horses and their capricious maladies had honed him to startling alertness. She didn't know about Dathne yet, but chances were the child slept just as shallow. And since just now she needed quiet and time alone with her own bleak thoughts, it was best she played the mouse.

She lit a single candle, then the fire in her stove to boil the kettle. Outside the window darkness mantled her yard, the forest, the mountains. Barl's Wall was a whisper of gold, lost amongst the stars. Sometimes it was easy to forget it was there. Or that she was here because of it, tied to a scattered group of not-quite-strangers whose lives she could end with one unthinking mistake. Who knew her but not each other and willingly lived with danger for the sake of an ancient prophecy and a life that had vanished centuries before they were born. Their courage had her weeping, if she let it.

Guardianship of the Circle had come to her three months before her thirty-sixth birthday. Married at twenty to a lovely boy whose face she no longer remembered, widowed childless at twenty-three, she'd not had the heart to woo or wed again. At least, for a long time she'd thought it was sorrow.

After her Great-Aunt Tilda had died, though, leaving her a mysterious box and a legacy she still had cause to curse, she wondered if that wasn't Prophecy working its will upon her. Dabbling its fingers in her private doings long before it needed her. Keeping her ready for the day when it did.

For this day, when dark decisions must be made so that an even darker future might not come to pass.

The kettle took a deep breath and started whistling. She whisked it off the stove top and made her mug of tea. Cradling it between fingers just beginning to feel the pinches of age, she sank into a chair at the table to rest her elbows and brood on matters like to break her heart.

After sending Matthias and Dathne to their beds scant hours earlier, she'd reached out to another Circle member, Gilda Hartshorn, to confirm the truth of Dathne's scrying. A seamstress in Dorana City, Gilda sewed often for staff up at the palace and in the City guardhouse. She had a genius for gossip and inspiring confidences.

*It's true, it's true, all true*, Gilda had told her. *Asher's due to die at midnight Barl's Day. A proclamation from the new king, Conroyd Jarralt.*

Prompted by unfathomable instinct, knowing they'd need all the help they could find to rescue him, she'd told Gilda the truth about Asher. Shocked, then tearful, Gilda had demanded, *But he's guarded day and night and there's a crowd around him no matter what the hour! Veira, Veira, what shall we do?*

Gilda knew no more of Dathne and Matt than they knew about her, and still it was best things stayed that way. So she'd settled the seamstress's fears with a calm assurance three parts a lie, then climbed in her bed to sleep. She was sixty-three years old now, and nowhere near spry. And the journey to collect Dathne had shaken her bones to aching.

Sleep hadn't come, though. She'd told Dathne she had an inkling of an idea on how to save their Innocent Mage, and she did. But that idea was dreadful. Merciless. Uncaring of hearts broken, lives lost, futures trampled. Doubtless it came from Prophecy itself, which accounted for its coldness. It also might account for coincidence: that of all the people who could be the key to Asher's freedom, it was her flesh and blood. Her sister's son. A boy grown now to manhood who she'd brought into the Circle against her will. Against all bonds of family. Against the voice in her heart crying, *No. Don't. Choose another.*

She hadn't. Couldn't. Like Dathne, like her nephew Rafel, she'd been chosen as Prophecy's tool. She might rail against destiny from dawn till dusk but it made no difference. Rafel was part of the pattern. Part of Prophecy. And so she'd called him to her, and willingly he'd come. Listened to her fantastic tale of omens and promises and dead men's dreams, and smiled.

*'Of course I'll help you, Veira. What am I meant to do?'*

Then, not knowing, she couldn't tell him. Now, suspecting . . . she couldn't bring herself to think of it.

From the henhouse outside in the yard, a babbling of girlish chicken voices and the rooster's lusty crow. Lifting her head, she realised the sky outside had lightened. That tentative sunsingers in the forest's foliage were warbling in chorus. It was day, and she had chores to do. Decisions to make. Plans to devise.

Prophecy to obey.

She was sixty-three years old, and nigh on sick of Prophecy.

Her mostly untouched tea was cold now. Wrinkling her nose, she tipped it down the sink then crept back to her bedroom. Pulled on thicker socks and extra woollens and lifted her coat from its hook on the back of the door. Matthias would be rousing soon, and maybe Dathne as well. She wasn't ready to face them yet.

A walk in the woods was what she needed. Solitude,

for the strengthening of heart and will. She'd take the pigs.

Pigs were good listeners, and they never talked back.

When Asher stirred again it was to a rising sun whose winter heat barely warmed his chilled and stiffened body. Far beyond caring about such niceties as privacy, modesty, shame, he pissed into the straw. The few remaining yellow stalks turned pink.

In the Square, the diminished crowd stirred and muttered and stamped its feet. A few half-hearted eggs cracked open on the cage roof. These ones were hardly rotten at all. Pale yellow yolk dripped onto his face. He opened his parched mouth and swallowed, because his belly was empty and rumbling. That small act of self-sustenance stirred his audience to anger. Someone shouted. Someone else threw a rock. Two rocks. Four. Five. One hit him, drawing blood. He threw it back, swearing.

The next thing he knew it was raining rocks, until the guards stepped in and stopped the sport. Not out of pity; they just didn't want an accident that might prevent his keenly anticipated beheading. Or to get hit by mistake themselves.

Adrift on a shifting sea of memories, swaddled in a sharp glass blanket of pain, Asher let himself float, praying that the next time he opened his eyes he'd be dead.

Gar woke to the sound of curtains rattling along their thick brass rods and an unwelcome voice. 'Your Highness? Your Highness.'

He rolled his head on the pillow then frowned. What? That wasn't right. Since when was his pillow made of wood? Someone had crept into his bedchamber and turned his pillow into *wood*. And then they'd rolled it *flat* . . .

He opened his eyes, blinking in the pale morning sunshine laid over his face like gauze. Oh. This wasn't his bedchamber, it was his library. The pillow was actually his desk, where he'd fallen asleep at some point during the night while continuing his search for Barl's diary.

His fruitless search. If the diary existed he'd failed to find it amongst Durm's books. It must be in Durm's study. If it existed . . .

He was starting to think it didn't. That the diary was nothing more than a figment of Durm's dying mind. That hope for him, for Asher, for the whole kingdom, was truly dead.

He sat up, groaning as every muscle protested his unorthodox mattress. His eyes were gritty, his mouth tasted like old socks and his head hurt as though it was spiky with nails and the sunlight was a hammer, pounding . . .

'Your Highness, really,' fussed Darran. 'You hardly touched your dinner!'

He rubbed his eyes. Glanced at the abandoned tray on the floor with its burden of congealed roast lamb and soggy carrots. 'I wasn't hungry. What time is it?'

'A quarter after seven,' said Darran, retrieving the tray. 'Now, sir, I've drawn you a bath. Please take it, and by the time you're finished breakfast will be ready.'

He felt his stomach roil. 'I'm still not hungry.'

'Hungry or not, Your Highness, you can't miss dinner and breakfast!'

He groaned again. 'You're turning into an old woman, Darran, right before my eyes.'

Darran sniffed. 'Well if I am, sir, you're hastening the transformation. Come along now! Up, up, up! Your bath water's getting cold.'

Clearly there was no escape short of dismissing the old man. A tempting thought, but no. Glowering, he shoved his chair back from his library desk and staggered upstairs to his bathroom, where there was indeed a hot bath waiting. Darran had even laid him out fresh clothes.

He didn't know whether to laugh or cry.

Still. The hot bath, scented with oils, did feel good to his cramped and tired muscles. He let himself sink beneath the fragrant water and waited for the heat to suffuse him. For his headache to subside and his aching tension to ease.

But no. With wakefulness and silence came more uncomfortable thoughts. If Barl's diary did exist and was hidden somewhere in Durm's study instead of his book collection, could he hope to find it there? Without falling foul of Conroyd? Without alerting the bastard to his unpermitted wanderings and causing his limited freedom to be reduced altogether? He tried to imagine guards in Conroyd's pay cluttering up his Tower, counting every step he took, every breath, and was forced to stop. Just the idea of it made him sick.

But he had to take the chance. If he didn't it meant he truly was Gar the Magickless again, forever, and faced a life of virtual imprisonment in a kingdom ruled by the wrong man. A life of unbearable guilt and sorrow. No matter what it took, no matter what it cost, he had to believe the diary was real, and contained a means of rescue for them all.

His bath was getting cold. He stood, dripping. Wrapped himself in a towel and staggered into his bedchamber where Darran was fussing over a small dining table. Odd. He couldn't recall having a dining table in here half an hour ago.

'I hope you don't mind, sir,' said Darran, buffing silver cutlery with a linen cloth. 'But I thought if you ate in here it might reduce the number of rooms to clean.' He looked up, stricken. 'Not that I begrudge the task, sir! I don't! But—'

'I know,' he said. 'It's a sensible plan, Darran. Whatever I can do to make your life easier, consider it done. And don't forget to set yourself a place too. We're in this together, old friend.'

Darran's sallow cheeks turned pink. 'I . . . I thought an omelette for breakfast, sir. With ham and asparagus. A little creamed cheese. I'll serve it momentarily, if that's agreeable.'

Gar sighed. Darran was trying so hard, and his own life was just as disarranged. Lay in equally smoking ruins. Through no fault of his own he'd been reduced to housewifery in the service of a disgraced and impotent prince of nothing. After a lifetime's exemplary royal service he'd earned much better than this ignominious exile.

Eyes suddenly stinging, he smiled. 'It's perfect. Thank you.' The smile swiftly faded, though, as another unwelcome thought stabbed. 'I can only pray Asher is treated so well.'

Something in the quality of Darran's silence made him stare.

'What?'

'Oh, sir,' Darran's expression was anguished, his voice a strangled whisper. 'I don't know how to tell you . . .'

'Tell me what?'

'About Asher.'

His heart thudded. 'For Barl's sake, just say it, man.'

Darran was wringing the linen polishing cloth as though it were a chicken's neck. 'I went and saw him last night.'

'Asher?'

'Yes.'

He felt his emptied lungs constrict. 'Why?'

Very carefully, Darran smoothed out the throttled cloth and laid it on the table. 'I was . . . concerned. I thought you'd want to know if he was all right.'

He didn't.

He had to. 'And was he?'

Darran shook his head, mute misery in his face. 'No. He's in a cage, in the Square. On public display like an animal. Lord Jarralt – the king – has hurt him.'

'The king is a cruel and wicked man.'

'Yes, sir,' Darran whispered. 'I'm most afraid you're right.'

Towel still clutched about his drying body Gar moved to the window, pulled aside the curtain and stared down into the grounds below where cheerful gardeners no longer worked. With an effort he kept his voice steady. 'And Asher. Did you have the chance to speak to him?'

'Briefly, sir. He asked me to give you a message.'

A message. The sunlight hammer resumed its pounding, and the nails drove into his brain. 'There's no need, Darran. I can imagine what it was.'

'No, sir,' said Darran. His voice sounded closer. 'In fact, he asked me to say he forgives you. He understands the kingdom must come before all personal considerations, and that in denying him you did what had to be done so Lur might remain safe and at peace. He begs you not to blame yourself for his death.'

'Oh,' he said eventually. 'I see.' Slowly he turned from the window and stared into Darran's pale, composed features. 'That doesn't sound like Asher. Was he lying?'

Darran shook his head, vehement. 'No, sir. Every word he said to me was the truth.'

Well. If Darran believed it – and clearly he did – then he'd believe it too. 'How was he?'

'His spirits are low,' Darran admitted, reluctant. 'Which is only to be expected. I think he's afraid, though he'd never admit it. But he loves you, sir. I was wrong to think he never did.'

A big admission from Darran. Gar nodded and turned back to the window, unwilling to trust his face, his self-control, to another's scrutiny.

*He forgives you.*

And did that make things better or worse? He wasn't sure. Might never be sure.

'You should get dressed, sir,' Darran said gently. 'I'll be back in a trice with your omelette.'

But when he returned some ten minutes later, he brought with him not breakfast but Willer. Smirking, resplendent in sky-blue satin embroidered everywhere with House Jarralt's falcon emblem, the horrible little man strutted into the room as though he owned the world.

'I'm sorry, sir,' said Darran stiffly. 'He insisted.'

Gar looked at his former employee. 'What do you want? You must know you're not welcome here, Willer.'

The smirk widened to a fatuous smile. 'On the contrary, *Gar*. As an emissary for the king I am welcome everywhere. His Majesty sends me to say: surrender the Weather Orb and such books and papers removed unwisely from dead Durm's apartments.' With a flourish he produced a sealed note and held it out.

Gar, forced to step towards him as though in supplication, raised a hand at Darran's hiss of outrage and took the missive without comment. Opened it and frowned. 'This is from Conroyd?'

'From the king, yes. And mind you address him as such, with all his due respect.'

Ignoring the little slug's snide tone, the temerity of his scolding, he continued to frown at the note. It was signed *Conroyd the First* and its contents betrayed both character and knowledge. *To quote yourself to yourself: 'I disobey, and others suffer.' Heed my emissary's demand without delay.*

It was Conroyd's handwriting, no question of that. And yet . . . and yet . . .

'Well?' said Willer, grown even fatter with arrogance and pride. 'Must I tell His Majesty you kept me waiting? Fetch the Orb at once!'

'Ignore him, Darran,' said Gar as his secretary choked on a breathless imprecation. 'He's a cur dog yapping from the shelter of his master's shadow.'

'Sir,' said Darran, and subsided, still bristling.

The Weather Orb was here, hidden safely in his bedchamber. He'd intended to take it back to Durm's apartments then changed his mind in case the Weather Magics transfer to Asher had failed, or faded, and they needed to perform it again. In case he found his cure and was able to resume his role as Weather-Worker.

One thought unnecessary, the other forlorn. He retrieved Barl's gift from its hiding place at the bottom of his blanket box and held it out. 'Durm's books and papers are unboxed and scattered. I'll need time to ready them for – the King.'

Willer took the Orb's box gingerly, as though it were

alive and may bite him. 'One hour. House Jarralt servants will come to collect them. Be advised – don't make them wait.'

Gar smiled thinly. 'And when you give King Conroyd the Orb, Willer, give him this message with it: he would do well to reconsider keeping Asher in a cage. Such unkindness sets a tone for his reign that some might find disconcerting.'

'You are the only one who thinks so,' retorted Willer. 'Didn't Darran tell you? They're lining up ten-deep in the Square to get their look at the traitor from Restharven and pelt him with the refuse from their dinner tables and byres.'

A lifetime of controlling his feelings in public kept his face from revealing any pain. Contempt, though; contempt he'd reveal, and gladly. 'And I suppose you couldn't wait to join in, could you? You must feel very proud.'

Willer flushed, lifted his twice-doubled chin. 'Durm's books and papers in one hour . . . or deal with His Majesty's wrath.'

'I'm so sorry, sir,' said Darran once Willer had departed. 'I'd have kept him out if I—'

Gar held out Conroyd's note. 'What do you make of this?'

Baffled, Darran took it. Read it. 'I . . . I'm not sure I know what—'

'It's Conroyd's penmanship. After two years on the Privy Council I'd know it anywhere. So should you by now. But . . .' He shook his head. 'Don't you think there's something *odd* about it?'

Darran examined the note again. 'I'm sorry, sir. No.' He frowned. 'Perhaps it's a trifle unsteady—'

'You do see it, don't you?' Gar said. 'It's Conroyd's

hand . . . and yet it's not. As though . . .' And then he stopped. The idea was too fantastical for words.

'Yes, sir?' Darran prompted. 'As though what?'

He took back the note. 'As though someone else's hand was laid over Conroyd's as he held the pen to write.'

'Oh,' said Darran. 'I see. Yes. Well. That would be very odd, sir.'

'Never mind,' he said, and crumpled the paper. 'I'm imagining things. Darran, I need your help.'

'Certainly, sir,' said Darran. He sounded relieved. 'Doing what?'

'Durm's books and journals. I want to go through them one last time before I have to give them over to Conroyd. I don't know. It's a slim chance but I keep thinking I might have *missed* it.'

'Missed what, sir?'

He took a deep breath. This secret was a luxury he could no longer afford. 'As he was dying, Durm told me he'd found a diary. Barl's diary. He seemed to think it was important. I want to find it. I want to keep it out of Conroyd's hands.'

Darran's eyes were opened wide. 'Sir! If it's true – why, it might change everything!'

'That's what I'm hoping for,' he said, and pulled a face. 'Praying for. Durm called the diary our only hope and its *my* hope he was right. He warned me against Conroyd. Somehow I think he knew disaster was brewing. But we've only got an hour. Breakfast will have to wait, I'm afraid. All your hard cooking . . .'

'Breakfast can burn, sir, for all I care,' said Darran firmly. 'Let's get at those books.'

# CHAPTER TWENTY-SIX

When Dathne woke in the trundle bed Veira had made up for her, she saw through the partly closed sitting room curtains that the sun had crawled high in the sky. Around her, the cottage felt uninhabited. As she blinked muzzily, trying to arrange her frothy thoughts, she heard the ringing crack of an axe blade against wood coming from somewhere outside.

After using the chamber pot and dragging on fresh clothes, she poked about the rest of the cottage, just in case her feelings had fooled her and Veira was there to talk to after all.

But no. The cottage was empty of both Veira and Matt, so she let herself outside through the kitchen door and into the cottage's tree-fringed back yard.

Where Matt was chopping firewood.

He glanced at her. Not angrily, but not in a friendly way either. 'Veira's taken the pigs for a walk,' he said, lining up a fresh round of timber on the block. 'There's no saying how long she'll be gone. I left oatmush on the hob for you.'

'I smelled it,' she said, and perched herself on a handy tree stump. The thought of food was revolting. Her belly was greasy, rolling with nausea. 'Maybe later.' She kicked her heels against the stump; the three black and white chickens scratching the grass nearby took frightened offence and scattered, squawking.

He nodded.

Drenched with regrets she watched him continue his chopping, distant and entirely self-contained. The man she'd known in Dorana was vanished. In his place stood this stranger with hooded eyes and a grim mouth and no exasperated pleasure in her company. In the mid-morning light the chasm between them looked no easier to cross than it had last night in Veira's kitchen.

Before drifting off to sleep she'd replayed over and over in her mind the sequence of events that had brought them to this time and place. The decisions she'd made, the choices she'd discarded in favour of silence and subterfuge.

Try as she might she'd not been able to imagine herself doing anything differently. And whether that meant that as Jervale's Heir she'd been right and was guided by Prophecy, or as her plain self she'd been nothing but a stubborn slumskumbledy wench, she had no idea at all.

In heavy silence the haphazard pile of wood dwindled as Matt reduced the rough lumps of seasoned timber to tidy logs and kindling, his horseman's hands gripped tight around the axe handle, his weathered face severe with concentration. The useful stack of firewood grew taller and wider and still he did not speak, and neither did she. Her heart and head were aching; she wasn't sure she'd ever been so sorrowed or felt so helpless in all her life.

Because it hurt so much to look at this shuttered and newly unknowable man she looked at her surroundings instead. A goodly garden had been created around the back of the cottage. There was a vegetable patch sprouting carrots and tomatoes and suchlike. Three scraggly apple trees. A riotous herb bed and a hodge-podge of flowers. A clovery lawn patched the spaces between cottage and cultivation. Veira's pony cropped grass in a small paddock attached to a tumbledown stable off to the left, and on the right was a mildly odorous pigpen. Next to that the henhouse, its jaunty red paint faded and peeling. It was all very . . . rural.

Aside from the sound of Matt's wood-chopping, the sharp calls of hidden birds and the answering cackles of Veira's hens, the forest hush was absolute. Unsettling, after the steady humming bustle of the City. But there was a kind of peace in it too. A balm to her lacerated soul. On any other morning she'd have revelled in the solitude and thought of this interlude as a holiday, embracing it with passion.

But all her passion had died. She'd killed it, with arrogance and pride and a refusal to consider she might be wrong. That Matt could be right. That being Jervale's Heir did not make her infallible.

She wanted to tell him that. To say she was sorry and beg his forgiveness. But his shuttered face defeated her. Made her more tongue-tied, and unfairly angry. So she sat unspeaking and watched him cut wood.

Eventually there was none left. Matt buried the axe blade in the chopping block with one mighty swing and said, sweating, 'Could be you were right after all.'

For a moment she could only look at him, slum-guzzled into silence. Then she found her meagre voice and said, uncertainly, 'What do you mean?'

He inspected his palms for blisters. Found one and popped it, frowning. 'I mean about not telling Asher the truth.'

*Asher*. Images from the scrying basin swam across her inner eye. She felt her heart constrict and her mouth suck dry. 'How so?'

'What you saw was done to him ... the way that Jarralt hurt him ...'

She thrust away the bloodshed and the haunting echo of screams. 'What about it? How can that mean I was right?'

Matt looked elsewhere, into the distance of tangled trees. 'Who's to say what a man can know and not talk of when that kind of thing's being done to him? With all the will in the world, if he'd known who he is and what we're about, it's more likely than not he'd have told it to that poxy Doranen bastard and then where would we be?'

She shook her head. 'No. Asher's strong. He'd never have broken.'

'You can't know that for sure. So the way things fell out it's best you held your tongue and made me hold mine.' He glanced at her. 'That's the only thing you were right about, mind. As for the rest of it ...' Faint colour tinged his face. 'The futtering ...'

'What about it?' she said tiredly, feeling her own face heat. 'You deny Asher's charge that you're jealous 'cause he's known me and you haven't, and never will. But how can I believe you? You act like a man feeling robbed.'

For some time he didn't answer. Then he shrugged. Glanced at her again then let his gaze slide sideways into the woods. 'Believe me, Dathne, if ever once I loved you I got over it soon enough.'

And that hurt, not because she wanted him to love her, at least not like that, but because there was a hardness in him now that before this moment she'd only ever noticed in herself. She'd done that to him, and wasn't proud to learn it.

'I do love him, Matt,' she said, worrying at a pulled thread in the fabric stretched over her knee. Needing him to believe her. 'It's not an excuse for what I did, but I suppose it is a reason.'

He nodded. 'I suppose.'

'I'm not sure *why* I love him, mind. The purpose behind it, I mean, not the bits and pieces of him that make me soft round the edges. And there must be a purpose, Matt. Mustn't there? Prophecy wouldn't have thrown us together for so long and in such a way that we fell in love if there wasn't a purpose?'

'You're asking the wrong man. I've never much understood Prophecy or its workings.'

'And yet you've followed it all your life. Followed *me*. Why?'

He gave her a painful smile. 'Why does a dog chase rabbits, Dathne? Because it's in his nature.'

In all the years she'd known him she'd never heard him sound so defeated. 'We can't afford to doubt now, Matt. We've come too far. Risked too much, and sacrificed more. We must see this through to the end no matter how bitter it might be.'

'I know that,' he said tersely. 'I'm here, aren't I?'

She longed to touch him, but was afraid he'd rebuff her. 'What I did with Asher . . . it was never a trivial thing. I meant what I said about us being sworn in marriage, Barlsman or no Barlsman. His heart is mine, Matt, and mine is his, no matter what.'

'I know,' he said. 'If I thought it'd make a difference, I'd say I wished you happy.'

She felt tears well, burning her tired eyes. Never before last night had she cried in front of Matt. It had been a matter of pride and, she thought, necessity. But such things seemed pointless now so she let them fall. 'It makes a difference,' she whispered, fisting her fingers in the folds of her skirt. 'Never think it doesn't make a difference.'

'Good,' he said. 'I'm glad for that.'

'I can't believe he has their magic,' she said. 'He made it snow, right under my roof. How can an Olken do that?'

Matt shook his head. 'I don't know. Unless . . .'

'Unless what?'

'Could he have Doranen blood in him?'

The idea was outrageous. 'How? Our peoples don't mix, it's forbidden!'

That made Matt snort. 'Olken magic's forbidden, Dathne, yet here we are. Aren't you the one who says all things are possible with Prophecy?'

'Yes, but . . .' She shook her head. 'It doesn't matter. He has their magic and I didn't feel it. How could I not feel it? It's my business to know the Innocent Mage better than he knows himself! And now because I've failed him he might die!'

Matt moved to her then, and folded her in his strong, sheltering arms. He smelled of sweat and leather, his jerkin warm beneath her cheek as he held her against his chest. 'You mustn't lose faith, Dath. We have to trust in Prophecy.'

'I do,' she sobbed. 'I do. Oh, Matt, I'm sorry I sent you away. I'm sorry I've always been harsh with you, keeping you distant. I thought it was best. I thought I was protecting you.'

'I know that,' he said, and rested his cheek on her unruly, unbound hair. 'I always knew. And even though it irked me sometimes I never begrudged you your snappishness. It's a sore burden you've been carrying all these years, Dath, and my only true sorrow was in knowing I couldn't carry more of it for you.'

'You carried a lot, Matt. You'll never know how much. There were times I thought I could never keep going. I'd have despaired if you hadn't been with me, encouraging. I owe you so much. I owe you my sanity and I never once told you. I'm sorry.'

'Hush now, hush,' he chided, rocking her gently. 'You're Jervale's Heir, you've a task laid on you like nobody else. Especially now, in the Final Days.'

She pulled away a little and looked up into his face. 'I may be the Heir but you're the Heir's conscience, her wisdom and her strength. Is there anything you can tell me, Matt? Is there anything you've felt that can show me a way out of this mess we're in?' She let out a long and shuddering breath. 'That I've put us in?'

He smoothed a tangle of hair from her face. 'I wish there was. What do your visions tell you?'

'Nothing,' she whispered. 'Ever since I lay with Asher they've stopped coming and I don't know why. I've never been so blind in all my life and it scares me.'

'Well,' Matt said slowly, 'could be they've stopped because they'd led you where you needed to be. With him. Could be you're right and Prophecy planned it all along.'

'For what purpose? How does me lying with Asher get us through the Final Days? They must be close now, for Asher's revealed as our Innocent Mage. Oh, Matt, are you *sure* you don't know anything?'

'Veira's asked me the same question,' he said, 'and all I can do is give you the same answer I gave her. There's something amiss with the magic fluxes, but I don't know how or why. It's in the City, because as soon as I left there the uneasiness faded, but beyond that . . . If I went back I might be able to tell more.'

She tightened her arms around him. 'No. You can't go back. With Asher arrested they'll want his friends next, and we're his two closest. You're safe here.'

'For how long?' Gently, he pulled away and began pacing. 'There's not a man, woman or child in all of Lur who'll be safe when Prophecy's finally fulfilled, Dathne, and your dreams become our reality. Our job's not over yet. We still have to save this kingdom from destruction.'

'How?' she cried. 'For that we need Asher and I can't help him! Can you? Can anyone?'

'I can,' said Veira's voice from behind them.

They turned. Stared. Dathne folded her arms about her ribs and held on tight. 'How?'

Veira walked out of the forest fringe and across the cottage yard to join them, her brown wool trousers soaked to the knees and her stout leather boots mired in mud. In one gnarled hand she gripped an old tramping stick and at her heels snuffled two enormous mud-covered pigs, tame as dogs. Her wrinkled-apple face was grim.

'With heartbreak, and sacrifice, and a mortal lot of danger,' she said. 'But we must act swiftly. I had word from the Circle last night: Asher's appointment with the axeman is set for midnight Barl's Day next.'

Dathne turned to Matt. 'I can't believe the king is doing this. Asher's his dearest friend!'

'If by the king you mean Gar then that's more bad news,' said Veira. 'Lur has a new king now.'

'Not Conroyd Jarralt?'

Veira nodded. 'Yes.'

'Barl protect us,' said Matt, and rested his hand on

Dathne's shoulder. 'There won't be an Olken safe anywhere.'

'Only if we fail,' said Veira, grimly. 'But if we are to save the Innocent Mage from dying and taking us all with him to the grave, you must do as I say without fratching. What's to come will come. Must come. Prophecy demands it.'

Matt frowned. 'I don't like the sound of that.'

'You're not asked to,' Veira snapped. 'Dathne, put these pigs back in their pen, child, and see they have a good breakfast. You, Matthias, fetch knife and bowl from the kitchen. Cut me two sprigs from every herb and planting in the last row of the garden there. Tie a strip of cheesecloth over your nose and mouth, be sure to put on gloves, and whatever your opinion of what you see and cut, keep it to yourself. Don't bring the cuttings inside either; leave them on the ground beside the back door. When you're both done, amuse yourselves in the kitchen by making soup for lunch. All the fixings are in the pantry.'

Bewildered, Dathne looked over at the herb bed. 'Cheesecloth and gloves?'

Veira's severe expression eased, just a little. 'For precaution only. I'd not put Matthias in danger.' She pulled a face. 'Not from herbs at least.'

As she stumped past them on her way back into the cottage Matt said, 'And I like the sound of that even less.'

Troubled, Dathne nodded, watching as the cottage's back door closed behind the old woman. 'Nor do I. But we'd best do as we're told, I think. Whatever it is she's planning, it's near torn her heart from her chest.'

Despite her village isolation and solitary cottage lifestyle,

Veira kept her Circle Stones out of sight, in a hidey-hole she'd dug beneath her bedroom floor and lined with discarded tiles from the village pottery. The neatly rejoined floorboards with their betraying finger holes for lifting stayed hidden beneath an old, fraying carpet.

Alone in her bedroom with the door safely closed and curtains drawn she rolled back the carpet, hoisted up the hidey-hole's lid and leaned it against the bed. Forty Circle Stones winked up at her in the flickering lamplight, looking no more important than a random collection of pretty quartz crystals, a magpie's play-things.

Forty stones, forty friends – no, *family* – forty oaths solemnly sworn. So few, to stand against the coming darkness.

She hunkered down beside the hidey-hole, grimacing as her knees protested. Rafel's stone, a blue as pale as fresh-skimmed milk, drew her gaze like a magnet. She picked it up, cradled it in her palm and called to him. When he answered, tears sprang to her eyes.

'It's time.'

For long heartbeats he said nothing. Then she felt him sigh. *When we heard of Asher's arrest I thought it might be. He is the one, isn't he? He's the Innocent Mage?*

She'd told no one save Gilda. Trust Rafel to guess the truth.

'Yes,' she said. 'It's him. Darling—'

*Don't say it.* She thought his smile might kill her. *You're crying . . . and besides, I've had strange dreams.*

'If there was any another way . . .'

*Perhaps I wouldn't have been born.*

'We have little time,' she said through her tears. 'You'll need to meet me tomorrow where the West Road runs into the Black Woods Road on its way to the City How soon can you get there?'

*By mid-morning or not long after.*

'You must invent some reason for leaving. Tell as few as possible and depart without an audience; say you go anywhere but to the City. Travel light and as fast as you can without drawing undue attention. Let no one see your sorrow.'

*I understand.*

'I'll see you tomorrow, then.'

*Tomorrow*, he said, still smiling, and out of love was the one who broke the link.

Some time later, after she'd won back composure, she again reached out to Gilda through the rich green stone that kept them in contact. Nearly ten long minutes ticked by before their connection was made.

*Sorry, sorry*, said Gilda, flustered. *I was with a customer, I couldn't get away*.

'No matter, Gilda. My friend, I have a task for you. And not to plunge you into deep dismay I must say this: upon your success lies the future of our kingdom.'

The link between them trembled with Gilda's uncertainty, then firmed again. *Of course, Veira. What do you need*?

'I'm coming into the City for the execution and I need you to save me bench space for three beside you, right down the front. Directly before the block.'

*Beside me*? said Gilda, faltering. *So close?*

'Yes. Can you do it?'

*Of course.*

'Bless you, dear. I'll see you before midnight this Barl's Day.'

She replaced Gilda's stone and selected another, this one dark blue-black.

'Rogan. I have a task for you.'

Rogan agreed without question, as she'd known he would. Next she contacted Laney Treadwell, whose family business was most useful, and finally she reached out to the ten best-placed and strongest magicians in the group, on whose shoulders she must place a heavy burden. Resolute, they promised to join her in Dorana and carry out their task.

Jervale bless them all. Without such staunch supporters she'd not have the heart to go on.

With all the arrangements in place, and tired almost beyond speaking, she replaced the last Circle Stone, the hidey-hole lid and the carpet that covered them. Eased herself groaning to her feet, and went out to the kitchen.

The soup was on the stove top, bubbling aromatically. Dathne and Matthias sat in silence at the table, each lost in private meditation.

'Please, Veira, what's going on?' said Dathne, looking up. 'The herbs you had Matt cut for you—'

'Are deadly,' she said shortly. 'I know it.'

Matthias stirred in his chair. 'Then why do you need them?'

She moved to the kitchen window and stared out into the garden beyond, with its undisciplined winter roses and riot of ravenberries. 'To serve Prophecy.'

'Serve it how?' said Dathne.

'I'll keep my own counsel on that. The less you know, the better. At least until you must.'

'And who decides when that is? I'm not a child, Veira, whatever you like to call me! I'm Jervale's Heir and—'

'And you'll learn to follow another's instructions!' she snapped, turning away from the window. Then, seeing Dathne's strained and peaky face, seeing the fear imperfectly smothered, she softened. 'Child, child – for that's what you are to me, married lady or not – stop fretting on things you don't control. We've enough worms in the apple without you making room for more.'

Dathne looked to Matthias, who shook his head and ventured a brief smile. 'No fratching, remember?'

Defeated, Dathne slumped. 'All right.'

'Good,' Veira said briskly, and moved to the stove. 'Now let's eat.'

Afterwards, once the soup had been consumed in silence and Matthias was sent outside to check Bessie, her shoes, her harness and the rackety old cart, Dathne turned her hand to washing dishes.

'I'm not fratching, truly,' she said, her hands in soapy water. 'I just wish you'd tell me who those herbs are for.'

Veira sighed. Letting the dish towel dangle from her fingers she said, 'No-one you know, child. I promise.'

'But someone you know?'

Grimly, she held her tears below the surface. 'Yes. Someone I know.'

'Then let me brew the potion.'

Oh, it was a tempting thought. Kind and loving too. 'No,' she said, and touched her hand to Dathne's shoulder. 'Though you have my thanks for offering.'

Mettlesome as always, Dathne took the refusal as criticism. 'I am capable! I have more herb lore than—'

'Herb lore has nothing to do with it. No woman with child should touch those cuttings.'

Shocked silent, Dathne stared at her. Pulled her hands from the soapy dishwater to flatten them against her belly and press, softly. 'With child? What do you mean?'

Veira snorted. 'I'm old, child, not blind or deaf or stupid. I might not've birthed my own but I've done my share of midwifery over the years. There's a look a woman gets. And I felt something different in you too.' Then she sighed. 'You didn't realise?'

Dathne shook her head. 'No. At least . . . I wondered . . . for a moment . . . but I *can't* be. We only lay together twice and I took precautions both times.'

'Then could be Prophecy had other ideas.'

'Why? What good can come of *this*?'

Veira reached for another plate to dry. 'There's always good in the birth of a baby.'

'When our world's about to end in flood and fire? *How*?'

'Perhaps to remind us not to give up so easily.'

'I'm not giving up!' said Dathne, stepping back. Soap suds dripped heedless to the floor. 'I'm lost! I'm frightened! I used to trust myself, trust Prophecy, to believe I was given what I needed to prevail! Instead I'm a fugitive and the man I was born to guide and protect awaits his death. And now there's a *baby*?'

The child was losing hope. Time for a little sharp prodding. 'In other words you *are* giving up.'

Dathne turned away. 'Perhaps I am,' she whispered roughly. 'Perhaps it's the best thing I can do for all of us. Give up. Walk away. Leave his fate to those who've not made such terrible mistakes.'

'I doubt that's best for Asher or his babe,' said Veira, and put a snap in her voice. 'You're Jervale's Heir, Dathne. You cannot walk away. And besides, who amongst us has never made a mistake? Not me. Not Matthias either. Making mistakes isn't the problem, child. It's not doing our best to fix them after that leads to ruin. And we don't know there's been any mistakes. Could be all of this is what Prophecy planned from the beginning.'

'Then Prophecy should've thought of a different

plan!' Dathne retorted, flushing with temper. Then she turned back to the sink, seeking refuge in housewifery. 'You haven't told Matt about this, have you?'

Raising an eyebrow, Veira held out her hand for the next dripping bowl. 'Could be he already knows. Handled enough pregnant mares in his time, hasn't he?'

'Well, he hasn't handled me!'

'Peace. I've not told him, child,' she said gently. 'And I won't. Time and your belly will tell him soon enough. And he's got himself a full plate already, I'm thinking. I don't need to force-feed him anything more to chew on.'

Dathne nodded, frowning, and reached for the soup pot to scrub. 'We're going back to the City, aren't we?' she said after a moment. 'To try and rescue Asher.'

Well, not 'we'. But she was too tired for more arguments, at least right now. So instead of telling Dathne the truth, she said, 'Yes. Later tonight, after dark. But there'll be no trying about it. The Innocent Mage will be rescued . . . and Prophecy will continue.'

Asher was dragged from a wonderful dream of Dathne by the sound of banging hammers. Cursing, he rolled painfully onto his other side, closed his eyes and tried to recapture sleep.

She'd been in a green and sweetly smelling place, her fragrant hair unbound, her thin face lit with a smile. There were trees all around her, and pigs, and hens.

He opened his eyes.

*Pigs* and *hens*?

Barl bloody save him. He was finally going mad.

With some of the novelty worn off, enough of the crowd had returned home or to their temporary lodgings in the City's hotels and hostelries for him to see what all the hammering was about. Brawny palace staff were building a dais on the left-hand side of the Square.

Ox Bunder, condemned to guard duty, noticed him noticing and leered in typically unfriendly fashion. Probably he was grudging because now he'd never get paid that three trins owed to him from their last game of darts down at the Goose.

Ha. Praise Barl for small favours.

Ox wandered over, planted his pikestaff like a walking-stick and leaned. 'Going to be a big crowd to see you get your comeuppance, midnight tomorrow,' he remarked. 'I hear the general councillors are near to drawing straws to see who gets the best view from up on that dais they're building. I hear Guild Meister Roddle's been offering money to make sure he's seated right down the very front.'

If he said nothing, Ox would stop leaning and hit him with the pikestaff. If he said something, anything, Ox would stop leaning and—

He sighed.

'Midnight tomorrow, eh?' he answered, as though he didn't know. 'You reckon it's goin' to rain?'

Ox stopped leaning and hit him with the pikestaff.

Spitting blood and a broken tooth, Asher rolled his face into his folded arms and took refuge once more in sleep. He didn't dream this time, of pigs or hens or Dathne, or anyone else at all.

Blessedly alone in Conroyd's townhouse, with Ethienne at long last noisily departed, the household staff dismissed and Willer sent to oversee arrangements for the impending Olken curfew, Morg sat in a chair in Conroyd's library and gave himself over to thought.

The Weather Orb, dutifully delivered, sat in its box

on a table before him. Teasing. Taunting. Tantalising. All that magic but a thin skin's thickness away.

There *had* to be a way to get at it.

Imprisoned within, Conroyd raged. Unlike Durm, whose guilt-stained soul had wept and wailed and begged Barl for mercy, for aid, Conroyd seemed more affronted than anything to find himself a captive inside his own body. The first shock passed, he now jabbered ceaselessly in the background, demanding explanations, insisting upon answers, offering help.

*Help* . . .

The fool, to think Morg required the help of a sheep. That he was in any position to bargain, wheedle. Make deals. *Arrangements*.

Morg reached out and stroked the Orb. Its quiescent colours swirled, sensing him. Rejecting him. His flesh belonged to Conroyd, but the spirit within was his own. The Orb would never give him access. *Never*.

Unless . . .

An idea, glimmering. A flickered spark of inspiration. He held his breath lest even a gentle exhalation extinguish hope. Could it be managed? Was it *possible*? Could Morg and Conroyd merge into a single entity just long enough for the Orb not to recognise Barl's bitter enemy? To grant him her Weather Magics that he might use them to bring down her Wall?

It would never have worked using Durm. Even with all his maudlin despair the fat fool had been far too strong. And their minds, at the core, were ultimately incompatible. The only way to control him had been to keep him safely, rigorously caged. Letting him out, even a little, would have been fatal.

But Conroyd? Ah, Conroyd. Here was a soul of a different stripe. One with faint echoes of his own darkness. Even better, he and Conroyd were blood related, ties of family whispering down the centuries. They belonged in each other, as he and Durm had never belonged.

And Conroyd was accepted by Barl.

Sitting back, closing his eyes, he reached inside and touched small Conroyd's mind, gentle as sunshine.

*You desire to help me, cousin? You wish to sip from the cup of power only I can hold to your lips?*

Little Conroyd whimpered, suddenly uncertain.

*Have no fear, blood of my blood. You were born for greatness. Born to raise the Doranen to the heights of all known mastery. Help me and together we shall birth an Age of Glory never before known in this land!*

Little Conroyd's greed and ambition flared like a torch at midnight.

*Come to me, Conroyd*, he whispered. *Let us mingle for a moment.*

Conroyd came to him, unthinking and unaware. Morg lowered the bars of the cage around him. Let him out. Let him *breathe* . . .

. . . and at the same instant breathed him in. Melted Conroyd like butter and soaked him through all his nooks and crannies, flavouring his spirit with the essence of Jarralt. Hiding himself like a fox evading hounds in running water.

Conroyd shrieked once, and was silent.

Time passed. At length something not quite Conroyd, not quite Morg, sat upright in its cradling chair. Removed the Weather Orb from its wooden box and held it in its hands. Sighing, it smiled at the glorious swirl of colour. The promise it held of death and destruction. The spell required to transfer the magic from Orb to waiting mind remained, a legacy from Durm. All it needed to do now was recite the words. Trigger the act of Transference. Steal the bitch whore's precious power.

The part of this new thing that was Morg took a moment to prepare. To ensure that he continued safely entwined with Conroyd. Satisfied, he sank beneath the surface again and the thing held up the Orb before its shining eyes. Spoke the words of the Transference incantation . . .

. . . and waited for victory.

Within the Orb the colours swirled. Deepened. Took on lustre and life. The creature watched, exultant, as they poured out of the Orb and over its hands. Into its hands. As they sank inside it, filling it with knowledge, with power. With the key to this kingdom's destruction.

And then . . . hesitation. The pulsing Orb trembled, the colours shifted. Darkened. Crimson and gold changed to purple and black and began writhing as though alive, furious, and in pain.

Barl's long-dead voice cried: *No! No! This is not for you, Morg! Never for you!*

But still the Orb tried to empty itself of magic, sensing yet the presence of an untainted vessel. The thing surged to its feet, howling, as the flesh of its fingers seared. Sizzled. As the darkness inside the Orb flooded outside, up its arms and over its body like a wave of foul black ink.

Morg wrenched himself free from Conroyd's cloying presence. Threw back his head and screamed in furious desperation. 'Bitch! Whore! You won't keep them from me again, Barl! *I will have them*!'

*No, Morgan*, her whispering voice replied. *No, you will not*.

The Orb burst into flame. Within heartbeats the air in the library was thickened with the stench of charred flesh and charred magic.

Morg screamed and dropped the ruined Orb. It fell to the floor and smashed into pieces. He collapsed a moment later, crushing its blackened shards to powder beneath his convulsing body as oblivion came to claim him.

It was Darran who found the diary. Fussing, fusspot Darran with his passion for order and symmetry, his determination that things must be just *so*. His busy fingers felt the irregular thickness in the aged leather binding of a text on primer exercises for junior magicians. His critical eyes saw the difference between the front and back covers and made him wonder . . .

Sitting beside him on the study floor, Gar slit the book's apparently untouched stitching with his dagger and eased the diary out of hiding. Held it in hands that trembled and wondered if he was dreaming.

'Barl save us,' breathed Darran, astonished. 'There really is a diary!'

Barl save them indeed. And in her own words, no less, if the diary was truly once hers. Was it the miracle he'd been waiting for? Hoping for? Believing in against all expectation of fulfilment?

If it wasn't, it was the closest thing he'd found.

He let the diary fall open. Stared at the swift, untidy writing, the faded ink strokes, the imprints of history. Struggling, he made sense of the first few lines.

*It saddens me to think of the magics we*
*must leave behind, but in this new land*
*magic must be a thing of order and discipline,*
*not an everyday indulgence or—*

'Gracious,' said Darran, peering. 'It looks like a lot

of old chicken scratchings! Do you think you can read it, sir?'

Gar let his fingertips caress the page. Inhaled the scent of musty dust and time, feeling hope's candle flare. He smiled.

'Yes. I can read it.'

Darran released a gusty sigh. 'Praise Barl for small mercies,' he said. 'But might I suggest you read it later? The king's men will be here soon, wanting these books. And for once I'm inclined to believe what Willer says: we don't want to keep them waiting.'

So he hid the diary at the back of a bookshelf and hurried to help Darran pack away the rest of Durm's collected life and learnings. When they were done, and the books, papers and journals were neatly boxed and stacked by the Tower's front doors he made himself stand still in the middle of the tiled foyer floor for a moment and breathe, just breathe.

'What now, sir?' said Darran.

'Now?' He shook his head to clear it. Wiped away sweat with his forearm. 'Now I have work, Darran. And if Barl is merciful and truly hears our prayers there'll be something in these pages that can not only save this kingdom but Asher as well.'

'Then you'd better get started, sir,' said Darran. 'And have no fear. I'll see you're not distracted or disturbed.'

Gar spared him a quick smile. 'Good man.'

As Darran's tired, drawn face lit up with an answering smile, Gar turned and headed for the spiral staircase. Took it three treads at a time, thinking:

*Please, Barl. Please. Be merciful, just this once.*

# CHAPTER TWENTY-SEVEN

Pellen Orrick sat at his desk and frowned at the reports spread before him. *No sign . . . no sign . . .* no sign . . .

Dathne the bookseller and Gar's former Stable Meister, Matt, were nowhere to be found.

He drummed his fingers on the desktop and frowned more deeply. What did their disappearance mean? Was it a coincidence? Unlikely. Were they merely dismayed that their friend had been revealed as a traitor? Possible. Or were they mired hip-deep in blasphemy beside him, and desperate now to save their own wicked lives? Also possible. Maybe even probable.

Which meant King Conroyd was right and this was a conspiracy. It was a horrifying thought, with implications and consequences too dreadful to imagine. Except that he was the Captain of the City and it was his job, his duty, to imagine them.

Chilled, Orrick sat back in his chair and stared out of the window towards the Square. He could just see the top of Asher's cage over the press of bodies still gathered to marvel and gloat. With the word gone out to all and sundry on his crime and imminent death, the City was as full of visitors now as it had been during the month of mourning for the late royal family. The inns were full again. The hotels too, and all the rustic hostelries.

Death was a booming business these days.

*Conspiracy*. How far did its tentacles spread, then? How deeply was its rotten abscess buried within the flesh of Olken society and how much blood would be shed in the attempt to cut it out? Would Asher's be sufficient? Or must the guards of the kingdom unite to spill blood enough to make a river?

Starting with Dathne's and Stable Meister Matt's.

Abruptly sickened Orrick left his office, left the guardhouse, and made his way across the Square to Asher in his cage. The four guards on duty dipped their heads in polite greeting and withdrew as far as they could, to give him privacy.

He addressed the prisoner without preamble. 'Your friends Dathne and Matt are missing. If you love them, tell me where they would go so I might bring them in sensibly and ask them myself how they assisted in your crimes.'

Asher's eyes were dark-rimmed and sunken, and all his wounds had festered. Without bothering to lift his head, or look up at all, he croaked, 'Piss off, Pellen.'

Despite the vile stench from the cage, the straw, Asher's unwashed body, Orrick stepped closer. 'If I tell the king I can't find them he'll order a reckless search. Innocent people might be hurt or arrested for all the wrong reasons. In the end you know they'll be found, Asher. There's nowhere they can run to or hide where I or someone like me won't find them. And then it won't be me and mine asking the questions, it'll be His Majesty . . . and you know best how that will go. So tell me where they are. Not for me, or for him. For them.'

Now Asher did stir and look up. 'I don't know where they are and any road, they were never involved and Jarralt knows it. If he wants them it's to hurt me, nowt else. Not that you'd care.'

'That's untrue!'

Asher laughed, a harsh and rasping rattle. 'Is it?'

'You think you have cause for complaint?'

Lifting one raw and weeping wrist, jangling the chains that bound him, for the first time Asher looked him full in the face. 'Wouldn't you?'

'You don't think you deserve this? You don't think it's fair? Why not? You were eager enough for justice when it was Timon Spake facing the axe!'

Asher flinched. 'Timon Spake was never hurt with magic. You didn't chain him up like an animal, or put him on show like an animal. For all he was a criminal you treated Timon Spake with decency!'

Orrick clenched his jaw, offended by more than just the stink. 'I take my duty seriously, Asher. Your arrest is lawful, your guilt beyond doubt. You *admitted* your crime. However . . .' He tightened his hands behind his back and lowered his voice. 'If the choice were mine, you'd have awaited execution in the guardhouse.'

'Really?' said Asher. 'Well, I guess that means we're friends again, eh?'

He looked away. 'We were never friends!'

'I know,' said Asher, softly. 'But we might've been.'

This was a mistake. Tugging his tunic straight Orrick said briskly, 'Reconsider your silence on Dathne and Matt. The longer they stay fugitive the harder I must search for them, and the worse things will be once they're found. If they're innocent—'

'Innocent?' said Asher. 'There ain't no *innocent* here, Pellen. Our new King Conroyd's got the bit between his teeth now. He's bolting towards turning all us Olken into cattle, and if you can't see that you're blinder than I thought. You let him get his hands on Dathne or Matt, it'll just be the start. Next thing you know, anyone who ever smiled at 'em will be under suspicion. You wait. It's all rollin' downhill from here.'

'And if it is?' said Orrick. 'Who's to blame for that? Who was the one caught dabbling with magic?'

Asher slumped into his filthy straw. Frowned at his manacled wrists. 'I know.'

'For the love of Barl, Asher, tell me where they are. You might be saving their lives!'

'You are blind,' said Asher, and closed his bloodshot eyes. 'Blind and bloody stupid. The best hope they've got is if I never mention their names again. So I won't. Now piss off, why don't you? I'm a very busy man.'

Rebuffed, nonplussed, grudgingly moved and resentful of that, Orrick stood there for a moment, just staring at him. Then he turned on his heel and went back to the guardhouse.

The new king awaited his report . . . and he had yet to decide what it would say.

Conroyd's townhouse was filling with shadows when Morg returned to himself. He felt pain. Confusion. A bizarre disorientation, as though he were trying to be two people at once. For some time he remained on the floor, struggling to piece together what had happened. The memory of Barl's voice sighed through his pounding head.

He lifted his hands before his eyes and stared. Charred flesh. Blistered meat. Revolted, he healed himself with a word and sat up. Barl's voice faded, chased away by buzzing Conroyd. He sank inside, retrieved all the melted thinness of himself and banished Conroyd deep within.

And felt . . . different.

Startled, as he had not been startled in centuries, he examined the difference. What was it? What did it mean? Was he still himself? Or had Barl's attack damaged him somehow?

*Damn* Barl. Had he loved her? Worshipped her? Wanted to spend eternity with her? He must have been mad.

Subduing the flesh emotion he waited for his startlement to pass. Conjured glimfire and considered himself. His surroundings. His beautiful clothes were smeared and stained – *the Weather Orb*!

Crumbled to ash and memory, ground into the carpet beneath him. Almost, almost, he wept.

More time passed. Self-control returned and intellect reasserted itself. Yes, the Orb was destroyed and with it his hope for a swift victory. But at least no other Doranen would have the Weather Magics now, and use them to keep Barl's golden Wall strong. And when Asher died, the last living Weather Magic would die along with him.

But failure to gain it for himself and his own ends meant he was still trapped here. Must wait weeks, months, for the magics to fade and the Wall to collapse beneath the weight of its gradual decay. And waiting meant he must somehow keep the other Doranen at bay, his borrowed body safe, until victory came limping to him.

Assaulted, intellect trembled. It was intolerable. *Intolerable*. He staggered to his feet, healed hands clenched into fists. Opened his mouth to shout aloud his fury, frustration and lingering pain – and gasped.

There was new magic in his mind.

Tentatively, he reached towards it. Brushed his senses against it, feeling it slowly unfurl, and laughed.

*Weather Magic.*

Not complete. Not all that had been contained in the Orb had passed to him. And what had escaped Barl's clutches was damaged now by the black flames. But it was Weather Magic all the same. This must be the difference he had felt. This, his longed-for victory.

'See, bitch?' he shouted to the empty room. To her lingering, vanquished memory. 'You did not beat me! You have not won!'

He now possessed just enough Weather Magic to let him see into the heart of her precious Wall. To show him its weft and warp and how he might tease its threads undone. Tease at the fabric of her genius, unravel it, and so unravel the world she'd made in defiance of him and the sacred vows they'd sworn to one another.

But not here. For such deep seeing he required the Weather Chamber.

He rode there on the back of peasant Asher's silver stallion. Like its former master the animal resisted him at first, but not for long.

Nothing and no one could resist him for long.

He travelled the City streets unnoticed, cloaked in a spell of distraction. Entered the palace grounds unremarked by the guards and turned the stallion's head towards the old palace grounds where Barl's final monstrosity squatted amongst the trees. The closer he got to the Chamber the more strongly could he smell it. Six centuries dead and her magic continued to hold sway. He hated her, *hated* her, and marvelled at her mastery.

Breaking through the trees at last he found himself

in a clearing, face to face with the ancient Weather Chamber. Bastion of Barl's magic and seat of his undoing. Teeth gritted, he dismounted and looped the stallion's reins over a handy branch. Lathered, pocked with spur marks, the animal drooped its head to the ground, panting and dripping bloody sweat.

After conjuring glimfire he opened the reluctant door and climbed the stairs two at a time, revelling in his athletic ease. The door at the top of the stairs was open. He shoved it wider, stepped into the chamber and was once more soaked with the drenching stench of Barl's Weather Magic. Faint echoes of her presence stirred like fading, rancid perfume.

He tipped back his head. Stared through the crystal ceiling and into the gold-washed sky. 'Do you see me, bitch?' he whispered. 'It's Morgan, dearest. Your husband's home.'

Unanswered, he turned his attention to the centre of the chamber, and the sympathetic model of Lur so skilfully tuned to the fabric of the kingdom. An unfamiliar emotion speared him: regret. The map was a miracle only Barl could manage. Oh, what they might have accomplished if only she'd stayed faithful.

Sinking to the parquetry floor he stretched out his hands above the model. Closed his eyes and opened his mind to the stolen incantations that writhed in his head like golden snakes, letting Barl's stinking magic suffuse him.

And then, at last, he understood. Everything that until this moment had been opaque was perfectly, beautifully clear. He understood it all . . .

*In this fecund land power flows through all living things, a part of them and indivisible. Not hard and sharp and brilliant like Doranen magic, to be forged into weapons and servitude. Olken magic is soft and slithery, nourishing like blood. Destined to slip through the fingers of any who might think to crudely grasp it. Barl sees this. Accepts this. Comes to realise that her purpose requires a marriage of magics. Night and day she labours to give the union life and so protect her new home forever. In the weather lies the key. She weaves magic like a tapestry, combining Olken and Doranen power into whole cloth. This thread for rainfall, that thread for snow. Here the colour of sunshine, there the shadows of wind. The power builds, feeding into the Wall she is creating, flowing from it to the fertile earth and back to the Wall again. It is an endless cycle of give and take, replenish and diminish and replenish once more. An act never-ending, demanding an endless sacrifice. And at its heart lies the WeatherWorker, living conduit of power and pain. The WeatherWorker is the weaver, with the Wall's separate and delicate skeins threading through fragile fingers of flesh and bone. The WeatherWorker controls the magic, is the magic, weaves the tapestry. Maintains the Wall. Constantly creates and keeps the balance between Olken and Doranen powers. And woe to Barl's beloved kingdom should the WeatherWorker snap a thread . . .*

Morg opened his eyes, struggling to remember how to breathe. Blinked and blinked and blinked again until the chamber resolved itself into the familiarity of hard lines and solid surfaces. Before him pulsed the map of the kingdom, its beating, vulnerable heart.

Which now he had the means to crush.

With the stolen Weather Magics incomplete he would be forced to move slowly. Torture! After interminable waiting he longed to rip Barl's Wall to pieces with teeth and taloned fingers. Sink his power into its entrails and gut it like a rabbit. Fall upon the magic-soaked model-map and pound it to splinters with his fists. Grind it to powder beneath his heels.

But no. Confined in flesh, denied access to his untrammelled powers and her complete incantations, he must still bide his time. Pick apart his dear Barl's tapestry thread by slow and sticky thread. Wait a little longer before being reunited with the best and most of himself, held in limbo on the other side of the Wall.

Morg smiled and soothed himself. Patience . . . patience . . . after these six centuries, what were a few weeks more?

By the time the hour came for them to leave the cottage, bent on Dorana and Asher's rescue, Dathne was almost numb with fatigue and dread. Filled with a churning horror, reminded sickeningly of Timon Spake and the orris root, she'd sat in the kitchen and watched Veira concoct her poisonous potion. Seven different plants were used: drogle, witcheye, lantin, dogsbane and bloodweed she recognised; the other three she'd never seen before and didn't dare query. One word out of place and she knew Veira would banish her from the room. And this wasn't something the old woman should do on her own, even if all the help she'd accept was a silent, sympathetic witnessing.

Once the poison was mixed, poured carefully into a small jar, stoppered and wrapped twice against spillage, Veira disposed of the leftover muck and went to walk in the forest again. With Matt still pottering outside and not needing help, he said, Dathne went back indoors,

But couldn't. Her hand kept drifting to her belly and her thoughts wouldn't turn from the miracle – the mistake, whatever Veira said – now growing deep inside her.

*A baby . . . a baby . . . a baby . . .*

What was Prophecy *thinking*?

What did *she* think?

As Jervale's Heir she'd never imagined becoming a mother. Not even a wife, given the danger of the life she lived. The last married Heir had died unhappily two hundred years ago, nearly; Dathne had taken that lesson to heart and sworn never to risk herself or her duty in the name of frivolous love.

But then had come Asher . . . and suddenly love didn't seem so frivolous. Love, without warning, became as needful as air.

Would he be pleased to discover he'd soon enough be a father? Would she even have the chance to tell him? If this rescue failed, if evil triumphed . . .

*No.* She wouldn't let doubt touch her. They'd rescue Asher unharmed – Prophecy wouldn't let it be otherwise. She'd see him again and he would forgive her the lies and the silences and when his task for Prophecy was done they'd settle down and be a family in the brand-new Lur they'd helped create.

Tears prickled, blurring her eyes. She was going to have a *baby*.

Outside the cottage, shadows lengthened. Dusk descended. Matt came inside, looking for dinner. She put the book back on its shelf and gave him some carrots to peel. Veira returned with two fresh rabbits already gutted, skinned and jointed. She set them to frying in butter and sage and so night fell upon them.

With dinner eaten and the dishes done, Veira announced they'd depart at midnight, then retired to her bedroom. Matt retired to his. Dathne returned to the sitting room, tried again to read, gave up, and blew out the lantern to sleep a little before they had to leave.

Sleep eluded her. Eyes open or closed, all she could see was that bottle of poison and the look on Veira's face as she'd stoppered it. Terrible sorrow. Dreadful resolve.

For Asher to be rescued, someone had to die.

The thought was appalling. Haunted her unmercifully so that she gave up the idea of slumber and ventured back to the kitchen instead.

Veira was packing bread and cheese and biscuits into a rough-weave hamper. 'There you are, child. I was about to come and rouse you. Matt's outside, harnessing Bessie.'

'Good,' she said, and looked for a mug. 'Is there time for tea?'

There was the slightest hesitation as Veira searched the drawer for a bread knife. 'Not for me and Matthias. We must leave in the next quarter-hour.'

She looked up. 'And me.'

Straightening, knife in hand, Veira shook her head. 'No, Dathne. You're staying behind.'

'Behind? I don't think so! Stay here alone while you and Matt run all the risks of rescue?'

'You won't be alone,' said Veira. 'You'll have the pigs for company. And the hens too. Don't forget to feed them or they'll raise a mighty ruckus. Few things as tetchy as pigs and hens if they're made to go to bed without their supper.'

'*Veira*!'

'It's too dangerous, child. You know they'll be looking for you.'

'And for Matt!' she protested. 'But he's going back, so why can't I?'

Breathing deeply, Veira tucked the bread knife into the basket. 'It's best if you don't. I've a little trick practised to keep the guards from spotting Matthias, but I'm not strong enough to play it on both of you.'

'Then show it to me and I'll play it on myself!'

'No,' said Veira flatly, and kept on packing the basket.

'No?' she echoed, and felt a flooding rage. 'I am Jervale's Heir! You don't say "no" to *me*, old woman!'

The kitchen's back door opened, revealing Matt. 'Don't fratch at her, Dathne. If she says you can't come, accept it.'

She turned on him, venomous. 'Not without a damned good reason!'

That earned her a scorching look from Veira. 'Because I say so is reason enough! You may be Jervale's Heir but Prophecy's brought you here and here is where *I'm* in charge! So hold your tongue if you've nothing of use to say with it, and finish off stocking that basket. It's a long trip back to the City and we'll have no time for stopping on the way.'

That said, Veira stalked out of the kitchen. Quietly cursing, Dathne did as she was told, flinging biscuits and fruit scones from their tin onto a clean cloth and then into the basket. Lifting hard-boiled eggs from their saucepan on the stove and tossing them in after. Hotly aware of scrutiny she looked up, and met Matt's understanding gaze.

'Veira's right,' he said, still standing in the doorway and letting the cold air in. 'She's the Circle Guardian. We must be guided by her, no matter how hard that is.'

'Veira's a bossy old besom and don't you try telling me otherwise!'

His lips quirked in a tiny smile. 'Actually, she reminds me of you.'

'Did I ask your opinion?'

He sighed. 'No. So I won't give it. And since the wagon's ready, I'm off to harness Bessie.'

'Fine,' she muttered through gritted teeth as the door banged shut behind him. 'I hope she stands on all your toes and breaks them.'

'Not a very charitable wish, child,' chided Veira from the other doorway. A padded dark blue coat was folded over her arm. 'You ride too roughshod over that young man.'

Dathne felt her face warm. 'He's got broad shoulders,' she said defensively. 'He can carry a few harsh words from me.'

'It's not if he can,' said Veira. 'It's if he should, and we both know the answer to that.'

Abandoning the basket, Dathne dropped into the nearest kitchen chair, watching as Veira put down the coat she carried and picked up the swaddled bottle of poison from the benchtop. The old woman's expression was unbearably sad.

Abruptly, anger died. 'Veira . . . don't take that with you. Rescue Asher without it.'

'We can't,' said Veira, not looking around. 'This is the way it has to be. One life . . . for another.'

'Why? It's *murder*!'

Three of Veira's hairpins were coming loose. She put down the poison and poked and prodded them back into place. 'It's sacrifice. There's a difference.'

'Asher wouldn't like what you're planning, Veira. He wouldn't want to be rescued like this. I know him, and he wouldn't want it!'

Veira turned, her kindly, wrinkled face now hard with purpose. 'I don't much care for what he wants, child. Or what you want either. This is about Prophecy, not personal desires. You may have forgotten that but others haven't.'

The barb was unexpected; for a moment she could hardly breathe, let alone speak. 'That's unfair.'

A scornful snort. 'Life's unfair, child.'

Which was, unfortunately, true. She picked up the thread of her original argument, loath to let it go. 'As Jervale's Heir I should be coming with you. Please, Veira, don't make me stay behind!'

Veira shook her head. 'Behind is where you belong.'

It was like telling a tree not to grow, or the sun to rise upside down: pointless. But that didn't stop her from trying. 'But, Veira, I need to be there. Asher might not trust you or Matt. He will trust me.'

With a sharp sigh Veira took a step closer. 'Child, child, emotion is addling your wits. What wise housewife puts all her eggs in one basket? Should this rescue fail, should we be discovered or Prophecy thwarted somehow by the darkness struggling to defeat us, you must pick up the Circle's pieces. You must become Heir and Guardian both. In my bedroom, on my dresser, I've left you instructions. Should the worst befall us, follow them exactly. Do what you can to save as many as possible. Save yourself. Bear your child. For it too is a part of Prophecy's plans and doubtless has some grand destiny whose purpose we still don't know.'

All without warning, Dathne felt herself flooded with tears. '*Damn* . . .'

Veira's eyes were brimming too. 'Have faith, child. Trust in Prophecy. Between us, Matthias and Rafel and I will bring your Asher home.'

'Rafel?' she whispered.

Veira nodded. 'The man we go to meet on the way.'

The man who soon would die. Had she really wanted

a name? Yes, but now she regretted knowing it. Names were real. Names belonged to the living and called to mind the dead. Feeling unsteady, she forced herself to her feet. 'When you reach this Rafel, tell him thank you. Tell him I'm sorry. Tell him I wish there was another way.'

Solemn, sorrowful, Veira reached out a hand and touched cold fingertips to her cheek. 'I will, child. For all of us.'

Dathne looked so forlorn, so abandoned, as she stood waving them goodbye from the cottage's front gate that Matt almost asked Veira to reconsider and let her come with them after all.

But only almost. Because he was in truth quite glad she wasn't coming. Was instead left safe behind in the middle of the Black Woods where no harm would come to her if this mad plan to rescue Asher fell all to pieces, as it seemed most likely it would.

Sunk equally deep in blankets and silence, Veira sat beside him on the little wagon's bench seat and let him get on with the driving. Bessie, a good-natured animal, seemed quite happy to venture out in the dark. Didn't take much driving at all, just the occasional 'hup-hup' and rattle of reins to keep her up to the bridle as she jog-walk-jogged along the empty road. For that he felt a little sorry. More energetic driving would give him less empty time to think about things he'd rather not consider.

Veira still hadn't revealed the details of this trip. All she'd said was they'd be travelling without stop until they reached Dorana, except for picking up someone else from the Circle. Someone, he suspected, he'd not long have the chance to know.

It was just one of the many things he didn't want to think about.

Slowly, steadily, the miles unrolled behind them. The night grew colder, marching towards sunrise, and he wrapped an extra blanket round his shoulders. Held the reins in one hand so he could warm the other in his armpit, and swapped them over time and again.

Eventually the morning came. Veira stirred and fed them from the basket. They were well along the Black Woods Road now. Sheep grazed on either side and rabbits scuttled white-tailed as they creaked on by but otherwise they were quite alone. Veira ordered him into the back of the wagon to stretch out and sleep properly. Happy to obey her he lay down, tucked the blankets around him and fell into a dreamless oblivion.

She woke him some little time later and he sat up, stiff and yawning. They stopped long enough to take turns ducking behind some convenient bushes, eat a little more and give the pony a short rest, and then resumed their travelling.

The sun had climbed almost to ten o'clock when they reached the West Road intersect where a man stood patiently with his eyes shaded, staring in their direction. At first, ridiculously, Matt thought it was Asher and his hands tightened on the reins.

Beside him, having a rest from driving and dozing with her eyes half closed, Veira tapped him on the knee and said, 'No. It's not him. But looks-wise it could be.'

He nodded, feeling suddenly ill. He was beginning to make out the bones of this rescue. 'And that's why you chose him?'

'Prophecy chose him, Matthias. Not me.' Veira sighed. 'Does it ever make your blood run cold with wonder? That we're in dire trouble, needing some kind of a miracle, and here's a young man who looks like another young man near enough to be his mirror self, or a brother, and he's one of us and willing to say, "Take me to do what's needed"?'

He swallowed bile. 'Everything about this business makes my blood run cold. I doubt if it's with wonder. How well do you know him, this young man?'

It took Veira a little time to answer. She smoothed the sleeves of her padded coat. Tucked her hair behind her ears, then tugged it free again. Chewed on a ragged fingernail, making it worse. He waited, not patient, but knowing he hadn't a choice.

'His name is Rafel, and I know him well enough. His mother was my youngest sister,' Veira said at last, sighing again. 'When Timon Spake died, and then his father Edvord, the Circle required a new member. Prophecy pointed its finger at Rafel.'

Shocked, he stared at her. 'And you heeded it? This man's your own flesh and blood, Veira. And in your pocket you carry—'

Her sideways look at him was bleak. Reproving. 'I know what he is, Matthias, and what I carry. So does he. He comes to this quite willing.'

'And you?' he whispered. 'How willing are you, Veira, to kill—'

'Be silent!' she commanded. 'Don't you understand yet? Prophecy must be served without fear or favour or it can't be served at all! Did you think this would be *easy*? Did you think we'd save our Innocent Mage without we pay a *price*?'

He wrapped his fingers round her wrist and gently drew her from him. 'Not one this costly.'

'Then you're a fool, Matthias, and I wonder if I can use you at all!' she retorted.

There were tears in her eyes. Seeing them, he felt ashamed. He was a fool to think she didn't know what she was doing, to think her blind to the consequences of their actions. She'd lived with them longer than he'd been alive. He picked up her hand and kissed it.

'I'm sorry. I'll not question you again.'

That made her smile. 'Of course you will. I think that's why Prophecy chose you. It's your job, and you do it well. Now hush. Rafe's close enough to hear us and we don't want him to see us brangling. What's waiting in Dorana will be hard enough. Let's not have him thinking we've anything on our minds but the gift he's agreed to give us.'

# CHAPTER TWENTY-EIGHT

Rafel, who so eerily looked like Asher and shared family blood with Veira, appeared remarkably cheerful for a man going to his death. Up close Matt could see he was younger than Asher by maybe a year or two, and not quite so heavily muscled. He wondered if that would make a difference. Rafel swung himself and his knapsack easily into the cart as it stopped beside him and settled himself behind the driver's seat, with his arms folded neatly along its back.

Veira kissed his cheek, unsmiling. 'Rafe.'

He nodded, eyes warm with affection. 'Veira.'

'You ready then?'

'I'm ready.' He had a clear, light voice. Not like Asher's gravelly growling at all. Neither of his eyebrows was scarred. Hopefully Veira had brought some scissors, to make a quick adjustment. 'So. Do you know yet how—'

She pressed a finger to his lips. 'Let's not think on that just now. Best you don't have the details to dwell on till they're needed.'

His smile was swift and wry. 'Maybe so.'

Matt knew he was staring. Couldn't help it. 'I'm Matt.'

'Good to meet a fellow Circleman, Matt.'

Hesitant, he shook Rafel's proffered hand. 'Likewise.'

'You hungry, Rafe?' asked Veira. 'Give me the reins, Matthias, and dig out some food from the basket. I'll have an egg. Peeled, if you please.'

So he handed over Bessie's reins and peeled them both an egg. Offered one to Rafel, but he refused.

'Strange days,' the young man said, and shook his head. 'I never thought I'd live to see them.'

'None of us did, Rafe,' said Veira sadly, and dabbed salt from her fingers with her tongue. 'But it's why we're here. Why the Circle was formed. Sooner or later these days were bound to arrive.'

'That's true,' agreed Rafel. A small silence fell, bloated with words unspoken. He broke it, eventually, saying, 'And it's really him? The Innocent Mage?'

'Yes, Rafe,' said Veira. 'It's really him.'

Matt felt his throat close. He couldn't imagine what this young man was feeling, or know the depth of his courage. His honour. Turning a little so he could see that disconcerting face he said, 'I'd like to thank you, Rafel.'

The young man looked at the sun-splashed passing countryside. 'No need. We're all born with different things to do. This is mine.'

'There is need. Asher – the Innocent Mage – he's my friend,' Matt said. 'You're saving my friend. I wanted you to know that, is all.'

'Ah,' said Rafel, and smiled. 'That's good. That's nice. Saving a kingdom's a grand thing to do but it does feel a tiddle bit impersonal. Saving your friend, though. That makes a difference.'

'You won't be forgotten,' he insisted. 'He won't forget you, although you'll never meet.'

'None will forget our Rafel,' said Veira, a warning note in her voice. 'I'll take the pony now, Matthias. You forage in that basket again and find me some sweet plum cake. And from here on in, I think we'll get used to calling you by a different name. No sense advertising who you are.'

'Changing my name is easy,' Matt said. 'But what about my face? I'm well known in the City. Even with a hooded cloak and darkness to hide in, there's a chance I'll be recognised. I heard you tell Dathne you had some trick?'

Veira nodded. 'That I do. But I'll wait a while before I play it. I'm not sure how long it'll hold.'

That didn't sound encouraging, but she was looking so sad he didn't have the heart to press further. Instead he smiled and nodded, saying, 'Whatever you think best, Veira.'

She dug his ribs with her elbow. 'I think plum cake's best. Didn't I say so? You're a bit young to be deaf, aren't you?'

As Rafel chuckled and Veira pretended flouncy offence Matt handed over the reins and dragged the basket into his lap. 'Here you are, mistress,' he said with mock servility, and dropped a lump of moist cake in her lap.

'Why thank you, Meister . . . Meister . . .' Her lips pursed as she thought about it. 'Maklin, I think,' she finished at last. 'I knew a Maklin once. A right silly fool if ever I met one, and definitely hard of hearing.'

Matt swallowed a snort. Exchanged amused glances with Rafel, and took the reins back from Veira so she could enjoy her cake.

Darran was industriously polishing the staircase banister when Willer returned to the Tower. The foyer doors flung open without so much as a knock and the horrid little man sauntered in reeking of arrogance and pomposity.

He flung down his polishing cloth, not bothering to hide his contempt. 'In Barl's sweet name, Willer, what do you want *now*? We gave you all Durm's books, I promise!'

'I've a message for Gar,' said Willer, smirking. 'From His Majesty King Conroyd.'

He nearly slapped the smug and shiny face in front of him. Had to pinch his fingers together behind his back to stop himself. 'Not Gar,' he said icily. 'His Royal Highness, the Prince. Call his name like a commoner one more time and you'll live to regret it.'

Willer's eyes narrowed to ugly slits. 'Threaten me one more time and you'll not live at all,' he hissed. 'Bolliton has no relevance now. You're an old man serving a destitute and deluded outcast cripple, while *I* am personal assistant to the king. His strong right arm. His trusted companion.'

'His lackey, you mean,' scoffed Darran. 'His scuttling errand boy. What's this message then? Give it me and I'll take it to His Highness.'

Willer went to push past him. 'I'll tender it myself. Stand aside, old crow. Don't interfere with the king's own business unless you fancy sharing cold straw with Asher.'

Blocking him, Darran leaned his face close. 'His Highness is sleeping and I'll not see him woken. Not by the likes of you. And as for threats, Willer? I make you no threats. Only this promise. Harass my prince unduly – cause him a heartbeat's more pain – and you'll never know another day's peace. I will destroy you and no one shall touch me for doing it.'

Whatever Willer saw in his face then, it must have been convincing. The little worm turned sickly pale and stepped back a pace. 'Very well. Take him the message yourself, it's of no account to me. His Majesty commands Prince Gar's attendance at the execution of the traitor Asher. A carriage will be sent here half an hour before midnight tonight. The prince is advised to be ready and waiting.'

'I shall so inform His Highness,' Darran said. 'Now get out.'

For a long time after Willer's huffy departure he stood in the foyer, feeling ill. Feeling old, and helpless. Then, because delay was fruitless, he climbed the staircase to Gar's apartments and prayed he would not weep.

'What is it?' said Gar, not looking up from Barl's diary. He was covered in ink: his fingers, his face. Long blue streaks in his hair. He'd wiped his hands on his lovely rose silk weskit, ruining it forever. The desktop was scattered with scribblings, the floor littered with discarded notes. He looked stretched thin as a wire.

Standing in the library doorway, afraid to step in closer, Darran cleared his throat. 'A message, sir. From His Majesty.'

Gar kept on writing, one inky finger tracing a line in the diary, his brow deep-furrowed with strain. 'I'm busy. Tell me later.'

'I think, sir,' he said carefully, 'I should tell you now.'

'Then tell me and go away!' Gar shouted. 'Can't you see what I'm doing?'

Darran told him. Quickly, to get it over with, then watched, unwilling but unable not to, as the meaning and the meanness of Jarralt's command sunk into Gar's understanding. The prince's fingers trembled and dropped the pen.

'So,' he murmured, unseeing. 'It's not enough that I condemn him. I must also watch him die. Oh, Conroyd, Conroyd . . . is *this* how much you hated us?'

Darran withdrew and closed the door before it was impossible to pretend he hadn't seen Gar's grief.

By early afternoon Bessie's unflagging walk-jog-walk had carried them without incident to the turn-off onto the main City road. Now there was traffic. Carriages and dogcarts and saddle horses, all bearing Olken, all flowing in a steady stream towards Dorana.

Still driving, his back aching now, Matt stared at them, stabbed through with a furious dismay. 'What's the matter with them?' he muttered to Veira. 'Don't they know it's bloodshed and murder they're going to see?'

'Judicious murder,' said Veira. 'There's a difference.'

'What difference?' he retorted. 'The blood spilled's not as red?'

She shook her head. 'It's not red at all, Meister Maklin. It's black. Black as the heart of the bad man who's dying.'

'You don't believe that!'

'Of course not. But they do.' She patted his knee. 'They have to. If they let themselves think for one moment this might not be just . . . well. Folks like to put an untroubled head on their pillow at night, don't they? And it's harder still for us Olken. If we don't condemn a dabbling in magic, it's the same as shouting we'd like to try it ourselves.'

It made him so angry he could easily have shouted himself. Behind them, in the back of the cart, Rafel snored softly, curled up beneath a canvas coverall. It was no use; he had to ask.

'When the time comes, Veira, how will you do it?'

'Kindly,' she said, after a moment. 'There's herbs in the brew I concocted as will ease him gently on his way. When all's said and done, Matthias, it's not so different from a dog or a cat that's aged past saving.'

Except that it was, and she knew it, and so did he. Nor was it the answer he'd looked for . . . but it wasn't in him to press her further. This time he patted her knee, then took her hand in his to hold, and squeeze. She didn't pull away.

He guided Bessie onto City Road and let silence fall again for three more miles. Then, still holding her hand, he said, 'It could be me, Veira, but I think Dath's not looking like herself.'

She grunted without comment and started poking in the basket for a cake crumb she'd missed the last six times she'd looked.

'She had more colour to her, the last time I saw her,' he added. 'Of course it might just be the worry . . .'

'Might be,' agreed Veira. 'There's a lot to be worried about, I know that much.'

'And she wasn't eating.'

'Worry can do that to an appetite, I'm told.'

Wretched old woman. She wasn't going to say. If he wanted to have his suspicions about Dathne's condition confirmed he'd have to ask the question outright, and even then he thought she'd probably feign sudden deafness. He chose another topic instead, one equally as vexing. 'If we manage this, Veira, if your mad plan works and we get Asher out of Dorana with his head still attached and ours, too, for that matter . . .'

She gave him a hard look. 'He'll be grateful.'

'For how long? Will he still be grateful when he finds out the truth and how it's been kept from him all this time? When he learns how I've lied, and Dathne's lied, all to make some Prophecy he's never heard of come true?'

'He's the Innocent Mage,' said Veira, quietly fierce. 'He's got Prophecy in his blood and bones whether he knows it or not. He'll do what he's born for, never you fear.'

She was the Circle Guardian, wise in things he'd never even thought of, but still he was driven to disagree. 'We've all been so set on what we want. How he fits into our plans. But, Veira, what about his plans, and what he wants? Magic's meant nothing but hardship and heartbreak for Asher. Look what it's doing to him now! I don't know if there's enough gratitude in all the kingdom, let alone one man's heart, to dull the pain of these past days. Or douse his anger when he finds out how he's been duped . . . and who's done the duping.'

He was making her angry. Her lips tightened and her fingers fisted in her lap. 'He loves her, Matthias.'

'And she loves him, I know,' he sighed. 'But she lied before she loved him, while she loved him, after she loved him. Is it 'cause you're both women that you can't see the blow you'll deal his pride?'

She fixed her gaze to the carriage up ahead. 'Pride's of no consequence where Prophecy's concerned.'

He shut his mouth. Could be she was right and he was wrong. Could be Asher would take it all in his stride, forgive the lies, the manipulation, the nudgings here and there to put him where he was wanted and when. Could be he'd embrace Prophecy and all its mysterious workings as willingly as he'd embraced Dathne when he thought she was only a woman who once worked in a bookshop.

If he did, well and good. And if he didn't . . . what could they do about it anyway? They lived their lives at the mercy of Prophecy and Prophecy, as always, would do as it willed.

'We'll not discuss it any more,' said Veira. 'What's done is done and there's no turning back. Why don't you climb in with young Rafel and get a little shut-eye? You need to be rested for what lies ahead.'

'What about you? You need rest too, and—'

The smallest flash of teeth, as she smiled. 'And I'm old? True enough, Meister Maklin. But I'm old like Bessie's harness leather is old. Tough, well looked after and hard to break. Rest. I'll wake you when we're closer to the City and it's time to play our trick.'

She'd have her way, he could see that, so he clambered over the driver's seat and into the cart's cramped belly, trying not to tread on snoring Rafel. How the man could sleep, knowing what lay ahead for him, was a mystery.

Even though she was right, and he was very tired, Matt doubted he would sleep . . . but a moment after he'd closed his eyes to think on Veira's words the old woman was shaking his shoulder and urging in his ear, 'Meister Maklin! Meister Maklin, come along now! Dorana's in sight. Wake up, it's time to fix your face.'

She was in the back of the wagon with him. Opening his eyes he sat up and saw the sun had set and the night was flickered with torches. Four burned brightly at each corner of their wagon. Rafel, taking his turn with the reins, had guided them to the side of the road; traffic had dwindled to a trickle and they were, for the moment, alone. Lit up with glimfire the City walls gleamed in the distance, no more than half an hour away. He hadn't thought to sleep so long.

'Lie on your back and keep your head down,' Veira told him softly. 'And no matter what happens, don't cry out. This shouldn't be downright painful but you might well feel a tingle or two.'

'Why?' he whispered, lowering himself to the wagon floor. 'What are you planning? What's this trick you've come up with?'

'To be truthful, dear, I'm not quite sure. Something to take the edge off your fine good looks, I'm hoping.' She settled on her haunches beside him. 'Now close your eyes and let down your defences. I need you quite open for this.'

Nervous, but trusting her, he settled into himself, loosening the fetters he kept round his mind, sinking into the fabric of the world around him . . . and nearly choked on a scream of pain and surprise. It was like breathing in fire, or poison, or something of both.

'What is it? What's happened?' demanded Rafel, peering over his shoulder.

'Matthias? Matthias!'

Veira's voice was an anchor, a saving grace. He clutched at her, desperate for the touch of wholesome flesh beneath his fingers. His mind felt fouled, smeared, contaminated with evil. Gasping, he fought the urge to empty his belly all over her. 'It's back! Veira, can't you sense it? Dark – sticky – *wicked*! Worse than ever I felt it before. Stronger – almost *alive*.' He pressed his fists against his mouth, to hold the horror inside. Struggled to regain his balance, his serenity, when the thing he could feel pulsing at the heart of the kingdom's magic wanted nothing more than chaos and destruction.

Veira's hands were cradling his head against her belly, she was holding him, rocking him. 'All right, all right, just you breathe easy, child. Make sure you're all closed up again. Maybe it's alive and maybe it isn't, but we don't want to go flapping our hands in front of its face if it is, now, do we?'

Heartbeat by heartbeat the awful feeling passed and he was able to sit up. 'That was horrible.'

'It looked it,' said Rafel, shaken. 'Are you sure you're all right?'

'I will be.' He stared at Veira. 'I think it's what Prophecy warned of. The thing we must fight in the Final Days.'

She pulled a face. 'I don't doubt that at all.'

'I don't think we can fight it, Veira,' he whispered, starting to shiver. 'Not that. It's too big. Too black, and hungry. If this is what Dathne's been dreaming . . .' A wave of revulsion engulfed him. 'I don't know how she can live with it. I don't know how she's not *mad*!'

'She's Jervale's Heir,' said Veira. 'It's what she was born for. And saving Asher's what *we* were born for so we'd best be on about it. Lie down again, Matthias, and this time don't open your mind. I'm going to try my trick another way.'

Reluctantly he did as she bade. Eyes closed, he felt her fingers spread across his face. Beneath their touch his skin grew warm. Hot. Burning. It twitched and crawled and seemed to seethe. He could hear her whimpering. Whimpered a little himself.

'There,' she said at last, sounding exhausted, and pulled her hands away. 'I call it blurring. Rafel, what do you think?'

'Jervale save us,' Rafel said, hushed and fearful. 'How did you *do* that? That's not his face!'

'Which would be the idea,' said Veira, acerbic. 'Matthias – can you hear me?'

He grunted. 'Yes, and see you too. Your nose is bleeding. What have you done to my face?'

'Nothing much,' she said, fishing in her pocket for her kerchief. 'Rearranged the furniture a bit. Made sure no one in that City will look at you twice.'

'How? I could feel you channelling energy, shaping me, but . . .'

Veira dabbed the kerchief at her lip and frowned at the bloodstains smeared on the cotton. 'To be truthful I'm not quite sure how it's managed. The idea came in a dream. I practised on my own face a time or several. Gave myself a nasty fright, looking in the mirror. It's not the way our magic's normally used and I wouldn't recommend it as a parlour game. But it'll do the trick tonight and that's all I care about. Rafel? Get this cart back on the road, young man. We've work to be getting on with.'

As Rafel obeyed her, Matt sat up and explored his face with his fingertips. It was definitely . . . different. Pockmarked. Fatter. His lips felt rubbery and his nose was an awkward shape.

He sighed. 'You couldn't have made me handsome?'

Veira just laughed and patted his knee.

The rest of the journey was completed in silence. They reached the City's outer stone wall. Passed beneath the shadow of its gates. Trundling by Pellen Orrick's guards unrecognised, unchallenged, Matt felt his crushing sense of dread ease so he could breathe again.

'We've a horse stall saved for us in a private yard down the back of the Livestock Quarter,' said Veira. 'Matt, you'd best drive us from here. You know where you're going.'

So he took the reins from Rafel and guided Bessie and the cart through the crowded glimlit streets to the livestock district, past smelly pens of goats and sheep and yards crammed full of cattle and horses, where Veira directed him to an empty double stable decorated with a flapping green ribbon. Stiff and hungry, they shunted the cart into hiding, unharnessed the pony and saw her safely settled with hay and water.

'Now,' said Veira, hefting her bag on her shoulder, 'I'm for a chamber pot, 'cause my bladder's a-bursting and I'll bet yours are too. Then we'd best find our places in the Square and settle ourselves for a long and fractious wait.'

Matt watched her march away, suddenly numb. Then he turned to Rafel, who hadn't bothered to pull his own knapsack from the cart.

Well, why would he? He wasn't going to need it again.

'Are you sure you want to go through with this?' he asked Veira's calm-faced nephew. 'It's not too late to change your mind.'

Rafel smiled, softly and sadly, not the kind of smile he'd ever seen on Asher's face. 'Thanks, Matthias . . . but it was always too late to change my mind.'

After that there was nothing left to say. Without thinking, Matt embraced him. Felt Rafel's fear and trembling courage. Then, side by side and silent, they followed in Veira's footsteps.

# PART FOUR

# CHAPTER TWENTY-NINE

*Damn*, thought Gar, and threw down his pen. Ancient Doranen grammar was a quagmire, and he was rapidly sinking. Remembering his blithe assurances that he could *easily* read the books they'd found in Barl's hidden library, he winced. What a shame there was no way of getting back in there. Perhaps his ancestors had thought to bring some school texts with them – an introduction to basic Old Tongue, for instance . . .

But the long-lost vault's door was warded against him, and there was no way now of breaking in. And besides, he *could* read all the other books he'd taken from those dusty shelves. It was only Barl's diary that was proving a challenge. A deliberate attempt to foil prying eyes? Or was tortured self-expression just one more thing that made her unique?

A tentative knuckle-rap on the chamber's closed door interrupted his profitless inner complaints. He looked up. 'What is it?'

The door swung open on soundless hinges, revealing Darran. Gar bit his lip, pinched with conscience. The old man looked tired. It was asking too much for him to caretake this whole Tower by himself and Conroyd knew it. Bastard. Instead of sitting warm and cosy in this library he should be helping Darran, prince or no prince, but nothing was more important than translating Barl's diary.

Not even an old man's precarious health.

'I'm so sorry to disturb you, sir, but I thought you should know: the carriage will be here in an hour.'

An *hour*? Was it that late? Had he really been sitting here without stirring for nearly seven hours? Startled, he looked at the clock on the fireplace mantel and saw that yes, he had.

Seven hours, and only five more pages deciphered to show for it.

Abruptly he was aware of muscles aching. Of a belly growling for food and a bladder in need of emptying. Stifling a groan he pushed his chair back and stood, hands pressed into the small of his back.

'I thought you were going to bring me dinner?'

Darran sighed. 'I did.'

Oh yes. So he did. And there it was, still untouched on its tray, which he'd ordered be put down somewhere, anywhere, just get out and leave him to work! Darran had left it on the side table next to the armchair.

Shuffling out from behind his desk, Gar spared him a swift, apologetic smile. 'Sorry.'

As he reached out a hand to filch a slice of pinkly tender beef, Darran swooped. Snatched the tray beyond his reach and retreated. 'It'll be stone cold by now, sir. I'll just go and heat it up for you.'

He nodded. 'Fine. And while you do that I'll attend to my appearance. When you come back make sure to bring a jug of icewine with you. Unless of course Conroyd saw fit to confiscate my cellar along with everything else?'

'No,' said Darran after a moment's hesitation. 'No, you've still a supply of good vintage yet.'

'Obviously an oversight on Conroyd's part.'

'Obviously,' said Darran, sniffing, and returned to the kitchen.

His head full of obscure phrasing and past-participal constructions, Gar drifted upstairs to his bedchamber and set about putting himself to rights. Made sure to keep pondering those recalcitrant participles, because provided he remained focused on the subtle differences between 'having' and 'keeping', then he was sure not to start thinking about why it was he had to bathe and shave and change his clothes.

If he let himself think about 'why', there was a good chance he'd drop in his tracks like an arrow-struck stag and never get up again.

By the time he returned downstairs, clean and refreshed and impeccably attired in black, efficient Darran had contrived to reheat his neglected dinner and unearth a particularly splendid jug of icewine.

Swigging it straight from the jug would be ungenteel, so he poured the icewine neatly into a paper-thin crystal glass – something *else* Conroyd had neglected to steal? Really, the man was slipping – and drank without pause until it was empty.

Assaulted with alcohol, his head spun a little. He smiled and poured a second glass.

This time Darran had pointedly left the dinner tray on his desk, after tidily putting all his scribbled notes to one side.

Gar sat down, speared meat with his fork and ate without tasting as he considered again Barl's diary and the entries he'd transcribed so far.

*I am afraid,* she had written. *In the madness of war we slipped away, but I know we can't hide forever. Morgan brooks no interference, nor leaves unpunished the slightest transgression – and my crime against him is not slight. We swore an oath together and he'll hold me to it or see me dead. By his reckoning he loves me and Talor forgive me, I love him. Loved him. Loved the man he used to be – not the monster he's become. I must find a way to defeat that monster, else surely we are doomed. And all the world with us.*

There was no indication when or where she'd recorded that entry. Most likely it was during the terrible flight from Dorana. Before she and her fellow refugees stumbled into the sleepy land of Lur.

Another entry, some time later:

*Two more of our children died today. We buried them in an Olken graveyard. These simple people are good, and kind. I can't repay them with bloodshed and destruction. There must be a way to keep this fertile land safe.*

And another, still later:

*He is coming, he is coming, I can feel it. Tabithe and Jerrot say I'm just dreaming, they say Morgan is dead, must be dead, the mage wars were unsurvivable . . . but I know otherwise. I've not told a soul of the power we discovered, the key to immortality. If I told them they'd see me as Morgan in their midst and I'd be killed out of hand, I'm certain. And if I die, there'll be no stopping him.*

Immortality? Gar pushed his dinner aside and poured himself more wine. It seemed no more likely on this second reading than it had the first. Immortality was a myth. A dream. Not even the ancient Doranen, magicians powerful beyond the imaginings of their tamer descendants, could aspire to such a feat.

Could they?

She'd said more about it, further on . . .

*There is some risk, in the making of this Wall. Not great, however, and I am a master magician. Morgan's equal, though he was always loath to admit it. When it is done and Lur is forever sealed safe behind it I think I shall honour my oath to Morgan and transmute myself immortal. Not for any base desire for power, or to feed some gross appetite for worship. I am not Morgan. I'll do it because I know he lives, and will change himself soon if he hasn't already. Then he will find us, no matter how long it takes to search each corner of the world. When he does I must be waiting for him. Ten years. One hundred. One thousand. He will come and I must face him. Defeat him. No other magician lives who might stand in his way.*

Gar sat back in his chair, shaking his head. Poured himself a third glass of wine and drank it faster than such a superb vintage deserved. Insanity. What he'd translated was insanity, the exhausted ramblings of a woman in shock, in mourning and soaked to the marrow in grief. No one could live a thousand years – which was a shame, really. To speak with Barl? A historian's dream.

'Sir?'

Rudely jerked from gentle fantasy, he looked up. Darran again. Hovering like a – what was it Asher used to call him? A constipated scarecrow? – in the library's open doorway.

Asher. *Damn.* And he'd been doing so well, not thinking of him.

'Sir . . .' Tentatively, Darran entered the room. 'I'm sorry. Lord Jarr – His Majesty's carriage awaits you.'

'Does it?' He flicked a glance at the mantel clock: it was a half-hour till midnight, exactly. Slowly, deliberately, he poured himself more wine. Lifted the glass and admired the way the firelight shafted through the pale green liquid within. 'How prompt he is. A man of his word.'

'Yes, sir,' said Darran. 'Sir . . . please . . . you have to leave now.'

He let his gaze shift to Barl's secret diary. His last hope of salvation. Asher's last hope of life. Hours of work and he was only halfway through it, with no answers found. No miracles revealed.

And now time had run out.

He emptied the fresh glass of icewine down his throat in one long, burning rush. Darran's expression was disapproving, but that was just too bad. If he thought his prince could get through this night sober he was very sadly mistaken. With delicate precision he placed the wineglass on the desk and stood for Darran's inspection.

'Well? How do I look? Don't say drunk.'

Darran's face was rigid. 'You look very proper, sir.'

He smiled, as bright and brittle as the icewine churning in his belly. 'Are you sure you won't come with me? I expect there'll be room for one more.'

Darran flinched. 'Thank you, sir, but no. I'm content to forgo the pleasure.'

'And it will be a pleasure. For many.'

'Alas, sir, yes,' said Darran, and stepped backwards, hinting, 'Sir . . .'

'I know, I know!' he snapped. 'The carriage is waiting.'

Darran followed him downstairs and opened the Tower doors for him. Ordinary torchlight spilled inside; he could've asked Conroyd to arrange for glimfire, but knowing how much pleasure refusal would give he'd refrained. Even though it meant more work for Darran. At the bottom of the Tower steps there was indeed a carriage, blazoned with House Jarralt's crest. The falcon now wore a thunderbolt crown. For a moment he thought he was going to lose his bulwark of icewine down the front of his black silk tunic.

Seeing him, one of Conroyd's lackeys jumped off the carriage's rear travelling step and opened the nearest door.

'I'll wait up for you, sir,' said Darran, standing back from the door. His eyes were anxious.

Gar started down the steps. 'Don't bother. I might be some time.'

'It's no bother,' Darran called after him.

At the point of entering Conroyd's ostentatious carriage, he paused and looked back. 'Fine. Suit yourself.'

He climbed inside. The lackey slammed the door and clambered back onto the travelling step. A whip-crack. A creaking of harness and wood. Then they were moving.

Gar let his head fall against the cushions and wished he were dead. Or really drunk.

The Square was a solid sea of Olken spectators wrapped warm against the midnight chill, packed on three sides around the space in the middle that still contained the cart, and the cage, and Asher. Conspicuous in blue and crimson, stationed at every opportunity amongst the crowd, beside the cage, wherever there was space to stand, and armed with both pikestaffs and truncheons, were Pellen Orrick's City Guard. Looking keyed-up. Looking grim.

The Square's fourth side was taken up with an unusually elevated dais reserved for the king and such dignitaries as still remained in the City. Most of them were Olken too. Gar, staring through the carriage window as it rolled slowly to a halt, saw how few Doranen sat with them and frowned. Odd. He'd imagined they'd be the most eager of all to see the upstart Olken die.

The carriage door opened and he got out, a few paces from the foot of the stairs attached to the dais. Heart uncomfortably thudding, he let his gaze touch the Square and the people, but not the cage or its inhabitant and only briefly, sickly, the block and the straw and the hooded man in black beside them, holding a sharpened silver axe. Was it the same man who'd dealt with Timon Spake? He couldn't tell.

Everything was lit as bright as day by the enormous balls of glimfire hovering overhead. There was a hissing snap as one of them shivered, showering sparks. A moment later a second followed suit. Then a third. A few cries went up from those folks stung by the spitting magic.

Payne Sorvold stood nearby in conversation with Nole Daltrie. Two of Conroyd's closest friends; of course they'd make sure to be here. Doubtless they expected high office in the new Doranen court. Seeing the uncertain glimfire, hearing the loud protests from the crowd, Sorvold broke off his amused rejoinder to some quip of Daltrie's and reinforced the stuttering magic.

Turning back, Sorvold noticed Conroyd's carriage and then the newest arrival. Excused himself to Daltrie and approached, his expression smoothed to a scrupulous politeness. 'Your Highness,' he said, offering a token bow. 'His Majesty asked that I greet you and escort you to your seat. He will be here himself momentarily.'

'Hoping for a grand entrance?' said Gar. His head was pounding; he'd not drunk nearly enough wine. 'Typical. What's wrong with the glimfire?'

Sorvold's eyes had widened at his comment, and his tone. He said, sounding wary, 'Nothing, sir. There's a lot of it up there, and larger than would normally be called, but you've no need for concern.'

'Did I sound concerned?' he said.

Sorvold took refuge behind formality. 'If you'd like to come with me, sir?'

'Oh, Payne,' he sighed. 'There is nothing I would like to do less.'

'Sir?'

'Never mind,' he said curtly. 'Let's go.'

As he fell into step beside Sorvold he caught sight of Pellen Orrick, resplendent in crimson, standing some ten feet away with his attention focused keenly on the crowd. Feeling eyes upon him, the captain turned. Acknowledged the royal presence with a nod. Gar nodded back, wondering what went on behind that cold, composed face. He'd had the impression Orrick and Asher were friendly, but if Orrick was disturbed by any of this he didn't show it.

But then, nobody with any sense would show sorrow here tonight.

He climbed the dais stairs behind Sorvold and followed him to the seat so thoughtfully reserved for him. Right down the front, of course. Beside the elegant, elaborate chair clearly intended for Conroyd. The good and ignorant people of his dead father's kingdom saw him, and a roar went up that threatened to rattle the stars.

'Gar! Gar! Barl bless our Prince Gar!'

He responded because he had no choice, nodding and waving and pretending he cared, that their wild acclaim meant something and he was glad to be here. Then, as the cheering died down, he took his seat. Breathing deeply, he let his face become a mask. He could feel the speculative glances of those few Doranen lords and ladies who'd decided to attend the entertainment. People who once had begged his attendance at their parties and dances, who'd dreamed of him as a match for their daughters, who now doubtless wished he'd died along with his family. Who found him inconvenient. An embarrassment.

Not one of them spoke to him, or even approached. Which suited him perfectly.

Some minutes later Barlsman Holze arrived, decorated in his most costly clerical robes. The still-jittery glimfire sparked and flashed on the rubies and sapphires sewn into his white brocade tunic. At his heels trailed Willer, swathed in dull green silk. The little man's air of self-importance bordered on the obscene as he shuffled himself into one of the seats to the rear of the dais, where apparently the Olken belonged. Holze sank into the chair on the other side of Conroyd's empty imitation throne. Gar glanced down at the Square, and frowned. Holze up here . . . and no sign at all of a Barlspeaker's presence amongst the guards. Did this mean Asher was to be denied the consolation of a clerical attendance? No prayers, as there'd been prayers for Timon Spake?

It seemed there was no end to Conroyd's casual cruelties.

'Your Highness,' Holze said with an almost imperceptible nod.

Gar unclenched his jaw. 'Barlsman.'

Behind them a low buzz of voices, as the other attendees distracted themselves with conversation. Holze leaned a little closer. 'I hope you're reconciled to tonight's event. There can be no suggestion of . . . ambivalence.'

'You think me ambivalent?' He smiled. 'You're mistaken.'

A new roar from the crowd below killed Holze's cold-eyed reply.

'The king! The king! Barl brings us the king!'

So Conroyd arrived in a sound-storm of rapture that threatened not only to rattle the stars but rain them down on all their heads. He was the king. He was their saviour, the glorious golden Doranen who'd rescued them from a royal house well loved but bled utterly dry of magic. He arrived draped in crimson, dappled with rubies, studded with diamonds. Riding Cygnet, the beautiful silver stallion Asher loved.

For the first time since climbing out of Conroyd's carriage Gar looked in the cage. Saw Asher, on his knees and staring with eyes gone hollow in a wounded face gone hollower still.

He had to look away.

Overhead the glimfire furiously sparked and sputtered. Four balls extinguished themselves entirely and were hastily rekindled by Sorvold and Daltrie, still in attendance on the ground. All the while Conroyd sat on the fretting silver stallion and waved, laughing, drinking the applause avidly, gluttonously, as though too much could never be enough.

Just as Gar thought he must be sick, Conroyd

dismounted and tossed his reins to a waiting Olken servant. Lightly leapt up the stairs to the top of the dais and stood before his empty chair. Not once did he acknowledge his former king's existence.

'Good people!' he cried, and the crowd fell silent. 'Your love moves me to tears!' Mellifluous, musical, his glorious voice bathed them all in beauty. 'Midnight approaches. Justice awaits. Let it be done, and let all gathered here bear witness to Barl's mercy and might! Captain Orrick!'

Pellen Orrick appeared before him and bowed. 'Your Majesty.'

'It is time, Captain. Do your duty!'

The crowd shouted, drumming its heels to show approval. On the dais behind Gar no such vulgar display; but the mood of self-satisfaction swelled. He watched, sickened, as Orrick walked with slow deliberation across the Square to the cage holding Asher. In one hand he held a large key.

To distract himself Gar turned to Conroyd, seated now, and said softly, 'It was supposed to rain here today. Did you forget?'

Conroyd smiled, his attention on Orrick. 'Be silent.'

'Or haven't you even taken the Weather Magic yet? Conroyd, you mustn't delay. The people depend—'

'Be silent,' said Conroyd, 'or lose your tongue.'

He flinched. Was it his imagination playing tricks or was there something wrong with Conroyd? Something different about him. His eyes? The way his skin stretched over his face? There was something . . . . . and it made his skin crawl.

Three more balls of glimfire expired and one exploded. Before Sorvold or Daltrie could act, Conroyd replaced them with a wave of his hand. Nodded to

Orrick, who unlocked the cage and handled Asher ungently into the Square. Asher moved slowly, painfully, his chains clanking in the sudden hush. He looked up and as their eyes met Gar felt his heart seize. Freeze.

Darran had *lied*. There was no forgiveness in Asher's thinned and bloodless face. No understanding or acceptance. Only hate and hate and hate.

*Damn* Darran. Damn Asher, too. And Conroyd. The crowd. Above all damn himself. He'd wanted so much to believe in Asher's absolution, he'd deafened himself to the small voice within whispering *what you do is unforgiveable*. Had allowed himself to be deceived . . . because deception was so alluring, and so desperately desired.

And now was dead. As Asher would soon be dead.

Orrick escorted his shuffling prisoner to the block. Steadied Asher before it and impersonally helped him to kneel. His kneeling broke the taut silence; the crowd shouted. Cheered. Drummed their heels again, ecstatic. Some of them sat so close to the block they were in danger, surely, of being soaked in spraying blood. Of having their clothing ruined. Did they realise? Did they care? Or was it deliberate? An attempt to gain some kind of revolting keepsake?

Remembering the horror of Timon Spake's beheading, Gar couldn't comprehend this lust for blood and death. These Olken who howled for Asher's murder were the same men and women who, scant weeks ago, had fought to call him friend. To buy him ale. To boast to their cronies: '*As I said to Asher himself, just the other day . . .*'

A touch to one shoulder, and Asher put his head on the block. Gar wanted to close his eyes but couldn't. He owed his friend this much, not to close his eyes.

With his hands and ankles chained Asher couldn't

keep his balance. He kept slipping sideways off the block; a final obscenity. Orrick looked up and Conroyd nodded. The chains were removed. Asher once more lowered his head and Orrick stepped back, well out of the way. The executioner came forward. Raised his axe. A gasp of indrawn breath ran round and through the waiting crowd—

– and all the glimfire went out.

Plunging darkness. Screams. Confusion. Conroyd, swearing. One minute passed, and then one more. A ball of glimfire bloomed. Another. Then another. Light returned, revealing Asher still kneeling at the block, passively awaiting death.

'*Kill him*!' screamed Conroyd, leaping to his feet. '*Kill him now*!'

The axe fell. Blood sprayed. The crowd shrieked. A ball of glimfire directly overhead erupted into shooting flame and sank, igniting the bloody straw and Asher's sundered body. Panic, as those closest to the carnage tried to get away. Some of them were on fire. Panic spread and the crowd stampeded.

Forgotten, held fast in some kind of frozen stillness, Gar watched as chaos held sway. Orrick and his guards tried and failed to maintain order. Barlsman Holze shouted prayers and pleas for sanity. Conroyd's guests tumbled pell-mell off the dais, in fear for their lives. Willer was squealing.

Gar couldn't help it; he laughed out loud.

Conroyd turned on him, his altered face livid. The glimfire's dying flames reflected in his eyes. 'Is this *your* doing, eunuch? *Is it?*'

Despite his danger, he smiled. 'Mine? How could it be? I'm a cripple, remember? Perhaps it's Barl, expressing her displeasure.'

Conroyd struck him so hard that a ruby ring opened the flesh along his cheekbone. 'If I find this is you, runt, your pain will last *forever*!'

Blood was pouring down his face. He groped for the kerchief Darran insisted he carry and pressed it to the wound. 'Are you mad, Conroyd? To assault me in *public*?'

There was madness, or something worse, seething beneath the surface of Conroyd's chalk-white face. 'With me!' he grunted. 'Now!'

His arm bruised in an inescapable grip, Gar found himself dragged from his seat, from the dais, down the stairs and into the Square where the stench of charred straw, blood and human flesh was hideous. He gagged. Retched. Brought up all his swallowed icewine in a frothy puddle at Conroyd's feet.

Conroyd threw him to his knees in the middle of it. 'Look there!' he commanded. 'You know him better than any man alive. Is that him? Tell me if it's him! And if you lie I'll see it and no mercy known shall save you!'

The body and its head had caught almost the full brunt of the flaming glimfire. The face was blistered, bubbled, oozing thick boiled blood, but it was Asher's. The rest of the torso and its limbs were roasted, its clothes burned almost away. Only one small section of flesh was left seared but unblackened: the right arm, from shoulder to inches above the wrist. In falling, the body had sheltered it from the worst of the flames.

Gar stared at the smooth, unscarred length of limb. Looked again at that terrible face, still recognisable, and then again at the unscarred arm.

Like immortality, this was impossible.

'*Is it Asher*?' said Conroyd.

Churned with confusion, with the beginnings of a

hope too great to admit, Gar pressed his hands to his face and let a sob burst from his throat. 'Damn you, Conroyd. Of course it is. He's dead. You've killed him.'

Cruel fingers tangled in his hair, dragging his head backwards to break-neck position. 'You swear it?' said Conroyd, his terrible eyes on fire. 'On pain of every punishment I've ever promised, and many more besides?'

His slashed cheek was burning. 'Yes, yes, I swear it!' he said. 'Look at his face! See for yourself! It's Asher!'

Conroyd looked. 'Yes,' he said at last, in almost a whisper. 'It is him. I've won. My exile at last is ending!' His grasping fingers loosened and he backed a pace away.

Gar climbed unsteadily to his feet, certain of one thing only: that *none* of this made sense. He stared at Conroyd, who for all his familiar cruelty yet seemed subtly unlike himself. And even as he watched, something rippled across that hated face, some alchemical change that suggested, for a single impossible moment, that he was looking not at one man but two.

As Gar opened his mouth to shout, Pellen Orrick came running to join them, his uniform torn and filthy. 'Your Majesty! Your Majesty, forgive the interruption. Asher's friend – Stable Meister Matt! He's taken.'

Stunned shock congealed into pain. 'Let him go, Conroyd!' he said. 'Asher's dead now. It's over. Please, let him go.'

Conroyd turned on him, wholly himself again. 'Get back to your Tower and stay there, runt! I'll know if you're straying and you won't like my wrath!'

Matt. *Matt*. Anguished, despairing, Gar turned away without looking again at the burned body at his feet. The Square was almost emptied now, the dais entirely deserted. The carriage that had brought him here was waiting a little distance away, the golden crown on the falcon's head flashing in the guttering glimfire. He climbed inside and let it take him home through the thronged and noisy streets. His wounded cheek throbbed, unmerciful.

True to his word, of course, Darran was waiting up for him. Took one look at his cut and bloodstained face and cried out in alarm. 'Sir! Sir, what's happened? You're *injured*!'

Either he needed to get properly drunk, right now, or he should never touch icewine again. Ignoring Darran's outstretched hand, his peppering of incoherently anxious questions, Gar paced around the foyer floor. Struggled to make sense of events that were incredibly senseless. Totally impossible. He was brought up short by Darran, who abandoned a lifetime of protocol, grabbed him by the arm and dragged him to a halt.

'Sir! Sir, you're *frightening* me!'

Shocked, Gar looked at the old man. Saw that yes indeed, his secretary – his friend – was frightened. 'I'm sorry. I didn't mean to.'

Appalled at himself, Darran unclutched his fingers and stepped back. 'Please, sir. I understand how you feel. What's happened is a tragedy. But it's not your fault and you mustn't go on blaming yourself. Asher's death—'

Gar held up a silencing finger. Leaned close. Whispered, 'Asher's not dead.'

From the look on the old man's face it was clear Darran thought he'd lost his mind. 'Oh, sir. Please. Let me take you upstairs. Help you lie down and find medicine for your wound. You've had a terrible shock and—'

He seized Darran's black-clad shoulders and shook him. '*Listen* to me. Asher's not dead. Someone is. Someone died tonight, cruelly and bloodily. But that someone *wasn't Asher*.'

Dumbly, Darran stared at him. 'Wasn't Asher?' he said at last. 'How can you be—'

Shuddering, he saw again that burned and blackened body. Smelled the wrenching stink of fresh-cooked flesh. 'A missing scar. You've seen it – on his right arm. An injury he got as a boy. The man killed tonight didn't have it. He wasn't Asher.'

'Then who—'

'I have no idea,' he said, and let Darran go. Began pacing again, his head pounding with thoughts and ideas and pain. 'But it can only mean one thing. Asher was rescued.'

'*Rescued*? Oh, sir, I mean no disrespect but—'

He spun about. 'Matt's arrested. He was there, Darran. He was involved somehow. I *know* it.'

Looking uncomfortable, Darran cleared his throat. 'Don't you know? Asher and Matt parted uncivilly, sir. At the risk of sounding ghoulish, isn't it possible that Matt returned merely to witness—'

'*No*!' Frustration was a fire, burning. Perhaps if he banged Darran's thick head on the nearest wall he'd see what had to be seen. 'At least – yes. It's possible. But I don't think it's the answer. I can't explain it. Call it intuition. Desperation. Whatever you like. But I know Matt was here to rescue Asher and he didn't come alone. Asher got away, helped by people who wanted to keep him alive. And I doubt they were Doranen.'

'Olken?' Darran whispered. 'You mean . . . more of our kind like Asher?'

'I don't know about that. I don't know who they are,

or what they want. All I know is we have to find them, somehow. Because they can lead us to Asher!'

'*No*, sir!' Darran was so upset he didn't seem to notice he'd raised his voice to his prince. 'It's too dangerous! If Asher's alive then I'm glad of it, for his sake. But you *cannot* meddle further! To do so could mean your life! You could *die*!'

'And if I *don't* meddle, Darran, it could mean the death of this kingdom!'

Darran's face crumpled with despair. 'Oh, sir. Sir. Why won't you accept it? The kingdom's dead already. At least, it's dead to you. Conroyd is our king now. Lur's livelihood rests with him.'

Again, he took the old man by the shoulders and this time held him gently, as though his bones could break. 'You don't understand Darran,' he whispered. 'There's something wrong with Conroyd.'

Darran snorted. 'Forgive me, sir, but I've known that for quite some time!'

'No, no,' he said, still whispering. Too afraid to give his thoughts full voice. 'I saw something. Tonight. In him. Saw . . . some*one*.' He took a deep and shaking breath. Let it out. 'Someone who wasn't Conroyd. For a moment, he . . . he wore *two faces*.'

'Your Highness . . .' Now Darran was whispering. Looking afraid. 'I don't know what you mean.'

He stepped back. 'Neither do I.'

'What you're saying . . . it sounds fantastical.'

'I know that. Insane too.' He forced a smile. 'But I'm not crazy, Darran. Witnessing that execution hasn't robbed me of my wits or filled my head with wild imaginings. I know what I saw. And I know this too. Since the moment we opened Barl's library – since Durm found her hidden diary – something's been wrong in this kingdom. I don't know what but I intend to find out.'

Still fearful, Darran stiffened his spine. 'Yes, sir. But how?'

Gar glanced up, as though he could see right through the ceiling and into his library. 'The answer's in that diary, Darran. I can feel it in my bones. I must finish translating it and there isn't a moment to lose. Very soon now, I fear it will be too late and Conroyd – or whoever, whatever, he is – will bring us all to ruin.'

He headed for the staircase, almost running. Darran called after him. 'And me? Your Highness? Can't I do something?'

'Of course you can,' he said, turning on the staircase. 'You can think of a way to rescue Matt!'

# CHAPTER THIRTY

'Conroyd?'

Morg kept his entranced gaze on the blood-soaked straw around the executioner's block. The glimlit Square was almost emptied of Olken now; a handful of industrious individuals were plucking wet, scarlet wheat stalks from the ground, darting in quickly before a guard could interfere with their relic-taking. The body was already removed, bundled into sacking and taken away to the guardhouse to await its promised ignominious destruction. Willer had gone with it, eager and gloating.

All in all, a good night's work.

Behind him, the cleric shifted restlessly. '*Conroyd.*'

Sighing, he turned. Considered the old fool coldly. 'Your Majesty.'

Holze's pale cheeks coloured. 'Forgive me. Your Majesty. Sir, we need to speak.'

He turned away again, this time resting his gaze on the guardhouse wherein languished an Olken of great interest. One who'd been held in firm affection by dead Asher, and might, with judicious winnowing, reveal some knowledge of Asher's unexpected abilities. Just in case there was some other inconvenient Olken somewhere who could yet interfere with his plans.

'Tomorrow, Holze.'

Standing at a discreet distance, ever-hopeful Sorvold and Daltrie waited to see if their friend and king required anything more of them. Holze spared them a wary glance and stepped closer. 'I'm sorry, but it can't wait,' he said, his voice insistently lowered. 'Tonight sees the end of an era for our kingdom. An era that has died with bloodshed . . . and a certain amount of unexpected excitement. As Lur's oath-sworn caretakers it is urgent that you and I confer. In private. Between us, as Barl's chosen instruments, we maintain the spiritual and temporal balance in this land. What we do next will set the tone for generations of Doranen and Olken to come.'

Well, no. Because Lur's current crop of milk-and-water magicians was its last and the Olken were irrelevant. But since he was, for the moment, forced to continue his charade as the dutiful, dedicated king he couldn't let Holze suspect that.

And, in truth, there was no desperate need to question the captured stable meister immediately. Obedient Orrick had him safely locked away. This Matt would keep a few hours longer – and a night spent stewing in fear would doubtless render him more pliable. More likely to speak without encouragement. Searching Asher's mind had nearly killed the Olken untimely, and Asher had been an Olken stronger than most. It might well be unwise to kill this one too quickly, and with magic. Orrick's inconvenient ethics might prompt him to whisper in the wrong ears.

He favoured Barl-sot Holze with a smile. 'Efrim, your wisdom as ever prevails. Indeed, let us talk.' With a raised eyebrow he summoned Payne Sorvold to his side.

'Your Majesty?'

He acknowledged Sorvold's bow with the slightest of nods. 'Ah, Payne. Barlsman Holze and I have weighty matters of state to discuss. See that my horse is taken to the Barl's Chapel stables.'

Sorvold bowed again. 'Certainly, sir.' His public face was impeccable; Morg almost laughed to see the churning disquiet behind it. The barely leashed desire to partake in those weighty state discussions. Sorvold's ambition stank like rotting flesh.

For desultory amusement he touched his fingertips to Sorvold's forearm. 'Patience, friend,' he murmured. 'Walking, one still reaches the desired destination . . . and with far less risk of a fall.'

Sorvold's greedy eyes glittered. 'Indeed, Your Majesty.'

As Sorvold and Daltrie withdrew, conferring, Holze made a little noise of disapproval. 'I confess I had thought better of Payne Sorvold. Such naked self-interest is displeasing to Barl. Those of us privileged to be in the upper ranks of Doranen society should care more for her desires than our own.'

Drivel, drivel, drivel. Was there no end to the man's pious platitudes? Suppressing contempt, Morg smiled. 'As you say, Efrim. But a king is confined to the counsel at hand. And if Payne Sorvold's voice is a part of the choir we must assume he sings with Barl's blessing, yes? Her choice may seem dubious to us but is it meet that we question it?'

The rebuke stung fresh colour into Holze's cheeks. He bowed. 'Your Majesty.'

Morg smiled. 'And now let us retire to your rooms,

Efrim, that we might best decide how together we can steer our beloved kingdom to its rightful destiny.'

'Indeed, Conroyd,' agreed Holze. 'Let us.'

Fuelled by desperation, Gar returned to his study of Barl's diary. There was no more time for a measured, methodical deconstruction of her memories. He had to risk haste, risk racing through each entry in his search for the key words and phrases that would help him explain their current predicament. Had to subdue the historian, whose love of language and detail cried out for a leisurely perusal, and let the king's needs hold sway.

*The king's.*

Yes. In his heart, though his magic was now a bitter memory, he believed he was still Lur's rightful king, its guardian, its protector, in a way that transcended magic and WeatherWorking and trappings of power. The transience of an externally bestowed authority.

His father's words, spoken so long ago, echoed in his mind like thunder. '*Barl has a destiny for you, my son.*'

This was it. Finding her diary. Learning its secrets and using them to save Lur from a danger he could not define but knew was upon them. That was connected intimately, inexplicably, to the fate of Conroyd Jarralt.

Ignoring the spiking pain between his eyes, indifferent to the dull ache in his shoulders, his spine, uncaring of the throbbing in his face where Conroyd's ring had cut him open, Gar bent all his energy to those secrets' uncovering. Every time he lifted his gaze from the diary's ancient, faded paper and ink the image of Conroyd's dual face rose before him, spurring him on.

Wisely, Darran left him alone.

The answer came hours later, as the first intimations

of light appeared in the sky beyond his library window. Not dawn, but dawn's harbinger.

Exhausted, he'd had no choice but to slow the speed of his reading. The diary's later entries were scrawled hastily, haphazardly, as though Barl had been as pressed for time then as he was now. They were almost illegible. The incantations she'd recorded were of no use to him, of course. Not any more. But if he could find Asher . . . prevail upon him for assistance one last time . . .

The Doranen arcane heritage was appalling. No wonder there'd been a war. No wonder Barl had hidden the diary, and Durm after her. No wonder such magics had been erased from his ancestors' memories. The thought of such magic unleashed during Trevoyle's Schism . . . unleashed now by Conroyd against any who dared oppose him . . .

Sickened, his fatigued eyes burning, acutely aware of the fast-approaching day, Gar flogged his tired mind onwards.

Barl had written:

*But while a locked room is safe, without a key it is also a trap. So I have fashioned one and in time I will use it to open a window in the Wall, that I may see what has become of the world beyond. And if it be safe then we will go home. I swear it, I swear it on my life. One day we will all go home.*

A window in the Wall?

Thrumming with tiredness he slumped in his chair and let the implications of Barl's words unfold in his mind. Fragments of her earlier comments resurfaced and clicked into place, part of the puzzle he was trying so desperately to piece together.

*I've not told a soul of the power we discovered, the key to immortality . . . He is coming, he is coming, I can feel it . . . He will find us, no matter how long it takes to search each corner of the world . . .*

A window in the Wall.

Was *that* the answer? Had *Durm* read Barl's diary from cover to cover? And had he, in all his pride and arrogance, opened Barl's window? Breached their safe, sealed kingdom and placed them all at risk?

He heard again Durm's harsh and dying words: '*Borne . . . forgive me. I couldn't stop him . . .*'

Gar dragged his fingers over his face, struggling to understand.

Stop *who*? Stop . . . *Morg*?

No. *No*. It couldn't be that. Morg was dead, *had* to be dead. Immortality was a dream, not reality. There was another explanation, one he hadn't thought of yet.

Behind his closed eyes he saw once more that rippling alchemical change cross Conroyd's face. Remembered the oddness in his writing, as though another hand had guided the pen. Remembered the gaping hole in the fence at Salbert's Eyrie, where horses and carriage had plunged over the edge without any attempt to swerve or stop. Taking with them three powerful magicians without a fight.

A window in the Wall . . . and an immortal warrior mage, steeped in evil, bent on revenge.

'*Darran*!'

The old man appeared in the doorway a few moments later, shaken and breathless. 'Sir? Sir, what is it?'

Gar pushed to his feet, clutching at the desk to keep from falling sideways. 'Get down to the guardhouse. Now, before the City starts stirring. Find Pellen Orrick and bring him back here.' He pounded a fist against his head, trying to rattle coherent thought free of crippling exhaustion. 'No! No, not here. It's too dangerous. Take him – take him to House Torvig's crypt. I'll meet you there.'

Darran looked as sleepless as Gar felt. In rumpled clothing, his hair awry, he wrung his hands in agitation. 'Sir? Has something happened?'

Slowly, acutely aware of all his aches and pains and his swollen cut cheek burning. Gar nodded. 'I think I've figured it out, Darran. I think I know what we're up against. *Who* we're up against.'

Darran swallowed. 'And do I want to know, sir?'

He shook his head, feeling sick. 'No. No, Darran, you really don't.'

Pellen Orrick jerked upright in his chair with a snort, furious with himself for dozing, and looked to his prisoner to make sure he was still there and breathing.

He was. Curled on his side against the cell's far wall, draped in a blanket, the stable meister watched his captor with silent wariness.

Perhaps not surprisingly, given the execution and the malfunctioning glimfire and the general air of unrest, the guards who'd apprehended Matt last night had been heavy-handed in their methods. Enthusiastic in their eagerness to restrain him. They'd brought him in unconscious. Now, in the murky just-dawn light, Orrick saw that the man was a patchwork quilt of cuts and bruises. None life-threatening but all uncomfortable . . . and with more discomfort still to come.

Creaking a little, Orrick got to his feet. Stretched, hearing all the bones in his neck go *pop*, then stared down at the silent, unmoving prisoner on the floor before him.

'His Majesty sent word late last night. He'll be here later today to interrogate you himself. If you're wise you'll tell him whatever you know, and quickly. Asher resisted and paid a heavy price.'

Matt blinked his swollen, blood-crusted eyes. 'I don't know anything.'

'For your sake I hope not. I warn you, Matt, since you're a man who to the best of my knowledge has done no harm: our new king is ruthless in the pursuit of justice. He'll use magic to tear the truth from you, just as he used it on Asher.'

'Magic?' said Matt, and sat up, wincing. 'But that's forbidden. You're the Captain of the City, how could you sanction—'

'Captains don't sanction,' he replied. 'Or object.' Not when a king commands. Even when their conscience pricked them. Even though they had grave doubts. And was that duty or cowardice speaking? An uncomfortable question he wasn't sure how to answer. 'Tell him what you know, Matt. Put an end to all this misery.'

'I told you,' said Matt, and closed his eyes. 'I don't know anything.'

Well, if the stable meister was telling the truth surely he had nothing to fear, magic or no magic. And if the man was lying the king would soon dig the truth free. Either way, it was out of his hands. He was weary, and hungry, and needed an hour or three at home.

The guardhouse was empty, save for Bunder on front-desk duty and young Jesip filling out reports. All the other lads, on active duty or recalled for special circumstances, were out patrolling the City, maintaining order after last night's tumult and hastening all the sightseers back to their homes, either in Dorana or beyond it. He sent Jesip out back to keep a close eye on their prisoner and paused for a word with stolid Ox.

'I'm off home for a bit. Stay alert and send for me if there's fresh trouble.'

Letting himself out through the guardsmen's entrance he saw that the day promised fair, with flushes of pink on the rim of the horizon. Smothering a yawn, he turned for the small gate leading into the alley . . . and was accosted from the shadows alongside the guardhouse building.

'Captain Orrick! Captain Orrick, a word!'

He knew that whispering voice. It was the prince's secretary. Darran. A good man, if a witterer. 'Sir?' Orrick said, approaching. 'Is something wrong? Come out into the light where I can see you.'

The old man didn't move. 'Captain Orrick, do you love this kingdom?'

And what kind of a question was that? He scowled, feeling fratched and fractious. 'Meister Secretary, it's been a long night and I'm in no mood for games. State your business or be on your way. It's a grave offence to loiter on guardhouse property.'

The old man inched forward until just his face was visible. His gaze darted left and right, seeking eavesdroppers. 'Captain, we must speak in private. Will you come?'

'Come where? And why? What do you want to speak of?'

Darran eased a little further forward. He looked exhausted. Terrified. 'I can't say, Captain. Not here. Please, I beg you. Come. In the name of our beloved King Borne.'

That name stilled his tongue. He looked more closely at Darran. Recognised honesty, and desperation. 'I was on my way home,' he grumbled. 'I've been on duty now a good long time, sir.'

'I know that,' said Darran. 'I'd not ask if it weren't important.'

He sighed. 'How important?'

'A matter of life or death,' the old man said. 'For all of us.' He held out a bundled cloak. 'Wear this. Pull the hood low over your face. We don't want you recognised.'

Orrick took the cloak and shrugged it on as the old man settled the hood of his own cloak over his greying head. 'If this is not urgent but a trick or, worse still, some lawless skulduggery . . .'

'Come with me, Captain,' said Darran, 'and see for yourself.'

Groaning, sighing, Orrick went with him.

He wasn't surprised to find he'd been taken to meet with Prince Gar. The choice of meeting place was more unexpected: House Torvig's family crypt. Chilly, and filled full of candles. And bodies.

The prince looked sleepless. High-strung and backed against an invisible wall. The cut on his cheekbone was scabbed over, the flesh around it bruised and puffy. 'Thank you for coming, Captain. Pellen. May I call you Pellen?'

Orrick nodded. 'Of course.'

'Pellen, I need your help. Lur needs your help. Can we count on you?'

His spine snapped straight. 'I am an officer of the crown. My loyalty has never been questioned.' Well. Not reasonably anyway. Or more than once.

The prince smiled. There was something ghastly in his eyes. He stood beside his dead sister's coffin, his fingers caressing her – *the effigy's* – cold stone foot. 'I know that,' he said. 'But you're also an officer who's never been asked to face what we are facing. To accept what will sound to you like the ravings of a madman.'

Careful . . . careful . . . Orrick moistened dry lips. Glanced once at the old man who'd brought him here, standing now in the corner, then settled his attention on the prince. 'And what is it we're facing, Your Highness?'

'I believe – the destruction of our kingdom.'

Well, yes, that did sound like the ravings of a madman. And he was so damned *tired*. 'Sir, you'll need to speak more plainly. You *believe* that we're in danger? From whom? From what? And where is your proof?'

'So speaks the City guardsman.' The prince shook his head. 'I'm not sure you'd call it proof, Pellen.'

Orrick glanced again at Darran. The old man's eyes didn't leave the prince's face. From his expression he at least believed what Gar was saying. Or did he just want to believe it? Hard to say.

Looking back at the prince, he thought for a moment, choosing his words carefully. 'Your Highness, have you told the king of your concern?'

The question provoked a harsh, choked-off bark of laughter. 'Pellen, dear Pellen. Conroyd is my concern!'

'You're talking treason. I can't hear this,' he snapped, and burned Darran with a look. 'You shouldn't have brought me here, old man. If you love your prince, take him away. Now. And I'll do my best to forget the three of us ever spoke.'

Spinning on his heel, chaotic with regret and sorrow and fury, he headed for the door.

The prince said harshly, 'I lied about Asher.'

He stopped. Listened to his thudding, hammering heart. '*Lied*, sir?'

Footsteps behind him. A gentle hand touching, tugging him round. The prince's face was stark. No royal mask, no polished public presentation. Raw emotion only, with everything laid bare. He flinched.

'What he told you was true. All of it,' the prince said, as softly as though they were in chapel. 'I asked him to do magic.'

His reply was automatic. 'Olken have no magic.'

The prince smiled sadly. 'Asher does. Did. I can't explain it, but it's true. And he used it to protect this kingdom. When my own powers failed I gave him the Weather Magics myself, willingly. He never conspired to steal my crown. He was the truest subject a king could ever have. The truest friend. In every way that matters, Asher was innocent.'

All his life a guardsman. He'd learned – thought he'd learned – to tell when truth was spoken. 'But you renounced him!' he said, incredulous. 'You signed the execution order yourself!'

The prince nodded. 'I had to. Even though I'd sworn to protect him, I had to sign his death warrant. If I refused, Conroyd said he'd slaughter your people. I believed him.'

Could a living man be turned to stone? It felt like it. He swallowed, struggling against the pain in his throat, his chest. 'He was *innocent*? But I *killed* him!'

'No, Pellen,' the prince said. 'The law killed him.'

'It's the same thing!'

The prince looked to Darran, then. As though he were seeking advice . . . or absolution. The old man shrugged. 'I think you must, sir. We've come too far not to.'

The prince sighed. 'You're no murderer, Pellen. Asher isn't dead. The man who lost his life last night was unknown to me. Asher lives, somewhere, and if we're to save our kingdom from destruction you have to help me find him.'

Orrick felt his legs give way. He stumbled sideways, fending off the hands stretched out to help him. Fetching up against a cold brick wall he pressed a hand across his face and fought to catch his ragged breath.

'This is madness,' he muttered. 'The rotten fruit of overwork. I must be dreaming.' He lowered his sheltering hand and looked at the prince. 'Tell me I'm dreaming!'

'If you are, Pellen, it's a nightmare. And the rest of us are snared in it with you.' The prince reached inside his buttoned coat and pulled out a battered, leather-bound journal. It looked ancient. 'This is Blessed Barl's diary. Durm discovered it and hid its existence. It contains our long-lost magics . . . and an incantation that opens a window in the Wall.'

'A *window*? Your Highness—'

'I know,' the prince said quickly. 'I know how this sounds, but please, bear with me. I believe Durm used this spell.' His face twisted with bitterness and regret. 'He was always a curious man. And an arrogant one. Convinced he was never in danger, no matter the risks he took.'

Orrick stepped away from the wall and clasped his hands behind his back. Buried beneath confusion and bewilderment there was shame, that he'd let himself be so undisciplined as to show such open dismay. 'Very well. A window. But what has that to do with Asher? With anything?'

The prince slipped the journal back inside his coat.

'Everything. When Durm opened that window in the Wall, I think something climbed through it after him and is here with us now, bent on malevolent destruction. I think it killed my family and wants to kill us all. That's why I have to find Asher. He's the only one with magic I can trust to fight against it.'

'Against *what*, sir? Nobody knows what lies beyond the Wall! Nobody knows who lives there!'

'We know who used to live there.'

It took Orrick a moment to work out the prince's meaning. When he did, he almost fell down. '*Morg*? Sir, you are raving!'

Gar shook his head. 'I wish I was. Pellen, Morg knew how to make himself immortal. Understand: he was a magician with powers we can't begin to comprehend. The Doranen of Lur are mere *shadows* compared to our ancestors, and what they could do. Did do. It's all in the diary and I tell you, it's terrifying.'

Was madness contagious? He was starting to believe the prince . . . 'If you're right – if Morg really is among us – how is it nobody's noticed?'

'Because he's clever. He's hiding.'

'Hiding where?'

The prince's gaze dropped for a moment. He took a deep breath. Let it out. Looked up and answered. 'Inside Conroyd Jarralt.'

Orrick turned away, one fist pressed to his aching chest. Barl save him . . . Barl save him . . . but he believed it. Last night. In all the mayhem. He'd seen King Conroyd's face as he demanded Asher's beheading. Seen him afterwards, gloating over the body. Something inhuman and unnatural lurked there, deep inside his bones.

The prince said softly, 'I'm the last living member of

House Torvig, Pellen. For hundreds of years my family has shed its blood for the keeping of this kingdom. By all that's holy, in this sacred house of rest, before countless generations of my witnessing family, I swear, I *swear* I've told you nothing but the truth. *Please*. Will you help me?'

Orrick stared at the ground. Time stopped, hanging on his answer.

He looked up.

'Yes, Gar. I'll help you. And if it proves we're wrong may Barl have mercy on our souls.'

Ox Bunder looked up in surprise as Orrick walked back into the guardhouse. 'Captain? Something wrong?'

Only everything. Still reeling from the prince's revelations, from his own mad decision to follow him blindly, break the law, *free a prisoner*, he called upon his twenty-eight years of guarding experience and showed the man nothing but a sheepish smile.

'I tried to sleep but all my leftover paperwork kept tapping me on the shoulder,' he said. 'You know how I am.'

Ox grinned. 'Yes, sir, I do.'

'No trouble from the prisoner?'

'No, Captain.'

'Jesip's still with him?'

'Er . . .' Bunder looked discomfited. 'No. You know his mother's poorly? He just wanted to see if she'd spent the night all right. I didn't see the harm, sir, he's been on duty for nearly two days. I checked the prisoner myself not ten minutes ago and he was out to the world, snoring.'

'I see. Well, I suppose that's all right.' He headed for the rear door leading to the cells. His heart was pounding so hard he was amazed Bunder couldn't hear it. 'But I'll have a quick look at him myself before I go upstairs. Carry on, Ox.'

Praise Barl, the guardhouse's other prison cells were empty, all impulse to petty criminalities swallowed by the enormous events of the past few weeks. He hurried along the cell-lined corridor to the room at the end where Asher had been briefly held. Where Matt now waited in equal danger. He opened the outer double-locked door—

—and found the prisoner trying to hang himself with the torn-off sleeve of his shirt.

'No, damn you! *No*!'

With shaking hands he fumbled the keys from his belt, jammed the right one in the lock and wrenched the cell door wide open. The stable meister was on his knees, swaying at the end of his improvised noose, wheezing, choking, his battered face suffused with blood and turning purple.

Orrick lunged at him. Tore frantically at the knot around his neck but had no hope of loosening it. Instead he got his shoulder under the man's heaving chest and bellowed for Bunder.

'Get me a knife!' he ordered as Ox skidded into the outer cell. Gaping, Ox bolted out again and returned moments later with a dagger. Together they freed the strangling prisoner.

'Captain, captain . . .' Bunder stammered, horrified.

'Never mind that now, Bunder – we'll talk about discipline later!' he growled, watching Matt's face fade from purple to red. His mind raced, seeking a way to turn this near-disaster into success. It wasn't easy. He was the Captain of the City; he spent his time putting people *into* prison, not thinking of ways to help them *escape*.

'This man should have a pother,' he said at last.

'There's a pothery two streets over,' said Bunder, eager to make amends. 'I'll—'

He shook his head. 'No. This is an important prisoner. He'd best be seen by the king's own man. Go to the palace and fetch Nix here. But *slowly*!' he added as Bunder made a dash for the door. 'After the hullabaloo last night the townsfolk don't need to see you careering through the streets like a scalded cat. Walk there and walk back again. Like you're out for a stroll. With a friend.'

'Walk back?' said Bunder, confused. 'But doesn't the pother have a carriage?'

'A very nice one, I believe, with royal bits and pieces painted all over it,' Orrick said. 'Humour me, Ox. Walk. This City's been in a ferment for far too long. It's our job now to set a calm example.'

'Yes, sir,' said Bunder, still confused but trained to the teeth. 'I'll be back with the pother directly.'

But not too directly, Orrick hoped, as the sound of Bunder's retreating footsteps diminished. Well. He'd bought himself some time. Now to spend it wisely . . .

Matt was breathing more easily now, slumped on his side, his face almost human again. 'You shouldn't have stopped me, Captain,' he croaked, looking up through slitted eyes. 'I'm going to die anyway.'

Orrick glared. Dragged the fool upright and leaned him against the wall. As a precaution he picked up the dagger and stuck it through his belt. 'Well done. You've almost ruined everything. Sit there and do *nothing*. I won't be long.'

Turning his back on Matt's bewilderment he hurried to the rear of the guardhouse and opened the door. Beckoned to Darran, once more hiding in the shadows.

'Hurry! One of my lads could return any moment!'

Darran stared in alarm. 'Where's Matt?'

'Inside. The damned fool tried to hang himself and besides, there's his escape to be covered! Come *in*!'

Wittering, Darran came. Matt's swollen jaw dropped when he saw the prince's secretary.

'*Darran*? Are you another Circle member? Is Orrick?'

'I haven't the faintest idea,' said Darran, kneeling beside him and speaking quickly. 'Now hush up and listen. I'm getting you out of here. Prince Gar's orders. The kingdom's in danger and we need your help to save it.'

'I don't understand,' said Matt, rubbing at his bruised, chafed throat. 'If you aren't part of the Circle why—'

Orrick kicked him, just hard enough to get his attention. 'Can you take them to Asher?'

Matt's face stilled. 'Asher's dead.'

'He's not and we all know it. Do you know where to find him?'

'Please, Matt,' Darran urged him as the stable meister continued silent. 'This isn't a trick, I promise. We're trying to save you. Trust us, we're your only hope. The kingdom's only hope. His Highness is *counting* on you.'

A riot of uncertainty in the injured man's face. An agony of indecision. They were running out of time . . .

Orrick snatched the dagger from his belt. Hauled Matt up and onto his feet then shoved the weapon into his hand.

'Stab me.'

'*What*?'

'No one will believe this unless I'm wounded! Stab me, you fool, and be quick about it! Do you want the king to find us? Could be he's on his way!'

Matt lifted the dagger in front of his face, looking at

it as though he'd never seen one before. 'Say I do it. Say I stab you. Then what?'

'Then we run, Matt! To Asher!' said Darran, on his feet again. 'His Highness is outside hidden in a donkey cart. We have to go now, man, before it's discovered we're missing from the Tower!'

But Matt just shook his head, still dazed. 'I can't – I don't know—'

Orrick looked at Darran. 'This won't work, he's addled with shock. You've got to get out of here, back to the Tower. Think of another way to—'

'There is no other way!' said Darran. His face was flushed, his eyes alight with desperation. 'Oh sweet Barl, forgive me!' he gasped. Snatched the dagger from Matt's unresisting fingers and struck.

Orrick choked as the blade sank deep into his shoulder. Magically tempered steel sliced muscle. Scraped bone. The pain was immediate. Shocking. Hot bright lights danced before his eyes and the small cell spun, sparkling like glimfire. Without his permission his knees buckled and he sagged to the floor.

Darran's hands were pressed to his face. 'Oh dear . . . oh dear . . .'

Oh dear was right. There was sweat on his face, icy as melted snow. His shoulder was on fire. Damn. Who'd have thought such a stringy old man would have such strength in him? 'Go,' he croaked. His right hand hovered over the jutting dagger hilt. If he pulled the damn thing out would he bleed to death right here on the floor? 'Now. Flog that damned donkey till it drops in the road and don't look back. Nix is on his way, I'll be all right. Tell His Highness, good luck. Tell Asher, I'm sorry.'

'Yes – yes—' said Darran, shaking, and took hold of Matt's arm to drag him from the cell.

Matt pulled free. 'Wait.' His dazed confusion had cleared. Beneath the bruises and bloodstains he looked himself again, the calm and competent man who'd run a prince's stables. 'We'll never get out of the City unrecognised.'

'We might do!' cried Darran. 'We must risk it!'

'No,' said Matt, and turned to Darran. Spread his hands wide and pressed them to the old man's face. 'Stand still. This won't take a moment . . . I hope.'

Pounded with pain, Orrick watched as Matt's battered face contorted and he lost his last colour. Beneath his pressing hands Darran cried out, protesting.

'What are you doing? Stop it! Stop it!'

Matt lowered his hands. Staggered a little, and would have fallen if not for his shoulder pressed hard to the cell wall. 'Did it work?' he muttered. 'I've never done it before. Just had it done to me, once.'

Shocked speechless, Orrick looked into Darran's changed features. A moment earlier they had been thin. Straight-nosed and sharp-chinned. Familiar. Now Darran wore the face of a stranger ten years younger, placid and pouchy, with a bulbous nose and a spider-working of veins across his cheeks. He found his voice and whispered, disbelieving, 'It worked. You're disguised, Darran. With magic.'

Darran gasped. 'Barl have mercy! Not you too, Matt!'

Still leaning on the cell wall Matt pressed his hands to his own face. Groaned aloud, a sound of extreme distress, and nearly slid to the floor, retching. When his hands fell away they revealed a second stranger.

'It's called a blurring,' he said hoarsely. His new face was grey and sweating. 'But we'll have to hurry. It won't last long.'

'Then go,' said Orrick fiercely. 'Now!'

They bolted. Alone and bleeding he sprawled face-up on the prison-cell floor. Before he could wonder if he'd done the right thing, the world around him turned scarlet, then black. His last clear thought, as consciousness left him, was something like a prayer.

*Sweet Blessed Barl . . . don't let me be wrong.*

# CHAPTER THIRTY-ONE

Morg woke late in his unattended house, and for some little while indulged himself in the luxury of silence. Silence was an antidote to the memory of Holze's insistent yammering . . .

*'Conroyd, you must show yourself the Weather-Worker in public. Conroyd, you must move into the palace. Conroyd, you must recall the lords and ladies now dallying in the country. Appoint a Privy Council . . . soothe the worried populace . . . decide upon an heir . . . name a Master Magician. Conroyd . . . Conroyd . . . Conroyd . . .'*

He intended to feed the cleric to his demons *personally* when at last the Wall came down.

His regrettably unavoidable meeting with the man had lasted hours. Through it all he'd nodded and smiled and indicated approval, agreement, whatever was required to bring the audience to an end. But it seemed Holze had been storing up an inexhaustible supply of opinions . . . and he couldn't risk taking action. A swift and surreptitious examination of the prosing cleric's mind showed him a man peculiarly proofed against easy tampering. More of Barl's interference? He couldn't tell.

Didn't care; in the end it would make no difference. With gritted teeth he'd survived the lecturing and so had Holze, barely, what he needed now was to bend his will towards the only thing that mattered: the next step in his undermining of Barl's infernal Wall. That exquisite task completed, he would examine the stable meister taken by Orrick's men after the execution and—

The execution.

Beneath his cosseting blankets Morg stretched with delight like a cat.

Interfering, unexpected Asher was dead.

Gar had wept; recollection of the mewling cripple's grief bathed him in more pleasure, leaving him languorous and replete. He was aware, too, of Conroyd's pleasure in that brutal death. Conroyd had hated the Olken with a passion nearly matching his own. Not that his docile prisoner said as much. Subdued at last, run out of words and curses, Conroyd sat silent in his cage now; but his feelings were as loud as any shout.

The glow of sunlight behind the bedchamber's drawn curtains reminded him the day was ageing rapidly. He rose, bathed, dressed, summoned food from his cookless kitchen and then rode Asher's cowed stallion back to the Weather Chamber.

Holze had been right about one thing, damn him: to allay suspicion he must show the people of Lur their expected weather. So he made it rain, but with the magic corrupted, the spell altered, so that every drop of water falling from the sky pulled free a thread of the tapestry binding together the bitch whore's ancient barrier.

Ancient . . . but not immortal.

Overhead, the golden Wall trembled. Shuddered. Staring through the Weather Chamber's clear glass ceiling Morg laughed and laughed to see it. Rode away light-hearted towards the City Guardhouse where waited the prisoner Matt, ripe for plucking.

But instead of the cripple's former stable meister he found chaos.

'It's a nasty wound, Your Majesty,' Pother Nix informed him on the threshold of Orrick's office. 'The captain has lost considerable blood. He'll mend, but – Your Majesty, he's not ready for – Your Majesty, I must protest! My patient—'

Thrusting the fool aside, ignoring his irrelevant gabble, Morg confronted Orrick on his makeshift sickbed. 'Well? What happened? And why was I not informed immediately?'

Stripped to the waist and swathed in scarlet-stained bandages, Orrick regarded him weakly. His skin had turned sickly and his eyes were rimmed with red. 'Your Majesty . . . forgive me . . .' His voice was a whispering trickle. 'I failed you.'

One of the guardsmen, a hulking brute, stepped forward from the background huddle of uniforms and bowed. 'Your Majesty, the prisoner tried to hang himself. Captain Orrick sent me to fetch him a pother and while I was gone the prisoner stabbed him near to death. He's escaped.'

For one blinding moment his rage was absolute, so that he nearly wiped them from existence with a word: Orrick, Nix, the brutish guardsman.

'Your Majesty . . .' Orrick again, barely audible. 'I'd hoped to find him quickly. Avoid the need to trouble you. I've many men out searching. He'll be recaptured, I swear it.'

Rage subsided. So the stable meister was missing. But did it really matter? Attempted suicide suggested secrets worth hiding, true . . . but equally it could have been fear. Asher was dead and WeatherWorking had died with him. The Wall even now was crumbling. What matter the fate of one Olken, destined soon for fire wherever he'd run to?

Not that he'd say so. Keeping all eyes focused on recent events would mean less attention paid to him. He smiled, magnanimously forgiving. 'Very well, Captain. I accept your apology. Continue your hunt for the miscreant. I trust implicitly your diligence shall find him in the end. Meanwhile, your men can enforce the Olken curfew and the other restrictions arising from this new and criminal action. My man Willer shall advise you of the details.'

He left behind him uneasy silence and a horrified exchanging of glances. Inwardly he smiled.

Downstairs in the guardhouse reception area he was accosted by ubiquitous Willer, damp from the still-falling rain and puffing from his minimal exertions. 'Your Majesty! Your Majesty! Oh, at last I've found you!'

'For what purpose?' he asked coldly. The little toad had pretensions, and required regular squashing.

Willer stepped improperly close. 'I have an urgent message, sir.'

He had no interest in messages. Frowning at the repellent creature he said, 'Did you do as I bid, Willer, and see to Asher's remains?'

Willer stepped back. 'I supervised their disposal first thing this morning, Your Majesty, exactly as requested. The dead dogs are burned now, and their ashes scattered. The traitor is no more.'

'Excellent. And your message?'

'Your Majesty,' Willer's voice was lowered to a sibilant hiss. 'Lords Sorvold and Daltrie request an urgent audience.'

Of course they did. Puling lickspittles, desperate for advancement. 'Inform them I am unavailable for audience.'

Willer swallowed, convulsively. 'Yes, Your Majesty. Your Majesty, they seemed quite . . . determined. They'll ask me to ask you again. What shall I tell them?'

'Tell them a king does not account himself to his subordinates. Subordinates account themselves to their king.'

Willer looked less than convinced. 'Yes, Your Majesty. Er, Your Majesty?'

In the midst of leaving he stopped and turned. Let his displeasure fully reveal itself and waited for Willer to cease his cringing. '*Yes*?'

Faltering, stooped as though avoiding a blow, Willer crept close again. 'There is just one more thing, sir. The palace provisioner was wondering when you thought to—'

'For all I care, Willer, the palace provisioner can drop dead of an ague!' he snapped. 'Delay me no further! I am fatigued with WeatherWorking and must recover my strength. The damage wrought by the traitor Asher is greater than even I imagined. Would you have me weak and incapable of fulfilling my sacred duties? Of saving this kingdom from his black and ugly business?'

Willer blanched. 'No, sir! Oh no!'

'Then desist your childish blatherings! And tell those who would tax me with trifles to quickly follow suit! I return now to my townhouse. If you're wise you'll see I'm not disturbed.'

'Your Majesty,' said Willer, his obeisance folding him in half.

Sweeping out of the guardhouse Morg ignored the murmured reverent acknowledgements by guards and visitors alike. Paused on the steps he savoured the slurry of rain splashing from the greeny-grey clouds he'd called with a thought. Olken and Doranen in the street beyond the guardhouse gates stopped to bow or curtsey. He ignored them too. Stared instead at Barl's great Wall, clinging tight to the mountains.

Was it his imagination or did the glowing gold seem . . . tarnished? And along its very top – was that a hint, the merest suggestion, of a tatter? A hem, unravelling?

He rather thought it was.

A lackey brought him the silver stallion. He mounted, smiling, and rode away.

Just as dusk was falling Dathne heard the cottage's side gate creak. She dropped the book she'd not really been reading, convinced at first it was a dream. Three false alarms she'd raised already. Was near worn out with hope and waiting. But this time it wasn't her frantic mind playing tricks. This time there was the sound of a tired horse – no, two tired horses – plodding along the track outside the cottage and the glimpse through the window of a cart rolling past, driven past a bent old woman wrapped tight in a blanket.

*Veira.* Veira was home. Which meant Asher—

She bolted into the kitchen so fast she banged into the rickety table and nearly fell flat on her face. Rubbing her hip and cursing she shoved the back door open and tumbled into the midst of Veira's vigorously scratching hens. They fled, cackling. The sun was sliding towards the brooding treetops and a chill wind was up, rattling their branches.

Veira slumped alone on the wagon's driving seat, her face half hidden in the hood of her cloak. Little brown

Bessie had been replaced by two tall raw-boned greys, and the wagon they pulled was different too.

'Veira!' she cried. 'I thought you'd never get here! Did it go right? Do you have him? What happened? And where's Matt? Quick, quick, tell me, quick!'

Veira pushed the hood back on her shoulders. In the fading light she looked exhausted. So, for that matter, did the two strange horses. They were splashed with mud to their bellies and their heads hung almost to the ground.

'Matt and me got separated. I swapped Bessie and my old cart for faster new horses and a wagon with a hidey-hole in it. Now stop your questions, child, and give me a hand with our Innocent Mage.'

All she could do was stand and stare. 'What do you mean, you got separated? Did you leave Matt behind? *Veira*!'

'Dathne!' the old woman snapped. 'I can't lift Asher out on my own! *Help* me. I'll tell you what I can once he's safe inside!'

The bony grey horses stood patiently as Veira clambered down from the wagon and began fiddling with the side of the box seat. Muttering under her breath, she poked and prodded while Dathne watched, feeling sick.

'Asher's in there?' she demanded. 'He'll be suffocated!'

Veira ignored her. Poked and prodded some more, then said 'Ha!' with a tired satisfaction. The side of the box seat dropped open and Dathne saw the soles of two bare and dirty feet.

Asher.

She leapt forward and helped Veira drag him slowly from his prison until his toe-tips touched the grassy ground and she could wrap her arms around his unconscious body. The weight of him had her staggering.

'He's drugged,' said Veira, leaning against the wagon and catching her breath. 'It was safer, and easier.'

Drugged. That was unlikely to please him. She could feel his slow and heavy breathing, warm between her shoulderblades. The rank smell of him caught in the back of her throat. 'Let's get him inside, then,' she said. Her voice was rough with pent-up tears and barely realised relief. 'Before he wakes and causes a ruckus.'

Veira put her arm around him from the other side and together they half carried, half dragged him into the cottage.

'My room,' Veira grunted.

They lowered him onto the sagging mattress in Veira's tiny bedchamber and took a moment to recover their breathing. Then, as Veira lit her bedside, lamps, Dathne looked into her husband's face.

'Oh, *Veira*,' she whispered.

'I know, child, I know,' said Veira. Shockingly, she sounded on the verge of tears. 'I'd best go see to those horses and the wagon. And the chickens.' She sniffed, looking disappointed. 'You might have done right by my chickens, child.'

Dathne flushed. 'I'm sorry, I—'

'And what about my pigs? Did you forget about my pigs as well?'

'No! No, I didn't forget, I just . . . I've been waiting, worrying. I . . .'

Veira sighed. 'I'll see to the pigs then, too. You stay in here. Make Asher comfortable and sit with him till I'm done outside. Then we'll clean and physick him. In the meantime, if he wakes . . .' She frowned. 'But I doubt he will. I gave him enough grobleroot to—'

'*Grobleroot*?' said Dathne. 'Veira, how could you risk—'

'Because I had to!' the old woman retorted. 'And it didn't kill him, so let it be. We've bigger things to worry about than whether or not I slipped him a sleeping draught!'

Dathne realised then how close Veira was to collapsing, and felt ashamed. 'I'm sorry,' she murmured. 'Of course you know what you're doing.'

Veira nodded. 'And mind you remember that. Now I'll be back directly.'

The bedroom door banged shut behind her. Dathne frowned at it, then turned her attention to the heavily stuporous Asher. First things first: get him out of his stinking horrible clothes. She'd only undressed him twice before, and both times were occasions for joy.

Now, though . . .

When she saw the extent of his injuries she wept a little, for what had been done to him. What he'd endured. And what he had yet to face, once consciousness returned. She threw the stained and filthy shirt and trews on the floor, settled his head more comfortably on the pillows, drew a light blanket over him and waited for Veira.

The sun had set completely by the time the old woman returned to the bedroom carrying her medicine tin, a bowl of warm water and a bagful of rags. Working silently, swiftly, they washed the dirt, dried blood and caked pus from Asher's bruised and crusted skin. Spread his wounds with salves and ointments, acridly healing. Now Dathne was glad of the grobleroot because they must have been hurting him. Through it all, Asher failed to stir.

At last the nasty task was done. Clean and physicked,

dressed in an old nightshirt and coddled with blankets, Asher slept on. Veira touched her arm. 'Into the kitchen, child,' she whispered. 'I could do with some tea.'

She smoothed Asher's hair a final time and followed Veira from the chamber, unspeaking. Watched in continued silence as the old woman waved her to a chair, refusing her assistance, and put the kettle on the hob. She looked pale. Moved slowly, painfully, as she dribbled honey into their steaming tea cups and tipped butter biscuits onto a plate.

'The important thing is,' she said as she finally settled down at the table, 'we got him here safely.'

Yes. Yes, that was important. It was everything. Dathne sipped her scalding tea cautiously, but didn't risk a biscuit. Her occupied belly was unforgiving now. 'Please, Veira. Tell me what happened. Rafel. Is he—'

Veira nodded. 'Yes. He's dead. Just as I planned it.'

'I'm so sorry.'

Staring into the depths of her mug, Veira seemed not to hear her. 'Rafel's dead and Asher's alive and good Matthias is missing. I wonder if this is what Prophecy wanted.'

Matt was *missing*? 'I don't know,' Dathne whispered. Reached out and covered Veira's hand with her own. 'Why don't you tell me all of it and I'll see if I can't answer.'

Not lifting her eyes Veira nodded again, then haltingly began to speak.

'He smiled at me, you know,' she whispered. 'When I gave him the potion and bade him to drink. He smiled, and kissed my cheek, and . . . and *thanked* me, for the chance to do such service.' Tears wet her cheeks, unheeded. 'I held him as best I could while the poison worked its will on him. I thought I'd made it painless but . . . at the end, he felt it. Not badly, and not for long, but I was looking into his eyes at the last and I saw—' She shuddered, and released a ragged breath.

'Don't think about it,' Dathne urged. 'It's over now, and he's at peace. What happened next?'

It sounded incredible, like something from one of Vev Gertsik's improbable novels. Circle members hidden in the crowd, tampering with Doranen glimfire. The hooded axeman one of their own, striking the head from a man already heart-stopped so living Asher might be whisked away in the shouting confusion. Fire. Alarm. Hysteria.

'I thought for a moment we'd not survive it,' Veira admitted after another swallow of tea. 'There was screaming. Trampling. I couldn't see a foot in front of me and if I'd fallen no one would've stopped to lend a hand. Our people there saved us. Bundled us into blankets and spirited us to the Livestock Quarter right under the noses of the guards. It was all such pandemonium I didn't even realise Matthias wasn't with us until we'd reached the horses and wagon and it was time to go.'

Her hand still on Veira's, Dathne tightened her fingers. 'It wasn't your fault. You said it yourself: saving Asher was the most important thing. Matt's a strong man, and resourceful. He'll find his way back to us. I know it.'

But she sounded more confident than she felt.

Veira pulled her hand free and pushed slowly to her feet. 'I'm sure you're right, child. But what say we see for certain, eh? I'll sleep easier knowing he's on his way here.'

'Let me. You're too tired to scry tonight, Veira.'

Veira frowned. 'And you're with child.'

'You mean there's danger?' Dathne said, alarmed, and

leapt from her chair, palms pressed to her still-flat belly. 'I scried when I got here! Have I harmed the baby?'

'No, no, I shouldn't think so,' said Veira, and pressed her back in the chair. 'Tanal's not a poison, Dathne. Chewed and not swallowed it does no harm. But better safe than sorry. Besides, I'm old and I'm tired but I'm not so decrepit I can't find our Matthias this once.'

'Then at least let me fetch what's necessary. Sit down and finish your tea. Eat another biscuit. You'll need your strength.'

Pretending to grumble, Veira obeyed. Dathne gathered the basin, the water, the herbs. Laid them neatly before the old woman then withdrew to lean herself against the sink, one ear cocked in case Asher should wake and make a sound. She was too nervous to sit again until she knew Matt was all right.

*Jervale, are you listening? He'd better be all right . . .*

Unhurried and methodical, Veira readied herself for the scrying. Chewed the tanal, spat it out. Closed her eyes, and waited.

It seemed to take forever.

'I have him,' Veira whispered at last. A slow smile spread over her tired, wrinkled face. 'He's safe. He's coming. And with company . . .'

'Company?' Dathne leapt to the table and stared into the scrying water even though she knew she'd see nothing. 'Who?'

'An old man – Olken – and a handsome young Doranen fellow. They're travelling in a donkey cart.'

A handsome young *Doranen*? Could it be – 'Gar?' she said, incredulous. 'He's bringing *Gar* here? *Why*?'

Veira shrugged. 'No doubt he has his reasons, child.'

'Not good ones!'

'Who's the old Olken man, do you think?'

'I don't know for certain. But if the Doranen is Gar then that has to be Darran. The royal secretary.' Dazed, she paced the kitchen floor. 'I don't believe this. What is he *thinking*?' Her pleasure at Matt's survival was doused now with ire. 'Once it's realised Gar's missing Jarralt won't rest till he's found him! He'll peer under every blade of grass in the kingdom! We'll all be discovered. When Matt gets here I'll *kill* him!'

Slowly Veira opened her eyes and eased herself out of the tanal's cloying grasp. 'No, you won't, child. You'll listen to his story with your tongue behind your teeth. There's been enough killing for now.'

That silenced her. When she could trust her temper again she asked, with restraint, 'How long till they reach us?'

Veira shrugged. 'The countryside is the same for miles and miles between us and the City. I can't quite tell where they are. They'll be here by and by, child. That's all I can say for certain.'

Suddenly queasy, Dathne dropped into a chair. 'Good. That's . . . good.'

But what Asher would say when he found himself in such a houseful, she hadn't the faintest idea.

'Our Mage'll be waking soon, I'm thinking,' said Veira, clearing the scrying things away. 'And it's nigh on dinnertime. Cook us a meal, child, and I'll sit with Asher till he stirs.'

Dathne nodded. She wanted to feel angry at Veira's high-handedness. To feel outraged and proprietary and indignant for her rights where Asher was concerned – but instead, she felt relieved. And then guilty. She was desperate to see him. She was frightened to see him. All the hidden truths would soon be laid bare . . .

'It'll be fine,' said Veira. Her eyes were warm and knowing. 'If we trust to Prophecy, it'll be just fine.'

In his dreams, Asher was sailing.

*The sky was a blue bowl overhead, with little scudding clouds and the sun playing peekaboo behind them. A salt-stiffened breeze snapped the sail against the masthead, the shirt on his back, the hair on his head. The fishing smack, not brand new but seaworthy all the same, gaily green and blue in her fresh coat of paint, plunged and curvetted like an eager young filly, dipping low into Restharven Harbour with the heaving weight of her nets and the bounty they promised. Her name was Amaranda. Laughing, he reached out his hands to haul the first net back on board. Laughing, Da joined him and together they cracked their muscles, smiling with the effort, as the catch came over the side in all its wet-scaled flapping glory . . .*

'Da!' said Asher and sat up in his bed.

'Easy now,' said a comfortable voice to his right. 'You might find your head's gone all a bit whirligig.'

It had. Dizzy, he flopped back on the pillows and waited for the spinning to stop. The voice was female. Old. Unfamiliar, as was the room. 'Where am I?'

'Safe.'

There were no lamps lit; he couldn't see the speaker's face. 'Where?'

'In my house.'

'And who are you?'

'A friend. The friend of friends. Be easy now. Your enemies are behind you and they'll not find you here.'

He touched clumsy fingers to his neck. 'I ain't dead.' It came as a kind of discovery, and a welcome surprise.

A breathy chuckle. 'No, child, you ain't.'

•

His mind was a jumble of memories. The cage. The Square seething with sound and faces. The executioner with his axe. The glimfire, which kept on sparking. How the wooden block felt pressed against his throat. The pain in his wrists and ankles as he walked towards his death. The stink of his own piss and sweat. Pellen's grim, unfeeling face.

Gar.

He tried to sit up again. For the first time in forever his body was free of pain. 'How did I get here? What's goin' on? Sink me, woman, who *are* you?'

A rough-palmed hand reached out of the darkness and held him down. 'People call me Veira.'

His muscles felt like soggy bread. 'What people?'

'Just people.'

'The folk who rescued me?'

'That's right.'

He wished there were a few more candles burning, so he could see this Veira's face. 'I want to meet 'em.'

'You can't, child. Not yet. But one day soon, I hope. Prophecy willing.'

Prophecy? What was prophecy? 'Who are you to say no to me? I want to meet 'em, I said!'

'And I said not yet!' she snapped, her voice hardening.

Another snatch of memory: loud screaming, and a harsh, urgent voice in his ear demanding: '*Do you want to live*?'

Then he did sit up, never mind his weakened body or the hand still pressed against his shoulder. 'I remember you now! You were there! You saved my life!'

'A lot of people saved your life, child,' the old woman said. She sounded suddenly sad. 'And one man in particular. I'll tell you about him, by and by.'

He sank to the pillows again, his body a traitor. 'Call me Asher. I ain't a child.'

A breath of amusement. 'You are to me. To me, at my age, you're a spratling.'

*Spratling*. 'That's a fishing word.'

'And you're a fishing man. Or you were, and hope to be again. But if you want that dream coming true there's a thing or two you'll need to do first.'

'Show me your face,' he said, suspicious. 'Why are we sittin' in the dark? Can't you light a lamp or somethin'?'

'Light one yourself,' said the aggravating old besom. 'The glimfire's in you, along with everything else.'

He stopped breathing. Didn't start again till his lungs began clamouring for mercy. 'That ain't funny.'

'And I'm not laughing. The time for hiding is past us, young Asher of Restharven. Though that's not the name I know you by.'

He wasn't going to ask how she knew him. Knew any of it. Wouldn't say another word until she lit a lamp and showed him her face and explained what he was *doing* here.

She answered the unasked question anyway. 'For six hundred years, Asher, me and mine have known you as the Innocent Mage. Prophecy named you in the days of Barl and the making of her Wall. When she sowed the seeds we're reaping as weeds today. You've a birthright, child. And the womb of the world is ready at last to spit you out in blood and pain.'

He shook his head. 'You're crazy.'

'Am I?' she asked him. He heard a whispered word and felt a tremble of power. A tiny bloom of glimfire appeared hovering above her palm like a firefly. It illuminated the softly folded planes of her face and turned her dark eyes to gemstones. 'You see?' she said, smiling. 'You aren't the only one after all. But you are the very best . . .'

He was too astonished to speak.

She frowned at the glimfire. 'Believe it or not this used to be ours. The Doranen took it, of course, just like they took everything else. And our fool elders let 'em. Made their short-sighted bargain and dropped us all in a stinky, stinky soup.'

He found his voice at last. 'I ain't got the first idea what you're witterin' about. You called *glimfire*. I thought I was—'

'Alone?' The old woman chuckled. 'No, child. Not alone. Every Olken's got magic in him. What did you think happens at your Sea Harvest Festival? You think the fish rise for a Doranen, singing? No. They answer the call of the Olken. Lur's fisherfolk using the power they were born with, all unknowing.'

'*What?* What d'you mean, what—'

She raised her other hand. 'Hush now. There's not much time for story-spinning, so pin back your ears and I'll tell you what's most needful.'

The last time he'd let someone tell him a story he'd ended up with his head on a chopping block. He kicked back the blankets. 'Don't bother. I ain't interested. And I ain't stayin' neither.'

She made no move to stop him. Just watched as betrayed by weakness he crashed to the rug-covered floor. Banged and bashed about finding his feet. Staggered to the bedroom door. Grabbed its handle. Wrenched it open—

'Hello, Asher,' said Dathne. Smiling. Shaking. 'Please don't go yet. We've a lot to talk about.'

* * *

After hours on the road the elderly donkey was exhausted, so they climbed from the cart and walked for a while. Matt kept to the poor beast's head, guiding its tottering footsteps along the rutted roadway. Gar and Darran followed behind. It was the dark of the moon and the starlight was faint. Close ahead of them were the Black Woods and the mountains. This near to the Wall there should be a glorious wash of gold to help them find their way, but . . .

Cold, hungry, plagued with blisters and longing for this journey to end, Gar looked around. Apart from themselves the road was empty; it should be safe to speak. 'Are my eyes playing tricks, Matt, or does it seem to you the Wall has . . . faded?'

Matt's voice floated back to him out of the dark. 'No tricks. If what you say is true – if Morg is really among us – then it's my belief he's working to bring down the Wall from inside the kingdom.'

Envy prickled. Matt had already explained his peculiar sensitivities. His . . . magic. It was all he'd explained; up till now the journey had been conducted almost in silence. 'You can feel that?'

'I can. Now, Gar, it's best we hold our tongues. Sound travels easier than we do, this time of night.'

Beside him Darran bristled, deeply disapproving of his prince's instruction that Matt abandon formality and get used to calling him 'Gar'. He chewed at his lip for a moment, debating. But it had to be said . . . before they reached their destination, which promised little relaxation. Now seemed as good a time as any.

He lowered his voice. 'You lied to me, Darran.'

Limping just a little, likely nursing blisters of his own, Darran kept his gaze pinned to the road. 'I'm sure I never did, sir.'

'Don't make it worse, Darran. You lied. Asher doesn't forgive me. He hates me. I think he'd kill me if he could.'

A fraught pause, then Darran rallied. 'His Highness is mistaken. I distinctly recall—'

He raised a finger. '*Don't.* Not if you truly love me.'

Silence, save for the creaking of the cart's wheels, the thudding of their feet onto the road's packed clay and the donkey's laboured breathing.

'I only sought to ease your pain, sir,' said Darran eventually, harshly whispering. 'Asher was about to die, I saw no harm in—'

'I know why you did it,' he said, biting back impatience. 'And I'm grateful that you care. But it doesn't change the truth. Asher trusted me and I betrayed him to his death. He hates me for that . . . and I can't say I blame him.'

'Well, I can!' said Darran, indignant. 'You did what you had to, what any king would—'

'Exactly. I acted like a king . . . but what Asher needed was a friend.'

'You've been a friend without peer, sir! He was a nothing, a nobody, when he came to Dorana!'

Gar shook his head. 'And now he's a fugitive, destined for death if he's discovered, and all because of me. I swore on my life I'd protect him, Darran, and instead of keeping my word I abandoned him. I just pray that when we see him again he'll not let his hatred of me stand in the way of helping us against Conr – Morg.'

'He won't,' said Matt from the gloom ahead. 'He might hate you but when he hears what you've got to say, he'll do what's needful. What's right.'

'How can you be so sure?' he said, shivering.

'Because he's the Innocent Mage.'

He frowned. 'And what *is* that, exactly, Matt? I think

it's time you told me what's going on. You do know, don't you?'

Darkly silhouetted, Matt nodded. 'I do.'

'In the guardhouse you mentioned a circle. What did you mean?'

'I meant I'm not alone,' said Matt. 'Me, Dathne, the folk who helped save Asher – we're magicians. Not like the Doranen. Our magic's different. But we have a power, like your people do. We're joined in secrecy and silence, bound to serve Prophecy and Asher. The Innocent Mage.'

'And does Asher know this?'

'He didn't, but I'd say there's a good chance he does by now. By now he likely knows everything.'

When last Gar saw him, Asher was kneeling with his head on a block, waiting for a sharpened axe to fall. Remembering that stark, cruel moment he felt his bowels constrict. What would happen when Asher came face to face with the architect of his torment and near destruction?

Matt seemed certain he'd forgive and forget. For himself, he wasn't anywhere close to confident. He had his own suspicions and they threatened to drop him where he walked.

He increased his pace till he fell into step beside his former stable meister. 'I think, Matt,' he said, letting his concern show, making it an order and not a request, 'that if we want to make sure Asher's with us, not against us, it's time I knew everything too.'

# CHAPTER THIRTY-TWO

Bundled back into the saggy single bed by that bossy Veira, Asher stared at Dathne as though she were a ghost. Nasty suspicions were stirring in his mind. Roiling in his belly.

It didn't help she was having trouble meeting his eyes.

'Dath?' he said softly, willing her to look at him. 'Dath, what are you doin' here? What's goin' on?'

Still she kept her gaze pinned to the floor. Now a lamp was lit and he could see her clearly. She looked frightened. He'd never seen her frightened before. Angry. Impatient. Uncertain. But never rigid with fear like this. She stood with her back pressed hard to the closed bedchamber door, her fingers fisted by her sides.

Retreated to the bedroom's shadows, Veira sat like a pile of laundry in a ratty overstuffed armchair shoved in a corner and watched them.

He ignored her. 'Dath – *talk* to me. How did I get here? Who's this Veira and what's she to you? To me? *Tell* me!'

In her dark corner, the old woman stirred. 'Well, child, you started this. Seems to me you should finish it.'

Dathne looked up. Her eyes were enormous. 'Asher, do you love me?'

He scowled. 'I married you, didn't I? Though it's startin' to look like I made a mistake.'

She flinched as though he'd struck her. In a way he had. He didn't care. If she was frightened, he was terrified.

'I've a story to tell you, Asher.' Her voice was a whisper. 'Will you promise to listen, not judging, till you know all the facts?'

It was the first of Tevit's Principles of Jurisprudence. Anger burned him. Did she think it was *funny*, throwing Justice Hall in his face now? After everything he'd been through?

She saw her error. Reached out to him, alarmed. 'Please, Asher! Listen! You'll understand everything by the time I'm done.'

'Understand what I'm doin' here? What *you're* doin' here? How I escaped, and how *she* can do *magic*?'

Dathne crept to the chair beside the bed and slid into it. Looked where he was pointing, at the silently watchful old woman, and nodded. 'Everything. I promise.'

'Dathne . . .' He felt sick, his heart was beating so hard. 'Can *you* do magic?'

Tears flooded her eyes. Overflowed down her cheeks. 'I couldn't tell you, any more than you could tell me. Secrecy was the only thing that saved us. Remember that, before you judge me.'

She could do magic. Everything about her was a lie. He turned his face away. 'Reckon I'd rather forget.'

'You can't. You mustn't. Or the kingdom will fall into chaos and nothing you love will survive.'

Without another word spoken he knew what went

on here was dangerous. Madness. Worse than anything Gar had tricked him into. He didn't want to know more. Wished almost he was dead, his head and his body in two separate pieces. Fed to the dogs, as Jarralt had promised.

*Jarralt.*

As always, Dathne read him. 'You're safe, Asher. I promise. No one's hunting you. Conroyd Jarralt believes you're dead.'

Still he couldn't look at her. 'He'd need a body for that.'

'He's got one.'

Now he looked. 'You *murdered* someone?'

'Jarralt's the murderer, not Dathne,' said Veira from the shadows. 'Rafel was one of us. He gave his life willingly, because it was needful. And his birthright.'

He kept his gaze pinned to Dathne. 'So all this is part of a plan?'

She nodded. 'Yes. One set in motion centuries before either of us were born.'

'And me? What am I?'

She sat a little straighter in her chair. Unclenched her fingers and laid them softly on her knees. 'You are the Innocent Mage, Asher. Born to save the Kingdom from blood and fire.'

He couldn't answer. Could only lie there and stare at this woman, this stranger. Had he kissed her? Had he *married* her? He'd never seen her before in his life.

'I know this is difficult,' she said. 'It's not easy for me either. Things happened I should've . . . prevented.'

'Like spreading your legs for me?'

She blanched. 'Like falling in love.'

'Is *that* what you call it?' he said, and laughed. His stomach was full of acid, churning.

She turned her face from him. 'Matt warned me this would happen. I was a fool not to listen.'

'*Matt* warned—' He struggled to sit up. '*Matt's* a part of this?'

'We're all of us a part of it, child,' said Veira from the darkness. 'Whether we know it or don't. What's coming comes to everyone trapped behind the mountains. And unless we work together, no matter our pride and hurt feelings, the thing that's coming will kill every last one of us. Is that what you want on your conscience?'

'I don't know what you're talkin' about! I don't know what you *mean*!'

'Then let me tell you,' said Dathne. 'Forget what hurts I've done you and just listen to the words. I swear they're true.'

All the wounded places in his body were awake again, and burning. His head pounded. He wanted to flee but his legs were too weak. He was pinned beneath the blankets, captive. As he'd been captive one way or another all his damned life.

'Have I got a choice?' he said bitterly.

Veira answered him. 'Always, child. We can't compel you to do what's right.'

No, they bloody couldn't. They couldn't compel him to do *anything*, magic or no magic, and woe to them if they bloody well tried. He had a little magic of his own. As for right and wrong – Dathne had a hide to think she could give him a lecture on *that*. All these secrets . . . the people in his life he'd trusted, leaned on . . . and *none* of them what he'd thought they were.

Veira said, quite kindly, 'Your pricked pride is the least of our worries, child. Hear Dathne out then tell me we were wrong.'

Pricked pride? Pricked *pride*? He nearly flung the words back in her face, came close to kicking aside the blankets and getting out of there, no matter if it meant crawling on hands and knees . . . but curiosity won over outrage, just.

'Fine,' he grunted, and folded his arms. 'I'm listenin'.'

The Doranen who came over the mountains six centuries ago were nothing like the Doranen he knew today, Dathne told him. Those Doranen were a bright and brittle people, weary and battle-scarred and desperate for peace. Their magic was a thing of violence. With it they called nightmares out of hiding and gave them life, gave them teeth to bite and talons to tear. Flattened buildings. Razed whole towns. Slaughtered thousands. They were warriors. And in their eyes were memories of the homeland they'd left behind them. Memories of carnage, and what it had cost them to escape.

Led by a young woman named Barl, they'd fled their war-torn Dorana in terror, crossing countless miles of country burying loved ones as they came. Confronted by the mountains they'd not turned back but instead clawed their way over them and down into Lur. And there found the safe harbour for which they'd long been searching.

They had no intention of giving it up. Of struggling back over the mountains, losing even more of their friends and family on the way, so they might die in the monstrous mage war they'd so narrowly, so dearly, escaped. No matter that this new land wasn't theirs to take. No matter it already had inhabitants who loved it. They were a race for whom wanting became having without a second thought. And they wanted Lur.

The people they found here called themselves Olken.

They were a gentle race with magic of their own, an earthbound power tying them to the land, to green and growing things. To the ebb and flow of natural energies. They lived in loosely allied independent communities scattered from coast to coast, with no central government, no king or queen. They had no hope of defeating the warrior Doranen. No chance of resisting the lure of Doranen magic. It was splendid. Miraculous. There was nothing it couldn't do. It even let the Olken understand the beautiful invaders, and be understood in return.

Not long after her people's arrival Barl gathered all the Olken community leaders together and explained about the conflict in her homeland, about Morg, and how defenceless they were against him . . . how he would not rest till he found her and her people and punished them for fleeing, and then take every Olken as a slave, or worse . . .

It so happened that in that time the Olken people were suffering. Drought and famine gripped their land and not even their strongest earth-singers could save them. Barl saw their dilemma and made them a glittering offer. Share their homeland with the Doranen – abandon their meagre magics and any memory of them – and she would create a paradise safe not only from Morg but from all the natural sufferings their earthbound lives were prey to. The Olken and Doranen would live together in perfect harmony, perfect peace, safe, secure and prosperous, hidden from the rest of the world beyond the mountains, until the end of time.

Dathne stopped talking. The room was so quiet Asher thought he could hear the spiders breathing. 'This ain't the story my ma told me when I were a spratling.'

She nodded. 'It wasn't. That story was . . . a lie.'

'But you know the truth?' he sneered. 'How, if the Olken agreed to forget it? Or is this just another lie, made up to get you what you want? From me.'

He could see his words hurt her, and was glad. He'd meant them to.

'One Olken voice spoke out against the bargain,' she continued, her hands folded tightly in her lap. Her eyes were bright in the dim lighting. 'His name was Jervale and I am his last living heir. Inheritor of his visions and the prophecy they foretold.'

Jervale was known in his own small community as something of a seer. A man whose dreams had the knack of coming true. As a small boy he'd had visions of a golden-haired people who'd bring the Olken to ruin. He didn't know who they were or when they'd come or what form that ruin would take. Years passed, he grew up, and the visions faded from memory.

Then the Doranen came, and with them returned his foreboding dreams. They told him the heart of the sweet fruit they offered was rotten . . . and that one day it would lead to his people's death.

'Jervale tried to warn the Olken elders but they were too Doranen-dazzled to listen,' Dathne said. She sounded sad, regretful. 'They didn't know him, or have reason to trust in his prophecies. In this prophecy, the most important of all. With children dying of hunger and thirst the Doranen were the answer to our prayers, or so it seemed.'

'Seemed?' he said. 'Sounds like they were, if folks were starvin' to death! Sounds to me like your precious Jervale didn't give a fart about that?'

'Of course he did! But he could see further than a season's shortage of food. He knew Barl was right: something dark and dreadful *did* lurk beyond the barrier of mountains. And he knew this, too. That for all their fearsome magic the Doranen would not be able to stand against it. Somehow *Olken* magic would have a part to play in protecting Lur. One day an Olken would be born whose destiny was to save us all in the Final Days. He named him the Innocent Mage.'

He stared at her, unconvinced. 'And you reckon that's me?'

She nodded. 'Yes. You are Prophecy's child, Asher. Born to save the world as Jervale foretold.'

Born to save the world? *Him*? It sounded so ridiculous he was hard-put not to laugh out loud. But he didn't, because her expression was so serious. Clearly she believed every word she'd said and right now he was at her mercy. One word in the wrong ear from her or the old woman in the corner and he'd be back on his knees before the chopping block. Besides, there were still things he wanted – needed – to know.

'And what about you?' he said. 'How do you come into this, eh?'

She glanced at Veira then rested her gaze on the foot of his bed. 'I am Jervale's Heir, his descendant, inheritor of his visions and knowledge. I've dreamed you most of my life, Asher. Knew you for who and what you are long before we met.'

Dreamed him? *Knew* him? Oh, he didn't like the sound of that. Didn't like it at *all*. 'And Matt?' He pointed at the old woman, brooding in her corner. 'Her? How do *they* fit in with your precious prophecies?'

Now her fingers laced themselves together to still their trembling. And well she should tremble, too. What she'd *done* . . .

'When he realised his warnings would not be heeded, Jervale went home and gathered to him his closest friends,' she said. 'Those who knew his visions could be trusted and believed his prophecy would come true. Together they swore an oath to hold the Olken's magical heritage in sacred trust, generation after generation, until the Innocent Mage was born and needed Olken magicians to stand with him in the Final Days. Together they devised a way to protect themselves from the Doranen's purge. They called themselves the Circle. Veira, Matt and I are all of the Circle. There are others, scattered throughout the kingdom, but only Veira knows who they are. Like me they are descended from the Olken of Barl's time. Like me, they've lived their lives with only one purpose: to defeat the evil that will come in the Final Days. That *has* come, Asher. The Final Days are upon us now.'

He shook his head, rejecting her and everything she'd said. Prophecies. Visions. Secret societies of Olken magicians. It was crazy. *Crazy*. 'You're mad,' he said, scathing. 'Stark staring moonstruck. You expect me to *believe—*'

'You have to believe it!' she cried. 'Every word is the truth!'

'The *truth*?' Scalded with sudden fury he kicked back his blankets and lunged off the bed at her, seizing the arms of her chair and prisoning her in it. 'You wouldn't know the truth if it bit you on the arse! You been lyin' to me since the day I turned up in Dorana!'

Despite his rage, she didn't shrink back. 'No, I haven't! Withholding information isn't telling lies. I was *protecting* you, Asher!'

'Protecting me?' he said, incredulous. 'From what?'

'From accident! From yourself!'

He leaned even closer, till he could feel her panting breath on his cheeks. 'The only danger I been in is from *you*. You should've found someone to protect me from *you*, Dathne.'

'That's not fair!' she cried. 'You were *never* in danger from me!'

He flung himself sideways and half rolled, half staggered to his feet. 'Of course I bloody was!' He could see it all, now; how she'd duped him, dudded him, played him like a puppet. 'You arranged everything, didn't you? I don't know how, but you did. Me savin' Gar's horse that mornin' in the market. Him thinkin' I was right to be his assistant. You practically *dared* me to take the job, when I knew in my guts I shouldn't! Was it you made him think of me in the first place, one day when you were sellin' him a book? It was, wasn't it? For why, Dathne?' He pulled down the neck of his borrowed nightshirt, baring burned flesh to the light. 'For *this*?'

She stretched out an imploring hand. 'No, no, of course not! I never *dreamed* you'd come so close to dying!'

He stepped back. The touch of her now would make him vomit. 'I don't believe you.' A cold thought struck him, then. 'How much does Gar know? Are you in bed with him too? Did you dream this up together, you and him, with the sweat of your futtering still wet on your skin?'

Tears streaming, she leapt to her feet. '*No*! How can you say so? How can you *think* it?'

Another thought, colder still. He made himself look in her face. '*Timon Spake*.'

Bewildered, smearing those pouring tears, she shook her head. 'What?'

'They caught him trying to do magic!' he shouted. 'Was he one of yours? Was he part of your precious Circle?'

As Dathne struggled for words – for lies – Veira

answered. 'He was, child. A good boy, Timon, but foolish.'

He turned on her. 'And you didn't save him? You let him *die*?'

The old woman stood and came forward into the light. 'We couldn't save him. Timon knew that. He died with courage, and will be remembered.'

Courage. That poor sickly boy, and all the blood in him, spilling. He stared at Dathne. 'He was never your cousin. That was another lie.'

Her stricken gaze flicked to Veira, and back. 'Forget Timon. Timon's dead. We must—'

'Why'd you bully me to let you see him, Dathne? What was so important?'

Veira took a small step closer. 'What's he talking of, child? When did you see Timon?'

'Beforehand. Briefly,' said Dathne. 'But that's in the past. Asher, *listen*—'

And now he understood. 'You were scared he'd talk out of turn. You thought he'd betray you.' His breath caught hard in his aching throat. 'What was in them cakes you took him?'

'Cakes?' said Veira, frowning. 'You made no mention of cakes, child.'

'They were nothing,' said Dathne. 'Nothing that matters anymore.'

No, they were something. The memory was there in her dark brown eyes. Eyes he thought had looked on him with love. His belly cramped, rejecting. 'They were poisoned. Weren't they?'

'Poisoned?' Veira echoed. 'Child, is that true?'

'Damn you, Asher!' cried Dathne, and turned to the old woman. 'I'm *sorry*, I *had* to! I couldn't trust he'd keep the faith and stay silent!'

He was so sickened now he could hardly see straight. 'But Spake did. You were wrong about him, Dathne, and you're wrong about me. I ain't your Innocent Mage. I'm a fool as was diddled by sweet talk and lies. Yours. Matt's. Gar's. Everyone's.'

'No, no,' said Dathne, breathless. 'Please believe me. I love you. We need you. You're Prophecy's fulfilment, this kingdom's only hope!'

She reached out her hand to touch him and he knocked it away. Knocked her sideways as the power inside him drew breath like a dragon and threatened to set him on fire.

'Get away from me, bitch! Get her out of here, old woman, or I won't be responsible. Get out, get *out*!'

The magic ignited. Burst from eyes, mouth and fingers in a roar of burning snow and flaming rain. He let it consume him . . . didn't care if it killed him. Or Dathne, or Veira.

Didn't care about anything.

Sobbing, Dathne let herself be pushed through the cottage and into the kitchen. She heard the door slam shut and felt Veira's hand press her into a chair.

'We . . . we . . . have to go back to him. We have to *stop* him!'

'He'll stop himself soon enough,' said Veira, filling the kettle. 'Best he gets it out of his system before we try another sensible conversation. I've dampened the bedroom, child. He'll do it no damage.'

She hiccuped, struggling for self-control. 'Dampened it? When?'

'While you were talking.'

'You expected this?'

'A tantrum?' Nodding, Veira put the kettle on the

stove top then opened the stove's front to rouse the coals with a poker. 'Of course. Didn't you?'

'It's more than a tantrum! That's not a fair word. He's angry, Veira, and he's every right to be. I did deceive him. In a way, I did lie.'

Veira sniffed. 'You did your duty as Jervale's Heir.'

'He doesn't think so,' she whispered.

'He will, in time.'

She felt her eyes fill again. 'He called me a bitch.'

'And so you are,' said Veira tartly. 'And so am I. You think this a business for gentle folk?'

She held Veira's challenging gaze for a moment, then looked away. 'I'm sorry about Timon Spake. If there hadn't been an accident – the cakes ruined – I'd have told you what I did.'

Veira shrugged. 'As you say, child. It's in the past. And after Rafel, who am I to judge you?'

On the stove top the kettle bubbled, burping steam. Veira set out mugs and milk and frowned at the almost empty jug. 'First thing in the morning you could make yourself useful, if you like, and wander along to the village. Get me more milk, since I'm almost out and we've got company coming.'

Oh, yes. Incredibly, she'd forgotten. Matt, and Gar, and Darran. Would they be here soon? She hoped so. 'Why don't you keep a cow? Or a goat?'

''Cause there's only me, that's why,' said Veira, adding tea leaves to the pot. 'And my few cuicks help the milkman. Will you go? I'll give you directions. It's easy enough to find.'

She nodded. 'Trying to keep me out of Asher's way?'

'I think it's advisable,' said Veira, making the tea. 'For the next little while at least. You can bring back more bacon too. Maybe some ham. There's carrots and greens in the garden and a big jar of pickled cabbage. Lots of eggs. I think provisions will stretch.'

She took the mug that Veira offered, 'Won't the villagers be curious about me?'

'Curious, yes. Rude, no,' said Veira, smiling briefly. 'Tell them you're my niece come to visit, that'll answer.'

The tea was hot and sweet, a welcome relief to the cold lump in her middle. *Asher*. She swallowed greedily, not caring that it burned. 'Will it be much longer, do you think? Before the absolute end?'

Veira blew on her own tea, brow furrowed with thought. 'No,' she said at last. 'Not too much longer.'

It was what she thought herself. Didn't know whether hearing the suspicion confirmed made matters better or worse.

'So what now?'

'Now, child, we'll have us some supper. Then you can go to bed and I'll sit up for Asher. And tomorrow will bring us what it brings.'

She wasn't hungry or tired but there was nothing else to do. She even managed to doze a little. She heard no alarm from Veira's bedroom. Its door opened and closed three times, and she caught the merest murmur of voices, but no one called for her to come. Asher stayed safely within.

At first light she rose, bathed, dressed and saw to the livestock. The chickens cackled, the pigs snorted, the raw-boned horses snatched for their hay.

Well. At least someone was glad to see her.

She heard the cottage's back door bang and put her head round the corner of the stable. Asher. He was dressed in drab brown jacket and trews Veira must have had stored or brought with her from the City. Grim-faced, he strode across the back yard, kicked open the gate to the forest and kept on walking. She almost ran after him, shouting. The Black Woods were dangerous. There were bears. Wolves. People. He shouldn't go in there alone . . .

The kitchen door opened again. Veira stood in the doorway and watched the forest's shadows swallow him. Said nothing as he disappeared among the mossy tree trunks. She was calm and quiet. Peaceful, almost. As though she'd reached a place of balance and was happy to stay there for a while. Dathne held her breath, half hoping Veira saw her, half hoping that she didn't.

She did. Nodded, acknowledging, then went back inside. Dathne sighed and followed her.

'Is he all right?'

Close to, Veira looked exhausted. Slumped in a chair, head propped in her hands with her silver hair all whichway, she nodded. 'Right enough. And will be better, by and by. He needs more time alone.'

'He won't run?'

Veira snorted. 'Run where? We're his only haven and he knows it. Make us breakfast, will you, child? I'm almost too weary for breathing.'

She cooked them eggs with cream and dill. Settled Veira in the sitting room with tea and a blanket, then went on her little trip to the village. It was surprisingly pleasant, marching through the forest with only a basket for company. A little balm for her lacerated soul. The air was fresh and clean, scented with pine. Unseen birds whistled and called, sounding cheerful. She kept one eye out for Asher but didn't see him. Finding the little forest community without mishap, she told all who asked that she was Veira's niece. As Veira predicted, they seemed happy with that. Gladly they sold her milk and meat and gave her a jar of honey in welcome.

She felt like a fraud, accepting.

Walking back was a slower affair; the provision-filled basket was heavy. There was still no sign of Asher. As she reached the cottage gate she paused and stared down the road, hopeful but not expecting—

Someone was coming towards her. Several someones. And a donkey. And a cart.

She dropped the basket and ran.

'Matt! *Matt*!'

Startled, he jogged to meet her halfway. 'Dathne, Dathne, what's amiss?'

She held him like a long-lost sweetheart, hugging his ribs to breaking. Cradled his hurt face gently in her hands and scolded him without mercy.

'I'm all right, I'm all right!' he soothed her, alarm and pleasure mingled. 'Is Asher here? Is he all right?'

'Yes.' It was all she dared to say.

Matt looked into her face and sighed. 'You told him.'

'Yes.'

'And now he's angry.'

She saw again that terrifying torrent of magic. 'Very. I know . . . I know . . . you warned me.'

A tentatively cleared throat turned her head. It was Gar, looking fragile. She hadn't even seen him. She stepped back from Matt and managed a half-hearted curtsey. 'I'm sorry, sir. Your Highness.'

He shook his head, faintly smiling. 'Gar.'

'And Darran,' she added, nodding at the old gentleman as he leaned against the rickety donkey cart. 'Forgive me. You both must be exhausted. Come inside. Veira will want to—'

The cottage's front door opened. 'Greet her visitors,' said Veira, and joined them. She kissed Matt's cheek and touched a finger to his bruised, rubbed throat.

'Welcome back, Matthias. You're a little the worse for wear.' Looking Gar up and down she added, 'And you'll be our late king's son, then?'

Gar nodded. 'At your service, Veira. Matt's told me all about you.'

'Well,' the old woman said, lips pursed, 'not *all* about me, I'm guessing.' She turned to Darran. 'And who might you be?'

Darran managed a tottery bow. 'His Highness's secretary, madam. Good morning.'

'This is Darran,' said Gar. 'A dear, dear friend, and all that's left of my family.'

As Darran choked back unseemly emotion, Veira again considered Gar with a narrow gaze. 'And why have you come here? To hide? If so, you're doomed to disappointment. There'll be no hiding for anyone in the long dark days ahead.'

Gar met her appraisal unflinching.

'I've come to help,' he said. 'And also . . . to make amends.'

Veira reached out and laid her palm against his pale thin cheek. Stared deep into his eyes. 'Good. For you've a lot you can do and much to be sorry for.'

Matt cleared his throat. 'Not that much. Gar helped me escape the guardhouse. Darran, too, and Captain Orrick.'

'Orrick?' said Dathne, startled.

Matt's smile was tired. 'It's a long story. I'll tell it properly later. After I've spoken with Asher.'

'I don't think that's wise. He's angry with you too, Matt. He knows you've a part in the Circle, and all that's happened.'

Veira closed a warning hand about her wrist. 'You'll find him in the woods yonder, Matthias,' she said, pointing behind the cottage. 'Working out a thing or two on his lonesome. Might be he could use some company round about now. He's had a tricky night.'

Matt nodded. 'I heard. I also heard he's—'

'Aggravated?' said Veira, eyebrows raised. 'It's not surprising. A man has a right to be aggravated when he learns last of all he's born to save a kingdom. We'll see you inside directly, child. Dathne, tend to the donkey.'

As Veira ushered the prince and his secretary into the cottage, Dathne rolled her eyes at Matt. 'I think she and Asher spent half the night talking.'

'Well, he has been hardly done by, Dath,' said Matt, determined to be reasonable. 'He had his head on the axeman's block before we saved him. That'd give any man pause.'

She winced. 'I know.'

He dropped an unexpected kiss on the crown of her head. 'Go coddle the donkey, Dath. I'll see you inside, by and by.'

Unwilling to let him go, she twisted her fingers in his shirt front. 'Be careful, Matt, please. He really is angry – and there's a power in him you can't imagine.'

He kissed her again, this time on the cheek. 'I'll be fine. Stop fratching.'

And he walked away, without looking back.

Slumped at the foot of a twisted honey-pine, aching and hollow, thrumming still, hours later, with the echoing remnants of power, Asher heard footsteps approaching and scowled. If he had to hear one more story about dear young Rafel he was going to puke. Or worse, do someone a mischief.

'Piss off, ole woman,' he said unkindly. 'After listenin' to you jaw at me all last night my bloody ears have gone numb. I ain't interested in anythin' else you got to say.'

'That's a fine greeting for a friend,' said a hurtfully familiar voice. One that once would've been welcome. 'If I am a friend. If you're willing to forgive me.'

He scrambled to his feet. Felt his hands clench into fists, and didn't unclench them. 'Matt.'

The stable meister looked terrible. Hollow eyes, sunken and bruised-looking. Charred patches on his face and a livid purple bruise around his throat. He stood at a distance, a little worried. A little wary.

As he should be.

'I hear you're feeling . . . aggravated.'

He smiled unpleasantly. 'You might say that. You might say aggravated don't even come close.'

'I don't blame you,' said Matt. His battered face was sympathetic.

He sneered. 'That's right generous of you.'

Sighing, Matt slipped his hands in his pockets. 'I wanted to tell you months ago, Asher. I wasn't permitted. If I say now I'm sorry, will it make a difference?'

'What's the point? Sorry won't undo what's done.'

'You're right. It won't,' Matt agreed. Hesitated, then took two steps closer. 'But neither will sulking out here in the woods. You are what you are, Asher. I didn't make you a mage. Neither did Dathne, or Veira, or anyone else. It's what you were born. What Prophecy meant you to be. Needs you to be.'

'I reckon,' he said conversationally, 'if one more person says the word "prophecy" where I can hear it they're goin' to be bloody sorry.'

Matt's lips quirked into something near to a smile. 'I can understand that.'

Bastard. Matt was talking the way he used to talk to

fractious yearlings. Calm. Gentle. Soothing. Any minute now he'd reach out a hand to pat him on the bloody forehead . . .

Asher folded his arms across his chest. 'So. Everything those bitches told me. Magic and history and dreams. What I was born for. You reckon it's true, do you?'

Matt frowned. 'Don't call them bitches.'

'*Is it true*?'

'Yes.'

But then, he knew that already. He'd felt the rightness of Dathne's fantastic tale humming in his blood and bones, even as he'd rejected it. Veira had told the truth too, talking gently and softly throughout the long night. But it had taken him till now to admit it.

*Sink* the truth.

'I could walk away,' he said, belligerent. Daring Matt to contradict him.

Matt nodded. 'You could.'

'I could walk away right now and no one could stop me. Not you, not Dathne. No one.' He bared his teeth in a Conroyd smile. 'I'm a man of power, Matt. I could burn you with a *look*.'

'I know it,' said Matt, unmoving. 'I felt the change when that power woke within you. Like a thousand roaring furnaces devouring a million trees, it was. You could burn this whole kingdom with a look, if that's what you want. Is it?'

'*I want to be left alone*!'

Matt sighed. 'To do what? Go where? There's nowhere to go, Asher. For better or worse, this kingdom's all we have. And unless you do what you were born to do we won't even have that.'

Asher raised a hand above his head, despairing. 'I'll tell you what I *don't* want, Matt! *I don't want this*!'

A thin stream of fire poured out of his fingers and flamed into the sky, singeing the honey-pine's fragrant foliage. Birds rattled upwards in a panic, screeching. Raggedly panting, not knowing how he knew it, knowing only that he could, he pulled the power back into himself. Slowly lowered his arm and stepped sideways to sag against the honey-pine's crooked trunk. His heart pounded and his blood burned. He spread out his fingers and looked at his hand. His shaking *magician's* hand.

*I used to be a fisherman.*

Matt was staring at him, wide-eyed but unflinching. Asher scowled. 'So what happened to your throat?'

For the first time Matt looked uncomfortable. 'In the chaos after your rescue, I was taken. I . . . tried to hang myself.'

'*Hang* yourself?'

Matt shrugged. 'Jarralt was coming to question me. I was afraid I'd talk. Tell him everything. Endanger you.'

'*Jarralt.*' He felt his fingers clench to fists. 'I want to kill that bastard, Matt, with my two bare hands. I want his bones for *toothpicks*!'

Matt's lips twisted in a wry smile. 'Stand in line.'

'How'd you escape him?'

'Pellen Orrick helped me.'

*Orrick*. Another name with spikes in. 'That bastard.'

'He knows now he was hoodwinked,' said Matt. 'I owe him my life, Asher. Don't judge him too harshly. He didn't have all the facts.'

*Facts*. 'So he's on your side now?'

'Our side. Yes.'

He pulled a face. 'Who says there's an "our side", Matt? Who says I'm goin' to join you? You savin' my life don't mean I aim to join you!'

Matt dragged a dirty hand across his unshaven face, wincing as calluses scraped burned and blistered skin. 'Look, Asher, I wish there was time for you to think on this,' he said impatiently. 'I wish there was time for a lot of things. But there isn't. You can't see it here, we're too deep into the Black Woods, but you can see it from the road leading in and elsewhere in the kingdom.'

'See what?' he said roughly. 'What are you on about now?'

Matt looked up, as though his gaze could pierce the forest's ceiling. 'The Wall,' he said. The faintest tremor was in his voice and his expression was bleak. 'Asher, the Wall is falling. The Final Days are here. And without your help – without the Innocent Mage – not a man, woman or child in this kingdom stands a chance of surviving.'

# CHAPTER THIRTY-THREE

Asher stared at him, dumbfounded. 'What am I s'posed to say to that? What d'you want me to *say*?'

Gently distressed, Matt spread his hands wide. 'Honestly? That you'll do it.'

'Do *what*?'

'Accept your destiny. Fulfil Prophecy. Save us.'

'How? How am I s'posed to save you? Does your precious bloody prophecy tell me *how*?'

Now Matt looked uncomfortable. 'No. Not in so many words.'

No, of course it bloody didn't. That'd be too easy, wouldn't it? 'Then what does it say?' he asked, struggling with temper. Old Veira had tried to tell him last night but he'd refused to listen. Now, though, he thought he'd better. 'Or is the bloody thing so vague you can't even remember it?'

Matt let out a hard breath and his gaze lost focus. '"In the Final Days shall come the Innocent Mage, born to save the world from blood and death. He shall enter the House of the Usurper. He shall learn their ways. He shall earn their love. He shall lay down his life. And

Jervale's Heir shall know him, and guide him, and enlighten him not."'

'"Lay down his life"? You mean *die*?' He backed away, shaking his head. 'Matt—'

'I know, I know, but think about it,' Matt said quickly. 'In a way you've done that already.'

Sharp pain. A furious, bewildered resentment. 'Wrong. Somebody else did that.' Not that he'd ever asked for it. Not that he ever would.

'But you were about to die,' Matt insisted. 'It was intended. And you helped Gar knowing it could mean your life. If you look at it that way, Prophecy holds.'

He turned away. 'Prophecy's a crock of shit, Matt. It can mean whatever you want!'

'Then forget Prophecy and trust in your senses!' Matt urged him. 'Barl's Wall is unravelling. I can feel it. You'd feel it too, if you'd let yourself. Don't be afraid of what's inside you, Asher. Embrace it. Extend your senses and feel the world around you. You'll see I'm right. You'll feel what I feel. Do it! Now, before it's too late! Before we're all beyond saving!'

In a different lifetime, he'd called this man 'sir'. Spurred by Matt's pleading he fell back on old habits. Did as he was told. Closed his eyes and opened his mind.

Darkness, seething. Malevolent power. Stuttering light. Thrashing feebly, Barl's Wall dying . . . black rotting patches like mould, like slime, smeared across its shimmering surface . . .

Gasping, he wrenched himself free of the vision – the dreaming – whatever had snared him. That part of himself he'd never dreamed existed, and didn't want to possess.

'You see?' said Matt. 'Dathne was right. The Final Days are on us. And you're the Innocent Mage.'

*Dathne*. More anger, more pain. 'That's what she says,' he muttered. 'Take my advice, Matt. Don't go believin' everythin' you hear.'

Matt's hard horseman's hand closed about his arm and roughly pulled him around. 'Dathne was born with a destiny too,' he said fiercely. 'To carry Prophecy in her heart and mind. To deny all womanly desires, her dreams of hearth and home. To risk her life, every day, safeguarding Prophecy first and then you. And she did it willingly because she knew it was needful. Even though it hurt her. Even though she knew she was falling in love with you, and what would happen when she finally told you the truth.'

Asher broke Matt's grip and retreated. He didn't want to hear this. Didn't want Matt to stand there *defending* the bitch. She'd lied to him, made a fool of him, coaxed out his heart then cut it to ribbons.

'Something evil has entered the kingdom, Asher.' Matt's voice was quiet now, ferocity subdued, or spent. 'Something you were born to fight. That only you can fight.'

No, no, no, he didn't want to *hear* this. Not from Matt. He'd heard enough of it last night from Veira and it was all a load of ole cobblers. 'I'm a fisherman, Matt! I ain't a warrior! This evil of yours, you want me to fight it with trout guts?'

'Of course not,' said Matt, impatient. 'You'll fight it with magic.'

'You fight it with magic!' he retorted. 'You and your damned Circle! You're the ones been practisin' for the last six hundred years. Me, I ain't got the first idea what I'm doin'!'

'If we could we would, believe me,' said Matt. 'But Olken magic isn't strong enough, and none of us can wield Doranen magic. Without your help we're doomed.'

'Why does it have to be *me*?' he shouted. 'Why can't you find someone else?'

'There *is* no one else! There's only *you*! That's why you're the Innocent Mage!'

'Well, I don't want to be the Innocent Mage! I never asked for it! I've a bloody good mind to just walk away right now! Walk away and never look back!'

Matt met his gaze unflinching. 'Yes. You can walk away, Asher. I'm not strong enough to stop you. No one is. You can walk away and all of us can die. It's not fair, it's not just, but it is that simple. If you walk away, the rest of us will die.'

Badgered, cornered, backed against the wall of his inconvenient conscience, Asher stared at his blunt, square hands. Beneath the surface of his skin the power simmered. If he closed his eyes he could almost see it: a river of fire, flowing through his veins. Ever since his outburst last night his awareness of it refused to fade. He took a deep, resentful breath, and eased it out slowly. He could still feel the sticky touch of darkness, fouling his mind.

'It's askin' a lot, Matt,' he whispered. 'One man against that kind of evil. One man all on his lonesome.'

'You're not on your lonesome!' Matt said sharply. 'You've got me. Dathne. Veira. The rest of the Circle.'

He snorted. 'Thought you said Olken magic was nigh to useless?'

'I said it couldn't defeat the evil we're facing. But there's still work for us to do. All of us have sworn to aid you, Asher. We'll give our lives if that's what's needed.' Matt stepped close again, his face a riot of unhappy emotions. 'I wish there was another way. I wish we could've told you sooner. I wish you hadn't suffered what you've suffered. When this is over, if you want to punish us for lying, or deceiving, walk away then. Never speak to us again and we'll understand. But I'm begging you, Asher: don't walk away now. Not when we need you. Not when you're all that stands between us and destruction.'

Silence, as though the Black Woods was holding its breath. Deeper in, a fox barked. Once. Twice. A predator, prowling. Searching for its next kill, and all the little rabbits unsuspecting . . .

Matt was right, the bastard. It weren't fair and it weren't just. But it was simple. Maybe he was this Innocent Mage, and maybe he wasn't. That weren't really the point. At the end of the day he was his da's son, and Da had never once in his life turned away from someone in need. Wherever he was now – if he was anywhere – he'd expect his youngest to follow that example.

So he would. But that didn't mean he had to like it, or play nice.

'Wait!' Matt called after him, as he stomped away in the direction of Veira's cottage.

'Thought you said we were runnin' out of time?' he snarled over his shoulder. 'You want to get this done or don't you? Make your mind up, Matt!'

'But there's something I haven't told you, Asher! Something you need to—'

'You told me enough! Now are you bloody comin', 'cause I ain't got all day!'

After ten minutes tramping he reached Veira's clover-patched yard. Scattering chickens he marched across it to the cottage, shoved open the back door and went inside. The kitchen was empty, but he could hear voices murmuring from along the narrow corridor. He followed the sound to its source: Veira's tiny excuse for a sitting room. It was crowded with bodies. Veira. Dathne. Darran? And—

'Hello, Asher,' said Gar.

He felt smothered. Disjointed. The room was suddenly hazy with red. A voice – his voice – said thickly, 'Get him out of here.'

Behind him Matt said, 'No. Wait. You don't understand—'

'Get him out or it's *over*!'

As Veira, thunderous, opened her mouth to say something he didn't care to hear and she might well regret Gar stood, dropped the leather-bound book he was holding onto the faded carpet and tugged at his travel-stained weskit. Then he glanced at all their horrified faces.

'I'd like a moment in private with Asher.'

'I got nowt to say to you.'

Gar held his hot gaze unflinching. 'All right. Then I'll talk and you can listen.'

'Hear him out,' Matt said, his voice low. 'Please.'

The river of fire burned hotter still. It was almost sweating out of him. 'Why should I?'

'Because we need him – and he saved my life.'

He wasn't expecting that. Startled, he looked at Matt, who nodded. Something must have changed in his face then, because without a word Dathne and Veira and Darran got out of their chairs and headed for the sitting-room door. He stood aside to let them pass. Refused to meet Dathne's anxious eyes or give Darran the satisfaction of acknowledgement.

Matt nodded. 'Thank you.'

Then he was gone too, the door was closing and it

was just him and Gar. He felt sick, his vision still clouded with scarlet.

'You got two minutes,' he said. 'Then I walk out of here and you don't exist any more.'

Gar's pale lips pressed tight, then he sighed. 'You hate me. I understand that. But don't let hatred blind you to the truth. Matt's right. You need me, Asher. You won't defeat Conroyd without my help.'

'Conroyd?'

'Well . . .' Gar bent to retrieve the dropped leather-bound book and frowned at its mottled cover. 'The thing that used to be Conroyd.'

He didn't want to ask . . . he didn't want to ask . . . 'What are you bloody on about?' he asked roughly. 'What's Jarralt got to do with this?'

Gar held up the book. 'This is Barl's diary. Durm found it but didn't tell anyone. He used an incantation in it to breach the Wall. Morg was waiting on the other side. He—'

'Morg? The magician your ancestors ran away from six hundred years ago?' He laughed. 'You're crazy.'

'I know it sounds fantastic,' said Gar. 'Impossible. But it's true. He came through the breach in the Wall Durm foolishly opened and masquerades now as Conroyd Jarralt, Lur's king and WeatherWorker. I think he's the evil your prophecy spoke of.'

'It ain't *my* bloody prophecy!'

'Well, whoever it belongs to it's about to be fulfilled. The Wall is falling, Asher. Matt feels it, and I'll bet you feel it too.'

The last thing he intended to discuss with Gar was feelings. 'You're mad. How can Morg be Conroyd Jarralt? Don't you reckon someone would've *noticed*?'

'He's lived six hundred years, Asher! He's skilled

beyond imagining! And it is him. Conroyd's no longer himself, I've seen . . . changes. And Durm tried to warn me before he died. I didn't understand him then but I do now. I think Morg used him to begin with. I think he's why my family died. How I got my magic, and why it failed. Morg is behind it all.'

Asher rubbed a hand across his tired face, his stinging eyes. 'And you want me to confront him, eh? The most talented, vicious magician your people ever bred. One strong enough to survive for six centuries. Strong enough to bring down Barl's Wall, all by himself. Me. An Olken fisherman who can make it rain, at a pinch, and then has to sit around snivellin' for two hours after.' He turned for the door. 'You're out of your sinkin' mind.'

'No! Wait! I haven't finished!' said Gar, and leapt forward to clutch at his arm.

Without thought, without planning, he let the barely leashed power boil out of him. Let it rip Gar's fingers from his sleeve and smash him across the room, knocking an armchair sideways and hurling him into the wall.

Coughing, choking and running with blood, Gar staggered to his feet. 'Asher . . . please . . .'

'Don't you touch me!' he ordered, shaking with rage. 'Don't *ever* touch me!'

The sitting-room door flew open and Veira tumbled in.

'What are you doing? What's going on here?' she demanded.

'It's nothing!' Gar answered, wheezing. 'I'm all right. A misunderstanding. Please, Veira. Leave us to talk.'

'There's nowt left to say, Gar. You've had your two minutes,' he spat. 'And now you don't exist.'

Veira stood in the doorway, blocking his exit. 'What

nonsense is this? Two minutes? Pah! You'll stay here and listen for as long as need be! Until you've heard all Gar has to say!'

'I ain't interested in what he's got to say! Listenin' to him landed me in this mess to start with!'

She slapped his face. 'Prophecy landed you in this mess, child, six centuries before you were born! Were you listening last night or did I talk myself hoarse for nothing? Did my Rafel die for nothing? Prince Gar is a part of this business! He's of the Usurper's House! And you will hear him, do I make myself clear?'

Ears ringing, cheek burning, he stared at the angry old woman. 'You might want to think twice, hittin' me, since I'm the only one as can save your wrinkly hide.'

'Child, child, I'll hit you as many times as it takes to drive sense into your fool stubborn head! Don't you know we're out of time?'

Sticky with blood, his legs unsteady, Gar stepped forward. 'What do you mean, Veira? What's happened now?'

She didn't answer. Just turned on her heel and stamped along the corridor towards the kitchen end of the cottage.

'Asher,' said Gar, his hands upturned. 'We should see what she's talking about. It sounded important.'

Itching to hit Gar again, he turned on his heel and stalked after Veira. Gar's footsteps followed him, sounding uneven, as though he were hurt.

Good. Let him be hurt. He deserved a few bruises and a whole lot more.

The kitchen's back door stood open. The others were outside already, scattered about the yard. Seeking solitude, he moved over to the henhouse. Gar joined Darran by the pigpen and rested a hand on the ole crow's shoulder. Seeing the blood on him, Darran made to protest. Gar smiled and shook his head. Not dismissive but reassuring. Watching them, Asher scowled. Something had changed there. Some balance had shifted. He looked away. Good luck to 'em, the miserable bastards. They bloody deserved each other. Veira, her tatty cardigan pulled close to her body, had joined Matt and Dathne a stone's throw from the stable.

All of them, silent, stared at the sky.

The morning's blue brightness had almost disappeared. Now the air above the Black Woods was bellicose with clouds. They seemed too close to the ground, low enough nearly for a tall man to touch. Grubby white and dirty grey, they whirled and streamed and jostled like live things. With a kind of mean-spirited deliberation.

'It looks like Westwailing,' Gar said, hushed. 'Weather run amok. Power without form or purpose.'

An ominous rumble trembled the air. Birds exploded from the treetops, flapping away. The horses crammed in the stable whinnied in sudden loud fear. There was a crash as hooves kicked timber. The donkey in its little enclosure off to the side echoed their distress with a nerve-shattering bray.

Asher rubbed the prickling skin inside his shirt sleeves. 'The Weather Magic's unravelling. The threads binding it to the earth, the mountains, are comin' undone.'

Dathne turned. 'You can feel that?'

He kept his gaze pinned to the curdling clouds. The unwanted knowledge inside him, transferred from the Weather Orb to that secret place in his mind, was chiming loud alarms. Setting his teeth on edge. It was like standing on the headlands watching a bad storm roll in over Dragonteeth Reef: the air alive with lightning, with wildness. Contemptuous of kings and their magics. Determined to lash without mercy.

It was just like that . . . only a thousand times worse.

He looked at Matt. 'This is just the beginning, I reckon.'

Another rumble of thunder, louder this time. This time the ground beneath their feet grumbled a reply. Matt clapped his hands to his head, groaning. Asher closed his eyes. Letting his woken instincts guide him he stretched his mysterious senses into the air. What he found there made him gag. It was worse now than it had been in the woods. The world around him smelled rotten. Rank and putrid, like a carcass blown with maggots.

He opened his eyes. Spat sour saliva onto the grass. 'I can stop this, maybe. I got the Weather Magic in me. I could fight it, stitch up the worst holes, buy us some time—'

'No!' said Gar, alarmed. 'Don't you understand? Morg will sense it. He'll know you're alive. The only way to stop this is to stop him. Kill him. And quickly, before it's too late. Before the land tears itself to pieces. The Westwailing storm will be nothing, *nothing*, compared with what's coming.'

'Aye, well, you'd know,' Asher drawled. 'Bein' a cripple and all.'

'How dare you!' shouted Darran, pushing forward. 'Ungrateful peasant! After everything he risked coming here to you! Endangering his life! Walking for miles! Just to bring that wretched diary where it might do the most good!'

'Good? What's it good for, Darran? Arse-wipin'? Or maybe I should throw it at Jarralt. Could be it'll knock him arse over eyeballs and dash out his brains. Maybe that's what it's good for!'

Lifting a placating hand at Darran, Gar answered. 'It's good for more than that, Asher. You didn't let me finish, inside. Barl's diary is full of spells. Incantations. Weapons of war that can bring Morg down. And I can teach them to you.'

Asher laughed. '*You* can?'

'All right then,' said Gar, flushing. 'Perhaps "teach" is the wrong word. I can translate them. Explain them. Show you in theory how they're performed. I was a magician, Asher, if only briefly. I've not forgotten everything yet. If your friends here are right about you, that might work. You're strong enough to use the Weather Magics, after all. You might be strong enough for this.'

'He is,' said Veira bleakly. 'He has to be. Else Prophecy's misled us and all that's left is death.'

'Prophecy hasn't misled us!' said Dathne, angry. 'Don't you dare lose faith, Veira. You're the Circle Guardian. You don't have the right to lose faith.' She turned to Gar. 'These war spells. How long will it take you to translate them? How fast can they be learned?'

Gar shrugged. 'Learning them's up to Asher. As for the translations, I'll need at least a day. The language they're written in is archaic and complicated. I think Barl used some kind of verbal trickery, in case the wrong person chanced to read them.'

'What does that mean?' said Veira. 'Is there danger?'

'Not to me,' said Gar, pulling a face. 'I no longer have the means to activate the incantations. But if I mistranslate them and Asher tries to use them . . . well. It might get very . . . messy.'

He snorted. 'Wouldn't be the first time you tried to kill me.'

Veira turned on him. 'Stop that! Is there time for your petty bickering when we stand beneath a sky like *that*?' She jabbed a pointed finger upwards, and they tilted their heads to look.

The thickening clouds had darkened like a bruise, sickly green and purple. Some were turned scarlet, like blood blisters. As they stared, silenced, scattered drops of rain plummeted groundwards, stinking of sulphur. Stinging where they struck exposed flesh.

'Time to get organised,' said Veira, and made shooing motions towards the cottage. 'Matt, get that donkey undercover then see to making those horses and the wagon as roadworthy and weatherproof as possible. I should have enough canvas and timber tucked away in the shed there for the makings of a wagon cover. Dathne, set to work in the kitchen preparing provisions. We'll be heading back to the City soon.'

'The City?' he said. 'Why go back to the City?'

'Because that's where Morg is,' Veira answered. 'That's where you must confront him.' She turned away. 'Darran, you help Dathne. Gar, get to work on those translations. Asher—'

He scowled at the old woman, disliking her intensely. 'What?'

'You come with me, child. We've Circle business to see to.'

Another roll of thunder. A vivid crack of lightning. The last ragged peepholes of blue sky disappeared entirely.

'Hurry!' shouted Veira as the rain fell down in earnest, and they scattered to do her bidding.

Aware of Asher's furious resentment, Veira ushered him into her bedroom and calmly closed the door. Smiled at him gravely and patted his arm. 'Have a seat, child.'

As he threw himself into the furthest armchair she rolled back the carpet, revealing her Circle Stone hidey-hole. Glancing up she caught a glimmer of interest in his eyes, quickly stifled. With a grunt she lifted the hidey-hole's lid and set it aside. In the dim light the Circle Stones glistened. Beyond the bedroom window the rain lashed down hard.

'Here is the Circle,' she said, and drifted her fingers across the stones. They felt warm. Comforting. 'Each crystal a person, sworn to wait and serve. Dedicated to you, Asher. Dedicated to your fight. Your destiny. Each one would die for you, as Rafel died, if it meant the defeat of evil. No – don't reject them,' she added as he shifted sharply in his chair. 'They chose this, Asher. No one forced the burden upon them. They are special, as you are special. Don't hurt them by denying their gift. There is no greater service than service performed on behalf of the Innocent Mage.'

'Even though I never asked 'em for it?'

'You didn't have to. Prophecy asked and they answered. That should be enough to satisfy you.'

He scowled at her. 'And if it ain't?'

'But it is,' she said softly. 'Why else do you think you're so angry?' She patted the floorboards beside her. 'Come sit with me. I think it's time you met them, child. They've a part to play in the battle upcoming and it's best not to fight beside strangers.'

Grudgingly, he joined her. 'They're all goin' to the City too?'

She shook her head. 'That's not possible. We're too far-flung.'

'Then how are they s'posed to help me?'

'By lending you their strength when you need it.' She

touched his knee. 'Don't worry. It'll all be clear soon enough.'

She reached into the hidey-hole and withdrew the one crystal she'd never yet used. Unwrapped its soft silk covering and held it carefully in one hand. It was the most beautiful crystal in the kingdom, one of a kind, forged from shards of all the other Circle Stones by Jervale himself. She closed her eyes and sank into a light trance, acutely aware of Asher beside her and the multi-faceted crystal nestled warm and waiting in her palm. With her other hand she touched each Circle Stone, calling to its owner, summoning them to the link. Not one by one, but all together. Showing each to the other for the very first time in the Circle's history. Three stones she left untouched: Rafel's, Dathne's and Matt's. Rafel had already done his part – while Dathne and Matt would lend strength in different ways.

At last the remaining Circle members were united. Through the shimmering, shadowed link she saw their beloved faces. Felt their curiosity and fear. Their excitement and their trepidation. Let it flow through her like a river, like a soft breeze, like a sigh.

*Veira . . . Veira . . . Veira . . .*

'My dear friends,' she greeted them. 'Welcome. I've called you now, in this time and to this place, to share with you completely what many already suspect or know. The Final Days are upon us. The Innocent Mage is revealed. The evil foretold has risen . . . and we are all that stands between it and the end. Now comes the time for the Circle to join hand in hand and deny evil its dominion. Are you with me?'

Thundering through the link, all their separate voices singing as one. *We're with you, Veira. We're with you. Tell us what to do.*

Blindly she reached out and took Asher's hand. Felt his brief resistance, then felt him surrender and submit. Heard him gasp as he was admitted to the shadow world of Circle communication.

'Behold, friends, our Innocent Mage. Young, and fiery, and full of ire. The evil we battle has touched him already. Bravely he carries the scars. Bid him welcome, and share with him your hearts.'

*Welcome, Asher. Welcome, our Innocent Mage. Know we stand with you. Beside you. Behind you. No matter what may be.*

She felt Asher's hand tremble in hers as the Circle's love poured through him. Heard his ragged breathing. 'Speak, Asher,' she whispered. 'The Circle will hear you.'

'I don't – I can't – what do I say?' he muttered.

'Whatever comes to mind.'

'I don't know why I'm chosen,' he said at last, hesitant. 'Can't believe there ain't nobody better than me. But since I am, since it don't seem there's anyone else, I'll fight this evil best as I can. Can't promise to win. Just that I'll fight.'

*Bless you, Asher. And we'll fight with you, never fear.*

Veira squeezed his fingers. 'And so we will. Dear friends, this Circle forged will stay unbroken. Go about your daily lives until I call you. And when that call comes stop what you're doing wherever you are and pour all your powers, all your strength, into this binding link. Pour it into Asher, that he might in the end prevail.'

*Call us, Veira, and we will come.*

Withdrawing from them was a wrenching pain that sprang tears to her eyes. Reverently she laid the crystal on the floor then looked at Asher, stunned and silent by her side.

'You see?' she said softly.

He nodded, his anger softened, his face pliable with understanding. 'Aye. At least . . . I reckon I'm startin' to.'

'Then will you not find a way to make peace with Gar? To put aside the hardships he's caused you, knowing it was all in the service of Prophecy?'

He pulled his hand from hers. 'That's got nowt to do with this. What's between me and Gar is between me and Gar. You keep yourself clear of it, Veira. Clear of me and Dathne too. Since I got no choice I'll be your Innocent Mage. I'll fight your battles for you. But that don't mean you got leave to dance in and out of my life on a whim. Understood?'

She sighed. 'Understood, child.'

Tucked away in the corner of her hidey-hole was a felt-wrapped bundle. She pulled it clear and laid it on the floorboards.

'What happens now?' said Asher. Polite enough, but with hidden flint sharp in his voice.

She looked up, and deep into his eyes. 'Do you trust me, Asher?'

He shrugged. 'I'm still here, ain't I?'

She unwrapped the bundle, revealing a hammer and a knife. The hammer she lifted and, before she could hesitate or waste time with regrets, struck it sharply to the forged-crystal Jervale had made.

Asher cried out in protest as it shattered into myriad pieces, glittering with all its colours.

'Don't fret,' she told him. 'The Circle's unbroken. This is just the next step.'

Swiftly she sifted through the shards, searching for the perfect piece. Finding it, she put it to one side then again turned to Asher.

'Bare your breast to me, child,' she commanded. 'On the left. Above your heart.'

He stared at her. 'What?'

'You said you trusted me, Asher. I swear I'll do you no harm.' Then she pulled a small face. 'Well. No great harm, and not lasting either.'

He wanted to refuse her, she could see it in his eyes. But some lingering memory of the Circle persuaded him. Scowling, he pulled open his shirt. Scowled harder when she lifted the knife. Its sharp blade glinted wicked in the lamplight.

He sucked in a deep breath. 'Veira – Veira—'

She struck without mercy, slicing open the thick muscle of his chest directly above his heart. Sliced lengthways then dropped the knife and thrust in her finger, tearing apart the muscle's long fibres, creating a hole. Blood made her fingers slippery. His harsh breath was hot in her face. She picked up the crystal shard and pressed it into the wound, forcing it deep inside the tissue. He was gasping now, grunting with the pain. With indignation, and shock.

She leaned towards him. Put her forehead hard to his, clasped the nape of his neck with her left hand and pressed her bloodied fingers to his chest.

'Breathe with me . . . breathe with me . . .' she whispered. 'Come, child, it's nearly over. And what is pain but a mere sensation?'

Hidden words rose tumultuous to her tongue. Words she'd been given long years ago but thought never to be called on to speak. His wounded flesh heated. Moulded. Grew cool. She let her hands fall free of him. Sat up straight and smiled into his face.

'Done, then. And well done too. Good boy.'

'You bloody mad crazy ole woman!' he shouted,

scrambling to his feet. 'What d'you think you're doin'? Carvin' me like a Barl's Day roast? What kind of craziness is this?'

Bone weary now, and emptied, she looked at the flesh of his chest. No wound there any more. Not even a scar. Just a faint irregularity, where the crystal shard was hidden. 'You're one with the Circle now, child,' she told him. 'They're a part of you, unremovable. When the time comes and the power is called for you'll have it at your fingertips. In your blood and bones.'

Those fingertips were scrabbling at his chest. 'What? What? What are you talkin' about?'

'Quiet your mind,' she advised him. 'Sink deep inside yourself. Can you feel them, Asher? All our good friends of the Circle? Can you hear their heartbeats, waiting?'

Startled, he stared at her. Closed his eyes, then jumped as though stuck with a pin. 'Sink me bloody sideways!'

She chuckled. 'What I told you last night of our magic, Asher, is only the beginning. There's more to learn yet and much you could teach me, if we had time. There's magic in you I doubt I'll ever understand. But that's how Prophecy wanted it, and who am I to question Prophecy? Have a look in my top dresser drawer, will you? There should be a blue felt drawstring bag in there.'

Bemused, bewildered, he found the bag she wanted and tossed it to her. She gathered up the other broken pieces of the hammered crystal and slipped them safe inside.

'Now what?' he said, still rubbing at that place on his chest, though she knew he had no more pain there.

'Now you go clean yourself up. And don't mention this to the others. I'll tell them myself when the time's right.'

He snorted. 'There's only Matt I'm talkin' to.'

'Then don't tell him,' she snapped, impatient. 'Go and see if he needs help with the horses. Or the wagon. Make yourself useful, at any rate. When those war spells are ready for you to practise, everything else must be done.' She looked to the bedroom window, out at the pouring rain. 'There's precious little time left.'

He nodded. Went to the door, then stopped. Turned. All of a sudden he looked young, and uncertain. 'Veira. Can I do this?'

She poured all her hope and believing into a smile. 'Yes, child. You can.'

He smiled in return, swift and wry. 'Crazy ole woman,' he muttered, then left her alone.

Heart aching, she creaked to her feet, tidied up her chamber then went to the kitchen to help.

# CHAPTER THIRTY-FOUR

In the City unsummoned water poured from the sky, alarming its insect inhabitants. Morg lounged on his townhouse balcony and watched the stinking rain fall, listened to the jabbering insect voices in the street below and savoured the swelling sense of alarm.

In the distance, Barl's dying Wall shuddered.

Blubbery Willer came panting to see him. 'Your Majesty – Your Majesty – Barlsman Holze craves an urgent audience! Shall I send him away too?'

Morg smiled. He'd been wondering how much longer he'd have to wait before the Barl-sot came bleating. 'No. Show him into the drawing room, Willer.'

He lingered a few moments longer, just to appreciate his handiwork, then sauntered downstairs to join Barl's little champion. On his entrance the cleric leapt to his feet. He was looking harried, distressed, no flowers in his Barlsbraid. There was a stain on the front of his workday robes.

'Conroyd!' he said, his reedy voice unsteady. 'I confess all my hopes were pinned upon not finding you here. Upon the frail hope that these inclement conditions were the result of your WeatherWorking inexperience and the lack of a Master Magician. But as you are here, and not at work in the Weather Chamber . . .' His voice trailed off and his hands clutched each other convulsively. 'Conroyd . . . you must have seen the Wall. Do you have an explanation?'

It was too soon yet to reveal his true face, so he arranged his expression into a mask of sorrow and disciplined alarm. 'Efrim, dear Efrim, indeed you've read my mind. I was about to send for you, as it happens. I need your help.'

'Anything! Anything!' said fool Holze fervently. 'Just tell me what I can do! Tell me what's gone wrong!'

He took a turn about the room, pretending to an agitation he was very far from feeling. 'I've not said this to another soul, Efrim, and I must ask you to keep it secret. If word gets out I fear for the people's safety. Barl's Wall is damaged. Not beyond my power to heal, of course,' he added as the cleric stifled a shocked moan and sank into the nearest chair. 'But certainly it will take some time. Blessed Barl's Weather Magics have shown me how to effect a remedy and I'm doing all I can. In time, I will succeed. But there will be more rain, and other unpleasantness, before I have completely undone the damage.'

'Asher,' said Holze, uncommonly vicious. 'This is the doing of that renegade Olken.'

Morg bowed his head in feigned sorrow. 'Yes. I fear so.'

'Have you spoken to that idiot Gar?'

'No,' he said after a moment. 'Why would I? Gar Torvig is a private citizen now. Irrelevant and unnecessary.'

'Yes, but he was there when Asher tinkered with the weather,' Holze said eagerly. Filled with a sudden, false hope. 'Perhaps he can tell us exactly what the criminal did, in detail. Perhaps that will help you put things right!'

An ingenious thought, if pointless. But interrogating the cripple would give Holze something to do. Keep him out of the way. He nodded. 'Bless you, Efrim. I should've thought of this myself.'

'No, no, Conroyd. You are pushed to your limit!'

Morg nearly laughed aloud at that. 'I'm afraid, Efrim, all the wonderful plans we hatched the other night will have to wait a little longer. Unless I rescue us from Asher's perfidious treachery we'll have no glorious future.'

'Of course, of course!' agreed Holze, standing. 'Nothing is more important than the repairing of Barl's Wall. That is your sacred duty, Conroyd!'

He nodded. 'Precisely. Now, as it happens, you can serve me in two other matters. Firstly, keep the City's population occupied with prayer. You need not be specific, a supportive exhortation on my behalf should be sufficient. I thought it might help allay the people's worries and let them feel they can contribute to the well-being of our beloved kingdom. It will also stop your subordinate clerics from speculating unwisely.'

Holze nodded. 'Of course. What else?'

'Until this crisis passes I think it would be wise to suspend all council activity, Privy and General.'

'Are you certain?' said Holze, frowning. 'There is still the business of the kingdom to conduct.'

'But will it be profitably conducted while the weather remains . . . unbalanced?' Morg shook his head, as though it mattered. 'I think we both know the answer to that. The guilds will agitate and our Doranen brethren will press for some arcane involvement. As it is, Efrim,

I turn away unsubtle requests for an audience every hour.'

Unhappily, the dodderer nodded. 'Yes. Yes. I fear this latest transition of power has upset a great many people.'

Upset? Morg turned away, hiding a gleeful smile. The insects had yet to learn the meaning of the word . . . 'I'd take it as a great personal favour, Efrim, if you could announce my decision in an emergency council session. I'll have Willer notify the councillors. Make sure you exhort them to pray hard for our kingdom's delivery.'

Holze bowed. 'Of course, Your Majesty. Be assured I will see to it.'

Concealing his distaste, Morg embraced the gullible cleric. 'I trust you implicitly, Efrim. Go now and minister to our kingdom. Use Willer as you would a servant of your own.'

'You won't need him?'

Need *Willer*? 'It's a sacrifice I'm ready to make in the service of beloved Lur,' he said gravely. 'Barl's blessings go with you, dear friend.'

Alone again, gloriously alone, Morg stretched out on the study sofa, closed his eyes and listened to the music of thunder as it rattled the vulnerable windowpanes.

Beyond Veira's curtained sitting room the wind howled mercilessly, without surcease. Unrelenting rain hammered the ground outside and hail the size of hens' eggs thudded against the cottage's thatched roofing. Gar glanced up, frowning. He'd heard it smash a window earlier but hadn't gone to look. Someone else would deal with that. He had to stay focused on his own task: the accurate translation of Barl's hoarded, horrible spells. Some half-dozen he'd completed already, and handed over to Veira so Asher might learn their dangerous intricacies. Perhaps a dozen more remained for him to decipher.

They made his head hurt.

The door opened and Dathne came in. 'Soup,' she said, balancing a tray. 'And bread. You've been cooped up here for hours. You should eat something.'

Behind her kind concern, deep sorrow. Her eyes were hollow, her lips deeply bracketed with lines of pain. He pushed aside his papers and took the tray from her. Steam wafted from the soup bowl, fragrant – but still unappetising. She went to the window, tugged apart the faded curtains and stared at the pitiless downpour.

He put down the tray, picked up the spoon and made himself swallow a little broth. Chicken. As a child it had been his favourite. He said, watching her, 'I take it that where Asher's concerned, you've ceased to exist too?'

She flinched, just a little. 'I'd rather not talk about it.'

'Fine,' he said, and swallowed more soup. Chewed on the bread, which was stale. 'What's everyone else doing?'

'Matt's cluttered the kitchen with harness, and he and Darran are oiling it.'

He choked. 'Darran's oiling harness?'

'He's determined to be useful.'

Dear old man. 'And Veira?'

Dathne hesitated a moment. 'She's outside in the shed with Asher. Helping him learn your war spells.'

His spoon dropped into the bowl. 'Veira can do war spells?'

'No,' said Dathne, turning away from the window. 'But since Asher refused to let you help him practice she's just . . . keeping an eye on him. You know. In case . . .'

In case he accidentally killed himself. 'I see.'

'But he's doing fine. Veira says you'd think he'd been summoning war-beasts since before he could walk.'

'Did you know that about him?'

'I knew nothing about him, beyond he is the Innocent Mage.' She rubbed her hands up and down her arms. 'It's cold.'

'It is,' he agreed. 'The trip back to Dorana will be miserable, I think.' In more ways than the merely physical.

She nodded at Barl's diary, shoved to one side on the little work table he'd been using. 'Can an arrogant dead woman's scribblings really save us?'

'I don't know,' he said, stifling a prickle of anger that Barl should be described so. Then he shrugged, his fingers caressing the diary's mottled cover. 'I hope so. Or at least, help Asher to save us. If he can. If he really is what you think.'

'Of course he is,' she said sharply. 'Or do you doubt me now? And Veira? And everything else you've seen and heard?'

He smiled at her, feeling sour. 'Dathne, with everything that's happened these past weeks, if you told me my name was Gar I'd feel a moment's doubt.'

Her face softened. 'Yes. I suppose you would. So many things turned topsy-turvy.'

So many things. 'I'm sorry. I didn't mean to sound critical. If we do survive the coming days – if Lur survives them – we'll have you and your Circle to thank for it.'

'And Asher.' She bit her lip, turning back to the window and the bleak view beyond it. 'Will it never stop raining now, I wonder?'

'What did your visions show you?'

She shivered. 'Horrors I'd rather forget.'

'Yet they showed you Asher, too. Can we have one without the other?'

'Who knows?' She pulled the curtains closed again, hard, then hugged herself tight. 'Not me.'

'It appears between the two of us we don't know much at all,' he said, and tried to make a joke of it.

Unamused she stared at him, her eyes large and dark. 'How could *you* not know, you Doranen?' she said, face and voice accusing. 'You're the grand magicians, the ones with all the power. Your father was the *king*, Gar, the *WeatherWorker*. You and your family had Morg in your midst, breaking bread with you, breathing the same air! How many hours did you spend closeted with him, studying your precious magics? How is it none of you suspected who and what he was? How could you not *know*?'

'Do you think I've not asked myself that question?' he retorted. 'Do you think an hour goes by that I don't look back on every hour, every minute we spent in Morg's presence and wonder how it was we were so blind? You can't blame us for our failures more than I do, Dathne, believe me! All I can say in our defence is that Morg may once have been Morgan, a flesh and blood man, but whatever he is now it's something beyond Doranen comprehension. Not even your Prophecy could name him, could it? Nor all your vaunted visions.'

'At least we *had* our visions!' she retorted. 'Six hundred years ago Jervale knew you and yours were a mistake, but your precious Barl shouted him down! How better might we be prepared for this day if—'

His fist thumped the tabletop. 'You can't know that! Dathne, finger-pointing is pointless. What's done is done. My people came, yours accepted us, and so your fates were bound to ours. It's history and unchangeable. We have to focus on the future . . . and hope against hope for a miracle.'

'We have a miracle,' she said fiercely. 'His name is Asher.'

'I hope you're right,' he said, suddenly tired. 'I hope he's everything your Prophecy claims him to be. For if he's not, this kingdom's doomed and every soul within it damned.'

'I'm right,' she said, then nodded at the tray with its burden of half-drunk soup and partly chewed bread. 'Are you finished with that?'

He nodded. 'Yes. Thank you. I'm sorry I couldn't do it more justice.' As she moved to take it away, he held up a hand, pausing her, and sifted swiftly through his haphazard pile of papers. 'Here,' he said, and slid three sheets under the bread plate for safekeeping. 'More spells for our miracle to practise.'

She looked at them as though they might bite. 'When will you have finished all of them?'

'By tonight sometime, I think. I hope.'

'I hope so too,' she said, and glanced at the curtained window as a fresh wave of hail rattled the glass. 'Matt says the Weather Magic's unravelling faster by the hour. The Wall won't stand much longer now.'

He pulled a face. 'Then I'd best get back to work. Thank you for the soup.'

'You're welcome,' she said, and left him to his papers, and Barl's diary.

Cowering behind a pile of old boxes in her weather-beaten shed, Veira raised her voice above the wereslag's howling screech and shouted, 'Kill it! *Kill it!*'

Panting, Asher slashed a sigil through the air and

uttered the words of banishment. The wereslag's writhing orange tentacles burst into heatless flame; its eight clawed arms withered; it shrivelled and died, leaving only a ring of smoking dirt on the shed floor where its acid slime had dripped and boiled.

'Sink me bloody sideways,' he muttered, and sagged against a handy post. 'How many more, eh?'

Sidling out from safety, Veira shuffled through the sheaf of papers in her hand. 'That's the last of the spells Matt brought out before.'

'Then how many are left to come?'

'You'll have to ask Gar,' she said tartly, eyebrows lowered in a challenge.

He curled his lip and looked out of the shed at the drowned garden. At the fringe of the Black Woods, and the trees flogging themselves to death against the leaden sky. He was exhausted. Had lost count of the monstrosities he'd called forth with just a few words and the power of his mind.

It was a mighty uncomfortable feeling, knowing that things like wereslags and trolls and horslirs and gruesomes lurked just beneath his skin. If Da could see him now . . .

Unsettled, still glooming at the lashing forest, his fingers crept up to his chest and rubbed at the hard little lump of crystal nestled in his flesh. Every time he summoned his power – a feat that came more and more easily, something else he didn't much care for – the crystal tickled. Buzzed, as though woken from shallow sleep.

He'd asked and he'd asked, but Veira wouldn't tell him any more about its purpose. Just: 'You'll know when the time comes. Stop fratching me, child.'

She said now, close enough to swat his shoulder,

'Leave it be! We've more spells yet to conquer and it'll be too dark soon to go on.'

He groaned. 'Let a body rest a moment, Veira. I been at this for bloody hours.'

'And hours are all we have left before we must head back to the City. I—'

'Sorry,' said Matt, slopping into the shed from outside. He was festooned with oil-dark horse harness, head and shoulders soaked with the ceaseless rain. 'Didn't mean to interrupt.'

'You ain't,' he said, frowning. All Matt's colour was bled from his face, leaving it drawn and pallid. 'You all right?'

Matt let the harness slide free onto a cluttered bench. 'The unbalance of magic is getting worse. I'm feeling it more with every hour that passes.'

Asher nodded. 'Aye.' He could feel it too, like sharp fingernails digging into his brain. Scraping over his skin. 'You got to block it out, Matt, else it'll tear you apart.'

Matt pulled a face. 'I'm trying. But I'm not you.' He looked at Veira. 'Can you spare a moment to help me strengthen this harness? I've grown more used to needles and waxed thread than bindings – and I never was much good at them to begin with.'

'Course she will,' Asher said cheerfully. 'She ain't got nowt better to do just now, since I'm for a breather.' And he made his escape before Veira could shout, or slap him again.

He ran over the squelching grass to the cottage, shoved open the kitchen door and escaped inside, dripping.

The kitchen was full of more cleaned harness, cooking smells and Darran. Who took one look at his face, rummaged in a cupboard, pulled from it an anonymous bottle of something that looked promising, at least, and poured him half a glassful.

He swallowed it in one gulp then staggered around for a while coughing and wheezing and banging his chest.

'You're welcome,' said Darran. Flour daubed his weskit, his face, his hair. He was in the middle of rolling pastry. It looked suspiciously lumpy.

Asher held out his emptied glass and waited. Pinch-faced, Darran poured him a stingy second splash, ostentatiously recorked the bottle and returned it to the cupboard.

He wasn't a slow learner. Sipping this time, not gulping, he emptied the glass again and put it in the sink. Glanced at Darran, sighed, rinsed it and set it upside down to dry.

Darran returned to his pastry. 'Gar never meant to hurt you.'

Another sigh. He had no strength for this. 'It's been said before and nowt's changed. Let it be, ole man.'

Bang went the rolling pin onto the table. 'He saved your life!'

'You mean Matt's.'

'And yours. Don't you even care how? Or is hating him more important than knowing the truth?'

Asher looked at him. The ole crow's eyes were blazing with unfair hope and accusation. He didn't want to see that, so he slouched over to the window. Looked at the rain instead of this pleading old man who'd been nothing but a trial and tribulation to him from the first day they'd met.

'Aye,' he said, surly. 'Hate's a lot more important.'

Darran seized him. Pushed up his jacket and shirt sleeve to reveal the ragged scar from his madcap

Restharven childhood with Jed. 'The other man's arm was scarless. But Gar said it was your body burned in the glimfire. He knew it wasn't and he lied, though he could've died for it then and there. He said it so they'd believe you were dead. That *must* be worth a little forgiveness, surely?'

'No,' said Asher baldly. 'It ain't.'

'Why not?' demanded Darran, pleading. 'Have you never done anything you've not been sorry for after? That you did because you had to, even though it led to someone else's suffering?'

*Jed*. He skewered the ole crow with a scathing glare. 'I never went back on a promise. And if Gar'd done the same there'd have been no body to identify at all, now would there? Someone still died, Darran!'

Darran flinched as though he'd been struck. 'I know. The prince is most—'

'Good. Then maybe you can ask Rafel to forgive Gar,' he said bitterly. 'Just don't ask me again, Darran. You'll only be wastin' your time and mine.'

Darran picked up his rolling pin and attacked the pastry. 'Yes,' he said, clipped and cold. 'Yes, I quite see that I would.'

Furious he'd been goaded into saying more than he'd intended, Asher headed for the inside kitchen door, thinking to change his wet clothes. He hauled it open—

—and Gar was on the other side.

'What?' he said roughly. 'What d'you want?'

From the stricken look on his face Gar had been eavesdropping. Mute, he held out his hand. In it was another sheaf of papers covered in his quick writing. 'More spells,' he said, subdued.

'Fine,' Asher said, and snatched them. He'd worry about dry clothes later. Turning on his heel he stalked out of the kitchen. Into the rain. Back to the business of killing with magic.

Shaken, Gar ignored the pleading look on Darran's pale face and returned to the sitting room and Barl's diary. He had only a few more pages left to examine. Relief warred with a sharp, unexpected sorrow at the thought. With the diary wholly translated he'd be leaving Barl behind. Saying goodbye. It hurt, to think of that.

Barl . . . Barl . . . how glorious she was. A woman unmatched in the history of their people. Brave . . . dedicated . . . consumed with integrity. He could read her handwriting now as easily as his own. She spoke to him intimately, mind to mind, a whispering of desperate confidences. Betraying to him, and only him, the secret torments of her heart. Her doubts. Her fears. Her passionate longings. He understood her as no one ever had; certainly not her faithless lover Morgan.

Pulling the diary towards him he turned to the next page. Blinked a couple of times to clear his fuzzy vision, then focused on the hastily scrawled entry.

*Being an incantation I shall call the Words of UnMaking. This is a terrible thing, and only my overwhelming fears have led me to it. The seeds of this monstrous spell grew out of my work with Morgan, though it shames me now to admit it. I do believe that the Wall I labour to bring forth will protect us from him. I believe we will be safe behind it forever . . . but if my belief proves false, yet will I prevail against him. For the dread words recorded hereafter will undo him utterly. Yes, and they will undo the speaker also . . . undo me, for no one else shall have them.*

*If I must use them . . . if I must die . . . I shall be justly punished.*

Silence, as the carved wooden clock on the wall ticked away the seconds and minutes of what might be Lur's last days.

Mouth dry, hands sweaty, he read the diary entry again then looked at the recorded incantations. Noted the syllables and the sigils and the rhythms of the words and saw, his heart hard-beating, that victory was held here in his hands.

Victory . . . and death.

There were no more spells in the diary after Barl's Words of UnMaking. The spell that would ensure Morg's death, and Asher's with it.

He read it again. Again. Again. Marvelled at the simplicity of its structure, its exquisite elegance, so quintessentially Barl. Recognised its triggers and why without question it would work. With magic a fading memory in his blood he could barely feel the incantation's power. Faced with the potential of such dreadful destruction he felt briefly, guiltily relieved the burden of its utterance would never fall upon him.

And then – as he read the incantation for the eighth time – his disciplined, scholarly, educated mind went *click*. And suddenly he saw Barl's spell in a whole new light. Saw it for what it was . . . but also what it could be. Still victory. Still death.

And yet entirely different.

He slammed the diary shut. Shoved away from his makeshift desk and roamed Veira's small sitting room, banging from mantelpiece to sofa to window and back again. He was sweating. Could he do it? Did he even dare try? If the memory of magic wasn't enough, if his vaunted scholarship were faulty. If he misplaced just one single syllable . . .

He could kill everyone. Even perhaps leave Morg alive.

No. He couldn't do it. Shouldn't. The risk was too great. It was arrogance inconceivable to think of altering Barl's final, perhaps greatest work. How long had he been a magician? Mere weeks. It wasn't enough. If what he believed was true, if the powers he'd manifested had never been his but were part of Morg's plan, then he'd never been a real magician. Had never been anything but a magickless cripple. A pawn, used and discarded on a whim.

And yet – and yet – he could *see* it. *Feel* it. *Taste* the changes to her incantation, if only in his mind. He knew Barl as well as he knew himself, now. Knew how her mind worked, how it saw and shaped the world, as completely as he knew his own.

He could do this.

He flung himself back to the makeshift desk. Opened the diary. Pulled a fresh sheet of paper towards him and re-inked his pen.

'I can do this, Barl,' he said aloud, as though she was nearby, listening. 'I must do this. I know you want me to. And it's the only way to repay my debts. Sweet lady, help me . . .'

Outside the cottage the last of the daylight was washed away and a rain-soaked night fell. As the cottage clocks struck seven, Veira shepherded everyone into the kitchen for dinner. Just as they sat down to Darran's lumpy rabbit pie one of the villagers, braving the dreadful weather, came calling at the back door to see if she was all right. She shooed the others into the corridor where they hid and held their breaths until Gavin was persuaded she was coping just fine, thank you, and went away.

'Is there news from the Circle, Veira?' said Dathne, as they resumed their seats at the crowded kitchen table. 'What's happening elsewhere in the kingdom?'

Veira sighed. 'Nothing good, child. I've heard from everyone and every story is the same. Storms rage from coast to coast. There's flooding. Fires. Tremors that tear the earth apart, just as when King Borne was ill. Fear riots unchecked in village and township streets alike.'

'And what of my people?' said Gar. 'Are there no Doranen attempting to help?'

'A few,' she said, shrugging. 'But what can they do? They have no Weather Magic. I'm told most of them have gone into hiding on their country estates, panic-stricken like the Olken.'

As Gar looked at his plate, clearly distressed, Darran cleared his throat. 'What about the Doranen in the City? The kingdom's strongest magicians sit on council, surely—'

She shook her head. 'Morg's suspended council business. Barlsman Holze has sent out orders for everyone to pray.'

'So not even he suspects Jarralt isn't Jarralt?' said Matt, stabbing his fork into a potato.

Unwillingly, Veira shared her last titbit of gossip. 'All the trouble's being blamed on Asher.'

Asher snorted. 'That's convenient.'

'It's very clever – and *in*convenient. We'll have to work hard to make sure you're not noticed once we get into the City.' She sat back in her chair, appetite defeated. 'We leave at first light. 'I'd be happier going soon after supper but the roads'll be too treacherous in the dark and we can't risk glimfire.' She looked at Gar. 'You all done with your translating, then?'

Gar put down his knife and fork. His expression was wary. Watchful. She didn't like the look of it. 'Done?' he said. 'Yes, I'm done. But the last spell isn't like the others. It's not a summoning for war-beasts.'

'Then what is it?' said Dathne.

'A spell that Asher can say only once. A spell I'll have to teach him myself, on the road to Dorana.'

For the first time, Asher looked at him. 'You ain't comin' with us. You can teach me it tonight.'

'I'm too tired tonight,' said Gar, flushing. 'I've been working all day and this is a desperately complicated incantation. Much harder than the others.'

Seated beside him, Veira put her hand on his arm. 'Why?'

He took a breath. Let it out. 'Because it's a killing spell. Powerful enough to destroy Morg himself.'

'And you're only just tellin' us *now*?' said Asher, glaring.

Gar held his hot gaze steadily. 'It was the last spell in the diary. Barl's final defence against Morg. I had to be sure I translated it properly.'

'And did you?'

'Yes. It will kill him.'

Still Asher stared. 'And what else? I know you, Gar, there's somethin' you ain't sayin'. Spit it out.'

'Unfortunately, it will also kill you.'

His words sparked a tempest.

'Then he can't use it!' cried Dathne. 'How can you even *think* he would—'

'There's got to be another way,' said Matt, pushing his plate away. 'Prophecy says nothing about—'

'I told you he was tryin' to kill me!' said Asher, indignant.

Veira slammed her hand hard on the table, making them all jump and fall silent.

'*Enough*! Nobody's said he has to use it. Might be we'll kill this Morg with an army of those monsters Asher conjured up this afternoon. But we can't afford to ignore any weapon handed us in this war. It's a kingdom and thousands upon thousands of lives at stake.' She looked at Asher, willing all kind understanding from her face. 'But in the end we're not the ones who'll be called on to use it, and die. That might be your fate, child. Can you bear it? If all else fails could you use *this* weapon . . . though it cost you your life?'

Asher shoved back from the table. Rubbed his hands across his face, then let them fall to his side. 'Why are you even askin', ole woman?' His cold gaze raked across all their faces. 'You got me to promise to help you, and you know bloody well I keep my promises – no matter what it costs me. Besides. There's some as might think I'm already dead. That all I am is a man livin' on stolen time.'

'Do you think that?' said Matt, into the red-hot silence.

Asher shrugged. 'Don't matter what I think. Nowt matters any more, save for stoppin' that monster in the City.'

'Yes,' Veira said, when no one else could answer him. 'No matter what it costs any of us, Morg must be stopped. Now let's all finish eating, shall we, then get ourselves some sleep. It'll be a mortal bad trip back to Dorana.'

Returned to the Weather Chamber under cover of darkness, Morg raged and raged round the Weather map till all the polish was worn from the parquetry and the mellow timber shone dim.

The bitch whore's golden barrier was pockmarked with weaknesses now, its intricate incantations fraying apace. Outside the chamber a shrill wind was howling. Trees lashed the cloud-clotted sky and lightning stabbed both air and sodden ground. The world bled rain.

The map itself was suffering too. Leprous patches of decay and destruction marred it from end to end. His listening mind heard a far-distant keening. He lifted his eyes and stared through the clear crystal ceiling at the writhing gold light above him.

'Yes, slut! Scream. *Scream*.'

An unheralded voice said somewhere behind him: 'Conroyd? Your Majesty? Might we have a word?'

Startled, he spun around. Stepped back, incredulous. Furious. '*Sorvold*? You vomitous excrescence, get out! All of you get out! You are not wanted here!'

They'd come in a gaggle, like geese. Sorvold. Daltrie. And uninvited back from the country, Boqur and Hafar also. Conroyd's dear friends and confidants.

As they stared at him, slack-faced with shock, he laughed his delight. 'You lackwits! Don't you know he *despises* you?'

Foolishly they'd braved the inclement weather. Wet, wind-tossed, plastered with tattered leaves, despite their silks and velvets and their pitiful little magics they looked like destitute vagabonds.

Payne Sorvold said, very slowly, 'Your Majesty, are you unwell?'

Victory was vintage icewine, burning in his blood. He spread his hands. 'Unwell? On the contrary, gentlemen. I am superb. I said *get out*.'

They exchanged uneasy glances. Sorvold spoke again.

'Your Majesty, we are here on behalf of your Council. Your people. The weather is . . . disturbing. The Wall itself seems – its appearance suggests – Your Majesty, clearly something is wrong.'

Boqur took a step forward. Neglected to bow. 'Conroyd, in plain language: you have refused to meet with us that we might form a proper advisory for you in these early, unquiet days of your reign. Against all precedent and sound precepts of governance you've suspended the kingdom's lawful Council. Anxious messengers pour into the City from districts throughout the kingdom, desperate to know how to proceed in the face of the weather's wildness. And an hour ago your assistant Willer informed us that our former monarch Prince Gar has vanished without trace.'

He laughed out loud. He hadn't heard. Didn't care. 'Vanished? *Vanished*? Oh, poor little runtling! Running and running with no place to hide!'

It was Hafar's turn to remonstrate. 'Conroyd, it's clear you're unwell. Perhaps the transfer of Weather Magic went awry. You should not have attempted it without a Master Magician to aid you. We did try to warn you, sir.'

'We must be honest, Con!' said bluff Nole Daltrie. 'Your kingship's off to a very bad start! Public executions, missing princes and now this dreadful weather! What are you doing to it? The City's in an uproar! Captain Orrick can barely maintain order. There's panic in the streets! Mobs at the palace demanding explanations! And hardly any Doranen are left to help control the population after your stupid wife summoned them to the country. It's an utter disaster and you're to blame! Now how are you going to fix it?'

He heaved a thundering sigh. 'Oh, Nole, Nole . . .

do rest that treadmill tongue of yours. I have no intention of fixing it. Everything unfolds as I desire.'

'As you *desire*?' said Boqur. 'Conroyd! Are you mad then, if not ill? Have you looked outside this chamber? The Wall itself's in danger!'

He smiled, rejoicing. 'The Wall itself is *falling*, fool. And soon you'll all fall with it.'

'Barl save us,' Daltrie whispered. 'I think you have gone mad, Con. Gentlemen, you heard him?'

'Indeed we did,' said Hafar grimly. 'We come just in time. His Majesty is unfit.'

Sorvold stepped forward, his expression rigid. 'You must accompany us, sir. Immediately. Whatever ails you, Pother Nix shall discover it and with Barl's blessings put you right again.'

'Pother Nix is a pus-pot. I am as well as I have ever been. Gentlemen, you're dismissed.'

'No, sir,' said Sorvold, still approaching. 'You are desperately ill. You must be, for the Conroyd Jarralt I know and admire would never—'

He stopped the idiot with a tender smile. Reached out and laid his palm, so gently, above the bleating fool's heart. Leaned close . . . and showed him his true self.

'But, Payne,' he whispered as Sorvold's face turned grey and his mouth sagged in horror. 'Can't you tell? I am *not* the Conroyd Jarralt you know and admire . . .'

A thought, and the labouring heart beneath his hand stopped beating.

'*Conroyd*!' the rest of the geese cried out. Daring to criticise, and question. So he slaughtered them like geese. Dropped their bodies where they stood, burned them to ash with an incandscent thought, then forgot they had ever existed.

## CHAPTER THIRTY-FIVE

The storm was worse come cock crow. Wilder wind. Heavier rain, gusting with hailstones and flurries of sudden snow. The fringe of Black Woods around Veira's cottage was battered and full of gaps where trees had been torn down through the night. The world looked desolate, beyond all hope. The sound of running water filled the sodden air.

As Veira battled through the deepening mud, freeing her pigs and chickens and the donkey, Asher helped Matt harness the unhappy horses to the wagon. Matt looked even paler this morning; instead of sleeping last night, as Veira had ordered, he'd spent hours cobbling together blanket-lined canvas covers for the animals to protect them from the rain and hail.

Checking buckles, tugging knots, Asher said, 'What d'you reckon we'll find once we get to Dorana?'

Matt shrugged. 'I'm trying not to think. Asher—'

He sighed, knowing what Matt was about to say. 'Don't. There ain't any point. If I got to say Gar's killing spell, then so be it. You want to get rid of Morg, don't you?'

'Of course I do! But not like—'

'Like what? Me dyin'?' he demanded. 'You mean to say you never thought it'd come to this? Even though your bloody Prophecy says as much?'

'No!' Matt protested. 'I never – at least I hoped—'

'Hope? Since when did hope save lives, Matt? I could stand in the middle of the City Square and hope till my head falls off that Morg'll drop dead at my feet, but it ain't goin' to happen unless I *make* it happen.'

'That doesn't mean—'

'It prob'ly does,' he said. 'And you've always known it. Don't go insultin' my intelligence now, Matt. Not after all we've been through.'

Matt stared at him, stricken. 'Dathne told me not to be your friend. She always knew how bad things might get.'

*Dathne*. He turned away. 'You should've listened.'

Frowning, Matt eased himself round to check the nearside horse's tail, tied up to keep it out of the mud. 'You should make your peace with her. This silence is killing her, Asher.'

He felt his heart hitch. 'That's my business, Matt.'

'You're being unfair!'

'You want I should stop talkin' to you too?' he said, dangerously close to snarling. 'Leave it, Matt. I got enough to give me headaches without personal claptrap on top of it!'

The horses tossed their heads and stamped, unsettled by their edgy voices as well as the howling rain. Matt reached out a hand to them and murmured, soothing. Then he nodded, and sighed. 'All right, Asher. Whatever you want. It's just a shame, is all. I'll say this for the last time then I'll not say it ever again: she loves you.'

Over his shoulder, walking away, Asher answered,

'Don't you know, Matt? Love's the bloody least of it.'

They left the cottage soon after that. Matt driving, with Dathne on one side and Veira the other. In the back of the wagon, under the makeshift canvas covering drummed with rain, Asher, Gar and Darran and their baskets of supplies. The old man tucked himself up in a blanket and quickly fell asleep, a bundle of snoring bones.

'I fear it's been too much for him,' Gar said, fretting. 'I should've left him behind in the Tower.'

Asher snorted. 'You should've done a lot of things, I reckon. Bit late now though, eh?'

Gar looked down at the paper in his hands. His face was closed-off. Unreadable. The way it used to be in the early days, when Gar was still 'Your Highness' and friendship never thought of. 'I hope not.' His fingers smoothed over the paper's creased surface. 'I hope with this I can put everything right.'

'That's what you call killin' me, is it? Puttin' everything right?' He laughed. 'It don't bother you at all, eh?'

Gar's eyes glinted. 'What? That this spell I've translated will destroy you? If I said yes, would you believe me?' He let his head fall back against the wagon's temporary canvas wall. 'Of course you wouldn't. You've made your feelings plain, Asher. Let's not belabour them now. You've agreed to do this, and I've agreed to help. Let's leave it that, shall we?'

Asher pulled his knees up to his chest and wrapped his arms around them. Glanced up as, overhead, the sky, invisible, was rumbled through with thunder. 'Aye. Let's.'

'Good,' said Gar tightly. 'Now shall we get to work

on the incantation? I know we've hours to go till we reach Dorana but this isn't a task for skimping.'

'And how am I meant to practise the bloody thing if sayin' it's goin' to kill me?'

'Credit me at least with some intelligence,' Gar snapped. 'I've broken it into sections. We'll work through them one at a time, out of order, and leave the sigils till last. Once you've committed each section to memory I'll show you the proper order they come in. All right?'

Grudgingly, he nodded. 'Aye. Fine. All right.'

'Good,' said Gar. 'Now pay attention . . .'

Dathne huddled inside her enveloping blanket and kept her gaze pinned to the horses' wet, canvas-covered backs. Poor things. They looked so miserable: ears pinned to their heads, snapping peevishly at each other every other stride, bound-up tails lashing. The waterlogged road unrolled before them, bordered each side with battered trees. The wagon's wheels slipped and slithered and the horses grunted with the effort of hauling it.

Beside her, Matt held the reins in hands reddened with cold. He was swaddled in one of Dathne's blankets too, but she could still feel him shivering. Suffering with the collapse of the kingdom's fabric of magic. Even she, never as adept as Matt, was starting to feel it now . . . a thin cold scream on the edge of hearing.

She felt like screaming herself. How much fear and sorrow could a body hold before it must spill out in a raging torrent?

Asher would not speak to her. Asher might well soon be dead.

She turned her head to stare at the slowly passing countryside, stuffing her knuckles in her mouth to dam the frightened grief. If he died . . . if he died without forgiving her . . . died believing their love was a lie, nothing but pragmatics and a cold, hard using . . . how could she go on after? What would she say to the child?

Their child . . .

Unbidden, her fingers danced featherlight across her belly. Was it a boy or a girl? Would it have his eyes? Would she see him in the way it walked? Hear him in the sound of its laughter? Would it even be born? Or was it, like him, destined to die? Did death await them all in distant Dorana?

*No.* She had to stop thinking like this or she'd be a drooling madwoman before ever they reached the City gates. There was hope, yet. There was always hope. She couldn't – *wouldn't* – believe that Prophecy had guided them so far only to abandon them at the end.

*Please, please, don't let him die.*

The clickety-clack of busy needles distracted her and she glanced past Matt to Veira. The old woman was knitting. *Knitting.* As though she was at home in her kitchen or in front of the fireplace and these were ordinary times.

Veira looked up. 'You fratched about our Mage and his friend tucked up behind us? Don't be. They'll not come to blows.'

'I know,' Dathne said. Tried to say nothing else, but the words were out before she could stop them. 'Veira – he won't have to use that killing spell, will he?'

In between them, Matt shook the waterlogged reins and kept his gaze pinned to the horses' backs. If he was filled with fears too, he wasn't letting them show. He'd gotten good at hiding his feelings lately. Once, she would've welcomed that, but now . . .

Now it just made her feel more alone.

Veira hissed over a dropped scarlet stitch. 'I hope not,' she said, making good her mistake. 'I've taken steps to join him with the Circle so they can lend him strength when he needs it most.'

That got Matt's attention; they exchanged startled glances. 'When?' Dathne demanded. 'And why aren't Matt and I included?'

'It's too dangerous for you and Matthias. The rest of the Circle is safe out of the way but we're like to be in the thick of things, child. You'd just be a distraction to him.'

'Then how can we help him?' said Matt, frowning. 'We can't do nothing.'

Veira patted his knee. 'I don't know yet. We'll just have to wait and see once we get there.'

Wait and see . . . wait and see . . . yes, but what? Victory, or a bloody defeat? The thought of Asher saying the terrible spell of UnMaking made her want to vomit. Damn Gar, anyway! Why did he have to find it? Why did he have to tell them?

*Send me a vision, I beg you, Jervale. Show me he's not going to die.*

She closed her eyes then, and waited, but Jervale refused to oblige. *Bastard.* Eyes smarting, throat clogged with tears, she folded her arms across her middle. Let herself slump on the wagon's uncomfortable seat and tipped her head sideways till it rested on Matt's shoulder. He didn't object.

She escaped into sleep, and restless unhelpful dreaming.

Dorana City was dying.

Morg stood on the roof of the emptied palace's residential wing and watched its distant death throes, smiling. Behind him, against a sky of tarnished silver, Barl's Wall was a coruscation of filthy, failing power, flogged in the wind like a tattered flag.

At last . . . at last . . . the bitch whore was beaten.

Beneath his feet, an ominous rumble. The rooftop trembled as the palace swayed drunkenly on its foundations. Below him, the sounds of windows, breaking, of bricks and tiles falling to shatter in the buckling courtyards. In the gardens mighty trees groaned and shuddered, their roots tearing asunder the rain-softened ground. After six hundred years the earth was waking. Shrugging its shoulders as the bonds of magic were finally freed.

He heard screaming from the rooftops around him. Saw a few frantic Doranen, many more Olken: former councillors and advisors, palace servants, housemaids, butlers, running to and fro as their gentle world fell to pieces around them. They saw him.

'Your Majesty! Your Majesty!' they screamed, like children. 'Help us! *Save us*!'

He raised a fist and stopped their heartbeats, each and every one. The noise was distracting. He wanted to savour victory uninterrupted.

A shadow touched his face and he looked up to see fresh clouds roiling, forming out of nothingness, out of the air, born of the wild and undirected Weather Magic he'd unbound from Barl's Wall. They clotted the face of the faded sun, turning day to murky dusk.

With a grinding rumble the earth heaved again, vomiting gouts of steam and boiling mud. In the distance, in the City, he saw more buildings tumble. Imagined the horror, the terror, and was suffused with a blinding joy.

'Your Majesty? Your Majesty,' a small voice croaked behind him.

Without turning he said, 'Go away, Willer.'

'But, Your *Majesty* . . .'

So he did turn, impatiently,' and looked at the pathetic thing bowing and scraping its way across the rooftop towards him.

'What?'

Willer stared at him, blotchy with fear and reeking of ale. 'Captain Orrick sends an urgent message! Many streets are running like rivers and the water's scouring everything from its path. There's drowned dogs – wrecked carriages – furniture—' He choked on the horror. 'People. *Children*.'

He nodded. 'Good.'

'*Good*?' Stunned silent, the little worm groped to understand. 'But, but, you're the king! You're the WeatherWorker!'

'Fool,' he said, contemptuous. 'I am neither. I never was.'

Tears rose in the fat man's eyes. 'Please, Your Majesty. Captain Orrick begs you to come. Barlsman Holze, too. Survivors are gathered in the Square – they're praying – but they need you.'

He sighed. 'Go away, Willer.'

Sweating, weeping, the worm wrung its feeble hands. 'Are you unwell, sir? Shall I fetch you a pother?'

Morg considered him. Witter, witter, witter. The bleatings of a sheep. 'I wonder, was there a reason for you to be breathing?' he mused.

Willer goggled. Began to back away, very slowly. 'Your Majesty?'

'No,' he decided. 'No, you've served your tiny purpose.' He pointed a finger and froze the maggot where it stood. 'But before I despatch you, would you like to know what you've done? What miracle your little mind and petty jealousies have wrought in this misbegotten kingdom?'

Lifting his finger, he set the worm adrift in the damp and stagnant air. It shrieked. 'No! No! Somebody! Help!'

'Look at it, Willer!' he invited. 'The might and the majesty of your blessed Barl's Wall! Do you see that it's failing? Do you see that it's *falling*? Do you know that you're to blame?'

'*Me*, sir? *No*, sir!' the bobbing creature protested.

He laughed at the horror in its face. 'Oh, yes, sir! For the only man with the power to stop me was Asher of Restharven, and thanks to you, he's dead!'

The worm began flapping its arms, trying to force itself back to the roof. It looked ridiculous. 'King Conroyd – *King Conroyd*!'

'Not Conroyd,' he advised the worm gently. 'Morg.'

Willer shrieked. '*Who*? No! You *can't* be! That's *impossible*!'

Breathing deep of the sulphurous air he flared power round his body in a crimson nimbus. Laughed aloud at the terror, the dawning belief, in the little man's eyes.

'Stop this, *stop* it!' the fool worm babbled. 'Before it's too late! Don't you see? You're killing the kingdom!'

'Of course I am. To be reborn all things must die.'

'No! No! I don't *want* to die!' the wretched thing wailed. 'Please don't hurt me! Please put me down!'

'Put you down?' he echoed, smiling. 'Certainly, Willer. Whatever you desire.'

And with a flick of his finger he spun sobbing Willer over the roof's stone balustrade then released him to fall to the flagstones below . . . where he burst in a welter of blood and fat.

Overhead, the first bright spears of scarlet lightning

lanced the billowing clouds, striking flesh and buildings with lethal force. The lurid sky writhed – and Barl's dying Wall flailed in useless defiance.

Dreary in the daylight gloom, the wagon trundled onwards. The cloud-filled sky stretched on forever, spitting rain and snow in gusts and eddies, sometimes furious, sometimes sullen. The hours unspooled equally sullen. The wagon's shivering passengers dwindled to silence. They saw not another soul as they travelled through the blighted, sodden countryside towards Dorana City.

Matt unhappily kept the horses moving, stopping only to let them drink and snatch a mouthful of grain. Morning surrendered to midday, surrendered to afternoon, surrendered to night.

'We won't stop again till we reach the City,' decreed Veira, lighting torches to leaven the dark as Matt ran his hands over the tired horses and the others staggered about in the puddles and slop, stretching their tired legs and trying to get warm. 'If you're hungry, raid the baskets. If you must piss or otherwise, do your business quickly and run to catch up. There's no time left for niceties or coddling.' She frowned at Darran. 'Sorry, old man, but there's no help for it.'

Darran nodded. 'I understand,' he croaked, and climbed back in the wagon, out of the blighting wind.

'And when will we reach the City?' asked Dathne weakly, rattled almost to pieces and leaning against a wheel.

'An hour or two past sunrise, I'm thinking,' said Veira, and pulled a face. 'Though I doubt we'll be able to see it.'

For Asher, filled to bursting with the prickly magic

of Gar's killing spell and trapped in the prince's unwelcome company, that end couldn't come fast enough.

No matter it might bring with it his death.

For the first and likely last time in his life, Pellen Orrick felt desperate. Staring through his office's broken windows he rubbed his pain-burned shoulder and struggled to hold back tears.

The dawn of a new day: the worst of his life. His beautiful City, elegant gracious Dorana, spread smashed and trampled before him. Every second building, it seemed, was collapsed or burning or burned out complctely, belching greasy smoke, spilling ruined wares through splintered doorways and shattered shopfronts, even as dirty water swirled around the floors and up the doorjambs. Bulls and cows and horses and sheep and goats, once safely penned in the Livestock Quarter, milled and lowed and bleated through the streets with no one willing or able to pen them up again. Some of them slipped, plunged head first into running water or gaping cracks in the ground, and didn't get up again.

There were more dead people than he'd thought to see in all his life. Crushed and smashed by falling masonry, bludgeoned and drowned by the rivers of debris-choked rainwater raging through the narrower streets. Some of the bodies were abandoned, others clutched hard in the arms of weeping loved ones. Olken and Doranen, this madness had spared neither. Nor had magic saved them.

Most of his guards had deserted their posts. Some had fled the City with family and friends, certain that just beyond the next bend, in the next town or village, lay safety, and sanity. The few who'd remained were dead or had gathered in the Square to pray, ignoring his pleas to uphold their duty and their oaths.

He couldn't really blame them. If he'd had a family he might have discarded duty too. Run away or joined with the crowd crammed into the Square where Barlsman Holze all yesterday led beseeching prayers for deliverance.

But deliverance didn't seem to be coming. Dorana was doomed, and the kingdom with it.

Weary almost beyond walking, he made his way downstairs to the guardhouse's deserted main hall where Ox Bunder held steadfastly to his post.

'Captain!' Bunder frowned. 'Where's your sling, sir? That shoulder's nowhere near to healed yet.'

'My shoulder's the least of my troubles,' he replied tiredly. 'Ox, you've a young family waiting. Why don't you go? I'll stay here, for all the good I can do.'

'No, sir,' Bunder said. Stubborn to the last. 'I've got my duty.'

Before this he'd never much cared for Bunder; now his heart broke for love of him. 'No, my friend, you've got your family. Go to them. That's an order.' He held out his hand. 'And good luck.'

Torn between guilt and relief, Bunder clasped his wrist. 'Yes, sir. All right.'

Orrick walked out with him. His lovely City stank of burnt bones and death. Stopping at the guardhouse gates, he patted Bunder on the back and watched the man force his way through the milling throng, the frightened animals, the puddles and debris.

Scarlet lightning split the sky, spearing the ground with random vengeance. The Golden Cockerel burst apart. A score of people died then and there, pulped and broken by flying brick even as they ran screaming for shelter. But in the centre of the Square, citizens with more faith than sense stood their ground, eyes fixed firmly on Holze on Barl's Chapel steps, as they stubbornly followed the cleric's desperate prayers.

Some folk even climbed into Supplicant's Fountain. Clustered round Barl's greenstone statue, they stroked and stroked her hands, her feet, the folds of her robe. Begged her in high, shrill voices to protect them, save them, forgive them.

Forgive them for what? What sin could merit such harsh retribution? He was a guardsman, he knew crime when he met it. The people of Lur had done nothing, *nothing*, to warrant the horrors he'd witnessed. The carnage yet to come.

All his life he'd thought himself a man of faith. But what was it he believed in? A cold stone statue? A woman who'd died over six hundred years ago, at an age almost young enough to be his daughter? Magic?

For six long centuries the Olken had been told the Doranen were different. Stronger. Better. But the streets were littered with Doranen dead, as well as Olken. Their magic hadn't saved them.

It wasn't saving anyone.

And neither were the prayers.

Even as he watched, another scarlet javelin lanced from the sky and blasted Barl's statue to rubble. Shards of shattered greenstone whipped through the crowd. There was screaming. Blood. More dead, more injured.

Fleetingly, he thought of Asher – but help from that quarter was clearly a forlorn hope. Asher wasn't coming. Asher was probably dead. Struck by lightning, drowned in a ditch, swallowed by the hungry earth. Asher's survival would be some kind of miracle.

Only fools believed in miracles, and Pellen Orrick had never been a fool.

Numb with despair he stumbled to the ruined

fountain. The remains of the poor fools who had believed in miracles, who needed his help, for all the good he could do them now. But he was a guardsman, help was his duty, and duty was all he had left.

'It's no use!' shouted Veira as the panicked horses reared and plunged, threatening to smash the wagon and everyone in it. 'We'll have to walk the rest of the way!'

Squashed beside the old woman on the wagon's seat so Dathne could get some rest in the back, Asher could scarcely hear her words above the howling wind. They were halted where the Black Woods Road met the main thoroughfare into Dorana. In the distance they could see the foaming River Gant, its banks burst, spreading like a lake on either side. A flood of carts and carriages poured past them fleeing the City, drivers and occupants blind to the mad folk standing still on the side of the road.

Dorana was a scant two miles away now. Behind it, the terrible Wall thrashed to ribbons against the stricken sky. Asher groaned as his guts thrashed in sympathy. There was a vice clamped around his head, its screws turning tighter and tighter with every heartbeat. Nothing could save Barl's Wall now, it was shredded beyond repair. He felt like he was shredding with it, all the power in him curdling and boiling, bubbling like engraver's acid sat on a naked flame.

'Hold on, child,' said Veira, her cold lips pressed against his ear. 'Not much longer, now.'

He pulled her to him, shoving her face against his chest, as fresh hail pelted from the sky. He heard the wagon's makeshift canvas covering tear, and someone's stifled shout as the jagged ice found naked flesh; it sounded like Gar. Then the air was full of sound and soaking splinters as a barbed spear of lightning struck the heart of a towering djelba tree, too close to their right. The horses bellowed again, ploughing the mud beneath their maddened hooves.

'Please, Veira, you got to let me *do* somethin'!' he begged. 'We'll never make it to the City at this rate!'

He felt her shake her head. 'No, child,' she answered; even muffled, her voice brooked no argument. 'He'll hear you and all surprise will be lost. Don't fratch yourself. Prophecy's protected us this far, it won't abandon us now.'

More red lightning whiplashed the air, struck the ground, the river, somewhere out of sight in the midst of the fleeing City folk.

'Don't listen,' said Veira fiercely, as he jerked his head towards the terrible screaming. 'Your job's ahead, not here. We have to go!'

'She's right!' Matt shouted, holding the horses with all his strength. 'Now help me get these damned animals unhitched before they flip themselves over and squash us all to mincemeat!'

Asher let go of Veira and leapt to the ground. As his boots touched mud the earth trembled and shuddered, heaving as though something monstrous and living surged just beneath the surface, battling to be free. The wagon lurched forward as the horses tried to run.

'Get to their heads, Asher!' yelled Matt. 'Hold them till I reach you! Veira, down! In the back there, get out!'

Skidding in the slimy mud, Asher reached the nearest horse's head and wrapped his fingers in the bridle. Willed the bloody animal to stand, stand, *stand*, you *bastard*. Digging in his heels he hung on till he thought his arm would tear right off at the shoulder. Then Matt was with him and there was a knife in his hand, sharp blade flashing, severing harness and traces. The horses, sensing freedom, struggled even harder. The knife slipped. A horse squealed. Blood churned into the mud underfoot.

Then the last length of leather surrendered to the steel. Mindless with fear the horses bolted, bridles still intact, canvas blankets slipping and sliding and flapping like sails. Gasping, grunting, Matt and Asher propped each other upright and watched the animals disappear into the gathering murk.

The lowering clouds pressed lower still, and belched a blizzard of snow.

'Come now!' said Veira, chivvying like a shepherd with her flock. 'We'll freeze to death and turn into snowmen standing here, and besides, we've work to do!'

Asher straightened. Managed a wry grimace in Matt's direction, then turned his face towards their destination. Felt his guts spasm all over again, protesting the death of Barl's magic.

'You all right?' said Matt.

He nodded. 'I'll manage. You?'

'I'll manage.'

There was pain in Matt's face, echoing his own. 'Let's go then, eh?'

Staggering and stumbling as the uneasy ground beneath them shuddered and the freshly rising wind flung hail and snow in their faces, with newly bleeding Gar supporting Darran, Matt lending a strong arm to Veira, and Dathne stubbornly alone, they started doggedly towards the City. Towards the failing Wall, which drew them like a magnet.

When he'd done all he could for the dead and maimed of Supplicant's Fountain, and finally convinced that fool Holze to get the people praying *inside* the chapel, even if it meant they had to stand on each other's shoulders and dangle from the ceiling, Orrick stayed in the streets doing whatever else was needed.

Indifferent to the danger, to spears of lightning, squalls of hail, and snow, the wind and stinking rain, abruptly collapsing buildings and lethally panicked livestock, he clambered over chunks of masonry and spars of timber, splashed through red-tinged puddles and stepped over rents in the cobbles, because what else could he do? Go back to his office, his desk, his *paperwork*?

He was trying to force his way into a half-tumbled dress shop in Lace Lane, one street back from the Square, to see if anyone was inside injured when a clutching hand closed round his good elbow. 'Pellen!'

He turned. '*Asher*!'

It was him. Whole, alive and not alone. Behind him, shrouded in cloaks and hoods, huddled Matt, Dathne, Darran, the prince, with blood on his face – and a wrinkled old woman he'd never laid eyes on before.

'Asher!' he said again, and was flooded with a complication of emotions. The ending world blurred briefly. 'How did you—'

Asher shook him. Pain flared, but he didn't care. 'Where's Jarralt? I mean, Morg?'

He pressed a hand to his wounded shoulder. Felt fresh blood, seeping, and a fresh chill of horror at the sound of that name. 'No one's seen him. No one knows.'

Another crimson whiplash of lightning, shrill and shrieking. The hideous screaming of horses, the bellowing of bulls. A thudding rumble as the Musicians' Guildhouse collapsed. Out of nowhere an icy wind, howling and whirling and tearing the bruised clouds to pieces.

A frightened, ragged cry sounded beyond the line of the lane's wrecked shops. Orrick looked at Asher and unspeaking they ran, splashing and reckless, back to the square. The others followed.

When they reached the open rubbled space at the City's centre, what they saw stopped them in their tracks.

'Barl have mercy,' moaned Darran.

The few remaining threads of Barl's miraculous Wall flapped uselessly against the green and purple sky. Once proud and gold and mighty, it was now a ripped and raddled mockery of itself. Even as they and the fools still out in the open watched, pieces of magic tore free of the anchoring mountains, setting fire to the trees at their top.

Then Asher and Matt cried out together, staggering, as the last stubborn links of Barl's great Wall snapped. A booming thunder of enormous energy, released, shivered shaken buildings to ruins. Pressed flesh to brittle bones. Beneath the City's cobblestones the earth turned over in one last, massive protest. Every person standing was thrown to the ground, shouting, and all the sensible folk who'd taken refuge in the chapel came running out again, down the steps and into the Square, to see for themselves what had happened. Holze came out behind them, braid flying, to stand on the top of his precious chapel steps and weakly call them back.

The wind fell silent. No rain. No snow. No pounding hail. Gasping, Orrick and the others clambered to their feet. Orrick looked around him, tried to see what fresh damage was done to his poor dying City. If anyone else was killed. His heart stuttered. Heedless of the pain, he flung up his injured arm and pointed. Shouted.

'Look! *Look*!'

The sorcerer Morg was coming.

# CHAPTER THIRTY-SIX

He floated on air, on power invincible, high above the wrecked, rubbled City and over the crowd-crammed Square.

'Barl, my beloved! Your Wall has fallen and I am here!'

A voice assailed him. 'Conroyd! If you are indeed Conroyd! In the name of Barl and all things holy, I command you now to leave!'

Ah, Holze. Barl-sodden, mumbling, bumbling Holze. He floated to the chapel, the last refuge of dead men, where the shaking old fool stood on the steps and defied him to the last.

'There is no Conroyd,' he said, smiling down at him. 'Conroyd is dead.'

'I don't believe you!' Holze quavered. 'Return him to us, whoever you are, and get you gone from here!'

Still smiling, he reached down and touched Efrim's cheek. Withered flesh scorched and melted. 'Efrim, Efrim. Recall your scripture. You *know* who I am.'

As the cleric fell backwards, screeching, he turned in the air and faced the vanquished mountains. Shivering with pleasure, with a ravenous hunger, he opened his mind and summoned his power, *all* his power, all of himself that he'd left behind, that for too long had been denied him beyond Barl's Wall. Summoned his glorious victory and received—

*Nothing.*

The shock was so great he fell like a stone. Plunged into the midst of four-legged cattle. Before they could trample him he turned them to ashes with fire and hate, then took again to the fretful air. Horror was a living thing, beating him almost to blindness.

*Nothing*? *Nothing*? How could there be *nothing*? He was Morg, the most powerful magician undying! He was a *mountain* of power, an *ocean* of power, a *sky everlasting* of power!

He opened his mind a second time, strained beyond the confines of flesh, of blood, this outgrown borrowed body—

—and touched his sundered self. Felt it tremble, as he now trembled. Yearn, as he was yearning, to be complete again.

And then it recoiled. Repulsed him. He felt revulsion, rejection, an utter repudiation of his mind and his mastery – as though he were a stranger and this not a coming home.

Deep inside him, Conroyd was laughing.

*Morg, Morg, what did you think? That I, Conroyd Jarralt, would lie down and die? How could you swallow me yet not know my flavour? You're far too late, cousin, and too long changed. Our minds are one. Our flesh is one. I am you, and you are me, and there is now no going back. The Wall is fallen and still you are trapped.*

Deaf and blind, Morg hung in the air. Trapped? *Trapped*?

He opened his mouth and screamed.

* * *

Forgetting he hated her, Asher grabbed Dathne's hand and ran, trusting the others to follow. As Morg dangled helpless above them, keening like a creature in torment, he headed for the nearest safe shelter: the Butchers' Guild common house, half of its roof missing and part of one wall, but with most of its front awning still intact. They scuttled inside and collapsed to the ground, panting.

'The guardhouse would be safer,' said Orrick. The shoulder of his tunic was wet with blood. 'And I've lots of weapons there.'

Asher shook his head. 'Truncheons and pikestaffs won't hurt that thing. Veira? What's happenin'?'

Seated on a big chunk of brickwork, the old woman dabbed a kerchief to her bleeding arm. 'Don't know. But it's useful. Everyone all right?'

Everyone was. Even Darran beside her, though he looked the worse for wear, pasty-faced, and breathing like a bellows. Gar, his hail-damaged cheek puffed and scabbed with blood, had an arm tight round the old man's shoulders, holding him shakily upright. Matt crouched beside them, and Dathne next, with Orrick closest to the street and trouble. Of course.

He shouldn't have let them come. They couldn't help him, and all their lives were in danger.

Gar let go of Darran's slumped shoulders and wriggled closer. 'Asher. I have to talk to you. Privately.'

Bits of broken masonry dug sharply into his knees. Ignoring the small discomfort, he didn't take his eyes from the Square. From Morg. 'What for? There's nowt left to say.'

Gar had never known when to shut up. 'Yes, there is. The killing spell—'

He spared the little shit an impatient glance. 'I've learned it. I know it. You did your job. Now hold your tongue, why don't you, so's I can do mine. I'm tryin' to think here, if it's all right with you.'

'But you don't understand! I—'

Lunging sideways past all the rest of them he shoved Gar hard and sent him toppling. The bastard's head hit the wall with a thud. *'There's nowt left to say!'*

As Darran protested and the others fussed over Gar, Veira leaned over and touched his hand.

Her hood was down, her silver snake of hair rain-soaked and tumbling round her shoulders. 'I'll call the Circle to you now, child. Let them in. Let them help you. Don't be afraid.'

He wasn't afraid, he was bloody terrified. With the Wall's demise the grinding pain in him was almost faded, but in its place something darker flowed bitter and sluggish through his veins, sticky like tar. The foulness of Morg. From the sick look on Matt's face, his friend was feeling it too. But not as keenly as he did. Or as intimately. Matt weren't the Innocent Mage.

*He ain't . . . but I am.*

For the very first time, he truly accepted it. Did that mean he accepted death too?

Veira's finger poked him. 'Asher! What is it? What's amiss?'

He waited until his heart stopped galloping and he could trust his voice not to crack, his feet not to run him away from there without asking permission first. 'Nowt. I'm fine.'

'Then be still and silent, and I'll summon the Circle.'

Asher watched as she fumbled in her pocket. Pulled out that blue felt bag and withdrew a shard of crystal. It shimmered in the lowering light, then was hidden between her palms. Her eyes closed . . . her lips moved without sound . . . and the crystal shard she'd buried in his flesh burst burning into life. In his mind a chorus of voices, echoing.

*We're here, Asher. We're with you. Use our strength when you need it. It's yours for the taking.*

Fear faded, and with it some of the blackness in his blood. He felt his power stir, untainted. Felt the remnants of pain ease. A comforting heat was in him now, centred above his heart. Within the crystal.

In the Square outside their shelter, Morg's horrible screaming stopped.

Asher stood. Ready or not, want this or not, his time had come. 'Best finish this, I reckon.'

The quality of silence behind him changed. Lost outrage. Acquired sorrow. Became heavy, full of unspoken last words. He didn't want to hear them. He was doing this because they'd asked him. Begged him. Because no one but him could do it. Because he'd promised to help them no matter the cost and unlike some people, he kept his word.

Didn't mean he wanted a scene.

'What are you doing? Don't go out there!' said Dathne. 'Fight him from here, in safety!'

Pellen Orrick answered her. 'How can he, Dathne? There are people in the way.'

The Square was full of Olken and a handful of Doranen. Folk who'd had nowhere to run to, or thought they'd be all right. Some of them wore faces he'd known once, surely, when he'd been a different man. Dazed and stumbling they crawled amongst the rubble and debris, the aimlessly milling livestock, the fallen bodies. Some struggled to reach Barlsman Holze, the last authority left in the City. The cleric sprawled on his Barl's Chapel steps, unmoving.

'*Asher*!' Dathne cried as he took another step.

He stopped, fingers tight on the ragged brickwork. *Don't look, don't look, there ain't no bloody point!*

He looked. He had to.

All her love was in her face. Seeing it, something brittle inside him broke, or was broken. He summoned a smile for her. 'It's all right, Dathne. The bastard won't touch you.'

There were tears in her eyes and on her cheeks. 'There's something I have to tell you, I—'

He went to her and dropped to one knee. Let his fingers trace the gentle upswing of her eyebrow, her severely curving cheekbone, and lips.

'Tell me later.'

'But—'

He stood, and she fell silent. With a final smile he turned his back on her. On all of them: Veira, Darran, Pellen, Matt, and Gar. Stepping out of their meagre shelter he looked at the creature spinning and spinning and spinning above him, oblivious to everything save its private pain.

But for how long . . .

In his mind, the Circle waited.

He ran haphazard to the steps of the chapel, dodging livestock, ignoring the fallen who needed his help, even the children. Holze was stirring now, sitting up. Seeing him, the cleric gasped. '*Asher*?'

He held out his hand. Above their heads Morg dangled, moaning. 'Holze.'

Five charred fingerprints marred the side of the cleric's pain-twisted face. 'You're *alive*?'

'No, I'm a ghost,' he said, and helped Holze to his unsteady feet. Despite the dirty past they shared he felt a grudging respect: Holze could've bolted, and didn't.

The Barlsman's pale lips tightened. 'Do you know what *that* is?' he asked, pointing to Morg.

'Aye. Do you?'

'I think I might,' Holze said, frowning. 'Though my mind can scarce believe it.'

He snorted. 'Believe it, Holze. That's Morg.'

The last hint of colour drained from the cleric's face, leaving the fingerprints livid, and he kissed his holyring with fervour. 'Barl save us.'

'If you say so.' Asher turned and looked at the dazed people in the square. 'These folk can't stay out here. Can you get 'em back in the chapel?'

'Yes, yes, of course, but why? What are you going to do?'

He jerked his head upwards. 'Kill that.'

Holze choked. 'How?'

'How d'you reckon?' he snapped, and conjured flame. Not tame and gentle glimlight but the cruel, greedy heat of warfire. One of the many tricks to be found in Barl's diary, which he could so easily have lived without.

'What is this *blasphemy*?' Holze demanded, staring at the fire leaping from Olken fingers. 'That's no magic known to me! How do you come by it? Who taught it to you? *Morg*?'

He grinned, feeling vicious. 'No, Holze. Barl.'

Holze came close to falling head first down the steps. 'No – no – that's not *possible*!'

With a flick of his wrist he extinguished the flame. 'We can argue what is and ain't possible when this is over, provided we're both still standin'.'

Shaken, Holze looked again at Morg. 'You can't kill him, Asher. There's Conroyd to consider.'

He could've hit the ole fool. 'Of course I can! I have to! And if Jarralt's still in there I'll be doin' him a favour.

Now get these idiot folk out of here, would you? I've seen enough dead bodies to last me a lifetime!'

He turned his back on the protesting cleric, trounced down the chapel steps and picked his way across the Square until he was directly under Morg's undulating body. Ignoring the danger, he closed his eyes, and for the first time called willingly to the power within.

The flames leapt, burning away the last of Morg's taint. Crimson, gold, silver, azure: the colours of his peculiar magic poured through his veins like a waterfall. And joining them, power of a different hue: earthy brown mixed with grassy green. Pure Olken magic, from the Circle. Suddenly he was connected to the natural world with a strength he'd never felt before. As though he were a mountain himself, forged of living rock.

Dimly, through the rainbow haze, he heard shouts. Cries of surprise and wonder. He stopped his ears to them. Looked inwards only, gathering the strands of his multicoloured talent, preparing it for battle. Barl's fierce war spells seethed beneath his surface, straining to be set free.

A woman's scream, abruptly silenced. Wrenched from his trance he opened his eyes – and stared at the face of death itself.

'*Asher*!' cried Morg, hovering before him. Jarralt's beauty contorted, distorted and spittled with hate. 'Not dead *yet*?'

He lashed out his mind, fingers blurring the air with sigils even as the words he needed tumbled from his tongue. Somewhere, softly, he felt the Circle's shock and surprise.

Spitefully laughing, Morg deflected the power. Sent the red flame splashing left and right, igniting helpless Olken who stood too close, like statues of stone.

Except statues didn't burn.

Sickened, he turned on the rest of them. 'Run, you idiots! *Run*!'

Gleeful, malevolent, Morg whirled above them. 'No, no, *don't* run! *Change*!' He pointed his fingers and shouted a string of terrible words, syllables to clot the blood and crawl the skin. Power poured out of him, black and stinking. The fleeing Olken it sullied fell screaming to the ground . . . and altered.

Became demons.

'*Jervale's mercy*!' cried Veira, watching. 'Prophecy protect us!'

Dathne watched, shaking and sickened, as vulnerable flesh boiled and bubbled, stretched and strained, grew fangs and talons and snouts and horns. Became scaled. Sprouted bristles. Thickened, hardened, and lost all humanity. She gasped as the milling livestock mutated with the people: grew steely wings and claws like bill-hooks and teeth as long and sharp as daggers.

Nothing living touched by Morg's foul magic was spared.

Forced now to focus on Morg's creations instead of Morg himself, Asher tried to stop the terrible transformations. He hurled his own magic after Morg's, light at the dark. The sorcerer extinguished it and flicked him aside with contemptuous ease. Catapulted him through the rancid air and crashed him to the puddled ground where he lay winded and feebly struggling.

'Asher!' said Matt.

Dathne clutched his sleeve. 'Don't. You can't help him. We can't fight – *that*.'

'Then what good are we, Dath?' he demanded. 'What are we *here* for?'

Veira turned on him. 'We've done our part, Matthias. We've kept the secret of the Innocent Mage, and brought him to the place he was always meant to be. Dathne's right, we're not made to fight this evil. That's why *he* was born!'

'It's not enough!' Matt shouted. 'I can't just sit here and let him face that alone!'

'He's not alone! The Circle's with him!'

'Aren't *we* the Circle?'

'Not any more!' said Veira, sharply. 'Our part is played. To interfere now is to put all at risk!'

Pellen Orrick stared at the monstrous things lurching and clattering and flapping and growling into life all over the Square. 'But I'm Captain of the City! I should be out there fighting!'

'If you go out there he'll try to protect you!' Veira told him. 'Which will likely get him killed. So hold your tongue and stay out of sight! All of you! That's the best we can do for our Asher now!'

She was hurtful, but right. Dathne exchanged stricken glances with Orrick, Gar and Darran, then turned to Matt, anguished beside her, and touched his hand. 'He'll be all right, Matt. We have to believe it. We mustn't lose faith, for his sake.'

'I'm trying, Dath,' he whispered. 'Jervale knows I'm trying.'

He looked so unlike himself, lost and frightened, it was easier to stare outside than at him.

Dazed and unsteady, Asher was back on his feet. Consumed with vengeance Morg sizzled the air above his dreadful creations. 'Kill him, children!' he shouted, pointing. 'Kill them all!'

The bestial, grunting, roaring things that moments before had been people, livestock, turned on Asher, slavering. Beat their wings. Lashed their tails. Crashed their tusks against their hides – and charged.

Asher flung out both hands and called forth Barl's war-beasts. The air around him shimmered and seethed as monsters worse than the demons attacking him burst into life from thin air. Creatures torn from the heart of nightmare, towering, stinking, yowling for blood.

Morg howled his fury as Asher's monsters attacked his creations. He called forth his own war-beasts, equally dire. The world filled with the sound and stink of violent death: the living demons' black blood gouted, poured sulphurous to the upheaved ground. The magical war-beasts burst into clouds of stinking acid.

Dathne watched, barely breathing, as Asher fought to destroy the cruelties Morg sent against him. From a vast distance she heard Gar name them: *brilbeests* . . . *dog-trolls* . . . *wereslags* . . . *ruunsliks* . . . an endless litany of foulness and decay.

Asher held his ground . . . but only just.

And then shrill screaming wrenched her head around. Not all the demons were trying to kill Asher. Some were in pursuit of other prey. She saw something that once had been a horse, now with eyes of fire and bony spikes all over its scarlet-scaled body, leap through a ruined shopfront then back out again with a Doranen youth in tow, his arm clamped in its teeth. The beautiful blond boy was crying, flailing at the creature with his inadequate, watered-down magic. The demon released him, reared up high, red hooves waving, then pounded his body to pulp on the cobbles.

More screaming, this time from the chapel as its doors burst open and four bull-demons chased a horde of Olken out of their refuge. Most were children. Holze staggered behind them, drenched in blood, but his wounds overcame him and he collapsed to the ground, dead or unconscious she had no way to tell. Asher saw the children – couldn't help them—

And Matt burst shouting from their pitiful shelter. Ran straight at the demons, waving his arms. At his heels, Pellen Orrick, just as demented.

'Come back, Matthias!' Veira shouted after him. 'Don't do it! *Come back*!'

Dathne leapt after them. Felt the brush of Veira's fingers as the old woman tried to catch her arm, and shook her off. Heard a curse as Veira followed. She didn't look back, saw nothing but Asher – Asher—

He'd seen Matt and Orrick. They'd reached the first of the running children and were pushing them desperately left and right behind anything that might hide them from the monsters pursuing.

The leading bull-demon reached the slowest of the little ones and gored her. Asher killed it with a spear of fire. Matt and Orrick kept on snatching children, throwing them to safety.

And then Morg attacked. Swooped from the sky like a falcon to the kill, his face a rictus of fury and hate.

Asher flung a massive ball of warfire at him. The writhing flames engulfed the sorcerer, cartwheeling him backwards and sideways into the majestic carved front of Justice Hall. Shattered masonry plunged to the ground, stained glass splintered and smashed and fell. Stunned and burning, Morg plummeted to the unforgiving marble far below and lay there, unmoving.

Slipping in mud, in bloodied water, hurdling rubble and bodies, Asher tried to reach Matt and Orrick and the fleeing children, throwing warfire at the demons as he ran. One of Morg's monsters reared up behind him.

'*Asher!*' cried Dathne, and he turned and killed it.

He saw her – faltered – brandished his arms – *get back! get back!*

Then his face changed. Someone shouted: '*Veira! Look out!*'

Dathne staggered round. Saw Veira, hobbling, her frail strength spent. Saw Pellen Orrick running back to her, a long spar of timber in his hands like a javelin. Saw a giant bull with bloodstained horns thundering behind the old woman. Gaining . . . gaining . . .

Veira tripped, went sprawling. Orrick lunged and thrust his makeshift weapon into the creature's gaping maw. It bellowed, gouting blood, and crashed to the ground—

—crushing Veira beneath it, and Pellen Orrick too.

Asher cried out and dropped to his knees, hands clawing at his heart, his head, oblivious to the battle raging round him.

'*Veira*!' Dathne shouted, and started running. Children forgotten, Matt ran too.

They reached Veira and Orrick together. Flung themselves to the blood-slicked street and reached for her hand – a way to free her.

No use. She was dead. Her eyes, half-open, stared at the red-hazed sky. Spilled from her fingers a shard of crystal, cracked now, its beauty charred.

'Veira!' Matt whispered. 'I'm sorry – I'm sorry—'

A groan, then, filled with pain and confusion. Grief-struck, Dathne looked over the lumpen carcass of the demon-bull and there was Orrick, leg-pinned and living.

Matt pushed to his feet. 'Help me, Dathne. I'll lift this monster – you drag him free—'

But they couldn't do it unaided. She looked back to the shelter for Gar, who should be helping—

'Dathne! Watch out!' Matt yelled, and knocked her

brutally sideways. She fell across a pile of rubble, feeling her skin tear and blood spill, crying out as her head struck something cruelly hard.

Matt had leapt forward, waving his arms. He danced himself sideways, away from her, shouting like a madman. What – *what*—

An enormous armoured-winged demon, snouted and bestial and no longer human, was lumbering towards them.

'Here! Here!' her crazy friend shouted – her compass – her anchor – her candle in the dark. '*Here*, you evil bastard!'

'No, Matt! Run! *Run*!'

But her voice was reduced to a whisper and around her the world was fading fast . . .

. . . but not quite fast enough.

Morg's giant, dagger-clawed monster seized Matt in its massive arms and tore him limb from limb. Hot blood sprayed in a mighty fountain, splashing the cobblestones scarlet.

On his knees and devastated by the sundering of the Circle, Asher heard Matt's desperate cry. He looked up. Through blinding pain saw the demon. Saw Dathne, in danger. Saw Matt shove her to safety – confront the monster – and die in blood and futility.

Time stopped, and the whole world with it.

When it started again he was back on his feet. Raging, weeping and lusting for death. War-beast after war-beast boiled into existence around him. He set them loose to rampage – and then leapt forth to join them.

*Kill – kill – kill*—

His first victim was the thing that slaughtered Matt.

When it was over, and all Morg's monsters were slain

or destroyed, there fell a silence, shot through with the sound of someone sobbing and someone else groaning. The Square was drifted with sulphurous smoke. Slicked underfoot with pools and puddles of blood, thick black and red, looking like a slaughterhouse with the sundered carcasses of demons and the broken bodies of children and their elders. Tired beyond imagining, Asher raised a hand as heavy as lead and banished his surviving war-beasts to nothingness.

Then he staggered to Dathne. Gar was with her, seemingly unhurt, helping her sit up. He didn't give a rat's arse about Gar.

'I'm all right, Asher,' she insisted, though there was blood on her face and her eyes were unfocused. 'Leave me. *Finish* this. Destroy Morg and end the nightmare.'

It nearly killed him, but he left her. Ignoring Gar, who shouted his name.

Morg the sorcerer lay still as death on the steps of Justice Hall.

Brimmed with pain Asher walked to join his fallen enemy. Reaching down, he rolled Morg over. Conroyd Jarralt's unmarked face was as handsome as ever. He was breathing yet.

On his belt, neatly secured in its lavishly jewelled sheath and barely flame-touched, Conroyd's knife. Asher slid it free and hefted it in his palm, admiring its weight and balance. Admiring the Olken craftsmanship. Odd that Conroyd chose an Olken-made dagger, given how he despised all things not Doranen.

Odd . . . and immensely gratifying.

He felt the merest flicker of sorrow, then. Conroyd Jarralt was a bastard but it was unlikely he'd asked to be consumed by Morg. And now he was going to die. Had to die, so Lur might live.

He shook himself. *Don't think on that, don't think on it. It's him or you and everyone else. You're savin' lives, remember?*

And not by spending his own, after all. When he wasn't so tired and full of pain, and this day's doings were a good ways behind him, he might crack a smile about that.

But not now.

He ripped apart Conroyd's blackened clothing. Bared Conroyd's unburned chest to the air. Blanked his mind, his imagination, and plunged the knife through muscle, between bones, deep into Morg's black rancid heart and twisted with all the might left in him to summon. Flesh quivered. Blood flowed. The sorcerer exhaled once, and died.

Incapable of walking anywhere else, even back to Dathne, Asher let himself slump to Justice Hall's steps. Dropping his forehead to his knees he let the trembling take him.

It was done, then. Done and done. Prophecy appeased. Outwitted, even, since he still lived. The mad world righted. Now he could go home to Restharven. Start a new life with Dathne. His wife. His beloved.

Eyes closed, shaking like a man with ague, he saw the sun rise over the harbour, smelled the salt air, felt the sea spray wet on his cheeks. A sob rose hot in his aching throat. *Home . . .*

Beside him, Conroyd Jarralt's body coughed.

No. No. That weren't bloody *possible . . .*

On his feet again and staring, sucking air like a man half-drowned, he watched the knife push slowly but surely out of Conroyd's blood-slicked chest to fall with a metallic thud on the marble steps. Watched the wound seal closed as though it had never been and the rib cage rise and fall, rise and fall. Saw the eyelids flicker a dreadful warning.

Shit. *Shit.* Morg was proof to killing steel, and now he had no choice: he'd have to use Gar's bloody spell. Seemed Prophecy weren't outwitted afterall.

It wasn't fair, it wasn't *fair*. He wanted to go home!

The words of the UnMaking spell were in him, and waiting. He called them to the tip of his tongue. Turned his head, just a little, just far enough to see Dathne, on her feet at the edge of the Square with Gar nowhere in sight.

Dathne. *Dathne.*

He nearly howled out loud.

*This wasn't bloody fair!*

At his feet Morg sighed, and shifted.

Now or never. Time was up.

With a right hand that trembled only a little, with a voice that cracked only just at the edges, he signed the sigils, spoke the spell, and closed his eyes.

*Here I come, Da . . . here I come . . .*

Nothing happened. No surge of power. No flash of light. No death, for him or Morg.

Disbelieving, he opened his eyes. 'Sink me bloody sideways!' he shouted, spinning about. '*Gar*!'

'This way, Asher!' the little shit called out, beckoning from deep shadows off to the left. 'Quickly! Here! Before he wakes!'

Head spinning, rage like a red mist clouding his vision, Asher slipped and slithered down the steps to join Gar in the narrow walkway between Justice Hall and the City chapel. Grabbed him by the shirt front and shook for all he was worth.

'You said it were translated! You said it'd bloody work!'

Gar fended him off with difficulty. 'It is! It will! Let me go, Asher! *Listen*!'

'To *you*?' he demanded. 'I'm done listenin' to you! I listened to you and look what it got me! Sink me, *sink* me, what do I do now? The bastard won't die! I stuck a knife in his heart and he still ain't dead! And your spell – your damned bloody spell—'

'Won't work unless it's channelled through me.'

He took a step backwards, staring. '*What*?'

Gar's face was bloodless, his eyes hollowed and bruised. 'I changed Barl's incantation, Asher. Not a lot. Just a little. Now I'm an integral part of the magic. The power must flow through me before it can kill Morg.'

Was Gar raving? Deluded? Had the past weeks' strain unhinged him completely?

Reading the questions in his face, Gar sighed and shook his head. 'I'm in my right mind, I promise you, Asher. And what I've said is the simple truth. It's what I tried to tell you before you tried to dash out my brains.'

'You altered the incantation? *Why*?'

'I had my reasons.'

Stunned almost speechless, Asher turned away. Turned back again, still struggling. 'But . . . but that means you'll die too, don't it?'

Gar shrugged. 'What do you care, so long as Morg is dead?'

'You are mad,' he whispered, retreating until his shoulderblades met cold damp bricks. 'Stark, staring suntouched.'

'You know I'm not. Morg must die and this is the only way.'

'It can't be!' he shouted. 'You're the smart one, the scholar, the historian! Think of somethin' else! I've already had one man die in my place, Gar, I ain't about to make it two!'

Gar shook his head. 'That choice isn't yours. It's mine, and it's made.'

'But *why*?'

'Why does it matter? You don't care about me.'

No, he didn't, but that weren't the point. 'Pretend I do and tell me *why*!'

Gar let out a sigh, and stared at the ground. 'I promised Fane I'd not seek her crown, and broke my word. I promised you I'd keep you safe, and broke my word again. I promised Barl I'd protect her people with my life – and that's one promise I intend to keep. I may be a magickless cripple but I'm still Lur's king. I'll not have my legacy a string of broken promises. My father taught me better than that. I told you once, I have a destiny. Do you remember? Well, this is it.' He looked up, then, his face as stony as any effigy. 'Don't try to stop me, Asher. I'll hate you if you do.'

'And if you make me go through with this, *I'll* hate *you*!'

A twisted smile touched Gar's lips. 'You hate me now.'

'Then I'll hate you *more*!'

Another shrug, uncaring. 'Hate me as much as you want. It changes nothing. Asher, there's no other way and we're running out of time . . .'

Trapped. He was trapped, with no escape. The bastard. The *bastard*. 'I'll never forgive you for this, Gar,' he whispered. 'Never not *ever*.'

'I know that already,' said Gar. 'Now shut up and listen. We only have moments. Everything I taught you in the wagon holds true. All that's different is the spell's delivery. You hold my shoulder and *you don't let go*. Understand me? If you let go the spell fails and Morg lives *forever*.'

He was numb. Dizzy. 'Over my dead body.'

'No,' said Gar, unsmiling. 'Over mine.'

He had no answer to that.

Still unsmiling, Gar reached inside his jacket and pulled out the age-mottled journal that had started this mess. Bits and pieces of ragged paper were slid here and there between its pages. Looking at it, his expression softened to tenderness. 'I brought Barl's diary with me. It comforts me, somehow, though I know that makes no sense to you.' He held it but, his hand unsteady. 'Take it. Care for it. It's the last the world has of a grand and glorious woman who gave her life for something bigger and better than she was. Don't let her be forgotten. Please.'

Grudgingly, he took the proffered diary and shoved the bloody thing inside his weskit. Gar's unguarded face was too terrible to look at. 'Now what?' he muttered.

'Now you put your hand on my shoulder . . . and we finish what Morg started.'

'And you're sure this'll work? You said it yourself, you're a magickless cripple, what if—'

Gar's chin lifted, his face full of pride now and nothing uncomfortable. 'You said it better. I'm the scholar. Trust me, Asher. This will work.'

Side by side they walked to the mouth of the passageway.'

'Begin the incantation,' Gar whispered. 'But keep us concealed till the very last word. Then we'll confront him. Don't forget: you must see his eyes. And for Barl's sake, Asher—'

'I know, I know, I bloody know! Whatever I do, don't let go!'

The words of the spell were still there, still waiting.

He took a deep breath. Let it out softly. Tightened his fingers on Gar's steady shoulder.

'*Senusartarum*!'

Sketch the first sigil.

'*Belkavtavartis*!'

Sketch the second, and the third.

'*Kavartis thosartis domonartis ed—*'

This time it was different. The magic ignited, dark and dreadful, setting his bones on fire. Left arm raised to shoulder level, fingers spread and pointing, Gar stepped smoothly out of the shadows. Shaking, burning, Asher stepped with him.

Morg stood posed at the top of Justice Hall's steps, clothing mended, immaculate and glittering. He saw them and laughed, burnished with power.

'So *there* you are! And look at you! *Look*! The little cripple and his tame brute Olken holding hands on the brink of death! How poetic! How *romantic*!' He lifted his arms and threw back his head. Baleful green fire crackled around him, igniting the sullen air. 'Oh, what a *wonderful* way to die! You two first, then whoever is left. Or should I leave you till last?'

Gar was shivering. '*Finish it*, Asher! Quickly, *now*! Before he kills anyone else!'

Yes, yes, more than time to finish it. He could barely contain the maelstrom within. On a choking breath he lifted his head to look deep into Morg's mad shining eyes. Opened his mouth and whispered: '*Nux*.'

Killing magic seared through his veins. Out of his fingers clutched to Gar's shoulder, into Gar's body and down Gar's arm to burst from his fingertips in a stream of pure gold fire.

It struck Morg hard in his knife-proof heart, transmuting him to a pillar of flame. Gar sagged to the ground, gasping, shuddering. Not loosening his grip, Asher followed him downwards as the spell of UnMaking flowed like blood from a mortal wound.

For five slow heartbeats, Morg burned incandescent. Then came a crack of ear-splitting sound. The golden fire bloomed. Blossomed. Swallowed the sun.

Morg disappeared, and his dead demons with him.

Without a word Gar slumped to the cobbles. Fell face upwards, green eyes staring at the cloudy sky. The sky with no Wall. Asher fell with him. He mustn't let go, no matter what happened.

Gradually, he became aware of feet, hurrying by him. Sound, as rubble was kicked away. Voices shouted orders, called for '*Help here, help*!' He wanted to answer but his head was hurting and he was oh, so very tired.

Footsteps stopped beside him. He opened his eyes. *Dathne*. At her shoulder, Darran. Not dead then, the ole crow, even with a groggy heart, and in his face such a ravagement of grief . . .

He managed to smile as Dathne knelt beside him, her hand pressing hard to his cold, wet cheek. 'You were goin' to tell me somethin',' he whispered, his voice a sickly croak.

Her eyes were brighter than any star. 'I was, love, wasn't I?' Her forehead came to rest against his. 'We've made a baby,' she told him softly.

A baby. A *baby*? How had *that* happened?

He turned his head and said to his friend, 'Did y'hear that, Gar? I'm havin' a *baby*!'

But Gar was dead, and couldn't hear him.

Darran sobbed then, a thin, broken sound. Asher sat up with Dathne's help, and stared at the rotten ole crow in fury.

'Don't you blame *me*, you bloody ole man! This ain't *my* doin'! It ain't *my* fault!'

His blunt and brutal handprint was burned into the shoulder of Gar's blue coat.

'It *ain't* my fault,' he said again. '*I* never thought of it. *I* ain't the scholar. It were *his* idea. All his. Not mine.'

He lowered his forehead to Gar's still chest.

'*I forgive you*, Gar,' he whispered. '*I forgive you. Please . . . now you forgive me, too . . .*'

Silence. And then a long slow weeping of rain.

# EPILOGUE

After the moist heat of the high summer afternoon, the shadowy coolness of House Torvig's royal crypt came as a welcome relief. Asher took a deep breath, tossed a ball of glimfire into the air and let it light his way along the corridor to the place he'd not stepped foot in since the funeral. His palms were damp and his heart was racing.

Sink it, he'd sworn he wouldn't let nerves get to him.

The chamber was cramped. Crowded with memories as well as coffins. As he pressed past Borne, then Dana, and finally Fane he touched a fingertip to his forehead in greeting. Looked into the marble serenity of their faces and with affection recalled them, living.

'Majesty. Majesty. Highness.'

They were the last royal family of Lur. The end of a long and proud tradition. One day they'd be nowt but old-fashioned portraits staring down from a wall. Engravings in a history book with no one left alive who'd known them.

One day.

But not today.

He reached the fourth and final coffin. Shoved his

hands in his pockets and took another deep breath, then let it out slowly, hoping the ache in his chest would ease. It didn't.

'So,' he said, into the somnolent silence. 'Here I am. Bet you thought I'd never make it, eh?'

By some kind of miracle he'd managed to get Gar's effigy pretty lifelike. Even though Darran kept insisting the nose was wrong.

Bloody ole crow.

Staring at Gar's proud stone profile he felt a wave of melancholy. A grinding echo of grief. Dathne said he shouldn't come here. *Let the dead lie and the living dance.* That was her motto. But he'd put it off for long enough, so here he was.

With a snap of his fingers he conjured a stool to sit on. No reason he couldn't be comfortable, was there? Heart still heavily thudding, he tilted it onto two of its legs till he reached a precarious balance.

'We had some rain this mornin'. Rain that fell all on its lonesome, without any meddlin' from me.' He shook his head. 'Rain without magic, like everyone's agreed to. Did you ever think we'd see the like? No more WeatherWorking. Now there's a thing . . .'

The City folk had danced in the street like children as the dove-grey clouds summoned by no one unburdened themselves without spite or fury. He and Dathne had smiled to see it. He smiled again now, remembering, then swiftly sobered; harsher memories lurked close to the surface. Sometimes he thought they'd never sink.

'Everything's different now, Gar. Everything's changed. For the better, I'm hopin', though I don't deny it's still a mite unchancy. Bloody politics. There's lots of you Doranen of the mind things should go right back the way they were. Seems they're havin' a deal of trouble gettin' used to Olken magic. Good thing I got Holze on my side. Good thing Nix and some healers from the Circle patched him up and kept him breathin'. He's the royal Barlsman. Folk listen when he speaks. He's kept the kingdom together, I reckon, him and his clerics. Kept folk from goin' mad.'

He thudded the stool back to the flagstoned floor. Got off it, arms folded over his chest, and started pacing.

'We lost a lot of people, Gar. Yours and mine. The storms savaged every inch of the kingdom, just like the Circle said.' Pulling a face he added, 'All of Conroyd's family perished. Sad, but I don't deny it's made life easier. Ain't no squabblin' over crowns any more. And it seems I got no brothers left but one. There were waves, you see, from the falling of Dragonteeth Reef. Ferocious, they were, folks say. Taller than treetops and faster than a galloping horse. They washed in from the harbours, up and down the coast. Restharven's most gone now, and Westwailing. Rillingcoombe. Struan's Cove.'

The playgrounds of his childhood, smashed to rubble and firewood. He'd not gone down to see them yet. Wasn't sure when – or if – he would. Getting the kingdom back on its feet was a full-time job, and besides, all those survivors, searching for answers. What could he tell them? How could he explain?

Not even the Innocent Mage could save everyone.

He shook his head. 'Jervale alone knows how Zeth survived, but if anyone was goin' to, it'd be him. I sent a message sayin' he and the rest of the family could come here. That they was all welcome. Folks as spoke for me said he just spat and walked away. Aye, well. That's bloody Zeth for you.'

With a shrug and a jerk of his chin he put that memory to bed.

'And Jed survived too, bless 'im. He's livin' here now, with us. Potters round the stables and pastures most days. Cygnet and Ballodair follow him like overgrown dogs. He won't stop feedin' 'em apples no matter how often I ask 'im not to.'

Was that glimshadow, or Gar secretly smiling? He smiled himself, a little. Right or wrong he found it hard to grieve for his brothers. But if he'd lost Jed . . .

'We're rebuildin', slowly. Got a new Council. Dathne's on it, and Pellen Orrick. Me. Holze, of course, and Nix. Lady Marnagh, too; she's a woman with sense. There's talk of makin' Orrick mayor of Dorana, but I don't know if he'll do it. He was born a guardsman, Pellen. Dathne's overseein' all to do with Olken magic.' He grinned. 'You should hear her speechifyin'. Scares the trousers off me. Veira'd be right proud of her, if she was here. Matt, too.'

His breath caught a little at the sound of their names, and his fingers pressed the lump of crystal still buried in his flesh. It was a talisman, now. A part of him, memory, as they were part of him and always would be.

'Bloody Darran's in his element. Fussin' and organisin' and bossin' folk about. Truth is I'd be lost without him, but don't you bloody tell 'im. The ole crow's puffed up enough as it is.'

He scratched his chin and watched, for a small while, glimshadows dance on the chamber wall.

'It ain't smooth sailin', not by a long shot, but we ain't quite capsized yet.' He snorted. 'Some fools want to make me king but I won't let 'em. I *ain't* a king, I'm a bloody fisherman. Just 'cause I got some powerful magic . . .'

Suddenly tired, he dropped back on the stool. 'I don't much care for magic, Gar. Don't like what the wrong person can do with it. Ain't too proud of what *I* did with it, even though I had to. I've kept Barl's diary, like you asked me. Read it, at least what you managed to translate. Your bloody handwriting – I nearly went cross-eyed. I'll keep it safe, no need to worry. But I reckon I'll keep it secret, too. Barl hid the thing for a reason, and I reckon she was right. No one should have that kind of power. Not for any reason.'

He'd told not even Dathne he had the diary. He had a duty to safeguard the future, just in case another Morgan – or Barl – was born.

Gar's effigy glowed warmly in the light of the yellow glimfire. In the stone face a silent agreement. Seeing it, he breathed a little easier.

'There's talk started up of crossin' Barl's Mountains, and I reckon we will go, one day. But there's work to do here first. That's what we need to think on now, not rushin' about from here to there, sightseein'.'

He stood again, then, and unkinked his back. 'Speakin' of work, I'd better go. Just wanted to tell you what's happening, is all. Figured you'd like to know.' His fingers touched Gar's shoulder, briefly. 'I miss you, my friend. Ain't a day goes by I don't think . . .' He stopped, his throat closing. It was done, it was done, and nowt could undo it. 'Anyways. I just wanted you to know this: I promise I won't waste what you gave me. What you gave all of us. I should've said thank you, Gar. I should've said a lot of things. Sorry. Guess I am bloody rude after all.' He heaved a sharp sigh. 'Don't know when I'll have a chance to visit again, but I will. I promise. Wait for me, eh?'

With a flick of his fingers he sent the glimfire bobbing towards the crypt's doorway. As he reached Fane's tomb he stopped. Shook his head. Turned back.

'Nearly forgot,' he said. 'About the baby. If it's a boy we thought we'd call it Rafel. That's a bit more personal than a mouldy ole statue. If it's a girl, Darran says we got to call it *Gardenia*.' He grinned. 'Darran can suck on a blowfish and die.'

And he left the crypt, still grinning.

The recently opened Garden of Remembrance was full of fountains and flowers and flitting, jewel-coloured birds. Asher came out of the crypt into warm sunshine, where families strolled and boys and girls, black-haired and yellow, threw balls of glimfire, squealing with laughter.

Dathne was waiting for him, round as a full moon.

'All right?' she asked, her hand on his arm.

He kissed her cheek. 'Aye. All right.'

'Good,' she said, and tugged him along the path. 'Now walk with me.'

As he turned, obedience personified, he caught a glimpse of Darran hurrying towards them from the direction of the palace. The light of battle was in the ole crow's eye and a dozen scrolls were clutched to his chest. He groaned. He never should have mentioned he was going to the crypt . . .

'What?' said Dathne, alarmed.

'Nowt, nowt,' he assured her blithely. Slid his arm around her shoulders and matched his stride to hers as they strolled between the budding pink cantimonies. With luck she wouldn't notice . . .

But Dathne glanced to her right and cursed. 'Oh, for Jervale's sake! Can't he leave us alone for five minutes?'

'Doubt it,' he said. 'Darran lives for his paperwork, you know that.'

She gave him a look. 'Since when are you so tolerant?'

'I ain't. But you're the one said bygones were bygones and these are brand-new days. *And* you said I had standards to set. Can't hardly show my aggravation in public, can I?'

'Maybe not,' said Dathne, and raised her hand. 'But I can.'

The scrolls of paper leapt out of Darran's sheltering arms. They heard his wail of dismay quite clearly.

'That weren't very nice,' he said. Glancing over his shoulder he saw Darran stooping and scooping the scrolls from the ground, and grinned. 'Then again, neither's this. Rat's arse to good examples!'

With a whispered word he set the scattered scrolls to dancing. The children, seeing a better game afoot, abandoned their balls of glimfire and joined in the chase. They thought it enormously funny.

Darran didn't.

'*Asher*!' he shouted, his voice carrying on the lively breeze. 'You *reprobate*. You *ruffian*. You *sorry* excuse for a king!'

Asher shook his head in sorrow. 'What a mouth the ole man's got. And all in front of the baby, too.'

'Disgraceful,' Dathne agreed, smiling. Took his hand and placed it tenderly on her burgeoning belly.

With Darran disposed of they wandered amongst the flowerbeds and past the statues in the Bower of Heroes: Gar and Matt and Veira and Rafel. The sun shone softly in an eggshell-blue sky. Birdsong drifted from the trees around him. And a lone skirling eagle rode the thermal currents above the top of the Black Woods, up the face of Barl's Mountains . . . and beyond.